Necroscope:

THE LOST YEARS

Brian Lumley

NECROSCOPE:
THE LOST YEARS

TOR®
A Tom Doherty Associates Book
New York

For Bonnie Jane Johnson, who took me to new heights,
and Zahanine for her name's sake (if not her namesake);
but mostly for Silky—so necessary to my way of life . . .

NECROSCOPE: THE LOST YEARS

A Tor Book
Published by Tom Doherty Associates, Inc.
175 Fifth Avenue
New York, N.Y. 10010

Tor® is a registered trademark of Tom Doherty Associates, Inc.

Library of Congress Cataloging-in-Publication Data

Lumley, Brian.
    Necroscope : the lost years / Brian Lumley.
        p.   cm.
    "A Tom Doherty Associates book."
    ISBN 0-312-85947-3
    1. Vampires—Fiction.   I. Title.
PR6062.U45N43   1995
823'.914—dc20   95-23536
                                                        CIP

First Edition: November 1995

Printed in the United States of America

0 9 8 7 6 5 4 3 2 1

CONTENTS

HARRY KEOGH:
A Résumé and Chronology.

CHRISTENED "SNAITH" IN EDINBURGH IN 1957, THE INFANT HARRY WAS THE son of a psychic sensitive mother, Mary Keogh (herself the daughter of a gifted expatriate Russian lady), and Gerald Snaith, a banker. Harry's father died of a stroke a year later, and in the winter of 1960 his mother remarried, this time to a Russian dissident, Viktor Shukshin. In the winter of '63 Shukshin murdered Harry's mother by drowning her under the ice of a frozen river; he escaped punishment by alleging that while skating she'd crashed through the thin crust and been washed away. Shukshin inherited her isolated Bonnyrig house and the not inconsiderable monies left to her by her first husband.

Within six months the young Harry "Keogh" had gone to live with an uncle and his wife at Harden on the north-east coast of England, an arrangement that was more than satisfactory to Viktor Shukshin, who could never stand the child.

Harry commenced schooling with the roughneck kids of the colliery; but a dreamy and introspective sort of boy, he was a loner, developed few friendships—not with his fellow pupils, anyway—and thus fell easy prey to bullying. Later, as he grew toward his teens, Harry's daydreaming spirit, psychic insights and instincts led him into further conflict with his teachers.

His problem was that he had inherited his maternal forebears' mediumistic talents, which were developing in him to an extraordinary degree. He had no requirement for "real" or physical companions as such, because the many friends he *already* had were more than sufficient and willing to supply his every need. As to who his friends were—they were the myriad dead in their graves!

Up against the school bully, Harry defeated him with the telepathically communicated skills of an *ex*-ex-Army physical training instructor, an expert in unarmed combat. Punished with maths homework, he received extra tuition from an ex-Headmaster of the school. But here he required only a little help, for in fact he was something of a mathematician himself. Except Harry leaned more toward the metaphysical; his intuitive grasp of numbers was lateral to the point of sidereal; his numeracy was as alien to mundane science as his telepathic intercourse with the dead was to speech.

In 1969 Harry gained entry into a technical college, and until the end of his formal (and orthodox) education, did his best to tone down the use of his extraordinary talent and be a "normal, average student." Aware that he must soon begin to support himself, he began writing, and by the time his schooling was at an end several short pieces of his fiction had seen print.

Three years later, he finished his first novel, *Diary of a 17th-Century Rake*. While the book fell short of the bestseller lists, still it did well. It wasn't so much a sensation for its storyline as for its historical authenticity; hardly surprising considering the qualifications of Harry's co-author and collaborator—namely a 17th-century rake, shot dead by an outraged husband in 1672!

By the summer of 1976, Harry had his own unassuming top-floor flat in an old three-story house on the coast road out of Hartlepool toward Sunderland. Perhaps typically, the house stood opposite one of the town's oldest graveyards; Harry was never short of friends to talk to. But by then, too, his headmaster of a few years ago had discovered his grotesque secret, and passed it on to others more secretive yet . . .

Blithely ignorant of the fact that he was now under wary scrutiny, Harry let his talent develop. He was *the* Necroscope, the only man who could talk to the dead and befriend them. Now that his weird talent was fully formed, he could converse with exanimate persons even over great distances; once introduced to a member of the Great Majority, thereafter he could always contact him again. With Harry, however, it was a point of common decency that whenever possible he would physically attend them at their gravesides; he wasn't one to "shout" at his friends.

In their turn (and in return for his friendship), Harry's dead people loved him. He was like a *pharos* among them, the one shining light in an otherwise eternal darkness, their observatory on a world they'd thought left behind and gone forever. For contrary to the beliefs of the living, death is *not* The End but a transition to incorporeality and immobility. Great artists, when they die, continue to visualize magnificent canvases they can never paint; architects plan fantastic, continent-spanning cities that can never be built; scientists follow up research they commenced in life but never had time to complete . . .

At his flat in Hartlepool, when he wasn't working, Harry entertained his childhood sweetheart, Brenda. Shortly, finding herself pregnant, she became his wife. But a shadow out of the Necroscope's past was rapidly becoming an obsession. He brooded over dreams of his poor drowned mother, and in nightmares revisited the frozen river where Mary Keogh had died before her time. Finally, Harry resolved to take revenge on his evil stepfather. In this as in all things he had the blessings of the dead, for knowing only too well the horror of death, coldblooded murder was a crime the teeming dead could never tolerate.

In the winter of 1976–77 Harry tempted Viktor Shukshin out onto the ice of the frozen river to skate with him, as once the murderer had skated with his mother. But his plan backfired and they *both* crashed through the ice into the bitterly cold water. The Russian had the strength of a madman; he would surely drown his stepson . . . but no, for at the last moment Mary Keogh—or what *remained* of her—rose from her watery grave to drag her murderer down!

And with that Harry had discovered a new talent; or rather, he now knew how far the teeming dead would go in order to protect him—knew that in fact they would rise from their graves for him . . .

The Necroscope's weird abilities had not gone unnoticed; a top-secret British intelligence organization known as E-Branch ("E" for "ESP" or ESPionage), and its Soviet counterpart, were both aware of his powers. But he was no sooner approached to join E-Branch than its head, his contact, was taken out, "with extreme prejudice," by Boris Dragosani, a Romanian spy and necromancer. Dragosani's terrible "talent" lay in ripping open the bodies of dead enemy agents to steal their secrets right out of their violated brains, blood, and guts!

Harry vowed to track Dragosani down and even the score, and the Great Majority offered him their help. Of course they did, for even the dead weren't safe from a man who violated corpses! What Harry and his friends couldn't know was that Dragosani had been infected with vampirism. What was more, he had murdered a colleague, the Mongol Max Batu, to learn the secret of his evil eye. The necromancer could now kill at a glance!

Time was short; Harry must follow the vampire back to the USSR, to Soviet E-Branch Headquarters at the Château Bronnitsy south of Moscow, and there put him down . . . but how? A British "precog"—an esper whose talent enabled him to scan fragments of the future—had foreseen the Necroscope's involvement not only with vampires but also with the twisted figure 8 or "eternity" symbol of the Möbius Strip. In order to get to Dragosani, Harry first must understand the Möbius connection. But here at least he was on familiar ground; the astronomer and mathematician August Ferdinand Möbius had been dead since 1868—and the dead would do anything for Harry Keogh . . .

In Leipzig Harry visited Möbius's grave and discovered him at work on his space-time equations. What he had done in life he continued, undisturbed, to do in death; and in the course of a century he had reduced the physical universe to a set of mathematical symbols. Möbius knew how to bend space-time! Teleportation: an easy route into the Château Bronnitsy.

For days Möbius instructed Harry, until the Necroscope was sure that the answer lay right there in front of him—just an inch beyond his grasp. But the East German GREPO (the Grenz Polizei) were watching him, and on the orders of Dragosani tried to arrest him at Möbius's graveside . . . where suddenly Möbius's equations transformed themselves into doorways into the strange immaterial universe of the Möbius Continuum! Using one of these doors to escape from the GREPO, finally Harry was able to project himself into the grounds of Soviet E-Branch HQ.

Calling up from their graves an army of long-dead Crimean Tartars, the Necroscope destroyed the château's defenses, then sought out and killed Dragosani. But in the fight he, too, was killed . . . his *body* died; but in the last moment his mind, his will, transferred to the metaphysical Möbius Continuum.

And riding the Möbius Strip into future time, Harry's identity was absorbed into the as yet unformed infant mentality—*of his own son!*

August 1977

Drawn to Harry Jr.'s all-absorbing mind like an iron filing to a magnet, Harry Keogh's identity was in danger of being entirely subsumed and wiped clean. His only avenue of freedom lay in the Möbius Continuum, which he could only use when his infant son was asleep. But while exploring the infinite future time-stream, Harry had noted among the myriad blue life-threads of Mankind a scarlet thread: another vampire! Worse than this, in the near future he'd seen that red thread crossing the innocent blue of young Harry's!

The Necroscope investigated. He was incorporeal, yes, but so were the teeming dead; he could still communicate with them, and they were still in his debt. In September of 1977 he spoke to the spirit of Thibor Ferenczy—once a vampire—at his tomb in the Carpathian Mountains; also to Thibor's "father," Faethor Ferenczy, who died in a World War II bombing raid on Ploiesti.

Harry was cautious. Even when dead, vampires are the worst possible liars, devious beyond measure. But the Necroscope had nothing to lose (literally), and the vampires had much to gain; Harry was their last contact with a world they had once planned to rule. Thus, by trial and error, playing oh so dangerous cat-and-mouse word-games with the Wamphyri, he pieced together the terrible truth: that in the late 1950s Thibor had "infected" a pregnant English woman, Georgina Bodescu, who later gave birth to a son. And Thibor's spawn, Yulian Bodescu, was the source of the threatening red thread!

In Romania, Alec Kyle and Felix Krakovitch, current heads of their respective ESPionage rings, joined forces to destroy the remains of Thibor in his Carpathian mausoleum. There they burned a monstrous *remnant* of the vampire, but not before Thibor sent Yulian a dream-message and a warning. Thibor had hoped to use his English "son" as a vessel in which to rise up again and resume his vampire existence. But since his last physical vestiges were now destroyed, instead he would use him to take revenge on the Necroscope, Harry Keogh.

As for killing Keogh: that should be the very simplest of things. The Necroscope was incorporeal, a bodiless id, his own infant son's sixth sense. Only remove the child and the father would go with him . . .

Meanwhile in the USSR, Alec Kyle stood falsely accused of murder. Russian espers were using a combination of high technology and ESP to drain him of knowledge . . . literally *all* knowledge! This process would leave him raped of his mind, brain-dead, and physical death would soon follow. And in England Yulian Bodescu was on the prowl. Intent on destroying Harry Jr., he headed for Hartlepool.

His trail was bloody and littered with dead men when finally he entered the house where Brenda Keogh lived and climbed the stairs to her garret flat. The mother tried to protect her small child . . . she was hurled aside! . . . Harry Jr. was awake; his mind *contained* Harry Keogh . . . the monster was upon them, powerful hands reaching!

Harry could do nothing. Trapped in the infant's whirlpool id, he knew that they were both going to die. But then:

Go, little Harry told him. *Through you I've learned what I had to learn. I don't need you that way any longer. But I do need you as a father. So go on, get out, save yourself!* Harry was free; the mental attraction binding him to his son's mind had been relaxed; he could now flee into the Möbius Continuum.

And what the father could do, the son could do in spades; he was a Necroscope of enormous power! And in the cemetery just across the road, the dead answered Harry Jr.'s call. They came up out of their graves, shuffled and flopped from the graveyard into the house and up the stairs. Bodescu the vampire attempted his first and last metamorphosis: adopting the shape of a great bat, he flew from a window . . . and took a crossbow bolt in his spine.

And as he crashed down within the grounds of the cemetery, so the incorporeal Necroscope instructed the dead in the methods of eradication: the stake, decapitation, the cleansing fire . . .

Harry Keogh was free, but free to do what? He was a mind without a body. Except he now felt a different force, an attraction other than his infant son's magnet id, a vacuum seemingly eager to be filled. Exploring it, Harry was sucked in irresistibly—into the aching emptiness of Alex Kyle's drained mind!

Employing ultra-high explosives to blow the Château Bronnitsy to hell, and his powers as a Necroscope to correct other anomalies, at last Harry could take the Möbius route home. His work, for the moment, was at an end. It was the late autumn of 1977, and he had taken up permanent residence in another man's body. Indeed, to all intents and purposes, and to anyone who didn't know better, he *was* that other man! But he was also the natural father of a most unnatural child, a child with awesome *super*natural powers.

So now Harry must face up to other, more mundane duties: those of a husband and father. But how might he perform those duties with the face and form of a different man? What of his poor wife, Brenda, who had already suffered more than her fair share of strangeness and horror? How could he ask her to share her life with a husband who wasn't the man she knew? Finally, what of the child . . . *if* Harry Jr. could still be considered a child?

But perhaps the most difficult questions the Necroscope must ask himself were these: how much greater than his own talents were his son's? How *different* were they? And perhaps more importantly: how did he intend to use them? Thus the world of Harry Keogh was a vastly complicated place—

—Which wasn't about to get any simpler . . .

The story that follows concerns itself mainly with certain episodes of the Necroscope's life, between the previously chronicled *Wamphyri!* and *The Source*. But it is not alone Harry Keogh's story. For without that the Wamphyri were there before him (and despite the paradox of their springing *from* him), it could even be said that Harry himself would not have been necessary: without a disease there's no need for a cure.

In short, this story is also theirs: part of the lost history of the Wamphyri . . .

PROLOGUE

T HE POWERFUL, SILVER-GRAY STRETCH LIMO, FAMILIAR IN ITSELF HOWEVER unusual—but less than unique—on an island of ancient Fiats and sputtering Lambrettas, bumped carefully over shifting cobbles under a baroque stone archway into the courtyard of Julio's Café and Restaurant in the eastern quarter of Palermo. The lone survivor of a World War II bombing raid, the walled enclosure was once the smallest of four gardens containing a middling villa. The other three gardens were rubble-strewn craters; only their outer walls had been repaired, to create something of an acceptable façade in the district of the Via Della Magione.

The courtyard was set out like a fan-shaped checkerboard: square tables decked with white covers, standing on black flags of volcanic stone; the whole split down the middle by a "hinge" of vehicles parked herringbone-fashion on what was once a broad carriageway. A palm-fringed gap in the wall at the point of the quadrant marked the vehicular exit into the dusky evening.

Some three dozen patrons sat eating, drinking, chattering, though not too energetically; a pair of sweating, white-aproned waiters ran to and fro between the tables, the bar and kitchens, each serving his own triangle of customers. Even for the third week in May the weather was unseasonably warm; at eight-thirty in the evening the temperature was up in the high seventies.

The east-facing wall of the courtyard contained what was left of the old villa: a two-storyed wing three rooms wide and three deep, with a balcony supported by Doric columns that more than hinted of better times. The central, ground-floor room was fronted by a marble bar which spanned the gap between the pillars; kitchens to the left of the bar stood open to the inspection of patrons. Amazingly, in this bombed-out relic of a place, wide arches in the wall to the right displayed the sweep of the original grand marble staircase winding to the upper rooms and balcony. Better times indeed!

On the balcony—whose tables were reserved for "persons of quality"— Julio Sclafani himself leaned out as far as his belly would allow to observe the arrival of these latest, most elevated of all his customers: Anthony and Francesco Francezci, come down from the high Madonie especially to eat at Julio's.

It was *wonderful* that they came here, these men of power, ignoring the so-called "class" restaurants to dine on Julio's simple but worthy fare. And they'd been doing it for six weeks now, ever since the first signs of improvement in the weather. Or . . . perhaps it was that one of them, or even both of them, had noticed Julio's Julietta? For Sclafani's youngest, still unmarried daughter was a stunner after all. And the Brothers Francezci were eminently eligible men . . .

But what a *shame* that she wasn't at her best! It must be the pollution of Palermo's air. The fumes of all the cars and mopeds, the stagnation of all the derelict places, the breathing of dead air and the winter damp that came drifting in off the Tyrrhenian Sea. But spring was here and summer on its way; Julietta would bloom again, just as the island was blooming.

Except . . . it was worrying, the way she'd come down with—well, with whatever it was—just four or five weeks ago; since when all of the color had seemed to go out of her, all the joy and vitality, everything that had made her the light of Julio's life. To be back there on her couch, all exhausted, with an old biddy of a sick-nurse sitting beside her—"in attendance," as it were—as at someone's deathbed! What, Julietta? Perish the thought! As for the old crow: Julio supposed he should consider himself lucky to have obtained her services so reasonably. All thanks to the Francezcis, for she was one of theirs.

But here they came even now, smiling up at him—at him!—as they mounted the marble staircase. Such elegant . . . such *eligible* men! Julio hastened to greet them at the head of the stairs, and usher them to their table on the balcony . . .

Almost exactly one hour earlier, Tony and Francesco Francezci had departed Le Manse Madonie in the mountain heights over Cefalu en-route for Julio's and the supposed gourmet pleasures of the café's "cuisine." The quality of Julio Sclafani's food was, ostensibly, the sole reason for the Francezcis' weekly visit to the crumbling, by no means decadent but decidedly decayed city. Ostensibly, yes.

But in fact the brothers didn't much care for the food at Sclafani's, nor for the eating of common fare anywhere else for that matter. They could just as easily dine at Le Manse Madonie, and do far better than at Julio's, without the bother of having to get there. For at the Manse the brothers had their own servants, their own cooks, their own . . . people.

And so as Mario, their chauffeur, had driven the brothers down the often precipitous, dusty hairpin track from the Manse to the potholed "road" that joins Petralia in the south to the spa town of Termini Imerese on the coast—where according to legend the buried Cyclops "pisses in the baths of men, to warm them"—so Francesco had turned his mind and memory to the real reason for their interest in Sclafani's piddling café: the fat man's daughter, Julietta. Francesco's interest, anyway . . .

It had been six weeks ago to the day. The brothers had been in Palermo to attend a meeting of the Dons: the heads of the most powerful Families in the world, with the possible exception of certain branches of European Royalty and nobility, and other so called "leaders of men" or business, politicians and industrialists mainly, in the United States of America and elsewhere. Except there's power, and there's power. That of the Francezcis was landed and gilt-edged . . . and ancient, and evil.

It lay in the earth (in territory, or real estate); in the wealth they'd been heir to for oh-so-many, *many* years, plus the additional wealth which the principal and their unique talents had accumulated and augmented; and not least in those peculiar talents themselves.

For in fact the Francezcis were advisers. Advisers to the Mafia, *still* the main force and power-base in Italy and Sicily; and through the Mafia advisers to the CIA, the KGB, and others of the same ilk; and through *them* advisers to those governments which allegedly "controlled" them. And because their advice was invariably good, invariably valuable, they were revered as Dons of Dons, as every Francezci before them. But to actually *speak* of them in such a connection . . . that would be quite unpardonable. It was understandable; their social standing . . .

As to that last: they had the reputations of the gentlest of gentlemen! Their presence had been requested—even fought over—for every major social event on the island for the last fifteen years, ever since they came into their inheritance and possession of Le Manse Madonie. And their bloodline: there had been Francezci Brothers for as long as men could remember. The family was noted for its male twins, also for a line that went back into the dimmest mists of history—and into some of the darkest. But that last was for the brothers alone to know.

Thus the immemorial and ongoing connection of the Francezcis with certain of the island's (and indeed the world's) less savory elements was unsuspected; or if it was it wasn't mentioned in polite circles. Yet in their role of freelance intelligence agents for the Mob or mobs—as advisers in the field of international crime, various kinds of espionage, and terrorism—the Francezcis were an unparalleled success story. Where or how they gained their intelligence in these diverse yet connected fields: that, too, was for the brothers alone to know, and for others to guess at. But to the Dons it seemed obvious that they had corrupted the incorruptible on a world-wide scale . . .

. . . Francesco's thoughts had strayed from their course. As the limo glided, or occasionally bumped, for the junction with the A-19 motorway into Palermo, he redirected his mind to that evening six short weeks ago:

After their meeting with the Dons (whom they had advised on such problems as what or what not to do about Aldo Moro and his kidnappers the Red Brigade, in Italy, and President Leone, who had become an embarrassment) the hour had been late. Driving back through Palermo and turned aside by a diversion where road works were in progress, Tony had noticed Julio's Café and suggested they pause a while for refreshments.

Indoors in the room of the marble staircase, the brothers had ordered Julio's "Greek Island Specialities." They'd picked at spicy sausages, stuffed vine-leaves, and various dips prepared in olive oil—*but no garlic*—all washed down with tiny measures of Mavrodaphne and a chaser, the brackish Vecchia Romagna, sipped from huge brandy-bowl glasses. By nine-thirty the kitchens had closed; the brothers dined alone. Julio had excused himself—a toothache! He'd called a dentist who, even at this late hour, had agreed to see him. His daughter, Julietta, would see the brothers off the premises when they were done.

Perhaps Francesco had drunk a little too much Mavrodaphne, too large a measure of brandy. Or it could be that in the gloom and drafty emptiness of the place, with the picked-at food gone cold on their plates, and the knowledge of lowering skies just beyond the arches, the woman had looked more radiant, more luminous . . . more pure? Whatever, Francesco had looked at her in a certain way, and she had looked back. And Anthony Francezci had gone down to the limo on his own, while his brother . . .

At which point the silver-gray hearse of a car had swerved to avoid a dead animal in the road—a goat, Mario thought!—and again Francesco had been shaken from his reflections where he lolled in a corner of the back seat. Perhaps it was as well. They had been passing close to Bagheria; in a moment they'd be making a sharp right turn. Oh, yes, for Tony would surely want to park a while at a place he was fond of: the Villa Palagonia.

"What, drawn to your monsters yet again?" Francesco's comment had been petulant, almost angry; he was irritated that his mood and memories had been broken into.

"*Our* monsters!" Tony had answered immediately and sharply. For it was true enough: both of the brothers knew the inspiration behind the lunatic array of stone beasts that adorned the walls of the villa. The carved dwarves and gargoyles, the *creatures* with human hands and feet, and other Things that defied description. Some two hundred years ago the owner of the villa, Prince Ferdinando Gravina, had insisted upon visiting Le Manse Madonie, home to the Ferenczinis, as their name was then. Rich as Croesus, he had been interested to discover why the equally wealthy Ferenczinis were satisfied to dwell in such an "out-of-the-way, austere, almost inhospitable sort of place." And Ferdinando's mania for grotesques—or his mania in general—had later emerged as a direct result of that visit.

But in any case Francesco had shrugged, saying, "According to Swinburne, these sculptures have their origin in Diodorus's tale of the freakish creatures that came out of the Nile's sunbaked mud." And before his brother could answer: "Perhaps it's better if that legend prevails? It was a long time ago, after all. *Too* long ago, for such as you and I to remember!"

At which Tony had scowled and answered, "Ferdinando looked into the pit, brother—the pit at Le Manse Madonie—and we both know it!" And then, sneeringly: "Let's be discreet by all means, but in the privacy of our own car in a place like this, who is there to eavesdrop?"

Then, as at a signal, Mario had driven on for Palermo . . .

And now they were there, at the Café Julio, and the fat little sod seating them at a table on his precious balcony and detailing his odious "cuisine," from which list they ordered this and that: a few items to pick at, a carafe of red wine. All a sham, a show; the brothers moved the food about their plates, waiting for Sclafani to mention Julietta. And eventually, returning upstairs from some small duty in the kitchens:

"Gentlemen, I'm eternally in your debt!" Julio bowed and scraped, plucked nervously at the towel over his arm as he sidled up to their table. "Er, I mean with regard to your kindness in providing a . . . a *companion* for my daughter. I cannot bring myself to call the old lady a nurse—can't admit to any real sickness in my girl—but the woman *is* a godsend nevertheless. She fetches and carries, sees to my daughter's needs, and I am left free to attend my business."

"Julietta?" Francesco contrived to look concerned. "Your daughter? Is she no better, then? We'd wondered why she wasn't around . . ." He looked down over the balcony into the courtyard, casting here and there with his dark eyes as if searching.

Julio turned his own eyes to the night sky and flapped his hands in an attitude of despair or supplication. "Oh, my lovely girl! Weak as water and pale as a cloud! Julietta *will* get better, I am sure. But for now . . . she reclines upon her bed, with shadows under her eyes, and complains about the sunlight creeping in her room so that she must keep the curtains drawn! Some strange lethargy, a malaise, a weird photophobia."

The brothers looked at each other—perhaps quizzically—and Francesco finally nodded. And to Julio: "Sclafani, we have business tonight. A man of ours returns from an important trip out of the country. Meanwhile we're out for a drive, passing a little time. It's a very pleasant evening, after all. Alas, we may be called away at any moment, which is why we didn't order more extensively from your menu. But this thing with Julietta: we find ourselves . . . concerned for you."

"Indeed," Tony nodded. "We Francezcis are delicate that way ourselves—with regard to strong sunlight, I mean. Which is why we're not often out and about when the sun is up."

"And," Francesco went on, thoughtfully, "—who can say—perhaps we find ourselves in a position to be of further service?" (Julio could have fainted! What, the Francezci Brothers, of service to him and his? Of *further* service?)

"You see," said Tony, "in three days a man will fly from Rome. A doctor, a specialist. You are right: there is a certain malaise or anaemia abroad. Servants of ours in Le Manse Madonie are laid low by it; we ourselves feel a definite lethargy. Our blood seems . . . weak? But at least in the heights we have the benefit of clean air! While here in the city . . ." He shrugged.

Open-mouthed, Julio looked from one brother to the other. "But what do you propose? I mean, I scarcely dare presume—"

"—That our doctor friend should take a look at Julietta, and perhaps keep her under observation a while?" Francesco cut him short. "But why not? He's our own private doctor and comes with the very highest recommendation! Moreover, he's been paid in advance. In such an arrangement, surely there are no losers! So, it's settled." He nodded his head as in final confirmation.

"Settled?"

"We shall send our car for Julietta three evenings from now—Saturday, yes. And the old woman shall stay with her at all times, of course. But that is to look on the gloomy side, for in the event that she should recover between now and then, which naturally we hope she will . . ."

"I . . . am stunned!" Julio choked out the words.

"No need to be," said Tony, delicately dabbing at his mouth. "Take our card. If your Julietta shows signs of recovery, call us. Otherwise look for our car Saturday night. After that, you may inquire after her at your convenience. But remember: we're private men. Our telephone number is restricted. And rest assured, Julietta will be attended to in every circumstance."

It was done. Hardly believing his stroke of good fortune, the fat man went about the night's business in a daze; the brothers, apparently unmoved, continued to pick at their food . . . until Julio was observed busying himself at the tables in the courtyard below. Then: "Watch the stairs," Francesco said. "If he comes up, issue a warning or distract him." But as he stood up and moved back a pace from the balcony:

"Now who is being indiscreet?" Tony smiled up at him with eye-teeth that were white and needle-sharp in a too-wide mouth.

Francesco leaned toward his brother—leaned at a peculiar angle—and answered through clenched teeth in a voice that was suddenly as black and bubbling as tar, "What, but can't you *smell* that bitch back there?" In another moment he straightened up, coughed to clear his throat, and continued in a more normal tone of voice. "Anyway, we need to be certain the fat fool will accept our offer. So drink your wine . . . and watch the stairs!"

He turned away. Two paces took him across the balcony and through a curtained archway into a corridor. He passed a gentlemen's toilet on his left, a ladies' on the right, and entered a door marked "Private" into Julio's office. Skirting the desk, he passed through a second door into Julietta's sickroom. And there she lay, with the old biddy Katerin, eighty years old if she was a day, in attendance. The crone was nodding. Startled, she glanced up at Francesco through rheumy eyes. "Who? What?" Then, recognizing him, she smiled, nodded and made to rise.

"No, stay," he told her. "Best that you're here, in case that oily little fat man should look in." Katerin nodded again and sat still. In the dimness of the room, the grandam's eyes were yellow as a cat's watching her master.

He sat half-way up the wide couch where Julietta lay, and his sudden weight woke her. Or perhaps she'd already been awake . . . waiting. Her eyes opened big as saucers; her jaw fell open; knowledge and horror painted themselves with rapid strokes upon her lovely, oval, oddly pallid face. But in no way odd to Francesco. And before she could cry out, if she would:

"Did you think I would desert you? Ah, no!" he told her. And his hand crept under her blanket, under her nightgown, to her thigh, so that she could feel his fingers trembling there. "No, for having loved you once, I shall love you all the days of your life." But he did not say *"my* life."

As his hand climbed higher on her thigh, so Julietta's mouth closed and her fluttering breathing steadied; she began to breathe more deeply—of *his* breath. His essence was in it, as it was in her. And his eyes were uniformly jet, like moist black marbles in his face and unblinking, or like the eyes of a snake before he strikes. Except he had already struck, on that night six weeks ago. And the poison had taken.

He smiled with his handsome, devil's face, and the horror went out of her as she lifted her arms to embrace him. But that could not be. "Soon," he told her. "Soon—at Le Manse Madonie! Can't you wait? A day or two, my Julietta. Just a day or two, I promise." Her sigh, and her breathing suddenly quickening;

the long lashes over her dark eyes fluttering, as Francesco's cool hand discovered the inside of her hot thigh. Then her nod, and a gasp of weird ecstacy as her head flopped to one side in sudden shame, or defeat, or surrender, and her thighs lolled open.

He held her lips open with his thumb and smallest finger, and let the middle three elongate into her. His hand was quite still, but the three central fingers stretched with a caterpillar's expansion, throbbing with the effort of metamorphosis like a trio of sentient penises, with pouting lips opening in their tips. And into her body they crept, while his thumb and smallest finger closed on her bud, to gentle it like a nipple.

And with the old crone watching and *knowing* everything—laughing silently through a gap-toothed mouth whose eye-teeth at least were still sharp and white—so Francesco found the artery he sought and used his fingers to pierce and sip at the soft center of Julietta's sex where the marks, if he left any, would never be found, and the blood, if any continued to flow, would have its own explanation.

Then, in a few seconds, a minute—as the girl went, "Ah! Ah! Ah!" and turned her head this way and that, until her eyes rolled up—slowly Francesco's jaws cracked open in a grin or a grimace, allowing a trickle of saliva to slop from a corner of his writhing lips. In that same moment his own eyes turned to flame, and then to blood! Julietta's blood. But:

Brother! It was Anthony; not a call as such (for the brothers were not gifted with the true art), but a warning definitely. A tingling of nerves, a premonition. Julio was coming!

A moment to withdraw from Julietta, and another to lean forward and kiss her clammy brow. Then he was out of the room, flowing from Sclafani's office into the corridor, and the door marked "Men" closing softly behind him. And his penis steaming as he plied it in the privacy of a cubicle, once, twice, three times, before it spurted into the bowl. And even his sperm was red where Francesco pulled the chain on it . . .

In the corridor, Sclafani was waiting for him. "Ah! Forgive me! I supposed you would be in there. Your brother asked me to tell you . . . Your man has returned from England . . . And your driver, Mario? . . . A radio message?" He fluttered his hands, as if that were explanation enough. Which in fact it was.

Francesco was cool now. He smiled his gratitude, and made for the balcony with Julio hard on his heels. "It's been such a pleasure to have you," the fat man was babbling. "I can't possibly bill you. What? But I'm already too deeply in your debt!"

At the table, Mario stood by in his uniform and cap while Tony spoke into a portable radio-telephone. Francesco wheeled on Julio and almost knocked him over. "My friend," he said hurriedly. "This is a private conversation. You understand? As for the bill: the pleasure was all ours." He pressed a wad of notes into the proprietor's hand, more than enough to cover what they had *not* eaten. As Julio waddled off, Tony was standing up.

"ETA in forty-five minutes," he said. "Even if we go right now, still the chopper will beat us to the Manse." He shrugged.

Francesco nodded and said, "I'll speak to Luigi *en route.*"

* * *

In the limo Francesco sat up front beside Mario. Outside Palermo the static cleared up and he was able to make himself understood on the car's communication system. "Your patient?"

"Sedated," came back a tinny, almost casual voice. "Threw up a little . . . doesn't seem to travel too well. The sedative, I suppose."

From the back of the limo Tony said: "Well, purging can't hurt. They'll be seeing to that anyway, at Le Manse."

Francesco glanced back at him. "I left instruction, yes." And into the radio: "Any problems at the other end?"

"None. Smooth as silk. Everything should be that easy!"

"Good," Francesco was pleased. "And this end? Control?"

"They've cleared me on to Le Manse Madonie. No problem."

(Of course not. The Francezcis' man in Air Traffic Control at Catania had picked up more than a year's wages for this!)

"Our people at the Manse will see to your patient," Francesco finished. "We'll be along later. Oh, and well done."

"Thanks, and out," the unseen pilot answered. There were no frills, not on the air . . .

At Le Manse Madonie, the brothers looked on while their people saw to the girl from the helicopter. Still sedated, she'd been stripped and bathed by the time they got there. The rest of it would take most of the night. They watched for an hour or so—the enemas, the operation of the pumps and mechanically forced voiding, the "purification," as it were—but after that they lost interest. The manicuring of nails, the cleansing and polishing of teeth, application of fast-acting fungicides to her various openings (lotions to be removed later in a final bathing), all of that would go on and on. Clinical but less than beneficial: health wasn't the object of the exercise. Only cleanliness.

"And all wasted," Tony Francezci shook his head in disgust as they made for their apartments about midnight. They wouldn't sleep but merely rest; time for sleeping when it was over.

"Wasted?" his brother answered. "Not at all. Well, the girl herself, maybe, but not the effort. He likes them clean, after all. And she can't lie to him, can't hide anything. *Outside* her mind, we could merely prise for clues. *Inside* it . . . he can lay everything bare down to the electrons of her brain and patterns of her past, the memories in the mush of her gray matter."

"Poetic!" Francesco's brother seemed appreciative, but his voice almost immediately turned sour. "Ah, but will he *divulge* what he discovers? Or will he obscure and obfuscate, as he's so wont to do? He gets more difficult all the time."

"He'll tell us something of it, at least," the other nodded. "It's been a while and he's hungry. He'll be grateful, and she'll make a rare tidbit. Why, I could even fancy her myself!"

Tony gave a snort. "What? But *you* could fancy old Katerin, if that's all there was!" And as they parted company at the top of a flight of stairs and made for their own rooms: "Oh, and on that same note: did you have Julietta, in Julio's backroom?"

"Something like that," his brother leered back at him. "If you're asking will we be sending for her . . . yes, we will. Why? Would you perhaps like her for yourself?"

"Not really," Tony told him. "For you've been there before me." There was no malice in it, nor in Francesco's answer:

"It never stopped you before," he said, evenly . . .

In the hour before dawn, the Francezcis met again in the secret heart of Le Manse Madonie. Beneath extensive cellars and ancient foundations, at a place deep in the bedrock—a place known only as "the pit"—they came together to attend personally to the final stage of the operation: the lowering of the girl into an old, dried-out well.

The mouth of the well was maybe fourteen feet across, wall to wall; the walls were three feet high, and of massive blocks of old hewn masonry; a "lid" of electrified wire-mesh in a circular frame was hinged to the walls on opposite sides, covering the opening like a grille. But the pit was silent for now, sullen and sinister even to the Francezcis. Down there somewhere, at a depth of some eighty feet, it opened into a cyst that had once contained water. Now it housed their father.

A mechanical hoist stood to one side, its gantry reaching out over the pit. Suspended by chains, a metal table slowly rotated. The girl lay naked on the table, with her hands folded on her stomach. In her entire life she had only once been cleaner, less toxic: in the womb, in the days preceding her birth before the first human hands were lain on her. Now *in*human hands would be lain on her. But first the interrogation; not of the girl but the Old Ferenczy, the monstrously mutated Francezci in his pit. Only the brothers were present; it wasn't work for lesser, more easily influenced or corrupted minds. But then, how might one corrupt the Francezcis?

The cavern containing the pit was a natural place, made *un*natural only by its grotesque inhabitant. Rocky ledges swept back into darkness, but the pit itself was illuminated: a bank of powerful spotlights shone down on it from the nitre-streaked dripstone walls. Where the shadows crept, stone steps had been cut back into a shaft that climbed in a spiral to the Manse—the aerie—high over-head. At the foot of the steps an electrified pneumatic "door," a grille of two-inch steel bars, guarded the exit. The door's control panel was set well back within the brightly lit shaft. Like the cover over the old well, this door to the exit shaft wasn't designed to keep anyone or thing out.

Yet the place wasn't specifically a prison but more properly a refuge, a sanctuary . . . an asylum. And just this once, perhaps the Francezcis were of a single mind where they stood at the rim of the well and Francesco quietly commented:

"It's as if the 'Mad' in Madonie were deliberate . . ."

Tony at once cautioned him: "Always remember, brother: he can hear you. Even when you're sleeping—or lost in your lust with some slut—*he* can be there. And he's here even now."

And the other knew it was true. Down here their father's presence was everywhere. It was in the echoes of their voices; and despite the glaring lights—or because of them—it was in the movement of the blackest shadows back there where there should be no movement. It permeated the very atmosphere, as if the place were haunted. But the Old Ferenczy was no ghost. Nor would he ever be, so long as he was their oracle.

Francesco looked at his brother. "Well, are you ready?"

Tony licked his fleshy lips, and nodded. He wouldn't ever be "ready," not really, but what must be must be. He had always been the Old One's favorite, "spoiled" by a father who had had time for him. As for Francesco: he had been too precocious; his father had *never* had time for him! Knowing something of the future—indeed, of most things—perhaps the pit-dweller had foreseen the time when Francesco would relish his . . . *incapacity.*

The electricity was off, the grille safe. "Father," Tony leaned over the rim of the old well and gazed down through the mesh on a receding funnel of massive blocks of masonry. "We've brought you something. A small tribute, a gift—a girl!"

A girl . . . a girl . . . a girl, the well repeated, an echo carried on the miasma. But a miasma, here? A wisp of mist, anyway, rising from the pit. The heat of the spotlights vaporized it, turning it to stench. The thing below might not be especially active, but it was there. It was breathing, and . . .

". . . Listening!" said Francesco, who was sensitive to such things. "Oh, he hears you, all right!"

"Father," Tony leaned out more yet. "We've brought a gift for you, but we have our needs, too. There are things we need to know . . ." For a moment there was nothing, and then the well seemed to sigh! It was physical—in that a gust of foulness rushed up from below—but it was also mental: the Old Ferenczy's telepathy, which in the brothers' case had skipped a generation. And despite that they were not mentalists, still their father's power was such that finally they "heard" him:

Only ask, my son . . . after you have sent me my tribute.

But if the message was simple, its delivery was dramatic. It reverberated in their heads like a shout, and was accompanied by a tumult of tittering, crazed background "voices" that were all their father's. He had concentrated *part* of his mind on his answer, but the rest of it was engaged in its own activity . . . the way a madman might often seem calm on the outside, while in fact he seethes within. And the many personalities of the thing—his diverse identities—were like a bickering, uncontrollable, heckling audience to the efforts of the part which now attempted to communicate with the world outside itself; in fact with the thing's son.

Tony reeled at the rim of the pit; his brother caught his shoulder to steady him; the mental babble subsided, along with the "echoes" of their father's true or "sane" voice. And:

"Dangerous!" Tony muttered. "He isn't in control."

"Or is he simply playing with us? Francesco scowled. "His split-personalities, multi-identities: it wouldn't be the first time he'd used them to confuse us . . ."

Tony nodded, grimaced, and called down: "Father, plainly you are not yourself. The girl will keep, and we'll try again later." He made himself believe it—*in his mind*—in case his father was listening. But then, as they reached for the metal platform hanging over the pit, as if to swing the girl aside:

NO! came that enormous mental grunt from below. *NO, WAIT!* And a moment later—less forcefully, almost pleadingly now, as they paused—*Does she come of her own free will? Is she pure? Is she . . . clean?*

And the brothers grinned at each other, nodding in unison. For this time there had been no background "static," no babble of crazed, secondary voices. When the thing in the pit desired it, he could control himself and shut them out.

Tony waited a moment, then said, "She has no will. As for purity: it's hard to find, father, in today's world. But clean? She's as clean as we can make her, yes. Except . . ."

Yessss?

"She knows things, which we would know. She's yours, but before you use her, will you not first examine her? For us?"

For a long moment there was silence, until: *But . . . why don't you examine her, my son? Before you give her to me?* The old thing's mental voice was sly now, wickedly intelligent.

"He knows," Francesco grunted, coldly furious. "He knows that we *can't* ask her, that even the best drugs won't open her up, because she's been forbidden to speak! Her mind's been tampered with, locked from inside, and only he can get in. And he knows *that,* too! The old devil wants us to beg!"

And: *Oh, ha! ha! ha!* laughed the thing, as the "miasma," his breath, thickened. *Oh, but I hear and know* you, *my son, my . . . Francesco?* The laughter ceased and the mental voice turned cold as ice. *And still you have no respect . . .*

"Hah!" Francesco scowled. "He thinks he's a Don!"

"He was," Tony reminded him. "A Don of Dons, one of the first. So don't annoy him; don't even *think,* but let me handle this!" And directing his thoughts and voice into the pit:

"Father, it was *you* who gave word of a certain threat. We acted on your word. For two centuries we have acted on it, and at last we have a lead. This girl has secret knowledge, buried in her mind. Nothing we do will give us access. But you . . . ?"

And in a moment—when they could almost hear the brain below working, and the body seething—*I can do it, yessss!*

"But will you?"

Yessss! Send her down.

"She must not be wasted," Tony cautioned. "Her knowledge can't be lost. It was risky bringing her here; we paid for her; we may never see another opportunity like this. And always remember, father, what threatens us threatens you . . ."

I understand, yessss. Send her down.

"But you are hungry, we know, and occasionally . . . impatient? And if—"

SEND HER DOWN—NOW!

There seemed nothing else for it. Francesco operated the gear to open one flap of the grille, and together they maneuvered the platform and girl into position over the open half of the pit. Finally Tony broke an ampoule under her nose, and she groaned and shook her head a little. But before she could wake up more fully, they sent her on her way to hell.

Her weight was measured on a dial on the control console. She sank sixty, seventy, seventy-five feet . . . and her weight became zero. "Get it up!" Tony croaked, as Francesco reversed the gears. The platform came up empty. But down below:

Suddenly the mental emanations—the blasts of raw, terrible emotion—were like a gale blowing in their heads! The brothers reeled, recovered, quickly closed and activated the grille. While in their minds, despite that they were scarcely gifted in the art, and that for once they were glad of it:

Flesh, bone, and bloood! The openingsss of her body, her face! The entrancesss to heaven, to hell! Oh, I am a monster! Yesss, for a man could never do thisss! But I am not a man! I am Wamphyri! Wamphyyyrrriii!

And above it all, a scream, just one—but a shriek to end all shrieks—as the girl came awake and felt . . . *what?* Her cry of shock, outrage, disbelief, was a sound to grate on the nerve endings forever. It came and went, as her mouth, ears, nostrils and head entire were crammed full of the thing, filled to brimming with him, as was her body.

And not only the hammerblows of the Old One's thought processes, but pictures to accompany them: *of a creeping, flowing, foaming* something, *never a human being, but with hands—oh, a great many—and mouths, and eyes, all converging on, soaking into, and expanding* within, *the girl.*

Then the bloating, the stretching, the rending!

And the mist over the pit gradually turning pink, stinking where its molecules came in contact with the grille . . .

A while later the Francezcis were surprised to find themselves close, touching, trembling, and slowly disengaged. Minutes had ticked by; the cavern was quiet again, or unquiet, and the pit . . . was just a pit, an old well.

Francesco looked at his brother quizzically, but Tony shook his head. "I won't, couldn't, talk to him right now. So let him rest. Later, maybe . . ."

But as they made to pass out through the steel-barred door into the exit shaft:

HE'LL BE UP! HE WILL BE UP! HE WILL BE UP! It was almost a cry of triumph, but quickly turning to sick terror. *H-h-he* will *be up, yes—in just a few years, three, or four at most—and then . . . then he'll seek me out . . . seek us out . . . seek us all out!*

"Who will?" Tony tried to ask. But dazed as he was from the mental blast, his voice was a croak. It made no difference, for he already knew, and his father had heard him anyway.

Who? came a fading, awed, even frightened whisper in their minds. *Who else but Radu? Who but Radu Lykan, eh?!*

And then a ringing cry like a soul in torment, or one lost forever in outer immensities: *Raaaddduuu!*

And once again a whisper: *Raaaddduuuuuu! . . .* that shivered into a shuddering silence.

PART 1

The Necroscope...
Harry Keogh?

A DEVIOUS THING.

GETTING UP IN THE MORNINGS WAS THE WORST OF IT, WHEN HE WAS OBLIGED to leave his dreams behind. For in his dreams he was usually himself, while in his real life the Necroscope Harry Keogh had become someone else entirely. Or not *entirely*, for on the inside he was still him. But on the outside . . .

. . . It was confusing, dizzying, frightening, maddening . . . especially maddening. And not only for Harry but for his wife, too. Indeed, more so for Brenda, for she could not and did not want to understand it; she only wanted things back as they had been. As for her baby son, Harry Jr.: well, who could say about that one? Who knew what *he* was thinking, planning, working on? But then again, who but a fool or a lunatic would believe that an infant of eighteen or so tender months was capable of working on anything?

Oh, he worked on getting fed or changed or attended to the same as any baby: by screaming for it. And he worked on collecting his audience of admirers the same way, too: by burping and farting and smiling in that gormless-innocent way that defenseless infants have, with their fat little faces seeming to slide off to one side, and their eyes getting crossed, and the drool dripping down off their wobbly little chins. Completely disarming, and utterly charming, of course. At a year and a half most of that was over now, but as for defenseless . . .

Harry Jr. was an angel—but one who had come face to face with the devil, and won! Him and his father both. But that had been only one battle; the greater, bloodier wars were still to come. Right now neither one of them knew that, however, which was just as well. Were it otherwise, they might not want to go on. The future has good cause to guard its secrets . . .

But as his father was more than just any man, so Harry Jr. was more than just any baby. It was when he was being . . . well, the *other* thing—when his expression was other than a baby's, and his thoughts more than the groping, fuddled demands or inquiries of an inchoate mind in an untrained body—that the espers of E-Branch were especially interested in him. It was when they felt, sensed, experienced the awesome, alien power washing out from him as he experimented, or did whatever it was he did, that they knew for sure he wasn't *merely* a baby. And when those baby-blue eyes of his lit with a faraway expression seen previously only in his father's eyes, and they knew that he conversed with a teeming majority no one else but he and Harry Keogh could hear and talk to . . .

Getting up mornings, the Necroscope would think of these things and, like Brenda, remember when it had been very different; when the world was a different place and he'd been a different person. It was easy to remember, for in his dreams he was still that other person. Hell, he *was* that person, even when he was awake! But only on the inside; which is to say, inside his head. For outside—in Harry's body and face and entire external appearance, and especially in the mirror—he was someone else. A man called Alec Kyle. Which took some getting used to.

That was probably why he clung so tightly to his dreams and was reluctant to let them go: because they were a form of wish-fulfillment, a place and a time when the world was a different world and the Necroscope a different person; himself.

This morning was the same, or should be . . .

For some, especially the young, waking up to a new day is a renewal, like being born all over again: the first day of the rest of their lives. Despite that Harry seemed to have done an awful lot of living, he was still very young: twenty-one years old. But his body—or Alec Kyle's body—was ten years older. And knowing that this was what he must always wake up to, Harry really didn't want to. It wasn't that he was suicidal about it; the fact that he now inhabited an older and alien body scarcely made him long for death (not the Necroscope Harry Keogh, a man who'd had it from the horse's mouth more than once what it actually *felt* like to be dead, who knew what it really *meant* to be incorporeal!). It merely made him reluctant toward life, made it safer to be asleep and dreaming—

—Well, sometimes. It depended on what you were dreaming about.

Currently he was given to dream a recurrent theme of life (but *his* life, before all this) where, like the proverbial drowning man, he clung to the straws of his past existence only to feel them grow waterlogged and slip one by one from his straining fingers. Each straw was a scene from the times he had known and the life he had lived, the chronological story of his oh-so-strange adventures. So that *like* a drowning man facing his imminent, inescapable death, the dream-drowning Necroscope saw it all skipping before his eyes like a scratched, comically accelerated, badly edited monochrome film.

His childhood in Harden, on the north-east coast of England, where he had attended primary and secondary schools with the roughneck colliery kids; his retreat from the mundane world of the living into the minds and "lives" of the Great Majority; his secret being discovered by Sir Keenan Gormley, then Head of E-Branch, and his subsequent return to "the real world" . . . his acceptance of his condition, the fact of his unique talent, and his willingness to use that talent by taking sides against the monstrous evils rooted in the USSR and Romania.

And superimposed on these accelerated glimpses out of the past, his life-long relationship with Brenda, a simple colliery girl whose love had formed the strongest single link between Harry and the orthodox world, one of the few things that kept his feet planted firmly on solid ground when often as not his mind was under it. And superimposed even over this, a glowing picture or memory of his mother—radiant as any loving mother as visualized by her child: her soap and rose-petal scent, the sweet warmth of her sigh, a golden aura all around her, as if the sun had risen behind her to diffuse her brilliant silhouette—all too soon snuffed out by a maniac, who in his turn had been snuffed by Harry.

Which was always the point where the Necroscope's blue, poignant dreams turned a dark, vengeful red. For after Viktor Shukshin there'd been Thibor Ferenczy, Dragosani, Yulian Bodescu, Theo Dolgikh, Ivan Gerenko . . . The list was a long one. And what of Faethor Ferenczy, that "father" or grandfather of vampires? Faethor had been dead for a long time now, true . . . but so had Thibor before him, and even a dead and buried vampire is a threat. Harry still couldn't be one hundred percent certain that the Old Ferenczy hadn't left other remnants (or revenants?) to fester in the earth like Thibor, waiting out their time until a grand return . . .

Colored by his fears and anxieties, the Necroscope's dream was quickly becoming confused. His mind was Harry Keogh's, but the brain that housed it had once belonged to Alec Kyle, a precog for E-Branch. Harry's truths—*his* thoughts, memories and emotions—dwelled now in those same vaults of complex, convolute cerebrum once Kyle's, where still the odd crevice or corner remained, not yet conforming to Harry's contours. Kyle's weird talent had been governed by the "shape" of that brain; his precognitive glimpses had used to come to him during those vague, confused periods of mental hiatus between dream and waking proper, at that point in time where the conscious and subconscious minds separate, allowing a dreamer to surface to reality. Nothing was left of Alec Kyle now, but the shape of his brain had not yet changed entirely; perhaps some small part of his talent lingered on.

For on the point of waking, suddenly Harry's dreams underwent a rapid transformation, mutating into sheerest nightmare! And because precognition is the dubious art of seeing the future—and the future is *not* a dream but a series of as yet unrealized events—it was as if everything that the Necroscope experienced was real as life. And the difference between these two dream-states was . . . electrifying! Most people, including Harry, "know" that they are only dreaming, but on this occasion he didn't.

As before it was a kaleidoscope of scenes, fast-fleeting, over which he had no control. But *where* before he'd considered himself accustomed to strangeness . . .

He stood in a place that wasn't of this world, at the rim of a desiccated plain of boulders that sprawled in one direction to an aurora-lit horizon, and in the other merged with foothills climbing steeply into mountains. Close by, a huge luminous dome was set in a walled crater like the eye of some fallen Cyclops in its buried skull, giving off a cold white light. The dome was like an alien pharos—but for what weird travelers? On high, the disc of a tumbling moon was lit half with the gold of an unseen sun, half with blue starshine; its surface pattern was in a state of flux, caused by the eccentricity of its orbit and rotation.

Clinging to what he knew of the geography of his own world, Harry's instinct told him that the aurora signaled north; odd, because that meant that the unseen sun lay far beyond the mountains in the south. But this was after all an alien world—

—To which he'd been sent . . . been sent by . . . by Faethor?

Here his reasoning faltered. To see the future is dangerous enough, but to try to remember *what is yet to be . . . !*

Yet for a moment Harry had known that Faethor Ferenczy had sent him here, that his being here had at least been advised or guided by that father of vampires, that Lord of Lies. And also . . . by Möbius? But for what reason? A quest, obviously—but why obviously? And if a quest, then for what, for whom?

He looked all about. The mountains on the one hand and the seemingly endless boulder plains on the other, and between them the enigmatic Gate, its cold white light flooding outward to silhouette the scattered, menhir-like boulders, casting unevenly concentric rings of shadow out into the Starside night.

The Gate? Starside? But these words, concepts, were meaningless to him . . . weren't they? Now what the—!?

In the north-east he spied distantly rearing stacks, fantastic rock formations crowned with . . . turrets? Towers? Tessellate stonework? . . . Battlements? Or was the effect simply the work of an alien Nature? Harry thought not, for there were lights up there. Smoke curled from tall chimneys; motes moved with purpose in the dark air around the upper levels. At this distance they were motes, anyway . . .

Suddenly Harry was aware that someone watched him. Spinning on his heel he fell into a crouch. On the boulder plain, only a short distance away, there stood a figure, slim, male, with a face of gold, burning in the reflected glare from the Gate. He held up a hand, gestured, said something, but Harry heard nothing. He was allowed to see but not to know . . . the future guarded its secrets.

Harry knew instinctively that there was no danger here, not from this one, at least. And filled with strange emotions, he moved toward the other. Yet while he would have approached him anyway, his motions were involuntary, the flowing, maddeningly ungovernable mechanics of dream—or rather, of precognition. But the golden-faced one had commenced to make urgent gestures, pointing into the sky to the east. Harry looked.

And now there was danger here! Those motes circling the great stacks—but no longer motes! Dark blots, rapidly taking on grotesque outlines, descending out of the sky from the direction of the aeries, and—

—Aeries?

Within his dream-self, Harry recoiled from the word. But his future-self continued to move toward The Dweller.

—The Dweller?

Finally he accepted that he was not given to know everything and concentrated on reaching the one who waited for him. But looking back he saw that the things in the sky were fast approaching, and that they were like nothing he had ever seen or nightmared before. One was winged, shaped something like a manta. The other was . . . incredible, monstrous, gigantic! It squirted through the sky like a squid in water. And now Harry could see that the first creature had a rider—Shaithis of the Wamphyri?—and knew that the second was one of his constructs, a warrior.

Harry was close to The Dweller now . . . Shaithis aboard his flyer was swooping down out of the sky . . . the wind from the flyer's mighty manta wings blasted dust and grit up from the plain into Harry's and The Dweller's faces . . . the creature's shadow fell on them as it shut out the stars!

The Dweller held up a wing of his cloak. Harry looked at him, at his golden mask, the scarlet eyes behind it, the mind behind the eyes . . . and knew *that mind! Yet he couldn't* possibly *know it! And for all the strangeness, still he was unable to stop himself as he stepped—or flowed—forward into the shadow of The Dweller's cloak, and felt it wrap about him . . .*

. . . And the kaleidoscopic picture changed. Harry had known *what would happen next—except it didn't! Instead of finding himself in The Dweller's garden (whatever that might be) Alec Kyle's wild talent had snatched him into yet another possible future, or the same one but further down the timestream.*

Now he was in the last great aerie of the Wamphyri . . . Karenstack? And furtive as a thief, he pursued the Lady Karen as she descended to her larder. Sinister and silent as smoke, Karen flowed in through a dark doorway; following her, Harry kept to the shadows while she activated a trog and brought it out of its cocoon. He watched her lead the shambling, comatose neanderthal to a stone table where it lay down, stretched itself prone and bent back its ugly, prehistoric head for her.

Then the Lady's jaws opened . . . opened . . . gaped! Blood slopped from her crimson mouth; scythe teeth sprouted, poising over a sluggishly pulsing jugular. Her nose wrinkled, flattening back on itself, and her eyes burned as red as lanterns in the twilight room.

"Karen!" Harry heard himself attempting to cry—in the moment before the kaleidoscope scene changed, taking him forward again in time, but only a little way this time . . .

. . . The Necroscope sat absolutely still, waiting . . . (for what he didn't know, couldn't say, only that he felt tense as never before), in the deepest darkest shadows of the aerie. And eventually it came: Karen's vampire! By what route it had left her body, Harry neither knew nor wanted to know; sufficient that it was here, where he . . . where he wanted it? It was a long leech, corrugated, cobra-headed, blind—and it had pointed udders, a great many.

Swaying its head this way and that, it inched forward . . . then sensed him and commenced a hasty retreat! Curling back on itself, it wriggled like a blindworm; for now it must get back to safety, return itself to Karen's undead flesh. But the Necroscope wasn't about to let that happen.

Using his flamethrower, he burned it . . . dying, it issued eggs, dozens of them, which spun and skittered, vibrating over the stone flags toward him. Sweating, but cold inside, Harry burned the eggs, too, every one of them. And as if from a million miles away—as if from someone else's dream—he heard the awful screaming, which he somehow knew was Karen's.

Then, abruptly, leaving him dizzy, disoriented, the scene changed yet again:

To a high balcony where he leaned out and looked down, and knew why he was dizzy: the terrible height! And way down there, crumpled on the scree, the Lady's white gown . . . no longer entirely white but red, too.

Karen (or what he and the future-Harry thought was Karen), was inside it. And terribly, achingly, none of it made sense to him, or fleeting sense at best—there one minute and gone the next.

* * *

Another jump:

Cold liquid burned his face, got into his throat and stung him, caused him to cough. It was . . . alcohol? Certainly it was volatile. It smoked, shimmering into vapour all around him. And . . . he saw that he was lying in it!

He struggled to his hands and knees, tried not to breathe the fumes, which were rising up into some sort of flue directly overhead . . . A blackened flue . . . Fire-blackened? Harry kneeled in a basin or depression cut from solid rock, kneeled there in this pool of volatile liquid.

Impressions came quickly: he must be in the very bowels of the castle (but what castle?), down in the bedrock itself . . . a huge cave. And against the opposite wall where rough-hewn steps climbed to unseen higher levels . . . there stood Janos Ferenczy, Wamphyri, watching him! The monster held a burning brand aloft, its fire reflecting in his scarlet eyes.

Their eyes met, locked . . . Janos's lips drew back from his unbelievable teeth in a hideous grin. He spoke . . . but the Necroscope couldn't hear him, could only sense the threat. Janos's gaze transferred to the torch in his taloned hand, then to the floor. Harry looked, too: at a shallow trough or channel cut in the rock, which ran from Janos's feet, across the floor, to the lip of the basin where Harry kneeled. And Janos was slowly lowering his torch!

Jesus! Harry must use the Möbius Continuum—but couldn't! His power had been taken away from him! He was no longer master of Möbius space-time! Again Harry knew this without knowing how he knew. His deadspeak was still available to him, but . . .

. . . Deadspeak? Since when had it been called that!? But no, he mustn't attempt to remember that which had not yet happened! Best if he simply accept it: that while the Möbius Continuum was no longer a viable proposition, still he had his deadspeak, his ability to talk to the dead. Wherefore, why not use it? Why not ask them—the teeming dead, the Great Majority—what all of this was about?

Too late! Janos's torch touched down and fire came racing in a blue-glaring blaze! Searing heat gouted up in a whooshing tongue of shimmering flame, roaring into the chimney overhead. Liquid fire singed the hair from Harry's head and face and set his clothes ablaze.

Leaping erect, he cavorted like a human torch!

Until yet again—perhaps mercifully this time—he felt himself snatched a little way into the future . . .

. . . To where he stood in antique ruins as dark as night, yet clear as daylight to him! For while he was scarcely aware of it, the Necroscope was a changeling now; an alien Thing was inside him.

He waited warily, patiently in the ruins of Castle Ferenczy; waited there with . . . with a dead man! With the resurrected Thracian warrior, Bodrogk.

Briefly, momentarily, flickeringly, Harry knew why they were here. His precognition told him that much, at least. And in a little while two women came up from below. One was Sofia, Bodrogk's wife of centuries, who flew into her husband's arms. Both Sofia and Bodrogk were dead; they had been called up from their ashes. But they were not as dead as the other woman! She was Sandra and was or had been Harry's woman—and later Janos Ferenczy's! The difference now was all too obvious.

For Sandra came ghosting in the way of vampire thralls, her yellow eyes alive in the night. But Harry knew in his way that she was less than Sandra now. Or more. Once she had loved, or lusted after him, for himself; now she would lust after all men—for their blood!

She flew into his arms, sobbed into his neck. And holding her tightly—as much to steady himself as to steady her—he looked over her sallow shoulder to where Bodrogk and Sofia embraced. If only their embrace could be the same. But of course, it couldn't. For Sandra's beautiful, near-naked body was cold as clay where it pressed against him, and Harry knew there was no way he could ever warm it.

She sensed his intention and drew back a little, but not far enough. His thin sharp stake, a splinter of old oak, drove up under her breast and into her heart. She took a final gasping breath, a staggering step away from him, and fell.

Bodrogk, seeing Harry's anguish, did the rest.

And Harry jumped again . . .

*T*his time it was different, for the dream-Harry wasn't in it. Or he was, but stood apart from it, watching it happen to his future-self. Which was probably just as well, for surely this had to be the end of him? Yet despite that in this instance he was merely an observer, still he was given to understand something of what was happening . . . and wished that he wasn't.

For in Starside, close to the glaring hemisphere Gate, the Necroscope Harry Keogh was burning. A vampire, finally he paid a vampire's price for a fatal mistake: to have let himself get too close to the Wamphyri!

He burned inside and out: fire on the outside, and a burning, consuming hatred within. For Shaithis, who even now took the Lady Karen (but Karen . . . ?) by force right there in front of Harry's cross. She seemed exhausted where Shaithis savaged and ravaged her; she resisted not at all as he tore at her.

The dream-Harry would go to their assistance . . . except he was rooted to the spot. He was an observer, forbidden to interfere. And as the flames licked higher around the Necroscope's funeral pyre, so Shaithis taunted him—but all in silence, like some hideous form of mime—while the fire ate at Harry's lower trunk. It was perhaps the cruellest thing that the dream-Harry had ever seen or could ever have imagined.

Perhaps too cruel—for even as an observer he was beginning to feel his own future agony!

Events speeded up, became a blur—a fury of fear, fire, and frenzied flesh!—and light! *Blinding light!*

The Gate was its source: a ball of silently expanding but all-consuming light. It ate Shaithis, Karen, the Necroscope—the entire scene—and it sent the dream-Harry . . .

. . . Elsewhen.

*A*gain Harry and his future-self—the one a dreamer, and the other a physical if future reality—were in the metaphysical Möbius Continuum, hurtling down a past-timestream, rushing back through times that were long gone and forgotten, among the myriad blue, green and red life-threads of Sunside-Starside, into their remote beginnings.

And again the dream-Harry was the observer, who couldn't help but observe that his future self was dead. Neither asleep nor undead but dead, truly dead (in this manifestation anyway), and gone forever . . . or going. Going where no one would ever be able to find him, into the far past of an alien, parallel vampire world. But being the Necroscope, the dream-Harry knew that it wasn't like that: the body of his future self was dead, yes, but the mind *would go on. Except this time . . . well, who could say where it would go to? Or perhaps this was the very end of the road, albeit right back at the beginning. A paradox— but wasn't everything?*

Horrified, because he knew that this was or would be him, the dream-Harry watched his own future-corpse where it tumbled head over heels into past time. Fire-blackened and smouldering—with its arms flung wide and its steaming head thrown back in the final agony of death—it was the one grim anomaly in a darkness shot through with the thin neon bars or ribbons of blue, green and red life-threads; for where they sped forwards in time, the dead Harry fell back. Then . . .

. . . An astonishing thing! For as that burned caricature of himself fell away from him—in the space it left behind as it tumbled from view—a glorious bomb-burst of golden splinters, like sentient spears of sunlight, breaking up and speeding out of this place into . . .

. . . Into a hundred different worlds and times!

Harry knew it without knowing how he knew: that while the Necroscope was gone, still he had gone on. Knew that he—the dream-Harry himself—would go on!

But as for now:

Still plunging headlong down the timestream—a dreamer, incorporeal—he went only into the past. But . . . the future-Harry's past? Which of course could only lead to his own present! Even by a dream's standards, it was confusing . . .

The present, the now, his *now. (Or if not now, then the immediate future. For of course his dream was precognitive). And this time Harry was himself. Not merely part of—or an observer. of himself—but* actually *himself. And the action was happening to him.*

The immediacy of the thing stood his hair on end, caused a cold sweat to break out on his face and neck. This was real, and he was . . . the victim? So far, in almost everything he had been allowed to see—in each phase of it—there had been a victim. And Harry suspected that the same general theme would apply here, too. Or more than suspected; it was just the feel *of everything, enough in itself to bring on these symptoms of extreme anxiety.*

Very well: a victim. Probably. But of what? He could only wait and see.

As to his location:

It was subterranean, a great cave, but not too far underground. Beams or curtains of light, however dim, filtered down from several diverse sources, setting disturbed clouds of dust glowing like small silver galaxies in their faint searchlight rays.

Harry was in motion; he moved with purpose if a little uncertainly through the gloom of the cavern, to a spot where the light was stronger. Looking up, he saw a rough-contoured ceiling of unusual stratification, as if the pressured bedrock had been tilted almost on end. Up there, like rows of jagged teeth set in the closed jaws of the ceiling, several harder, impervious layers projected downwards where softer strata had fallen away. Higher still, where even more loose stone had weathered out, narrow, uneven gaps reached up to day- light—or as Harry now saw, to starlight. These crevasses, filled with mainly unwinking stars on a backdrop of diamond-sprinkled sky, were the light-source. The lack of scintilla- tion could be caused by the Necroscope's subterranean viewpoint, or by a thin atmosphere, or both. He was loath to hazard a guess.

Still sweating (despite that he sensed the coldness of the place), Harry looked around on his own level. And now that his eyes were more accustomed to the smoky gloom, he could make out massively slanting columns, walls and chimneys of rock that climbed from floor to ceiling, and slabs of fallen rock tumbled into tiers and tangles in every direction. The cave was a veritable labyrinth of upended, mainly fractured strata; a geological freak whose ceiling seemed held aloft only by those mighty columns formed of harder layers. While around and through this Giant's Causeway of natural, angular supports—glooming over the rubble of shattered rock like empty, stony eye-sockets—a network of fissures, leaning lintels and gaping crevices formed doorways to uninviting, unknown routes through a forbidding and probably treacherous maze of doubtful extent. In a nutshell, it would be an easy place to get lost in.

Except . . . Harry seemed to know where he was going. Certainly he did; for if this was a precognitive glimpse, then he had already been here—but in some near-distant future time. Not so strange; for time, as the Necroscope was well aware, is relative. But in any event he had no time to ponder it, for he was moving on. On through the jumble, seeming to drift in his dream-state over the debris of fallen ceiling stones which had been deliberately rearranged, laid in a rough-and-ready crazy-paving style to form a pathway or ways through the great maze. And because it seemed the safest way to go, Harry followed the main pathway.

And suddenly he was there, at his destination . . . his rendezvous? A place where the tiers of fallen slabs and columns of rock formed a natural if jumbled stairway up the inwards-curving wall of the cavern to a level area some eighteen feet wide by twelve deep, where stood—a table? An altar? Some kind of neolithic sarcophagus?

But Harry knew that his last "guess" was right, and that it hadn't been a guess; knew that he had been here before, and that indeed this solid-seeming block of stone standing central in the levelled, paved area under the alcove in the rough rock wall was . . . a massive stone coffin!

Now his sweat ran colder still; it stood out in droplets on his brow, and stuck his shirt to his back between his shoulder-blades. He paused to look around, to hold his breath, listen, absorb something of the atmosphere of the place. He had a feeling that he wasn't alone, and was offered evidence to confirm his suspicion; evidence, at least, that someone else had been here, and recently.

As dreams (even precognitive dreams) are wont to do, this one was unfolding itself sequentially, adding details along the way. Now Harry saw the torches—or became aware of them—in their brackets in the walls, and especially at the base of the great stone coffin. Oil or resin-soaked faggots, bedded in gaps in the flags of the floor, and burning so close to the sarcophagus that their flames were blackening its base.

And there was this sweet smell in the air. A scent remembered from . . . Zante? Or Samos? From the Greek Islands, definitely. It was in the smoke: a smell of . . . pine forests? Well, at least the torches accounted for the smoky atmosphere. As to who had set them burning: that would soon be made clear, Harry was certain. They would be back, those . . . worshipers? Those acolytes, anyway. Back to witness the "Great Return."

What? A Great Return?! The Necroscope grimaced and felt a strengthening of his resolve. Hah! The reanimation of an alien abomination, more like—the resurgence of an ancient evil. And that was why he was here: to prevent it! Moving more naturally now, but sweating still, and anxious, he commenced climbing the jumble of stone to the dais and sarcophagus—and was arrested by a mournful sound echoing in the confines of the great cave. Mournful, yes . . . a sobbing ululation . . . a howling! At which he felt the short hairs at the back of his neck stiffening in spontaneous recognition.

Time was short and Harry forced himself to climb faster. The steps leaned this way and that, some of them almost as tall as himself, so that he must actually and physically climb *them, and at each level adjust his stance and balance. But forty feet up the log jam of fallen blocks and toppled columns, finally he stood at the corner of the ominous mausoleum.*

Where the high dais backed up to the side of the cave the wall was formed of a series of black, near-vertical stacks compressed together into the almost crystalline forms of hexagonal columns. A horizontal fault had caused weak sections to topple, creating zig-zagging chimneys and, deeper still, cracks or windows passing right through the rock to the open air of the outside world. The rims of these vents or fissures were lined in pallid starlight, so that Harry imagined the entire cavern complex as located at the edge of a crumbling ravine. Except . . . he more than merely imagined it, he knew—

—That he was in fact in Scotland, somewhere in the high Grampians, the Cairngorms east of Kingussie!

The knowledge came . . . and was gone again, as quickly as that. But the Necroscope's urgency—those sensations of nameless anxiety—remained the same. And as a second bout of howling sounded, he gave a start, ran his tongue over dry lips and approached the great stone coffin. The heady smell of resin was much stronger here, curling up in the smoke from the torches at the base of the sarcophagus.

It was then, for the first time, that Harry noticed the "decorations" of two-inch diameter holes bored through the bottom edges of the four slabs that made up the coffin's sides. He saw them, and at once recognized their function: not merely as a crude decoration, but as outlets for the contents of the sarcophagus. There were six of them along the nine-foot-long coffin's front edge, and three along each of its almost five-foot-long end panels. Warmed to a thick fluidity by the heat of the torches, a glutinous yellow substance *was oozing from the rows of holes, dripping down the base of the sarcophagus, gradually filling the cracks in the paving and forming gluey puddles on the floor of the dais. And this substance was the true source of the evocative "scent"—warm resin, of course.*

The sarcophagus was almost five feet high; the Necroscope took up one of the central torches from its niche at the front of the great box, and leaned over to look inside. What with the gloom, the smoke, the heady reek and all, his eyes were watering badly; it was hard to make out the contents of the coffin. But the very terms he'd applied—"sarcophagus," and "coffin"—had in themselves been sufficient of a clue or forewarning. For what else would one expect to find in a tomb, but a corpse or corpses? Except, and as Harry Keogh was only too well aware, there are corpses and corpses.

The scattering of torches in the walls cast their flickering light down; the brand in Harry's hand set the surface of the translucent, semi-solid resin in the coffin glowing like burnished bronze; the vague outline of . . . of something, *but something grotesque almost beyond belief, suddenly became visible. Which was when what had started as a dream—a precognitive glimpse—turned into sheerest nightmare!*

The figure trapped in the resin was at least seven feet long, two and a half broad at the shoulders, and narrow at the waist and hip. Still only half-discernible but obviously a huge man, still there was that about it that smacked of the un-, the in*-human. It lay on its back, arms folded across its chest, and despite its dimensions Harry felt that it was somehow shriveled, reduced, as if time had taken its toll on it. As to the precise nature of the thing:*

Quite apart from the earlier phases of his dream, Harry was acquainted with the Wamphyri. Indeed the Necroscope knew more about vampires—real vampires—than any other man in the world. He had seen Dragosani at the end of their bloodfeud, in the fullness of his Wamphyri change, and he'd also been face to face with Yulian Bodescu, in the very flux of metamorphosis. He knew exactly *what a fully-fledged vampire looked like; that in fact it looked something like . . . like this! And yet this was like* nothing *he'd ever seen before. But one thing for certain: it exuded evil as surely as its great sarcophagus exuded pungent resin.*

And now it seemed the precognitive nature of the Necroscope's dream was over, and that purest nightmare was taking full sway. At least he hoped so; for if the rest *of it was a glimpse into his future, then he wanted none of it!*

Suddenly aware that shadows were creeping where no shadow had been, Harry stepped back from the sarcophagus, fell into a crouch and looked all about. There had been furtive movement, he was sure, there on the paved causeway where it passed under crazily tilting lintels . . . and in the shadows along the walls . . . and among the countless jumbles of fallen rock. Gray shadows, flowing, fleet-footed . . .

. . . And a renewed burst of howling, near-distant at first, but then answered from close at hand. Very close at hand!

Harry's left hand held up the flaring torch; his right was on the rim of the sarcophagus. And even as he looked again into the coffin, at the barely discernible yet unmistakable outline there, something came bubbling up out of the gluey mess to grab his wrist!

It wasn't a hand, or barely. Clawed, black, trembling and shriveled, yet strong with some inner fever, it was half-hand, half-paw, all horror! And it drew on Harry with an irresistible strength until in a moment he found himself half-over the stone side of the coffin and into the resin. But at the last his wits were returned to him, and drawing back with every ounce of his strength, finally he broke free of the thing that held him. Or rather, it broke free of its arm!

How Harry danced then, with the alien hand still clasped around his wrist, as he tried to disengage, free himself from that unearthly grip. But he'd hauled so hard that he'd dragged the owner of the shriveled claw erect in its great coffin. And, God help him, the triangular eyes in its resin-dripping, half-mummified head were slowly opening . . . and its dog's jaws were splitting apart in a monstrous grin!

"Jesus! Jesus!" *Harry yelped as the Thing reached for him. And:*

"Jesus?" *it replied, its awful voice a surprised cough, a snarl, a bubbling-up of centuries-trapped phlegm and mucus. And tilting its head sardonically on one side:* "Ah, no, not Jesus!" *it told him.* "If you would call me anything, call me Lykan . . . Lord Lykan, of the Wamphyri! Or perhaps, in your case—" *(its great arms were folding him in, while its eyes blazed like yellow lanterns, branding his soul as it growled),* "—in your case I shall make an exception. Aye, for it were best if *you* call me . . . father?"

Harry did no such thing. Starting awake he called out for his Ma, all mud and bones and weeds in her watery grave nearly four hundred miles away in Scotland. For cold and terrible as *she* might seem (to anyone else), she was the warmest, safest thing in Harry's world.

But as has often been stated, the future is a most devious, difficult thing, and not much given to displaying itself to common curiosity. Even the Necroscope, the least common of men, could not be allowed to know or remember too much. And as is frequently the way of it with dreams, this one was already fading from the eye of memory. In a moment all that remained of it was the *fear* of it, whatever it had been. That and the cold sweat, and Harry's tumbled bedclothes.

And his sweet mother's anxious query, sighing in his metaphysical mind across all the miles between: *What is it, son?*

Harry stopped panting, took a deep breath and let it out slowly, and told her, *Nothing, Ma. Just a dream, that's all. A nightmare.*

And: *Well,* she said after a little while, *and isn't it to be expected?* (He could picture her troubled frown.) *After all, you've known some strange times, Harry.* Oh, yes, she was right there! And there were also times when the Necroscope's Ma was the very master (or mistress) of understatement. But:

Strange times, yes, Harry answered quietly, wryly.

Then, in a moment, seeing her son was all right, she was lighter at heart. *When will you come to see me, Harry? You've always a home here with me, you know.* Her words might easily have chilled another man to the bone, but Harry felt only her warmth.

Soon, I think, he told her. *Pretty soon. But right now . . .* He sighed and shivered a little, for the sweat of fear was beginning to dry on him. *Oh, you know . . . there are problems.*

He sensed her nod of understanding. *There always will be problems, Harry, among the living. And, as you know well enough, even among the dead! But whenever, I'll be waiting here, knowing that soon you'll be close to me . . .*

Her incorporeal voice faded slowly away.

Problems among the living, and among the Great Majority. And all too often their problems were Harry's. His nightmare had disappeared completely now, forgotten, sunk back into the depths of his subconscious mind . . . but however briefly, his mother's words had struck a chord there.

Problems among the living and the dead.

And . . . the undead?

BUT WHERE IS HARRY KEOGH?

ER, HARRY?"

Darcy Clarke stuck his head round the door of the Necroscope's E-Branch "suite": a long, narrow room, really, fitted out like a small hotel room for Harry's convenience, until he could find the time and opportunity to look round for a place for himself and his family in London . . . *if* he could convince his wife to stay. Right now, though, the way it was going with Brenda and all, Clarke considered it a hell of a big if . . .

In fact, in years gone by when this entire top-floor complex had belonged to the hotel below, Harry's apartment had *been* one of the rooms. In front, it was simply an overnight bedroom some four or five paces square. At the rear, partitioned behind a sliding door, there was a wash-basin, a shower and WC. The floor space of the main room was occupied along one wall by a computer console with a swivel-chair and space beneath for the operator's feet; it was of little or no use to the Necroscope, who had his own unique ways of solving problems. In a corner a wardrobe stood open. Some items of Harry's clothing were hanging there; others lay folded on shelving to one side.

Harry had been about to shave. He wore a towel round his waist and foam on his face, and was leaning over the wash-basin with a plastic shaver in his hand. And he looked just a little sick: pale and sick and tired. *Well,* Darcy thought, *he's looked pale ever since I've known him . . . ever since I've known him as Harry, anyway!* Because of course that had only been for seventeen months; but he'd once known him a lot longer than that as someone else. It was that previous person whom Darcy was looking at now—on the outside, at least.

Harry was only twenty-one, but his body (or Alec's) was ten years older. The Necroscope's hair was russet-brown, plentiful and naturally wavy; but even in the last few months a lot of the luster had disappeared, and the odd strand of gray hair had appeared among the brown in the temples. His eyes too were honey-brown; very wide, very intelligent, and (strange beyond words) very innocent! Even now, for all they'd seen—for all that he'd experienced and learned—they were innocent. Darcy knew it could be argued, however, that certain murderers have the same look. But in Harry the innocence was mainly genuine. He hadn't asked to be what he was, or to be called upon to do the things he'd done—but he *had* done them.

His teeth were strong, not quite white, a little uneven; they were set in a mouth that was unusually sensitive but could also be cruel, caustic. He had a high brow, a straight nose, cheeks that seemed just a fraction sunken. Not surprising, that last, for the Necroscope had lost weight. Alec Kyle had been perhaps too well-fleshed—once. With his height it hadn't mattered much. Not to Alec, whose work in E-Branch had been in large part sedentary. But it mattered to Harry Keogh. It had been bad enough carrying around those extra years, let alone the extra weight! He was trying to find time to get his new body in training, bring it to its best possible condition. *He'd be better off,* Clarke thought, *if he got his mind sorted out first!* He suspected Harry's mind must feel something like a nervous cat in a new house—prowling around and trying to get used to the layout. But it was already more than a year.

"What is it, Darcy?" the Necroscope asked, his voice listless as his looks—listless, but not lost. The man might be little more than a boy, but still he carried a lot of mileage. And his tone of voice, the depth of his penetrating gaze, his obvious intelligence, carried a whole world of authority.

But his looks, Harry Keogh's *looks!* They were the stumbling block, and not only for Clarke but for every esper in the Branch. The fact that each time they spoke to Harry—or even thought of him—it was on the tip of every tongue to call him Alec, just as Clarke had barely avoided doing a moment ago. And this despite that he'd been deliberately rehearsing to himself, *Harry, Harry, Harry,* all the way down the corridor.

Clarke forced himself back to earth. "It's late," he said. "And, well, one or two of the gang just happened to mention you mightn't be . . . you know, feeling too good?" He came in, closed the door behind him and sat on Harry's tumbled bed.

The Necroscope gave a shrug of his shoulders and offered a mirthless, *"Huh!* They just 'happened' to mention it, right? I mean, it's not that these espers of yours have been into my mind or anything. Hell no! But they just kind of 'suspected' I might be a bit down this morning." He frowned and gave a snort of derision. "Christ, give it a *rest,* can't you, Darcy! I mean, surely you know I've been feeling them groping away in my head morning, noon and night every day for well over a year now!"

Clarke flopped his hands uselessly. "But they're . . . well, *espers,* Harry!" he said, making it sound like an apology. "And they do manage to keep their talents pretty much to themselves. I mean, we have our code, you know? But we can't help worrying about you . . ." *Or thinking about you, and about Alec. Wondering what kind of a freak you are; how you feel about it. And what about that poor girl downstairs; how she feels. Because we told her you were dead! And now you're alive, but no longer you! And as for Alec, he's gone forever. We know how it was—you've told us how it was, and Ben Trask has corroborated it—but we wonder anyway . . .* The Ben Trask of Clarke's silent reflections was another Branch operative, a human lie-detector.

The Necroscope looked at Clarke and he looked back: at a man he'd known as the precog Alec Kyle. Or rather, he looked at the *shape* of Kyle with

Harry's mind in it. And so back to that again: a complete fuck-up of a situation! And Clarke thinking: *But if it can fuck me up like this, what must it be doing to him and his family?*

Clarke continued to look at Harry where he'd scraped the first tentative swath through the foam—and where he'd immediately stopped shaving, and was now staring at his reflection in the mirror over the bowl. Clarke couldn't possibly *know* what the Necroscope was thinking (telepathy wasn't Darcy's talent), but he could take a stab at it: *Looking at himself and wondering who he was . . . and where he was! Knowing that in fact the Russians would have cut the real him up long ago, to study his guts and brains. And that they'd have done a far more thorough job of it—and certainly a more clinical one—than the necromancer Boris Dragosani had ever done on one of his victims.*

Trying to concentrate on what he was doing, Harry crooked his mouth and said, "You know, sometimes when I cut myself I'm surprised it hurts? It's true: I'm having to learn to be a lot more careful with myself. It's like when you borrow a book out of a library: you don't much care how you handle it because it isn't yours. Except this time it isn't like that, because now it *is* mine and I have to look after it. And I'm not just talking about a book but a body: *my* body, now! And not even a snowball in hell's chance that I'll ever get another. So I have to take care of it—despite that I don't much *care* for the damn thing!"

He finished shaving: a patchy job, but he hadn't actually cut himself. Tossing the shaver into the basin, he splashed his face, patted it dry, and stepped into the bedroom. And letting the towel fall paradoxically *unselfconsciously* from around his waist, as he started to dress he asked: "So what do you think? How do we look, Darcy?" Darcy knew it wasn't a so-called royal we. The Necroscope was asking about the two of him.

Well, of course, the recently elected Head of Branch could lie, but he chose not to. "How do you look?" He shook his head in unfeigned concern. "Not too good, Harry. In fact, you look like shit!"

And finally Harry had to grin. *He* looked like shit. This from Darcy Clarke! Not that Darcy looked like shit, no—but then again he didn't look like much of anything! For Darcy was possibly the world's most nondescript man. Nature had made up for this physical anonymity, however, by equipping him with an almost unique talent. He was a deflector: the opposite of accident-prone. Only let him stray too close to danger, and something, some parapsychological guardian angel, would intervene on his behalf. He had no control over the thing; indeed he was only ever aware of it if he stared deliberately in the face of danger. Or occasionally when danger came creeping up on him.

The talents of the others—telepathy, scrying, precognition, oneiromancy, lie-detecting—were more pliable, applicable, obedient; but not Darcy's. It just did its own thing, which was to look after him. It had no other use. But because it ensured Darcy's longevity, it made him the perfect man for the job. Continuity was important in E-Branch. The anomaly was this: that he himself didn't quite believe in it until he felt it working. He still switched off the current before he would even change a light bulb! But maybe that was just another example of the thing at work.

To look at Darcy Clarke, then, no one would ever suspect he could be the boss of anything—let alone head of the most secret branch of the British Secret

Services! A job that Darcy hoped against hope he'd soon be able to hand over to Harry. Of middle-height, mousy-haired, showing early signs of a slight stoop and a small paunch, he was middling in just about every way. He had sort of neutral-hazel eyes in a face not much given to laughter, and an intense mouth which you just *might* remember if you remembered nothing else, but other than that there was a general facelessness about him which made Darcy instantly forgettable. Even the way he dressed was . . . conservative.

And indeed looking at him, Harry thought: *He's a very ordinary, extraordinary man!* And however much the Necroscope might dislike the situation, it was a very difficult thing to dislike someone like Darcy Clarke. So: "What's on the menu for today?" he asked him, glancing at his watch. It was 9:45 and Darcy was right: it was late. By now, the rest of E-Branch would be buzzing. But before Darcy could reply to Harry's first question, he followed it up with: "And what about Brenda? Did you see her yet this morning?"

"We had breakfast together, downstairs," Darcy answered. "She's . . . well, fine." But he didn't seem too sure about it. And more hurriedly, eager to change the subject: "The baby is just beautiful! I mean, he's really coming along . . ."

Harry stared hard at him. Right now he wasn't interested in the baby. "She still doesn't want to see me, right?"

Darcy flapped his hands. "Harry, it's only been—"

"—A year and a half," the Necroscope cut him off. And he was right. Time had flown.

"Okay," Darcy nodded. "But give Brenda—give *yourself*—a little more time! I mean if you, we, aren't used to this yet, how can you expect her to be? She's just a girl, and she went through a hell of a lot."

The Necroscope continued to stare hard at him for a long time, then nodded, shrugged, gave a deep sigh. Darcy was right, he knew. Life had to go on, and Harry's life for the moment was here at E-Branch. He had to involve himself, become part of it. He'd be okay as long as there was something to do. Well, apart from these endless fucking debriefings!

It was as if Darcy had read his thoughts. "We think there may be work for you, Harry," he said, beginning to breathe easier as he sensed the Necroscope's spring winding down a little. "Work that should suit you right down to the ground."

But Harry only wondered: *And below it?*

Much in accord with Harry's own deliberations, it was the general consensus of opinion in the Branch that if they could keep the Necroscope busy, it would be best for him and everyone else concerned. They had a telepath, Trevor Jordan, who despite the mainly unspoken Branch code occasionally came into contact with Harry's jumbled, anxious thoughts; a locator, Ken Layard, whose talent drew him to the Necroscope like a moth to a lantern, so that his mind kept bumping into him; and an empath, Ray Betts, who couldn't help but sense the Necroscope's overwrought emotions. But these were only the special cases; *every* E-Branch member was affected by Harry's presence one way or another. For to a man or woman, and in their own ways, all Branch operatives were talented, and all must feel for a fellow psychic.

They knew what the Necroscope was; they were aware of his awesome, even frightening powers. But they also knew what Harry had done for them, for the world, and how he was paying for it. If they could keep him with them, keep him working, it could be he'd eventually get over the multiple traumas of past and present. Certainly he was the type who worked best under pressure. Making use of a case that only the Necroscope could possibly handle, Darcy Clarke was about to apply just such pressure. In his office at the end of the corridor, the recently appointed Head of Branch waved Harry into a chair and told him, "This . . . could be a nasty one."

Harry nodded and said drily, "*My* kind of work, right?" He waited for Darcy to get on with it. But before he could begin:

The intercom came cracklingly alive and blurted an urgent, "Sir?" Simultaneously, an alert button on Darcy's console began flashing red. Keying all-points connections with the Duty Officer, he said:

"What is it?"

"One for us, I think." The DO's voice was tense.

"Put it on screen," Darcy answered. And a moment later his desk screen displayed a communication from the Minister Responsible. Harry, seated opposite, saw Darcy's jaw drop as his face almost visibly paled. *"Christ!"* Darcy hissed.

The Necroscope stood up, paced to Darcy's side of the desk, glanced at the screen:

Origination: MinRes.
Destination: Director INTESP.
Duty Officer INTESP.
All Agents INTESP.

IRA Alert! A few minutes ago the Metropolitan Police received anonymous advance warning that a device will be planted in Oxford St., set to detonate at 10:25 today. Any chance you can do something, Mr. Clarke? Sorry for short notice. No reply required—action will suffice . . .

"Your Minister Responsible has a sense of humor!" Harry's tone was dry. Then . . . the Necroscope blinked, staggered, and grabbed the edge of the desk to steady himself! Darcy scarcely noticed; made breathless by haste, he was already getting back to the DO:

"Is Trevor Jordan in?"

"He's on it," came the immediate answer. "I caught him on his way to the office and diverted him."

"I'm on it, too," Darcy snapped. "But no one else! Get me a car, then get in here and take over."

"There's a car waiting out back."

As Darcy left his chair and headed for the door, the Necroscope said, "How about me?"

Darcy skidded to a halt, whirled around. "No way! There's only one you, Harry, and this is—"

"—Dangerous?" Harry was himself again; he grinned, however coldly. "I've seen a lot worse places than Oxford Street, Darcy."

Darcy shook his head. Speaking rapidly but precisely, he said, "*You* can be hurt, Harry. You can be killed! But with me, it's not very likely. My talent won't even let me get close to that bomb, which means I can help the police find it. Where my legs won't take me, that's ground zero! As for Trevor Jordan: he knows the risks—but he also knows the mind of just about every IRA bomber working in England! If this bloke's still out there on the street, Trev can probably find him. But you—"

He might have gone on, but Harry held up a hand. "You've made your point. Don't let me hold you up."

In the next moment, Darcy had wheeled and disappeared out into the corridor. In his wake he left an old-fashioned wooden coat-stand teetering where he'd grabbed his overcoat. It swayed first one way, then the other. It might even have toppled; but coming from nowhere, a sudden swirl of air straightened it up.

The door hadn't yet slammed shut behind Darcy's back; his running footsteps were still echoing in the corridor; his communications screen still carried the Minister Responsible's cry for help. But already his office was quite empty.

Against Darcy Clarke's orders, against all logic, and definitely against commonsense, the Necroscope had taken a Möbius shortcut to Oxford Street. For to Harry it didn't feel like he was putting *himself* at risk at all. And he could hardly be putting Alec Kyle at risk, now could he? For Kyle was already dead . . . wasn't he?

And his talent, too?

But if so, then what was it Harry had seen, experienced, in the moment after reading the Minister Responsible's message on the viewscreen? How to explain what had come and gone in the briefest possible time, like a crack of lightning illuminating some secret part of his brain and causing him to stagger?

For he'd seen . . . a Möbius door, *but horizontal!* A Möbius door, shimmering, hovering lengthwise in mid-air, superimposed on reality. Then, as quickly as it had come, the extraordinary vision had disappeared. But in its split-second existence, the Necroscope had seen the door shaken, had seen it writhing like a ring of smoke in a sudden draft—

—And he'd seen what it vomited, like some monstrous volcano, high into the suddenly darkening sky!

Harry scarcely knew London at all. Despite that the Necroscope was much, far, and extremely strangely traveled, London hadn't been an extensive part of his itinerary. He had visited Oxford Street, however, and so knew several co-ordinates; enough that he wouldn't emerge in the middle of the road in heavy traffic, anyway. Not that that ever happened; in doubt, he could always look out through his exit door before stepping through it. But as for the street itself, its junctions, idiosyncrasies—its "personality"—he really didn't know one end from the other.

He emerged in the entrance of a shoe store perhaps midway along the street. An extremely tall man in spectacles, leaving the shop in a hurry, bumped into him, looked surprised, and at once apologized. But Harry was already looking around, getting the feel of things.

It was mid-week but there were plenty of people about. Up and down the street, he saw policemen; already they were thick on the ground. And somewhere out there would be Trevor Jordan, probably in the company of a couple of plain-clothes officers. As for Darcy Clarke: he wouldn't even have reached his car yet. But once at the driving wheel he'd be here before you could say boo! And he'd very probably be mad at Harry, who couldn't even say why he'd come here against good advice.

A sign said Hyde Park to the west, Oxford Circus, Holborn, and Central to the east. Looking along the street toward Hyde Park, Harry saw that police activity was hotting up. There was no panic as yet, but things were happening: barriers appearing as if from nowhere, being dragged across the road; traffic being diverted, stopped from coming this way. Wherefore the suspect area must lie to the east, toward the city center.

Sure enough, in the direction of Holborn, traffic and pedestrians alike were being diverted off the main road down side streets, and several of the police down there were using loud-hailers. A great many of the people on the street seemed used to it all; they began to move a little faster but were still mainly unhurried. Most of them looked irritated by the disruption of their everyday routines, but were nevertheless obedient to the law as police activity grew in proportion to the number of officers arriving on the scene. On the other hand, some paid little or no attention to it all but went about their business as if there were no interference whatsoever.

A string of six red-robed Hari Krishna types with shaved, bowed heads, beads galore, and their arms folded up their wide sleeves went single-file, in an almost mechanical pitter-patter shuffle, along the pavement. With their heads down like that—the way they seemed intent upon their own feet and moving with that rapid, rhythmic, apparently blind locomotion—it astonished Harry that they somehow managed to avoid collision with anyone or thing in their way! Their leader, and the one bringing up the rear, carried tiny golden bells that chimed in time to their precise, almost clockwork motion . . .

Except Harry wasn't here as an observer of life but as a foil against death. Fine, but how to go about it? So he stood there undecided, until a young policeman of about his own age approached and said, "Best to get well away from the barriers, sir. We'll be clearing the whole street in a little while."

Harry looked him in the eye and said, "Look, some friends of mine—E-Branch people, Trevor Jordan and Darcy Clarke?—are helping you blokes out. Now, it's possible you never heard of these people, but your seniors very definitely have. Since I fancy my friends are a lot closer to the action than I am right now, that's where I need to be. So I'd be obliged if you would, well, direct me? Where's it all happening?"

Listening to Harry, the policeman had at first looked surprised; then his eyes had taken on a blank expression; now they went hard and his eyebrows came together in a frown. "E-Branch? Sorry, pal, but you're right: I never heard of it. Press, d'you mean? But in any case, and since it isn't in my orders, I have to ask you to move on."

The pavement was still alive with people. Harry pointed at them, saying, "What, just me? I mean . . . can't you get this lot moving first? What about the Hari Krishna types?"

Now the young officer was really ruffled. His lips tightened and he said, "Look, *chummy,* we have to start somewhere and you're it! So just leave out all the lip and move your backside out of here!"

Harry refused to display his annoyance. He simply nodded, conjured a Möbius door and stepped through it. He wasn't there any more. The young officer started to say, "And if I can give you a word of advice . . ." and stopped short. He wasn't speaking to anyone and people were starting to look at him. He turned a couple of stiff-legged, complete circles, looked for Harry and failed to find him, finally shuffled sideways into a shop doorway and out of sight . . .

The Necroscope emerged from the Möbius Continuum at the junction of Oxford Street and Regent Street, and knew that he must be pretty close to the venue. Policemen in uniform were everywhere, working frantically to clear the street. Glancing at his watch, Harry saw the reason why: it was 10:16. If indeed a bomb had been planted, it was due to explode in something less than nine minutes' time.

Caught in a crush of people being shepherded down Regent Street, he stepped to one side and looked about. Then, just as he was about to be caught up again, he spotted Trevor Jordan on a traffic island in urgent conversation with two uniformed senior policemen. Sidestepping the cordon, he ran toward Jordan, shouting, "Trevor, can I be of help?"

Jordan saw him and quickly spoke to the inspectors; one of them waved off a policeman who was hot on Harry's heels. And as he skidded to a halt, Harry was apologetic. "I . . . just thought it might be a good idea to be in on this," he gulped.

Jordan shrugged and said, "Right now I don't see what you can do, but since you're here . . ." He shrugged again. Jordan was the easygoing sort generally, but it was obvious from his tone of voice that in the current situation he saw the Necroscope as an encumbrance. There weren't any dead people to talk to here . . . not just yet, anyway.

A seasoned if occasionally variable telepath, Jordan was thirty-two years old. His looks fitted his character precisely: he *was* usually transparent, open as a favorite book. It was as if he personally would like to be as readable to others as they were to him; as if he were trying to make some sort of physical compensation for his metaphysical talent. His face reflected this attitude: oval, fresh, open and almost boyish. He had lank mousy hair falling forward above gray eyes, and a crooked mouth that straightened out whenever he was worried or annoyed. Mostly, people liked him; having the advantage of knowing it if someone *didn't* like him, Jordan would simply avoid that person. But, rangy and athletic, it was a mistake to misread his obvious sensitivity; there was plenty of determination in him, too.

Harry asked him: "Is this where it will happen?" He scanned all about, trying to work out what was going on.

In his time (just seventeen months ago), the Necroscope had been the author of a considerable amount of bombing of his own, but he told himself that

that had been different and even necessary. Or was it all in the eye of the be-holder? Well, maybe, except this wasn't a nest of mind-spy thugs and megaloma-niacs in some nightmare-riddled château in the USSR, but a busy thoroughfare in the heart of London. The people who could get involved, hurt, killed here, were innocent of any crime other than being here. And there were still far too many of them.

A flood of shoppers was even now issuing from stores both east and west, adding to the crushes down Regent, Portland and New Bond Streets. And police activity had grown even more urgent. There were dog-handlers, with sniffers straining at their leads; loud-hailers boomed to left and right, issuing raucous instructions; motorists were leaving their blocked-in cars and hurrying on foot in what they hoped was the safest direction.

"Chaos!" Harry said, guessing that Jordan hadn't answered his question because he didn't know.

"The name of the game, sir," one of the police inspectors harshly an-swered. "The three D's. To cause as much disruption, death and destruction as inhumanly possible. Chaos, yes. But if you're with Mr. Clarke's Branch—and if this is new to you—where've you been?"

"Oh, places," Harry looked at him in a certain way of his, and was glad that Alec Kyle had been the sort who kept himself to himself. And turning to Jordan: "There are only six minutes left, and people all over the place!"

But Trevor Jordan wasn't listening. He was half-collapsed in the back of a squad car parked on the traffic island, with a pained expression on his face and his hands to the sides of his head. The policemen looked at each other, went to question him. Harry stopped them, saying, "He's at work. Leave him."

The police cordon in Regent Street had let a car through the crush. It slewed across the road, bumped up onto the traffic island alongside the squad car. And Darcy Clarke got out. He saw Harry at once and began to protest, "Jesus, Harry—!"

But the Necroscope had gone down on one knee beside Jordan, who was muttering: "It's . . . it has to be . . . Sean!"

"Sean?" Harry gripped his shoulder, stared hard into his squeezed-up face.

"Sean Milligan," Darcy hissed in Harry's ear. "He's one of their best, or worst!"

"Armed," Jordan gasped. "And with more than just a bomb! He . . . he hasn't primed it yet. Too many police around. Sean knows he'll be spotted, knows they'll get him. He's thinking of . . . of creating a diversion. Yes, that's it, a diversion!" Jordan's eyes blazed open. "Oh, fuck! *Now* he's primed it!"

"Primed!" Darcy snapped at the two officers, who at once turned away and began speaking into walkie-talkies. Up on the roof of a building, Harry caught the glint of metal as a marksman took his position behind a parapet.

"Primed, yes . . ." Jordan's eyes were squeezed tightly shut again, and sweat rivered his face. "And he's set the timer for . . . just one and a half minutes!"

"God!" Darcy was trembling; he looked like he might make a run for it, which told him—and Harry Keogh—a lot.

"Trevor," the Necroscope spoke softly. "With only ninety seconds left, Sean has to be on the move. Which way's he heading?"

But Darcy Clarke babbled, "Oh, I can tell you that!"

And Harry continued to speak to Jordan: "Has he still got the bomb?"

"Yes!" Jordan's gasped answer, as he squeezed his temples more yet. "But he knows he must get rid of it, and now! Jesus, fifteen pounds of semtex!"

"Christ!" Darcy suddenly yelped. "Let me in the car. I've got to get *out* of here!" He made to scramble for his car, tripped and went sprawling across the back of the police vehicle.

And it happened. A tall thin man with a pale, badly pock-marked face, wearing a loosely flapping overcoat and carrying a sausage-shaped holdall, came at a run down the middle of the road. Jordan looked up, saw him, yelped: "Sean!" And the recognition was mutual. Not that Milligan recognized Trevor Jordan, but seeing the squad car, the senior policemen, and three civilians all grouped on the traffic island—and all staring at him—he did know that he'd been made.

The right-hand side of his coat went back and the snout of an ugly, short-barrelled machine-pistol swung into view. Harry sensed hasty movement on a roof, the re-alignment of a weapon; Milligan sensed it, too, and the gun in his hand swept up, his thin lips drew back, and both he and his machine-pistol snarled their abuse! Bullets chewed the high parapet of the building, causing the marksman up there to duck down out of sight. And over the chatter of Milligan's gun, Harry heard Jordan cry out:

"Getaway! He's looking for the getaway car!"

Milligan was maybe forty feet away, pointing his gun here, there, everywhere, trying to choose a main target. A secondary crowd of people had come bursting out of a large store onto the street, but they weren't a threat to the IRA man. On the other hand, the sausage-shaped holdall in his hand was definitely a threat to them. And it was rapidly becoming one to Sean Milligan, too.

As the Necroscope glanced again at his watch and saw that there was something less than a minute to go, two things happened. Darcy Clarke had finally got into his car, started the motor, and was making to drive away. His car had just lurched off the traffic island onto the street when a second car, low, dark, fast and mean, came careening through a traffic barrier in a tangle of twisted metal. The two vehicles collided; Darcy's car was thrown back onto the traffic island and the rogue car glanced off, smashed through a pair of bollards, mounted the curb and nose-dived through a store window. Sean Milligan wouldn't be making his getaway after all.

He knew it, and it was time to apply the crazed logic of the total terrorist. The sniper on the roof couldn't get off a shot at Sean because of the people on the street; Sean had to get rid of his holdall in the next twenty seconds and then make one hell of a run for it, but first he had to get these people out of his fucking way and he couldn't shoot them all. He aimed his gun at the parapet hiding the sniper, pulled the trigger and stitched the wall of the building with a tracery of bullets. Then, as the milling people scrambled for cover, Sean chose his target. Not so difficult, for there was only one target after all: the City Center itself, and what could only be a bunch of top-ranking officials and police officers.

By now he should have been shot dead, and he knew that, too. Which meant there were no armed policemen on the ground in the immediate vicinity. So maybe he stood a slight chance after all . . . *if* there was still time.

Panting, sweating, cursing, he ran toward the group on the traffic island

and, pivoting like a discus-thrower, whirled the holdall. Which was when he saw Harry Keogh. Harry had come forward onto the road, putting himself between his friends and Sean Milligan. Still pivoting, preparing to release his deadly missile, Sean let rip with a burst of wild fire from his gun.

Harry had guessed how the other would react; he'd already conjured a Möbius door between himself and Milligan. Stray bullets ripped past him, but Sean's arc of fire was restricted by the door, which no one else but the Necroscope could see. The main stream of bullets crossed the threshold and passed right out of this universe. While up on the roof, the sniper finally had Milligan in his sights and fired one hurried shot.

Hit in the hip, the IRA man tripped and went flying. Him and his holdall both, flying right in through Harry's door!

And the Necroscope knew what he must do. If he simply collapsed the door there'd be questions, because people just don't vanish into thin air like that. But Harry had a picture in his mind that he couldn't shift, which told him how it must be. And with only three seconds to go, he tilted the door on its side.

His mind wrestled with the alien, metaphysical math of the thing . . . and won! And as if the invisible door's top edge were hinged, it swung upward through ninety degrees into the horizontal. And the Necroscope hurled himself backward away from it as it blew!

Fifteen pounds of semtex in the Möbius Continuum, a place where even thoughts have weight, and a spoken word can be deafening. And only the frail however savage shell of a human body to take the blast. With one exception it was exactly as it had been during that split-second of precognition in Darcy Clarke's office; the exception was sound. For even though the Continuum acted as a baffle, still there came the subdued roar of the explosion, as the immaterial frame of the door buckled and warped and finally blinked out of existence.

But not before the Continuum had rid itself of a hideous contamination, and a jet of wet red stinking human debris had erupted like a volcano, flinging the guts and brains and shit and shattered bones of a man up and outward against the high walls and windows of the street.

And then the slimy, spattering rain, that smelled of cordite and copper and many a crime corrected . . .

It was over but as yet the street was still and strangely silent. Street-cleaning vehicles had been ordered up and were on their way; somewhere in the near-distance police and ambulance sirens wailed their unmistakable dirges; a handful of unfortunate uniformed officers were picking up . . . whatever pieces were large enough to be gathered off the street. A man, staggering and bloody, was being led away from a shattered store window, where the rear of his car stuck up at an odd angle.

"You," one of the police inspectors said to Harry, with a hand on his shoulder, "are a hell of a lucky man. You were the closest to it when that bomb went off." But suddenly his voice was very quiet. "What did you . . . see? I mean exactly what was it that *happened* there?" Carefully, he dabbed specks of blood and other matter from his forehead.

Darcy Clarke was fully recovered. Breaking into the conversation with what he hoped would be a useful lie, he said, "I saw everything. When Sean was shot he fell on top of his hold all. Then there came the explosion. His body muffled the sound but took the full force of the blast. He just . . . flew apart."

Harry nodded. "Something like that," he said. "Actually, I was looking away from it."

As luck would have it, most of them had been looking away from it. But behind the parapet wall of a tall building, white-faced and wondering, a police marksman examined his weapon and thought, *what the hell . . . ?* For it was one thing to shoot at a man, but quite another to hit him and see him fall—and then watch him disappear right out of this world!

Not fifty feet away from the group on the traffic island, Harry's Krishna types huddled in a shop doorway. For once immobilized, they stared at the scene of what could have been an enormous disaster. Harry saw them looking. Their sandals might have been stilled for once, but their slanted eyes were still full of the action that had been, and that they'd seen. One of them—their leader?—was lowering a camera. Harry couldn't help wondering what he'd been photographing, and why . . .

Amazingly, Darcy's car looked like it might still drive, however dangerously. The senior lawmen seemed uncertain about it, but before they could advise Darcy against it he'd bundled the Necroscope and Trevor Jordan inside and driven off. On the way to E-Branch HQ, he said, "It seems we should never underestimate you, Harry. I don't know what you did, or how you did it, but I do know it was you."

And Jordan said, "My telepathy seems like a toy by comparison!"

"We all played our parts," Harry shrugged. "We've worked together before, and it's starting to look like we make a good team." But before they could misinterpret that, and perhaps his future intentions, he added: "Well, *this* time it worked out, at least."

Darcy made a derisory noise in his nose. "But sometimes I feel like such a . . . such a bloody *coward*, that's all!"

"I shouldn't if I were you," Jordan told him. "Oh, it was Harry who saved the day, right enough, but was it *all* him? How do you know he wasn't prompted by that guardian angel of yours, Darcy, taking care of you as always?"

Which gave them all something to think about on their way home . . .

Back in Darcy's office, after he and Harry had cleaned up and things were quieter, the Head of E-Branch took up the conversation with Harry where it had been interrupted by the Minister Responsible's call for help:

"Harry, we know that we can't overload you. By that I mean we know you could give us the solution to every unsolved murder there's ever been, certainly to the ones where the victims knew their murderer. Except—"

"—Where they *know* their murderers, you mean," Harry cut in, correcting him.

And Darcy knew he was right. For Harry was the Necroscope and talked to dead men. To him, when a man died, he didn't just stop. His *body* stopped, yes, but his mind went on. And Harry's talent gave him access to such incorporeal minds. Any ordinary policeman must find clues, discover evidence to bring a killer to justice. But Harry could have it "straight from the horse's mouth," as it were. To him the dead weren't, well, departed—not all the way—but moved aside. As if they were in another room, where he could speak to them across the threshold of his amazing talent. He could simply *ask* a victim who had done it!

. . . Or perhaps not so simply. No, definitely not simply. This thing he had was almost unique; it would still *be* unique, if Harry Jr. hadn't come along. Which was the problem in a nutshell: how do you use a unique talent to best effect? For example, you surely wouldn't employ Albert Einstein as an accountant! And what of the Necroscope, Harry Keogh? In a world where brutal murders and terrorist atrocities were now "commonplace" crimes (God help us), Harry might easily find them his life's work! Was that why he had been born into this world and time? His only reason for being? Was that *all?* Darcy thought not.

"What I'm saying," he continued, "is that you—we, the Branch—can't be expected to do the work of the police. Well, not all of their work. We do some: a lot of big-time crime, or the occasional case that's so abhorrent someone *has* to be made to pay for it. Or sometimes an 'urgent' job, like today's thing in Oxford Street. But in the main we're spies . . . mind-spies. It isn't so much individuals we protect as the country, our way of life—'western civilization,' if you like—from forces that oppose it. But I know you've heard all of this before, and from someone far more eloquent . . ."

Harry nodded, knowing that Darcy meant Sir Keenan Gormley, first Head of E-Branch, who had recruited him into the service. By coincidence, that had been just such a case. Abhorrent, yes, to say the least . . . for Boris Dragosani had butchered him! But without Sir Keenan, without having spoken to his remains, Harry might never have gone on to his discovery of the Möbius Continuum, and to his *re*-discovery of life, in the brain-dead body of Alex Kyle. Except he *must* stop thinking of it in that way, because Kyle was no more while he, Harry Keogh . . . was.

"So currently you're worried I might think that this job of yours, whatever it is, is beneath me, too mundane," he said. "You think I might reckon it's just a red herring to divert my mind from other, more personal problems—and that's probably exactly what it is! But you and I are on the same side in more ways than you think, Darcy. The fact is, I *need* this job, whatever it turns out to be. That's why I got myself involved down in Oxford Street today—yes, I know, against your best advice—because it was a diversion . . . Well, and maybe for a couple of other reasons, too. Okay, so this other job you're talking about is no big deal. At least it will keep me busy. That's my reasoning, anyway. And it's yours, too, I fancy. So why don't we just get on with it?"

Darcy nodded, seemed relieved. "Okay. But it isn't just a coincidence that I mentioned the police. This time they've actually asked us for our help. Oh, we get requests from them . . . fine! Like today, when they know we have someone who can help. I'm talking about Jordan, whom they've used frequently enough in the past. But even to the top brass in the police he's just someone with a weird knack, a lucky guesser. That's how they view us: as a pack of fortune-tellers, literally 'psychics' in the popular or worst possible meaning of the word. As if they see us sitting around a table holding seances or something—which isn't too far from the truth, I suppose! Anyway, we're always their last resort."

"But not this time," Harry nodded. "Because this time . . . is it something that involves the police directly?"

Darcy looked him straight in the eye. "Right. It's because they're getting murdered, Harry. By a madman. And I mean *literally*, a genuine dyed-in-the-wool lunatic! A serial killer with a grudge against policemen."

The Necroscope thought about it, and finally said: "There must be a lot of people holding grudges against the police."

"Just about every criminal in the book," Darcy answered. "That's what makes it so hard to catch the bastard! The files are crammed with people this could be. Suspects? Everyone who ever committed a violent crime! And thirteen thousand reported in the last twelve months! So you see, this could be the break we've been looking for with the police. We already have a good record of co-operation with Special Branch and the other secret services, but we were never on a sure-footing with the common-or-garden 'Bobby' on the beat. If we can show them that we've really got something here, not just an old lady called Madame Zaza with a crystal ball in a Gypsy caravan . . . I mean, there could be all sorts of weird stuff the police bump into and we never get to hear about it. This could be a breakthrough."

"Weird stuff? I thought you said this was mundane."

"No, *you* did. If you want to call grotesque, bloody murder mundane, then yes, it is. Except . . . it just *could* be something else. If I sound hesitant, it's because we're not quite ready to believe that this is . . . what it's made out to be."

Harry frowned. "Then you'd better tell me what it's made out to be. Why are you holding back?"

Darcy answered frown for frown, finally glanced away. "Oh, I don't know," he answered at last, but his voice was much quieter now, darker, even a little shaky. "But maybe—just *maybe*, you understand—this really is your sort of thing, after all . . ."

DEAD RECKONING.

IT ALWAYS HAPPENS AT THE FULL MOON," DARCY SAID.
"What does?" And now Harry was quiet, too.
"The murders," said Darcy. "They happen at the full moon. And after each murder a bout of howling, and the bodies of the victims are found . . . torn."

"Torn?"

Darcy nodded. "As by an animal. A big dog, or maybe a—"

"—A wolf?" The Necroscope finished it for him, yet could never have said what had prompted him to cut in. Just that Darcy's mention of howling, and a big dog, had seemed to set something in motion. It could be something he'd dreamed. But if so it was gone now, and only its echo left to trouble him. Taking a deep breath, he tut-tutted; perhaps significantly, he didn't grin. "What are we talking about here, Darcy? A werewolf?"

"Someone who *thinks* he's a werewolf," Darcy shrugged. "Or wants us to think it." He relaxed a little, feeling pleasantly surprised that the Necroscope had got straight to the heart of the matter. Harry Keogh had always been precocious, of course, but there was a lot more than that to him. There was his history, too, his knowledge of the darker side of life.

"And we don't believe in werewolves, right?" (Was there a touch of sarcasm in the Necroscope's voice?)

"We're E-Branch." Darcy went on the defensive anyway. "We can't afford to simply disregard or disbelieve anything—not after what we've seen and what we know. But in this case, it's more that we'd like—"

"—That you'd like some proof? That you've simply *got* to know one way or the other? Because if this *is* the unthinkable, you can't let it go on?"

Again Darcy's shrug, a little nervous but in no way careless. "Two years ago we wouldn't have turned a hair. But since then . . ." He let it tail off, and of course Harry knew why. For since then there'd been the Necroscope and everything that went with him. Namely vampires! Upon a time, people hadn't believed in them either.

"But a werewolf is . . . something else," Harry was thoughtful now, his gaze sharper, less soulful. And staring at Darcy: "You said you think these murders are the work of 'someone who *thinks* he's a werewolf.' But as you also pointed out, this is E-Branch. So what do *you* think?"

Now Darcy's face was grim, even gaunt-looking. His eyes, suddenly vacant, seemed to scan the past. "It feels like only yesterday," he answered. "I can hardly believe it was—what, eighteen months ago?" Again Harry knew what Darcy was talking about: the Bodescu affair.

"I was in on most of it, down there in Devon," Darcy went on. "I saw . . . saw what *became* of poor Peter Keen. Hell, I was the one who found him, or what was left of him! But you know, we never did make up our minds just what did that to him? Yulian Bodescu? Well, maybe. Or was it that godawful dog of his, that *Thing* that was more than just a dog? I don't mind admitting, I still have night-mares about it, Harry, and I suppose I always will. We thought we had Harkley House contained. *Huh!* How wrong can you be? Yulian escaped, and his bloody dog very nearly got out too! But that was only at the end, the *finale*. And what I've been asking myself ever since, is—"

"—I know," the Necroscope cut him off again. "You know how hard it is to kill such things. You're wondering if something—something like that dog, maybe?—might have escaped *before* you moved in for the kill, before you razed Harkley to the ground."

The other nodded, then changed his mind and said, "Well, not really. We were fairly well satisfied that we nailed down everything that could be nailed down. But the Dragosani thing, then the Bodescu affair and all—the whole chain of events—seemed designed to make us aware that we espers aren't the only different things in creation. We're one side of the coin, yes, but for white there's black, and for good there has to be evil. We knew that, of course, but we weren't aware of the different *bands* of evil. I mean, we didn't know just how dark they could get."

"So now that you know, what *do* you think? About this so-called werewolf, I mean."

"Personally? It's like I said. I think, I hope, that he's a man—but *only* a man! A lunatic, affected by the moon at its full, trying to murder as many police-men as he can before they get him."

"But why policemen? Why should a 'werewolf' discriminate in that way? When his blood and the moon are up, surely a victim is a victim? That is, if our understanding of the 'legend' of the beast is correct."

"But that's *why* I think it's a man!" Darcy nodded. "It's one of my reasons, at least; I mean quite apart from logic and commonsense telling me it's a man! This is someone who *reasons* and *discriminates*, someone who knows the police will hunt him down. So if he must kill, who better to take out than the ones who are looking for him, threatening him?"

Harry found himself interested, and no longer just because it was some-thing to keep him occupied. For of all men, the Necroscope had experience of the strange things of the world, and knew that some of them shouldn't be al-lowed to continue.

Finally: "Okay, I'm convinced," he said. "Convinced that something needs sorting out, anyway. So how about the details?"

"We don't have any," Darcy shook his head. "Just a set of utterly senseless murders. On the one hand a couple of police officers already down in the ground, and a third in the morgue waiting to go. And on the other hand their friends, colleagues and families mourning them, grief-stricken. And dead-center, a yawning great gap called 'motive' and 'evidence.' I mean, it's an old cliché, I know, Harry, but this time it's also a fact: we just don't have a clue."

"But we do have somewhere to start," said the Necroscope, grimly.

And in fact he had three somewheres . . .

*S*ometimes *I can take it,* Jim Banks told Harry. *I tend to sleep a lot, like I'm emotionally exhausted, you know? But it's when I'm "awake" that it's rough.* They *try to comfort me . . . I have that at least. But even so, it's hard. Oh, I know I had a long way to go and a tough road ahead. My life wasn't easy, and it wasn't about to get any easier, but it* was *a life!*

Banks had been one hard copper; the Necroscope could sense the sob behind his unbodied voice, but Banks never once let it break through to the surface. Harry supposed he'd done most of his crying and cursing earlier on, when finally the dead—and his situation—had got through to him. The "they" he had mentioned *were* the teeming dead, of course, the Great Majority of mankind who were there before him, "laid to rest" in the cold, cold earth, or gone up in smoke into the sky.

Banks was of the former variety: buried in a north-London cemetery under a marker that gave his name, dates and a motto, and a sad farewell from his family. The motto was in Latin and said, *Exemplo Ducemus.* Harry wondered about that.

I was an MP, a Military Policeman, for twelve years, Banks explained. *SIB: Special Investigation Branch. That's the Corps motto,* Exemplo Ducemus: *By Example We Lead. Now, in this place, I'm just another follower—following all the poor bastards who beat me to it! Maybe I should have stuck to a simple* Requiescat in Pace, *eh?*

Except, as Harry knew well enough, the dead don't rest all that easy but find ways to occupy their incorporeal minds. Jim Banks's way would be to keep on doing what he'd done in life. A cop, currently he might easily be investigating his own murder, if only in his incorporeal mind. He *would be* investigating it, certainly—or at least trying to think it through—but just like his colleagues in the world of the living he didn't have much to go on. Only the fact that he'd been very close to something. Too close by far.

"But you'll tell me as much as you know?"

Not much to tell, Harry. A month ago I was the detective in charge of investigating a ring of car thieves. I got as far as a pub in the East End one night, and that was where my lead petered out. But after that until he got me, whoever he is—I don't know, it was . . . weird! I had this feeling I'd been made, that someone had cottoned on to me. Yet I had no reason to feel like that! I hadn't even known I was that close to anything!

Scanning the ranks of old headstones, some leaning, Harry looked around. His gaze followed the tracks of wandering, white gravel pathways between dreary rows of markers, to a high stone boundary wall. Beyond the wall, a distant hill stood silhouetted against the smoky evening sky, where lights were just beginning to come on in a clump of darkly huddled houses. The cemetery was located in a quiet backwater; well in keeping, distant traffic sounds hung faint as ghosts on the greasy air. It was a late February night, damp and miserable as only

London ever gets to be. On the other hand, Harry had to admit that it was peaceful here. Well, to anyone else . . .

But there was pain in the earth, the Necroscope knew, and in some of its inhabitants. Banks was one of them, and already Harry had made up his mind that Jim Banks must be avenged. For only the teeming dead—and the one man privileged to talk to them—knew how truly precious was life, and how terrible the act of stealing it away.

Harry's thoughts, except when he shielded them, were just as audible to the dead as his spoken words. Banks had overheard him, and was quick to point out: *This mad bastard didn't simply "steal it away," Harry! If you mean he was stealthy, well, yes, there was that in it. But there was a lot more than that. Something strong and fast and furious. Something that slid into my chest like the tines of a pitchfork, to puncture my heart and stop it, and me, dead!*

"Do you want to show it to me?" The Necroscope knew that it could be easier that way. "If you don't want to talk about it you can just . . . let it happen. That way I get more of the flavour of it."

Flavour? Banks's incorporeal voice was suddenly sour. *It wasn't ice cream, Harry.*

"Bad choice of words," Harry said, by way of an apology, and he cursed himself roundly. But it was okay; Banks would do anything he could to help bring his killer to justice.

You want to feel something of it, right? You want to get the mood of it?

"Just the night in question, the start of it," Harry told him.

He had forgotten for the moment that he was talking to an ex-policeman, but Banks was quick to straighten him out: *You'd better have what led to it, too,* he said. And Harry gave a nod, which he knew the dead man, long gone into corruption, six feet deep in his grave, would sense. *Because I have this feeling it all sprang from that night in the pub where my lead gave out on me. My lead ended there, yes, but I think that's where* he *must have picked me up! Looking back on it, I reckon my mistake was a simple one. The thing is, I wasn't looking for violence, you know? I was hunting car thieves, not some crazy, vicious, murdering bastard! So . . . maybe I was a little loose with my inquiries.*

"You gave yourself away?"

The Necroscope sensed a sigh from the immaterial mind of the man in the grave. *Yes, probably . . . No, better than that, I know I gave myself away.*

"How? I mean, I'm not a policeman, Jim. If I know what it was you did to attract attention to yourself, maybe I can duplicate it and swing a little action my way."

The other was at once alarmed. *What? You'd use yourself as bait? No way, Harry! Jesus! I had the training, I knew what to expect. But I never expected this sod! All right, so you're the Necroscope. But you've just admitted you're no James Bond. And you're certainly not Muhammad Ali!*

"No, but I do have a lot of . . . friends? You know what I mean? I'm never alone, Jim, and I'm not above accepting a few tips from those who went before. Believe me, I can look after myself."

Really? Well, so could I, or so I thought. Banks had settled down again, but he was bitter and angry . . . with himself, not with Harry. Harry was only the trigger, a reminder of what had been lost, the fact that there was still a decent world up there with *some* decent people in it at least. Up there beyond the final darkness, yes. And so:

Okay, this is how it started . . .

A nightclub owner's Porsche had been stolen. Banks hadn't felt too bad about the theft because he'd known that the owner, one Geordie King, had a lot of previous himself; he'd been a right old Jack-the-Lad in his time, a gangland hoodlum from the good old days. That was a long time ago, however; now he was a "businessman" and "going straight."

But, still having contacts in the underworld, Geordie King had done a bit of investigating of his own. What he'd managed to turn up wasn't much, but it was better than nothing. An informant who owed Geordie a favor had told him he should watch out for a man called Skippy, who could be identified from the spider "or something" tattooed on the back of his right hand. A spider with five legs and a sting. What's more, this Skippy was from "up north": Geordie's old patch in Newcastle, where the "used car" business was all the rage. His thick northern accent would give him away at once—especially to a fellow "Geordie."

So King had put it about that he was interested in having a chat with a certain Skippy bloke from up North; various contacts in the pubs and clubs had kept an eye out for the spider tattoo; soon the reports had started to come in— in the form of ominous warnings! Skippy was only one member of the gang, and they weren't the sort to mess with. In other words, collect on your insurance, Geordie, and let it go at that.

At the same time, however, King had heard on the grapevine that Skippy was known to frequent a boozer not far from his own East End club.

Well, despite King's checkered history he was well past his sell-by date. So he'd taken good advice and from there on kept his nose out . . . but it hadn't stopped him passing on the information to the Old Bill, namely Jim Banks. It was a matter of principle, so to speak. Honor among thieves, and all that.

Which was how Banks had happened to drop in on the pub in question that night just a month ago . . .

"But you hadn't told anyone about your lead?" Harry found it a bit odd.

Banks's incorporeal shrug. *Rivalry. It was my case. Maybe I was out of line, out to prove something—out of touch? But this is England, not the USA, and there was a time when policemen didn't get killed too often in the line of duty, you know? And as far as I was concerned, I was still investigating a gang of car-thieves. Maybe I should have taken a leaf out of Geordie King's book and stepped a bit more cautious.*

"You think there's more to it, then? More than just auto theft?"

No, I think they're car-thieves, plain and simple. Mainly young and crazy, and probably into drugs, too. And, fairly obviously, at least one of them doesn't give a kiss-my-arse about human life! Especially the lives of policemen . . .

"Tell me about the night in question," said Harry.

I thought you wanted to "see" it?

"Can we save that until later? Like . . . the end?"

And after a pause: *My murder?*

"It it's not too—oh, shit!" (For Harry had almost said "painful.")

He sensed Banks's grin, however grim. *Hey, don't sweat on it, Harry! Let's face it, I don't choose my words any too carefully either!* Then, quickly sobering, he continued:

It was a civvies job, which goes without saying. I mean, I haven't worn a uniform in a long time. Nothing fancy, though, because this pub had a rep as a bit of a rough-house. The night was miserable: rain, sleet and all sorts of shit hammering down out of the sky. It was a Friday and the bar was packed with all kinds of sub-human specimens. I had a rum to warm up and bought one for the barman, then asked him if Skippy was in. Good question—bad timing!

A bloke just three stools away straightened up like someone had stabbed him in the back! I'd already checked him out in the bar mirror: about twenty-six or so, pale and pimply, white and ugly, long-jawed, loose-lipped and shifty-eyed, and a crew-cut like the bristles on a shaving brush. Hardly inconspicuous! Put it this way: you wouldn't want your sister dating this one. But his hand stayed wrapped round a beer on the bar. And that's what settled it.

And it dawned on me: "Skippy" was probably a foreshortened version of a nickname that must have sounded a bit over-the-top—a bit too Hollywood?—for this bloke's Newcastle chums. So they'd cut "The Scorpion" down to Skippy.

That's what was on the back of his hand: not a spider but a scorpion. Five legs *(what, artistic license?) stretched their hairy joints down his four fingers and thumb; the beady eyes of the beast were located on his index- and third-finger knuckles, to make them stand out when he clenched his fist; its sting was at the end of a segmented body stretching four inches along his wrist.*

And some other stuff: Skippy was in paint- and oil-stained overalls. His hands were dirty, and there was fresh paint under his fingernails. But from the moment I mentioned his name he'd been looking at me—glaring at me—in the mirror. Suddenly the hand disappeared, and Skippy with it. He was out of there.

Well, like I said, the bar was crowded; I couldn't really take off after him like Kojak. (One, it would give me away completely. Two, the bloke was young and fast—probably a sight faster than me—and he would know where he was going. Three, I was sure he'd have some previous; I could find out all about him from police records in Newcastle or New Scotland Yard). So . . . I had another drink, hung about for fifteen minutes or so, finally went back out into that lousy night.

And I think that was my second mistake. I should have got straight out of there. See, these new gangs are more audacious than the old crowd. In Geordie King's day if a perp thought the filth had locked-on, he'd head for the hills and keep right on going. But nowadays . . . I'd made him, so he *would make me.*

As Banks paused, Harry turned up his collar against a sudden squall of wind and drizzle. It had occurred to him that if anyone should see him sitting here on this slab and talking to himself, they'd think he was out of his mind and probably call the police!

I am *the police,* Banks reminded him, with an entirely immaterial, totally humorless grin that Harry sensed rather than saw. *And you probably* are *out of your mind! Why didn't you come to see me in daylight?*

"Because I wanted to get on with this," the Necroscope answered. "See, I've got problems of my own, and this should help me to forget about them. For a while, anyway."

So talking to dead people is therapeutic, is it? . . . But in the next moment, in a far more conciliatory tone: *What sort of problems are we talking about, Harry? Bad ones?*

"Not desperate," Harry told him. *Not as bad as being dead, anyway!* Even though that last thought was full of his usual compassion, still it might sound flippant; and so Harry kept it to himself. And: "Go on with what you were telling me," he said.

When I left the pub I had a tail, Banks went on. *I wasn't sure about it then, but I am now. I mean, I've had lots of time to think things out, you know? And that was when it all started to go weird on me. It was like . . . I don't know . . . in a way it was pretty much like this, like talking to you. It felt like—how can I explain it?—like I wasn't alone . . . inside!*

"Inside?"

Inside my head.

"You were talking to someone in your mind?"

(The shake of an incorporeal head). *No, not talking,* listening! *And not me, someone else. As if someone—a stranger—was in* there! *Sitting there grinning to himself, in a corner of* my *mind, listening to me think and . . . watching me! That's what it felt like, Harry: I just* knew *I was being observed! It was a feeling that grew on me from then until . . . well, right to the bitter end. Weird, eh?*

In his time Harry had come across weirder things; for the moment he would keep *those* to himself, too. But having listened carefully to all Banks had told him so far, it struck him that Darcy Clarke was probably right, and on both counts.

For one: he was already engrossed with the case, to such an extent he was sure it would divert his mind from the psychological pitfalls of constantly querying who or what or where *he* was. And two: it looked like this really was something he would have to follow through to the end, a job that only the Necroscope himself (but *himself*, Harry Keogh's self) was qualified to handle.

And the more he listened to Jim Banks—and felt of his shock, his horror—the more convinced he would become . . .

That was how it started, and pretty much how it stayed, Banks continued in a while. *It wasn't with me all the time, only when I was actually working on the case. But the closer I got, the more I was aware of its presence. Except it wasn't an "it," it was a him! Someone as real as you are, Harry, and as real as I . . . was.*

"You're talking about a telepath," Harry told him. "A mentalist. Someone who can get into a man's mind like that has got to be—"

"—*A figment of his own imagination? Yeah, I know,* Banks stopped him short. *Or I thought I did.* But:

"Not . . . necessarily," said Harry, thoughtfully. For the Necroscope remembered Boris Dragosani's story: how the vampire Thibor Ferenczy, the old Thing in the ground, had invaded his mind in order to sway Dragosani to its will. Also, he knew the mind-spies of E-Branch were capable of just such mental eavesdropping. Telepathy was real, not just an idea out of fantasy or a figment of wild imagination. Why, his own thoughts on the subject, on this occasion, were a form of the selfsame talent; which was something else that Banks overheard, of course.

So I was right, he said in a while. *Call it by some other fancy name if you like, but what you're doing right now is the same sort of thing.*

"Well, not exactly," Harry answered, with a shake of his head. "As far as I know there are only two of us who can talk to the dead. The other one is . . . my son! The talent seems to have passed down to him from me. And plainly *we* are not spying on you! You *know* I'm here and you're not obliged to talk to me or even suffer my presence. True telepathy, on the other hand, is mental communication between the living . . . *And sometimes the undead?* Which was a thought he also kept back; pointless to further complicate matters.

"Also," he went on, "telepathy doesn't have to be intrusive; it can provide genuine two-way communication. I have certain friends who mind-spy, yes—for the protection of society, our way of life, just as you through your work protected those same ideals—but the way these friends of mine describe their skills, they aren't in any way this sinister thing that you experienced."

No, because that was *intrusive!* Banks declared emphatically. *And more than that, it was also frightening. If it hadn't finished when it did, the way it did—I don't know—I think I might well have gone crazy.* Hah! *Instead I went . . . dead! But at first, I really was starting to believe that I was suffering from some sort of persecution complex! I thought it was* all *in my head! I mean literally! It was only afterwards, recently, that I saw it as something else.*

"As what, then?"

As . . . a distraction! Banks answered.

"Someone was deliberately crowding your mind, in order to distract you from your investigations? Is that what you're saying?"

Like an irritating smokescreen, yes, Banks was convinced. *But I fought it, pushed on, kept coming. And since he couldn't* frighten *me off, finally he—*

"—He killed you off."

Yes. But even at the end he was helped by this telepathic trick of his. I mean, he knew *when I was going to come for him, and where from! And so he beat me to it . . .*

"So what did you find out about him? This fellow with the scorpion tattoo, I mean?"

Harry sensed Banks's nod. *As I'd suspected, he had lots of previous. But all petty stuff. He'd done time up north, plenty of it, all short term. But I did get something useful: Skippy was on a year's probation, but they'd let him move down to London to take a job in his cousin's garage in the East End. Some sort of cock-eyed rehabilitation program: see if giving him a decent job would straighten him out. I mean, Jesus, Harry! This shit's "therapy" was to do face-lifts on stolen cars!*

"The paint under his fingernails?" Harry lifted a querying eyebrow. "It was all coming together for you."

Too true!

"So what next?"

Next? Have a look inside that garage, what else? It was the bottom floor of a condemned municipal car park. The upper stories had been made safe, reduced to a towering metal skeleton, but the ground floor and basement had been converted into workshops, inspection pits, paint bays and what have you. All the gear: your typical auto-repairs garage on a grand scale. I figured most of the work would be legitimate, a front for the real earner: the conversion of stolen cars. But it would have to be a superfast turnaround.

Tea-leaf a posh motor, give it a quick face-lift, and ship it out. Ten to twelve hours maximum, most of it at night, after hours.

"And did you check it out? And is that what got you . . . ?"

. . . No. I didn't have time. Just thinking *about doing it, and getting ready to set the thing up, is what got me killed! Because* he, *the gang's—what, mindspy?—wasn't about to let it go that far. He was on me all the way, and it happened the night before I would have taken out a search warrant.*

"And before you could let anyone else in on it . . ." Harry was quiet but couldn't keep a tone of censure—and of anger, at the waste of Jim Banks—out of his voice.

Banks accepted it. *I was out of line. I just wanted this one for myself, that's all. Rivalry, like I told you. It would have been a feather in my cap. But instead—it was something that felt like a pitchfork in my heart!*

"And that's why there were no clues to your death—well, other than the ones you've given me. Because you chose to play it close to your chest?"

Right. Banks was downcast. It was in his immaterial voice, and Harry could sense it wasn't just because he'd paid the ultimate price for his errors. Banks was privy to his thoughts, of course, and at last released a sob that no one in the world but the Necroscope Harry Keogh could ever hear. *You pays your money and takes your chance, Harry.* But the voice in Harry's mind was racked with . . . what, guilt?

"Jim, don't torture yourself," Harry told him. "You didn't do anything wrong."

And my family? My wife and kids? Were they guilty of something? But still they're paying, Harry. And . . . and the others, and their families? What about them? But no, I had to play the loner, always the loner. I wouldn't feel so bad if I'd paid for it the same way, on my own. But those poor guys had to pay for it, too. Because of me!

"Because of you? I don't see it, Jim. You were only doing your job, and when you'd gone someone picked it up where you'd left off. You had nothing to do with—"

—But I did! And now I ask myself over and over again, if they'd had the whole *story, would it have been different . . . ?*

The Necroscope shook his head. "I don't understand. What do you mean, 'if they'd had the whole story?' Your colleagues? But they didn't have any of it, did they?"

Do the names Stevens and Jakes mean anything to you? The dead man was somehow managing to keep himself under a semblance of control, but his anguish was lying just beneath the surface.

"The other victims?"

Bank's incorporeal nod. *Those two were the closest I had to friends on the force. I mean, I had friends, you understand, but those two were . . . close. I asked them if they'd like to be in on it when I closed down the biggest auto-theft gang in London. And like a fool I told Derek Stevens, who was closest of all, about the garage. And all the time that bastard thing was in my head, listening to everything!*

Now Harry understood Bank's stored-up grief. Not for himself but his friends. And he sensed the dead man's nod of confirmation. *I told them too little too late. Just enough they'd be sure to try to square it for me after . . . after I . . .*

But for the moment he couldn't go on. So Harry finished it for him. "After you'd been murdered?"

Yes, (a fading sob).

"They'd investigate the garage without knowing how dangerous it was, and so put themselves in the firing line?"

Yes . . . God, yes!

"And they wouldn't know a thing about this mentalist, his telepathic trick, because you yourself hadn't known. You said it yourself, Jim: that you thought you were going crazy."

Don't look for excuses for me, Harry.

"I'm not, because you don't need any. You were only trying to uphold the law, and so were they—and so will I." He was in now, like it or not. "Okay, Jim, you've given me enough to go on. A starting point, anyway. But now I need to feel it: your pain, your anger. I need to feel angry enough to want to put it right. Call it incentive, for want of a better word."

The night it happened? How it happened? What I saw?

"All of it, yes."

Give me a moment, Banks told him. And in a little while, in direct contact with the Necroscope's metaphysical mind, he began to think it through, relive it exactly as he'd experienced it that night.

And Harry was with him all the way . . .

Banks's place was a stone's throw from Peckham High Street. It was nothing special: a tall, terraced house with a yard at the front, a balcony on the first floor, a small round window spying out from an attic room, and a vegetable patch at the back, crushed between neighboring gardens. All of the houses in the terrace looked the same, with only slight variations of exterior décor. But the rooms were big and high-ceilinged, and there was plenty of space for the kids.

No space for Banks's car, though; his garage was one of a dozen in a low, asbestos-roofed block of badly constructed concrete boxes at the end of the terrace. This made for a walk (or a run when it was raining) of a hundred yards after he'd locked up. And when the weather was *really* bad, as tonight, it pissed him off to have to go rushing into the house spraying droplets like a hosed-down dog.

These were some of the thoughts that occupied his mind as he switched off the motor, snatched his keys from the ignition, rammed the door open with his elbow and made a dash for the up-and-over garage door. And this was another:

Fuck it! Why can't I ever remember to take the garage key off the fucking keyring? Now (as usual) he'd have to start up the car again to drive inside! Standing under the leaky garage guttering, he finally fumbled the correct key into the release handle and turned it—only to discover when he yanked on the handle that he'd *locked* the damned thing!

But even as warning bells commenced their mental clamor, as suddenly and as sinisterly as that, *he* was there again! That ominous presence watching and waiting, his silent snigger grown to a snarl now in the back of Banks's mind!

God! Banks thought in a moment of panic. *I must really be losing it!* And: *Bastard, bastard, bastard!* as he concentrated on what he was doing, turned the key the other way, and hauled on the handle to swing the door into its up-and-over position. Inside the garage it was night-dark, cluttered with household junk at the back. And the light switch . . . wasn't working!

Shit and damnation! But it was okay; the car's headlights would give him all the light he needed to park up. But . . . was that movement back there?

A pair of dark figures moving forward, silhouetted against the greater darkness behind them; and Banks frozen to the spot, transfixed by the utterly unexpected! But in that single moment he put the whole thing together, and the warning clamor in his mind—and the sniggering—went up several decibels.

The garage door: he *always* checked twice that he'd locked it. But you could buy these fucking cheap keys in any hardware store. And the light: he'd replaced that bulb just a week ago! And that sniggering in his mind: it wasn't *in* his mind anymore but . . . but right here in front of him! First the sniggering, and then a low warning growl!

Banks unfroze . . . but too late. The figures coming toward him out of the darkness of the garage converged with him, fastened on him! One of them, briefly illumined in the rain-lashed glint of a street lamp, was Skippy, Banks would swear. But in the next moment an arm went round his throat, and the scorpion-tattooed hand swept a glittering knife on high! Then—

"No!" said the second figure. "He's mine. This piece of . . . *filth* is mine!" But the voice itself was filth—full of bile and phlegm and hatred—and Banks knew that this was the nameless mental intruder. No longer a bodiless, spying, sniggering specter but a living, breathing reality. And to corroborate it, coming to him in his mind again, but audibly now:

Your balls are mine, you stinking cop scumbag!

Then Skippy's knee in Banks's back, thrusting him forward onto something that ripped him open like a paper bag. Pain! Unbelievable pain! And the slash, slash, slash of silver-flashing steel as sharp as razors . . . the hot surging wetness of Banks's blood from his face, chest, belly and genitals as he went down. In just a couple of seconds he lost pints of blood. That alone would suffice to stop him, the shock alone: of feeling his face torn open to the bone, his belly in ribbons, his manhood shorn from him in a tearing of upward-swinging scythes!

And the slashes not stopping but continuing to rain down on him where he slumped, then crawled, then collapsed. But the pain . . . miraculously the pain was going away, like a dull ache receding; so that only the tearing of shuddering but no longer protesting flesh remained to remind him of his murder. Because Banks knew that that was what it was: The End of him, with all his blood leaking out onto the floor, to mix with the rain and the oil-clogged dirt . . .

He lay just inside the garage, looking out. After a while (it might have been hours but could only have been seconds), his eyes focused one last time on the rain-blurred street lamp. It was either that, a focusing, or the mucus of his eyes drying on the nerveless eyeballs to sharpen his dying vision. But as his brain prepared to switch off, someone or thing—a face, anyway—leaned down and looked him in his own torn and bloodied face.

But God, that the last thing he would ever see should be *that* face! It wasn't Skippy; it wasn't human; it wasn't *anything* Banks might ever have believed in. But it *was* as monstrous as the death it had delivered. So that he didn't just die but went out screaming, however silently.

And as if in mocking answer, the last thing he ever *heard* seemed to be a distant howling . . .

. . . Banks was still doing it, silently screaming—but in the eye of memory now, a scream of rage and frustration as well as horror—as that rabid wolf visage gradually faded from his mind, and the drizzle worked its way inside Harry's collar, and Bank's sobbing from beyond lit a fire in the Necroscope's guts that he knew couldn't be extinguished as long as this went unresolved, unpunished.

Until he'd "seen" the face of the wolf for himself, Harry had almost forgotten what Darcy Clarke had told him: the werewolf theory. *Having* seen it, his senses were as shocked as the dead mind's that transmitted the pictures, as stunned as Banks had been on the night of his murder. He couldn't help but wonder if he would have fared any better. Probably not, not then, but he would now. It was all a matter of knowing what you were up against.

Gathering his composure and his thoughts, he finally said: "Two of them, then. Skippy and . . . *that,* whatever it was." His voice was colder than the grave itself, so that Jim Banks knew Harry wouldn't let him down even if his own life were forfeit.

And: *Well, what do you think?* The dead man was able to ask him at last. *I mean, was I crazy, Harry? Or what?*

"You're as sane as I am," Harry told him. And to himself: *Which right now isn't saying much!* "But what do you reckon?"

Banks shook off the last remnants of his own horror, and answered, *What do I reckon? Dead reckoning, eh, Harry?* But his words contained little or no humor. *All right: I think it was a bloke dressed up as a wolf. See, a wolf or big dog goes on all fours, but this bloke was* leaning over me! *So . . . why the disguise? I mean, if I'd survived they were goners anyway. I had already identified Skippy. So why that crazy horror mask?*

"Work on 'crazy,' " Harry told him. "A lunatic, Jim. Someone influenced by the full moon, who *thinks* he's a werewolf."

Really? The single word sounded like a sigh of relief to the Necroscope. Even dead, Banks was pleased to know that his mind hadn't been cracking up.

Harry squared his shoulders, tucked his collar in more yet and prepared to leave. "I have some people waiting for me," he was apologetic. "But before I go I want to thank you, Jim, for what you've told me. It wasn't easy for you, I know. I mean, *I* really do know."

It's okay, the other told him. *Just don't forget to let me know how it turns out, right? It might make all of . . .* this, *a little easier to get used to.*

"Be sure I'll let you know," Harry told him. "One way or the other, I'll let you know . . ."

Beyond the gates of the cemetery, Darcy Clarke and the locator Ken Layard were waiting in a Branch car. Darcy was at the wheel and Layard sat slumped in the back seat, half asleep, his mouth lolling open. As the figure of the Necroscope loomed out of the wreathing mist, Darcy opened the front passenger door for him.

He got in, looked at Darcy, said: "You know, there's really no need. Transport is the last thing I require. You could find a lot better things to do with your time."

Darcy gave a shrug and started up the motor. "Harry, the way we see it you're our most valuable asset. We can't be sure how or even if it will work out, but eventually, if it's feasible, we'd like you to take over as Head of Branch. Except, as you know, we've already lost two heads in the last two years! So—"

"—So you intend to keep your beady eyes on me . . . yes, I know."

As they pulled away from the curb, Layard jerked awake in the back, said: *"Huh*—?" And, "Oh, Alec!"

Harry felt Darcy cringe down in his seat beside him, and turned his pale face to glower at Layard where the locator was already biting his lip. But whatever the Necroscope might have said, Darcy beat him to it. "Ken, were you just born stupid or does it take a lot of practice?"

"I . . ." Layard said, glancing at Darcy, then looking into Harry's face. Finally he shrugged and sighed, "I guess I was asleep. What can I say? I'm sorry . . . Harry." Following which he tried to change the subject. "Anyway, how did things go? I mean, did you get to . . . well, speak to him?"

The Necroscope hadn't been in a good mood to start with; now he wasn't in any sort of mood at all. "Yes, I . . . 'well, got to speak to him,' " he mimicked the others' hesitancy. "I'd never met Jim Banks in life, but we got on pretty well. Funny thing, but for a total stranger *he* knew my name right from the word go! And he'd only had a few minutes—which is a lot less than eighteen fucking months!" It was perhaps unfair of him, but that was the way he felt.

In any case, nothing more was said until they reached their second destination. Nothing that Darcy or Layard were privy to anyway . . .

KEENAN GORMLEY, AND OTHER VICTIMS.

BANKS HAD BEEN THE FIRST MAN TO DIE; OR RATHER, HE'D BEEN THE FIRST *policeman* to die. But on the way to the second graveyard, this time in the Muswell Hill district, as the Necroscope tried to relax in the front passenger seat, closed his tired eyes and settled down into the worn leather upholstery:

Harry? The dead voice was one he would know anywhere, any time: it was that of Sir Keenan Gormley, first Head of E-Branch. *Harry? Harry, my boy! I can't tell you how good it is to know you're alive and well . . . again. Word has reached me about what you're working on. You're the Necroscope and your thoughts are very strong; sometimes we can't help but overhear them. And of course we've been, you know, "holding our breath," as it were, since discovering that you were back in the land of the living. In fact I've held back—oh, for a long time—from contacting you, for I knew you'd be busy. But as of now I want you to know that if there's anything we can do . . . ?*

"Sir Keenan?" The Necroscope spoke under his breath, the merest whisper of sound, drowned out by the car's motor. "It's good to know you're still around, too." (What does one say to someone who was cremated more than two years ago?) "I suppose you know that I'm . . . what? Not the man I used to be?" Conversing with the dead could be complicated.

We know about it, yes. Sir Keenan's incorporeal voice was sorrowful, for Alec Kyle. *And also something of your problems, Harry. Your discomfort? But you know, Alec's case was one in a million. He was* totally *lost, to the living and the dead alike. But without him we wouldn't have you. So you see, your problem is our blessing. Where would we ever have been, what could we ever have done, without the Necroscope?*

"And for that matter, what can you do now?" The way Harry said it, it wasn't a thoughtless question. The Great Majority were his friends and very important to him; he simply referred to their incorporeal condition. Or rather, their usual condition, without that they were engaged in any . . . *activity* on his behalf. But as well as having certain conversational difficulties, communication with the teeming dead (much like telepathy) frequently conveys more than is actually said, and Sir Keenan understood that the Necroscope was only showing his customary concern and humility.

Well, for one thing, we can tell you that the deaths you're currently investigating weren't the first of this maniac's murders! There have been a dozen here in London, all occurring near the time of the full moon; maybe a day or so before, during, or after. But it must be said that the victims were no great loss to humanity . . . nor of any special benefit to us! In fact, and to be frank about it, they are mainly of the criminal element.

"Ganglanders?" Harry wasn't surprised. There had always been gang wars in London and there always would be, mainly for territory. "From the East End?"

In almost every instance, yes. But what a close-mouthed bunch, Harry! Honor among thieves and all that rubbish! And of course there was nothing they could do about their lot anyway. Ah, but that's all changed now that you are on the case! You're the Necroscope; which is to say you're not "filth," not the law! With you, they don't consider themselves informants; it's not like "grassing" in the normal sense of the word.

"How good is their information?" Harry was eager now. For the fact was that he didn't have a lot to go on.

I'm afraid there's not that much I can tell you, the dead man answered. *And most of it is conjectural anyway. But surely anything is better than nothing?*

Harry gave a mental nod. "Tell me, then," he said, "and let me be the judge of it."

The murders had all happened during the last three years, all of them around the time of the full moon, but not so many that the police would necessarily make the connection; there'd been a good many killings in that time-frame. Indeed the only thing that *might* have connected them lay in their uniformly unsolved status . . . In that, and in the fact that the last three murders (prior to those of the police officers) had been committed by a thing half-man, half-wolf, or by someone in the guise of such a creature. Which would seem to indicate that the maniac had only recently adopted his werewolf role. This last, however, the use of the wolf mask, was something that other *living* investigators couldn't possibly know; only the victims had seen their attacker's face. The victims, and now Harry Keogh, Necroscope . . .

It was the horrific *nature* of these last three murders—their *modus operandi*—along with those of Jim Banks, Stevens and Jakes, of course, that had finally alerted the authorities to what they now erroneously categorized as a series of serial killings. That these atrocities were the work of a lunatic was hardly in question, but "serial" killings? Sir Keenan Gormley and the Great Majority doubted it.

Harry had been right: the initial series of seemingly unconnected murders had been territorial. A homicidal member of a gang of car-thieves had begun taking out members of encroaching gangs one by one, almost systematically. But after a while, following his first half-dozen killings, maybe he'd started to enjoy it! Maybe he'd sensed his power, the advantage that his weird talent gave him, his ability to get into an enemy's mind and pre-empt his every move. A grudge against the police? Well, maybe. The urge to permanently remove any persistent adversary—very definitely!

An esoteric talent plus a diseased and generally criminal mind, equals gruesome murder. Lycanthropy: not merely a concept of fantastic fiction but a mania, a recognized and accepted psychiatric phenomenon. The madman's need to tear his victims to pieces like a wild animal, and his bloodlust at the full of the moon, when the lunar orb tugs at the fluid of his brain no less insistently than it lures the great oceans. His anguished howling when innermost passions are finally vented in acts of furious mayhem!

The madness of a rabid animal, then, in combination with the warped cunning of an habitual criminal. That was what the Necroscope was up against. And as yet he was still no closer to learning the murderer's identity . . .

"**S**o what do you suggest?" he asked Sir Keenan Gormley, as the car sped him ever closer to the Muswell Hill cemetery and his second liaison.

"Eh?" Darcy Clarke glanced at Harry out of the corner of his eye. "Did you say something?"

Harry gave a slight start, and muttered. "Er, just talking . . . to myself." He knew how the espers of E-Branch looked upon his talent, that even with their knowledge of parapsychology, still they found it disquieting. Settling deeper into his seat and switching to a mental mode, he said:

Sir?

And Keenan Gormley chuckling in his mind: *What do I suggest? Well, for one thing, if I were you I wouldn't let myself stray too far from* that *one! Darcy Clarke has to be just about the safest man I know—or knew. But quite apart from Darcy's talent, he was also a good friend. And better to have him as a friend than a foe, Harry, what with that guardian angel of his and all! You certainly wouldn't want to go up against* him *in a duel, now would you? So if Darcy wants to keep his eye on you, don't complain about it.*

I'll try to remember that, Harry told him. *But that's not what I meant. I wasn't talking about Darcy.*

No, of course you weren't. But I thought it worth mentioning, that's all. I'm just so glad to see that you're still with E-Branch. He fell silent for a moment, mulling the real question over in his incorporeal mind. Then:

I think . . . (Sir Keenan's disembodied voice was much more sober, thoughtful now) *that I would probably try to fight fire with fire. For talking to you about Darcy and the Branch brings back to mind some of the amazing talents you have at your command. Quite literally, yours to command. If you so desire them.*

Oh? Harry waited. And shortly:

Your quarry appears to be some kind of telepath, which so far has given him an advantage. But you have all the fully developed talents of E-Branch. So why not give him a taste of his own medicine, Harry? From what I know of you, that's your way, isn't it? An eye for an eye, and all that?

Harry was interested. *I should use an E-Branch telepath?*

Now that you know what you're up against? You'd be a fool not to! And Sir Keenan explained what he meant.

Harry thought about it a while and said, *Maybe, if that's what it comes down to. But right now I have to be saying goodbye. For shortly I'll be speaking to Derek Stevens, the second of this lunatic's three policemen victims.*

But Keenan Gormley had already drawn back; Harry felt him shrinking away, as from a scowl or a slap. And he felt obliged to ask: *Is there something I should know?*

He sensed the other's nod and eventually, hesitantly, his answer: *Sometimes . . . some people . . . just aren't ready for it, Harry. Some people don't get used to death so readily. And some . . . well, they don't get used to it at all, ever. When I found out you'd be handling this, I tried speaking to Stevens myself, just as I've spoken to others of the victims: in order to save a little time, you know?* (Harry sensed his sigh). *I'm sorry, my boy, but . . . Derek Stevens hasn't got used to it yet.*

Harry felt Darcy Clarke's elbow giving him a gentle nudge. Looking up, he saw that the car was at a standstill outside the Muswell Hill cemetery. And since they were here, it seemed only right that he should give it a try.

Well, if you must, I suppose you must, Sir Keenan Gormley told him, his ghostly echo of a voice fading to a distant whisper in the Necroscope's metaphysical mind. *But better you than me, Harry. Far better you than me . . .*

From this side of Muswell Hill, the fact that the district was elevated was obvious. Southward, the nighted streets of London sprawled like some giant, shimmering cobweb woven on the curve of the world. It had done raining for now, but in Harry Keogh's fertile imagination the cold glitter of distant street lamps in the moisture-laden air was the reflection of a myriad jewels of dew on the blacktop strands of the great web. And the vehicles crawling on the roads were Mama Spider's children, learning the skills of the silken tightrope.

But evocative though the vista was, it wasn't the Necroscope's reason for being here. As he penetrated the graveyard, the concerned, concerted, ever-burgeoning clamor of incorporeal voices sounding in his metaphysical mind brought him back down to earth—and below it—in a moment. Their *concerned* clamor, yes. Full of concern, for Stevens. They weren't talking to Harry (not yet, for they didn't know he was here), but to each other, and to Stevens. Trying to talk to him, anyway.

Discovering the dead man's plot wasn't difficult: it lay dead center of the physically silent but psychically noisy babble which, as Harry approached, grew louder by the moment. The brand-new marker, clean gravel chips and fresh flowers provided all the corroboration he needed. These things and Stevens's name, his dates, and his epitaph, of course:

> *A Man of Law & Order,*
> *—a Fighter to the Last—*
> *Struck Down by the Lawless,*
> *in the Pursuit of His Duty.*
> *Sorely Missed, but Alive*
> *in Our Memories,*
> *Always.*

A very sad thing. But the babbling creature in its grave was sadder by far . . .

It was just as simple as Sir Keenan Gormley had tried to forewarn: the dead couldn't console him. Derek Stevens couldn't come to terms with his demise, wouldn't accept it, wasn't going to lie still for it. And despite that he *knew* in his innermost being (or unbeing) that he was dead, still he fought against it and cried his horror of it, until his plot and the entire graveyard reverberated with his silent shrieking and his coffin wasn't merely a box but a cell in a subterranean asylum. An asylum in the worst possible sense of the word, that of the madhouse.

A madman? Harry asked of the dead moaning in their graves.

Driven mad by grief, frustration and horror, Necroscope! a shuddering voice answered. *For the living aren't alone in their capacity for grief. We also mourn—for the absence of all the loved ones we left behind, who don't know that we're still down here . . . and must never know! Else they'd sit by our graves all day, and their brief sojourn in the land of the living would be wasted no less than ours in the darkness of death . . .*

So taken aback by the sheer soulfulness of it, the doom-fraught *feeling* in the voice, for a little while the Necroscope said nothing. But then:

Excuse me, Sir, for I don't know you (Harry respectfully shielded his thoughts from the rest of the cemetery's dwellers in order to speak to this one alone). *But I do know that while you are* in *the majority, still you are of a minority: a defeatist among optimists. For while I've spoken to a great many dead men, I honestly can't say I ever before heard the . . .* condition *or the lot of the teeming dead expressed so mournfully, so hopelessly as you express it. Even vampires, who have lost not only life but undeath and immortality, too, seem a deal more accepting of their station than you are of yours! Which isn't so much to put you down as to inquire . . . well, what is it that's made you this way?*

For a moment the other was silent, perhaps shocked. Could this really be the Necroscope, whose compassion was universally acclaimed? Harry sensed the stiffness in the unquiet night, and to his relief felt its gradual easing. Until eventually: *You're right, of course,* said the unknown voice, but without its hopeless tremor now, stoic in the modern sense, yet submissive when faced with the truth. *You must forgive me my doubts and my regrets, Harry, my lack of conviction. Ah, but it comes hard for a preacher to be preached to, for a man of the Faith to discover himself faithless!* Made *to discover it, and by one so young at that! And yet you're so—*persuasive! *You put it so very well! Perhaps you should have taken the cloth and been a preacher? Or maybe you'd make a better philosopher. Have you studied philosophy, Harry?*

Some, the Necroscope answered, which was at least in part the truth. *Or rather, I've played a few word-games in my time. And with experts, too. I know how to argue, if that's what you mean.* He explained no further than that. But on the other hand, what the dead man had said to him explained a great deal.

All of his life this man had preached of a God and a life after death. But now, *in* death . . . where was He? Why had He not taken these souls to His bosom? Neither Necroscope nor preacher could answer *that* question; but in fact He had claimed them, or would eventually. Except Harry had always had his doubts, which this apparent delay in the promised deliverance only served to exacerbate. The whole truth of the matter was something he was yet to discover, albeit in another world, another time.

Harry's thoughts on the preacher's predicament were like spoken words, which the dead man answered. *Again you are right. For if I thought it hard to convince my flock in life, how much harder in death, when the anticipated resurrection is not?*

Harry nodded. *It must be difficult, yes. But you do still talk like a priest.*

I still think like one, deep down inside! It's just that now, well, my words seem so futile, so empty. Even to me, sometimes! And the worst thing is, I can't put a time on it, can't advise them of the hour of their salvation. But talking to such as you, and feeling your living warmth, I do believe, of course I do! For if there is nothing left but this darkness, this purgatory of sorts, then why have you come to remind us of the past—if not to provide evidence of a glorious future? For He was, He is, and He shall always be . . .

God's messenger? Harry didn't feel like one.

But you are! the preacher was insistent. *You bring light in the eternal darkness, Harry, and hope where no hope existed. You . . . rekindle the flame! Yes, and I think I know what brings you here: the soul-destroying cries of this demented one, taken before his time. You are here to comfort him. Tell me that I'm right?*

Not quite, Harry shook his head, and knew the other would sense it. *If I can comfort him, well and good. But in fact I'm here to question him. I want to know who killed him, so that I can right the wrong.*

Revenge? The voice of the preacher was far quieter now.

An eye for an eye, Harry growled.

You can't find it in you to turn the other cheek?

So that the murderer goes free to kill again?

It's not my way, Harry.

Nor mine, not really. But I'll do what I must.

And in doing so, lower yourself to the killer's level?

Tell that to the dozen or more he's *lowered six feet under the sod!*

I can't give you my blessing, the preacher shook an incorporeal head.

Give me access, that's all I ask. Call off the others, for they're doing no good and crowding me out.

It was true, Derek Stevens had them all in a state. Every single—inhabitant?—of the place, brought to the brink of what among the dead could only pass for nervous collapse. They knew no peace with him; they could neither converse nor hear themselves *think* for his noise; they flocked to him with gentle words, and the hardest of them with threats, but nothing they did brought surcease for he was inconsolable. To the world outside, the world of the living, the Muswell Hill graveyard would seem a hallowed place of peace and rest, but to the ones interred here it was now a Bedlam.

Well, Harry thought to himself, *Sir Keenan did try to warn me, after all.* But as he seated himself on a nearby slab the tumult fell off a little, and as the teeming dead felt his presence, they drew back and made way for him. Then gradually, the incorporeal babble tailed off to a hiss of whispers, and finally a welcome silence, as they waited.

Or almost a silence. For down there in the earth, unheard except by the dead and the Necroscope Harry Keogh, there was a sobbing. A heart not yet melted in corruption lay broken there, a soul with nowhere to flee suffered all the undeserved grief of the grave, and a mind bereft of control, cut off from man's five earthly senses teetered on the brink of total insanity.

In the eye of memory, fleetingly, the Necroscope pictured an illustration from some old book (perhaps the idea of Bedlam had brought it back to mind): of a man lying in a foetal position on a bed of filthy, vermin-infested straw over broken flagstones, with gaunt, drooling, hollow-eyed figures shambling to and fro, aimlessly, all around. Add to that scene all the protests and the pleading and even the threats of the Great Majority, and Harry couldn't help wondering: is that what it's like for Derek Stevens?

To the teeming dead, the unguarded thoughts of the Necroscope were perfectly audible. And:

Yessss! Stevens sobbed, and huddled to Harry in his mind, crushing to him for his living warmth!

Any other man would have recoiled at once. To be embraced, even in one's mind, by a corpse, isn't a thought to dwell upon. But Harry was the Necroscope, and the dead were his friends. He could no more shrink from Stevens in his grave than from a sick friend in a hospital ward. And so he instinctively wrapped the dead man in his warmth, and let him leech on it a while . . . but briefly, for something warned him not to let himself succumb to the other's incurable chill.

But as he drew away:

No! Don't go! Who are you? What are you? A nurse? A doctor? You're alive, I know that, because you're warm. I can feel your warmth! But the others in this . . . place, they're cold! So tell me, tell me, tell me . . . you've got to tell me they're lying! I have to know that I . . . that I'm . . . aliiiive! Right at the end it turned to a wail, a sobbing shriek that sank down as if into the earth from which it issued.

"*I'm* alive, yes," Harry spoke out loud, however quietly now, which was easier for him and made no difference at all to the Great Majority. "But this . . . *isn't* a hospital, Derek. I'm Harry Keogh, the one they call the Necroscope, and sometimes I wish I wasn't. This is one of those times." There was no other way to do it. His words spoke volumes, told far more than he'd said, but even in his ears they sounded like a betrayal.

Nooooo! The dead man's wail denied it. *My parents, wife, family, friends. My whole wooooorld! . . . Gone?* But this time the final word was a whisper.

"Not gone," Harry's face was wet with his own tears, and his voice rang with his own agony. "They're still there, Derek, everything, everyone. They have accepted what you can't accept. Because they saw, felt, touched you, and knew that they had to give you up. Their living senses made them to know that yours . . . don't work any more."

The sobbing had stopped now, and for long moments there was only a stunned, breathless silence. It was as if the dead held their breath, waiting for Derek Stevens to gather his, a renewal of his crazed raving. The Necroscope sensed it coming, and stopped it short:

"I can tell them you're okay now," he said. "Your family, your friends, Jim Banks and George Jakes. I'm the only one who can tell them. I can make it easy for them, reassure them, give them strength to carry on. Even those last two, who like yourself *can't* carry on, and have accepted it. Or I can say nothing at all. Or . . . I can tell them you're like this. But I'd really hate to do that, and leave them in the same sort of hell, going mad with worry over you . . ."

There couldn't be a "same sort of hell," not remotely! The dead man answered at last. But now there was that in his incorporeal voice that hadn't been there before, so that Harry felt like an inquisitor, as if he'd issued a threat or attempted to coerce the other. *But you did!* Stevens told him, with something of a sneer. *You threatened a dead man! So much for the "mercy" of the Necroscope! And if that was a lie, what about the rest of the bullshit they've been feeding me?*

At which Harry relaxed a little, and perhaps even smiled to himself through his tears. The word-game he was playing was going his way at last. And: "You're not crazy, Derek," he told the other. "Not if you can still reason as well as all that!"

Crazy? The other seemed surprised. *Was I supposed to be?* His voice was still bitter, but Harry sensed that he had definitely turned back from the brink. *Mad with grief, sure* (just as the preacher had said). *Tortured by frustration, naturally. But*

I wasn't crazy. Bull-headed, that's all: a bad loser, and unwilling to give up on a lost cause or argument. Well, hell, I've always been that way!

Of course. And how he'd always been in life was how he'd be in death. But even the worst loser must accept the verdict when he's finally down and out.

Harry felt the soft sighing of the dead, for *this* was an argument that was definitely going his way now. Except, as the Necroscope was well aware, it wouldn't go down well if he stuck the boot into an underdog. One should always leave a bolthole, so that the gallant loser may retire with grace. And so:

"Well, and you'll win this one, too, in the end," he said, however casually.

Eh? How's that? (Stevens was "back on his feet" again, the sob gone from his voice forever. It was the prospect of winning when all had seemed lost. But how could everything be lost when he was still here, still fighting?) *What? I can still win?*

"Can and will," Harry assured him. "Because in the end . . . why, we'll all be in the same hole! Everyone, eventually."

What? (Wonderingly).

"Death is a hell of a long time," Harry explained. "You've lost nothing, Derek. Or at worst, your situation is a temporary one. But everything and everyone you've said goodbye to, you'll be saying hello to in some distant future. Except by then, why, you may not want to!"

Not want to? (Astonishment!) *I won't want to be reunited with—*

"—You'll get *old*, Derek, and so will they. You'll be old in the ways of death, and them old in the physical sense. Which is something you won't have to suffer. They'll have new friends and be . . . different. And so will you. But who knows, who can say? Maybe they'll be *like* you, as rebellious as you have been, and need you to show them the way when finally . . . finally they get here. Just as the dead will show you the way, if you'll let them."

I can have new friends?

"Even old ones! Jim Banks isn't that far away. You should be able to talk to him, if you'll just reach out."

Have I been . . . selfish?

"No, just scared. And you scared the dead, too, because now and then they lose someone like you. Now and then, someone will retreat so far into his misery that he's permanently lost. They thought you were going that way, too, Derek."

And so they called you in . . .

Harry shook his head. "I didn't come to help you, but to *ask* for your help! Just as Jim Banks has helped me, and George Jakes too, I hope."

Jim, George, and me . . . Now the dead man knew what it was all about, what it had to be about, and Harry felt his excitement. *Now that really would be a way to finish a fight, right? To hit back from the grave! So what do you want to know?*

Harry told him, and what little there was he got: from a seat in the front row, as usual . . .

Afterwards, when the Necroscope had said goodbye to Derek Stevens and was leaving the cemetery:

Harry, said the preacher, *that was just . . . marvelous! And you really do know how to argue, don't you?*

"Told you so," said Harry. "But in fact I had an advantage over you. I knew something you couldn't know."

Oh?

"It was something I saw written on his gravestone, something that had been put there by people who knew Derek better than either one of us. It said he was 'a fighter to the last.' Except, as we've seen, the fight isn't over yet . . ."

The Necroscope had to make one more visit. And this time it was a venue and a meeting that he wasn't looking forward to at all: the police mortuary in Fulham, where George Jakes lay gutted on a slab waiting for him. For it's one thing to talk to the dead, but something else to converse with a mangled mess that simply isn't recognizable any more and smells of the blood, guts, and shit that used to lie *under* the skin!

Harry steeled himself to it, however, and on the way told his esper friends what Derek Stevens had told him:

"Less than Banks, I'm afraid. When Banks was hit, Stevens didn't automatically tie it in to what Banks had been investigating. Banks had been onto a gang of car-thieves, yes, but he had been killed by some maniac who was perhaps responsible for a whole string of previous murders. Maybe Banks had been doing some work on those, too? The only thing Stevens was certain of was that Banks had a lead on this East End garage. And he knew it was a job he had been keen to finish. So Stevens waited and watched, and got together and made plans with George Jakes. And because Stevens and Jakes had had close friendships with Banks, the investigation of Banks's murder was passed to another, more "impartial" team. Not that there was any real impartiality; a policeman had been murdered, and the police are clannish about that kind of thing. Anyway, Stevens and Jakes were out of it.

"But *if* there was some connection between Banks's murder and his theory about the garage and his auto-theft case, Stevens reckoned business would fall off a bit now; the gang would keep a low profile until they saw which way the wind blew. In which case it would be pointless to raid the garage right now, for the place would be 'clean.'

"And in fact, over the next three weeks to a month, there *was* a noticeable fall-off in reported car-theft. But that could be coincidental, and Stevens still couldn't tie Banks's murder to the suspect garage. In a month, however, the moon had waned and waxed anew; toward the end of that period the incidence of vehicle theft had risen again; the taking of a couple of Porsches clinched it, and a raid on the garage was on . . . and the moon was nearing its full.

"Meanwhile, Stevens and Jakes had looked the place over. A run-down, multi-story ex-municipal car park, the garage was huge and decrepit, a concrete skeleton. Upstairs it was a gutted ruin; only the ground floor and basement were still viable, and housed the garage proper. Access, however, was by no means easy. There were no windows on the ground floor and one of the two old entrance/exits had been blocked off. The remaining entranceway onto the disused ramps was controlled by a manned barrier and a motorized, steel-ribbed, retractable overhead door. There was no natural light in the work areas, only electrical, and the only visitors allowed inside were clients whose vehicles were in process of repair. A search-warrant was vital.

"But in the course of looking the place over, Stevens and Jakes had experienced the same kind of invasion suffered by Jim Banks: something, or one, had got into their minds! But a feeling so strange, unnatural, weird, that neither one of them more than mentioned it to the other! Maybe they suspected they might be cracking up a little—certainly Stevens felt shaky about it—but neither one of them made too much of it, not to his partner, anyway. In fact Derek Stevens put it down to an attack of nerves, and to the loss of Jim Banks. But I've spoken to both of them now, and I know that their symptoms were exactly the same.

"This wolf-thing, a self-designated lycanthrope, was into their minds. Maybe he'd been alerted by their giving the garage the once- or twice-over in preparation for their raid. Whatever, it never got that far . . .

"Five nights ago, a day before the full moon, Stevens was driving home from work on wet roads through a thin drizzle. He stopped at a red light controlling road-works at a bridge over a railway . . . but the truck following right behind him didn't! The only warning he got was that *Thing* in his mind, an obscene chuckle, and a gurgling mental voice that told him: 'Kiss your asshole goodbye, fuckhead!' Followed by a howling, like a madman trying to imitate a wolf.

"Struck in the right-hand rear, his car spun left, smashed through a makeshift 'safety' barrier, and fell thirty feet onto electrified tracks . . .''

Darcy Clarke nodded. "We read about it in the papers. That would probably have been enough—falling like that and crashing down on that live rail—but the commuter train that piled into him two minutes later left no doubt. It was a miracle the train wasn't derailed and there were no other injuries."

Harry nodded. "That was the extent of what Derek Stevens could tell me. And now I'm left with George Jakes. Or rather, with whatever is left of him!''

"Harry," Darcy was very quiet, "I know you've seen some stuff, but the police have told us that this one is, you know, ugly. Jakes didn't have any family, so they didn't pretty him up much. He's . . . just as our mad friend left him three nights ago. But the police are finished with him now and he burns the day after tomorrow. Jakes was a 'Green' and that's how he wanted to go, cremated. He reckoned we're short enough of space as it is, without filling the ground with dead meat—his words, Harry, not mine! So his boss told me, anyway."

Harry thought about it a moment, and said, "You're right, Darcy, I've seen some stuff. The Château Bronnitsy . . . was full of it! But thanks for the warning, anyway. I could probably contact Jakes from here, or from my room at E-Branch HQ, but that isn't my way. See, in my book, respect works both ways: if you want it, you've got to give it. So I'll go to see him anyway."

And in a little while they were there . . .

No two dead people are alike, Harry knew that. Jim Banks had been hard, but not really. Derek Stevens had been hard-headed; he hadn't wanted to admit defeat, wasn't nearly ready to quit, even when the chips were all the way down. With them, maybe it was like a suit of clothes you wear to impress. They were just people underneath, wearing policemen on the outside. Well, and that was them. But George Jakes was something else. George had been *hard* hard. And he still was.

And he was soft, too, in places. Or as soft as his rigor mortis would allow.

But on occasions like this, the Necroscope was adept at keeping his thoughts to himself . . .

Harry and his friends had been taken down into the Unnatural or Suspect Deaths room by a police pathologist in a white surgical smock—rather, it had started out white, but their guide had just finished an autopsy in another room. Chatting to them in a friendly enough fashion, he cleaned his hands on the smock as he led the way, then stripped off his thin rubber gloves to let the trio into the locked, refrigerated morgue. And leaving them, he told them, "Drop the key into my room when you're finished." Which was the only thing they actually heard. The rest of his patter had been drowned out, blurred to a mumble by the morbid aura of the place.

Clarke and Layard followed quietly behind Harry where he went from sliding drawer to drawer, examining labels. But when he stopped at a drawer marked "George Jakes" they stepped back a little. Darcy admitted to still being queasy from the mess in Oxford Street, and Layard didn't want to see stuff just for the sake of seeing it. But if Harry really needed them . . . ? He shook his head and let them leave, then slid open the drawer. And:

What's new, Necroscope? said George Jakes, with a grin of horror on his face that he'd wear forever, or at least until it rotted off. And before Harry could answer, but in a far quieter mode, as Jakes scanned his visitor's stunned thoughts: *Hey, is it that bad? Funny, 'cos I can't feel a thing! But I can remember it—and how! And seeing it in Technicolor doesn't really help. So what say you switch it off now, Necroscope? I mean, I was never a one for watching myself on home videos, either, you know what I mean?* By which time the humorous touch had disappeared entirely from Jakes's voice. And Harry realized that the dead man had been looking at himself through his eyes!

He quickly slid the drawer shut, groped for a steel chair to steady himself, sat down heavily in it and said, "George . . . I . . . What can I say? I'm sorry." It didn't seem much, but what else *could* he say?

Despite that the drawer was shut, Harry could still see its contents. They were printed on his mind's eye in all their gory details. But Darcy had been wrong: someone *had* done something of a job on the corpse, if only to make it bearable. The stitches were . . . less than cosmetic. Like a slipshod job on a torn hessian sack, Jakes's corpse seemed to have been sewn together mainly to *keep* it together, to stop him falling open or even apart.

Harry deliberately put the picture out of mind—to keep it from Jakes's mind—and took a deep breath. Then, remembering what Jim Banks had told him: "But at least you didn't feel all of it, George," he said. "You couldn't possibly have felt all of it."

I felt enough, Jakes answered. *More than enough to put me down among the dead men!* Obviously he wanted to forget it, but knew that he couldn't, not for a little while. So: *Let's get on with it, Harry. I know what you want, so let's get started . . .*

I had no family, (Jakes commenced his story). *The only real friends I had, and few of them at that, were on the force. I'd been a cop man and boy, since I was eighteen until a couple of weeks ago when I turned forty. And much like you, Harry, I was the one who always got the nasty cases. It just seemed to turn out that way: rapists and murderers and arsonists, pimps, perverts and all the slime that walks the streets, they all seemed to head my* way. Hence my reluctance to make more than a handful of friends, take a wife and raise a family. Being that close to all of the shit, I didn't like the idea of contaminating others. Or . . . maybe it was a matter of trust. So many people out there seem bent on making it, even over the bodies of the rest of us, that I wasn't willing to put myself in the firing line. I mean, I'd be the best sort of cop I knew how, sure, but I'd get along just fine on my own and not rely on anyone else. And I did.

And people—even other cops, unless they were close to me—didn't mess with me. I had this reputation: I smoked too many cigarettes, and drank too much cheap whiskey, maybe . . . but I got the job done. Especially if it was a job no one else wanted. And I was hard, for despite all my bad habits I kept my body in good nick. It would have to be one rough son of a bitch who put me down. And it was . . .

Normally I wouldn't have fallen for it, but these weren't normal times; I was feeling for Derek Stevens. I mean, one day there were two of us, and the next . . . he was gone! A lousy hit and run traffic accident, of all things. But at least it proved my theory: that a man's better off on his own, if only because he leaves no one to mourn after him when he's gone. I suppose I was bitter, you know? And no way I could tie Derek's or Jim Banks's deaths together, or connect them to Jim's work on the stolen car rackets.

But one thing for sure: warrant or no warrant, tomorrow I was into that East End garage. And nothing and no one was going to stop me! The trouble was, I thought these things while walking the street with my hands in my pockets and my fortieth cigarette sticking out of a corner of my mouth right there outside the garage, which I was looking at one last time before busting the place. And of course he was listening to me! I knew he was there, in my head, but figured it was just another symptom of the blues.

Well, you live and you learn, and then you die . . .

Before I left the place I saw a van rolling down the exit lane onto the road. There were two guys inside, and the van was giving out a blast of raw jungle-music, I mean like that calypso stuff that your namesake Harry Belafonte used to sing, but a hell of a lot wilder. Hey, I never got past Bill Haley, Little Richard and Fats Domino, so don't ask me to be specific! But it was Caribbean Island stuff: Jamaica or somewhere like that, for sure. And so was the front seat passenger.

He was Rasta as they come, greasy dreadlocks and all, and his eyes were black as his plaited hair where they stared at me as the van shot by. Those dark eyes seemed to be saying, "We'll be seein' ya 'gain, Honky!" And they sure enough did!

The guy driving was younger by three or four years; he was white—well, a dirty pale—pimply, sort of loose around the mouth like some kind of idiot, and wore a crewcut. Yeah, Harry, I know. What do you think, I've been lying here doing nothing? I've had a word or two with Jim Banks, sure, and this guy would have to be Skippy. But I didn't know that then. These guys were what?—Just a couple of yobs employed by the garage, as far as I was concerned. Yeah, a couple of yobs who were waiting for me in my flat when I got home.

Like I said, if I hadn't been so down I might have sensed it, I might have known something didn't smell right. But by the time I did smell it, it was too late.

My flat is on the ground floor and the other two tenants, upstairs, always work late. So the rest of the house was empty. It was—I don't know—something-to-seven by the time I got home. Outside, the street lights were already on. But as I turned my key (which seemed to stick in the lock a little), opened the door, stepped inside and tried to switch on the lights . . .

. . . Suddenly I knew! But it was already too late.

There was a little light from a street lamp right outside the main door of the house, which shone in through chinks in my curtained windows. But I hadn't been in there a minute before I knew they were there. Just a feeling, or a taste or smell; the fact that my lights were on the blink; and shadows where there shouldn't be any.

I don't know who or what hit me on the head. But the carpet was wet with my blood when I came to, and a spot behind my ear felt soft. I could only have been down a second or so, but as I stirred and tried to drag myself into a sitting position I heard this ugly voice say, "Tough bastard, isn't he?" in a broad Geordie accent. And another voice, deep and brown and guttural, and yet a voice in my head, *saying:*

"Yeah. But you'll be softer on the inside, won't ya, boy?"

And when I opened my eyes to catch a glimpse of that face, which I knew went with the voice . . .

. . . It was Jim Banks's wolf-face, of course, but the mad eyes staring out of the sockets were black and glinty as coal, and human . . . and inhuman! *Then I was kicked over onto my back, and the thing seated itself astride my upper thighs and showed me its claw: five surgical knives set in a swarf-glove that he wore over his hand!*

It was dark in my flat, as I've said; the only light came in through chinks in the curtains from the street lamp outside; but it wasn't so dark I couldn't see this Skippy character over the crazy man's shoulder; how pale his face looked, and how he couldn't bear *to look but must turn away!*

And then the pain as that Thing ripped into me, and didn't stop ripping . . .

But you're right, Harry, Jakes sighed after a while, *I didn't feel all of it. You can only take so much, you know? And funny, the last thing I remember thinking before I passed out and woke up here, was: "Jesus, my flat's going to look a real mess . . . !"*

Then he was quiet again, maybe turning it all over in his own mind. But as the Necroscope was about to say thanks, Jakes said: *Oh, and there's one other thing. It probably isn't worth mentioning, but I'll let you decide. There was this girl.*

"Girl?" Harry repeated him.

She was outside the garage, just walking up and down the street. I saw her there twice, and again on the night . . . that this happened. He shrugged the last off, was finally done with it. *She was a real looker. Tall, slim, slinky, yet natural with it. Maybe Eurasian? Could be, from the shape of her eyes: like almonds and very slightly tilted. And her hair, bouncing on her shoulders, seeming black as jet but gray in its sheen, with the light glancing off it. She was the ageless type, Harry. I mean, anything from nineteen to thirty-five. But a looker, oh yes!*

He pictured her for the Necroscope, who agreed with him: yes, she was definitely a looker. "A customer, waiting for her car to be fixed?"

Could be, Jakes shrugged again, and fell silent.

The interview was over . . .

R. L. STEVENSON JAMIESON, AND HIS BROTHER . . .

BACK AT E-BRANCH HQ IT SHOULD HAVE BEEN TIME TO CALL IT A DAY, OR A night, but Darcy had mentioned some paperwork he must see to before going home. Likewise Ken Layard; he also had work to attend to. And so they had ridden up together with Harry in the elevator and accompanied him to his door. Or perhaps the paperwork was just an excuse because they had sensed that the night wasn't quite over yet where the Necroscope was concerned.

The place was quiet. With the majority of esper personnel already checked out, the main corridor might easily be mistaken for any corridor in any better-class London hotel. But the Duty Officer had met the three out of the elevator, and as the Necroscope entered his room and made to close the door . . . suddenly it seemed he heard someone breathe his name! He immediately boiled over and, stepping back into the corridor, shouted, "Hey, look! If I'm involved, why not simply *involve* me? I mean, don't talk about me, talk to me! What am I, a social leper?"

Layard had already entered his office; but Darcy and the Duty Officer, an esper by the name of John Grieve—a bespectacled, balding twig of a man in rolled up shirt-sleeves, gray slacks and slippers, with a clipped, precise, military or "old-school-tie" sort of voice that Harry supposed might easily get him typecast as an Inland Revenue Inspector, which he was anything but—were standing with their heads almost conspiratorially close together.

"Well?" he snapped, as they turned puzzled faces toward him.

"Well what?" Darcy was plainly annoyed. "We weren't talking about you, Harry!"

"Er, but we *were* about to." John Grieve was less certain and fidgeted with the lobe of his right ear. "Or if not about you, about your wife. And you're perfectly correct: I should have included you. But I wanted Darcy's opinion first."

Now Darcy was looking at Grieve in the same puzzled fashion. "What? What's going on?"

"That's what I was trying to tell you. It's about Brenda." And quickly, before Darcy and the Necroscope could break into a bout of angry questioning: "We seem to have lost her—and the baby." In the Necroscope's mind, Grieve's dry, official, almost emotionless voice seemed to ring like an echo chamber; Darcy's, too. Perhaps it was an irritating effect of the empty corridor and rooms, he thought, and put it aside if only for the moment. But Brenda and Little Harry, missing? That was something else!

"Lost them?" he repeated Grieve. "My wife and child? What do you mean, 'lost' them?" The phrase seemed too well-chosen, too final. Harry's tired eyes were wide awake now, unblinking. "Have they . . . come to any harm?" He grabbed the DO's elbow.

Grieve looked him straight in the eyes and said, "No, not that we know of. Now, do you want to let go of my arm so I can talk to you in what's left of comfort?"

Harry gritted his teeth but released him. And waiting for Grieve to speak, he re-evaluated what he knew of the man. Grieve had two talents; one of them "dodgy," Branch parlance for an as yet undeveloped ESP ability, and the other very remarkable and possibly unique. His first gift was that of far-seeing: he was a human crystal ball. The only trouble was he had to know exactly where and what he was looking for, otherwise he could see nothing. His talent didn't work at random but had to be directed: he had to have a definite target. .

His second string made him doubly valuable. It could well prove to be a reflection of his first talent, but occasionally it was a godsend. Grieve was a telepath, but a mind reader with a difference. Yet again he had to "aim" his talent; he could only read a person's mind when he was talking to him . . . but if he knew the person in question, that *included* when they were talking on the telephone! Using John Grieve, there was no need for mechanical scrambler devices. It was one reason why Darcy used him as frequently as possible in the role of Duty Officer.

But . . . had it been something of Grieve's talent that the Necroscope had experienced just a moment ago? Was it even possible?

"You weren't talking about me?" Harry frowned and licked his dry lips, his mind returning to that peculiar sensation he had felt when he'd entered his room: the feeling that his name had been whispered. And then there was the echo chamber effect, which was still present: as if his head were hollow—or as if it were . . . what, occupied? By someone else? Someone who was spying on his thoughts? "Were you *thinking* about me, then? And if so, would I be able to *hear* you thinking?" Suddenly Brenda and the child had taken a back seat in Harry's order of priorities. Or if not that exactly, then he'd seen the possibility of a connection with their disappearance and this new problem. A remote one (he hoped and prayed), but a possibility.

Again Harry gripped Grieve's arm, then both of them, as he read the other's negative stare. No, he wouldn't have been able to hear Grieve thinking about him. And so: "John, I want you to read my mind," he snapped. "Go on in there and see what you can find. See *who* you can find! Do it now, as quickly as you can."

Almost instinctively Grieve looked, and recoiled at once! He wrenched himself free of Harry, took a stumbling step backward, said, "What . . . ?"

"Well?" Harry caught up with him and held him against the wall of the corridor. "What did you see?" (Perhaps not surprisingly, the echo had vanished now; the voices of everyone involved were remarkably clear and ordinary; there was no whisperer in the Necroscope's mind).

Darcy was looking worriedly from Harry to Grieve and back again. "What on earth . . . ?" he began to say. But Grieve cut him short with:

"Two of you?" (This to Harry). "A moment ago, two of you. But now, only one. Only . . . you!"

Again Harry released him, and turned tremblingly away. He had been invaded, his mind broken into. Just like Banks, Stevens, and Jakes before him. For long moments there was an electric tension in the air, until finally:

"Well, is someone going to explain?!" Darcy shouted.

At which Harry took them into his room and listened while Grieve reported the details of Brenda's and Little Harry's disappearance. Grieve didn't waste any time, but the Necroscope was now sensitive to every second ticking by. And as he listened to Grieve, he also found himself listening to—or for—something in his head. But it didn't return. Or not yet, anyway.

"She was shopping in Knightsbridge," Grieve started. "She had the baby with her. We had men on her, of course, three of the best. The same people who have watched out for her all the time she's been here, Special Branch and good at their job. Not espers but the next best thing." He shook his head. "If it were anyone else, I'd suspect their report was a whitewash. But not these blokes. They know what they're doing. And if they say she disappeared, she disappeared . . .

"But not into the crowd, you understand, though certainly there were plenty of people on the streets. But she took young Harry into a baby outfitters, and left the minders waiting outside. Where they waited, and waited . . . and finally went in to see what was wrong. Well, there was no exit from the rear, but Brenda and the kid—"

"—Were gone," Harry sounded much calmer now. "Yes, I get the picture. But what time was this?"

"Five-thirty or thereabouts. You two had already left the H.Q. with Ken Layard. I didn't want to cause a panic or divert you from what you were doing. There seemed every chance that we would pick Brenda up again. I mean, we're not looking after her because she's under threat or anything, but mainly because . . . well, because—"

"—Because sometimes she doesn't seem capable of looking after herself?" Harry cut in again. "It's okay, go ahead and say it. She has problems, I know." And to himself: *Problems, Brenda? That's saying the very least!*

All those weeks, months of debriefing following the Bodescu case and Harry's subsequent metempsychosis, his rehabitation of another's body. Indeed his very *being*, when Brenda had thought him dead. Wouldn't that be enough to . . . *unnerve* anyone? And gradually, during the course of all that debriefing, and Harry's rehabilitation, it had become increasingly apparent that Brenda was in real trouble. But surely that was only to be expected, and might even have been anticipated.

For after all, Brenda had only recently become a mother; she'd still been recovering from an uncomfortable confinement and problematic birth, when for a while her doctor had thought he might lose her. Add to this the fact of her husband's weird "talent," that he conversed with dead people, which Brenda had known about and which had preyed on her mind for months—and then the fact that her infant child seemed possessed of similar or even more frightening powers, so that even among the espers of E-Branch he was looked upon as something of a freak—and the fact that Harry was now (literally) a different person, one who *was* Harry, with all of his past, his memory and mannerisms, but living in a stranger's body; the fact of the absolute *terror* Brenda had endured on the night when she came face to face with the monster Yulian Bodescu, whose like she couldn't possibly have imagined even in her worst nightmares . . .

Little wonder her mind had started to give way under the strain. On top of which she hated London and couldn't possibly return to Hartlepool in the north-east; her old flat would be poison to her and full of monstrous memories. For it was there that the Bodescu creature had attacked her, attempting to destroy both herself and her child!

Thus, as her mental connections with the real world were eroded, Brenda's visits to various specialists and psychiatric clinics had increased. Until now . . . what had happened here? Had she decided that enough was enough? Or was it the work of some outside agency? Or could it be that the baby himself . . . ?

"Anyway," Grieve continued, glad to be off the hook, "it didn't work out like I thought it would and they're still missing. We have as many Branch agents on it as we can spare. They're out there in the city right now, doing whatever they can."

His words drew the Necroscope back to earth. "The address of the store?" The look on Harry's face was now entirely grim.

Grieve took Darcy and Harry to the Ops Room, punched up a street map of London onto the big screen. He showed the Necroscope the exact location of the store.

Harry said, "Okay, now I have something to do." Then, to John Grieve: "I won't be gone long, but in the meantime Darcy might like to tell you about the case we're on." And to Darcy: "I hope this thing with Brenda has nothing to do with our werewolf, but ever since we got back here—I don't know, I can't be sure—but I think I've been experiencing the same sort of mental invasion that Banks and the others described."

"Christ!" Darcy gasped as the meaning, or a possible meaning, of what the Necroscope had said sank in. "But if he knows you're on to him . . . do you think he'd take hostages?"

Harry held up his hands in a helpless gesture, but a moment later gave a grim shake of his head. "No, I don't think my son would *let* him! Let's hope it's just a coincidence. But one thing for sure, I daren't waste tonight. So while I'm gone perhaps you'd like to call in Trevor Jordan? Better still, let me have his address and tell him to wait there for me. It's something Sir Keenan Gormley recommended . . ."

Using several co ordinates that he knew, the Necroscope went to the store in Knightsbridge where he entered the premises using the Möbius Continuum. His arrival at once set off the store's alarms, but that didn't bother him; in the event that his plan worked, he wasn't going to be here very long.

In Harry's incorporeal days, before his "repossession" of Alec Kyle, he had been able to travel into the past and "immaterialize" there: he'd been able to manifest a ghostly semblance of himself on any bygone event horizon. Now, embodied and fully corporeal once more, this was no longer possible; it would create unthinkable paradoxes and perhaps even damage the temporal flux itself. He could still travel *in* time, but while doing so must never attempt to leave the Möbius Continuum for the real world.

Transferring back to the Continuum, he found a past-time door and floated for a moment on the threshold, gazing on time past. This was a sight that never failed to awe him: the myriad blue life-threads of mankind, twisting and twining in the metaphysical "vacuum" of a previously conjectural fourth dimension; those neon filaments that might best be likened to the "retinal memories" of time, the trails of human lives that had traveled here; or if not here, in the mundane world on the other side of the Möbius Continuum.

And way back there in the past, the blue haze of Man's origins, that supernova of human life, from which these streamers had hurled themselves into the ever-expanding future. It seemed to Harry that he heard an orchestrated, sighing *Ahhhhhhh* sound, like a single, pure note from some other-worldly instrument, or the massed voices of a magnificent chorus in a sounding cathedral; but in fact he knew that all was silence, that it was only the effect of his stunned mind. For if any man were to actually *hear* the tumult of the past, that would be a sound to blast his brain and deafen him forever.

Almost reluctantly, the Necroscope brought himself back to the task in hand. This was the place where his wife and son had disappeared just a few hours ago. Well, he had his own theories about what had happened to them; and now, one way or the other, he intended to prove them. And without further ado he launched himself down the past time-stream.

But here a curious and paradoxical thing. Because he had never existed in this particular space-time, Harry had no past life-thread to follow but must simply let himself plummet, and because this region of the past was now *his* present (and even his future!), his true life-line extended *behind* him and seemed to unwind from him like cotton from a bobbin back to the past-time door. And Harry found the knowledge that he could return to his point of entry via that thread very reassuring . . .

In a little while he had reached his destination, arriving at a point in past time where it would be proved eventually that his son, the infant Harry, had contrived to bring about an amazing, almost unique occurrence. But that was for the future, not the past!

He knew the life-threads of Brenda and her baby at once; he seemed drawn to them—sucked at by their rush—as they emerged like bright blue meteors out of the past, and hurtled by him on course for the true future. The one a mature blue nucleus at the head of a trailing thread, its pathway through all the alternatives of time, and the other smaller, but brilliant with new life! This was them, or their temporal "echoes" after entering the store, but what the Necroscope desired to discover was their course from here on.

Quickly reversing his direction of travel, Harry followed behind and gained on them; for he had the advantage of knowing that time is relative, and that in the metaphysical Möbius Continuum *will* is the single cause that brings effect. And indeed he willed himself to catch up with them, "just in time."

Speeding behind them, intent on following wherever young Harry might take his mother, the Necroscope was witness to an effect that would baffle even him, and continue to do so for a period of seven long years—or "lost years," as much of that time would come to seem to him. For Harry had forgotten a very simple fact: that what *he* could do with the Continuum, his son could do in spades!

It was simply this: that in the space of a single moment of time Brenda and the infant Harry's life-threads had come to an abrupt, totally unexpected, apparently violent end! Blinded by the sudden flash of twin bomb-bursts, Harry closed his eyes and sped on through what must surely be the debris of his family, scattered atoms of light occupying the "space" where they had been. But then, looking back, he saw that their termination had been too complete, too utter; that in fact *nothing* remained of them. Not in this world, anyway—

—Or rather, not in this place?

And so perhaps Harry could be forgiven for believing that his son had simply moved his mother to some other, safer place in the mundane world, and that he would experience little difficulty in finding them and going to them later.

But later can be a long time, as the Necroscope would discover soon enough. And in his case it might even be years . . .

Back at the baby outfitters, the alarms were still going off. As Harry paused there to get his co-ordinates, so the telephone started ringing. For a moment he ignored it, then gave it some thought. For who would be trying to call a baby store at this time of night? The answer seemed obvious.

Moving to the front of the store, Harry found the office, desk, and telephone, and lifted the latter from its cradle. At the other end of the line, Darcy Clarke said: "Harry?"

"Yes?"

"Good, I'm glad I caught you! Look, don't go to Trevor's place. I spoke to him on the 'phone and by now he's on his way in. But, er, he told me to tell you that he wouldn't—I mean, not under *any* circumstances—accompany you anywhere via *your* mode of travel. Is that understood?"

Harry grinned to himself however coldly, and nodded. "Yes, understood," he said. And: "Can you reach him in his car?"

"Yes."

"Then tell him to go to this address and meet me there." He passed on the address of the East End garage. "And tell him to keep a low profile."

"Harry, is this wise?" Darcy's concern came over loud and clear. "Do you think you should be following this up? I mean, tonight?"

"Probably not, but I didn't start it."

"What about police or E-Branch back-up?"

"Definitely not! Just Jordan, no back-up. In fact I want you to back off!"

For a moment there was silence, then Darcy asked, "Can I hear alarms ringing?"

"Probably in more ways than one," Harry answered, and put the 'phone down. And to himself: *Sirens, too!* Outside the shop, visible through the plate glass, a police car had screeched to a halt. Its siren was blaring and blue light rotating. A young policeman came to the window, held a hand over the peak of his cap and scanned the interior. He saw Harry walk out of the office, shrank to one side, began talking excitedly into his handset. Harry waved cheerily at him, then walked into the back of the store where it was still dark, conjured a Möbius door and took his departure.

Lawmen had irritated the Necroscope more than enough for one day. Time to let *them* do some explaining—and especially after they'd broken into the store for no apparent reason . . .

Harry took the Möbius route to the East End, and stepped from his door into a thin, penetrating drizzle that filled the night with its misery and turned the cobbles to gleaming jet. Turning up his collar, Harry walked a quarter-mile to the run-down district where the garage was located, and from a nearby street looked the place over. The garage was pretty much as Harry had heard it described.

Its supports and upper floors formed a concrete skeleton six stories high; the sections making up the outer safety walls had been knocked out, so that the floors were like vast lintels supported on giant steel and concrete stanchions. In silhouette against the night sky, the place might be a towering 20th-century Stonehenge, or some surrealist sculptor's "Ziggurat."

Below, at ground level, the ramps at Harry's end of the mainly derelict building had been removed, the entrance bricked up. But enclosed behind an eight-foot-high brick wall, a maintenance yard extended a further sixty feet or so beyond the end of the main structure. Ensuring that he wasn't observed, Harry made a quick Möbius jump into the yard to have a look . . .

. . . And retreated in double quick time when he discovered warehouse doors standing open at the end of the main building, emitting a blaze of electric light and the sounds of human and mechanized activity. Also, the yard was full of quality motors; he'd seen a handful of Porsches, even a Lotus! Obviously the people in the garage were working overtime, and the Necroscope knew what they were working on. He only hoped they wouldn't be working too late, and that Trevor Jordan wasn't going to take all night getting here.

For if the "werewolf" were on duty, sooner or later he'd be bound to discover Harry lurking out here, which could only result in complications. But Sir Keenan Gormley had advised to fight fire with fire, and Harry's answer to his unknown adversary's telepathy was Trevor Jordan's. Maybe Jordan could block the other out, giving the Necroscope the edge he needed. Which wasn't to say that Harry didn't already have an edge; he had a good many edges, and sharp ones at that, but he'd seen through the eyes of dead men what he was up against.

His plan was a simple one:

Get into the garage, check out some plates, engine block numbers and what have you, get out again and report the entire operation to the police. The Branch could pass on the information about the crazy wolfman, the murders he'd committed. And if there wasn't enough real, *living* evidence against that one . . . maybe Harry could think up some other way to settle the score. Maybe even to the point where he'd offer himself up as bait.

But the law is the law; despite that the Necroscope might occasionally seem scathing of red-tape officialdom, he wouldn't be playing the part of executioner just for the sake of it. He knew that the murdered men, especially Jim Banks and the other policemen, wouldn't want it that way. Well, not if it could be avoided. But if it couldn't—

—In that case, if there were no other way, then Sir Keenan Gormley's law would apply. Then it would *have* to be Harry's way. An eye for an eye . . .

Right now, however, deciding that his lone figure was too obvious standing there in the blurry, watered-down light of the street lamps, Harry made his way to an alley on the far side of the road and stepped into its shadows. No sooner had he done so than he realized that he hadn't been alone in what he'd thought was an empty street. Looking out into the night, he saw a figure, female, walking in his direction but on the other side of the road, in the lee of the garage wall.

Despite that she wore flat black shoes, she looked tall and lithe. Her gloves were black, too, as was her trouser-suit. Her hair was tied back in a pony-tail, and her manner was carefree as she swung a fancy black shopping bag, for all the world as if she were just returning from a jaunt to some fashionable outfitters for that special little item—and to hell with the rain! Harry couldn't quite make out her features but found himself wishing that he could, for he felt sure she'd be a looker . . . At which he remembered what George Jakes had told him.

Could this be the same girl? She fitted Jakes's picture, definitely. But if so, what would she be doing here now? Some sort of fancy lookout for the garage? It seemed likely.

But then, catching a glimpse of her dark, slanted almond eyes in a pale, heart-shaped face as the girl reached the wall of the maintenance yard and glanced across the street in his direction, the Necroscope drew back into the alley's shadows.

And as his back met the wall—at that precise moment of time—a well-known voice spoke suddenly, sharply in his mind: *Harry? Thank goodness I've found you! My boy, you move so fast, it's hard keeping track of you!* Sir Keenan had spoken to him at a moment of maximum concentration, when his nerves were at full stretch. So that there in the darkness Harry gasped and gave an involuntary start. The dead man felt it and said, *Oh, and what are you up to now? Why are you so jumpy?*

Harry took a chance and glanced quickly round the corner. But the girl . . . was gone? But how? There were no other alleyways close by, and the street was a long one. Yet from what he could see it was deserted end to end. Even an Olympic sprinter couldn't have disappeared at that speed! And it wasn't likely she'd gone over that wall . . . was it?

Well? Sir Keenan pressed him. *What's going on?*

Putting the problem of the girl aside to explain the more important details, Harry whispered: "So you see, while I was half-expecting some kind of mental intruder, I *wasn't* expecting you!" On the other hand, while he engaged in incorporeal conversation with Keenan Gormley, he wasn't likely to be overheard and intruded upon by any living mind. Even a telepathic "werewolf" can't intercept the thoughts of the dead.

Sir Keenan, however, could hear his thoughts well enough, and told him: *Harry, you know that normally I wouldn't bother you, but I believe this to be important. Indeed, I think it's what you've been looking for—the identity of the murderer!*

Harry stiffened at once and said, "I think I already have it. Or if not an actual identity, a description at least. But it would be good to have confirmation, yes.''

It happened after you visited Banks, Stevens, and Jakes, Sir Keenan told him. *Someone came forward.*

''A dead someone?''

Oh yes, a victim no less than the others. Yet if possible a worse crime *than the others, for this was the murderer's own brother!* The Necroscope sensed what would be the sad shake of Sir Keenan's head. Then: *Harry, now I'd like to introduce you to R.L. Stevenson Jamieson, and let him take it from there . . .*

Harry had become adept at discerning good from bad almost from the initial ''sound'' of a dead voice. And when this one spoke to him, at first tremulously, and then with growing confidence, he knew its owner for a good and honest man.

I reckon I was, yeah, the other agreed, but not without a degree of modesty. *As best I knew how, anyways. But my brother . . . wasn't. Like I means, he* isn't! *You want to hear our story, Necroscope? See, I think things is gone far enough. I has heard you talking to others 'bout this thing, and even though I was a ways off and it weren't me you talked to, still I felt how warm you was. So I know why the dead 'uns love you so. And God knows that should anything happen to you, my name and bones is cursed forever. Well, I don't want that! No way! So . . . does you have the time to hear me out, Necroscope?*

And of course Harry nodded his confirmation . . .

I'll keep it short (R.L. Stevenson began his story). *We were born in Haiti, Port-au-Prince. By we I means me and my brother, A.C. Doyle Jamieson. And before you asks: yes, our Poppy was a hell of a reading man! We had a older sister, too, Shelley. Or M.W. as we sometimes called her, 'cos Wollstonecraft is a mite long-winded.*

I was born in '46 and Arthur Conan came seven years later. So you see, he was my little brother. But out there in the Antilles it was much the same as here in England, or anywhere else in the world, I reckon: there's a hell of a difference in seven years! What I mean is, I was brung up respectful to folks, just like Shelley before me. But by the time Arthur Conan came along things was changing. For one thing, Poppy was getting old. He weren't much good at correcting anymore.

Ma died when Arthur Conan was born, and three years later Shelley got herself married and moved across to Jamaica. Which left just me, ten years old, Poppy, and A.C. That didn't help a lot neither, 'cos there was no women folk to teach A.C. his manners and put him right when he did wrong, just me and Poppy to do our best at spoiling him . . . which we did. By then Poppy was really old; A.C. had been his last spurt, so to speak, if you take my meaning.

About Poppy. He had obeah *blood in him; me too, a little, and A.C. a lot! You know the obi, Harry? Shoot, a 'course you does! Why, this thing you're doing right now is . . . well, it's obeah, right? Black magic! Obi! Those islands is still full of it, I hear. Whole regimes has risen and fallen on it! But more of it when A.C. and me was kids. It came with the black folks out of Africa, you know? The preacher used to say that obi was born in sin and bred in ignorance, and didn't have no place in a God-fearing world. But I always figured he was more a-feared of obi than God!*

Except, Poppy's obi was gentle stuff, for protection more than anything else. I mean, Poppy wouldn't a harmed a soul! He was just happy with his charms and love-potions, and never once messed with poisons or dead folks—I mean the zombies, Harry, begging your pardon! Protection, yeah! But Poppy did have something more than the simple stuff, and he coulda used it to make himself a big man. Why, whole governments have balanced on such as this, in Haiti and the Indies! Yeah! For Poppy had the power to look into a enemy's mind, and so know his every move.

Why, it was even better than that: he simply knew it when he came up against a bad one! This thing of his would kick in; right away he'd be reading any bad or dangerous thoughts aimed in his direction. And he'd know who was aiming them! Not that it happened too often, you understand, 'cos Poppy didn't have no enemies.

There was special times when Poppy would practice his obi, and the full of the moon was one of them. We had a little house and garden sheltered by the cliffs in a corner of a shingle bay near Port de Paix on the south coast. We kept a few chickens, a pig or two, and there was plenty of fish in the straits between Haiti and Tortue Island. What with green stuff out of the woods and the garden, we didn't do too badly at all. But as Poppy got older and A.C. grew up, I'd keep getting this feeling that my little brother wasn't satisfied. There was a whole wide world to play in, and our garden by the beach wasn't big enough . . .

We'd creep on up Poppy at full moon time. He had what he called his "obeah house": it was just a wooden shack at the end of the garden, where mostly he'd sit on a old rocker and tilt a jug. But sometimes he'd burn herbs, mutter a spell or two, turn in a circle and scan all around, to "feel" what was going on in the world. And the next day we'd have chicken for dinner, 'cos he'd a used a bird in his practice. But if he'd catch us spying on him, my, how he'd fly into a rage then! Obi was something he didn't want us having nothing *to do with! And he'd get me on my own and say:*

"You has a good aura. Robert, you is chocolate—which is to say, you's a natural thing. As a forest is green, and a fish is silver, you is chocolate. Like a log is brown, and the sky's blue, and the sea's deep green down under, you is the color of your soul, too. But son, I tell you your brother is dark. And I mean darker than just his skin! But Arthur's young and that can change—better had, too, else there's no good ending for him! Except I knows I won't be here to look out for him, so I got to leave all that to you. You is his brother, after all." And that was me stuck with it. Not that I minded much, not then . . .

But come the time A.C. was seventeen, I was a full-time working man and didn't have a lot of spare time for him. Poppy was on his very last legs; in fact, I couldn't see how the Old Boy was still hanging in there! And my brother . . . well, he be just a handful!

There was this girl in trouble in Port de Paix (not that that meant a hell of a lot, 'cos she had something of a reputation anyways), and A.C. was smoking a lot of the wrong stuff. Also, I suspected he was big in a gang on the wrong side of the law. And you got to remember, Harry, The Law out there in them days wasn't the same as here in England! No sir! Men was dying for their political beliefs, or just disappearing off the face of the earth, which amounted to much the same thing. But worse than these things, I also figured A.C. was doing some obeah, or trying to do it, anyways.

I spoke to Poppy 'bout it, and he said, "Son, it's what I feared. The blood will out. Obeah's in my blood, and in you and your brother's blood, too. Except I knows that if A.C. gets it he'll use it wrong. But I also knows that you is there to block him. So long as you is alive my obeah's split two ways, between you and your brother. So wherever he goes, whatever he does, be there to square it with the Powers That Be. I mean, the powers that govern obi. Just be there, and Arthur won't have full command of his skills. But son, I feel I has to tell you this . . . your brother is strong in obeah. I has known it for, oh, many a long year.

I reckon it's why I hangs on: 'cos I know he doesn't come fully into his own till I is passed on . . ."

Now Harry, that's a night I'll remember always, 'cos when I was leaving the Old Boy be in his obeah house, I saw a shadow sneaking away along the garden, and that shadow was shaped like my brother . . . Well, Poppy died a few days later, all curled up like an old leaf and clutching his belly as if he ate something that didn't agree. I had my suspicions, but God, I couldn't see A.C. doing that! I just couldn't . . . !

A couple years went by, and Poppy was right: his obi came down to me and A.C. But as I said before, I got a little and my brother got a lot—and all of what he got, bad!

A.C. was nineteen and wanted by The Law. Not for anything you could specify; mainly for being against the so-called authorities. If they'd got him he was a goner for sure, and A.C. knew it. That alone was enough to turn him against any kind of genuine authority from that time on. He wanted to smuggle himself out of the country, and he had the contacts to do it. All he needed was papers, which weren't hard come by to someone who could do a few favors, some obi tricks for folks, to get them. And he got papers for me, too.

See, I minded my promise to Poppy, that I would go along with A.C. wherever he went, and watch him whatever he did. He was my little brother, after all. So we came to England. I suppose we was illegal immigrants, since our papers were faked and all; anyway, they never did catch us. Luck—and obeah—were with us. And there's a lot of island folk over here, you know? There's always someone who be ready, willing, and able to protect an obi man. I suppose I was looked after 'cos people liked me, and A.C. 'cos . . . 'cos they feared him.

But trouble follows trouble, Harry, and here in UK, A.C. just couldn't keep his nose out of it, same as back home. Black gangs and what all, pilfering, drugs . . . he was just a bad lot; he was into everything! I would a given up on him for sure, but for my promise to Poppy. And I knew that he'd be a lot worse if I wasn't there to keep a balance. But it seemed my obi balanced his and kept him out of trouble. Well, out of the worst kind of trouble, anyways.

'Ventually we fell apart. I had me a job, a good one, too, and there was a girl . . . but never mind 'bout that.

One night A.C. came around to my place, and he'd had too much to drink. Said he wanted to talk. Well you know how drunks ramble. But there's rambling and rambling. My brother was looking at me sort of strange and breathing slow and heavy. And you know, Necroscope, I couldn't help but remember that night when Poppy told me about the balance between our obis, and how A.C. Doyle Jamieson wouldn't come into his own while Poppy was still alive; and how even then there'd be me to steer a path for him. And I admit I thought: "Well, looks like A.C.'s about ready to start steering his own path!" and I thought: "This boy wants my obi, too!"

Anyways, I asked him what was the trouble, and he told me the leader of another gang was after his skin. But A.C. could only catch a "glimpse" of this boy every now and then. I mean, an obeah glimpse, you know? Like when Poppy knew that a enemy was after him? But this was serious stuff, and A.C. needed to know this guy's every move. But he couldn't, 'cos my obeah was blocking his! And I had heard 'bout this boy and knowed he was real bad stuff.

Well, like a fool I told A.C. I'd rein back on it, and I did just that. I hadn't given my obi hardly a thought since my talk with Poppy, but now I concentrated on clearing the way for A.C. It weren't nothing physical, all in the mind. I just quit from giving off obi. I figure *you knows what I'm talking 'bout, Necroscope, 'cos you be like that. But . . . oh, I had bad dreams for a couple nights, 'til A.C. came to see me again.*

And by then it's been the time of the full moon, obi time, and I has seen in the papers how this other guy is dead and all tore up. And here's my brother, A.C. Doyle Jamieson, on top of the world, not like when I last saw him; 'cept just like before I couldn't believe that of him, not of my brother. But just in case, I lets my obi flow again; I send it out of me not just to guide but to counter Arthur! And he knows I done it, o' course. How? 'Cos he picked up on a enemy—me!

Well, a month went by . . . it was full moon time again . . . and after that . . . I mean it was then that . . . Harry, I was out of it! But don't ask me to tell you 'bout it, 'cos I won't. And you already had it from the others. And it's because you had it from them that I knows it were Arthur. See, the way it happened to them is how it happened to me. Just exactly. So in the end I has to face up to it; but like I always tells myself, A.C. was my brother, after all . . .

"**Y**ou will know, of course," Harry told R.L. Stevenson Jamieson in a while, "that the best your brother can expect is to be put away, probably for the rest of his days? And I do mean the very *best* he can expect."

And the worst?

"He thinks he's a werewolf, R.L., and to my way of thinking he won't be safe even behind bars or in a padded cell! But the worst is death. If he puts up a fight . . . well, he just has to lose. Because if he doesn't, other people will. They'll lose their lives."

He sensed R.L.'s nod. *I suppose I knowed that, deep down inside. Sure I did, 'cos if I hadn't, I wouldn't a come to you. But I figured if he got to go, best at your hands, Necroscope.*

"Not if I can help it, R.L.," Harry shook his head. "Not now I've spoken to you. But if it comes down to it . . ."

I'll understand, R.L. told him. *And Harry, if I can be of any help . . . ?*

"Well, perhaps you can at that." For out of the blue, the Necroscope had an idea. And: "How's your obi, R.L.?"

Eh? (And Harry could almost see the surprised expression on the other's face). *Why, it be gone down into the earth with me!*

"Oh, really?" For Harry knew it wasn't like that; he knew that whatever a man is or does in life, he'll usually continue to be and do afterward. Why, it could well be that R.L.'s obeah had helped keep his brother's identity secret even among the Great Majority!

You think so? R.L. obviously hadn't given it any thought. *Oh, my! You means, I was still looking out for A.C. even after he killed me?*

"It could very well be," Harry told him. "In a way you've kept right on protecting him—or his good name, at least."

Huh! said R.L. *His good name, indeed!*

"Yours, then," Harry answered. "And now, well, maybe you can protect me, too."

Eh? How's that? (Astonishment, this time!)

Harry explained, and R.L. quickly got the picture. He was dead and his obi with him . . . or maybe not. Through the Necroscope he could use it again, *for* the Necroscope! And in doing so deny its use to his brother. "But only if it comes down to it," Harry told him

—And in the next moment gave a massive start! There in the deep black shadows of the alley, he had been so caught up in his conversation with the dead man that he'd failed to hear the pad of soft, furtive footfalls as they approached him. Too late he *had* heard them—at the same time as a hand came down on his shoulder!

"Harry?" Trevor Jordan said, as the Necroscope gasped and lurched away from him. "Did I startle you?"

"Jesus Christ!" Harry whispered, falling back against the wall. "Trevor . . . Trevor, what do you think you're doing!?"

"What I was told to do," the other answered with a shrug and looked perplexed. "I'm keeping a low profile, what else?"

. . . AND ONE OTHER.

FREED OF HIS CONVERSATION WITH R.L., HARRY'S MIND BECAME A POSSIBLE target again, as did the telepath Trevor Jordan's. For of course he, too, was an enemy of A.C. Doyle Jamieson. The extra-sensory presence of both of them was too much; their combined esp-auras—undetectable to the great mass of mundane mankind—radiated out from them into the rainy night in every direction. One direction would have been more than sufficient: that of the garage across the road.

There came . . . an intrusion! Which the Necroscope felt at once. But instead of avoiding it or flinching from it, he answered back and tried to get into the mind that was getting into his. Trevor Jordan felt it, too, the blunt groping of a strange and strangely gifted mind, and said: "Wha—?"

But Harry held up a hand to still Jordan's inquiry, husking, "Listen in if you want, but be sure not to open your mind to it for now. I'll let you know when." And:

Huh? The intruder grunted like a pig in Harry's mind, no longer a mere whisperer but a sentience surprised that the Necroscope had recognized his presence and was reacting to it, but not in the way that the intruder had anticipated. Then, because he knew he'd been discovered:

You . . . again! There could be no mistaking the phlegmy, threatening quality of that voice, or the megalomaniac "superiority" of its owner. Any other man but a telepath born—and a practiced one, who had come into contact with deranged minds such as this before—must surely recoil from the stench, the mental slime of it, like a poison seeping in his mind. A telepath, yes . . . or the Necroscope Harry Keogh. For he had spoken with vampires, and not all of them dead ones. By comparison—and *strictly* by comparison—this mind was almost sweet. But as for the rest of it, the actual contact:

In fact, this mind-to-mind contact with a living person wasn't unlike speaking to the dead. Except Harry wasn't a true telepath; he couldn't "send," but only receive incoming information; any answers he might originate would only be "heard" by virtue of the *other's* telepathy—which in this case amounted to the same thing.

And this time the other—*none* other but A.C. Doyle Jamieson—had indeed heard the Necroscope's thoughts. But they were scarcely the thoughts of a frightened man, and definitely not those of one who doubted his own sanity! And:

Who are you? (There was anger in that voice now, and perhaps something of uncertainty if not downright fear.) *What are you? What the fuck . . . are . . . you!?*

"I'm the end of the road, Arthur," Harry told him. "I'm a big dose of your own brand of obeah bouncing right back at you. I'm a silver bullet heading for your heart. I'm the justice of all the lives you've taken held back way too long, pent up, and now about to burst out and enact itself on you!" But in Harry's metaphysical mind, irrepressible if not deliberately expressed, there was one other thought: *And I'm the one they call the Necroscope.*

A.C. got all of it, but especially the last bit. And even though he didn't know what a Necroscope was, it sounded threatening and he didn't like it. *Huh? Necroscope?* (The "scope" ending had stuck in his mind; finally made sense to him, albeit mistakenly.) *"Scope': a spy! A police spy? A raid? Oh, really?* A.C. was trying to sneer but in fact he was panicking now, and far more dangerous for it! Finally he broke and snarled: *Well, fuck your ass, bro!* His presence vanished abruptly from Harry's mind.

The seconds ticked by. Then:

Down the street at the other end of the garage, the overhead door began clattering up on itself, its long metal leaves concertinaing into the housing. It was easily sixty yards away, but in the quiet of the midnight street, even at that distance Harry and Trevor Jordan could hear hoarse, angry shouting. And as the darkness was suddenly slashed by headlight beams, a veritable convoy of vehicles came roaring down the exit ramp, one after the other onto the road. White and blue sparks lit the night where wings hit the walls of the ramp and chassis jarred down onto the shining tarmac as the cars and vans turned viciously, squealingly into the road, some heading in the one direction and others coming Harry's way.

He and Jordan ducked down, shrank against the wall of the alley, watched two cars and a van howl by, their drivers pale-faced where they crouched over their steering wheels. "Like a pack of rats deserting a sinking shit!" Jordan said in Harry's ear. Glancing at him, Harry saw that his eyes were narrowed to slits and his face creased in concentration. "But the shit who ordered them out of there is still inside!"

"What?" Harry frowned. "You're in contact with him? But I asked you to stay out of it! We're not sure what we're dealing with here."

"We're dealing with one powerful telepath, that much I'll grant you," Jordan answered. "Also a frightened one. Something is interfering with his talent. He's trying to locate you again but something is getting in his way. Not me or you but—oh, I don't know—something else. And anyway, I didn't deliberately ignore your warning, Harry. But with a talent as strong as this one . . . he's hard to avoid."

"R.L. Stevenson." Harry offered a grim nod. "That's what's bothering him most: his brother's obeah. I can almost feel it flowing through me!'' Which made little or no sense to Jordan; he couldn't get the meaning of it because he was busy *not* reading the Necroscope's mind.

But at that precise moment the intruder had chosen to return, and he *was* reading it. And:

What . . .!? (He issued a disbelieving croak.) *R.L.? But . . . he's dead! Listen, you white fuck, whatever you are: my brother is dead! Did you get that? He's dead! I know 'cos I killed him! For that matter, so are you dead, or good as . . . and the two you got out there with you!*

Two? And Harry wondered: *What? Can he feel R.L. too? Not just his obeah but . . . R.L. himself?*

Who you trying to shit, Fuckscope? There ain't no "feeling" R.L. 'cos R.L.'s dead! I mean your two friends out there! Enemies, all three of you—but only three of you. So come and get it, if you got the guts. I mean, three against one . . . what are you waiting for? But remember this: I got the moon on my side! His fading mental laughter was like the barking of a wild dog.

''He's not scared any more,'' Jordan hissed. ''He's just mad-angry—and mad as a hatter, too, of course!''

''He's picked up three enemies, but there are only the two of us,'' Harry was puzzled. ''If he's also reading R.L.'s talent, that makes him something of a Necroscope in his own right!''

''Whatever he is, he craves blood . . . namely, yours!'' Jordan answered. ''But also mine, if I've read him right! We should stop this right here and now and call in the law.''

Cowardly bastards! the thing in Harry's head roared. *Fuck you, then. We fight another day!* And Harry got a vivid mental picture of the intruder inside the garage, making for his vehicle. But the Necroscope had been challenged; worse, he'd been scorned, called a coward. And deep inside there was still this feeling that *he* wasn't at risk. Not the Harry Keogh he'd used to be, anyway.

Meanwhile, Jordan had locked on again, deliberately this time, and said: ''There's more than just him in there. He has a friend with him. Or . . . friends?''

''Skippy,'' Harry answered, jumping to the wrong conclusion, or one that was only half-right. ''They're both in there. And if they get away this time, who knows when we'll be able to bring them to book.''

Jordan saw what was coming next, and said, ''Harry, I . . .''

''Are you coming?'' The Necroscope held out his arms.

Jordan backed off. ''Your way? Not *likely!* I've seen inside your head, Harry. I know a little of what your Möbius Continuum is like! I'll go over the wall.'' Allowing no time for argument, he left the cover of the alley and made to run across the road, only pausing to turn and toss something back. It glinted blued-steel. Harry caught it: a 9mm Browning. ''Since you'll be there first,'' Jordan quietly called, ''you may need it.''

Reaching the wall, he looked back . . . and saw that he was right, Harry was no longer there—

—But he *was* inside the garage. And A.C. Doyle Jamieson knew it! The madman's astonishment was like triple exclamation marks in the Necroscope's mind, followed by a ripple of terror, and a barrage of inwardly directed questions: *What? Where? How? Who? . . .* and finally a renewed flaring of anger. His was a mind full of moon and murder. And Harry was his target for tonight.

There came silence, physical and mental . . .

Someone switched the lights off; Harry heard the switches trip. And now there was darkness. Only one small electric bulb, fifty or so feet away in the middle of a massive concrete ceiling, gave any light at all. And it cast shadows.

Moving shadows!

Harry saw or sensed movement . . . a metal object clattered as someone stumbled over it or kicked it aside. That was to the left. But to the right: a slithering of shadows, just a flicker but enough to bring the short hairs at the back of Harry's neck erect like a cat's brush. His eyes flickered this way and that, glanced upward. Overhead, a system of gantries supported rails and a motorized cabin and crane; heavy chains were still swinging a little on their pulleys. Or maybe they'd only just been set swinging?

A.C. and Skippy·. . . and who else? Harry remembered what Trevor Jordan had said only a moment ago: "He has a friend with him . . . or friends?" Well, great! But how many of them? Jordan was right: Skippy didn't have to be the only one.

Three! said a voice from the blue, or rather from the metaphysical darkness behind the Necroscope's eyes. And he at once knew its owner for R.L. Stevenson Jamieson. *Three enemies. But* whose *enemies is harder to say! Two of them is against you, for sure. As for the third . . .* Harry sensed the dead man's shrug.

"R.L.," Harry whispered, "you'd best be using your obi to damp down your brother's. I mean, you should save your efforts for that. Don't waste them talking to me."

You is there to put things right, Necroscope, and I'll do whatever I can to help you, R.L. told him. *Don't you be worrying 'bout my obi. It is working, believe me. And I just read in your mind my own brother boasting how he killed me! So I won't be holding you to no promises, Harry. Don't be holding off for my sake. You go get that son of a . . .*

Harry's eyes were now more accustomed to the gloom of the place. The shells of cars lay in various stages of repair, conversion, and reconstruction, in twin rows of bays equipped with inspection pits, overhead hoists, and various hand tools. Jacks and other wheeled machines stood abandoned in the central aisle, and chains dangled everywhere. The garage had been evacuated in a hurry and was now a mantrap. Even to someone well acquainted with the layout, any abrupt or hasty motion could prove dangerous to say the least.

Harry was shielded by one of the massive steel stanchions supporting the high ceiling; he was located just inside a repair bay, where he'd stepped out of the Möbius Continuum. Some forty or so feet to his left, the warehouse doors that he knew opened on the maintenance yard . . . had been closed! By now Jordan would be stranded on the other side of them, and that meant that Harry was on his own. And he knew that even if he took the Möbius route into the yard, still the telepath wasn't going to let himself be transported *that* way. But in any case what good would it do to get Jordan inside? None: it would only place him in greater danger. Of course, Harry could simply wash his hands of the whole mess and take himself out of here. But that wasn't his way.

And the trouble was that here in the dark and the danger, he was starting to feel more nearly himself; he was more surely aware of the jeopardy in which he had placed *him*self, the Harry Keogh mind if not the original body. But what the hell, it was all the same—wasn't it? It had now been brought forcefully home to him that this *was* him! And he really was on his own . . .

Not necessarily, Necroscope, said the near-distant voice of George Jakes, causing him to start a little. *Harry, use the—what, Möbius Continuum?* Jakes was excited, uncertain of what he'd "heard" Harry thinking. *By all means use it, but not just to cut and run! You need real back-up, Harry, and it just might be that I've got the answer.* Then, quickly (indeed, as quickly as that), he outlined his plan. And because George Jakes was a dead man, whom only the Necroscope could hear and speak to, no other prying, intruding mind was privy to it.

Harry listened, liked what he heard, acted upon it. The idea of placing an ally like Jordan in jeopardy had been sufficient to give him pause, true, but Harry was no fool; he knew he could use George Jakes without worrying about the consequences. And this way he would be keeping his promise both to R.L. Stevenson and to the teeming dead in general. He made a Möbius jump to the police mortuary in Fulham, and in a matter of seconds returned to the East End garage.

But coming back, he wasn't alone . . .

I got him! R.L. was triumphant, his incorporeal voice greeting the Necroscope even as he stepped from his door. *You was right, Harry. My obeah has come back to me, drawn back through you. It gives me strength and depletes A.C. He'll have a hard time finding you now. The balance is maintained; you is equals. At least as long as I can hold him.*

"My thanks, R.L.," Harry whispered; but in the empty, echoing garage his words were plainly audible! Almost immediately, there were furtive movements both left and right . . . and overhead?

Harry wasn't much disturbed by the movement on the right, which wasn't so much furtive as deliberate, purposeful. He knew the *sounds* he heard were the shuffling scrape of George Jakes's feet where he headed off alone on his mission of vengeance. But Jakes's *shape* and *shadow* were grotesque things, made even more grotesque by the glowing nucleus of the single dim light bulb, which silhouetted his lumpish figure in a pale aura, and cast his long freakish shadow on the angular machinery and dangling festoons of chains like that of some nightmarish spider on its web.

But the movement to the left? The door to the maintenance yard was that way. Had Trevor Jordan somehow managed to force an entry, or was someone waiting for him to do so there in the darkness? Harry conjured a Möbius door and jumped to the warehouse doors. Standing in the near-absolute darkness, scarcely breathing, he could hear nothing inside. But outside:

Harry? It was Jordan's telepathic whisper, the result of a gigantic effort on the part of the telepath. *Can you . . . let me in?*

No, Harry thought his denial. *Just stay in touch with me. Then, if anything happens, get the hell away from here and call the police!*

You've got it, and he sensed the relief in Jordan's mind. But they had also given themselves, and their situation, away!

Hey, you. Fuckscope! (In his mind, Harry saw a hulking, menacing outline moving in the mechanical labyrinth of the garage). *I know where you are, shithead.*

You're locked in and one other mother's locked out. And I'm coming for you, Fuckscope! The maniac bayed like a hound, but all in silence.

"Trevor, did you get that?" Harry spoke out loud through a knothole in a wicket gate set in the main door. "Can you pinpoint him?"

"Yes," Jordan's anxious whisper came back. "He's down in the basement where they keep their personal vehicles. But he's moving in your direction. He *is* coming for you, Harry!"

Yes, but A.C. isn't a Necroscope (Harry kept that thought to himself). *And he hasn't got the foggiest idea what's coming for him!* Neither had Jordan known it until he saw it in Harry's mind, and then he recoiled as if slapped in the face! *However,* Harry went on, *if A.C. Doyle knows where I am, then it's probably a good idea not to be here.*

Going on foot this time, using the repair bays as cover, he made his way back along the central aisle into the heart of the garage. But halfway back to the single source of electric light . . . suddenly it was snuffed! There came the soft tinkle of fragile glass breaking.

Harry froze. Whoever had smashed the light, it wouldn't be George Jakes. Because light or dark it would make no difference to him. Jakes was governed by . . . whatever he was governed by! Love of the Necroscope, mainly; or Harry's power over the dead, whichever way one chose to think of it. So, it could only have been A.C. or Skippy—or one other?

One other, Jordan told him. *But I can't read him . . . or her! This one has a funny mind. I've met the like before. You can't scan them any too easily. They sort of deflect telepathic probes. Like mindsmog, you know? I don't think it's a conscious thing, but—*

I get the idea, Harry cut him off, and made to release the safety on his 9mm Browning. But even as he did so, chains rattled almost directly overhead!

The Necroscope's gaze jerked upward. He saw eyes glaring down on him from the gloom of the gantry walkway. And sliding down the greasy chains, a lithe, black-clad male figure kicked the gun from his hand, not only disarming him but numbing his arm at the same time.

Shocked, caught completely off guard, Harry's thoughts flew in every direction. Fumbling, he made to conjure a Möbius door, tripped and went sprawling over an open box of tools into a pile of fresh swarf. He felt a leg of his trousers rip, felt his hands sliced as he scrambled to untangle himself. But suddenly the black-clad figure was standing over him, eyes burning in a black stocking-mask, and a dark gash grimacing where the mouth would be. Then the mouth formed words, and snarled:

"Just one more motherfucking copper who won't come snooping anymore!" A Geordie voice—Skippy—and the Necroscope could picture the writhing of the scorpion tattoo on his wrist as he drew back his arm for the killing stroke; but no need to imagine his weapon. Harry could see that well enough: the long ugly curve of a silver-glinting machete!

The blade went up, commenced its arcing sweep forward and down—

—And something struck out of the darkness, making first a vibrating thrum, then the vicious *whuuup* sound of cleft air! But it didn't cleave the Necroscope.

The machete flew out of Skippy's hand; his black silhouette was straightened forcefully from its killing, feet-apart stance, jerked upright and tossed back like a carelessly discarded puppet. He tugged at something sticking out of his chest, coughed a spray of black that Harry knew must be red, and went down into darkness without another sound. And stayed down.

A shadow moved sinuously close by. Harry heard a straining sound—like something being stretched under pressure—and the sharp *click* as a catch engaged. And being no stranger to crossbows, he knew what had hit Skippy. A moment later:

The bright beam of a pocket torch shone directly into his eyes. He was still tangled in cutting swarf, and dripped blood where he put up a hand to shield his eyes. But before the light snapped off he saw the Browning lying in the swarf and reached for it. This time, before freeing himself, he prepared the gun for firing. As he did so, he saw the shadow—a female shape, surely? and one that he'd seen before? but he couldn't be sure because his eyes were still dazzled—slipping away along the central aisle.

Think straight, can't you! Trevor Jordan snapped in his mind. And as Harry finally got to his feet, in a softer, more anxious tone: *How bad is it? Are you okay?*

I'll live, the Necroscope answered, hoping Jordan would hear him. *But things are getting nasty now and I can't rightly say what's going on. Get back over the wall and call for backup. Let's have the police in on it.*

HQ has been tracking us, Jordan answered. *I called for backup the moment you . . . what, went into shock? I thought it was all over for you, Harry!*

No, not quite, not yet, Harry answered. *Now for Christ's sake leave me be! I need to concentrate.*

And as Jordan cleared the telepathic ether, so Harry took over. He spoke to R.L. Stevenson Jamieson:

R.L.? I hope you've got your obi going full blast. A.C.'s going to be pretty mad when he finds out he's lost a bosom pal!

'Fraid not, Necroscope, R.L. came back at once. *You is on your own. My obi maintains the balance, that's all. But now the balance is all in* your *favour! And in case you is interested, I wants you to know we just welcomed a stranger into the ranks of the Great Majority. Or we will, eventually, when he quits fussing and screaming, and if he be worth it.*

Skippy? (Harry scowled, and knew that R.L. would feel the depth of his loathing, the way he shuddered in his soul.) *Well, he isn't worth it!* But in the moment of speaking, Harry sensed that the shuddering wasn't his alone. The intruder, A.C. Doyle Jamieson, was back. Except now he was whimpering like a whipped dog where he crouched in Harry's metaphysical mind—almost as if he were trying to hide there!

Get out of there, A.C., Harry quietly, coldly told him. *I don't want to share your pain with you when finally you die!*

Let me show you something, Fuckscope. The other's terror was transformed on the instant, replaced by rage and madness. Now he no longer panted his fear but his hatred and bloodlust. *Let me show you how it was for the rest of those bastards who tried to bring the werewolf to heel!*

But before he could begin: *No!* the Necroscope refused him point-blank. *I've already seen how it was, A.C. I know* exactly *how it was. So instead, I'd like to show* you *something:* (A mental picture of Skippy, transfixed by a crossbow bolt, stopped dead—literally—in his tracks, and sprawled in the bloody swarf where he'd fallen.) But because that didn't seem enough:

Harry opened up his metaphysical mind to display all the unknown depths, the gauntly yawning vacuum, the absolute *otherness* of the endless Möbius Continuum. A.C. saw how Harry was a part of it, linked to it, and finally sensed the preternatural chill of The Great Unknown creeping in his bones. Then, as the psychic ether slowly cleared:

Well? The Necroscope was very quiet now. *And are you still coming for me, Arthur?*

The answer was a howl—but one of anguish, of a diseased mentality frustrated to the breaking point—that reverberated in the darkness of the garage and went echoing off into a throbbing silence. No, A.C. wasn't coming for him; A.C. was running!

From somewhere below came the cough of a motor revved into tortured life, the scream of its abused engine, and Harry supposed that A.C. was heading out of here. There was only one way out, down the old car-park ramp and through the barrier. But if the barrier were lowered?

Harry judged the co-ordinates and made a hasty jump to the garage entrance, just inside the retractable doors. To his left he saw the dark tunnel of a two-lane down-ramp to the basement; down there, headlight beams swerved erratically, tires shrieked their shrill protest as the revving roar came closer.

Hurriedly, Harry scanned the walls on both sides of the exit for the button controlling the overhead door, to no avail. And it was too late to cover the thirty or so feet to the barrier's tiny control shack, switch on and lower the boom; A.C.'s vehicle was already roaring up the ramp from the basement! But:

Don't sweat it, Necroscope, said George Jakes's incorporeal voice in his head. *Didn't you hear the bugle sounding the charge? The cavalry's right here, Harry!*

Harry looked, and he saw, and even the Necroscope himself scarcely believed what he was seeing. But conversation with the dead often conveys more than is actually said, and Jakes showed him the whole picture in the time it took for the battered van to make it up the ramp; or rather, he showed him the picture as it had been just a minute or so ago:

A.C. Doyle Jamieson, tall, burly, decked out in his wolf-mask and wearing his glove weapon, lurching like a drunkard in the darkness of the basement, spewing obscenities like the madman he was as he made for his van. The vehicle was parked with its driver's door to the wall; A.C. yanked open the front-seat passenger's door and hurled himself headfirst inside the cab. But before he could reach the controls the motor coughed into life! Someone was in the driver's seat, hunched over the steering wheel, and A.C. knew it could only be one of his enemies! So why hadn't he been able to read him?

The answer was obvious, but of course A.C. couldn't know it: that only the Necroscope, Harry Keogh, can read anything of the dead!

The cab rocked as the van drew out into the central aisle and the driver gunned the motor, heading for the dim square of light that marked the exit ramp. Then the headlights blazed on and illuminated a figure standing dead ahead, a female figure with her arm and hand raised and pointing—or aiming—directly at the cab!

This was a concerted attack; they were acting in perfect co-ordination, all of A.C. Doyle's enemies together! He yelped, ducked, turned and struck with his honed steel claw all in one movement—struck at the face of the man at the wheel. And the face unzipped itself like a banana, its flesh flopping down in strips, then turned to grin at him with scarlet gums and reddened teeth and wet, pus-dripping eyes!

A.C. would have screamed then, but could only go "Urgh, urgh, urghhh!" as the Thing *beside him lay back its grotesque head and gurgled:*

"Ow-woooow, wolfman! It's silver bullet time!"

But in fact it was crossbow-bolt time: a bolt that came smashing through the windscreen and nailed A.C.'s shoulder to the padding of the seat, where its head jammed in the aluminum back-plate . . .

All of this from Jakes's mind as the van reached the top of the ramp and bounded onto the ground-floor level, and turned left, not right, to go revving up the skeletal ramp to the next floor, and the next, and the one after that. All the way to the top. And Harry seeing it through Jakes's dead eyes, but *hearing* it with his own ears even over the thunder of the van's engine:

A.C. Doyle's shrill, agonized, maniacal screaming, as it finally dawned on him that a man he'd killed was about to kill him! And:

Cheers, Necroscope! Jakes crowed in Harry's metaphysical mind, and he aimed the vehicle at the parapet wall six stories up. *Thanks for having me in on this. This is for Jim Banks and Derek Stevens, but mainly it's for me. The tank of this bucket is full, and I always wanted to go out this way: in a blaze of glory! Oh and by the way, here's the face of the ugly fuck who caused all of this:*

And he reached over with a dead hand to rip A.C.'s wolf-mask right off his head. Which was at the same time as the van hit the wall and went through it in a crumbling of rotten mortar and battered concrete, and a shrieking of twisted metal.

Harry staggered back against the wall in the entrance to the garage, flopped there with his jaw hanging slack, looking at A.C. looking at George Jakes. At the mad, black, screaming face; the claw-hand held up to ward off the very *sight* of the dead man; dreadlocks flying in the midnight wind as the van's door was shorn from its hinges. The mad eyes almost bursting from their sockets; the thick, foaming lips; the torso beginning to float in free-fall, but pinned to the backrest by the crossbow bolt whose flight stuck out from A.C.'s shoulder.

Let's talk again some time, Necroscope, said Jakes. *But right now I just want to savor the warmth . . .*

Harry shook himself, had time to straighten up and look out into the street . . . where even now something was crashing down in the center of the road. And Jakes was right: the van's tank must have been full to brimming.

Under a sky clearing of clouds, in which a bloated moon lit the wet-shining streets of London, A.C.'s van hit like a bomb, nose first, went off like a clap of thunder and blotted out the night with the abrupt brilliance of his funeral pyre. And of George Jakes's.

Which was the way one of them had wanted it, at least . . .

Harry shook himself again. His numb mind cleared, and he heard . . . police sirens? Of course, and they'd be here in just a few minutes.

Harry, are you okay? (It was Trevor Jordan, but faint now that the pressure was off.)

Yes, Harry answered. *Are you out of it?*

Well out of it, Jordan answered, with a mental sigh.

See you later, Harry told him, nodding.

But right now . . . there was something he had to do, had to know.

He had seen the girl outside the garage. Then he'd seen her inside (but couldn't be sure), when she'd saved his life. And he'd seen her a third time, in Jakes's dead mind, so that finally he *was* sure! Now he wanted to see her again, find out who she was, why she was here. Jakes had pictured her at the far end of the basement. To the Necroscope's knowledge there was no exit down there, and he knew that the maintenance yard doors on this level were locked. She had got in through those doors but couldn't get out that way. Which left only one escape route. She had to come this way. And she did.

She came panting, alert, aware of the growing clamor of the sirens. But Harry was waiting for her well inside the garage, at the landing where the down-ramp met the ground floor. She came up the ramp at the run, still carrying her "shopping bag." The Necroscope knew what was in it: her crossbow. She'd shot two bolts to deadly effect and was probably out of ammunition, else she'd be holding the weapon. But he still had the Browning. And he'd found the main switch for the lights, set back in a recess in the wall at the top of the ramp.

As the girl drew level he threw the switch, stepped into view. She gave a small cry of surprise, skidded to a halt and blinked in the suddenly bright light. "Who . . . ? What . . . ?"

"Don't be scared," Harry told her. "It's all over. I just wanted to thank you—for my life."

"Oh, it's you," she said, and breathed her relief. "I . . . didn't know which one of you to shoot! I was . . . just lucky, I suppose." her dialect was a distinctive, husky, even sexy Edinburghian brogue that Harry vaguely recalled and recognized from early childhood days in Scotland, and from later visits.

"Me too," he grinned, however wryly. "Very lucky!" And for the first time he felt the stiffness of his drying blood sticking his torn trousers to his legs.

"But the one in the stocking-mask," she continued, "well, he looked the most likely target." She licked her lips nervously and glanced this way and that, obviously seeking a way out. She had seen the gun in his hand.

"And the man in the van?" Harry was intent now, staring at her. "The passenger? I mean, why didn't you shoot the driver?" It would have made no difference but he wanted to know anyway.

Her eyes went this way and that. "I . . . I saw what looked like a big dog or wolf, sitting in the van, but it was a man in a mask. He attacked the driver, tore at him. And I . . . I—"

"—You fired at the one who looked the most dangerous," Harry nodded. "So . . . were you hunting them, or what?" He stepped closer to her but she didn't shrink away. Out in the night the sound of the sirens had grown very loud, and he could feel the girl's urgency radiating from her.

"Just one o' them," she replied, her brogue thickening as her anxiety increased. And now she moved closer to Harry. "Are ye the police?" The way she said police it sounded like "polis."

"No," the Necroscope shook his head, and at the same time made up his mind about something. This girl should answer questions—to the law if not to him—but she had saved his life after all. "I was hunting them, too."

"Well, and we got them, did we no? But now, I've to go . . ." She made to brush by him, and cars skidded to a screeching halt immediately outside the garage, where orange flames lit up the night and black smoke roiled for the moon.

"Tell me one thing and I'll help you," he gripped her arm, and she looked at his hand where he held her. "I promise, I'll get you out of this."

"Better make it fast, then," she gasped, as running footsteps clattered on the entrance ramp.

"Why were you hunting him?"

"Why were you?" She was drawing back from him, and she was surprisingly strong.

"They murdered friends of mine."

"And they placed good friends o' mine in . . . in jeopardy. But I'm afraid ye're too late to get us out o' here!"

Harry reached back, threw the master switch, and the entire garage was black as night. Then he conjured a Möbius door, and swept the girl through it. And: *Where to?* he asked.

Her thoughts were like a vastly gonging, cracked and echoing bell: *WHAT? . . . WHAT? . . . WHAT?*

Shhh! Harry told her. *Just cling to me, and tell me where home is. Where do you want to go?*

She clung to him, just as tightly as she could! And: "Anywhere out o' *here!*" she whispered hoarsely, a whisper that rang like a shout in the primal emptiness of the Möbius Continuum.

He went to a place he knew, exited from the Continuum, and held her upright until she felt the solid ground under her feet and stopped trembling. Then, gradually opening her eyes . . . she reeled for a moment, and abruptly sat down—

—On the rain-slick cobbles of the alley just across the road from the garage. But the rain was finished now, and a mist swirled ankle-deep like a river of white-glowing milk all along the alley, lapping into recessed doorways and swirling from the Necroscope's sudden resurgence.

Harry didn't want to answer any more questions right now, but later he might have some for her. "Now *I've* to go," he told her in her own brogue. "How can I find you again? I mean, if I wanted to. Or if you . . . wanted me to?"

He held out a hand, helped her to her feet. "I . . . I just dinna *believe* what happened then!" she gasped. "I really dinna believe it!" Her hands fluttered up and down the length of her thighs, brushed water from the wet seat of her trousers.

"I've really got to go," Harry told her, moving off along the alley away from a street that flared red and orange in the roaring firelight.

"B.J.'s," she breathed. "Find me at B.J.'s."

"Oh?" He looked back from the dark threshold of a recessed warehouse back entrance and cocked his head questioningly.

"A wine bar—I mean, *mah* wine bar—in Edinburgh." Her mouth was hanging open, and her words came out soft as breath.

But Harry had had enough of initials, A.C.s and R.L.s, and B.J.s included. "So what does it stand for? B.J., I mean?"

"Eh?" Her mouth was still open, and looked delicious. "Oh, mah initials? Bonnie Jean," she said.

The name rang a bell. Harry remembered an old musical he'd seen on the TV in his flat at Hartlepool—how long ago? Now he recalled the title, and the words of a certain song:

Go home, go home,
go home with Bonnie Jean.
Go home, go home—
—*IIIII'll* . . . go home with Bonnie Jean.

Well, maybe . . . but not tonight, Bonnie Jean. "Just like in Brigadoon!" he said.

She obviously understood his meaning. For now, accepting the weirdness of things, she closed her mouth, smiled however wonderingly, and said, "Aye, mah brave laddie, *exactly* like in Brigadoon. And your name . . . ?" But then, momentarily distracted when a police vehicle with blaring sirens went screeching past the mouth of the alley, she looked back over her shoulder.

And B.J.'s question hung unanswered on the damp night air, for when next she turned to Harry . . . all that remained of him was a swirl of mist, collapsing like an exorcised ghost on the spot where he'd been standing . . .

Harry made brief stops in several locations—graveyards, all of them—to report the results of the night's adventure. The principal details were already known, however, mainly through the efforts of one R.L. Stevenson Jamieson. Before returning to E-Branch HQ, Harry spoke to R.L. himself, and said:

"Well, a proven principle is shown to be working still. I mean, what you did in life you'll continue to do in death. And in so doing, you'll earn the gratitude of all the teeming dead. No need to worry about your name being cursed now, R.L."

You talking 'bout my obi, Necroscope?

Harry nodded. "You know I am. For in life, you took care of your brother as best you could—you kept the balance. Now in death you'll go right on doing it."

It don't take no effort, Harry, R.L. told him. *It's a natural thing. 'Specially now that I'm in touch with Poppy again! See, I didn't like to bother him with all this before. But now we is all together, so to speak—*

Again Harry's nod. "No shame attaches to you or your Poppy, R.L. And like I said, the dead will always be grateful to you for keeping A.C. in his place. What I mean is, when the teeming dead talk to each other it's voluntary; they don't need to feel anything like A.C. creeping in their minds!"

Oh, A.C. be no trouble now, Harry. The werewolf's gone for good. No more howling, just the whimper of a cold, lost little puppy. But he'll be okay, once he learns he's safe in the dark and the quiet.

And: "Fair enough," the Necroscope answered. "Let's leave it at that, then . . ."

PART 2

Searching.

FOR BRENDA, AND FOR HIMSELF.

DESPITE HIS SEVERAL DUTY STOPS, STILL HARRY BEAT TREVOR JORDAN BACK to E-Branch HQ. He found the place just as the telepath had advised: fully activated under Darcy Clarke and ready at a moment's notice to back him to the hilt . . . psychically if not physically. In the event, and with the assistance of newfound friends, he hadn't needed extra help; also, and right from the beginning, he had asked Darcy to keep out of it. Be that as it may, the Head of Branch had been ready, willing and able, and it said a lot for the value the espers placed on Harry.

Eventually the Necroscope was able to complete his report, and in the wee small hours he sat alone with Darcy in the latter's office. With his duties behind him, Harry at last found time to inquire after Brenda and his infant son. Not that his concern was any less than it should be, or his attitude in any way casual, but he knew that wherever his wife and child were, it was unlikely that they would come to any harm. For all that Harry Jr. was a babe in arms, he'd already displayed his ability to protect his mother from even the most dire threat, and Harry Sr. knew that whatever mundane things the infant wasn't capable of doing for himself, Brenda—or the Great Majority—would do for him.

And in answer to his, "Anything . . . ?"

"Nothing," Darcy shook his head worriedly. "Not a thing. Every man who wasn't on your case has been on the lookout for Brenda and the baby. They've all drawn blanks. Precogs, telepaths, hunchmen, locators: a dead end—if you'll forgive that expression. When Brenda first came here, it was Harry Jr. who brought her; we have to assume he's taken her away again. Why, and where to . . . is anybody's guess. Of course we shall go on searching for them, but right now . . ." His shoulders slumped a little. "I'm sorry, Harry. You've done so much, given so much of your time and energy for us, and we don't seem able to do a thing for you."

"Which means I'll have to do it for myself," Harry answered, but without bitterness. "Darcy, you must have known from square one that the main reason I let you talk me into staying here was for Brenda? You had all the contacts, and

I hoped the people you brought in would be able to do something for her. I knew she'd be safe here if there were any aftershocks from the work I'd been doing. But that's all over now."

Darcy saw what was coming. "You're moving out?"

"Lock, stock and barrel. E-Branch isn't for me, Darcy. I was always a loner, and that's the way I have to be. And after all—and as you've often enough said yourself—do I really want to spend my life slopping out mental sewers? I just can't see myself at the beck and call of the police, their 'pet psychic' who they can call on to solve every grubby little murder in the book! Oh, I know it wouldn't be like that, but it would be *something* like that, and it isn't what I'm cut out for. So, it looks like it's come sooner than either one of us expected. I'm moving out, yes."

"When?"

"I don't have any ties here. I mean, I'm not bosom buddies with any of the people here, or anything like that. I have friends here, yes . . . I hope you're *all* my friends. But no one I have to say goodbye to. Except maybe you. So, goodbye."

Plainly Darcy didn't know what to say. "You're our greatest asset—or you were."

"I'm just a man," Harry answered, and meant it. "And anyway, the Branch has enough going for it."

"But . . . lock, stock and barrel?"

Harry shrugged. "That doesn't amount to much. Nothing, in fact. What's in that wardrobe in my room can stay for now. Maybe I'll pick it up sometime."

"That's not what I meant. No contact?"

"Only if you find my wife and child. But in any case, I'll probably find them first." Suppressing a yawn but stretching a little, the Necroscope grimaced as he felt a scab break on his thigh under new bandages. His expression was wry as he looked at his hands, which were also bandaged.

"You should have had stitches," Darcy was concerned.

"I *hate* stitches!" Harry answered. "Not to mention scars! This way if I'm lucky there'll be no scars."

"So where will you go? And when? Not tonight, surely?"

"There's my flat in Hartlepool, which could use some tidying up before I sell. It's been empty for well over a year. And my inheritance up in Bonnyrig, that big old house. I think I'd probably like the solitude, and I would be that much closer to my Ma. As for when: what's wrong with tonight?"

"Look," Darcy said, suddenly anxious, "we're both tired. You especially. You look all in! And we don't see things right—nobody does—when we're tired. Spend the night here; have breakfast with me in the morning; make up your mind then."

Harry shrugged again. "It's made up," he answered. "On the other hand, you're right and I am tired. Okay, tomorrow is soon enough . . ."

Darcy looked pleased, said, "And you'll stay in touch—I mean, when you're settled?"

Harry sighed. "If you promise not to bother me . . . maybe. But let's have it understood right here and now—I'm through with E-Branch, Darcy. It isn't me.

I wouldn't have time for the Branch anyway, no time for anything, until I know about Brenda and little Harry."

Darcy nodded. "Very well . . ." And then, on an afterthought: "What will I tell the police?"

"Eh?"

"They found two bodies in that burned-out van. One was our werewolf, yes, but the other . . . ? They're bound to identify him, you know. And then there's the one inside the garage, shot dead . . . but with a crossbow?"

"Let's deal with George Jakes first," Harry answered. "The big question is going to be: how did George get out of a Fulham mortuary into a burned out van in the East End, right?"

"You're the last one who saw him, er, in designated situ, as it were. If we have to put a name on all of this—I mean, we won't, but if we had to—"

"It would be mine, yes . . ." Harry gave it a few seconds of thought, and said, "Tell them that A.C. Jamieson was an obeah man from Haiti. They should be able to prove that easily enough. He must have stolen Jakes's body so that he could use it to put some kind of hex on the police. As for why he chose to commit suicide: who knows? He was a madman, after all. Also, tell them to look for a shriveled or melted wolf-mask, and a claw glove. Then they'll have all they need."

"More than they need," Darcy agreed. "That garage was full of class motors, most of them knocked off!"

"As for the one inside the garage, 'Skippy' . . . maybe that was Jamieson's work, too. Sure he was a madman, but mad like a fox! Killing Skippy, he was covering his tracks. Simple . . ."

"And the murder weapon?"

"They won't find it," Harry shook his head.

"Something you haven't told me?"

"Something I might look into, eventually."

"Well, then," said Darcy, nodding thoughtfully, "it seems we've covered just about everything." Then the faint half-smile that had almost made it onto his face turned to a frown. "Still, I'm glad Jakes didn't leave anyone behind. Family, I mean."

"I know what you mean," Harry answered. "It would be hard to explain, right? But don't go worrying about Jakes, Darcy. I have it on pretty good authority that he doesn't feel sorry for himself, just glad that he got his man, albeit after the fact."

Thinking about it, Darcy's face went pale. He remembered the Bodescu case, Hartlepool on the north-east coast, and the teeming dead coming up out of their graves. But for the fact that he—what, *liked* the Necroscope? trusted him? knew there was no menace in him?—he supposed by now his guardian-angel talent would be howling for him to run the fuck away from the man!

"It just doesn't bear thinking about," he said, quietly.

"Well, if you must," the Necroscope told him, "then think of it this way: Jakes was only doing what he'd always done in life, and what he did best. He considers himself fortunate to have had another crack at it, and to have done it well. I say we should all be so lucky . . ."

"All I know," Darcy answered, "is that when I'm dead and gone, all I will want to do is lie *very* still!"

"Yes, but that's for now," Harry told him without emphasis, but with a strange light in those eyes that knew so much.

Darcy was scarcely listening to or looking at him, which was probably as well, but was still considering recent events. The dead thief and murderer in the garage, for instance. Harry was right: so far the police hadn't found the murder weapon—but they did have the actual instrument of death, the short, hardwood bolt. They had spoken to him about that, and it was worth mentioning at least.

"Are you sure you don't want to say anything else, Harry?" he said. "About this crossbow thing, maybe? I mean, a crossbow is in any case an odd sort of weapon. But forensic are looking at it and they're puzzled by the fluke, the arrowhead."

This was something new. Harry cocked an eyebrow. "So what about it?"

Darcy shrugged. "It's a steel arrowhead, as you'd expect. But silver-plated? You kill werewolves with silver, don't you?"

Harry was good at hiding his thoughts, his emotions, and this time his surprise. And coming to him as an extra surprise, it seemed he was getting good at telling lies, or half-truths, too! Never to the dead . . . but to the living? "I didn't know what I was going up against," he said. "Oh, sure, *we* had decided that this was the work of a . . . what, a lycanthrope? Some kind of lunatic? But what if we were wrong? There *are* strange things in the world, as we know only too well."

Darcy nodded. "You did kill him, then? Hence the missing weapon?"

The Necroscope looked away, finally muttered, "He's dead, isn't he?" But now it was definitely something he would have to look into . . . eventually.

He stood up a little unsteadily, and said, "I seem to be more tired than I thought—yet how am I supposed to sleep? I have a lot on my mind, going round and round. Sometimes I can't remember a time when I didn't have! A pity we can't just switch ourselves off, like machines."

Darcy gave a small start, as if he'd just remembered something, and said, "But we can! What, do you think that as head of this bloody outfit I leave sleep to chance? God, I'd *never* get any!"

Harry looked at Darcy as he opened a desk drawer, took out a small bottle, stood up and went to a water dispenser. "Do you have any allergies?" He dropped a single white pill in a glass and filled it with water. The tablet dissolved in a moment.

"No," Harry shook his head. "No allergies that I know of. But . . . sleeping pills?"

"Just one," Darcy told him. "Does the trick for me every time. Just switches me off."

Harry took the glass. "Maybe this once," he said, tilting his head back and downing the water. But as he drank, he didn't notice the fact that the Head of E-Branch seemed to be holding his breath . . .

After the Necroscope left to go to his own room, Darcy called a Branch "specialist" on his home number. Not an esper as such, still this was a man with an extraordinary talent. "Doctor Anderson?" Darcy inquired, when finally the 'phone was picked up. "James Anderson? This is Darcy Clarke . . ."

And in a moment, answering the tinny, tired voice at the other end of the line: "Yes, I do know what time it is, Anderson, and I'm sorry it's so late. But this is important. Do you remember that Keogh thing we spoke about? Well, it's come up."

And in another moment: "Just two minutes ago, yes."

And finally, before putting the 'phone down: "Good, I'll be expecting you."

After that there was nothing for Darcy to do but wait for Anderson to get there. That and to suffer feelings of disgust, self-loathing, like his substance had devolved to so much quaking, treacherous scum on the surface of a sucking swamp. On the other hand . . . well, duty and conscience didn't mix, not in his job. Darcy's first duty was to the Branch (the swamp?), and he knew it. His conscience would have to take a back seat . . .

Maybe the Necroscope's attitude had been too casual after all, or he had been too sure of himself. So E-Branch couldn't discover the whereabouts of his wife and child . . . so what? *They* didn't have the Möbius Continuum to work with. (Like a little kid refusing to let the other kids play with his ball—Nyahh! Nyahh! Nyahh! Or too possessive and much too pleased with himself that he had a ball in the first place.) But as the saying goes, what goes around comes around, and just like the little kid Harry had discovered that you can't play the game on your own. Especially not hide-and-seek.

From his rambling old house outside Bonnyrig, he called Darcy Clarke and poured out his frustrations; but Darcy could only tell him what he already knew, (else E-Branch would have contacted him first): "We haven't even the foggiest idea where they could be, Harry. It's like they've vanished off the face of the Earth!"

"A month, five weeks?" Harry looked at the telephone like he didn't believe what he was hearing. "You've been on it for five weeks, and nothing? What, E-Branch, with your locators and your hunchmen, your seers and scryers and precogs? You haven't the foggiest idea?"

Which got Darcy's back up more than a little. "What are you trying to say, Harry?" he snapped. "That you don't think we're trying hard enough? That you don't believe we're looking for them, is that it? Well, start getting it together and believe this: that we have as much interest in the kid as you have—if not for the same reasons!"

And while Harry didn't much like that last, still he knew it must be true. Of course E-Branch wanted to find Harry Jr. Just because his father had turned them down, that didn't mean the child would—*when it was his turn!* But maybe Darcy realized he'd said too much, and:

"Harry," his tone of voice was more even now, "I . . . don't want to fight with you. I mean, Christ, we shouldn't be fighting! We *are* looking for them, you know we are. And I was wrong to fly off the handle like that. What I said . . . wasn't what I meant to say."

"But you did say it," Harry answered, and he was quieter, too. "My son: the next E-Branch dupe! What, when he's fifteen, sixteen? And while you're waiting, you'll be standing off in the background, watching him grow up, measuring his skills, letting him develop? Or will you step in before then, recruit him like I was recruited: by showing him all the world's evil, and telling him that with him on the team E-Branch will have the power to change all that? And what then, Darcy? Will *he* be the one who ends up slopping out all of those mental sewers? Oh really? Not if I can help it . . .''

"And not if *I* can help it, Harry!" Darcy's voice was pleading now. "Look, you're not yourself or you wouldn't be talking like this. And I really *didn't* mean it the way it sounded. You want my word on it? You've got it: we'll never interfere with your son or his way of life. But Harry, the fact is that none of us will ever have *anything* to do with him, if we can't find him! and at the moment we can't.''

The Necroscope was silent for a while, then said, "But you will keep trying?''

"Of course we will.''

"Well, thanks for that, at least.'' And Harry put the 'phone down . . .

Down by the river bank, where the water swirled and eddied in a small bight, Harry spoke to his Ma. It was the first time since the day he'd come up here almost three weeks ago, after selling off his flat in Hartlepool, and the Necroscope's mother was beginning to feel neglected. But his mind had been troubled—oh, for a long time—and like any mother she'd sensed it. So despite that she could speak to him anywhere, any time, she hadn't intruded. And anyway, she knew how he liked to visit the people he talked to.

It was the middle of April, blustery but at least dry, and Harry was wearing his overcoat where he sat at the river's rim. *But you'll probably catch your death anyway!* she told him, feeling the cold breeze in his hair, and scanning the blurred gray mirror images of clouds scudding in the river (as seen through his eyes, of course). *It's no day to be out, Harry.*

She was down there in the mud and the weeds, her spirit at least, and probably her bones, too, even if the rest of her was long washed away. But typical of a Ma (of *any* mother anywhere), even though Mary Keogh no longer felt the cold for herself, she was still able to feel it for her son.

"I'm okay,'' Harry told her.

No, you're not. But she wasn't ready to push it, not yet at least. And because he didn't seem ready to speak: *Well, how are things with the world, Harry? The rest of the world, I mean . . .*

He recognized the ploy: to take his mind off his own problems by getting him to relate the troubles of the world in general. Now that the dead were all linked up and talking to each other from their graves and various resting places, they could get the news from recent arrivals, of course. But through the medium of the Necroscope it was that much more immediate; they could see it and perhaps even feel something of it, if not actually experience it. Harry was their one link with the living. And on this occasion especially he went along with it. For his Ma was right and he wasn't "okay.''

Not that there was much of good news. "Do you really want to know?''

Is it that bad?

"Well, it isn't wonderful!'' He pulled a face. "You'll have to judge for yourself.'' And recalling a recent newscast:

"Most of Africa is in turmoil: Zambia and Rhodesia, Mogadishu, Somalia,

Ethiopia. White 'supremacy' looks to be on its way out in Rhodesia, where they've just voted for black rule.''

But isn't that just right? Aren't all men born equal?

Again his shrug. "As long as the recently equal are happy to remain equal—I mean as long as they don't want to be *more* equal—I suppose it's okay . . ." And quickly, so as to radically change the subject before she could start protesting or moralizing: "And there's been an atomic meltdown at a place called Three Mile Island in the United States. It's a power station.''

Oh? (She scarcely sounded impressed.) *Something melted? Is it that important?*

Harry had to grin. When his Ma had died nuclear power was fairly new, industrially at least. "It's pretty important, yes. Dangerous stuff. It kills people, Ma. An unpleasant, invisible, silent death." The grin was gone now from his face, and his Ma knew why. She had gathered the rest of it—the seething horror of it—from his mind. And he felt her incorporeal shudder.

What else? she said.

"Well, there's been some pretty terrible stuff coming out of Cambodia, but—''

—But Harry couldn't possibly talk about *that,* not to his Ma! He at once bit his tongue and blanked his mind, wondering where in hell his thoughts could have been wandering that he'd ever mentioned it. Maybe it was because of the way *she,* his Ma, had died, but reading about that death-lake in Stung Treng had given the Necroscope nightmares: those two thousand bodies tied together with ropes and weighted with stones . . .

She had caught on from his first mention of Cambodia, however, and quietly said, *"Oh, don't worry, Harry. For we know all about that. And as for Pol Pot: well, he'll have to come to us, too, you know, in the end. But he can have no idea what's waiting for him down here.*

"What's waiting for him?" Harry had never thought of the dead as being especially vengeful. After all, what could they do?—well, without that he, Harry Keogh, the Necroscope, was their motivation?

Do? His Ma at once answered. *We'll do nothing, say nothing, have nothing at all to do, not with him. And he'll be so cold, lost, and lonely, it will be as though he has no existence, not even this kind of existence, whatsoever. And eventually he won't have. He'll simply fade away into nothing. But he will know why . . .*

For a moment Harry felt the icy chill of her words—the coldness of outer space, the blackness of inner earth—as if it had entered into his soul. But it quickly passed and she was warm again. Strange, but of all Harry's dead people she was the only one who ever "felt" warm! Or maybe not so strange. She was his Ma, after all.

"So, that's it then," he said after a while, and shrugged. "Oh, there's other stuff, but maybe it wasn't such a good idea to tell you what was happening in the world after all. I mean, when you think about it, that meltdown at Three Mile Island is probably the least of our worries!''

And she was glad to change the subject, too. *But if this . . . "meltdown?" is so dangerous, then why did they do it?*

"What?" (Was her understanding that limited?) "But it was an *accident,* Ma! They didn't do it on purpose!''

Oh! (She gave a little laugh.) *Then I suppose it can't be helped, can it?* But her laughter quickly died away, and it was time to be serious again. *So in fact nothing is very much different from what it always was: men go on making mistakes. And I don't suppose there's much help for that. But now you've got to tell me what* can *be helped, Harry. Tell me how I can help. And more especially, how I can help you . . .*

So finally the Necroscope's beloved mother, his frequently omniscient Ma (where he was concerned, anyway), had got to the point. She sensed it when his shoulders slumped a little, just before he sighed and told her: "I haven't found them yet, Ma—Brenda and my baby son. Oh, there are a million places I've not even thought to look yet, I know, but that seems a million too many to even know where to start!"

For a while she was silent, then quietly said, *Do you want me to ask among the dead, Harry? I mean, do you think it's possible that . . . ?*

Harry scarcely dared question her on the subject, but knew he must. "Surely not, Ma?" he said, almost pleadingly. "If that was the case, wouldn't you have known by now? If they were . . . ?"

Not necessarily, son, she said. *It depends where, and when. I mean, if it were* you *we'd know, be sure! And no matter where* or *when, for there's only one Necroscope . . . well, two now. And we'd know it at once, if your light went out. But death is generally a common affair: someone is born, lives, and dies. Inevitably. Brenda is Brenda, just another ordinary person, another life. And if she were to die in some far place, well that could take some little time to get back to me.*

"And your grandson, Harry Jr.? Is he just another 'ordinary' person? I don't think so—and not just because he's your grandson. He *knows* about you! You know about him! Wouldn't the Great Majority know it if his light was extinguished, too?"

But you have been with us for some time, Harry, she reminded him. *And the Great Majority didn't know about you, either, at first. Why, they didn't even know about each other until you came on the scene! Oh, I knew you were different, but then I was your mother! But believe me, it took quite a while to convince the rest. Finally, they believed; how could it be otherwise? They felt your warmth as you passed close by; they heard your dreaming, and sensed you trembling when you were afraid. In those days of your childhood, they sprang to champion you. Little did they know that one day you would be the champion of the dead!*

"You mean, they don't know him yet? He hasn't been around long enough? But in Hartlepool that time—what, a year and half ago?—they even came up out of their graves for him!"

For both of you, Harry. Oh, Harry Jr. called them up, but who did they come to save?

"Isn't he . . . *warm,* then? Like me?"

He's warm, yes. And the dead feel him like a small, kindly flame. But he isn't the light in their darkness, like you. One day, maybe, but not yet.

"You won't know it, then, if he dies . . ." It wasn't a question but a statement. And in a way Harry was glad. He wouldn't want to be apprised of his son's death, nor of Brenda's, ever. Neither by the living nor the dead.

I would know it . . . sooner or later, his mother told him. *But right now, I can promise you this much at least: nothing of that nature has reached me yet. To my knowledge, they are still among the living.*

Harry breathed a sigh of relief. If his mother said it was so, then it was so. And in all truth, that had only been a very small fear anyway; he had "known," been sure, that his wife and son were alive somewhere. But where?

His Ma heard his silent query, and asked him: *Where would you go, Harry, if you wanted to hide yourself away? Where would Brenda go? Surely you knew something of her secrets, her fantasies, her dreams?*

Suddenly the Necroscope realized how selfish he must seem. Because he hadn't been thinking of it from his wife's point of view, not really, but his own. And now his mother, in her way, had brought it home to him that Brenda was a person in her own right, with her own secrets, fantasies, dreams. With feelings and emotions and passions, all of them damaged now, or contaminated by contact with Harry's world, until she had only wanted to "hide herself away" from it. But:

That's not what I meant, son, his Ma told him. *You know it isn't! It was simply my . . . my manner of expression.*

Except Harry knew that speaking to the dead often conveys more than is actually said; so maybe he'd read something of his Ma's true thoughts, after all. And certainly she had touched a raw nerve in him. Perhaps deliberately? Ah, but she had a way of bringing things into perspective, his mother—and ways of bringing *him* into line!

But at the same time her approach to his problem had set the Necroscope thinking. For of course Brenda *was* different, a person in her own right with her own ways of thinking, her own likes and dislikes. So that now Harry wondered where *would* she be likely to hide herself away, if "hiding" as such had seemed the only course open to her? She had never been much of a one for the sun but always enjoyed the rain! She'd loved gardens, the wind in her hair, dramatic, misted landscapes. To sit in a window-seat in their garret flat and listen to the rain on the tiles . . . that had been one of her favorite things.

In which case, Harry's Ma chimed in, *this place would seem entirely suited to her purpose! This very place!*

"She never even saw this place." He shook his head.

But a place like *this one?*

"Maybe, maybe not. Certain coastlines seemed to appeal to her, rugged cliffs and rainy skies . . . and any garden; but more especially, a garden with a corner run wild. Long grasses, wild flowers, and a place where she could lie on her back and watch the clouds. And the stars: the brighter the better. She didn't know a single constellation, but she liked them anyway. A place of wildness—a wilderness—and a lot of stars in the clear night sky: that would suit her perfectly."

You're a poet and you don't know it! His Ma rhymed.

"I wonder where I get it?" Harry said. And she sensed that his mood was lifting a little.

I think it's about time you started checking on those million places, she told him. *For after all, we must have narrowed them down a little by now.* And Harry agreed.

They little thought or could ever have guessed that Brenda and Harry Jr. were in just such a place as the Necroscope's Ma had suggested, which her query had brought into vivid definition in his mind. A place of dramatic scenery, however alien; of long, misted nights, slanting, sunlit days, long grasses and wild flowers. And a garden quite beyond Brenda's previous expectations, her mundane imagination.

For the fact was that at this point of time it was beyond even the Necroscope's imagination, too, and would stay that way long after he'd given up any real hope of finding them . . .

But for now: first Harry reconsidered the places he'd already checked out, starting with Brenda's old home with her folks in Harden, a colliery village on the north-east coast.

The mine ("the pit") itself had been worked out and shut down for some time now, so that the place had seemed even more soulless than before, but the people were there as always. Of course, if Brenda or the baby were really trying to avoid him, if they were actually hiding themselves away from him—which he was forced to believe was true—then this would be the last place they'd go. Harry had known that from the start, but still he had looked. What he'd found had made him more miserable yet.

He couldn't simply approach Brenda's people as in the old days, for he was no longer him. What, go to them and tell them *he* was Harry Keogh, and try to explain? They'd never accept any of *that*, these salt-of-the-earth—and very much *down* to earth—north-east folks! Instead he'd approached Brenda's father in his local pub, introducing himself as a friend of Harry's, and asking what had become of him. Which had had a mixed result.

To make a long story short: Brenda and Harry had got married, and there was a child. Eighteen months ago, she'd taken the baby to London to join her husband. He was working there, writing a book or something. She was always very quiet about his work. Nothing strange about that; she was probably a bit ashamed that he didn't have a "proper job." What, Harry Keogh? Why, he hadn't done a stroke since leaving school—not physical work, anyway. But whatever he did, writing or whatever, he must be doing all right; she'd never been short of money.

But then, just a few weeks ago, she'd written to say that she was taking the baby "abroad" somewhere. And that was maybe a funny thing, for she hadn't mentioned her husband: just herself and the baby. Still, she'd hinted often enough that Harry did some kind of hush-hush job with the government; maybe that was it. They must have gone off somewhere overseas to some embassy or other. Maybe the writing hadn't worked out, so he was wearing his other hat now. Maybe the government had given him a job as one of these "special couriers" or something: someone who carries important documents or goods from country to country. Or perhaps the writing *had* worked out after all, and all of this was a tax dodge. Except . . . well, Brenda should *write* more often. That last letter had been—what? All of five or six weeks ago? And they were her parents, after all . . .

In short, they were obviously worried about her, no less in their way than Harry himself. And equally obvious, it wasn't a put-up job . . . Brenda wasn't with them and they really didn't know her whereabouts. He got the same story from all of her old friends. So Harden was out; she simply wasn't there, and no one knew where she was.

Then another thought had occurred, and one that really was worrying. The Necroscope had given the Russian E-Branch (known to Darcy Clarke and his lot as "the Opposition") a hard time of it in the last two and a half years. They'd lost three Heads of Branch over that same period, and seen their HQ outside Moscow reduced to so much rubble! What if this thing with his wife and baby was something they had been engineering ever since Harry's showdown with Boris Dragosani? What if they knew that he, Harry Keogh, was alive, despite that his body—his *original* body—was dead? If anyone was likely to have that information, it had to be the world's ESPionage organizations! The Opposition's top telepath, Zek Föener, had known it definitely . . . and following the destruction of the Chateau Bronnitsy, Harry had let her go free. Could Zek have told them? And had they then taken Brenda and the baby in order to facilitate the coercion of the Necroscope himself?

But no, a large part of that didn't make sense; he'd been incorporeal following his fight with Dragosani, and no one in the world would have believed that he'd *ever* be back, not even Harry himself! But on the other hand part of it *did* make sense. Right at the end of it, up in the Khorvaty region of the eastern Carpathians, Zek Föener *had* known that he was back. So she could have given him away after all; which would mean that her Russian superiors had put this thing together all in the space of . . . what, eighteen months? Even after he'd decimated their E-Branch?

No way; he hadn't left the Soviets nearly enough machinery to bring it into being! Which meant it had to be another dead end, and in a way the Necroscope was glad. He would hate to have to blame this on Zek Föener; partly because he had genuinely liked her, but mainly because his last words to her had been a warning never to come up against him or his again. If a threat carries no weight, then it isn't a threat. But this way he wouldn't have to enforce it . . .

So . . . where had Brenda ever been, that she might want to return to? Nowhere to mention. Where had she ever expressed a yearning to go? Again, nowhere. Since their early teens she'd only ever wanted to be with Harry. And he hadn't been the most responsive of sweethearts, either. Indeed, he'd asked himself a hundred times if he really loved her or if she was just some kind of habit. She had never known his uncertainty (he hadn't been able to tell her, because she herself had been so absolutely sure), but now he despised himself for it anyway.

But on the other hand, how do you tell someone who has loved you for so long—as long as you can remember—that you just aren't sure of your own feelings? Not so easy. And a lot harder when she's pregnant with your child.

Misted landscapes, dramatic scenery, cliff paths and gardens grown wild, and starry skies . . .

It brought a certain picture to mind, but of what? *High passes and mountain peaks, and stars like chips of ice glinting on high. And a plain of boulders stretching away to a far northern horizon under the weave of ghostly auroras.*

The picture came and went like . . . like an invention of his own imagination? It had to be, for he had certainly never visited such a place! But in any case it was already fading, melting into unreality like a fantastic dreamscape; which was probably as good an explanation as any: that in trying to visualize Brenda's ideal habitat, he'd evoked a leftover from some old dream. Not so old, in fact

. . . indeed so new that the actual *fact* of it—its basis in reality—was yet to happen. But the Necroscope couldn't know that, and in the space of just a second or so the picture had faded entirely.

The future was ever a jealous place . . .

A million places? Hell no, there were a *million* million places! Since Brenda had never been anywhere or done anything very much, she could literally be anywhere doing anything! But the north-east coast was where she'd been born and grown up, and it still had to be the best bet.

Harry had tried all the towns and villages between Harden and Hartlepool, and had then backtracked all the way to Sunderland and Durham City . . . to no avail. But he had been surprised how many small villages there were that he'd never heard of or visited before, and how easy it was to *try* to find a lost someone, albeit hopelessly. Housing and building societies, hotels and flats and bedsits, and temporary accommodations, these were the obvious places to check: Brenda had to be living somewhere, had to have a roof over her head. She wasn't registered at any of the agencies; the dozen or so girls with small babies who were registered weren't Brenda. And Harry wasn't greatly surprised, but he'd had to try anyway.

Somewhere abroad: that letter she wrote to her father had said she was going abroad, hence the million million places. For if there were a couple of hundred towns in the north-east that the Necroscope had never visited, and five thousand in the rest of England, then what of the rest of the world?

Somewhere abroad.

. . . *A garden in a fertile saddle between ruggedly weathered spurs, where dusty beams of sunlight came slanting through the high passes during the long daylight hours, and the stars glittered like frosted jewels at night, or ice-shards suspended in the warp and weave of ghostly auroras* . . .

The northernmost of the North American States? Canada? The frozen tundras of the northern Soviet Union? Switzerland? (Did they even *see* the aurora borealis in Switzerland—and why the northern lights anyway?) But Brenda was a British girl, naïve in most things even in her native country, even in her native *county!* And as the Necroscope rubbished his own inward directed queries, so that fleeting picture of some far, alien land once more retreated. Which was just as well, for search as he might he would never discover it on Earth.

Never find them . . . never find his baby son . . . never even see them again . . . not on Earth!

Harry started awake in a cold sweat, in his bedroom in the old house not far from Bonnyrig. A sweat of fear and frustration, yes, and a feeling of utter loneliness.

He lay panting in his bed, damp with perspiration, feeling his heart racing and his blood pumping. So that for a few brief moments it wasn't as if Brenda and the baby were missing at all but simply that . . . that *he* was the lost one! And of course the genuine Harry Keogh, the original Harry, *was* lost.

That again: his body, gone. And piece by piece his entire world going, too. Was that why he had to find Brenda, in order to find himself? In which case his search was useless, for she would only deny him.

Fuck it . . . that was why she'd run away in the first place! Because he wasn't him!

She'd run, or been taken away. By the baby or by . . . someone else?

The Russians? But he'd already been over that and it seemed very unlikely. So if not the Opposition, the much-ravaged Soviet E-Branch, then who?

As his sweat dried on him, so Harry's thoughts cleared and his mind seemed to sharpen and focus as he hadn't been able to focus it for quite some time. He went right back to square one: to that night at E-Branch HQ when he'd first been told that his wife was missing. At the time he had put aside the possibility that A.C. Doyle Jamieson—self-styled "werewolf"—could have been responsible for the double disappearance. But now?

The man *had* been into his mind, after all . . . but for how long? Harry had become his "enemy" the moment he became involved with the dead police officers and took up their case. Had A.C. been "listening" to him—to his thoughts and worries and problems—from that time on? In which case he would know about Brenda, Harry's one weakness. But surely if that were the case, *if* he and his gang of car thieves were responsible for Brenda's disappearance, then right at the end when A.C. himself had come under fire, he would have used her as a threat, to stand Harry off. Yes, of course he would—but he hadn't. So . . .

. . . So, damn it to hell, it was another blind alley!

After speaking to his Ma he'd come back to the house full of resolve, and now it was almost burned out of him again. But while his mind was sharp he must pursue the problem. It was so frustrating: to be equipped with his powers—the powers of a Necroscope—and no way to use them to solve his problem, except by trial and error.

He got up from the bed feeling stiff; this damned *body* of his, which wasn't nearly as flexible as it had used to be. Because it was a different one, naturally. Or unnaturally?

The light coming through fly-specked windows was gray as the day outside. He had been down only an hour or two. An hour or two wasted. Down and out. Wilting. Going to seed. Oh, really? And suddenly Harry was angry with himself. He had to shake himself out of it and get on with the search, get on with life. He was ten years older than he should be, sure, but he didn't have to settle for that, did he? His mind was still in shape, wasn't it? And the mind governs the body, *doesn't* it? Well then, he'd have to get the fucking body in shape, too!

He was dressed; he went out into his overgrown garden and did twenty furious press-ups, then felt ridiculous and sat hugging his knees in the deep grass and shivering from the difference in temperature between the house and the garden. And in a while he thought:

My Ma's right . . . I'll catch my death!

Death, yes.

Always a close companion of Harry's, death wasn't something he worried about. Not from a distance, anyway. Close up it would be different, of course. If ever death should attempt his stealthy (or sometimes abrupt!) approach, then like anyone else Harry would be galvanized—to life! But as for the *idea* of death and the dead themselves, he knew no fear. Indeed, he had a thousand dead friends, but not one of them who could help him now, not this time. While among the living . . . did he have any friends at all?

Well, some—like Darcy Clarke and his people—but even they weren't like the dead, because the dead were true friends and rarely demanded payment. As for the exceptions to the rule, the one or two monstrous members of the Great Majority who *had* demanded payment . . . but they were in the Necroscope's past now and couldn't resurface. At least he prayed not.

It was a morbid train of thought, which he tried to break by numbering his friends among the living. These were a handful at best; no, not even that, for he couldn't any longer approach them as Harry Keogh. They would "know" that he wasn't!

Depression, was that it? Probably. And Harry thought: *If I believed in psychiatry I might even go and see a shrink. But if he started to explore my past, how could I explain it. He'd be certain I was incurably insane! Or, if I liked strong drink, I might go and get drunk and see how I felt when I woke up. Except . . . I wouldn't know where to go to drink, and I'd probably feel out of place when I got there. But damn it, I really feel like I could use a good stiff drink! And a talk with a genuine friend. Yet I have no one to talk to but the teeming dead, and they're the only ones who give a damn anyway!*

A morbid train of thought, yes . . .

But now the entire *chain* of his thoughts, ever since he'd started awake in a cold sweat, began to join up link upon link. And there was one missing link, which was integral to the rest. He hadn't thought of it until now because it had seemed wrong, especially when he was searching, or trying to search, for his wife and child. But there might be something in it at that.

Initials writhed on the screen of Harry's mind. Not A.C. Doyle Jamieson and his brother R.L. Stevenson's initials, but someone else's. Someone the Necroscope had studiously avoided thinking of until now. But now . . . maybe he did have a friend among the living after all. Or someone who owed him, at least. And maybe, just maybe, it went a lot deeper than that. For one thing, the time frame was right: the disappearance of his wife and child had coincided precisely with this one's advent. And since that was true, mightn't there be a more relevant, more sinister connection?

Psychiatry? Maybe that was the last thing Harry needed. Maybe all he needed was a rest—from all of this, even from thinking about it! Or a change. Didn't they say that a change was as good as a rest?

Have a good stiff drink and sleep it off, sleep it right out of his system. Clear the air. Christ, he needed a drink! Or was it simply his body—or somebody *else's* body—that needed it? But . . . the mind controls the body, doesn't it? Well, yes, it does, except when the body has habits or needs that control the mind!

Suddenly things clicked into place in the Necroscope's metaphysical, his lateral-thinking mind. But *his* mind in another's body. And a little shakily—shaky with realization, albeit as yet unproven—he went back into the house, to the telephone.

Darcy Clarke was at E-Branch, and he at once sensed something of the excitement in Harry's voice. And in answer to the Necroscope's question:

"What, Alec Kyle? What did he do when he was under pressure?" Darcy said. "Well, he would just ride it out, Harry. When there was work to be done, or a problem to be solved, he'd work at it all the way until he'd covered every angle, almost to the point of exhaustion. And after that? What did he do for relaxation?" (Harry could almost sense the other's grin.) "Well, I'm not sure if I should mention this, you know? I mean—speaking ill of the dead and all that—but . . ."

". . . Did he like a drink?" Finally Harry forced the issue. And Darcy's answer lit up his mind like the crack of dawn on a summer day:

"Did Alec like a drink? Did he *ever!* When he was wound up, so tight it was the only way to unwind . . . *then* he would drink, yes! Usually at home, because there he wasn't risking anything and he didn't have so far to fall into bed. I remember one time he invited me round to his place and between us we killed a big bottle of Jack Daniel's. I stayed over, because I knew I wasn't going to make it to anywhere else. And I paid for it for three whole days. But Alec was just fine! That body of his could soak up hard liquor like a sponge."

"He wasn't an alcoholic, was he?" (Something of alarm now, in the Necroscope's voice.)

"God, no! Once in a blue moon, that's all. But when he did it, Alec did it right."

"Thanks," Harry breathed, and put the 'phone down.

And now he knew. Knew how to be himself again: by *not* being himself. Feelings of illicit attraction? Chemistry, that's all. Alec Kyle's chemistry. And the need to have a good stiff drink following a period of prolonged stress? Again, chemistry: the ex-precog's body doing its own thing—or rather the thing it had *used* to do. And there stood Harry smack dab in the middle, firm in his determination to get used to his new body, without giving a moment's thought to the fact that it must get used to him!

So maybe a night on the town wasn't such a bad idea after all. Maybe *then* he'd be able to get it all going—get body and mind working together—and figure something out. And come to think of it, he did know where to go to get a drink, and probably a free one at that. She owed him that much at least.

Alec Kyle's personal body chemistry? Illicit attraction? Sheer loneliness? Maybe it was all of these things. And initials, certainly.

B.J.'s . . .

B.J.'S

I T WAS 3 P.M. AND JUST AS GRAY IN LONDON AS IN EDINBURGH, AND EVEN darker for Darcy Clarke, who had been sitting at his desk for the last hour, ever since the Necroscope called him, still feeling bad about things in general and wondering what the hell this latest "thing" was all about. Alec Kyle's personal habits? Especially the fact that he'd liked a drink now and then? What in the world could *that* have to do with Harry's search for his wife and baby son? Answer: nothing. Which meant that Harry was still dealing with the same basic problem, still getting used to the fact of his new body.

And as if that weren't enough, Darcy thought, *I had to go and fuck about inside his head! Or get someone to do it for me, anyway.*

The "had to" part was the only thing that let Darcy live with it: the fact that E-Branch and the security of the people, the country, came first above all other considerations. But it had been inevitable from the moment the Necroscope had let him know that he would probably be moving on. Then, even hating it, Darcy had been obliged to set the thing in motion. But all the time he'd been hoping against hope that it would never have to be brought into being, and he'd kept right on hoping until the moment Harry had said he was through, definitely.

From then on it had all been down to Doctor James Anderson, whose business address was a consulting room and a highly rewarding practice in prestigious Harley Street. One hell of a step up for a man who only three years ago had been working the nightclub circuits as a stage hypnotist! But E-Branch had found and elevated him, which was about the same as saying that they owned him. And certainly he *owed* them. That was why he'd come in that night a half-hour after Darcy called for him, and why he had done what he'd done.

Sinister? But in a way it might be argued that everything E-Branch did had sinister implications for someone. Except this time it was being done to a friend. And that was what bothered Darcy the most: that this time the Department of Dirty Tricks had come down on Harry Keogh.

Yet for all that Darcy felt guilty about this thing, the fact was that he hadn't initiated it. That had come from much higher up, from a gray, almost anonymous entity known only as the Branch's "Minister Responsible." It had been Darcy's duty merely to let the Minister know how things stood, and the Minister's to order counter measures.

And (Darcy was pleased to remind himself) they could very easily have been much harsher measures, except he'd been able to advise in that respect, too. So Harry had suffered a degree of minor, or maybe not so minor, interference: so what? He was still functioning, wasn't he? Darcy gave a small shudder as he put what might have been to the back of his mind.

As for why it had had to be done:

Harry Keogh was potentially the most powerful force in the world, for good *or* evil. He was the Necroscope, and Sir Keenan Gormley had "spotted" him almost from scratch, and homed in on him with unerring instinct, recruiting him to E-Branch. But if Sir Keenan had "discovered" him, so to speak, couldn't a far less friendly agency just as easily find him?

For example the Russians. By now they must be keenly interested (to say the very least) in Harry's kind of ESP. It was a weapon he had used against them to devastating effect. Even though Harry "himself" was or might appear to be dead and gone, still the attention of all surviving members of the Soviet ESP-organization would be riveted upon their British counterparts' every move from this time on.

It was even possible (barely, but possible) that the Russians already knew about British E-Branch's "new" Necroscope! And wouldn't *that* be causing them some concern!? What, the ex-Head of Branch, Alec Kyle, back in business? Not brain-dead, or physically dead and blown to bits along with the Château Bronnitsy, but alive and well and living in England? Not drained of all intelligence on a slab in some necromantic ESP-experiment, or pulped in a holocaust of almighty proportions, but sound as a bell and consorting with his old colleagues in London? Good God! By now they'd probably be thinking that *every* Englishman was indestructible . . . and they'd be wanting to know why! And how . . .

Darcy found himself grinning at his own flight of fancy, but of all men he knew that there had never been so fanciful a flight as that of Harry Keogh, Necroscope. And the grin died on his face as he considered other possibilities.

Assuming that the Russians knew nothing—that they were still recovering from the Necroscope's onslaught—still there were other ESP-agencies in the world and Harry could conceivably fall into their hands.

And not only mindspies but crime syndicates and terrorist organizations, too. What a thief he'd make, what an assassin or terrorist! Barriers, borders and brick walls couldn't stop him; he could disappear almost at will; the teeming dead were in his debt and would go to any lengths, literally, to advise and protect him. And all the knowledge of Earth had gone down into the soil or up into the air, where it was written like lore in some mighty volume in an infinite encyclopedia for Harry to open and read. If he had the time, but he didn't because of his search.

Oh, yes: Harry would be invaluable in the hands of any one of a score of criminal elements. And it was still possible that his wife and child's disappearance was connected in some way to just such an organization. Which was why the Branch was indeed working flat out to discover their whereabouts. Oh, they were doing it for Harry, too, who had done so much for them and for the world, but they were also doing it for themselves, for "the common good." And it was for that same common cause that Darcy had called in Doctor James Anderson.

Anderson was the best, the very best there was: a hypnotist without peer in all the land, as far as was known. Working without anesthetics on patients lulled to a painless immunity under the weird spell of Anderson's eyes and systems, surgeons had carried out the most delicate operations; women had given effortless birth in exceptionally awkward circumstances; mentally traumatized and schizoid cases had shed their delusions and extraneous personalities to emerge whole and one from his healing gaze. And far more importantly where Darcy was concerned, Anderson was a master of the post-hypnotic command.

Darcy remembered how it had gone that night . . .

By the time they had entered Harry's room using a master key, the Necroscope had been dead to the world, and probably to the dead, too! The drug Darcy had given him had been a sleeping pill, but a pill with a difference. Distilled from the oriental yellow poppy—and as such an "opiate"—the principal active ingredient had the effect of opening the mind of the subject to hypnotic suggestion while he slept on. The hypnotist would then insert himself into the subject's dreams, his subconscious mind, implanting those commands which the subject would act upon and accept as routine long after the drug had dispersed and he was awake.

Darcy had obtained the pills from Anderson, who used them when he was treating mental cases. Not that Harry was a mental case, but it had provided an easy method of bringing him under Anderson's control without the Necroscope himself knowing what was happening. Since he wasn't a patient as such, it was imperative that he did *not* know what was happening. For rather than being a curative treatment, this was to be preventative.

Darcy had been present throughout and remembered the entire thing in detail. Especially he remembered his only partly covert, his almost suspicious examination of Anderson himself: the way he'd considered the hypnotist's attitude to be far too relaxed, too casual . . . well, in the light of what he was doing and who he was working on. Didn't he know who this man was? But then he'd had to remind himself: no, of course Anderson didn't know who or what Harry was. He was only doing what he'd been asked to do.

Anderson was young, maybe thirty-five or -six years old, tall, and good-looking in a darkly humorless sort of way; or perhaps more attractive than good-looking. But maybe that was residual of his stage days, when he'd used to portray himself as some inscrutable deity of inner mind. If so, then he'd succeeded very well indeed. With his high-arching eyebrows, full, sensual lips—that seemed *too* full and sensuous against the pallor of his face—and the sunken orbits of his eyes, dark as from countless sleepless nights; why, only give him a pair of horns and Anderson would be the very epitome of the devil! "A handsome devil," yes.

His hair was a shiny black, swept back and, Darcy suspected, lacquered into place. His chin was narrow, almost pointed, and sported a small neatly trimmed goatee; his sideburns were angled to sharp points midway between the lobes of his small flat ears and the corners of his mouth. And as if to underline or emphasize his looks, he wore a cloak, which to Darcy's mind was about as theatrical as you could get. Anderson's eyes, of course, were huge, black, and hypnotic. And his voice . . . was velvet.

Inside Harry's room, the doctor had wasted no time. Darcy remembered how it had been: first Anderson sitting by the Necroscope's bed, and lifting each of his eyelids in turn to check the dilation of his eyes. Then, when Harry's eyes stayed glassily open, the classic technique: a crystal pendant swinging on a chain, and the doctor's soft, smoothly insistent voice, commanding Harry that he:

"Watch the lights, the sparkle, the heart of the crystal. Feel the heartbeat as the crystal swings to and fro, and match it with your own . . ." Then Anderson's hand seeking and checking the pulse in the Necroscope's wrist, his nod of approval, and the pendulum's swing gradually slowing as the doctor's marvelous voice continued:

"Harry, you can close your eyes and sleep now. You *are* asleep . . . you are asleep but you will continue to hear me. I am your heartbeat, your mind, your very life and soul. I control you; I *am* you, and because we are one, you will obey me. You will obey *you*, for I am you. We are one, and we're asleep, but we hear our mind speaking to us, and we obey. Can you hear me, Harry? If you can hear me, you may nod . . ." The Necroscope had closed his eyes at Anderson's command. As he slowly nodded his head, so Darcy had found himself holding his breath.

"Harry Keogh, you are a rare man with rare powers . . . you are a man with rare powers . . . rare powers, yes. Did you know that? That you're a man with rare and wonderful powers?" Anderson hadn't known what Harry's "rare powers" were; only that he was following Darcy Clarke's instructions. And again the Necroscope's nod.

"If others knew of your powers, they would want the use of them. Others might want the use of these strange powers. Others might even use them against us, to harm you and me and the ones we love. Do you understand?" (Harry's nod.)

"Now listen," Anderson had leaned closer to the man in the bed, his voice more deep and sonorous yet. "We can only be safe so long as others know nothing of our powers. We are safe only so long as we protect our powers. Others must never know what we can do. We must never speak of our powers. *You* must never ever *mention* your powers to anyone. You must never *disclose* them to anyone. You must never *display* them to anyone. Do you understand?" (Harry's slow, uncertain nod.)

"You may use your powers as is your right, Harry, but you may *never* speak of them, or display them or otherwise disclose them to others. You may never, *ever* speak of them, or disclose or display them to others, no matter what the provocation, not even under the stress of extreme pain or torture. Do you understand?" (Harry's nod, more positive now.)

"Now listen, Harry. You are still you but *I* am no longer you. This is someone new speaking to you—someone you don't know! You don't know me, but you can hear me. If you *can* hear me, say yes." Harry's head had commenced its almost robotic, mechanical nod; but now it paused, stiffened into immobility, and his mouth fell open. His tongue wriggled a moment in the cave of his mouth, then stuttered:

"Y . . . ye . . . *yes.*"

"Good! Now then, my friend, my good friend. I've heard it said that you have amazing powers? Is this true? Answer me!"

The Necroscope said nothing—but his face grew pale, his eyelids fluttered and his tongue wobbled wildly. Which was the point where Darcy had begun to wish he'd never set this in motion, except the possible alternative had been unthinkable.

"Let's be reasonable," Anderson's oh so persuasive voice had droned on. "Let's have a normal conversation, Harry. Your throat is no longer dry; your mouth is salivating; your tongue is freed and you can talk normally. Let's *talk* normally, shall we? Now, what *is* all this about these powers of yours? You can trust me, Harry. Tell me about them . . ."

At that the Necroscope had seemed to relax a little. His eyelids had stopped fluttering; his mouth closed as he licked his lips; his Adam's apple bobbed as he moistened his throat. Then:

"Powers?" he said, inquiringly. "Whose powers? You have me at a disadvantage. I'm afraid I don't know you, or what you're talking about." (At which Darcy had grinned, for this was more like it. Harry didn't seem uncomfortable any more—indeed he *was* having a "normal" conversation. And he was lying his head off!)

Anderson had glanced at Darcy, nodded and said, "He was a difficult subject. I know it's hard to believe, that it looked very easy, but you'll just have to take my word for it: he *was* hard to get into, and I could feel him fighting me. I always know when they are fighting me, for I get these terrible headaches . . ." He used a handkerchief to pat several beads of sweat from his forehead. "And you can believe me, I've got a beauty right now! But let's put it to the ultimate test, eh? He knows you, right? He knows you for a good and trustworthy friend? So why don't *you* ask him about these wonderful powers of his?"

"What?" Darcy had been taken by surprise. "Just like that? I can . . . talk to him while he's under?"

And: "Wait," Anderson had told him, and turned back to the Necroscope. "Harry, you have a friend here, Darcy Clarke. Darcy wants to speak to you, Harry, and you will talk to him just as you have spoken to me: a perfectly normal conversation. Do you understand?"

"Of course," Harry had answered, a half-smile forming on his sleeping face. And without pause: "How's it going, Darcy?"

For a moment Darcy had been taken aback; he hadn't quite known what to say. Then words had formed and he'd said. "It's all going well, Harry. And you?"

"Oh, so-so. Better when I know about Brenda and the baby. I mean, when I know they're okay."

It was the lead Darcy had been looking for. "Sure. And as the Necroscope—I mean with your powers and all—it won't take too long, right?"

Harry's eyes had stayed closed, but he'd cocked his head inquiringly on one side. "Eh?" he'd finally answered, frowning. And: "It seems everyone is determined to talk in riddles today! Look, I hate to rush off like this but I'm—you know—busy? Do you mind?" And with that he'd rolled over in his bed, turning his back on both of them.

At which Anderson had grasped Darcy's elbow, saying, "Not even you! You see, he won't even talk to you about it—whatever 'it' is. Well, so far so good. But now I'd like to hammer the point home. I want to reinforce it and make absolutely certain that my post-hypnotic command is in place. Except I warn you: this is very repetitious stuff. I'm afraid I may bore you to death. Or if not that, I might certainly put *you* to sleep, too!" Anderson's success had pleased him, making him seem more warm and human.

Darcy had stayed, however, and seen it out to the end. And Anderson had been right: it was repetitious and boring, so that by the time he was done Darcy was indeed yawning.

"And now he can sleep it off," the doctor had told Darcy, as they turned off the light and let themselves out of Harry's room.

Then, in his office, Darcy had asked: "What next? Is there anything else I should do? I'm having breakfast with Harry tomorrow morning."

Anderson had shrugged. "He'll probably seem a little confused, reluctant. Whatever this big secret of Keogh's is, all of your E-Branch agents presumably know about it. It's simply that you're keeping it from the outside world, right?"

"That's right," Darcy had nodded his agreement. "We know about it, and Harry *knows* we know—"

"—Hence the confusion," Anderson had finished for him. "If I were you I wouldn't test it: don't even bring it up. Or if you must, then have someone else test it. Some 'stranger?' But well away from this place."

And Darcy had seen the sense in that. "And is that all? Nothing else I should know?"

Anderson had looked at him, pursed his full lips, said: "He's no longer one of yours?"

"That's right. He's moving on. He has things to do. But why do you ask? Is it important?"

Again Anderson's shrug. "There may be—I don't know—side effects?" But before Darcy could show his alarm: "I mean, I've been into his mind—or not *into* it, but I have opened it up a little. In some people the mind is like a door with rusty hinges. And as I told you, Harry's door was damned near welded shut! So I . . . applied a little oil. You see, it's not simply the drugs and my eyes and my voice, Darcy—it's also my mind. No, I'm not an esper like you and yours, but I'm special in my own way just the same. I mean, I can put certain people under just by snapping my fingers! But Harry wasn't one of them. He was difficult. Except now that I've oiled his hinges, so to speak, well, he could be easier the next time."

"The next time?"

"If someone did get hold of Keogh, it's possible—just possible, mind you— that they'd be able to get into his mind as 'easily' as I seemed to."

"They could undo what you've done?"

"Ah, no, I didn't say that!" Anderson had held up a cautionary finger. "What I've done is done, and as far as I know only I can break it. But the rest of Harry's mind might now be more accessible. *He* might more readily give in to hypnotic suggestion. However, that's a pretty big might. I shouldn't worry about it if I were you."

But in fact Darcy Clarke hadn't stopped worrying about it ever since, for close on five weeks. It was a terrible idea, a fearful concept: to have someone break into a man's id—into *him*—without his knowing it; to weaken him in ways he wasn't even aware of, then leave the doors of his mind flapping helplessly to and fro in the wind of some future mental intrusion!

Not that it was really as bad as all that, Darcy told himself, returning to the present. He was simply over-dramatizing again, that's all. It wasn't as if the Necroscope was likely to come up against another hypnotist, now was it?

But still, it wasn't the sort of thing Darcy Clarke himself would ever want to happen to him. Not likely! And of course, it couldn't *ever* happen to him, not as long as his guardian angel talent was watching over him.

On one of the last two counts Darcy was quite wrong, and on the other he wasn't quite right. But then, he wasn't a precog.

Which was perhaps just as well . . .

That same night Harry took the Möbius route into the heart of Edinburgh and hailed a taxi. It was raining and he didn't want to walk—and anyway he wouldn't know where to go, for B.J.'s wasn't in the book. But his taxi driver should know it.

"B.J.'s," he told the man, who turned, looked back at him, and shook his head sadly.

"There's a lot cheaper places tae get pissed, Chief, if ye must," he said. "But the booze in they damn wine bars costs a pretty penny, aye!" He was a "canny Scot," obviously.

"Thanks for the advice," Harry told him, "but B.J.'s will do."

"As ye say," the other shrugged. "Ah expec' it's the young lassies, aye." And they headed for B.J.'s.

The Necroscope quickly got himself lost as the taxi turned right off Princes Street into a maze of alleys, and the looming gray bulk of Edinburgh Castle, his principal landmark, vanished into a rain-blurred sky, behind the complex and merging silhouettes of shiny rooftops and arching causeways. The echoing canyon walls of bleakly uninteresting, almost subterranean streets and alleys sped by on both sides, and between squealing, nerve-rending swipes of the windscreen blades Harry could look ahead and see a pale glow of city lights reflected on the undersides of lowering clouds.

Time seemed suspended . . . he might even have dozed a little in the musty-smelling back seat. But eventually:

"B.J.'s," the driver grunted, bringing his taxi to a halt in a narrow street of three-story buildings whose shop-front façades were built onto or extended from the old brickwork of a gently curving Victorian terrace.

Harry shook himself awake, climbed stiffly out of the taxi and paid the fare, then turned up his collar and looked up and down the street. And as the taxi pulled away he saw that the area was more than a little run-down and shabby, and hardly the place he'd thought it would be. It scarcely matched up to B.J. or what he'd imagined of her. But just what *had* he imagined of her? What sort of place had he envisioned? A low, Moorish dive—but one with style—on the fringe of some Moroccan *Kasbah,* like a Rick's Café and Casino, magically transported from pre-war Casablanca? What, to Edinburgh? Oh, there were dives here, certainly—likewise in London, Birmingham, Newcastle, Liverpool, and

Leicester; and in Berlin, Moscow, Nicosia, New York, Paris, almost anywhere—
but as for style . . . that was about as far as it went.

Harry had no idea where he was, his physical geographical location, but he
did know he'd never have any trouble finding it again. He had instinctively absorbed the *feel* of the place—its aura, its "co-ordinates"—into his metaphysical
mind. From this time forward, using the Möbius Continuum, he would always
be able to come here.

The rain came squalling slantwise; the street was almost deserted; it was too
late for run-of-the-mill shops, and only one late-nighter was lit at the far end of
the street. A Chinese takeaway was open maybe half-way down, also a pub opposite the restaurant, letting out a little orange light from incongruous "antique"
bull's-eye windows. But where was B.J.'s?

For a moment the Necroscope thought his driver had simply dumped him
at The End Of The Known World, until he spotted the illuminated sign, no
bigger or brighter than a cinema's "Exit" sign, over a shaded door set back
from the pavement between a shoe shop on the one hand and a fish-and-chip
bar with a "For Sale" sign in the whitewashed windows on the other. The illuminated sign was in dull blue neon and simply said, "B.J.'s."

Harry moved into the shadow between the two shops, making for the door.
But as he did so, he sensed movement across the street. Turning his head, he
was barely in time to witness the brief electric glare of a camera's flash from a
dark shop doorway directly opposite. Now what the hell . . . ? Someone taking a
picture of him, outside B.J.'s? But who could have known he'd be coming here?
He hadn't known himself until this afternoon! And he certainly hadn't told anyone.

He turned toward the street and made as if to cross . . . and a slight, bent
figure came scurrying out of the shop doorway, heading down the street toward
the pub. Bird-bright eyes under a wide-brimmed hat glanced back at Harry, as
the figure made off in a slap, slap, slap of leather on wet paving slabs.

Harry wanted to get a better look at this one. Fixing the orange glow of the
pub's small-pane windows in the eye of his mind, he quickly stepped back into
the shadows and conjured a Möbius door . . . and a moment later stepped *out* of
the shadows of the pub into the street, and headed back toward B.J.'s.

The mysterious figure in the raincoat and wide-brimmed hat came almost
at a run, saw the Necroscope at the last moment and very nearly collided with
him. As the man swerved aside, Harry caught at his arms as if to steady him, and
so came eye-to-eye with him, however briefly. Briefly, yes, because even as Harry
stared at him, so the small man displayed a surprising strength and wiriness,
wrenched himself furiously free and made off down the street again. And this
time Harry let him go, all five feet four or five of him, watching him disappear
out of sight down a side alley . . .

Harry felt fairly certain he'd never seen the man before, and therefore that
the stranger didn't know and couldn't possibly have recognized him. As for
Harry's use of the Möbius Continuum: the stranger would never believe that the
man in front of B.J.'s was the same one he'd bumped into on the street just a
moment later! So, nothing much for Harry to concern himself over there. But
. . . what was it all about? Was it some kind of threat, something to worry over? Or
was it simpler than that?

Maybe Darcy Clarke had decided to have Harry watched—or watched over—for his own good. But if that was the case, how had Darcy known he'd be going to B.J.'s?

Maybe the explanation was even simpler:

Like, someone was watching B.J.'s for his own reasons. Or perhaps a private detective for someone else's reasons? Or the police? What if B.J.'s was a front for something else? And what kind of a girl—or woman—was this Bonnie Jean anyway, that she should go around shooting at men with a crossbow? But that last was a question Harry had asked himself many times before. It was one of the several reasons he was here: to find out if there was any connection between B.J. and Brenda's disappearance.

Walking thoughtfully back to B.J.'s in the rain, he considered the face he'd seen, or that glimpse of a face, before the—what, observer?—had wrenched himself free. That face on the little man, that startled face, that had decided Harry against any further action at this point. It wasn't that he'd felt afraid of the little man, just . . . surprised? Startled? Even as startled as the small observer himself? But by what?

There are looks and there are looks, and the little man had had one of those looks. Like a cornered rat. And everyone knows that it's best not to corner a rat. *Such* a look, on the face of the little man, had been enough to stall Harry— on this occasion, anyway. But if there should be a next time—then he might want to know more.

Approaching B.J.'s, he pictured that face again: that wrinkled old face with its rheumy, runny eyes. At a distance he'd thought of them as "bright bird eyes," but seen close-up they weren't. Those oh-so-strange three-cornered eyes that one second looked gray and the next shone dull silver, like an animal's at night . . . and the *next* turned gray again; or maybe it was a trick of the street lights. And the long, heavily veined nose, flanged at the tip; and the too-wide, loose-lipped mouth in its thrusting, aggressive jaws. And overall, the gray, aged aspect of the face generally.

Just a glimpse, yes, and not necessarily accurate. But it had been sufficient to give him pause . . .

Letting the picture gradually fade in the eye of his mind, the Necroscope was satisfied (but not pleased) that he wouldn't easily forget it. Indeed he might just ask B.J. about it. About its owner, anyway. For if she was aware of the little man—if she'd ever seen him—she'd certainly know who Harry was talking about.

It was just one of the several questions he had for her. As for the questions she might have for him . . . well, he'd do his best to avoid them.

So he told himself, anyway . . .

The door was heavy and banded with metal, and equipped with a buzzer, a peep-hole, and a speaker grille. Harry buzzed, detected slight movements within, and felt himself observed. Eventually a female voice asked:

"Are you a member, sir? If so, hold up your card. If not, state your business." *Obviously one of the club's "young lassies,"* Harry thought.

"I'm not a member," he answered. "I was invited—by Bonnie Jean."

There was silence for a long moment, then: "Wait."

Harry seemed to wait an inordinately long time, but when the door finally opened it was B.J. herself who stood holding it open for him. And again Harry wasn't certain what he'd been expecting. He had met her before, yes, but a lot had been happening at the time. Funny, but the best picture he had of her was the one George Jakes had given him:

A real looker . . . Tall, slim, slinky, yet natural with it. (The shape in Jakes's dead mind had been that of Lauren Bacall in that old Bogie movie where she says, "You know how to whistle, don't you?") *Maybe Eurasian? She could be, from the shape of her eyes: like almonds and very slightly tilted . . . And her hair, bouncing on her shoulders, seeming black as jet but gray in its sheen. The ageless type . . . Anything from nineteen to thirty-five . . . But a looker, oh yes!*

And now the reality. But still the Necroscope couldn't see her clearly enough, not in the dim light in the hallway inside the door. On the other hand, she could obviously see him.

"So, it's mah brave laddie in person," she breathed, smiling at him wonderingly with her head on one side. "Mah own wee man wi' no name." Then she straightened up, and was still two inches shorter than Harry. "And maybe no' so very wee at that! But I was beginning to think I'd never see you again! Come in, come in."

The hallway or corridor was wide, high-ceilinged, carpeted. Low music came from somewhere up ahead; pop music, Harry thought, late '50s or early '60s. He quite enjoyed all that old stuff. The corridor seemed a long one; there were pictures on the walls, large tapestries in gilt frames; but there were no doors leading off to right or left. A peculiar set-up.

"I know what you're thinking," B.J. said, leading the way. "I thought so myself the first time I saw it—a fire hazard, right? Aye, well the authorities thought so, too. But in the event of fire—God forbid!—there are escape routes enough at the back and out into the garden. And we are on the ground floor, after all."

"I wasn't thinking about fire," Harry answered, not looking where he was going, and bumping into her where she paused at a fire door. And: "Sorry," he said, as she raised a querying, perhaps amused eyebrow. "Clumsy of me . . ."

"But you weren't so clumsy the last time we met," she answered, with the hint of a frown in her voice. "Indeed, I might even say greased lightning!" If she was fishing for some kind of reaction she didn't get it. Harry merely shrugged, and continued:

"No, I wasn't considering the fire risk. I was just wondering: why such a long corridor?"

They were standing very close together. He could smell her scented breath when she answered, "Originally it was an alley between the buildings to right and left. When the shop façades were built at the front, the alley was roofed over to give safe access to the property at the rear—my place, now." Her Edinburgh burr had almost disappeared, replaced by something Harry didn't quite recognize. "Downstairs is B.J.'s," she continued, turning from him and pushing through the door. "Upstairs is my living area. And the garret . . . is my bedroom."

Harry followed her, commenting, "When you answer a simple query, you really do answer it in full, don't you?"

And giving him that look again, "Well, at least *one* o' us does!" she replied, and a little of the brogue was back. Then, with a wave of her arm: "B.J.'s," she announced.

Inside was definitely better than out. Shrugging out of his coat, which a pretty girl in a not-quite-*Playboy* outfit took to the cloakroom, Harry looked the place over. There was a longish mahogany bar with access hatches at both ends, behind which two more girls served drinks—or would serve them, presumably, but at the moment there were only one or two customers. And at the far end of the room another girl sat near the juke-box, an original Wurlitzer by its looks, flipping the pages of a magazine.

"A 'quiet' night," Bonnie Jean commented wrily, as Harry perched himself awkwardly on one of too many empty bar-stools, and she went behind the bar to serve him. "It's always the same when it's raining." There were two other customers ("club members," Harry reminded himself) at the bar, one at each end where they nursed their drinks and chatted up the girls, and a group of three seated at a table in a corner close to a darts board. B.J.'s clients were all over forty, well turned out, business types. Men with money, anyway. It looked like the taxi driver was right: this wouldn't be a cheap place to drink.

Harry continued to look the place over and decided: *It's a converted hole-in-the-wall pub.* And he was right. B.J.'s had been a fairly standard if poorly frequented public house at one time. The ancient pumps were still in place behind the bar, and the oak ceiling beams were dark-stained from genuine fire smoke. The open fireplace itself was still there, big enough to take a small table, but the flue had been sealed when central heating replaced the warmth of a real fire.

"That fireplace isn't Victorian!" he said: an awkward seeming statement—almost an accusation! But he was still finding his way, getting used to the place. And to B.J. To her presence. Or to his presence in her place.

She took pity on him and didn't smile, but answered what he now saw as a dumb comment with a reasoned reply. "You're right. This place isn't Victorian. It goes back a lot further—two or three hundred years at least. Remember, it's set back from the 'modern' stuff, the terrace that fronts onto the street. Twenty years ago it got annexed to all of that almost by mistake, when they started to convert the whole street on this side into some kind o' shopping arcade! But the builder went broke and it all fell through. And a good thing, too, for this old building was here first. More recently it was a pub, but too out of the way. When I bought it I couldn't afford to modernize it, and now I'm glad."

And before he could make another stupid comment (what the hell *was* it about this girl that so tangled his tongue, Harry wondered?) she went on: "This was once a huge living room. Why, it took up most of the ground floor! Now it's split in two by the wall behind this bar. Back there is a storage room, an original kitchen, modern toilets, and access to the garden. And the stairs."

"What's the difference?" said Harry.

"Eh?" She cocked her head, and he admired the angle of her jaw, but found that he couldn't look at her. It was disconcerting. He *wanted* to look at her but couldn't. It was as though he was a schoolboy again—his first fumbling approach to Brenda!

That brought him up short! What was this Bonnie Jean, some kind of Lorelei?

"The difference?" she said.

"Oh!" He pulled himself together. "Between a wine bar and a pub."

She nodded and smiled knowingly. "I had'na taken ye for a drinking man, and it seems I was right. But while we're on that subject, what would ye like?"

"Hmmm?"

"To drink!"

Harry shrugged. "I don't know. A short?"

"Vodka, gin, whiskey, brandy, rum—you name it."

"Er, brandy, I think."

"Cognac? Courvoisier?"

"Whatever you say."

"No, no, *no!*" She laughed. "It's what *you* say!"

The man at the closest end of the bar had been listening to their conversation. Now, sneeringly, he called out, "Seems ye've got yoursel' a real live one there, B.J.!" He was short, stocky, and seemed to have no neck; well-dressed but uncomfortable-looking. What, a rough diamond? A rough something, certainly.

Smiling along the bar at him, the Necroscope said, "A live one? I guess I am—for the time being." The other didn't know what to make of that; scowling, he turned back to his girl.

And in a lowered voice, Bonnie Jean said, "He chats me up from time to time. The protective type, you know?" She slid a glass of cognac in front of Harry, and said, "On the house. I . . . don't know your name?"

"It's Harry," he told her. "Harry Keogh. So what with him and me, it seems you're well protected, Bonnie Jean." he sipped at his drink, which hit him at once and in all the right spots. So now he knew what Alec Kyle's tipple had been; what his body's tipple still was!

"B.J.," she told him. "In here I'm just B.J." But she had known what he meant well enough, and quickly went on, "I still owe you for that, Harry."

"Well, you owe me an explanation at least," he agreed, and gave a shrug. "You know, of a couple of small things . . . ?"

"But not here," she replied. "Not now. And there's a good many things I don't know about you, either . . ."

Harry knew a word game when he heard one, and he was good at them. "Yes, but not here," he said, smiling. "Not now." Astonishingly, after just a sip or two, the cognac was loosening him up! But he'd better not let it loosen him too fast or far. And aware of her eyes on him, finally he looked back at her—and *looked,* and drank her in.

Finally he had her; her picture had firmed-up, taken on life. And she wasn't so much the looker that Harry and George Jakes had thought she might be. But undeniably attractive, yes—even to the point of magnetic. Those eyes of hers, their oh-so-slight slant—and their color, a deep, penetrating hazel flecked with gold: feral eyes. Her ears, large but not obtrusive, flat to her head and elflike with their pointed tips, not quite hidden in the swirl and bounce of shining hair. Her nose, tip-tilted but by no means "cute." *And* her mouth: too ample by far, yet delicious in the curve of its bow. As for her teeth: the Necroscope couldn't remember seeing teeth so perfect or so white!

But she had been studying him, too. "Funny eyes," she said. "Well, not funny . . . strange. Like someone else is looking out of them."

Harry could have answered that one, but he kept silent as she went on: "They look sort of sad, compassionate, and . . . I don't know, trustworthy? But deep down, maybe they're a little cold, too. Maybe you've been made cold, Harry. Have you led a strange life?"

"What, have you been reading my palm?" He smiled his sad smile, which was always a part of him and couldn't be changed, not even by Alec Kyle's face. "Maybe you've missed your calling, B.J. Maybe you should have been Gypsy Bonnie!"

"I . . . fancy I might have come from Gypsy stock at that," she answered. "But how close was I, really?"

"Maybe too close," he answered. "Maybe right now, you're too close."

Showing feigned alarm, she drew back a fraction. "Oh? And are ye big trouble, Harry?"

"I hope I'm not going to be," he told her, honestly. "And I hope you're not going to be. I do need to talk to you, B.J."

She drew back more yet, and meant it this time—not away from Harry, but from the man who had spoken to him just a moment ago from the end of the bar. He had finished his drink and now knocked a bar stool aside in his stumbling approach. There was an unpleasant something on his face: a question—an accusation—aimed at B.J. but intended for Harry. Now he gave it voice. "Is this creep botherin' ye, hon . . . ?"

And Harry thought: *Protective? More the possessive type, I'd have thought.* And seeing the ugly glint in the man's eyes, and weighing him up: *Two hundred and twenty pounds if he's an ounce, and every ounce a pain in the backside!*

HOME WITH BONNIE JEAN.

AND: *SERGEANT,* SAID HARRY TO A GOOD FRIEND OF HIS, WELL OVER A HUNDRED miles away in the cemetery in Harden, *I believe I have a problem.* His dead friend, an ex-Army physical training instructor, and an extremely hard man in his time, was into Harry's mind at once, looking out through his eyes and reading the picture he saw in the bar room. *The thing is,* Harry went on, while Sergeant got acquainted, *I don't want too much mess.*

Step away from the bar, Harry, "Sergeant" Graham Lane told him. *This lad's big and bold, but he's getting old. What, forty-five? And look at his gut: he drinks too much, and he's had too much tonight, too. The next time he speaks to you, if he really means to have a go, is when he'll make his move. Let me take it from there . . .*

Harry moved away from the bar into open space, heard B.J. saying: "Look, Big Jimmy, we were only talking. I've the right to talk to people in mah own place, have I no'?".

"It's the way he was lookin' at ye, lass," Big Jimmy answered, speaking to her but narrowing his eyes at Harry. "I just dinnae like his attitude, his flashy answers!" (Here it came):

"You!" Big Jimmy rasped, turning more fully to Harry. "So ye're a live one, eh?" And he started his swing. "Well, not for long, ye fucking *pipsqueak!*"

Sergeant was right there in the Necroscope's mind, directing him, almost controlling him. So Harry let him handle it his way.

The bar was on Harry's right, and Big Jimmy was moving along it from the left, still knocking aside bar stools. The man had swung with his right hand, a lumbering blow with lots of weight but nothing of speed. The Necroscope stepped forward *inside* the arc of the fist, caught Big Jimmy's wrist in both hands, turned and bent forward from the waist. The big man's impetus carried him forward; Harry's back formed the fulcrum and his opponent's arm the lever; he rose up, somersaulted, came crashing down on a table and reduced it to rubble. And Harry said:

Christ, Sergeant! I said no mess!

What mess? The other answered. *It's over! He's winded but that's all. And maybe he'll take it as a warning. Only a total moron would push it any further. He's seen how fast we are.*

Well, I hope you're right, Harry answered with feeling, as Big Jimmy got groggily to his feet.

"Why, ye—" The man took a stumbling step forward.

The Necroscope took a pace back, his arms lifting and extending forward as his hands commenced moving in an unmistakable karate weave. And cocking his head slightly on one side, warningly: "Don't," he said. Simply that.

"Huh!" The other grunted, stopping dead in his tracks. "So ye're a hard man, are ye?"

"You really don't want to find out," Harry told him.

And from behind the bar: "Ye're *leaving*, Big Jimmy!" B.J. snapped. "Right now, an' ye're no coming back!"

Big Jimmy looked at her through little red pig-eyes, cast one more murderous glance at Harry, and grunted, "Fuck ye'all, then!" As he swung around and headed for the door, one of the girls was hot on his heels with his coat; and B.J. shouting after them:

"Tear up his card! No one's ever tae let that pig in here again!" Her eyes stopped blazing and she looked at Harry, who was finishing his drink. And regaining a semblance of control, B.J. said: "Greased lightning, aye. Maybe ye're right, and I should'nae have tae do with ye."

"Too late for that, B.J." he told her. "We're already had 'tae do,' as you well know." He glanced round the room but no one was looking his way. They probably thought it best not to. One of the girls was clearing away the wrecked table. "We have to talk," Harry reminded B.J.

She pursed her lips, as if preparing to argue, but finally said, "Tonight, then, after we've closed. Midnight, right here. And now perhaps ye'll go? Ye're no' a member, after all. Ah've mah license tae think about."

And you should think a little more about your accent, he thought, *which changes like the wind round Edinburgh Castle!*

B.J. signaled for one of her girls to get his coat, then phoned for a taxi: "Just in case the Big Man's waiting outside for ye . . ." But he wasn't, and neither was the little man with the camera. Harry didn't need the taxi but took it anyway—as far as the town center. Then he took the Möbius route the rest of the way to Bonnyrig.

Back home he rummaged around until he found an incredibly ancient bottle of Scottish malt whiskey that must have belonged to his stepfather. There was still an inch or two of liquor in the bottom, and as he poured himself a large shot he couldn't help but wonder what Alec Kyle would have thought of it. Oddly enough, he still felt buoyed by the single shot of cognac he'd had at B.J.'s! So what was he to make of that? A warning?

And: *I've really got to get this body in training,* Harry thought. With which he poured the contents of his glass—and the rest of the bottle—away down the kitchen sink. Once you know your enemy, it's easier to deal with him.

And that was the end of that . . .

* * *

But maybe he should have taken a drink if only to lighten up a little. Doom and gloom were back by the time he used the Möbius Continuum to return to B.J.'s, a little after midnight, and the miseries were on Harry as heavy as ever. Also, he was somewhat upset by all this unnecessary hopping about; if B.J. had really wanted to talk to him, why hadn't she simply taken him into her back room and *talked* to him? Or . . . had she needed the time to set him up?

Whichever, he was alert as never before as he stepped out of the Continuum across the street from B.J.'s in the dark doorway where he'd seen the little man with the camera. If anything he was early; two of B.J.'s girls were just getting into a taxi at the curbside, and B.J. herself was seeing them off. She gave a wave from her doorway as the cab pulled away, then moved back out of sight. And the illuminated sign blinked into darkness.

Harry conjured a door of his own, moved across the street, rang B.J.'s bell. She hadn't had time to lock the door yet; he sensed movement, heard the rattle of a chain; the door swung open.

And seeing him: "Now how in all that's . . . ?" she said, and frowned her puzzlement. "You weren't here just a moment ago. I thought you weren't coming."

He shrugged. "I saw your girls leaving and waited. Didn't want anyone to get the, er, wrong idea."

"Oh, really?" she raised an eyebrow. "Well, maybe ye'd better come in then, before someone sees you!" And as he made to step across the threshold, "But Harry, you can believe me that they wouldn't get the wrong idea. So let's have it understood: this is strictly business. It's not that I *want* you here, but that you want to be here, right?"

His turn to frown, where he paused with one foot over the threshold. "You invited me."

"No," she denied it. "*You* insisted!"

"Well, I'm here anyway," he said.

"And do you still want to talk to me?" (She half blocked his way).

"If you'll let me in, yes!"

Smiling, she let him pass. And walking along the corridor while she finished locking the door, he wondered, *now what was that all about?*

The lights were low in the bar room; Harry stood waiting, until B.J. came in from the corridor and turned them off altogether. Then he stood in total darkness, until a vertical crack of light expanded into an oblong as B.J. opened a recessed door behind the bar and passed through into the back room. And looking back at him, she said: "Well, are ye no' coming?" She was in and out of that accent of hers like a hungry budgie in its cage, hopping to and fro from swing to swing!

Harry let himself through the bar hatch and followed her into the back room, or one of them. It was a storage room with a door to one side and stairs ascending to B.J.'s private rooms overhead. Here the Necroscope hesitated . . . until from the foot of the stairs B.J. said: "I see more than enough of that bar of an evening. So if we must talk, let's at least be comfortable."

Following her up the lighted stairs, he admired her figure and the natural swing of her backside in her sheath skirt, which was slit up one side oriental style. B.J. was slim and shapely . . . and classy, yes. Or was it just Kyle's body chemistry? Whichever, the Necroscope felt it; also their closeness: the fact that they were quite alone here. But (he was quick to reassure himself) it was all part of the search for Brenda.

"This is where I live," she told him, stepping aside on a landing that opened directly into her living room. "Go on in." And as he stepped by her into the room: "Do have a seat, Harry Keogh," she said.

Before doing so he looked the room over, and was pleased with what he saw. For where the bar below was a mixture of different styles, this room was all B.J.—it perfectly reflected her image, or the image that he still had of her. It was tasteful, yet exciting, too. It pleased the eye, and simultaneously satisfied the mind. Lacking pretension or ostentation, still it looked rich, looked real . . . like the woman herself?

The carpet was pile, patterned, and obviously wool. Harry could almost feel its warmth coming right through the soles of his shoes. The carpet's pattern was . . . what, Turkish? Greek? But Mediterranean, anyway. As were the varnished pine ceiling beams that formed spokes from the center of the ceiling, completing the wheel where they were joined up by curving members around the room's perimeter. Thus the room had a circular or at least octagonal look, while in fact it was simply a square room. But actually there was nothing "simple" about it.

The main lighting feature, a small round chandelier on an extending golden chain, depended from the hub of the pine ceiling-wheel; its crystal pendants served to contain the electric light from three egg-shaped bulbs, so that the whole piece was set glowing like a small soft sun. Its light was adequate, but could be supplemented by use of shaded wall lights, and by the reading lamp on its tall white stand near the circular central table.

The three inner walls were decorated with what looked like good quality old prints in modern frames, while in the corners narrow tapestry screens framed in bamboo added to the circular effect. In the exterior wall, a wide bay window and seat took up three-quarters of the space and opened onto a balcony overlooking the garden; the Necroscope could see the gently mobile tops of trees or shrubbery out there, gleaming a lush green in the rain, and a night-dark hill in the distance (the Castle's Rock, maybe, or Arthur's Seat?) silhouetted against a lowering sky.

A light-tan leather lounger faced two matching easy chairs across the polished top of the pine table, and a pair of tall, narrow, crammed bookshelves filled the gaps between the framed prints along one wall. A television set at the foot of one of the screens that flanked the bay window could be viewed comfortably from the lounger, while a music center on its stand occupied the space in front of the other screen. Behind all four of the screens small chests of drawers were barely visible; obviously Bonnie Jean kept her clutter in the drawers, well out of sight of visitors. She was one tidy lady.

To complete the picture, there was a rotating drinks cabinet on the open landing itself, where B.J. had paused, presumably to prepare drinks, and to inquire: "A Courvoisier?"

Harry almost replied in the affirmative, then remembered his vow against hard liquor and shook his head. "Thanks, no."

"What?" she said. "And am I supposed to sit here drinking by mahself!"

"Nothing hard," he answered. "I'm not one for hard liquor. Tonight was a one-off. If you hadn't suggested cognac, I probably wouldn't have thought of it. But look, since B.J.'s is a wine bar, why don't you offer me a glass of wine?"

That seemed to please her. "Actually," she said, "I think I'm glad ye're no' a drinker. Hard drink will make a fool of a man—like Big Jimmy, for instance. It'll put an idiot in your head and a braggart in your mouth, to think and speak for ye!"

The Necroscope was well able to appreciate that: the idea of other people in your head, speaking and acting for you. And it wasn't too far-fetched, either, except his people were anything but idiots and usually told the truth!

"As for the difference," B.J. went on . . .

". . . Eh?" he felt obliged to cut in.

"Between a pub and a wine bar," she smiled.

"Oh!"

"It's the license," she explained. "A pub's hours are controlled, and its clients often aren't! But my wine bar's a club whose opening hours are satisfactory *to me* . . . within the law, you understand, and with clients that I can pick and choose."

"Like Big Jimmy?" Harry sat on the lounger.

"It was Big Jimmy's first bad mistake," she answered, "and his last."

"You know," Harry said, "that was the first Jock 'Jimmy' I ever met? I know everyone *calls* everyone Jimmy up here, but are there really that many Jameses?"

She laughed, and explained: "It's like 'Johns' in London. Or 'Bruces' in Australia. If you don't know someone's name, you call him Jimmy, that's all. But Big Jimmy really was one."

Harry grimaced, and agreed, "He was one, all right!"

"I'll tell ye something, though," she said, sitting in one of the easy chairs opposite him. "You'd best be careful how you use 'Jock.' The Scots don't much care for it."

"Oh, I can tell you know about them," Harry said. "Despite that you're not one of them . . . ?"

B.J. turned her face away and busied herself pouring wine, generally hiding her momentary confusion.

She had brought a silver tray bearing a crystal decanter, a bottle, and glasses, from the drinks cabinet. Now she poured a glass of red wine from the decanter and a glass of liebfraumilch from the bottle. Taking up the sweet white wine, she offered a toast: "Here's to you, Harry Keogh." And the accent had quite disappeared.

Harry picked up his glass and looked at it. The glass was many-faceted; its contents were a light ruby red, but seemed misty. "The red's for me?" he queried. "But I thought red wine was supposed to give you a headache? What's this, the 'house' wine?"

"That headache stuff's a myth," she told him. "In fact I deliberately chose the red for you because it's not so strong. But it does have more than its share of sediment, which is why I decanted it. I managed to clear most of it. But if you don't like it . . ." she shrugged. "I can always make you a coffee, or something else of your choice?"

Harry took a sip. The taste wasn't unpleasant; there was a certain bite to it—a hint of resin, maybe? He took a stab at it. "You seem taken by things Mediterranean."

"Aha!" she said. "One minute an innocent, the next a connoisseur! But you're right: a friend brought a whole crate of it back from Greece for me. Probably very cheap local stuff, which might explain it's quality, but . . ."

". . . It's okay," Harry cut her short. "It tastes fine. And I'm grateful for your hospitality. But B.J., I do have to talk to you."

"I know," she said. "About that night?"

"Yes."

"Well good, because I want to talk to you, too."

"You probably saved my life," Harry went on, "and I'm not forgetting that I owe you for that. But what you did was still a killing, if not downright murder! Also, you nailed the 'wolfman' to his seat in that van, and so helped kill him, too. *And* you were very cool, calm and collected about the whole business—which worries me. I mean, it's not everyone who goes around shooting people with a crossbow, then shrugs it off like it's something that happens all the time . . ."

She waited until she was sure he had finished, then said: "You could have asked me all of these things that night, after you . . . well, after I found myself in the alley . . . when I was off balance? Let's face it, Harry, if I have a case to answer, so do you. You said you weren't a policeman, so . . . what were *you* doing there that night, eh? And then there's a really big question: namely, how did you get us out of there? I mean, I still can't believe that—"

"—Drugged," the Necroscope lied. "I drugged you." (He'd come prepared for this.)

"What?" Her eyes had narrowed to slits, increasing their tilt, making her look more feral than ever. "*You* . . . drugged *me*? How? When?" Disbelief was written plain on Bonnie Jean's face.

"When I took your arm. I squeezed your arm tightly, held you, but still you pulled away. The effort you exerted to free yourself concealed the fact that I'd administered a drug from a small device in my hand. It had been meant for the people I was after, but I hadn't had an opportunity to use it."

She let that sink in, and thought about it. And finally: "That . . . all sounds a bit far-fetched," she said. "What, you got me out of there, unconscious, on your own?" But Harry saw that she was uncertain.

"I wasn't alone," he went on. "I had friends in the yard at the back of that place. And I switched the lights off, remember? That stopped the police for a little while. By the time they went inside, we'd bundled you over the wall."

"Oh?" She cocked her head on one side. "And then you carried me across the road, in full view of anyone who just might happen to be looking, to the alley, where you waited for me to recover, right?" Her sarcasm didn't quite drip, but it brimmed, certainly.

"Yes," Harry nodded, delighted that she herself had supplied the answer to his biggest problem. "Exactly right. There was a lot of milling around; most of the police were inside, or gathered at the entrance ramp; their vehicles were all over the place, blocking the road. And there was the distraction of the blazing van, of course. Also, if we *had* been seen . . . well, the people I work for are powerful. And so you see it wasn't really difficult. The drug is quick-acting, and just as quick to disperse. After a few minutes you came out of it. You were a bit shaken but nothing serious. Surely you remember sitting down on the wet cobbles?''

B.J. looked very uncertain now; her eyes blinked rapidly as she attempted to absorb all of this. ''I was shaken up,'' she finally said. ''I . . . didn't know *what* to make of things, except that it seemed like some kind of magic. I went to my hotel and to bed. In the morning . . . well, it was all like a dream! And I had no way to contact you or even to know who you were. And I still don't.'' She looked at him accusingly.

''I shouldn't have helped you,'' the Necroscope continued, and took another sip of wine. ''It didn't do me much good with my superiors, the people at the top. I should have left you at the garage to fend for yourself, and that way the police would have had a suspect for the killings. But . . .'' He shrugged. ''You had saved my life, and I felt obliged.''

''So . . . you're an agent, of sorts?''

''Yes.'' (It wasn't too much of a lie. He *had* been one, at that time, anyway.)

''Working . . . for whom?''

''People,'' Harry shrugged again. ''When the police can't do something that needs doing—when the law defeats the lawful—then my people are there to help. Except they're not my people any more. I overstepped myself, with you.''

Her mouth fell open. ''You're out?''

''Yes,'' he answered. ''This is my last job: to find out why you were there, why you did what you did. Only answer a question or two, truthfully . . . you'll be in the clear. And I shall have squared it with my people.''

''They'll take you back?''

''No, but that's okay. I have other things to do.'' He sipped again at his wine, which was in fact excellent. It soothed a sore throat he hadn't even realized he had. And it was loosening not only his tongue but his mind, too, and making everything he'd said seem reasonable—even to him!

''So . . .'' (she was still uncertain). ''After you'd left me in that alley—and that was something of a swift getaway, too, if I may say so!—where did you go? And how did you disappear so quickly?''

''I went to my superiors and briefed them on what had occurred. They'd been after that gang for a long time. As for getting away quickly: there's a wicket gate in that warehouse door in the alley. I simply stepped through it.'' (Well, he'd stepped through a *kind* of door, anyway, if not a wicket gate.)

The frown was back on her face. ''I could swear that when I glanced away from you, then back again, you had simply . . . I don't know, disappeared?''

''That stuff I used on you,'' he answered. ''It has illusory effects, but they soon wear off. Also, it was very misty in the alley. Anyway, what are you suggesting? Where's the mystery? I get paid—I *used* to get paid—not to be seen, to arrive unannounced and depart without leaving a trace.'' Suddenly Harry was slurring his words. Not a lot, but sufficient that he noticed it. ''So what with the mist and all, and your disorientation . . .''

And there was B.J. refilling his glass. Had he emptied it that quickly? ''Now it's your turn,'' he said, stifling a yawn.

''Is my company that boring?'' B.J. smiled wonderingly. Or so he thought.

"Tired!" the Necroscope told her, feeling the weight of his leaden eyelids. Not surprising, really . . . all the chasing about he'd been doing . . . and the drink . . . and the big question mark still hanging like a sword over Brenda and Harry Jr.: their whereabouts, their safety. He leaned to one side, propping himself up with one elbow on the lounger, and asked: "Why were you there? Why the cross-bow? Why did you kill that Skippy bloke, and *try* to kill the one in the wolf mask? Just for revenge? You said that they'd put friends of yours in jeopardy." (The word "jeopardy" hadn't come out very well, but Harry continued anyway): "Which was enough to make you track them down and *kill* them? Well, all I can say is, you must really care for your friends! Why not start by telling me about that?"

"Are you okay?" she looked a little worried now, concerned for him.

"Me? I'm fine!" But the glass tilted in his hand a little. That was okay, there wasn't much wine in the glass anyway.

"Look, be comfortable," she said. "I've only just realized how wiped out you look! Here, let me fix that . . ." And before he could complain even if he'd wanted to, B.J. had placed a couple of pillows under his head. "You have hol-lows under your eyes a cat could curl up and sleep in!" she said. But the way she said the word "sleep" was like an invocation: he could actually feel his itchy eyelids closing, and was too tired to rub them open.

"Your . . . turn . . ." he said, lolling there—

—And barely felt her hands touching his shoulders, turning him on his back, and easing his head onto the pillows. And: *Damn it!* he thought, as he passed out. And a moment or an aeon later, even more idiotically: *I hope I didn't drop my glass!*

When she was satisfied that the Necroscope was well and truly under, taking her time and careful not to disturb him too much, B.J. unclenched his fingers from around the glass, removed the tray and wine and all back to the drinks cabinet, then returned to Harry and pulled down the crystal chandelier on its retractable cable and chain. His story hadn't been so wild after all. Not to someone like Bonnie Jean Mirlu, who had heard many wild stories and known many wild things in her long, long life. And what he'd said about drugging her hadn't come as too much of a surprise either, except for the fact that she hadn't been able to work out what he'd done to her at the time. But now? It was far easier to believe that than that he'd somehow conveyed her in the blink of an eye from one place to another, without covering the space between! What, like some kind of Genie out of the Arabian Nights?

Well, Bonnie Jean didn't believe in that sort of magic, but the "magic" of secret agencies, like MIs 5 or 6, and mindbending drugs especially, these were things she could *readily* believe in. Yes, for she had experience of the latter!

Indeed her red wine was a case—or a good many bottles—in point. The recipe for that had been old when the sciences were young, and when dabblers had been called alchemists. B.J. didn't know what the ingredients were, but she knew where they were cached and how to brew them up. And she knew some-thing of their origins, too: the islands of the Greek Sea—the "Mediterranean," as it was now—and the Bulgarian Empire (later Romania, or Eflak, or Wallachia). Oh yes, and even further afield; for certain of the ingredients had come from the Far East with the Hsiung-nu (later the Huns), in the form of precious balms and medicines.

Certainly the wine had been known in Manchuria and Sinkiang, and to the esoteric Worm Wizards of the Takla Makan Desert, and much later to Arab alchemists in olden Irem, the City of Pillars. In the 14th century it had been used by the Bulgars—who were good chemists and wine-makers both—and by the Serbians and the Ottoman Turks, to ward off the Black Death itself which also had its source in the east. After that, its secrets had been lost to mankind in the reel and roil and turmoil of a troubled world. Lost to mankind, aye, but not to Bonnie Jean's Master, who remembered all things and told them to her in the hours when she was called up to attend *Him*. For she was *His* watcher where *He* lay in state, the Guardian of *His* Place. And the hour of *His* calling would be soon now . . .

. . . *The howling in her mind, that would call her back even from half-way across the world—the cry of the Great Wolf in* His *secret den—that throbbing throat that the wild Carpathians had known when the Danube was a trade route and Alaric of the Visigoths was yet to sack Rome* . . .

Reluctantly, B.J. drew herself back from her mental wanderings in space and time. After all, these weren't her memories but those of her Master, and she was only privy to them through *Him*. But Bonnie Jean had watched over *Him* for two hundred years—like her mother before her, and hers before her—and was a zealous, even a jealous Guardian. And now someone was come who might, just *might*, threaten B.J., and in so doing threaten *Him* in *His* place.

Well, threats weren't new. They were old as earth, as old as her Master's being here; indeed, some of them had come here with him! But the nature of the threat was something else. Aye, for there are threats and there are threats. Now she must discover what sort Harry was, and decide how best to deal with it.

Kill him? Oh, that would be easy, so easy. She could have done it in the garage—she almost *had* done it—except she'd thought he was a policeman, and knew that the police don't give up easily when one of their own is murdered. She could even do it now, this very minute . . . Ah, but what would follow behind? What of these powerful friends of his, these men who could act when the law couldn't? And what was their interest in her? Was it just the way he said it was, or was there a lot more to it? No, killing him now would be stupid, dangerous. Especially if he had been sent here, as he alleged. Safer to find out about him—discover all there was to know—and then let her Master decide his fate.

By now the wine would be right through his system. It was time to begin. Bonnie Jean propped Harry up with pillows until he was in the half-reclining position. She drew curtains across the bay windows, turned down the chandelier lights to a softly luminous glow, and gave the spiral flex a gentle twist that set the pendants slowly turning. Winding and unwinding, they sent a stroboscopic flicker through the finely sheathing membranes of the Necroscope's eyelids.

And: "My turn, aye," she said softly, in a while. "Or are you no longer interested? Don't you want to listen to me then, Harry Keogh?"

His eyelids flickered and B.J. smiled. Oh, he could hear that hypnotic voice of hers, all right, as in some especially vivid dream. "No need to speak," she told him. "Simply nod, or shake your head, in answer to my questions. Do you understand?" B.J. couldn't know that this was a "game" he'd played before, and that therefore his resistance was weakened. Or should be.

He nodded, but his eyelids continued to flutter a little. "Would you like to see?" B.J. wondered out loud. "If so, then open your eyes. The light won't hurt you; indeed the crystals will help you see more clearly. They'll help both of us to see much more clearly."

The Necroscope opened his eyes, and Bonnie Jean was gratified to note that their pupils were dark pinpricks swimming on moist mirror irises. "Now listen," she said, ensuring that the soft spokes of light from the chandelier's pendants were wheeling directly across his eyes and forehead. "I want you to listen carefully and answer truthfully. You do want to answer my questions, don't you?" Her voice was now magnetic, utterly irresistible.

(A slight twitch of Harry's head: left and right, left and right. A shake? A denial? He must be stronger than she'd suspected! But no, he'd been asked a question and was only trying to answer it truthfully—just as she had demanded!) Then his Adam's apple wobbled, and he gurgled: "Y-your . . . t-turn . . ."

Why, he was continuing their "waking" conversation! A different reaction from anything she'd ever known before. Oh, he was a strange one, all right, this one! But: "My turn, yes," she agreed. And why not? Why not satisfy *his* queries here and now? Then, whatever his fate would be later, for now at least he'd be satisfied that she was innocent of any "ulterior" motives in connection with the killings in the garage. What she'd told him at that time—that her motive was pre-emptive, defensive—had been a lie concocted on the spur of the moment. She had hoped to gain his sympathy by telling him that those people had threatened friends of hers. That way he'd be more likely to see her as an instrument of his own revenge, which he had. And now was the ideal time, the perfect opportunity, to substantiate and reinforce his previous opinion.

And so: "My turn," she said again. "You want to question me, Harry? You want me to answer those questions you asked me before you fell asleep?"

(His slow, shuddering nod.) And B.J. wondering, *What sort of mind has this man, anyway?* A determined one, certainly!

"Very well." She went along with it. "Except . . . I shall expect you to believe everything I tell you. And no matter what I tell you, or say to you, you will only remember that I'm innocent of any crime. You'll only remember that I'm *innocent,* and anything else that I *require* you to remember. And in that respect, and with that regard to myself, you will only act when I desire it. At such times as I require, you'll follow any instructions I may give you to the letter. You'll follow any instructions I give you . . . to . . . the . . . *letter!* Is that understood?"

But his nod was tentative, trembling.

"If I'm to trust you with the truth, you must trust me," she insisted. "Isn't it only fair?"

"Y-yes," he said.

"Very well," she said. "Now pay attention, and let's try to have a normal conversation—except you will generally accept what I say. But you are allowed to point out any holes in the logic of my answers. So . . . can we try to talk normally?"

Harry's throat worked up and down as he licked his lips. His face relaxed a little, and he said, "Sure, why not?" in a perfectly ordinary speaking voice . . . but his pinprick pupils remained fixed unblinkingly on the slowly mobile pendants.

B.J. was frankly astonished: at one and the same time he was difficult and he was easy! Perhaps, when these "people" of his had trained him, they had somehow strengthened him against hypnotic suggestion. And post-hypnotic suggestion? If so, then he was a dead man. He mustn't be allowed to take any knowledge out of this room except what she desired him to know. But that was for the future, while for now:

"All right, then let's take it question by question," she suggested. "You wanted to know about my crossbow?"

"It's a weird weapon," he said, attempting a shrug.

"No, it isn't," she shook her head, despite that he wasn't looking at her. "It's a perfectly normal weapon which I use to hunt rabbits in the Highlands. I climb, hunt, and live off the land; those are my hobbies. But I know a crossbow's power, and that it will kill men as well as rabbits. Also, it's a *silent* weapon! Anyway, it served its purpose admirably, and it saved your life. Does that answer your question?"

"Yes and no."

"Yes and no? Then let's deal with the 'yes' part first. What do you mean by yes?"

"Your answer goes part of the way to explaining a coincidence."

"Which is?"

"That the man you helped to kill—the one in the van—believed he was a werewolf."

That hit B.J. like a fist! And forgetting for the moment that she was in control here, she even tried to cover her momentary confusion, which Harry wouldn't notice anyway. But then, regaining control: "Are you saying that you, or these 'people' of yours, actually believe in werewolves?"

"No, but the man you shot in the van did believe in them. He thought he *was* one. If you had believed it, too, you'd use either a silver bullet, or—"

"—A silvered crossbow bolt?" (She had seen it coming.)

"Yes. And you did."

She laughed, however shakily. "That bolt was ornamental! Both of them were. They were taken from the wall of a hunting lodge in the Grampians. They were decorations, hanging over a fireplace along with a lot of other old weaponry. The lodge was my uncle's place, and when he passed on I got one or two of his things. The heads of those bolts were silvered for easy cleaning, because silver can't rust!" It was all a lie; clever, but a lie. But she knew that because it at least sounded feasible, it would be that much more acceptable to her "guest," especially in his drug-induced trance. In any case, this was a "normal" conversation and allowed for normal responses. So perhaps Harry had been looking for just such an answer; maybe he'd even hoped for one. At any rate he sighed . . . a sigh of relief, it seemed to B.J.

Yet still she frowned and said: "But if you and these . . . these 'people' of yours don't believe in werewolves, what made you think I might?"

"I didn't say that we did," Harry answered. "It was just something that required resolution, that's all."

"And is it resolved now?"

"Yes."

"Very well, and now I have a question for you."

"Oh?"

"What else are you working on? You said you weren't concerned that you'd been dropped by your people because you had other things to do. What things?"

"I'm searching for my wife and child."

Stranger by the moment! B.J. thought. But he couldn't be faking it. His eyes hadn't blinked once; they were still fixed firmly on the crystal pendants where they slowly revolved, continuing to seek their natural balance. "Are your wife and child lost, then?"

"They . . . went away," he said. "From me, my work. The baby . . . he . . . it was a difficult birth. My wife's health suffered, mental as well as physical—or rather, mental *instead* of physical."

"Post-natal depression?"

"And other . . . problems, yes."

"So she ran away? With your baby?"

"Yes."

"But in your line of work, with your experience, you'll be able to find them, right? I mean, like you found me? I'm not in the telephone book, Harry."

"Neither is Brenda," he answered. "But I can't simply ask a taxi driver to take me to her . . ."

"That's how you found me?"

"Yes."

"So . . . where will you look for them?"

"Abroad. Canada. Maybe America. The West Coast. Seattle. That's where I'll start, anyway. Probably."

"And when will you go?"

"As soon as possible. Maybe tomorrow. But that's a lot of questions, and it's your turn again."

She nodded, despite that he couldn't see her; it was just that their conversation was that "normal!"

"You asked me if I'd killed or helped to kill those men in the garage out of revenge," she reminded him. "Well, I did. Revenge pure and simple. I told you it was because they had placed friends of mine in jeopardy, but it was more than that. I don't much like to talk about it, that's all." (She was lying again, but trying to make it sound good.) "You see, one of them used to come here, into my bar. He was chatting-up one of the girls, a close friend of mine. Later he called from London, asked her down to see him. She went, and didn't come back. But she left a note of the address she'd gone to. I waited, and eventually saw in the newspapers how her body had been discovered. After that, I felt it was all up to me. I look after my girls, Harry. Their welfare is very important to me . . ."

At least that last part was the truth, and B.J.'s story as a whole wasn't a complete falsehood. About a year ago, she had lost a girl on holiday in London. She simply hadn't come back and was still missing, B.J. presumed dead. The work of her Master's olden enemies? She prayed not . . .

Meanwhile, though she had finished speaking, Harry wasn't saying anything. So B.J. prompted him: "Does that sound reasonable?"

"Yes," he answered tentatively, "as far as it goes. Skippy was from Newcastle. Edinburgh is a short hop. Skippy was always on the run. He might have come up here to get away from trouble in Newcastle. But . . . you shot at two men."

"One because he was trying to kill you," she answered. "It was dark in the garage, and he was obviously a killer. And . . ."

". . . And the other?" Harry prompted her, his eyes as glassy and fixed as ever.

"Because I thought he was trying to run me down! I mean, I didn't actually shoot at anyone, just at the van . . . and I had to get out of there! I was frightened, Harry!" It was another clever lie. And while the Necroscope's drugged mind was absorbing it:

"Your turn, Harry," she said. "Just what is this organization you worked for?"

"It's called E-Branch," he said, flatly. "Part of the Secret Intelligence Services. The most secret of them all."

"And your job with this E-Branch?"

He was silent, but beads of sweat had formed on his brow.

"Well?"

"I was a field agent."

"Doing what?"

"You saw that for yourself. Those louts in the garage were murderers and thieves. They were responsible for the deaths of innocent people, including policemen, *and* your friend! I was—oh, a means of enforcing the law, where natural laws no longer applied."

"What?" She cocked her head on one side. "They'd given you a license to kill?" That wasn't *exactly* what he'd meant, but:

"Oh, I'm no stranger to death," he answered. And before she could respond, "But now it's your turn again. Why does an 'innocent' girl like you have access to mind-bending drugs—like the stuff you must have put in my wine? And why, if you're so innocent, are you afraid of being questioned? Instead of hunting this Skippy and his lycanthrope friend down, why didn't you give the police the girl's last known address in London, which you told me you knew? Last but not least, why is someone watching you or your place—*this* place? A shriveled-up little man with a face like . . . I don't know. Like a greyhound?"

But Bonnie Jean had had more than enough of this game now. And anyway, he was much too good at it. As for that last question of his: it had shaken her to her roots!

So: *Enough of this!* she thought. Now it was time to apply the real pressure . . .

HARRY: WEIRD WARNINGS.
BONNIE JEAN: SHE WONDERS AND WORRIES.

BEYOND THE BAY WINDOW, LOW OVER THE DISTANT HILLS AND GLEAMING palely on the rim of the clouds, the waning moon was five days past full strength. B.J.'s powers—or some of them, such as her metamorphism—had waned with it. But others had been hers from birth; they were hers by right. Her Master's greatest talents had been his mentalism and, upon a time, his metamorphism, of course; and B.J. was blood of his blood. She would have all that was due to her in the fullness of time . . . even if it took another two centuries for full development. But for now—

—She was a beguiler. That was her art: hypnotism. Aided by the wine, her eyes and mind would exercise such power even over this awkward subject, this Harry Keogh, that he would become as a toy in her hands: hers to command, to do with as she willed. And because she had never failed, B.J. never once considered the idea of failure.

In this she was surely fortunate, for Harry Keogh's metaphysical mind wasn't at its best. It resisted the Necroscope's contours; echoes of Alec Kyle's precognitive talents continued to shape it; its defenses had been undermined by previous tampering. But Bonnie Jean knew none of this.

Now, drawing the small table to one side, she positioned her chair so that the chandelier hung just to the right of her head, where its scintillant pendant crystals continued to turn to and fro but on a level with her eyes. And in this position she faced the man on the lounger across eighteen inches to two feet of space, and said, "Harry, now we'll do something else. When I tell you to, I want you to look into my eyes. Not now, but when I tell you. Is that understood?"

"Sure," he said. "But it's still your turn."

Oh, he had *willpower*, this man! But so did B.J., and she also had the wine—and powers other than will—to subvert the will of others. "But that game is over now," she insisted. "And at my command you *will* look into my eyes." And before he could answer, if he'd intended to:

"Harry, this is no longer a 'normal' conversation. Your mind isn't yours to control. You feel the effects of the wine. You feel ill as never before. Your brain is swimming. The room is spinning. Only I can stop it. Only my eyes can stop it!''

Harry's head began to loll on the cushions, to and fro, backward and forward. More beads of sweat stood out on his brow, forming damp spots in the permanent creases of forgotten frowns. But his pin prick pupils never once left the pendants, even though his eyes rolled to the motion of his face and head.

"You do believe me, don't you?" she went on. "You do feel those effects I've described?" In combination with her purring, persuasive voice, the action of the delusion-inducing, suggestion-enhancing wine worked on Harry's mind to the desired effect. He was pale as death, panting now and beginning to convulse. As rapidly as that, he displayed all the symptoms of physical illness; in a little while he might even be sick!

And: *Now!* thought Bonnie Jean, reaching behind her back to the top of her sheath dress, finding the zipper, drawing it down, down, and shrugging the garment off her shoulders. *Let it be now!* For a moment the dress clung to her breasts, then fell forward and exposed her to the waist. She stood up, stepped out of the dress as it fell, and pushed down her panties. And once again: *Now! Let it be now!*

This would take some effort; it wasn't her time; the full moon was B.J.'s time. But she needed more than her own strength now, more than the strength of her human eyes. Oh, Harry Keogh would listen to her as a woman, and obey her to a point. But as the *Other* she would be more powerful yet and have complete control over him, or so nearly complete that it wouldn't matter.

And seating herself naked before him, she turned her gaze on the chandelier and let its light fill her brain. It formed a softly glowing moon floating right there in her room, a gloriously *full* moon. A moon of strange powers, and one of change. And Bonnie Jean . . . changed!

It was as if her flesh *rippled;* it was as if her colors flowed, especially the color of her hair, out of her head and into her body. The gray highlights were highlights no more but solid color; *she* was gray, almost white. Her coat, pelt, fur, was white! And her eyes: their shape was angular now, triangular, or at least *framed* in triangles of white fur. And their size was huge, and their color—was blood!

And Bonnie Jean's lips . . . her mouth . . . her teeth!

It was metaplasia, but almost instantaneous. It was metamorphosis, monstrous and immediate. If the Necroscope had been awake, or other than entranced—if he'd seen it, experienced it—then he would have known what it was, would have known to cry out. And the one awesome word he would have cried:

Wamphyri!

But he hadn't seen, didn't know. And the breath he *might* have felt upon his face, which came from scant inches away now, was still sweet—not with the sweetness of perfume but an animal sweetness, or musk—and the words he heard when she spoke were more a cough, a grunt, a growl, but still *her* words which he must obey:

"My eyes, Harry. Only my eyes. If you would put an end to your sickness, your misery, then look into my eyes. Don't look at me . . . but only into my eyes."

And he did. Into her furnace gaze, into those eyes which had fascinated Mesmer himself, into a hypnotic whirlpool that was easily the equal of Doctor James Anderson's; except James Anderson had been here first, and his post-hypnotic commands still applied. They were buried deep, but they were here and they were still active.

And: "There," the creature that was Bonnie Jean husked, binding Harry to her gaze. "And all your pain is eased, your sickness is washed away, the whirling of your brain has been stilled. Now tell me, is it good, Harry?"

The Necroscope tried to answer but couldn't; his tongue was swollen, his throat parched. But she heard his sigh, and saw how the heaving of his chest gradually subsided. And finally, completely under her spell, he nodded.

And his pinprick pupils were like crimson motes burning in the reflection of her gaze, or tiny planets swayed by the lure of twin suns . . .

In the morning, starting awake from some instantly forgotten nightmare, Harry had a splitting headache and felt like death warmed up. Then he saw where he was, knew that he'd spent the night here without remembering a thing about it (well, except for the really important stuff), and felt even worse. B.J.'s living-room, her lounger . . . herself, emerging onto the stairwell landing in a toweling robe. She'd showered and her hair was still damp on her collar. The smells of coffee and toast came wafting from the tray she was carrying.

"God!" said Harry, sitting up and laying aside the blanket she had thrown over him. And he meant it when he repeated: *"God!"* For the last time he'd felt like this was on that morning in London, after taking Darcy Clarke's sleeping pill . . .

She smiled at him where he screwed up his eyes, fingered back his hair and gritted his teeth, and told him: "When you went, you went *really* fast and never knew what hit you. But I have to admit I asked for it. After all, you'd warned me that you weren't much of a drinker."

"The wine?" Harry grunted. "That stuff? How can anything that tastes so good be so wicked?"

"But isn't that always the way is it?" She laughed at his pained expression. "Anyway, it was either the wine . . . or the life of a secret agent is very, very strenuous!"

"Ah!" he said. "I told you about that?" (But how much? Had he been *that* drunk, or ill, or whatever?")

"Nothing specific—but I would have known anyway. I mean, you were so calm and controlled in that awful situation in London. You would have to be something special just to be able to get us out of that place the way you did!"

With which most of it came flooding back—or so the Necroscope thought. The words "that awful situation in London" were a mental trigger, a trip to release his stored "memories." And now they were there, dropping neatly into place . . .

. . . *Her motive had been revenge pure and simple. Her girls were very special to her, and she felt like a mother to them; in almost every case they'd been in need of care up until the time she employed them. Also, she had known that Skippy was "a bad one." If the police weren't able to pin the murder on him, he might easily put two and two together and work out that B.J. had fingered him. After that, he might even have come looking for her!* It seemed like a perfectly sound motive—to the Necroscope, at least. Because B.J. had *told* him it was sound.

And the silvering on the heads of the ornamental crossbow bolts? *Perfectly acceptable. Even the odd little chap who had been watching the place: the father of one of the bar's hostesses, maybe, checking that she worked in a decent place? Or perhaps a private detective following one of B.J.'s more dubious customers? Well, if she had any more clients like Big Jimmy, that would seem reasonable enough, too!*

And so his memories seemed whole, complete as some well-remembered tune, and not a single discordant note to jar his mind awake to its errors. As far as last night was concerned, that page of the Necroscope's mind had been re-written.

Maybe he frowned once or twice, and blinked as B.J. sat down beside him and poured coffee, but that was all. Harry's main concern right now was that he hadn't been bothersome to his lady host. For after drinking her red wine . . . well, the night's events were vague, to say the least!

"Have you decided, then?" B.J. broke into his thoughts.

Startled, he looked at her. "Decided?"

She nodded, sighed, said, "My, but you're having a really rough time of it, aren't you? Have you decided when you'll continue your search for your wife and baby! It was the very last thing you said to me before you, er, turned in? No, I can see that you don't remember. You said that you'd have to sleep on it. You told me it could be as early as today. But looking at you this morning . . . I can't say I'd advise you to travel *anywhere* too far too fast, Harry Keogh!"

"Too far too fast." The word sequence opened another door in the Necro-scope's mind. *Brenda and his son. He had come here to find out if there was a connection between Bonnie Jean and their disappearance. Forlorn hope! No, B.J. was just a strong-willed young woman who believed in taking matters into her own hands. And Harry couldn't deny that if he'd been in her place he would probably have done pretty much the same thing. An eye for an eye. Her connection therefore was purely coincidental.*

And despite his false memories, this time Harry was absolutely right: where Brenda was concerned, B.J.'s coming on the scene had been entirely coinciden-tal.

So, back to her question. "I'll think it over—think it out—a while longer," he said. "Well, for a couple of weeks, anyway." *(A couple of weeks? Yes, he was decided. Three weeks at least . . . to think it out.)* And fingering his scalp again: "That is, when I *can* think again! But I'll need at least that long to work out some kind of plan—won't I?"

She nodded and shrugged. "Well, it's none of my business, of course. It's just that I wish you luck. But whatever you do, you will stay in touch, right? Let me know how you get on?"

Harry wasn't looking at her; he was sitting there holding his head between his hands, blinking his stinging eyes and trying to focus them, looking at his left sock where it hung half off his foot. But her words rang in his mind like a bell:

"Stay in touch . . ."

He gave a slight involuntary jerk, was unable to stop his reaction, as a short, sharp series of vivid scenes flooded his mind:

A full moon, brilliant yellow, like burnished gold, sailing a clear night sky. That was all he should have seen, and he knew it—knew *something*—remembered some-thing however briefly, like a name on the tip of the tongue that comes . . . then slips maddeningly away: "When the moon is nearing its full, stay in touch!" That was all there should be, yes. But there was more:

A snarling visage: the merest glimpse of dripping fangs, salivating leathery lips, pointed ears and gray fur; and commanding eyes, red as sin—full of sin—carrying some secret message that Harry couldn't read. Then the moon again, showing the wolf's head in silhouette, thrown back in a silent, throbbing howl!

The kaleidoscopic scenes were there . . . and they were gone. And even the knowledge that they'd *been* there was gone, except for a fading shadow on Harry's metaphysical mind.

And of course he jumped to the wrong, or not entirely correct, conclusion: it had to be Alec Kyle, his precognition! But had it been a warning, or what? Or was it simply an echo not of the future but the past, a flashback to the madness and mayhem down in London? And if so, why? But already it was gone . . .

B.J. had seen him start; he could feel her watching him. He jerked up his head and looked at her, catching her off balance. There was a smile on her face—or the vestiges of one—that she hadn't quite managed to drop. And knowing she'd been caught out, as it were, she shook her head and said: "So there we have it: no drinking man, you, Harry! Man, ye're *rough!*"

So, she'd been smiling at his discomfort—right? But a very secretive sort of smile. Or maybe a knowing smile? Again Harry jumped to the wrong conclusion:

B.J. must see a good many heavy drinkers in her bar. Alcoholics even. Let's face it, you could find alcoholics in just about any bar anywhere in the world. Couldn't you? The trouble was the Necroscope didn't know much about them. Only what he'd heard. For instance: one drink is enough for some people, while others can drink all night and never show it for a moment. What kind of drinker had Alec Kyle been, really? A heavy one, maybe? Too heavy? A secret one? Secret enough to hold down his job at E-Branch? And here was Harry Keogh, lumbered with Kyle's body. *And* his addiction?

He looked at the tray where B.J. had set it on the pine table. The coffee looked good but he really didn't fancy anything to eat. His throat was sandpaper-dry and his brain felt like a wet sponge! But Bonnie Jean had asked him a question. God, he felt so stupid! What was it she'd asked?

"Won't I be seeing you again?" She obliged him.

"I . . . I have your number," he told her. "I'll know where to contact you." (But why in hell would he want to contact her, apart from the obvious reason? What *arrangements* had been made last night? He was sure that nothing had happened here.)

Mulling it over, he drank his coffee . . .

Half an hour later he left, walking off along the street into a dreary morning. And not long after that one of B.J.'s girls reported back to her and said: "I followed him, like you said. But . . . I lost him!"

"What?" B.J. was angry. She had obtained Harry's telephone number but that was all. It was a simple oversight, an error on her part. She'd wanted to know where he lived, how to get there and what it looked like—things that she could have asked him last night. It had seemed such a perfect coincidence: the fact that he had a place up here close to Edinburgh! But she'd known that Harry would "stay in touch" with her, and so hadn't really considered the possibility that he might be hard to locate. She had only sent the girl after him on an afterthought. Now, however, taking time to give it a little *more* thought:

Harry was (or had been) some kind of agent. What if this place of his wasn't "his" place at all but a safe house? Perhaps it was a good thing her girl had lost him. Perhaps these "people" of his had been waiting for him, to whistle him away, and the telephone number was merely a contact number. She knew it was listed, which meant she couldn't use it to discover his address. All very irritating! And because the girl hadn't answered her yet: "How *could* you lose him?" she snapped.

"He went into a newsagent's," the girl told her hurriedly. "I thought he'd be buying a newspaper and waited in my car. But he didn't come back out."

"Maybe he'd spotted you!" B.J. snapped. "I told you to be careful. He's no fool, that one."

"I thought I *was* careful," the girl looked bewildered.

B.J.'s attitude softened, and finally she said, "Maybe he went out the back way." And she left it at that. For after all, Harry was that kind of man. And in his line of work it must be second nature to take precautions against being tailed. Indeed, he had said as much. He was just good at his job, that was all.

Again she remembered that damp, dangerous night in London: the action in the garage, and how . . . *something* had happened to her, before she came to her senses in the alley; then how Harry had seemed to disappear into the mist. Oh, yes, he'd been good at his job, all right! But in any case, what difference did it make? For B.J. knew he would be in touch again, and even *when* he would be in touch: in just three weeks' time.

Glad to be let off the hook, B.J.'s girl went down to tidy up in the bar room. For in fact she, too, was lost for an explanation as to how she had so stupidly, even ridiculously, lost her target. Because as far as she knew—having checked and double-checked—the newsagent's shop in question didn't *have* any back way out!

Harry's coat was of the voluminous variety, a big heavy thing that John Wayne might have worn in some wintry Western. Shrugging out of it in the old house near Bonnyrig, he became aware of an oblong shape swelling out the left-hand side pocket, and of extra weight on that side. He would have noticed it sooner, except he wasn't up to noticing much of anything this morning. It was a small, flat bottle of B.J.'s wine; no label, but the same unmistakable red, and loaded with sediment.

A gift, obviously. What, from B.J.? But after last night anyone would think she'd know better. Red wine and Harry Keogh didn't mix! Maybe she'd simply dumped it on him before someone else suffered the consequences. Well, cheers, B.J.! He gave it no further consideration . . . because he'd been told not to.

There was something else that B.J. hadn't mentioned about her "Greek" wine: the fact that it was savagely addictive, far more so than any cocaine derivative. But even if the Necroscope had known, right then he wouldn't have been able to so much as look at the stuff. Not yet, anyway . . .

It was mid-morning, and Harry was still tired; he had a stiff neck from B.J.'s lounger, not to mention a hellish hangover. Taking aspirins, he tried to think straight. There were things he had to do this morning—if only he could remember what they were! But—

—*Call your superiors. The people you worked for. Get me off the hook. We don't want them carrying out any unnecessary investigations on an innocent girl, now do we?*

No, of course not. But . . . Bonnie Jean wasn't *on* the hook, was she? They didn't even know about her! Even as these pseudomemories and thoughts crossed his mind, Harry had picked up the 'phone and dialed Darcy's number. It was a Saturday, but still Darcy might be in his office. And he was.

"Harry? What can I do for you?" And more quickly: "If it's about Brenda, I'm sorry, but—"

"No, it's something else," the Necroscope cut in. And now he knew what it really *was* about. "Darcy, check and see if the police down there have an unsolved murder on their hands, won't you? An Edinburgh girl or young woman, murdered in London about a year ago? If they have, you can tell them the case is closed. Tell them it was down to Skippy or our would-be werewolf—or both of them."

"You're still working on that?"

"No, it was just something that came up."

"Oh. Well, thanks anyway."

"Oh, and you remember the silvering on the heads on those crossbow bolts? Well, it was ornamental. They once decorated a wall over a fireplace in a hunting lodge or something. The silver was to stop them from rusting."

"You *have* been working on it!"

"No," Harry sighed. "Just checking back on everything that was going on at that time, that's all. The time when Brenda and my son . . . you know."

"Sure," said Darcy. And: "Well, thanks again, Harry."

"Also," the Necroscope blurted, before Darcy could put the 'phone down, "you might be able to tell me something more about Alec Kyle."

"If I know, I'll tell you," Darcy answered.

"I asked you if he liked a drink. You told me he wasn't a heavy drinker, but that when he did take a nip, then he really went to town on it."

"That's right."

"Could he have had a problem that you didn't know about? I mean, is it possible he was an alcoholic and knew it, but he had it more or less under control? Except on occasion, when it would break out and he'd have to feed it? Wait! Don't give me your answer right off but give it a moment's thought. It could be very important, and I know how loyal you are, Darcy . . ."

Several seconds ticked by, then the other said: "Well, it *is* possible, of course. In this game I've come to realize that almost anything is possible! But I wouldn't have thought so. I never knew a steadier man, Harry. On the other hand . . . he was a precog, as you know. They all have this thing about the future; they're all a little scared of it—and sometimes a lot. If, and I mean *if,* Alec had a problem, he kept it pretty well hid. And *if* he had one, you can bet your last penny it would have to do with his talent. 'Talent': that's a laugh! I sometimes wonder if we're not all cursed!"

Harry thought about that, then said, "Thanks, Darcy."

"No, it's me, we, us, who should be thanking you," Darcy told him.

"You're welcome," Harry answered, automatically, and he started to put the 'phone down—then paused and said: "Darcy, I'll be up here for maybe three more weeks, then I'll probably be out of the country. I think they must have gone abroad. But when I go . . . I may be gone a while. I mean, I won't be coming back here each night. And I'll need funds."

"I can swing that," Darcy told him, without hesitation.

"No," Harry answered, "I'm not going to hit on you or E-Branch for money. But there is something you can do for me."

"Just mention it."

"Find out where the Russians keep their gold."

"What?" (Astonishment.) "Where the Russians—?"

"I mean, their repository? Like Fort Knox or something?"

As the last word fell from his lips, so Harry reeled. It was as if for a single second he was no longer in his room. It was just like that time in Darcy's office, in the moment following the warning of an imminent IRA attack. Except this time nothing had prompted it, there was nothing to explain why—

—*Why Harry stood in the open, somewhere else, in bright daylight, and craned his neck to look up, and up, at stark yellow and white cliffs . . . and at the squat, white-walled castle, mansion, or château that was perched there on the edge of oblivion. A fortress on a mountainside (from Harry's viewpoint), at the very rim of a sheer drop that must be all of twelve hundred meters to the sloping scree of a rubble-strewn gorge. The scene was . . . Mediterranean? All sun-bleached rocks, brittle scrub, a few stunted pines, and a salty tang from the unseen ocean.*

"Their repository?" Darcy answered, abruptly yanking the Necroscope back to the here and now. "Why, I'm sure they must have! And I can probably find out about it, yes. But—"

Harry quickly pulled himself together. It could only have been a manifestation of Alec Kyle's precognition. As to what it meant . . . who could say? He tried to carry on the conversation as if nothing had happened. "Or if not the Russians, someone or some outfit—maybe the Mafia, or some other organization like that, with bullion—who you'd like to see lose some big money? Maybe to our advantage? Like, gunrunners, or drug traffickers? I'm sure you know what I'm saying."

Darcy laughed out loud . . . but the Necroscope didn't even chuckle; he was still recovering from the effects of his inexplicable—what, visitation? Finally the head of E-Branch said, "*Ahem!* You know, if I didn't know better, Harry, I might accuse you of planning something decidedly illegal?"

"I suppose it depends whose side you're on. You'll do it?"

"If that's what you want, yes," Darcy said.

Harry nodded, despite that the other couldn't see him, and said, "Then do it soon. And Darcy—see if you can find someone who'll give us a decent exchange rate, no questions asked."

This time, putting the 'phone down, Harry *was* smiling despite his headache. Because he knew that on the other end of the line, Darcy Clarke wasn't.

But even as the 'phone settled in its cradle—

—*He was there again! But this time he was* up *there on the rim of the cliff, and the walls of the keep rising before him. Its medieval turret towers seemed semi-sentient—like stone sentinels—where he craned his neck to look up at them. And he felt his hair moving on his head, perhaps blown by the winds off the gorge.*

It came and it went, and Harry sat there beside the telephone again. With his hair still standing on end . . .

Bonnie Jean was worried. About E-Branch: how successful she'd been in throwing Harry, or "them," off her trail." About Harry Keogh himself, because she believed there was *still* something about that one that wasn't connecting. Where he was concerned, no sooner was one mystery cleared up than another surfaced!

Like how he moved so quickly and came and went the way he did, and the way he had eluded her tracker. As to the matter of his drugging her that night at the garage in London—the more she considered *that,* the more utterly ridiculous it seemed! But any alternative was even more ridiculous, indeed impossible! So it could only be true. If only she had been a little more thorough when he was in her power. She could have discovered a lot more about this E-Branch he'd worked for, for one thing . . .

And as if all of this weren't worrying enough, now there was the question of the watcher. A detective, or the father of one of Bonnie Jean's girls? She thought not. But from the description Harry Keogh had given her, B.J. believed she knew who—or what—it *might* be. Well, it had happened before, on several occasions down the decades. And now it could be happening again. She supposed she should be grateful Harry had brought it to her attention, except grateful wasn't part of the equation.

But forewarned is forearmed. If indeed this should prove to be the worst possible scenario come or coming to pass, then B.J. must look into it and, if necessary, draw *their* fire away from her Master. She had done it before—all of a hundred and seventy-five years ago—to lure *them* from the true spoor; and twice more in the years flown between. Inexperienced though she had been on that first occasion, still she'd won; and likewise ever since, else she wouldn't be here now! It was *why* she was here, after all; to guard over the dog-Lord in His immemorial sleep, where He patiently awaited the advent of the One Foreseen, the Mysterious One.

The *right* one, aye. And yet again B.J. thought of Harry Keogh, if only for a moment . . .

. . . And the time of the calling so close now, when again she must go to Him. But this watcher:

If he (or they) were that close, and if they had been allowed to follow B.J., all unbeknown, perhaps to the very lair? That was unthinkable—that she might so easily have betrayed a secret so well-kept for six long centuries! Well, at least it excluded Keogh's involvement with them. For if he were one of them he never would have offered his help in the first place. And when he had her under the influence of *his* drug, he could have done whatever he wanted with her; could have . . . *removed* her, and so dealt with her Master, too. For without B.J. what was her Master but a poor defenseless thing in a cavern tomb? But Harry had done nothing except bring her to safety.

But oh, what she wouldn't give for Harry Keogh's extraordinary skills now!

The way he seemed simply to vanish like that. Why, with him on her side, B.J. would have nothing to fear during the coming visit to her Master! Harry would lose any would-be trackers as easily as he'd eluded her girl.

With him on her side . . . or, him *by* her side?

Keogh . . . Keogh . . . *Keogh!*

Why was he on her mind so? For after all she, Bonnie Jean Mirlu, was the beguiler, with the power of fascination! And yet somehow this Keogh fascinated her . . .

Oh? And did that mean something?

His eyes, so warm and innocent: neither brooding, conniving, nor flirting (or flirting only a very little); not even especially beautiful, yet extraordinary in their depth, in the way they echoed the soul behind them. They were oh so soulful, those eyes of his. And at that B.J. gave an involuntary shiver, for the thought of his soul was . . . *delicious!* And if her Master were to give the word, why, she might yet taste it, steal it from him in one raw red moment! Aye, and *that* would put an end to his mysterious ways, for sure.

His *mysterious* ways . . . ?

Bonnie Jean started into shocked awareness where she sat thinking things out and brooding in a chair in her living-room. Harry Keogh: a mystery man appearing on the scene from nowhere, as if on cue. And B.J. feeling this attraction, a weird affinity that was hard to place, as if she already knew him. So much so that when she should have let him be killed—or killed him herself—instead she'd entrusted herself *to* him! Then, later, *he* had sought her out, to bring her a warning. This mysterious Harry Keogh.

What was she thinking? That he might actually be *that* mysterious one, *the* Mysterious One, for whom the dog-Lord waited? And if he was, and she had simply let him walk out of here . . . ?

Bonnie Jean had lived too long to panic, but for a moment that's what it felt like. Then logic took over. So Harry Keogh had come and gone . . . so what? He would be back, and she *knew* he would be back—whenever she called! Through her hypnotism, her fascination, he was now as much in thrall to her as she was to her sleeping Master. Except he didn't know it yet and probably never would. She could be with him—use him, deal with him, however she chose—and afterward he would remember only what she required him to remember.

Her immediate instinct, to call him on the telephone—now, at once—gradually eased. *He* was at her beck and call, and not the other way around! And anyway, he wasn't going anywhere for at least three weeks. And when he did he'd be going with B.J., to see her Master. Yes, and then all would be well. If by some miracle Harry should prove to be the one, then she would reap her reward, her Master's eternal gratitude. And if he was not the one, still she would be rewarded, and the dog-Lord's most urgent need satisfied. For it would also be the time of replenishment, the time of nourishment.

Bonnie Jean's time, too, as well as that of her Lord and Master and ancestor, the dog-Lord Radu Lykan . . . !

Meanwhile, she would put a watch on the watcher, and perhaps discover who or what he was. Using her girls, it would be an easy thing to arrange a roster of observers—a stake-out?—on the street outside the wine bar. A tiny garret window in B.J.'s bedroom looked out over the rooftops, but could just as easily look down across the street into the very doorway where Harry had seen him. A person might sit there, unseen and unsuspected behind the window's net curtains all day long, and keep watch on the street. All night long, too, if B.J. desired it. Then, if someone was watching the place, and if he should be a terrible someone, B.J. would soon know about it. And the next time one of her girls followed someone, be sure she would not lose *him!*

She would not *dare* lose him!

Not for her life. Not for all their lives . . .

It was that same afternoon. Some miles away in the study of his house outside Bonnyrig, the Necroscope Harry Keogh sat absorbed in—and occasionally nodding over—the list of faraway places which he'd spent hours compiling in the reading room of a local library. His "system" had been elementary, and flawed:

Take a modern World Atlas and track the lines of longitude west from the north eastern region of the British Isles to discover areas of similar climatic characteristics and habitability in the rest of the world; not forgetting the west coast of England itself, of course, but with all coastal regions given the same priority.

The idea sprang from what his Ma had said, and what he had later thought: that Brenda might have found *this* place, Bonnyrig, ideally suited to her personality. From which Harry had gone several steps further, extrapolating an imaginary—yet persistently "real"—world or place of dramatic scenery, misted nights, slanting sunlit days, long grasses, leaning trees and wild flowers. Indeed, a vast garden run wild, all hidden away from the eyes of men. Hidden from Harry's eyes, anyway.

So where to find such a place? And would the climate prove to be similar along the same lines of longitude? For the imagined scene—at least with regard to its weather patterns—wasn't especially dissimilar to the north-east coastal region of Brenda's childhood. And the Necroscope had simply extended that region one hundred and fifty miles north to take in Edinburgh and the Firth of Forth. And Bonnyrig, of course.

It gave him a band round the Earth bordered by lines of longitude 55 and 56 North, including parts of Antrim, Donegal, and Londonderry in Northern Ireland; which was something that Harry hadn't previously considered—that Brenda and his baby son could be as close as Ireland. It had given him pause, but not as much as the discovery that if he followed the same lines east, they would also enclose Moscow, several thousands of miles of frozen tundra, the Bering Sea, and Alaska!?

Which would seem to put paid to *that* theory, at least.

And Harry had shaken his head and grinned, however wrily, thinking himself a fool that he hadn't paid more attention in school. If only his knowledge of the world's geography was as good as his understanding of maths! But there again, the Necroscope's amazing skill with numbers had very little to do with his education. Nothing he'd learned from the living, anyway . . .

It was then, as he tossed his pencilled list aside to let his head loll against the back of his easy chair, that the telephone rang.

Harry sat up, reached for the telephone on the occasional table, paused and frowned. B.J.'s bottle of red wine was there, beside the telephone where he'd set it down. And the Necroscope was thirsty. He—or Alec Kyle's body—was thirsty. His eyes stung like there was a pound or two of grit in them; his throat hurt as if someone had wire-brushed it on the inside; his mind felt equally desiccated, dried out. And somehow he knew that a sip of the wine, just a sip, would ease everything and he'd be able to face up to things. But face up to *what* things? Just a moment ago he had seemed okay, and now . . . ?

For his life, Harry couldn't say why he had frozen like that, with his hand stretching halfway to the 'phone. But the room was suddenly darker, as if a storm was about to break. Or maybe it was just the grimy patio windows; he hadn't found the time or energy to clean them, and what little light forced its way in from the overgrown garden was usually gray.

The telephone rang again, insistently, drawing his hand just a few inches closer, to where it hovered nervously above the top of the dusty table. Yet still he held back from picking up the 'phone. He felt a chill on or *in* his back, as if a cold wind was blowing along the marrow of his spine, and shivered uncontrollably. In the last few seconds it was as if the whole room had gone cold as the grave! Now what the hell . . . ?

Pick it up, idiot! he heard his own voice demanding from deep inside his head. *Pick up the damn telephone! What in the world's wrong with you?*

But he wasn't expecting a call, was he? Or was he? There was something he should remember about the telephone, but when he went to think about it, it kept giving him the slip. Like a word on the tip of his tongue that he simply couldn't remember. And his brain was fuzzy from all the planning he was . . . well, *supposed* to be doing! *Was* he expecting a call? Maybe he was, but not yet, surely? And what call was it anyway?

The 'phone rang yet again, and this time—despite that he knew it was coming—it caused him to start in his chair.

So why not pick the fucking thing up, answer it and find out? But find out what? Something that he really wouldn't want to know? Maybe. And what had made him think *that*, anyway?

Questions, *questions!* And nothing in his head but a ball of fluff, or rather a tangle of barbed wire. His stinging eyes . . . his sore throat . . . and B.J.'s bottle of red wine sitting there oh-so-temptingly . . . and the—

Rrrr-iiiing! . . . Rrrr-iiiing!

—Damned telephone!

Harry went for it, curled his fingers around it, picked it up . . . and the room went dark as night, so that he knew it had to be a storm. *Now the thunder!* he thought. *Now the lightning!* But the thunder and lightning never came.

Something else came.

Almost involuntarily, Harry tightened his grip on the fur ruff of the telephone as he drew it from its cradle toward his face . . . the telephone that wasn't. *He* drew *it* at first, but in the next moment it was drawing him! A straining, bristling ruff that dragged on his arm as if he was walking an unruly brute of a dog. And he simply couldn't believe his eyes as he looked at his hand and saw what it was holding in check, but barely:

Not a dog, but a snarling, coughing, choking wolf's head, red-eyed with feral yellow pupils! The thing didn't have a body but grew out of the telephone's speaker. And the cable was like a leash that lashed with the living head's frantic motion, then stretched itself taut as the awful thing it anchored strained on it, turning Harry's arm inward toward his gasping, utterly astonished mouth! The head was trying to get at him, bite him, crush his face in its slavering, fetid mantrap jaws!

"Almighty G-*God!*" Harry gasped, tightening his fist to a knot in the ruff of coarse fur, trying to force the head back while bringing his left hand into play as he fought to protect his face. The wolf's gaping, snarling muzzle was black leather flecked with white foam; its unbelievable *teeth* were ivory yellow; its ears lay flat to its head, seeming to streamline the horror of its intentions as they pointed the whole gnashing, clashing monstrosity of a visage at the Necroscope. Then—

—That tunnel of teeth closing on Harry's flapping left hand, where he felt bones snap in at least three of his fingers, and the searing agony of flesh severed, shorn through!

And *paws* as big as his hands were elongating themselves out of the telephone's speaker, followed by a long gray slime-damp body, as if the telephone was giving birth to this *Thing!* And the jaws were clashing inches from his face; they slopped blood and bits of mangled, twitching finger! And the gray fur of the beast's ruff tearing in his right hand, coming out in scurvy, matted tufts!

He . . . he couldn't hold it off!

And worst of all, the *intelligence* in those yellow-cored, murderous, oh-so-knowing eyes, as the red-ribbed throat of the monster expanded to engulf his face, his head!

Harry screamed gurglingly but unashamedly, thrusting himself back so spastically, with such force in his driving legs, as to topple his chair over backward.

And as if from a million miles away, the heavy pattering of raindrops on glass, and a flash of lightning at last. Then thunder clattering mightily close by, and a gust of wind hurling open the patio doors.

Harry's Ma came rushing in through the doors, crying:

Harry! Good God, son . . . what sort of a dream was that!?

And his Ma was all mud and bones and weed, but that was okay because it was how she had always been. But he also knew she shouldn't be here, that she *wasn't* here except . . . except in his head . . . ?

Harry?

And, "Ma!" he gasped, panted, choked, where he lay sprawled on the floor, with the rain hissing in his face, and a wind howling from the garden, whirling his pages of loose-leaf notepaper in a dervish dance all around the room.

Dream? Of course it had been a dream! But had she really needed to ask what sort?

"A nightmare, Ma," he told her, where her drowned spirit lay deep in mud and weeds in a bight in the river that was her grave. "A f-fucking godawful n-n-nightmare!" For the first (and probably the last) time in his life, the Necroscope Harry Keogh had uttered a curse word in the presence of his beloved Ma.

But he needn't worry, for his Ma had "seen" his dream and understood. . . .

HARRY: PRESENTIMENTS AND PRECAUTIONS.
BONNIE JEAN: THE ROUTE TO THE LAIR.

MA," HARRY SAID, AFTER HE'D STOPPED SHIVERING. "DO YOU THINK IT'S possible I'm going . . . well, maybe a little crazy?"

Do you mean really crazy? (His long-dead mother was careful how she answered him.) *Do you mean mad? If so, then I think it's highly unlikely. If that were going to happen at all, son, then surely it would have happened some time ago? But after all you've been through—which really doesn't bear thinking about—I think it's very possible that you're suffering from stress, anxiety, pressure. And who knows? Perhaps you're physically ill, too. I mean, with an ordinary illness?*

"My eyes? My sore throat? The fluff in my head?" He blinked watering eyes and swallowed hard to try to ease his throat.

Flu, if ever I saw a dose! his Ma told him. *All the classic symptoms. You're suffering from the backlash of living down in London. I was only there once—oh, thirty years ago, when I was a girl—and then only for a few weeks, but it did the same to me! All that smog, the smoky trains and dirty railway stations. Not only that, but didn't I warn you against coming down to the river to talk to me? Not in this bad weather, Harry! Not when you could just as easily be warm and dry in the comfort of the house.*

Harry shrugged and told her, "But you know that isn't my way, Ma." Then he managed a wry grin, and added: "Anyway, that London you're talking about was some time ago! It's not as bad as that now. Don't I recall reading somewhere that if you fell in the Thames in the 'Forties, when you were a girl, you'd have to be really lucky to drown—because it was much more likely you'd die of any one of a dozen fatal infections instead?"

He sensed his Ma's incorporeal nod. *I think that's probably true, yes. But—*

"—But there are fish in the Thames now," he informed her. "Even salmon!"

Well, you wouldn't catch me eating them! she said. *And anyway, you've changed the subject. Because you know what's coming next.*

"I should go and see a doctor?" He hugged his overcoat more tightly to him, where he crouched at the rim of the bight, over the gray-gleaming, wind-ruffled water. But there had been something in the Necroscope's voice (scorn, perhaps? impatience? or sheer obstinacy?) that caused his mother to bridle.

Huh! She snorted. *And is that how you reward good advice? Well, your grand-mother used to say, "No one can help the man—"*

"—Who won't help himself," Harry finished it. "Yes, Ma, I know. And I also know you're right. So I'll go and see a doctor—tomorrow."

But why not today?

"Because it's late in the afternoon. Even if I could find a surgery open it's an odds-on bet there'd be a queue. And, Ma, these days you're not much appreciated if you call a doctor out for something like the 'flu!"

No, she said. *You wait until you die, right?* And before he could answer: *Harry, you're living* alone *up here, and you don't have any close friends! Well, not among the living. What if you should come down with something serious?*

He shrugged. "But I do have a teleph . . ." And he broke off.

And she said: *A telephone, yes . . . which you're afraid of? But I can't say I blame you. That was a very bad dream, Harry!*

"Or a warning, maybe?" He wondered out loud . . . then shook his head, and said: "No, Ma, I'm not afraid of the 'phone, just a little wary of it . . . And I'll stay that way until I find out what all of this means."

She picked up on the first part of what he'd said. *A warning? How do you mean?*

"Alec Kyle was a precog. That was his talent: he was able to catch these glimpses of the future. Usually in his dreams, just before waking. And I think he still does. Or rather . . ."

You do? (Sometimes she was quick on the uptake.)

"Possibly. That dream wasn't my first . . . what, warning?"

But isn't that all to the good? she queried. *I mean, surely it's better to know* something *of what to expect than nothing at all?*

"Maybe," he answered. "But just to know that something unpleasant is coming doesn't help me to understand it. Sometimes I do and other times I don't. That was how it worked for Kyle, too. Also, he . . ." And Harry paused again.

Yes?

"I think that Kyle may have been an alcoholic," he blurted it out. "He kept it under tight control—or as tight as possible—but it was there nevertheless."

Oh, dear! His Ma said, slowly and sadly. *And you . . . ?*

"I'll have to control it the same."

You've . . . experienced the need, the urge, to take strong drink?

"More than just the urge." Harry nodded ruefully, and knew she would sense it. "My thick head?" he sighed. "Not the 'flu, as you see." And quickly: "But I promise you I'll see a doctor anyway."

She was suddenly thoughtful. *So your dream wasn't necessarily poor Mr. Kyle's talent in action after all, then?*

"What?" But since speaking with the dead often conveys far more than is actually said, the Necroscope had her meaning well enough. "You mean, some kind of delusion?"

Delirium tremens (the nod of her incorporeal head). *Well, possibly. So as you see, Harry, that makes a doctor imperative!*

He hugged his coat tighter still, and sighed his agreement. "Yes, Ma, I suppose it does . . ."

It was coming in squally again and Harry headed for home. Home: the old house where his mother and stepfather, Viktor Shukshin, had lived, until the maniac Shukshin had murdered her, drowning her under the river's ice. Harry had been a small child, but he "remembered" that day well enough—and from his mother's point of view at that! So maybe this new "thing" was just part of an older skill; maybe he was an "observer of times," like some Old Testament wizard. For if he was able to so vividly visualize a past he had never personally known, then why not something of a future that *no* man had known—as yet? Perhaps these flashes of the future came to him via the Möbius Continuum and had nothing to do with Alec Kyle at all!

Thus Harry's metaphysical mind ran in contradictory, ever-decreasing circles, while he continued to get nowhere.

Home: a drab, unkempt sort of place at best. One day he'd find the time to do it up, starting with the garden that sprawled almost all the way down to the river. Except to call it a "garden" was to lend it an unwarranted respectability; in fact it was an overgrown and weed-infested wilderness!

As it started to rain again, the Necroscope hurried along a crazy-paving path to the fly-specked patio doors, swearing a vow along the way that the thorny bramble creeper that whipped at his legs would be the first to go!

Letting himself in, he saw the sky darkening over again as the wind came up to bend the trees bordering the river. A great day for a nightmare, no question. But Harry didn't believe that was all it had been. Despite its surreal quality, it had seemed *very* real at the time. And what if he'd ignored that other warning, down at E-Branch HQ in London? That had been a hell of a mess anyway, but if he hadn't been able to use his Möbius door as "foreseen"—it didn't bear thinking about. At least he had *understood* that warning. Which made this other thing, about the old castle, the place on the cliff, seem doubly suspect; it was something he didn't understand. Why, he could feel the hair on his scalp moving again at the thought of it! As for this latest warning, the telephone nightmare: whatever else he did, Harry knew he couldn't afford to ignore *that* one!

This time he locked the patio doors behind him and turned on the single ceiling light. And in the dusty jumble of his so-called "study," where a plywood packing case stood open in one corner, dribbling straw, and Harry's handful of "worldly goods" were strewn about willy-nilly, the mere fact that an easy chair still lay on its back where he'd left it in his rush to get out of here, and that the occasional table had been overturned, *and* that the telephone was still purring away to itself, where he'd spilled it onto the floor . . . these things would hardly seem to matter. They were just part of the general clutter, that's all. Except that *wasn't* all, for Harry knew that in fact they were the debris of his dream. Especially the telephone.

He picked the 'phone and cradle up and went to replace the receiver—and paused. What if it were to ring?

But how could it ring? No one knew his number, or next to no one. He hadn't been up here long enough, and his name wasn't even in the telephone book; and in any case, he'd asked for his number to be listed, ex-directory. B.J.

had it, yes (though for his life he couldn't think why he'd given it to her). But what the heck, she was just an innocent—if strong-headed, even wrong-headed?—young woman anyway. But fascinating, in a way.

And then there was E-Branch . . .

Was that it? Was he scared of getting a call from E-Branch, frightened of learning something that he really didn't want to know? Such as the death of his wife, or his child, or both? Or maybe being called in on something he couldn't ignore? For the fact was, that as part of the country's security services, the Branch had its own Dirty Tricks Department. And if they really needed him . . . he knew they wouldn't think twice.

Was that it? That his dream had been symbolic, colored by his recent experiences in London? That would explain this wolf fetish he seemed to be developing, which had combined with the warning to produce his nightmare. So it still remained his best bet that this was some sort of left-over of Alec Kyle's talent. He *was* seeing something of the future; he *had* been warned about receiving a call, most probably from E-Branch, that would prove to be dangerous; he *must* protect himself against it.

Well, that was easy. And more determined now, he placed the 'phone in its cradle and dialed the operator. But even so, and while he waited for her to answer, still he sweated and glanced all about the room. Until finally:

"This is the operator. How can I help you?"

"I want to change my number, to ex-directory," he said.

And after she'd checked: "But your number's already listed, sir. It *is* ex-directory."

"I want to change it anyway."

"Fine. I'll put you through to the service you require . . ."

It was as simple as that. As for Bonnie Jean . . . he could always give her his new number, if the need should arise.

And then, generally feeling a lot better, the Necroscope shaved, tidied up his study, finished the unpacking that he'd started a month ago, and made himself an evening meal . . . And thought about Brenda and his baby son, of course.

The way he worried about them, he could have set off right there and then, heading off aimlessly into the Möbius Continuum on some wild-goose chase that might easily last him the rest of his life. A wild-goose chase? Now why had he thought that? But of course he knew why: because his son had powers the equal of his own, and if he didn't want to be found, then Harry didn't stand much chance of finding him. His one trump card was that he knew more about the world and its ways; he was experienced as only an adult who has lived (and died?) can be experienced. While the baby . . . was a baby.

But in any case he wouldn't be going anywhere for, oh, at least three weeks? . . . He would need that long to work out his plan of campaign, surely? . . . And meanwhile he would stay here, warm and comfortable despite all the bad weather, safe in this big old house.

Harry shook his head and frowned. God, he was starting to think like his mother! Starting to worry about himself—promising to see a doctor and such! But, three whole weeks to plan some kind of search campaign? He shrugged, blinked watery eyes, rubbed at his sore throat. *And* the mental fluff was back, right there where his brain should be. So much for a rapid recovery!

As for getting a plan together: if three weeks was what it took, then that's what it would get. All he had to work out now was what to put *in* it!

But his throat was *so* sore! And his eyes: hot, and itchy as hell . . . probably through sleeplessness, or a night spent in a drunken stupor, tossing and turning on Bonnie Jean's lounger. At which he remembered her wine. It had been on the table—

—And was now on the floor, having skittered against the skirting board under a bookshelf when he'd knocked everything flying. He went scrambling for it without realizing how desperately he needed it, trying to convince himself that it might be just the ticket, just what the doctor ordered. Its warm, resin-laden, sleep-inducing glow, all ruby-red and swirly-deep in his glass. It would ease his throat, for sure.

A sip, that's all. Just this one small glass. After all, it wasn't *his* addiction he was pandering to, but Alec Kyle's. Except this time it really was for curative or medicinal purposes. He was just *so* tired! Damned if he didn't intend to get a good night's sleep tonight, at least!

And doubly damned if he did, too . . .

Two and a half weeks later, when B.J. could no longer resist it, and when she had decided that she couldn't afford to wait any longer, she did try to call the Necroscope—only to discover that he had given her the wrong number! But she knew he couldn't possibly have done it deliberately. Checking with the switchboard, she then found that he'd changed his ex-directory number. But since she'd given him no instructions to the contrary, why shouldn't he? She had simply failed to consider the possibility that he *might* do such a thing, that was all.

But all was not lost. He *had* been ordered to stay in touch with her, and B.J. knew he would and even when he would: just a few days before the full moon, Harry would contact her. He had damn well *better!* And meanwhile she had decided to do a little searching of her own, for him. For in the glaring light of the possibility that he might be more than a mere mystery man and in fact *the* Mysterious One—

—Harry Keogh had become very important to her. So important that perhaps it was time B.J. took a short "holiday." She had already closed the bar down and split her five girls into two teams: one pair of girls searching for Harry locally, and the second team staking out the wine bar in its immediate vicinity to see if they could sight this watcher Harry had warned her about and discover his business with her. Which left B.J. herself and one other girl. Well, now she had somewhere to go, with or without Harry Keogh, and couldn't risk being followed. And she knew exactly how to employ the last of her girls . . .

In the wee small hours of a wet and windy Sunday morning some four days before B.J. was due to hear her Master's call, she headed north. She felt sure that once she'd explained why she was early, Radu would understand her zeal in this respect.

She drove a hired car, a cheap, old, reliable but unspectacular model that wasn't likely to attract unwanted attention. Even so, she wouldn't drive it directly from the bar but took a taxi to the home of one of her girls, who had picked the car up for her. The girl lived in a northern district of the city.

It was a well-timed operation: Bonnie Jean left the taxi and paid the driver, got into the hired car and drove it away. And in the mirror she saw the girl—one of her "lieutenants"—following close behind in her own car. The girl wasn't just acting as a decoy; she would *become* a physical obstruction if B.J. should be followed. She would simply put herself and her vehicle in the way of the pursuer! But it was 2 a.m. and the weather was bad, and with the precautions B.J. had taken, she didn't think it likely that she'd be tailed.

To further bolster her confidence in that respect, there was the fact that despite all her vigilance there had been no further spying on her place as reported by Harry Keogh. So perhaps it had been a one-off sort of thing after all, a coincidence that hadn't involved her directly. Well, maybe . . . but B.J. was becoming less and less inclined toward coincidences, and in any case she hadn't been willing to risk it.

And now there was only one hazard, one gauntlet left to run: the Firth of Forth bridge, the only way into or out of the city from the north. If anyone had seen her leave home, and assuming they knew she would ultimately drive north, the bridge would be the ideal place to pick up her trail.

But the bridge came and went without incident, and so did B.J.'s escort. A mile or so beyond the Firth of Forth, heading for Perth, the headlights of the car behind flashed three times in her mirror, and she knew what the signal meant: there was no one in pursuit, no one to track her to the lair in its mountain fastness. But even so her lieutenant would park at the side of the road, and wait there a good hour, recording the details of passing cars and observing what she could of their drivers.

And the rest of it was all down to Bonnie Jean Mirlu . . .

Dawn found B.J. at "a friend's house" in tiny Inverdruie; she stayed there whenever she was up this way, which of necessity meant regular quarterly visits. But Auld John was always here, as his father had been before him. John "belonged" to her Master no less than Bonnie Jean herself, but his blood was not of *the* blood, and so he was merely a thrall—a watcher or sentinel—here on the approach routes to Him in His lair high in the mountains. But having been sworn to Him by moonlight, John was nevertheless his Master's true man.

B.J.'s route had taken her through Perth, Pitlochry, Kingussie and Kincraig, and finally across the Spey to Inverdruie. And as true dawn's light limned the misty horizon of the Grampians, so Auld John was there to greet the "wee mistress," as he thought of her, when her car pulled into his drive. And:

"Better garage the car, John," she told him, after a brief hug. "I've had snoopers at my place in Edinburgh, and we cannot afford such up here." And entering his small house where it was almost hidden from the road in a copse of birch, rowan and juniper, she waited for him.

"It was dire cold last time ye were here, Bonnie Jean," he told her, coming in and closing the door. "Me, ah could'nae hae climbed wi' ye. No this time. It's these old bones . . . mah fingers hae no grip in they!"

"You're for watching, John," she reminded him. "No for the climbing."

"Aye, but ah'd hae dearly loved tae see Him just one more time," he said. "Perhaps next time, come summer. But . . . surely ye're early, lass?"

"Snoopers, as I said," she nodded. "And maybe worse than snoopers. Things He should know, anyway. And a stranger, John. All very mysterious. But as for him: well, I've no doubt you'll be seeing him soon enough, if I've gauged it right."

The old man cocked his head. "A stranger? Here? And 'mysterious,' did ye say?" His eyes were suddenly bird-bright.

Again her nod. "Who knows, who knows?" She gave herself a shake, turned to the fire and warmed her hands. "Reasons enough to come up here a few days early, anyway."

Auld John was maybe sixty-five, but still spry for all his complaining. He was tall, gangling, walked with a woodsman's lope (an entirely *natural* one, the insignia of his calling as a gillie and tracker, if anything, and not rooted in any condition), and wore his long, thinning gray hair tied back in a clasp, to keep it from his weathered face.

He had on occasion accompanied Bonnie Jean high into the Cairngorms, to the lair. But *that* was a climb, and Auld John was no longer up to it. As for their relationship . . . that was strange as can be. For more than sixty years ago B.J. had used to bounce him on her knee! And here she was a young girl, and him an old man . . .

The blood is the life!

Auld John sat down opposite the wee mistress, reached out to put a log on the fire in the great wide hearth, and said, "A body grows auld. Truly auld."

"But slowly, John," she answered, "very slowly. And you'll outlive most men. Aye, and you've a lot to be thankful for. For after all, you've known Him."

"In His sleep, ah've known Him, it's true. But tae see Him up and aboot . . . ! D'ye think . . . ?" And now his voice was low and his eyes narrow in the firelight. Narrow and feral over a long flat nose.

"All things are possible in Him, John," she told him. "As the stars and mistress moon spin their tracks through space and time, slowly but surely His time comes around. He may not stay down forever. For just as your bones age and wither, so do His—and He has outlasted the centuries! I've calculated his time over and over again, and always it comes out the same."

"Four years, is it?" The old man's voice was low, almost a growl, yet pleading in its eagerness. "Is it down to just four years?"

Bonnie Jean nodded again, and repeated him, "Three or four at most, after six long centuries! A drop in the ocean, John."

"And then, and then . . . ?" It was an old story, but he would hear it again.

"Then, a legend born anew," she answered. "A new creature in the heights, along with the pine martens, the golden eagles, and the wildcats. But just think, John: in His horseshoe mountains, He knew the real cats: the last of the sabertooths!"

"A new creature in the high crags," he whiningly repeated her, his yellow eyes blinking his excitement.

"And in the cities!" Bonnie Jean added. "Don't forget the cities. Oh, our Master tried the other way—the secret way—all those many centuries ago. It didn't work then, and won't now."

"But," the old man protested, "only show a man something that's different—be sure he'll murder it! Come hell or high water, if it's strange and fails to conform, it's a goner. And if it's like Him up there?'' (A toss of his head, indicating the Cairngorms.) "If it's like the Master? War, Bonnie Jean, war!''

"Indeed,'' she agreed. "And as it was then, when He first came among us, so it is now. Except men have forgotten the old times, the old legends, and no longer believe. And by the time they do, it will be too late! Aye, and there's no Great Black Death now, John, to plague Him and His. And just as our Master was driven here, driven west, and north, by that black, devouring fire, so now *He* will light a flame and drive east. Except He'll not stop, but drive south and west too! For in His time the world was so small; why, there are entire *continents* that He never saw or knew about! But He will, He will . . .''

"The Black Death stopped Him, consigning Him to the everlasting dark . . .'' Auld John shivered.

". . . Not everlasting, John,'' she told him. "And when He's up, it's the Red Death that will light His way! Ah, but nothing from poor Mr. Poe, though certainly it will seem like it. No more hiding, John, when next He comes down from the mountains. And the name of the pack . . .''

". . . Shall be Mankind!'' (His turn to interrupt.)

"They shall be legion,'' she tossed back her hair, gray as Auld John's in the firelight. "And His enemies, who or whatever remains of them . . .''

". . . The true death,'' he nodded. "Neither undeath, nor any sort of sleep such as He has known, but death forever!''

"Amen to that,'' she said, and smiled.

"When will ye go tae Him?''

"Give me soup, your good broth, and tea to brew and a little strong, wild meat to take with me. Inverdruie sleeps; when she wakes I'll be long gone. You'll see me along the trail into the foothills, as always, then return and wait for me here. But I may be gone a while, so don't worry if I seem late.''

"I'll no worry,'' he told her.

"And my equipment?''

"Safe and sound. But, are ye sure ye need it?'' There was a chuckle in his voice. She answered with a laugh of her own:

"I could climb it blindfold, as well you know!'' Then her laughter stilled and she sobered in a moment. "Except I can't afford to slip. My life means nothing, but His . . .''

"Aye, lass, aye,'' he leaned across and took her hand. "He has lived too long to die like that: cold and alone, lonely in His lair.''

Bonnie Jean said nothing but stared into the fire. Shortly, John went to see to her food and make his preparations . . .

B.J.'s climbing skills were prodigious; working with enormous efficiency and at great speed, and using only her sense of balance, and the natural tenacity of long fingers and toes to defy gravity, she seemed almost to adhere to a rock face. And in all truth she scarcely required Auld John's ropes, pitons, karabiners, and similar paraphernalia of the professional climber. But she took them with her anyway.

It was as she had explained: as His guardian, His keeper, she simply could not afford to slip. For while to Bonnie Jean the climb itself was little more than a thrill—and her faith in her skill was absolute—still she *might* make a slip. Which to Him in His centuried sleep could easily mean the difference between undeath and the true death. For the balance B.J. was required to maintain on the rock face wasn't nearly so delicate as the balance of His continued existence.

Auld John knew all of this, and though he was silent on the woodland trail where they walked, still all of his thoughts were for Bonnie Jean and their mutual Master. "Ye'll take care, lassie, in the heights?"

"You know I will, John."

"There has been a rockfall or two."

"Good! I'm always on the lookout for new routes."

Early spring sunlight, sharp and bright, dappled their path through birch and Scots pine. B.J. didn't much like the sunlight; stepping aside from the larger yellow splotches, she felt glad that her climb would be mainly shaded by the bulk of the mountains.

Back in Inverdruie, most people were still abed, barely awake, tossing and turning . . . but mainly turning their backs on the light coming in through their windows on this fine but chilly Sunday morning. There'd be church, of course, and animals to feed at the nearby nature reserves: brown bears, bison, antelope, and reindeer. And maybe even a handful of visitors, tourists, at the gift shops in the villages. Nothing like the crush of a few months ago, when the snow was deep at Aviemore and the skiers dotted the slopes like a myriad brightly hurtling insects against winter's blinding white backdrop.

"Aye, and there were climbers, too," Auld John reminisced. "But no out this way." No, for this was the Cairngorms Nature Reserve: more than a hundred square miles of mountain heights and wilderness; the haunt of deer and wildcats, of foxes, otters, and other creatures of the wild—but rarely men. And it was John's domain, too. These were the trails where he was a guide, which made it easier to ensure that the most secret of the forest tracks remained secret. Oh, sometimes, even in the winter months, some idiot climber would ignore all the posted warnings to bring his team in here and stray this way . . . and sometimes they wouldn't make it out again. It rather depended on where they walked, and especially where they climbed—and also on who else might be climbing there . . .

Now the ground was rising. At a break in the trees Bonnie Jean and Auld John paused and looked back along the way they'd come, across Loch an Eilein with its crumbling castle. Bonnie Jean was well acquainted with a local tradition: that the old castle in the lake was much associated with the outlawed son of Robert II, called the Wolf of Badenoch; Badenoch being the area east of the Spey and along the Cairngorms foothills. Ah, but she also knew that "the Wolf" had been dead for a hundred years before the castle was built; which seemed to her to beg the question, just which wolf was remembered here—and just how well had diverse traditions kept themselves apart? Or how badly?

Among the trees, mossy granite outcrops began to show: "the tears o' the titan mountains," as Auld John was wont to call them. And at last they were through the foothills to the base of an almost sheer rock face. And: "Granite," Auld John informed unnecessarily, "an' more than four thousand feet of it, at that—perpendicular!" Well, not quite.

He had carried her pack; now he helped to transfer it to her person, tied back her hair with his own clasp, and filled a small pouch at her belt with chalk powder, to keep her fingers dry for the climbing. Finally: "Where the going's rough, use the rope," he advised, for he dared not order.

And up she went . . .

Four thousand feet of granite. But by no means perpendicular, not all of it. In places the going was flat, or very nearly so: scree-filled basins, domed plateaux, rocky re-entries and pine-clad saddles. Oh, in one or two places it was sheer, and in the worst place of all vertiginous to overhanging through five hundred feet of a traverse that would cause the best of climbers to blink and cringe back from it, if only for a moment or two, before the actual assault. But to Bonnie Jean's mind that was what climbing was all about: the challenge.

Not so much of a challenge to her, though, whose business, whose *duty* it had been to climb these rocks at least once in a three-month, every season of the year, for the last *one hundred and seventy years!* Some six hundred and eighty times now—she occasionally lost count—B.J. had pitted herself against these heights, and so knew each crack and crevasse, every cave, ledge and chimney along the way.

She knew where veins of rose quartz shone pink and purple in the grainy granite face, and a chimney where curious smoky crystals or "gorms" (cairn gorms) had weathered loose and lay in a neat pile, like a natural cairn. She knew where to avoid the aeries of the great Golden Eagles, especially now, in the mating and nesting season, and used as landmarks the bruised and rusted pitons of yesteryear, more often than not her own, out of times when she'd lacked experience.

And for every thousand feet she climbed, she would move laterally a kilometer or more, ever deeper into the mazy interior of the mountain system, where few climbers had ventured before. But in one hundred and seventy years—especially the last thirty—there had *been* climbers, some of whom had come too close.

Well, the Cairngorms were notoriously unforgiving mountains, and in places they were entirely inaccessible. Some bodies had never been, never would be discovered. But Bonnie Jean knew where the bones of a handful of them lay, at least; knew, too, what was become of their flesh . . .

Some two hours after midday, she rested on a ledge overlooking a dark ravine with a waterfall and white water that rushed down to the swollen, near-distant Spey. Almost all the snows of winter had melted down into the earth and the rocks now, to filter their way into falls and cataracts. The heavy rains of the last few months had added to the tumult, and the tumbling tributary four hundred and fifty feet below sent up spray to dampen the rocks. Higher up, a series of caves opened into a far greater cavern system: the lair itself.

B.J. could have—perhaps should have—chosen the "easy" route into the lair: up onto the plateau's shattered roof, and down through any one of several shafts into the dusty, rubble-strewn heart of the place. But this way had been a challenge, albeit a small one, for here the rock was rotten and given to crumbling. Thus it presented her with an opportunity to test secondary skills, this time with the generally despised apparatus of the professional climber.

And having eaten just a bite, and sipped a little water, then—for the first time during her climb—pitons and hammer, karabiners and fine, light nylon rope came into play. She used them all to form a hoist, then cranked herself up onto the last ledge, where a treacherously fractured "window" opened into the gloom of the lair. And leaning back with her feet on the ledge and every ounce of her weight suspended on the rope, she looked down through all that deadly height to where fangs of rock were blackened by the torrent, and the gorge was a snarling gash of a mouth more terrible than any dark beast's—

—Almost.

And so into the lair, which for all B.J.'s previous visits was at least as fearsome a step as the actual climb itself . . .

Once inside, after a brief scramble through shrouding cobwebs, accumulated dust and sharp, stony debris, B.J. wasted no time. With the ease of any night-sighted animal and most wild creatures, her eyes very quickly adjusted to the gloom. Had it been pitch-black, they would have served her just as well. So that even as she shrugged out of her harness, she was able to gauge fairly accurately her location in this cavern system which she had explored so many times before. She knew where she was, and therefore where He was.

And between them, maybe two hundred feet of pitfalls and crumbling pathways, jumbles of fallen, hexagonal pillars, and dizzy causeways over crevasses which, for all she knew, might well go down to the roots of the mountains. On this one level she had explored the lair, for this was His place. But as for other possible levels: she didn't know, couldn't say.

And apart from the natural obstacles of this great cavern, there was one other thing standing between B.J. and her Master. A *Thing*, yes, and she shuddered at the thought of it . . . even the "wee mistress" herself.

It was something of His, she knew, but still it was beyond reason. Beyond her reason, anyway. But it was sentient; it knew things, sensed things. It would know she was here, and it would stir when she passed by. *And* it would know why she was here . . . that it, the *Thing* itself, was one of her reasons. For just as B.J.'s Master hungered, so did His creature . . .

That would be the part she disliked, the one aspect of her duty that bothered her. Her Master's needs were one thing, but the needs of His creature were something else. She . . . *disliked* feeding it, even with beast's blood. Also, she never failed to be amazed by the fact that so little could satisfy so much. But would it be the same when the *Thing* was up? Surely He intended to bring it up, else what was its purpose? But Bonnie Jean had never inquired about it; it wasn't her business to question but to guard and inform, as it was her duty to obey.

The place was unquiet; only take a single step away from the crack of light gleaming through the dusty, irregular shape of the "window," and silence fell as if someone had switched it on—or switched all sound off—except for the echoes of the lair itself: the dripping of water in various unseen locations, and B.J.'s own breathing, her own muffled movements. Quiet, yet unquiet . . . But by no means a contradiction of terms. The tumult of the gorge was dead here; it couldn't find its way in; something shut it out.

There was some light, at least; rays or curtains of dim light filtering dustily down from various faults in a ceiling of ill-defined height and extent: the shafts through which she might have descended, if she'd chosen a different route. Light in *this* place, anyway, but not where He lay. For B.J.'s Master could no longer suffer direct sunlight. The moon was His light, and the full moon His glory! And it would be the same for B.J. in time to come, for she too was a moon child. So far as possible, she shunned the sun even now, though as yet it wouldn't kill her—not in her human form, at least.

And she had often wondered: why here? Why build a lair in this high place, when Radu might have found Himself a place of darkness utter? But as she knew well enough, it had been a matter of circumstance, not choice. And anyway, He had been used—in a different age, in a different world—to a lofty manse indeed. But then, He'd been used to many things in His time . . .

Carrying her pack slung over her shoulder, and following a trail of poorly arranged "flagstones" long since fallen from the ceiling, Bonnie Jean set out through the maze of stony rubble. In places the path was obscured, almost obliterated, where recent falls had crashed down and caved in the paving stones or hurled them aside, forming angular granite piles and jumbles of rock which were almost crystalline in their nitre-fused shapes. But "recent" in B.J.'s terms meant other than it would to persons of normal longevity. Indeed, it meant *any* time in the last ten decades! Still, it was as well that her Master's time would soon be up—that *He* would soon be up—for this place wouldn't last forever. And in this modern world . . . well, "repairs" were out of the question! Oh, there remained a handful of thralls in various parts, and B.J.'s girls, of course, but getting them up here safely and secretly would be nigh impossible, and the task itself utterly beyond them. This place had been "built" before B.J.'s time, and the thralls who had built it for Him had died at their work. But in that bygone time all the land around was a wilderness, when prying eyes were few and far between . . .

Thus her thoughts ran as she approached the place of the *Thing*, that dark cave to one side of the main cavern, where the light never reached and the silence was near absolute; the *physical* silence, anyway. But the atmosphere, or ether—if there really were such a thing—seemed to seethe here; she felt the oppressive weight of the place almost tangibly upon her shoulders.

B.J. was no mentalist (it was only the awesome strength of her Master's sendings that made possible communication with Him, let alone His creature!), but as always in this place, so close to the *Thing*, she sensed emanations of weird entity, the foetal fumblings of that which waited to be born. And because it was her duty, despite the fact that she hated it, still she turned from the path, however briefly, entered the cave of the *Thing*, and thus "announced" her presence.

And as her eyes adjusted to the greater darkness, so the aura of awful sentience—of a vacant yet savage awareness—grew more tangible yet . . . *and* the sure knowledge that she in her turn had been recognized.

An outline or silhouette took shape in the darkness, one which radiated its own almost imperceptible red glow, like the embers of an almost-dead fire in a dark room. It was a cylindrical shape formed of hexagonal granite columns standing on end like the staves of a barrel. At their bases these pillars were buried in rubble and buttressed with boulders to stop them toppling outwards; they formed the walls of a massive container or vat. But several of them were cracked, and others were slightly splayed or stood askew, or had been forced apart by the geological stresses of the mountains, allowing trickles of a resinous sealant or preservative to escape from within and form puddles hardening to amber at the bases of the surrounding boulders.

B.J. approached the vat, reached out tentatively at first, but finally placed her hands upon two of the columns. The stone was cold to her touch; it shouldn't convey anything but that it was stone; nothing of the nature of its contents should be apparent. But something was apparent. And B.J. thought: *It's like listening to the sea in a sounding shell. Except the sea has an entirely natural sound, with nothing of sentience and entirely oblivious to the rest of the world around it. It can't respond, except to ignore.*

But this *Thing*, her Master's creature, was not oblivious. And even as she listened to it, so it "listened" to her. And:

Thud! (Dully, like some far, faint vibration, felt in her fingertips.)

She had felt, heard or sensed it before and didn't recoil. In another five minutes, or fifteen, or twenty, if she cared to stand here so long, she would hear it again.

The slowed-down, almost-stilled, hibernating heartbeat of the *Thing*. No, not hibernating (she corrected herself) but suspended, indefinitely extended . . . waiting! And alive, oh yes!

Alive, in there, Her Master's future . . . what, guardian? Something to take her place, when He was up again? That was a thought she had thought before, even scarcely daring to think it. His own fierce creature, to guard Him in His lair . . .

Thud!

And this time, because she stood there rapt in thought—and perhaps unworthy thoughts, at that, because He had assured her often enough that she would always have a place with Him—Bonnie Jean was startled and snatched back her hands.

Was it intelligent, like Him, she wondered? Would it perhaps be jealous of her, this unborn *Thing?*

She moved quickly to the side of the stone vat, climbed a stairway of stacked slabs, finally gazed down into the solidified murky swirl of a mainly opaque, luminous resin reservoir. And with eyes feral in the darkness, she kneeled at the rim to peer through the crusted surface deep into the looser liquids beneath, at the foetal *Thing* that was curled there—

—That massive wedge of a head as seen in profile. Those long dog jaws. The dark orbit of an eye big as a platter!

The last time she was here, its heartbeat had been slower, and the great lid of its eye entirely closed, asleep. But now:

Thud!

The *Thing* quickened beyond a doubt, and the lid of its eye seemed gashed where a crack of yellow light glowed from within, brighter than its protective resin sheath . . .

Bonnie Jean stood up, descended the stairs, left the cave for the less fearsome labyrinth of the cavern complex, and finally ran breathlessly to her Master . . .

. . . To Radu Lykan.

PART 3

Vampire Genesis.

SHAITAN: HIS RISE AND FALL.
CANIS SAPIENS: THE WEREWOLF CONNECTION.

SHAITAN THE UNBORN CAME OUT OF THE VAMPIRE SWAMPS, OH, A LONG TIME ago. The first and worst of the Wamphyri—the first of the Great Vampires—Shaitan was the source of undeath.

He came out of the west and saw that the darkness of Starside was good, but he felt through the thinning mists the withering rays of a hot sun blazing through the high passes of the barrier mountains; it turned his skin rough and red. So he took the left-hand path round the mountains, and came upon the boulder plains of gaunt and gloomy Starside whereon dwelled nothing of any threat; while southward lay the sun which was injurious (and possibly even fatal) to him and all such as he would bring into the world. From which time forward he would always choose a dark and sinistral path through life . . .

When he knew a strange dark thirst, he drank of the sweet water tumbling down from the mountains; it quenched his thirst but did not truly satisfy him. When he felt a strange dark hunger, he ate grasses, herbs, some bitter fruits. These served to fill him but the hunger would not pass. It was the hunger of an evil spore, a leech, which had taken root within Shaitan, body, mind, and soul . . . if there had been a soul.

Shaitan was unclothed but unashamed, for he knew that he was beautiful; and he would display his beauty. So he compared himself to the beasts of the wild, of the swamps, foothills and mountains, and saw that their beauty came from their innocence. For which reason it was useless to display himself or even impose his will upon them. Unintelligent, innocent, they could not deny that he knew best; they would bend to his will too easily. Wherefore he would impose that will upon others of his own design. Except . . . where were they? Traveling east, he looked for them but discovered them not yet a while. And in his loneliness he took bats for familiars, whose flying skills he envied.

Eventually he came upon trogs, cavern un-men and -women, who were scarcely beautiful and not greatly like unto himself; but Shaitan corrupted them anyway, filling them with his vices, and making them sick and dead and undead. He took trog women to his bed, and there was issue. Such "children" as were born were hideous, insane, ever hungry! They suckled blood, not milk, and grew too fast. Their mothers lay on them to smother them. Shaitan devoured one, in order to taste of its flesh. It satisfied the hunger of his leech . . . barely, for a while.

So then, with the bats and the trogs Shaitan had gathered minions unto himself. But was this all there was? The parasite within him was mature now; it desired more; it lived on Shaitan's blood as he lived on the blood of others, but was not satisfied with its host's regimen. And so he would seek out other men, on whom to impose his will. Except he sometimes wondered: whose will was it? His or his parasite leech's? And from then on the question of free will, and integrity of spirit, became matters of great importance to Shaitan, even assuming dimensions of obsession in him. And in all subsequent vampires.

The trogs likened Shaitan to certain "men" on the far side of the mountains, in Sunside. He determined to conquer Sunside, which would be as subtle as all his works. First he would approach the Sunsiders as their friend, later as their master.

And so in the twilight before the night Shaitan went into Sunside, and in the gloamy foothills was drawn to the fires of hunters. East and west as far as his eyes could see, the fires lit up the night like beacons. The Sunsider tribes were legion! In his black heart Shaitan was glad, believing that at last he had found true men upon which to impose his will.

His dreams of conquest quickly evaporated. With Starside's trogs it had been easy, but these men (the "Szgany" of Sunside) were very different . . . and their women different, too. Unlike trog females, Szgany women were lovely creatures. Shaitan was the Great Seducer; he seduced—and he murdered! But his crime was discovered and he was hounded out of the Szgany camps.

His trackers set a wolf upon him, and for the first time Shaitan used metamorphism to change his shape and become more animal than the wolf itself! Furious in his rage, he slew not only the watchdog but certain of his human pursuers, and took others for his thralls. For as a dweller among Starside's cavern trogs, Shaitan had discovered his power over men: how his bite infected their blood with an incurable fever, until they became his thralls forever and ever.

And hidden in a vampire mist called out of his own pores and up from the earth, Shaitan and one of his thralls went up into the dark foothills, finding refuge in a cave. For the purple dawn twilight was fading, and a poisoned golden blister was poising itself even now on the southern horizon far across the forest. Shaitan's symbiont had become a two-edged sword—impossible to accept its advantages without its disadvantages.

Sunlight: it was a seething agony in his eyes and against his hide! It burned him, visibly steamed the moisture from his flesh, and sapped his great strength! He could go out from the cave for seconds, but minutes would deplete him horribly, and an hour would kill him and his leech both. He had suspected it, which was why he had gone into Sunside in the evening. But now he had proof positive: the sun *was* his mortal enemy.

The long day crawled endlessly by; more men of the Szgany whom Shaitan had vampirized came to him as thralls; when night fell he took these poor creatures over the mountains and down into Starside, where several trog thralls were waiting on the return of their master. Now his band numbered thirteen in all, and Shaitan named them his disciples (though in fact they were his blood-slaves). And thirteen would become a *number* of ill-omen from that time on, in more worlds than one . . .

Coming down into Starside, Shaitan saw a light shining up into the night, which one of his band said must be the fallen white sun that some called a gateway into hell. Shaitan was curious, and said he must see this hell-gate.

They climbed a low crater wall, stood on its rim and gazed down upon the dome of cold fire within. Blinded, the trogs staggered to and fro. One tripped, fell, landed on a ledge close to the white glare. Fearful of the strange light, he put up a hand to fend it off; his hand touched the dazzle's surface, and sank into it . . . he cried out in his guttural fashion, as the hellgate dragged him in and swallowed him whole!

And Shaitan said: "This shall be a punishment for any who would offend me three times. Three chances, for I am forgiving, as you see. And there shall be other punishments, aye. I am the Lord Shaitan, who can make men undead! Anyone who would do me harm, let him first think on this: I shall drain his blood and bury him deep in the ground. And he shall lie there and scream forever, or until he stiffens to a stone in the earth. And that land there to the north; I perceive it is icy cold and no fit habitation. Therefore, let him who would deny me beware. In my house there shall be no warm bed or soft woman-flesh for him; no kind master to guide and instruct him; neither wonders to be witnessed nor mysteries revealed. For I shall banish him north to freeze in the ice all alone. But for him who would obey me in all things, and be my true servant, a rich red life forever . . . aye, even unto death—and beyond! So be it . . ."

Lord Shaitan and his followers came to a region of giant stone stacks weathered out of the mountains. In their bases they were fortified with fallen scree jumbles; in their columns were fissures, ledges and caverns, many as vast as halls. Shaitan much admired these soaring stacks, which were very grand and gaunt. "One of these shall be my house," he said.

And a thrall told him: "They are like unto the aeries of the mountain eagles!"

"Aye," said Shaitan. "The aeries of the Wamphyri!"

He set to and built his house; the task was enormous; only a vampire and his thralls could ever accomplish it. Except Shaitan would build not only a house but an empire of vampires. He recruited trogs out of their caverns, and sent his lieutenants into Sunside to hunt Szgany. And in the bowels of his rearing house, Shaitan experimented with his own metamorphic flesh, to furnish himself with all of his requirements.

He bred trogs into cartilage creatures, whose minds were small and bodies elastic. From these he made leathers and coverings for the aerie's exterior stairways, or articles of furniture for his rooms. And all of his *materials* still living a life of sorts, gradually petrifying and becoming permanent in their places. He mated men with trog women, the issue of which was unseemly. He got foul, bloated things, all gross and mindless, which he bred into gaslings, for the heating of the stack, and into things-which-consume, for his refuse pits.

Shaitan took mindless vampire flesh and converted it; he would build flying creatures, and soar out from his aerie upon the winds like his familiar bats. At first he failed; later he provided his flyers with the altered brains of men, that they should have something (but never too much) of volition. All of which creatures, nascent and full-formed, were his thralls.

Word of his works went abroad into Sunside. Starside was now damned and shunned utterly—by men, at least. But by now the Szgany had problems other than Shaitan and his raiders. Far in the west the swamps were a spawning ground for monsters! Foolish men and innocent creatures went down to the scummy waters to drink, and things other than men and wolves came up!

And in the early years of Shaitan's ascendancy, a great many beings who were *like* unto him came over from Sunside to build their houses in the rearing stone aeries of the Wamphyri. And because they were even as strong as Shaitan and much of a kind, he made no protest but let them be. For in any case there was space enough among the great stacks and even Shaitan was unable to lay claim to all of them. Also, across the barrier mountains there was food and entertainment for all. Still, as a precaution, Shaitan fashioned fierce warrior-creatures, to fill any would-be enemies with terror . . .

And in the next two hundred years the Wamphyri became a great many. Too many . . .

On Sunside, the Szgany had become clans of "Travelers," moving nomadically from place to place by day, and sleeping in deep forests or caves at night. Even so, the Lords of Starside gave them no peace, and the toll in blood was monstrous!

Then Shaitan saw his error in permitting other Lords to wax so strong and so many. He determined to get bloodsons out of comely women, with which to whelm the other Lords and keep them down; and his sons and daughters were many. Of the latter: he used them in their turn, for his own flesh was the sweetest. Which would be the way of it with vampires down all the ages.

And as the Lords and Ladies of the Wamphyri proliferated, so they degenerated, going from evil to evil, and descending depth to irredeemable depth . . .

Eventually all of the greater stacks had masters or mistresses; the lesser aeries were occupied; there was no room left in all the heights for men and their sons, daughters, thralls and creatures. And so, finally, they warred for possession of the stacks, until Starside's skies were full of flyers and warriors fighting under the ice-chip stars and in the ramparts of the great aeries. Gongs sounded, wardrums pounded, and banners fluttered, displaying the devices of their masters. Vampire destroyed vampire—even fathers, sons and brothers—as the boulder plains and lands around were drenched in blood and littered with the grotesque, shattered corpses of fallen beasts.

Even Shaitan came under attack, but he was clever in the defense of his aerie, and went not out to war. But as various Lords were weakened in stacks close by, then he would swoop on them and put them down. In this manner a cluster of aeries all came under Shaitan's command.

When his strategy was seen, the others called a truce and came upon him as a single force, and Shaitan was almost trapped in Shaitanstack. Only his metamorphism saved him, when like the fallen angel he was he used it to develop a bat's design and glide from his highest ramparts to safety in a secret place. Meanwhile his forces had rallied and regrouped under his lieutenants, and Shaitanstack had not been taken . . .

The bloodwars lasted a hundred years; the fashioning of flyers and warriors became an art; Wamphyri numbers were decimated in all the reek and roil of mindless slaughter. It was the era in which Sunside's Szgany backed off from the abyss and breathed again, and reorganized their lives and what little remained of their society. Except it couldn't last.

For Shaitan was now the undisputed Lord of Vampires, the "high magistrate" to whom lesser Lords took their disputes for his judgment. And as the clamor of war subsided, so the period of mercifully infrequent raids on Sunside was over, and the nightmare sprang up again with renewed vigor. For now the Wamphyri must see to the provisioning of their ravaged and undernourished aeries, whose sustenance roamed on Sunside.

For sixty years this was the way of it, and Shaitan doled out hunting permits and took his tithe of trembling flesh from whatever the others brought back. But the lesser Lords loathed him and would whelm him if they could. He knew it and when the coup came at last was ready to put it down. All who had conspired against him, he brought to trial—even his own son, who he banished to the Icelands: the least of his punishments.

As for the others who had plotted to overthrow him, these were several, and their punishments various. Some were buried alive (or undead) on the boulder plains, to "stiffen to stones" in the shuddering earth. One, Nonari the Gross, was tossed with his entire court and the leaders of his Szgany supplicants into the Hell-lands Gate. And if this Nonari's bloodname, Ferenczy, had been a curse to the Szgany of this world, then it was destined to become just such a curse in another.

Likewise banished through the Gate were the Drakul brothers, Karl and Egon, who rivalled Shaitan in their evil, and one other who was a great thorn in Shaitan's side. For in the earliest days of Shaitan's coming he had tried to work his will on such as Radu Lykan, but all in vain; the gray brothers of the barrier mountains acknowledged no master but the Leader of the Pack and owned no mistress but the hurtling silver moon at her full. And Radu Lykan was of that sub-order of Wamphyri: a wolf, or more properly, a werewolf! Lord Shaitan abhorred such "dog-Lords," the sons of wolves, and even if there'd been no bloodwars he would have found a way to dispose of such as Radu.

So for a while there was peace again on Starside, and a truce between the Wamphyri Lords and Ladies. But *because* they were Wamphyri, it couldn't last. Greedy, jealous, territorial, they were a plague unto themselves. And eventually even Shaitan was whelmed and fell, and was driven from Starside into the cold and inhospitable Icelands.

All of these things are legends told aforetime. But what remains to be told was previously undisclosed . . .

Perhaps wolves, like men and bears, foxes and bats, and other species, were creatures of both worlds: Sunside/Starside, and the so-called Hell-lands on the far side of the Starside Gate. Perhaps, springing from the one cosmic germ, a universal soup of genesis, similar forms of life were preordained in the primal plastic of many worlds.

The fossil record of Earth suggests it was so. But unless some paleontologist was fortunate (or unfortunate?) enough to know exactly where to dig, he would never in all the world find anything remotely resembling the Wamphyri of Sunside/Starside. He would not discover them among the strata of Earth's prehistory, for in their beginning Earth was not the homeworld of the Wamphyri. But for an accident of Nature (the Gate on Starside, and later a second Gate, forged in error and ignorance by men), the Wamphyri could never have ventured here. There would have been wolves of the wild in our world, but not werewolves.

Of the latter:

It has been told how men and beasts went down to the vampire swamps to drink, and how creatures other than men—but most certainly beasts—returned from that place. Until they learned better, the gray brothers of the mountains were among the first victims of the swamp-born horror. Contaminated with a vampire spore, occasionally a sick wolf would return to the pack. But he would be different and changed forever. Like any human wanderer or explorer suffering the same fate, he would become an outcast from his own kind.

Men savaged by such an animal would usually die, to rise up again as vampire thralls—but without a master! Then they in turn must flee from their families and friends to wander as outcasts until their former brothers tracked them down, or the furnace sun found them wanting. Or they could cross the mountains into the dubious safety of Starside.

But they were different again from the victims of human vampires; not only did they fear the sunlight but revelled in the moonlight! For there was something of the gray brothers in them, whose mistress is the full and tumbling moon. Also, they were generally insane—lunatics—or at the very least, they lacked total command of their senses. As such and despite that they were dangerous, they fell easy prey to men, the sun, the human vampires of Starside. Thus, in the language and psychology of the world beyond the Starside Gate, it was such pitiful creatures as these who would have been the true lycanthropes: madmen who *thought* that they were wolves!

Except . . . there was another sort.

Paradoxically—and for all that it sickened such lifeforms as suffered its infection—vampirism was the source of an incredible longevity. For the sickness was spiritual and of the soul, while life was physical and of the blood. Which meant that rarely, mercifully rarely, a wolf infected with a vampire spore would live long beyond the years of a true wolf, and its leech . . . would mature! Then the real danger, when a wolf such as this should savage a man!

For the vampire is tenacious, and the bite of *this* wolf would carry a deal more than venomous spittle! Indeed it might even carry the egg of its leech, by means of which a true vampire extends something of itself down all the ages. And whether or no the victim died, he would rise up again undead and Wamphyri! Such men were. They *were* men—but the vampire egg of a wolf was in them, with whatever it had contracted or inherited of its former host's makeup.

And unlike the poor *lycanthropes* of a different civilization and world (whose blood might be infected however slightly with some faint trace descended from Starside?) the werewolves of that parallel world did indeed have the power of transformation: metamorphosis into their ancestral form. All it took was the moon flying full over the boulder plains, to transform man into beast-man, to turn certain Lords of the Wamphyri into men with the faces, forms, and ferocious *appetites* of wild dogs!

Homo sapiens, *Canis* sapiens, loup-garou . . . werewolf!

Radu Lykan—banished through the Hell-lands Gate by Lord Shaitan, as we have seen—was one such. But before he was a dog-Lord, Radu was a man. And this is his story:

Radu had been a loner, a mountain man . . . until he and his companion wolf had ventured east of the barrier mountains into the swampy badlands. He had been a man who rarely bothered with his own kind, favoring the company of a dog of the wild whose broken leg he had healed when he discovered the animal half-buried in sliding scree; since when they had been inseparable.

But where other Szgany loners were usually dull, slothful fellows—disinclined to the companionship of the camp, or to working alongside their gipsy brothers on Sunside; or defective of mind or spirit, which might tend to make them brutish, turning them into thieves, vagabonds, and finally outcasts from the camps of the Szgany by virtue of the fact that none would have truck with them—Radu was very different.

He had been born into the band of Giorga Zirescu, a bully of a tribal chieftain whose twin sons were no better than their father, made worse by virtue of Giorga's influence and protection. Ion and Lexandru Zirescu had grown up with Radu, or rather *he* had grown up suffering their constant brutalities—but no more or less than the rest of the tribe suffered under Giorga and his sons. For while the Szgany Zirescu were strong in numbers, they were weak in resolve and easily cowed by their chief. And despite that Giorga was loathed, he and his sons were huge men, as hard-headed as they were hard-fisted.

Radu's mother had died giving life to his sister, Magda; that had been when he was seven years old, following which his own childhood had been lost to caring for the small girl-child, while his father Freji hunted, gathered, or beat the bounds on the perimeter of Giorga's territory, in the lee of the barrier mountains where they commenced their gradual slump toward the western swamps and badlands. And in Freji's frequent absence, Radu fell prey to the Zirescu brothers.

The twins were two years Radu's senior, and their various torments ranged from trifling insults to major beatings. They would even have hurt little Magda, if Radu had not been there to redirect and absorb their spite, so protecting her. But he always was—which served to earn him yet more insults, when Ion and Lexandru were wont to catcall and name him "Radu the wetnurse," and so forth.

Radu was tall; indeed, and for all that his father was a slight man, Radu's height was extraordinary. Aged nine he was tall as a fifteen-year-old, yet lithe and willowy as a lath—or as "a lass," as Ion and Lexandru would have it! Perhaps it was his nature to be thin; more likely it was the lack of good food (and the fact that hard work was plentiful) that kept him that way. But he was not without physical strength, and likewise his character was strong, however repressed. His face was usually expressionless, with dark, deep-sunken and humorless eyes, long cheekbones and jaw, and strong straight teeth in a thin mouth closed as if clamped shut. For he had learned even as a child that it was best to say very little, especially in the company or presence of the Zirescu brothers.

As a child, Radu's hair had been black—black as night, black as jet!—but even in his early teens it had started to turn gray, and ashen streaks were prominent at his veined, sensitive temples. His nose was long but not severe . . . until Ion Zirescu broke it in a one-sided scuffle, and it healed squat at the base and hooked in the middle, lending Radu a hawkish mien tempered by self-imposed strictures of iron will, with which he held himself in rein. It was necessary that he exercise a firm control over himself, if only to appease his ailing father, who was a pacifist at best, a coward at worst, and no match for the Zirescus at any time. Which might explain why Radu usually lost his battles: (why, in his circumstances it might even be considered prudent to lose!). For while the Zirescu twins were trouble enough in themselves, their cronies among the tribe's young men were numerous and the times several when these had held Radu down while the brothers kicked and pummeled him. So the young Radu had learned to control himself, while events shaped which would be quite uncontrollable.

Into Radu's mid-teens, the bullying of the Zirescus went on unabated; the youth suffered many a bloodying, many a sore bone and broken face, but never once complained to his father, whose health had for long and long been failing. But if Freji Lykan was feeling the weight of his years and the weariness of many deprivations under his swine of a chief, then Giorga was likewise declining . . . except in his case it was the good plum brandy and surfeit of meat that were taking their toll. And of course his brutish sons looked on like the vultures they were, wondering where and when he would fall down for the last time, and who would bully the Szgany Zirescu when Giorga was no more. Perhaps both of them, if only out of mutual fear and suspicion. Oh, for they knew well enough how much they were hated among a majority of their people.

All of which brings us to a time approximate with the era of Shaitan, when he came out of the west on Starside and built his aerie on the boulder plains, and the swamps in the badlands seethed with vampire spores. But as yet the incidence of their evil manifestations on Sunside were few and far between. As in all mankind, however, other evils were ever present. And in the Szgany Zirescu, the evil was in the name of their most prominent family: the Zirescus themselves.

The morning came when Freji could no longer work. His eyesight was failing, and in any case he had never been much of a hunter. Now his back gave him such pain that he could scarcely walk, and it was his turn to go into the forest to gather nuts and fruit. In the Szgany Zirescu, a man worked till he dropped, then lay there while the tribe moved on, or until he found the strength to get up again. There were few drones among the Zirescus (with the exception of Giorga, of course, his sons and a handful of their cronies), and precious few old ones. And despite that Freji was half-crippled, his chief sent him stumbling off into the forest with a basket—from which task he failed to return. The Sunside days were worth four of those in a parallel world that lay all unknown beyond the Starside Gate, yet night fell and still Freji was not back.

Radu had had his own duties that day; likewise his sister Magda, now grown to a beautiful girl, even as beautiful as her mother had been. And when finally Radu left the camp and went off into the woods to search for his father, he went without knowing or suspecting that it would be Magda—or her beauty, or her loss—that would finally forge the iron in his blood into cold, hard steel.

Magda—and the Zirescu twins, of course . . .

But when he'd found his father's body, and seen the truth of his dying— that it had been no accident, and certainly not the natural end of Freji's life— then the rest of it had gone blazing across Radu's mind like some mad meteorite through Sunside's night skies!

For more than a year now the Zirescu twins had been paying court (of sorts) to Magda, not yet fifteen . . .

Giorga had said that eventually she must choose one or the other . . . Magda had scorned both of them; she knew that already they were a scourge among the Szgany Zirescu's girls and young, unmarried women—and among some of the married ones, too . . .

Her father, Freji, who had a parent's say in such matters, had been stalling the twins and their father, telling them that Magda was too young. But it was not uncommon among Szgany girls to take husbands at the age of thirteen, and Freji had known he couldn't delay matters indefinitely. Giorga had fumed, cursed, threatened! He wanted grandsons from his sons (real grandsons, and not bastards), to carry his name on. Freji Lykan had fumbled and fawned, but still he'd stood his ground . . .

The twins had poured scorn on Magda, and declared that she would end up an old maid, or a tart for any man. And deep down inside, Radu had bubbled and boiled . . .

And now this:

Freji stiff and dead—murdered and left to the flies in an area of the forest rarely visited. His body had been tumbled into dense undergrowth; Radu discovered it when a vixen started away from the corpse. Then, after lighting a small fire, he had seen the cause of his father's death: the long blade of an ironwood knife broken off and still buried . . . in Freji's thin back! A cowardly attack—typical of the backstabbing Zirescu twins. But Freji's wicker basket was missing, and never a sign of the fruit and nuts which he had surely gathered that morning . . .

Back at the Szgany Zirescu encampment, Radu went direct to the keeper of the foraging, called Provisioner Borisciu, and asked him if anyone had brought in food from the forest that day. But despite that Radu held himself under tight rein, perhaps Borisciu saw something in his face. Answering Radu's question carefully, he told him that it had been an extremely good day; but surely he must already know that, since he had been one of the hunters, hadn't he?

"From the forest," Radu repeated himself, clutching the other's wrist, however coldly. "I'm talking about greenstuffs, not meat, Provisioner." And now Borisciu was sure that there was something hard and cold and different in Radu's eyes.

"Fruits, aye," he answered. "But isn't the forest always good to us?" And quickly, as if to change the subject: "But the catch in fishes was exceptional! A good day at the river, Radu! Keep it to yourself, and I'll perhaps find you a fat trout for your sister to cook for you and your father's supper . . ." With which he'd paused, remembering that someone had told him Freji Lykan was late coming in.

"Fruits," Radu's grip tightened more yet, while his voice became a growl. "Tell me about the fruit, and nuts. Did anyone bring in plums, apples, almonds? A wicker basket of fruit, out of the woods? Tell me quickly!"

"Radu, I—"

"—Who was out gathering today? Do you know what I'm saying? Or were you in on this too, Provisioner Borisciu?"

"What?" Borisciu's mouth fell open. "In on something, me? Why, the Govasci family were gathering today, likewise Andreas Tuvi, and . . ." But here he paused again.

". . . And?"

"And your father, I remember now." But the Provisioner's eyes had suddenly gone very wide; he was frightened for his own skin. Something that had struck him strange earlier in the day, when the Zirescu twins had come in very quietly and secretively with a great basket of fruit, struck him even stranger now. Or perhaps not. And: "What is it that you are thinking, Radu?" He trembled in the other's grip. "What is it with your father?"

"Dead!" Radu hissed in answer, releasing him with a shove, so that Provisioner Borisciu staggered back behind his counter, against the side of his caravan. "Dead! Murdered in the forest, and his basket taken."

"By some enemy of the Szgany Zirescu, no doubt!" Borisciu gasped. "Would-be settlers, claim-jumpers, land-thieves—on Giorga's territory!"

But Radu cocked his head on one side and said, "Enemies of the Szgany Zirescu? Aye, it's true—the twins themselves!" At which Borisciu knew he'd been right, even though he'd scarcely dared admit it even to himself. And Radu saw it in the Provisioner's eyes.

Nodding slowly, grimly, the young man said, "Now tell me: did they bring in a basket of fruit?" His voice was cold as the wind through the mountain passes. Though his eyes showed little or no emotion, his lips were thin and pale; his chest rose and fell, rose and fell, as if from running. And suddenly Borisciu saw the right and wrong of it—the coldblooded murder of it—and could keep his peace no longer.

"They did," he gulped at last. "A basket laden with fruit and nuts. And I remember thinking it strange that for the first time in as long as I could remember, the Zirescu twins had done a little hard work!"

"Dirty work, aye," the other muttered, turning away. "They must be mad or half-witted, to bring that basket back here."

"Or they don't give a damn," The Provisioner called after him, quietly. "Because for too long they and their father have stood taller than any law, even their own. But you . . . you're grown to a tall one in your own right! Only go carefully, lad, and look for them at Hzak's brandy stall. They were halfway drunk when I passed by an hour and a half ago. By now they'll have had a skinful; they shouldn't give you too much trouble. But what's this? Will you go hot-blooded and without a weapon? I like you, Radu Lykan, even as I liked your father. I'd hate to see you dead, too."

Good advice. Radu went to the caravan of Freji Lykan, now his . . . and found it dark and still, the lamps unlit, the door swinging ajar in a night breeze. But an empty clay jug lay on the grass outside, and a whiff of brandy still drifting on the air: foul breath of the beasts who had been here before him.

Magda . . . was in the bushes close by, where they'd dragged her, used her, and left her broken and naked and dead. And Radu incapable of believing it; he could only sit holding her in his arms, rocking her and shaking his head. Until in a little while he grew cold, then hot, then bitterly cold again, and trembling as from a fever—or from the fury building inside, as he pictured in his mind's eye that which he *could not bear* to picture:

The blood under her fingernails, some of which were broken, a sure sign of the furious fight she'd put up. The coarse-weave scarf around her neck, with which they'd choked her screams and eventually her life. The bruises and other . . . *signs,* upon her tanned body. Many hands had gripped Magda's flesh, to hold her down (even as Radu had been held down, upon a time), their fingers digging in, to leave disgraceful, impure marks on what had been purest of all. And all of them had shared in her—shared *in* her! And there had been more than just the Zirescu twins . . .

Back to the caravan Radu went, his feet finding their own way, for his mind was somewhere else. To the box under his bed, where in the afternoon he had cleaned his crossbow, and wrapped it in an oiled rag until the next time. For now it *was* the next time, except he wasn't after goats now but pigs.

Then to the campfire, where the coarse, guttural laughter of drunken men—or louts—rang out loud in the red-flickering light; and a half-dozen of them sitting there, where decent men no longer sat, for the Szgany Zirescu were ashamed of themselves. But no shame here, only whispers and jeers and the mention of . . . of a name! Magda's name! But to have heard it from the rubbery, brandy-sodden lips of her violators and murderers! To have heard it in *such* a context:

"That's a *fuck* I'll never forget! And tight as the skin on a tambourine—well, until we were all done with her, anyway!" The speaker was one Arlek Bargosi. He burst out laughing at his own coarse wit—then coughed, choked, and lurched to his feet. The others looked to see what was wrong with him—

—And saw the flighted half of a crossbow bolt sticking out of Arlek's Adam's apple, and the red-dripping barb protruding from the back of his neck! Arlek clutched uselessly at the stout ironwood shaft, said, "Urk! Urk! Urk!" Then spewed blood and fell on his face in the fire. And as hot cinders flew this way and that, Radu Lykan stepped into view, stretched the gut on his weapon, and laid a second bolt in the tiller's groove.

But Radu was changed, his face no longer expressionless but broken in a nightmarish grin, his eyes reflecting the red firelight, and teeth bared like bars of white light where saliva foamed in the corners of his mouth. Taller and grayer than ever, he looked, and even more hawklike—except the hawk was blooded now, and stooping to its second prey.

The Zirescu twins shot to their feet. Bulky, bearded, red with booze, they were nevertheless sober in a moment. For this time, in the astonished silence, they heard the *thrum* as Radu released his bolt, and the *hiss* as it flew true to Ion's heart . . . or would have flown true, if another of their cronies had not stood up and put himself stumblingly in the way.

That one's name was Kherl Fumari, and Radu's bolt smashed through his spine and pushed out his jacket a little in front before it lodged there. And as Kherl gave a gurgling cough and crumpled to his knees, Ion Zirescu saw how close he had come. For Kherl clutched at him as he slid to earth, and looked up into his face with eyes already glazing over.

And there stood Radu grinning his mad wild grin, chill as the night but fluid as a river, nocking his weapon and sliding home his third bolt on the tiller . . . a shot destined never to be fired. Behind him, a massive figure loomed out of the darkness: that of Giorga Zirescu himself! A club was in Giorga's hand; he hefted it, then swung it with smashing force against the back of Radu's head. And that was that.

Giorga tossed the club aside, scowled at his dumbfounded sons and their stumbling colleagues. And: "Huh!" he growled. "As well I still have a friend or two—despite that I sired such as you two!"

"Father, we—" Lexandru started to speak.

"—Be *quiet!*" his father told him. "Do you think I don't know what brought all this about? Well, I do! I was woken from my sleep by a friend, as I said. And he had overheard you talking about it round the fire. Radu's sister, Magda—dead, and by your hands! Six of you, onto one girl! This pair of mangy corpses here, Kherl Fumari and Arlek Bargosi, and the Ferenczy brothers, Rakhi and Lagula," (Giorga glowered at the Ferenczys where they stood shuffling their feet and glancing sly-eyed at each other), ". . . and you two, of course!"

"Not all our fault," Ion shook his tousled head. "It was you who sent us after Freji, to do him in. Well, and there was that in Radu's eyes as told us he knew! He must have found his father out in the woods. As for the girl: that . . . *was* an accident. She wouldn't hold still."

Coming closer round the fire, the old man kicked Arlek Bargosi in the side so that he rolled over out of the embers. Smoke and the smell of roasting meat came up from Arlek's scorched corpse; his black face crackled and popped. Giorga stepped around his body, and paused where Kherl Fumari lay sprawled on the trampled grass. "Huh!" he said again. "A hell of a to-do, all this!" And to Ion: "Help me with Kherl."

Ion stepped forward—

—And met Giorga's fist like a rock, smashing into his face! "Never accuse me again!" Giorga stood over him where he fell. "Never answer me back in any way. Do you understand?"

And Ion could only look up dazedly at his father, dab at his bloody mouth and nod.

Giorga nodded, too, glanced from face to face, narrowed his eyes and muttered, "Now then, listen in and I'll tell you what's to be done."

The four gathered round him, and waited while he considered it. Then: "First the girl," he said, "where is she?"

Lexandru started to answer but Giorga cut him short. "No, don't bother telling me. I don't want to know. Two of you can collect her from wherever she is, take her into the woods and bury her. And bury her deep!" He looked scathingly at his sons. "Later, when everyone has their heads down, you two had better do the same for Freji Lykan. Except this time make sure no one can find him—ever! As for Radu: if that clout I gave him on the head didn't do for him, the river will. So drag him to the riverbank where it's deep, put a weighted rope round his neck and toss him in. In the morning we're moving on; the next time we come round this way, there'll be nothing of evidence left. That's it: a whole family dealt with. And our hands clean . . ."

Ion said, "And no one will ask questions?"

Giorga nodded. "Probably. But this is how it was:

"Radu went mad. He was always the weird one, as everyone knows, quiet and sneaky and what have you. So he was overheard arguing with his father. Then he must have followed Freji into the woods and done away with him. His sister guessed the truth of it and accused him. He threatened her and she ran off. Knowing that she might come back and tell what she suspected, Radu made to go after her. Before he could leave camp, Kherl Fumari and Arlek Bargosi, who had learned something of the story from the frightened girl, challenged him; Radu killed them—one in a cowardly fashion, from the rear—and ran off. As for the veracity of the tale: why, here's poor Arlek, all done to a turn, and Radu's bolt in his neck. And here's Kherl with another bolt in his back, and Radu's crossbow lying where he dropped it. And there were witnesses: you four.

"All of this was tonight . . . you must work out the finer details for yourselves, for from now on I don't want anything to do with it. But in any case, and since we'll never see any of the Lykans again, there'll be no one to deny your story."

As Giorga finished speaking, Ion and Lexandru looked at each other. A mutual message, however silent, passed between them: that they'd better have words with Provisioner Borisciu, too, to ensure that his lips were likewise sealed. Or maybe to seal them permanently, if they weren't already. And:

"Well, what are you waiting for?" Giorga wanted to know. "Best get to it, before this spreads any further."

And all four of them, they got to it . . .

Radu knew nothing of the fact that he was dumped in the river, and that a big rock dragged him down to the mud and weeds. But the Zirescu twins had been very sober by then and in something of a hurry; the knot around his neck was fumbled; it had slipped loose before he hit the bottom. Then the current found him, buoyed him up, and whirled him downstream.

Midnight found him on his back, where wavelets washed white pebbles at a bend in the river. He was tethered by weeds, supported by a mat of drifted branches. The swelling at the back of his head was large as a hen's egg, but apart from a handful of scratches and bruises he was in one piece, and felt all the better for it after he'd emptied his system of river water. He remembered . . . well, *something* of the night before (the vengeful killing he had done, certainly, and of being knocked down and dragged through night-dark undergrowth; fragments of whispered conversation) but precious little. Still, it was enough for now. Sleep and warmth were what Radu needed most, to give the soft spot at the back of his head a chance to harden up.

He managed to get a fire going, dried out his clothes and got back into them, built a bed of bracken and grasses to sleep out the night. And spent most of the next day in sleeping, too, and in trying to forget about his father and his sister. It was hard, but he tried anyway. Because by then he'd decided to forget about mankind in general and be a loner, one of the strange wild men who came down out of the hills now and then to sit by a campfire in the night. Except Radu would be a real loner; no campfires for him but his own, and no man's company, either.

All his life he'd known the brutalities of his "brother" men, and for all he knew it would be the same in any tribe as it had been with the Szgany Zirescu. With which Radu Lykan was gone from the Szgany of Sunside, and claimed by the forest and the wild mountains. He had no friend but himself (at least for a while), no cares but his own, no counsel but that of the sun, moon, and stars. For the first time in his life he was free.

And he moved from place to place and territory to territory as if there were no bounds to speak of, taking to the ways of the wild as if it had been preordained. Thus Radu became a creature of Nature, a man alone who went where his fancy took him. He left no tracks, and skirted or otherwise avoided the camps of men. But more especially he vowed to keep apart from the Szgany Zirescu, for he knew that if he returned to *them* it would be a bloody thing . . . his blood or theirs, whichever

But he also knew that having *tasted* the blood of his foes, he'd found it to his liking, which meant it could easily become a habit. Two of his had died, and two of theirs had paid the price. Let that suffice; let Giorga, Lexandru and Ion Zirescu, and the Ferenczy brothers, stew in the juice of their own miserable existence, and if they thought Radu was dead so be it, he was dead—to them, anyway.

East lay the territories of the Szgany Hagi, the Szgany Tireni, the Mirlus, Lidescis, and many another band or tribe. Radu often heard their babble, saw their fires reflected from clouds drifting low over the woods at night, read their boundary marks and crossed their trails; but other than that he had nothing to do with them, and they never once knew he was there.

So he wandered the length and breadth of Sunside's woods; he climbed through the foothills to the tree-line, turned west, and explored the passes and mountain heights. For a year, two, three, he was alone, until the day when he found a great white she-wolf trapped in the scree where the flank of the mountain had slipped a little. And it was a rare, strange thing . . .

Radu had been hungry and could have killed and eaten the wolf. It would have been easy; he'd stolen a good crossbow in his wanderings and could have put a bolt in her, then dug her out and built a fire to roast her joints. She was a dog, true, but she was meat.

But looking into her great, feral yellow eyes, Radu decided against it. He, too, had been crippled in his time—by apathy and cowardice, and by the shame of the Szgany Zirescu, unable to escape from the shadow of a shameless leader—but he'd freed himself, grown strong in his freedom, and survived. This she-wolf's crippling was a purely physical thing: a forepaw was broken where it stuck up awkwardly from the rubble and debris, and she was unable to drag herself free. But Radu saw parallels, and couldn't bring himself to kill her. It was one of those strange paradoxes; if she'd been running with a pack he wouldn't have thought twice about shooting her. But now:

He made his way out onto the dangerous sloping surface of the sliding scree, and patiently dug her free. And with every passing moment the treacherous rocks could have slipped and fallen away, grinding both of them into oblivion; or the bitch could have turned on him and grabbed his throat. But the mountain held its breath, and the she-wolf made no such vicious protest; finally Radu put a rope round her chest and dragged her to one side—

—At which the scree jumble gave a shudder and a mighty groan, and avalanched down onto Sunside!

Well, maybe she knew Radu had saved her life. But whether or no, she let him splint her paw, and accepted cooked food out of his hand when he shot and roasted a rabbit. And a day later, when Radu thought she could probably make it on her own and set off west again, the she-wolf came hobbling after him. For while her pack had forsaken her, this man had not, and she would not forsake him. After that, going from strength to strength, eventually she was fully recovered.

From which time on there were two of them.

In Radu's entire life, this incident was one of the very few good things that had ever happened to him. Who could have guessed that it would result in the very worst thing of all?

CHANGELING!

IN RADU'S DREAMS, HIS FATHER AND SISTER LIVED AGAIN, AND WALKED AND talked with him, reminding him of his past. Waking was invariably a bad time, when suddenly he would know that they were dead, of course, and discover himself a loner. And but for the company of Singer (so named for the fact that when Radu sang to himself of an evening, she would join in to serenade the moon), he suspected he might very easily lose his mind. Nor would he be the first loner to go mad from the solitude of his ways.

But Singer was there, hunting with and for Radu, constantly by his side, more of a friend and companion than any human creature he had ever known, except for the mother he had loved for so short a time, and his family which was no more. But despite the presence of the white she-wolf, ever more frequently he would find himself dwelling upon the fate of his father and sister, and the fact that he'd been thwarted in the hour of his vengeance. At the time, two for two had seemed satisfactory . . . now he felt the scales had been weighted against him, and knew how he'd been cheated. Looking down on western Sunside from the heights where the barrier mountains commenced to crumble to the swamps, he would fancy he saw the fires of Zirescu encampments. And despite his Szgany vow to be gone from the western forests forever, he would feel this oh-so-strong compulsion to return, for however brief and bloody a time . . .

He was a man full-grown now, firm in all his limbs, still lean but springy as a sapling, swift as a bolt from a crossbow and just as deadly a hunter, no less than his lupine companion. And he wondered how fat and idle were grown the Zirescu twins, Ion and Lexandru, and their loathsome father, Giorga; and how long, tall and pimply the Ferenczy brothers, Rakhi and Lagula? Perhaps Giorga was dead; Radu hoped so. But strangely, he hoped the Zirescu twins and the Ferenczy brothers yet lived. And when thoughts like that came to him, then he would run with Singer, and hunt to take his mind off things.

Until eventually, weary of the mountain heights in spite of all their grandeur (and perhaps afraid of his feelings when he looked down on western Sunside), he sought new horizons, new scenes and sensations. The far western lowlands lay mainly unexplored; Radu fancied there must be havens in the green fringes, where birds sang and creatures played, and fishes leaped in the cool clear water before it all ran to swamp.

But in any case he dreamed of the dark and misted forests he'd known as a boy, and once more walked with his father, sister and mother (despite that she had died when Magda was born) along old Szgany trails, and so would go down into the unknown badlands. If he dared, he would prefer to go down into the Sunside of his childhood, however unhappy that had been, but could not for reasons already explained. At the moment he was an outlaw, true, but to the best of his knowledge men didn't seek him for his life. All of which could change if he deliberately set himself against the Zirescus. And so it was the badlands, which were not named that way for nothing.

At first, all seemed well. Streams fell from on high, cascading into cool, misted depths, and Radu and Singer swam where the falls had formed basins in centuries-hollowed rocks. Vines and hybrid flowers flourished in the spray from the waters and the sunlight streaming from Sunside, and in fertile valleys between black, eroded spurs the foliage was lush and filled with living things. But then, as the course of their descent turned away from Sunside, abruptly things changed.

The warmth from the sun lancing overhead was still present, but now the rising mist was dark and dank, no longer silver-edged and glowing. The shrubbery was lush and tangled, but there were fewer and smaller flowers; the nights were cold, and Singer full of some strange uneasiness of spirit. Radu supposed it was because they had turned their faces from Sunside, and at his earliest opportunity turned south again while yet continuing his descent. The freshness of the heights never returned, however, and down in the western bottoms, where the mountains crumbled to a desert of mud, Radu found no such green fringes as he'd hoped for and never a haven to mention.

What he did find was a marshy bogland of fallen, rotting trees and low, thick-leaved, flabby gray shrubs, under an evil miasma which rose as a mist from the apparently endless swamps. Of croaking, hopping things there were plenty, and of snapping lizardlike things, too, but of the clean, warmblooded life of Sunside's forests . . . never a sign, except for the occasional slumped, black, unrecognizable carcass, rapidly turning to rot and become one with the swamp. It was like a different world, even a dawnworld, whose dwellers were primal creatures out of time.

And in the swampy margins were toadstools as black as tar, bursting underfoot and sending up clouds of red spores to drift in the foggy reek. It was as if the very air was poisonous, and something warned Radu to fasten a rag over his nose and mouth; but Singer went on all fours like the wild dog she was, drinking the water between patches of scum and breathing the spore-laden air. Then, as they began a retreat toward higher ground, they saw a ragged, mud-streaked fox stumbling in the mire, all bleary-eyed and three-quarters done for.

Radu was loath to waste a bolt on this poor emaciated creature, yet knew it would be a mercy to put it out of its misery. In the time he'd spent with Singer, some two years now, he had trained her in the hunt (though truth to tell, in certain aspects she had trained him!). Now he told her: "See to it!" Which was the order to kill.

Leaping out into the mud, she came upon the fox at once, to break his neck in her jaws. And shaking the poor thing, she let it fall on its side. That should have been enough, but in the next moment . . . an amazing thing! For the jaws of the fox yawned open and it snapped at Singer's face, and what with the spray of flying mud, and the snarling, snapping, and threshing of their heads where their jaws seemed locked, it appeared to Radu watching from the bank that something passed between them, from fox to wolf. Or it could have been that Singer had ripped out the fox's tongue to swallow it whole! Whichever, that signaled the end of it; the fox sprayed red from his mouth, sank down into the mud and gave up the ghost.

But it was not the end of it for Singer. Leaping to firm ground, she sprang this way and that, coughed and choked, and bounded in the air, until finally she collapsed. Unconscious, she lay with her sides heaving, then grew still, and only the faintest of heartbeats to let her master know she yet lived.

Dismayed, Radu sat with Singer a while, there by the rim of the swamp, with her head in his lap and her tongue lolling, until it appeared she wouldn't die. Then, draping her over his shoulders, he carried her out of that place, and in an hour or so she struggled to be put down. Shortly after that, to Radu's great relief, she seemed as good as new. She *seemed* that way, at least . . .

They explored for an afternoon and an evening—that was all, but more than enough in that place—before Radu headed south and a little east, to skirt the barrier mountains into Sunside. He knew it to be a route which must take him into Zirescu territory sooner or later, but by then he would have climbed back up into the mountain heights and so put temptation behind him. So he thought.

And when the ominous twilight failed and the long night fell at last, because the region was strange to Radu and possibly dangerous with hitherto unknown hazards, and the swamps alive with mosquitoes and other flying things, he found a cave in an outcrop at the foot of the mountains and built a fire in the entrance to keep injurious insects and other creatures at bay; behind which he and the now strangely withdrawn she-wolf sheltered and prepared for sleep . . .

. . . When down from the heights echoed a distant howling in praise of a blotchy yellow moon tumbling through the murky sky. And though Singer's nose lifted and her eyes lit with recognition, still she made no reply to the songs of the gray brothers on the mountain flanks. And even when Radu sang a low tune to himself (as he was wont to do in strange places), Singer held back from joining in; not even a growl escaped her, or a yawn of her long-jawed, soft-leather mouth. So that all in all Radu considered it weird, but perhaps a mood was on her, which in a place like this he could understand well enough . . .

During the night on those several occasions when Radu woke up to toss branches on the fire, stretch his legs or relieve himself, he discovered Singer awake, silent, staring out past the slow-burning fire into the night, or whining low in her throat, or shaking her head from some unknown irritation and pawing at the earth where she stood in the entrance of the cave.

Far more worrying, on the last such occasion, she was on her belly close by, forepaws outstretched in Radu's direction, peering at him intently through her feral—or sick?—yellow triangular eyes. Following which he felt it prudent to remain awake, and sat by the fire until the twilight before the dawn, then moved on with all speed toward the risen but as yet hidden sun somewhere on the far flank of the crumbling mountains. And it has to be said that Radu was glad the night was over . . .

As the Sunside/Starside nights are long, the days are longer still. But the territory was unknown to Radu, the rotting rock of the lower mountains was treacherous (so that he must go with care and patience), and there always seemed to be a new, higher ridge behind whichever false plateau he had just negotiated.

For he had made up his mind that instead of skirting the mountains, he would cut diagonally across their lower ramparts and so arrive in the western part of Sunside already aloft and in the heights. But because of the dangers and arduous nature of the route (which seemed far more difficult than the one by which he'd descended to the swamps), it wasn't until the twilight before the night, and after several camps, that at last he arrived over Sunside; and even then not nearly as high on the mountain flanks as he had intended.

The twilight before the night: a dull orange afterglow slowly fading over the far furnace desert, and the sky to the south banded from amethyst on the horizon to a dark indigo in the vault of the sky, where several stars were already evident. While over Starside the skies were long since jet, whose stars seemed like chunks of ice frozen in their orbits; but Starside itself was obscured by virtue of the mountain peaks. A myriad of Sunside's tiny bats, along with a handful of a larger species, *whooshed* and whirred on the air where they hunted, while down in the woods the scattered fires of Szgany camps lit the night, sending aromatic odors drifting on thermals of their own making.

And there was a conflict of longings in Radu hard to describe: the need to be among men again, oh yes—but good men, brothers, men he could trust—and the need to avoid them at all costs, for this was surely Zirescu territory. The need to sit in the glow and warmth of a campfire, and chew on a joint of meat with its juices hot and dripping, washed down with a jug of good Szgany wine . . . and the dark desire to glimpse a startled face by starlight (that of Ion or Lexandru, perhaps? Or Rakhi or Lagula?) and squeeze off an ironwood bolt at point-blank range. Oh, a medley of longings, wishes, desires and urges; but the certain knowledge, too, that to surrender to them must bring about the worst possible result, when he would not only be a loner but an outcast, too, from all men and for the rest of his days.

Well, and wasn't that his way? And wouldn't it suit him well enough? To be a loner, yes, but not to be pursued as a murderer, when in fact he would be an avenger of the weeping dead. (For in Radu's mind and memory, and in his dreams, his father and sister were given to weeping, causing him to cry, too.)

And so, as always, he put it from his mind, climbing up into the mountains while yet there was the light for it. And Singer with him as ever, but a Singer changed now and almost unknown to him. For now when she hunted the great white she-wolf kept her kill, and now when he would hug her she backed off from him, whining and showing her fangs. And whatever it was that was at odds between them, Radu knew that the difference wasn't in him.

Not yet, at least . . .

It happened quickly. Radu made camp that night in a delve in a cliff high over the foothills, where a great boulder had weathered free of the bedrock, rolled away and left a hollow behind. Scarcely a cave, still it was dry and would shelter him if the rains came. Soft heather made a passable bed, and a cured skin was his blanket; it would suffice. Normally he would have Singer, too, to snuggle close and keep him warm. But the she-wolf didn't want that now, and truth to tell, neither did Radu. She had a look about her, a light in her eyes, a flattening of her ears, that warned of further changes in the offing—

—Which came as he slept.

It was a sound that woke him: a whine, a snarl, a cough or grunt. One or all of these things, but a sound anyway . . . made by Singer. And sitting up in his bed of heather, backing away from her, Radu was astonished and horrified by this picture of a dog of the wild so patently torn between loyalty and strange, alien emotions. She crept toward him, shied away, whined as in some inexpressible agony . . . and was at once drawn back to him, slavering and showing her scythe teeth, where the soft leather of her muzzle was drawn quiveringly back. And Radu understood that she now saw him as prey of sorts—yet *remembered* him as her friend and master! He sensed that she was driven by something, and fought it with whatever remained of her former loyalty. He knew something of her torment, which must in a way be similar to his own. For while *he* lusted after the blood of certain men, still he remembered a handful of times when men had been good to him; and while *she* came upon him to kill him, she yet loved him with at least a spark of her old love.

And even as he drew back the string of his crossbow until it nocked, and even as he slid a bolt into the tiller's groove, Radu Lykan grieved over what he must do, for the companionship they had known together. But plainly Singer was mad and all of that was over now, and like the fox in the swamp she'd be better off dead and out of her misery.

He aimed direct at her forehead—her brain, to make a quick end of it— and knew he couldn't miss. For even though Singer had witnessed the power of his weapon, still she crept closer, and closer yet, almost as if begging him to kill her! And all the while she stared fixedly at Radu, pleadingly with eyes he knew yet didn't know, not any longer. She was almost upon him; her eyes were yellow lamps shining on him; powerful jaws yawned open! And:

"Goodbye, old friend," Radu told her, squeezing the trigger.

In the last moment Singer had lunged forward . . . only to be stopped dead by the ironwood bolt that chopped through her sloping skull into her brain; so that she fell twitching upon Radu's chest where he had jerked back away from her. Her jaws still gaped open, however; his, too, as he saw something writhing in the dark cavern of her mouth! Then, but too late, he once again remembered the diseased fox in the swamp: the thing he had seen passing from the one to the other, which he'd mistakenly thought was the fox's tongue, torn out at the roots by Singer.

It was the same now, but as the shiny-black, corrugated body of the leech-thing ejected from the wolf's mouth, and in the instant that it transferred to Radu's, he saw that it was no tongue! It lived—it thought, reasoned, or instinctively *knew*—and it moved like lightning as it sought . . .

. . . A new, better, stronger, more intelligent host!

Impossible to close his mouth! Such was the girth of the horror that his jaws were made powerless, like taking too big a bite of an apple and stalling on it—except *this* loathsome thing was no apple. Head-first, it *fed* itself to him, putting out hooks into his throat to draw itself down inch by choking, vile-tasting, stomach-heaving inch. Then . . . it was *in* him and he could breathe again. He did—gasping, coughing, and massaging his throat—and came lurching to his feet as he tried desperately to vomit, to rid himself of the nightmarish parasite within. And *it* knew that, too!

Radu would never know just exactly what the horror did to his insides then, but even as he blacked out he guessed it was the same thing that it had done to Singer's. And as incredible pain hounded him into a merciful oblivion, he could more fully appreciate how she had felt when she'd collapsed at the rim of the swamp . . .

. . . *And* something of how she must have felt when she came awake. His throat burned; it was dry, cracked, bruised inside from the thing's passage into his body. And so it had been no nightmare, no subconscious association of ideas lingering from his recent visit to the swamps, but the real thing. A real *Thing* had vacated Singer's body in favor of his! It was in there even now, hiding in his body, lodged there where he could neither see nor feel it, nor affect it in any way. Like the fox, and then Singer, he was now the host of this parasitic creature, this leech that he imagined to be similar to the tapeworms that occasionally got into the systems of the Szgany.

Well, Radu knew the cure for *that* well enough! He'd seen how the sufferers of such infestation submitted to starvation, and when they were almost dead of hunger allowed themselves to be tied down with their mouths propped open, so that the parasite could be lured out of them by the stench of rotting fish or meat! But that was something a man couldn't do on his own; the temptation to bite such a thing in half and spit it out as it disgorged must be overwhelming—not to mention a complete waste of time and effort! For only leave a segment of the creature inside the host body, an entire new worm would grow from it! Then again, the tapeworms Radu had seen were slender, many-sectioned creatures; they *could* be bitten in half!

But . . . he knew that *his* parasite was different. He knew it without knowing how he knew. He felt it: a malign intelligence of sorts, a sentience other than the basic, natural, instinctive hunting and breeding knowledge of beasts of the wild, or the higher spiritual or morality-guided intelligence of men. This thing would use the guile of the fox, the ferocity of the hunting wolf, and *his* superior knowledge and intelligence for its own! Except . . . there would be nothing spiritual or moral about it. And nothing remotely human.

These were thoughts that entered Radu's mind in his first waking moments, but he could hardly suspect that they were not his thoughts entirely, or that their source was not entirely his mind. But such was the case: by virtue of its metamorphic make-up, the leech's mutant DNA was already bringing about the most drastic changes in his own, and doing it in such a way as to link itself with his mind, his blood and bones, his very being. The thing would *be* him, and even though he would continue to believe himself master of his own destiny, *he* would be it.

Cold, it would kill off what was human in him while intensifying what was cold and inhuman. Devious, it would so dilute what little was left of human love and compassion as to remove these things entirely, while accentuating those baser emotions it could use to its own advantage . . . such as lust, greed, and hatred. Tenacious, it would cling to life—to Radu's life—even as it molded itself to his internal organs and spine. And there'd be no getting rid of it, neither by primitive medicine nor any method of man's devising. For Radu was the higher life-form it had searched for since its development from a spore to a leech in the body of the fox, and it was with him now for as long as he lived.

Ever ravenous, it would lust after the very source of life, the red-pulsing river of life, which flows through the arteries of men and beasts. Except a man has only so much life, only so much blood; so that in order to survive, Radu too must consume or be consumed. It was the burgeoning curse of the vampire, new to Sunside/Starside even as Shaitan the Unborn was new, so that as yet Radu knew neither of them. But he would, he would . . .

Day finally dawned, and Radu was ill. He carried Singer out of the cave, dropped her into a crack in the rocks, filled it with stones. Under normal circumstances the effort would be scarcely worth mentioning; now . . . it felt like a day's work. He knew he should hunt, for good red meat to fuel him through whatever was to come, but the sun had a furnace heat he'd never felt before, which raised angry red weals on his skin and crisped the hair of his forearms to small coiled cinders. Even with his back to the sun he could scarcely see to find a target! Plainly he was ill. But he knew he had a Thing in him, so it was hardly surprising. And the very thought of that Thing made him feel more ill yet.

He found water, a small waterfall with a pool, laved his scorched and rapidly roughening body and filled a skin, took up his clothes in a bundle and headed back to his cave. On the way he saw a rabbit nibbling the grass in the shade of a tree, and even in his condition couldn't miss such an easy target. Back in the cave he found himself ravenously hungry and ate raw red flesh.

This wasn't the first time Radu had had it red; now and then when it rained and the grass he used for tinder was damp, he might find it impossible to get a fire going. Then he would simply skin his catch, cut himself a good hindquarter joint and fill his belly. And of course Singer had been there to dispose of the rest of their kill, which she naturally preferred that way. But on this occasion there was no such excuse. The day was hot and dry; Radu had flintstones; he could easily have cooked his food—but he ate it raw anyway. Perhaps it was simply a question of expedience.

And perhaps not . . .

And he slept . . . and slept. Never such a long sleep in all his life. Never before, and never again. For this was the Sleep of Change. This was his leech's chance to complete the melding, and make itself one with him. Something of the fox's wiles went into him, but not a lot, for that poor creature had been out of its own environment; it had never been afforded the opportunity to display its skills. On the other hand, a great deal more of the great white she-wolf found its way into Radu; for the leech had liked her strength and ferocity, her sense of the wild, her sinuous shape and speed. Singer had been a child of the night, a hunter of lesser creatures, an eater of raw meat, who slaked her thirst on blood. Good!

But the man . . . *knew* things! He had something that neither fox nor wolf of the wild could ever match: a creative mind with the power to override instinct, to say "No!" or "Later!" to the normally irresistible hereditary urges and demands which alone command the actions of lesser creatures. And because he could guide and control his own actions, he could himself *be* guided and controlled.

Thus, even as Radu had trained Singer, now his leech would train him. And with filament extensions of itself rooted in his brain, the vampire leech lay with Radu where he tossed and turned in his cave through the long Sunside day, ignoring all the nightmares which its presence inspired, while "listening" with rapt intent to his dreams. And learning from them.

And determining how it would be . . .

Radu woke in the evening twilight and was himself again . . . so he thought. He stretched upon his heather bed, and there was a new suppleness in all his joints. His throat no longer gave him pain, and there was no aching in his bones. Whatever small symptoms of his solitary ways had been, they were no more. He knew a physical comfort—a sensation of real well-being—such as he had never experienced before. He was "a new man." And he was more than a man. And less.

During his recovery, Radu had defecated in a secondary cave that branched off from the main one close to its entrance; the smell of his shit would keep creatures at bay. Strange for it was something he had never done before. Singer had done it from time to time, but she was a child of the wild. Rather, she *had been* a child of the wild. Then, remembering that Singer was no more, Radu grieved a little while he dressed.

His short trousers of stitched skins seemed baggy on him; obviously he'd lost weight, but he didn't feel too hungry, not for his usual fare, anyway. Radu's sandals seemed too short for his feet, and his jacket failed to connect with his trousers or tie properly across his deep chest. And there were short, dark manes of hair on the backs of his hands, and trailing down his wrists. Astonished, he found twin pads of hair in the palms of his hands, too! Moreover his fingernails were longer, thicker, darker, and pointed at their tips like claws.

But . . . how long had he lain there? Why, he must have been delirious! These changes in him had surely taken longer than a single night. But they were natural changes, obviously: loss of weight, and some slight wrinkling and shrinkage of his clothes, and his hair and nails growing all unhindered by normal wear and tear. But a healing sleep, for sure. For there was such a *zest* in him that—

—Except here Radu's thoughts were arrested by an echoing, ululant, faint but concerted howling from the high plateaux and passes, as his gray brothers in the heights began to serenade a full and glorious moon where she tumbled through the darkening skies. But . . .

. . . *His* gray brothers?

Radu wasted no time puzzling over it, for now his zest had turned to something other than a human passion. Now he longed for the thrills of the wild: the hunt, the chase, and the kill. But again, his bloodlust was not for the blood of the wild but for that . . . of his own kind? Or those who had been his kind, at least. And down there in the western forests, that was Zirescu territory.

He paused for a moment in the mouth of the cave to sniff at his excrement. His, yes, but it was black. The black of the digested blood of the rabbit. And perhaps the digested essence of something else? What of the leech-thing? Was this it, liquified and turned to black shit by his juices? Radu thought not. But then why couldn't he feel it inside him, a Thing as big as that? He frowned and gave a shrug. What had been had been. What was become was become. And what would be . . . would be.

But up in the mountains his gray brothers were aprowl and howling, and Radu threw back his head and howled with them. It felt good, as good as the night against his flanks! And pausing beside the pool to go down on all fours and sip, and seeing his face reflected in moonlight, Radu scarcely wondered at the fact that his eyes were triangular and gleamed feral yellow, or that his long-toothed smile was the smile of a wolf. For in the silver light of the moon all was made clear to him, and he remembered his dreams of vengeance and knew that it was time. Except he would go among men as a man, so that they would know who he was and why he had returned . . .

In his descent into Sunside, Radu was quick and surefooted as a wolf, but a wolf with all the agility and climbing skills of a man. Head first, with his chest and belly close to the earth, he dug in the heels of his hands to brake himself, sliding and skittering where the way was treacherous. Upright but bent forward, he loped where the going was level and easy. Whenever he found his way barred by cliffs, he reverted to human skills and clambered like a man, and at all times he stuck to the shadows as much as possible. For his eyes were suited to the night; he saw as clearly as in daylight. Or better, for he was Wamphyri! But as yet he wouldn't have recognized the word, or known that it described his condition, even if he'd heard it shouted.

In the first quarter of the night Radu was down into the foothills. Now the night was dark, lit only by starshine, for the orbit of the hurtling moon had taken her beyond the rim of the world. Which was just as well; her gravity no longer enraptured Radu's mind, and he was more himself . . . or he would be, if not for his symbiont. And in fact his leech *was* a true symbiont, for it gave as well as took. Now, if Radu were wounded, the vampire would heal him. Now his strength was that of eight or nine men—even ten, if need be. Now he was near-indefatigable, not to mention near-immortal! For barring accidents or an attack of the utmost ferocity, or a disease such as leprosy which even his leech could not cope with, he would not die.

Not that Radu knew any of this; these were wonders he was yet to discover, mysteries as yet unfathomed—or irredeemable depths as yet unplumbed. All he knew was that he felt . . . *well*, fitter, faster, and fiercer than ever before, and that his body burned with an inner fire; also that he was a force to be reckoned with greater than he'd ever been, but not nearly as great as he would be. But mainly he knew that he had the ability to right several great wrongs.

Revenge, aye, against the Zirescus and the Ferenczys!

And this would be what he gave to his leech; this was his part of the unspoken, unspeakable, unbreakable pact: that what he *apparently* did for himself, he in fact did for the vampire. Radu knew how to kill, and now must learn how to enjoy it. His life had been governed by fear and hatred; now his own hatred, enhanced tenfold by his vampire, would be an instrument with which to *inspire* fear. His human passions, hitherto suppressed, contained within the dam of his humanity, could now spill over in an inhuman orgy of emotion and violence beyond the range of common men. He could feel it in his blood. *Wamphyri!*

And the weirdest thing of all was this: that not even his leech knew these things! All it "knew," and this by some alien instinct, was that its host was a strong one, and that through him it lived. And all it had was its metamorphism, its tenacity, its awful hunger. For the fuel of its degenerate, regenerative engine was blood—which was why that engine was geared to drive Radu's lust for life, and for death. Aye, even at the expense of every life he touched from this time forward . . .

Coming upon the camp of the Zirescus, Radu was cautious. The camp's watchdogs (wolves reared from pups) would be out in the dark forest, silent but alert. Trained, they wouldn't bark to scare an intruder off but simply tree him, then whine or howl till someone came to discover what was what. Or, if their victim should choose to fight, they'd just as soon hamstring him behind his knees, and bark to attract their masters. All very daunting.

Yet Radu was not overly concerned. For somehow he felt he understood the ways of wolves; he believed he could handle them even as he'd handled the great white she-wolf of the wild. Perhaps even better than he'd handled Singer . . . now.

Sure enough, when they came to sniff him out, Radu held out his arms to them, and after a moment they crept close and licked his hands where he stood in the forest's shadows. Then, when they would whine, he cautioned them with a low *"Tut-tut!"* Until they were silent. And while he could sense that they were worried, still they *were* silent. For all of this was at a time when the Wamphyri were unknown in western Sunside; as yet, and apart from the frightful campfire tales of the occasional lone traveler (old wives' tales at best), the Zirescus had no real knowledge of the terror out of Starside's towering aeries that even now ravaged in the eastern woods. Thus the Zirescu wolves had not been trained against such as Radu—but after tonight they would be.

The wolves were satisfied (half-satisfied, at least) that Radu was not a threat; he sent them about their business, then advanced upon the camp. The night was young and there were men about the central fire. Radu was more than well acquainted with the habits of the Zirescus; he knew where to find old Giorga's caravan on the outskirts of the encampment. That is, if the fat old bastard were still alive! Of course that last was as yet a matter for conjecture: what with the Old Zirescu's swinish eating and drinking habits and all, and the ungovernable nature of his temper. But *if* he yet survived . . . well, the future extent of his span was hardly conjectural at all! It would end right here, right now, this very night. And Radu's father would be waiting to greet him in hell.

Yet . . . Radu held back, waiting in the shadows a while to think things out. For it seemed somewhat bold to simply walk up to Giorga's wicker door, knock and wait for a reply. If the old man were to look out through a peephole, suspect something and cry out—what then? The stars were too bright, the night too clear. Better if there were a ground mist, to soften the sound of Radu's approach or the clatter of any brief scuffle. Better if the damp, fertile earth and the trees of the forest were to exhale the moisture they'd gathered during the day, and throw a soft lapping blanket of white over the entire camp. Except, the earth and the trees couldn't do that—could they?

In some worlds it would be thought of as witchcraft, magic, the supernatural. And perhaps in Radu's world, too. Yet in the Himalayas of Earth, Tibetan priests are known to test themselves by falling asleep in water turning to ice, and upon waking generate sufficient bodily heat to melt it! And the firefly turns on the lamp in his own body without burning himself, and by its light finds a mate. And certain creatures winter through in a state of hibernation where others would surely die a freezing death. But here in this world . . . despite that Radu knew little or nothing of such things, suddenly he sensed a measure of his power—of a *new* power, in Sunside/Starside.

Radu was like—no, he *was*, or would be if he willed it—a catalyst! His presence in these woods was alien, even as he himself was alien to mundane mankind; the very chemistry of his body, no longer a human or entirely natural chemistry, had the power to bring about changes in natural things. He felt it burgeoning within him; he had desired something and now would will it. He would *breathe* a mist, and cause the forest itself to reciprocate!

And with the metamorphic assistance of his leech, he did exactly that. The pores of his body opened and seemed to steam; the mist poured off him as if he were dry ice; his heavy breath issued from his lips as an expanding evil essence that billowed out from him and appeared to call lesser mists out of the woods and up from the very earth itself! And on the outer rim of the Zirescu encampment, Radu flowed within his mist to reach up and tap lightly on the wicker door of Giorga's caravan.

"Eh? Who?" (Radu would know that bass, grumbly, rumbling voice anywhere; the Old Zirescu *was* still alive.) "What is it? Can't a man catch up on a little sleep around here?" There came the sound of movement from within, a small barred window opened inwards, and a puffy, bearded, squinting and red-eyed face appeared behind the bars. Radu stood at the foot of the caravan's steps and kept his face averted. His vampire mist obscured him a little where it swelled, rolled, and sent up wispy tendrils, serving to hide his actual identity, but the sparse and ragged clothing of a mountains loner gave him away as a stranger. And:

"Eh?" Giorga mumbled again, but sharper now. "What, a wanderer, come at night to try the hospitality of the Zirescus? So why bother me? There are men at the campfire, I'm sure. Go sing for your supper there." Giorga was probably drunk; certainly his brandy breath was strong in Radu's nostrils. But before the old man could close his window:

"I haven't come to take anything but to *give* something," Radu told him, disguising his voice as best as possible—which wasn't in fact difficult, except now he must also disguise it from a growl! And continuing: "Giorga Zirescu, I bring a warning. But I can't talk out here—" And he glanced quickly this way and that, as if worried that he might be overheard. "—So let me in, and I'll tell you of the doom that hangs over you and yours even now!"

"A warning?" the other gasped. "A doom? Whatever can you mean?" And more harshly, commandingly: "Speak up, man, and perhaps I'll hear you out!"

Radu straightened up but kept his face averted. "I'm not one of yours, Giorga, that you can speak to me like an underling. I'm a loner, yes, a wanderer . . . ah, but the places I've wandered, and the things I've heard! They say that Giorga Zirescu grows old and fat and sodden, and his sons no better than young shads in the rut, and the Zirescu women all slatterns who would open their legs to dogs rather than take the pigs his men have become!"

"What!" Giorga's eyes bulged at the window. "Who says these things? Who dares issue these lies? I have no truck with neighbors, so who's to know that . . . that I . . ."

And Radu looked at him sideways, just a glance, but a look that said it all. "Yes, go on. Who's to know, that you . . . ."

The other calmed down a little, snarled, "I've no time for gossip. Sticks and stones may hurt me, but catcalling . . ."

"Sticks and stones, aye," Radu repeated him. "And crossbow bolts—and men who lust after your land, because they believe you're not fit to hold it?" And when that sank in:

"Eh?!" Again Giorga's gasp. "Is that it? Land thieves? But this is *my* land, as it was my father's before me! So someone's after me for my territory, is that it? A land feud? But no one has the right! Tell me more."

"I would, gladly," Radu answered with a shrug, beginning to turn away. "Except it would seem that the one they call the Old Zirescu is much too proud to talk face to face with a loner and wanderer. It seems he's too high and mighty! And should I stand out here in this damp and clinging mist, without even a sip of your good plum brandy to warm my throat? No, I reckon not. So now you'll just have to guess where they'll strike . . . and how many . . . and when. Well, and good luck to you . . ."

Turning his back on the caravan, Radu made as if to stride away. But:

"Wanderer, whoever you are, wait!" Giorga's voice was anxious now, all of the bluster driven out of it. "And yes, you're right: I'm an ungrateful old wretch at times! But come in, come in and warm yourself. Brandy, did I hear you say? Why, I could use a drop myself! And look, I've a jug of the very stuff right here!" The bolt was drawn back, and Radu heard the creak of the caravan's wicker door.

In another moment, soundlessly, he turned and was up the wooden steps, and something of his mist flowed inside with him. What's more, Giorga Zirescu had *invited* him in of his own free will!

Well, with a little help from Radu's lying leech . . .

RED REVENGE!

L AND?" GIORGA ASKED AGAIN, AFTER HANDING RADU A LEATHER JACK. "IS
that what this is all about?"

Radu took a sip of the sharp-tasting brandy—the merest sip—then put the
jack down. It had been a long time and he needed a clear head. "It's about land,
and life, and death," he said, and his voice was very deep, very gruff, as for the
first time he turned his face fully in Giorga's direction. And in the light from the
Old Zirescu's lamp, he searched for some sign of recognition, but found nothing in the red-flecked, boozy, bulging eyes of the other. If he had—if Giorga had
shown even a glimmer of recognition—then his time had come, be sure. His
night visitor had already determined that it had come anyway, but all in good
time, when Giorga had been given to know why.

"Well, we're face to face," the old man told him. And that was true enough;
in the close confines of Giorga's caravan they couldn't be anything else. "So
now let's have it: explain yourself. As for land and life and death, they're all one.
If a man must fight to keep his territory, then he fights. His land *is* his life, and
it's where he's buried when he dies!"

"And will his people fight with him, or will they run away because they hate
him?" Radu's voice was deeper yet, a rumbling growl issuing from his throat, his
suddenly chaotic emotions.

"No," the Old Zirescu pushed his face closer yet. "They'll *fight*—because
they fear him! Here in these western forests, since time immemorial, the Zirescus have always been strong. In my time, I, Giorga, have been strongest of all!
I had to be."

"In your time, aye," Radu nodded. "But do you mean strongest, or hardest? Were you strong with your people, or hard on them?"

By now the old man had sobered a little. His gaze was curious as he sat
down on the wooden frame of his bed and looked Radu up and down. If he'd
seen this man before he was sure he would remember him. What, a man as tall
as this; why, he must be all of six foot three! And his strange looks . . . those eyes

of his: yellow in the lamplight. And his gray hair, swept back like a mane to fall over his collar. His slightly pointed ears and long, hairy hands . . . Then again, the loners were all weird in their ways and looks—this one especially! Why, his words were almost . . . what, accusing?

And suddenly Giorga suspected that this wasn't about land, and likewise that he wasn't much interested what it was about. Simultaneously, he suspected it had been a mistake to invite this man into his tiny cramped caravan in the first place.

"Whatever I've been—and whatever I've done—it was my way," he answered at last, and placed his pillow as a rest for his back. But beneath that pillow he kept a long ironwood knife with a bone handle. Its edge wasn't so keen, but its point was sharp as a splinter.

"It was your way, aye," Radu growled, "and always for your own good: yours and your sons'. But never for the good of your people. They *do* hate you, Giorga!—even as I hated you, upon a time . . ."

"Eh?" Giorga sat up straighter, pulled the pillow round in front of himself, clasped the handle of his knife. There was a good crossbow hanging on the wall, but it wasn't loaded. Supposing it had been, so what? This man looked as fast as he now looked dangerous! "This isn't . . . it isn't about land?"

"Oh, but it *is!*" Radu answered, sitting down carefully at the other end of Giorga's bed and moving fractionally, inch by inch closer. And now his voice was a hoarse throb . . . of anticipation? "Indeed, for it's about a man who *worked* that land for you, who *hunted* it for you, and *beat the bounds* with you, year in, year out, and for payment suffered the jibes and insults of a fat, greedy old man and his loathsome sons. It's about how he was murdered because he stood in the way of his daughter going to one of your sons; and it's about the girl, too, who was as good as you and your lot were bad! She was held down, Giorga, raped time and time again, then murdered because her father—by no means a brave man—had not obliged the Zirescus by letting her go as wife to Ion or Lexandru!"

"I . . . I . . . I *know* you now!" Giorga pointed with his left hand. But Radu knew that the old pig was right-handed, and saw that treacherous right hand trembling behind the pillow in Giorga's lap. And indeed all of Giorga trembling: his fat belly, his chins, the very jowls of his face. And: "You're Radu, son of Freji L-L-Lykan!" he stuttered.

"Aye, Freji's son, and Magda's brother. That same brother who was outlawed—or who outlawed himself—when he avenged his father's death and his sister's rape and murder. Except he was stopped in the hour of his vengeance . . . by *you*, Giorga, I fancy! And was it Ion and Lexandru who also tried to drown me? And the Ferenczy brothers, likewise on your orders? Ah, I know it was! But as you see, I am not drowned, and not nearly dead! And it *is* about land, or soil, after all—*this* soil, Zirescu soil, where you've rooted like a pig all your days, and where you're now destined to die a swinish death. *This* earth, which the poisons of your loathsome gases shall turn putrid even as you're lowered into it! And no one to mourn over you, Giorga, even if they would. No, for your sons will be down there with you!"

Giorga lunged; his black ironwood knife was in his hand, upraised; Radu grinned as he caught the other's fat wrist in his own taloned hand, and held it effortlessly. And his grin was the grin of a wolf as his leech poured metamorphic juices through his system, causing his teeth to scythe upward from his raw red gums as his mouth yawned wider yet!

In the space of five heartbeats Radu Lykan had changed—changed before the Old Zirescu's bulging, disbelieving eyes—into something radically different from . . . from anything he'd ever seen before! The man was gone, and a monster crouched in his place. And the *face* on that creature: the flame-eyed, salivating, grinning, panting visage of hell itself! That monstrous, gaping mouth . . . !

Giorga sucked at the suffocating air, and opened his own mouth—to cry out! But too late. Pain snatched the cry from the circle of his rubbery lips, turned it to a yelp, a gurgle, a great *whoosh!* of expelled air, as Radu twisted his arm until it snapped at the elbow, closed a hand over Giorga's hand, and slid the knife home through unprotesting layers of fat and up under bulging ribs. Oh . . . it hurt, and it did great—even fatal—damage! But not immediately. Giorga's fat protected him; the knife's tip couldn't reach his heart, not angling up from his belly like that; his left hand ceased its fluttering and reached for the knife, clasping its handle where it protruded from his gut. And he panted, "Oh!— *ah!*—oh!" as he tried to draw it out, but couldn't because of the pain.

Then, still grinning, Radu towered over him, cocked his head on one side in the inquiring manner of a great dog, and looked him right in his cringing eyes, as if he were looking into his soul. And he said, "Farewell, Giorga!"—then caught his beard and yanked it up, and without pause drove his fangs into and slicing *through* the old man's windpipe!

Giorga flopped and vibrated in Radu's grasp, until the werewolf released him and let him topple from his bed to the floor, where he got jammed in the narrow space. It was over, this part of it at least. And the Old Zirescu bled and tried to scream (but had neither the air nor the strength for it), and flopped about in his own blood, and bled some more; great steaming jets of crimson, pulsing from his gaping throat and punctured gut. Air whistling in and out of his severed windpipe, where bright red bubbles formed a livid froth, but all slowing down now as life quickly ebbed.

Until finally it really was over . . .

Outside the caravan in a mist of his own making, Radu paused for the merest moment to spit Giorga's taste from his mouth. His taste and the last trace of his blood. For despite that Radu was hungry, and his leech *ever* hungry, Giorga Zirescu's blood tasted vile to him. Yet the memory of what he had done would always remain sweet—and sweeter still when the rest of it was over and done with.

Radu had taken down Giorga's crossbow. Now he loaded it and his own weapon both, hooked the one to his belt and took the other firmly in a paw-like hand. And as the woods and the earth continued to issue his wreathing mist, he headed direct for the communal fire's dull orange glow in the center of the encampment. For he had realized his strength at last; he knew his awesome power, and that he need not fear anything in man or Nature—not yet at least.

And loping low through the mist, his senses were alive with all the sounds, scents, and sensations of the night. He was a *child* of the night! He heard the rustling in the undergrowth that tracked the hunting shrew; sensed the hooded eyes of an owl upon him; detected an almost inaudible shrilling of tiny bats, sounding clearer than ever before in his vampire-enhanced ears. And he smelled blood, of course—the blood of the Zirescus and the Ferenczys! For Giorga's blood had not been enough. But that of his sons and their friends might yet quell the fire raging in Radu's veins . . .

The moon was up again, a full and brilliant disc shining like silver in the sky! Its beam fell in a swath, undulating on Radu's ground mist and lighting his way to the fire. Passing like a wraith between the innermost caravans and carts, he was almost there. Now he could see the ruddy faces of men in a huddle about the fire, and saw that they were frowning. Their conversation reached him; they talked about—the watchdogs, the camp's wolves!

For the wolves were there, those tame dogs of creatures; their tails were down and their ears flat, and they whimpered around the feet of their human masters. Aye, and if they could talk they'd be telling of Radu's presence, too! They probably were, in their way, but the men were too stupid to know it.

Except if the blood of men had a scent, so did the blood of the Wamphyri— Radu's blood! And now the wolves around the fire smelled it. Moreover, they smelled the death which he had so recently wrought. There were three of them; they quit their slinking about the feet of the seated men and as one creature turned in Radu's direction. Their ears pointed him out in the shadow of a caravan, and now that they stood in the company of men, they felt safe to issue a series of growls and yips.

"Eh?" someone said. "Is there something there?" And indeed there was something there. Radu loped forward more surely into the fire's glow, came to a halt and straightened up. Without pause he scanned the faces in the firelight— and saw that Ion and Lexandru were there! Also the Ferenczys, and three colleagues. As scurvy a handful as he could imagine, but he hated the first four above all other men.

All jaws dropped, all eyes were on Radu, who now grinned in his fashion and growled, "This is between me and the Zirescus—those two, Ion and Lexandru, rapists and murderers!" He pointed with his crossbow. "And also the Ferenczys," he pointed again. "I've killed Giorga and now I'll kill his sons and their friends. As for the rest of you: you don't have to die if you don't want to. Enough of talk; too much, even." No longer just pointing his weapon but *aiming* it, at Lexandru, Radu squeezed the trigger.

It started as quickly as that, without any warning other than that furnished by the watchdogs. Lexandru had come to his feet as Radu spoke, and as the bolt flew to its target he held up his hands in denial. The bolt passed between them and struck him in the left breast, burying itself to the ironwood flights. "Oh?" he said in a loud voice, as if he queried the thing. "And is it—what, Radu? Not dead? Well, there's a th-thing!" Then he coughed blood, crumpled to his knees and fell on his face.

But one of the men at the fire had sufficient wits about him to shout, "*Attack!*" to the wolves. And as Radu hooked the empty crossbow to his belt and levelled the other, the wolves at once sprang toward him. The leader fastened to his weapon forearm; snarling fangs bit deep; Radu grasped the wolf's mane with his free hand, whirled in a circle, and released the disorientated animal into the sprawling fire! Twin strips of his flesh and skin went with it, torn from his forearm by its eye-teeth, but Radu scarcely felt it. For he was in action, doing what he'd dreamed of doing for so long. Except for now Ion and the Ferenczys must wait, for the other wolves were here.

One of them was in mid-air, coming head-on, forepaws outstretched and muzzle slavering. Radu couldn't miss; he shot his bolt and ducked, and the skewered wolf yelped, passed overhead, bounced once and struggled to its forelegs, then collapsed and lay still. The third skidded to a halt as Radu fixed it with a feral-eyed glare and said growlingly, "Oh? And would you die, too? Come on, then, let's get done with it. For there's room in the fire yet." But the gray one had seen more than enough of Radu and backed off whimpering.

Radu sensed trouble, retaliation; he'd spent too long on these tame wolves! Quick as thought he fell to all fours, felt a crossbow bolt fly inches overhead even as he dropped, glanced across the fire at the knot of men. The Ferenczys had already bolted. Ion Zirescu was making off between the caravans, heading for the forest. The man who had shot at Radu was now readying his weapon for a second try. The others stumbled this way and that; startled out of their wits, they scarcely comprehended what was happening.

Radu loped to the fire, stooped to snatch up a burning brand. And as the man with the crossbow nocked his bolt, Radu let fly with the firebrand, which hit him full in the face. His beard went up in fire and smoke; in another moment his head was a ball of fire! Dropping his weapon, he danced, yelped and beat at himself, and went rolling into a patch of undergrowth close by. By which time the others were all fled. But Radu had seen Ion go, and knew which direction he'd taken.

The moon came up over the trees at the edge of the clearing, and seeing it Radu went to all fours, threw back his head and howled. It seemed the most natural thing in the world, despite that the sound it made was surely one of the most terrible. For although it was the cry of a beast, the howling issued from the throat of a man! And all of his pent-up passions went into it. It told of all the pain and frustration of a tortured youth remembered and stored, and now released in a torrent of monstrous pleasure as it burst like a flood over the last of those who had caused it. It cried all his years of torment relieved, or in the process of being relieved, at least.

For Ion Zirescu and the Ferenczy brothers still lived, and the fact of their living was itself a great torment. But their deaths would be a pleasure incomparable: like a sigh in the soul of Radu Lykan—a sigh of relief!—*if* he still had a soul. Ah, and the werewolf knew what he wanted from Ion! For he'd dreamed a dream from time to time, which he now believed was more memory than dream:

Of lying facedown in the trampled earth of a clearing, and hearing voices as if from a long way away, yet coming to him clearly through a darkness shot with brilliant flashes of light but otherwise devoid of sensation except for a terrible pain at the back of his head, and a great anger seething deep in his core, and a yearning even as great as his current yearning: to tear the living, smoking hearts out of the ones who spoke these words:

"... Radu's sister—dead, and by your hands! Six of you, onto one girl! This pair of mangy corpses here, Arlek Bargosi and Kherl Fumari, and the Ferenczy brothers, Rakhi and Lagula ... and you two, of course!" (*Unmistakably Giorga's voice. And the answer*):

"Not all our fault. It was you who sent us after Freji, to do him in. Well, and there was that in Radu's eyes as told us he knew! He must have found his father out in the woods. As for the girl: that . . . was an *accident,* for she wouldn't hold still."

That one had been Ion. And Magda's death had been an "accident," because she had tried to fight them off where they'd rutted over her like beasts!

Ah, but there are beasts and there are beasts, and the rest of it wouldn't be an accident, be sure! Giorga was dead, Lexandru, too, but Ion and the Ferenczys still lived. For *now* they lived, anyway. Again Radu howled—howled his bloodlust and a vow to the goddess of the moon where she floated on high: that Magda would be avenged in a manner befitting her ordeal! In answer, it seemed the moon lit his way through the woods by silvering the madly trampled, blundering trail of Ion Zirescu . . . to where the last of that loathsome family was hiding.

Later, Radu would scarcely remember tracking him, loping through the dark woods and falling to all fours to sniff the trail of freshly crushed grass and rootlets, the vile-smelling spoor of sweat and fear. But in a little while there'd been a clearing, with a stand of trees to one side, and breaking from the woods into the clearing Radu had sensed . . . stillness! All was still; neither a sound nor any movement; not even the hoot of an owl or the furtive creep of small creatures in the grass. Why? Because they had been *startled* to stillness by the sudden crashing of a fugitive? Possibly . . .

Radu's mist had subsided by then, but the moon was still full and high and his powers were still with him. Except they were new powers and he didn't know them; he wasn't experienced in their use. But listening to the stillness—keeping absolutely still himself and straining to detect even the slightest sound—he "heard" something that wasn't a sound! Instead, it was . . . a thought! *They* were thoughts! The terrified thoughts of Ion Zirescu!

At first Radu shook his head; he knew he was imagining it, this *listening* to another's mind. But as he concentrated even harder, so the thoughts came that much clearer, so that now he must heed them. And this was what he heard:

. . . *Followed me! But how? Is he a man or a dog, to track me so unerringly? Radu Lykan, alive! Or perhaps his vengeful spirit? But a ghost that kills? And his strength! His great speed! No, this is no ghost but Radu himself. We thought him a coward like his father, but the youth who killed Kherl and Arlek that night was no coward. And now he's back. But my father, Giorga, dead? Well, so what . . . Lexandru and I would have seen to* him *before too long! Ahhh . . . !* (That last was a gasp of horror, and it signaled that Radu had been seen.)

He closed his eyes and concentrated more yet, and saw . . . through another's eyes! Through Ion's, of course! Saw himself, or his shadow, poised at the edge of the clearing, head cocked forward, ears alert as they angled this way and that. And saw—and indeed *felt*—himself go down on all fours again, and aim himself at the stand of trees. For Ion's line of sight had given him away, and the shock of his thoughts confirmed it:

. . . *He's pointing at me, coming straight for me! But I have my machete . . . !*

Oh, yes, Radu was coming. Half-upright and leaning forward, he loped toward the stand of trees. But . . . Ion had a machete? Oh, really? And deep in a clump of gorse, Radu paused to ready his crossbow—four seconds at most—before continuing in a new direction, apparently *away* from Ion. And in his head:

. . . *He'll go right by me! He hasn't seen me!* (It was a sigh of relief, almost a sob—a pitiful "sound"! But there was no pity in Radu Lykan.)

And in the corner of his eye Radu saw Ion there, crouching in the shrubbery under the trees, behind a dense patch of brambles. But not dense enough. Radu whirled, aimed, and fired; Ion uttered a cry of shock, pain, as the bolt zipped through fringing undergrowth to take him in the right forearm, spinning him until his feet tangled and he went down. His machete had flown from useless fingers. And suddenly he was a man alone, unarmed, against a monster . . .

A shadow grew out of the night's darker shadows, and as the moon slipped behind a cloud Radu Lykan was there, his eyes like yellow lamps in the darkness. And: "Up," he panted, his voice a cough, a bark, a hideous threat. "On your feet, Ion Zirescu, or die where you lie." He nocked the last of his bolts.

Sobbing, Ion got up, and stumbled backward away from Radu until he backed up against a tree. And: "Perfect!" the werewolf Radu growled, as he pointed his weapon point-blank and squeezed the trigger. The ironwood bolt shattered Ion's left collarbone and nailed him to the tree; his cry of agony cut the night like a knife, and he would have blacked out but daren't. His weight would rip the muscle of his shoulder open, or stretch and tear the ligaments there, and cripple him for life. Radu heard his thoughts and inquired, "What life?"

"Kill me, then!" Ion sobbed. "Get it done with, if that's what you want." And with a bolt in his right arm, and another through his shoulder, holding him in place, he braced himself shuddering against the tree.

Radu's voice was a low rumble as he answered, "But that's not *all* I want!"

"Wh-what?"

"You murdered my father, then raped and killed my sister. Well, Freji's paid for: Giorga paid that debt. But Magda can't ever be paid for, for she was priceless. But you and your brother, the Ferenczys and those other two pigs, you held my sister down and took her again and again. Maybe two of you at a time . . . or maybe three? I saw her body, the signs you left, your stinking froth on Magda's skin. As well she died, for I don't think she could have lived with it. Well, neither can I. And neither can you."

His last words were a snarl; he hooked a hand like a claw in the front of Ion's trousers and ripped them open. Ion was caused to jerk a little, and the bolt in his shoulder dragged against raw nerves. He almost passed out, which wouldn't do at all. Radu pushed his wolf's face close, sniffed at Ion's parts and growled, "That worthless thing was the instrument of your torture, your . . . your pleasure?" As he closed his talon-like hand on his captive, Ion could do nothing but writhe and shudder against the tree. "And you and the others, all six of you, you took turns to rape her of her innocence. Now it's my turn. Except you're not innocent."

He crushed Ion to the tree, clenched his hand like a vise, used his vast Wamphyri strength to castrate and more than castrate the other. In a split second Ion lost everything, even the lower pipes of his body, dislocated, wrenched out of place, and left dangling. He lost consciousness, too, and would go on losing blood enough that he'd never again wake up. Well, and Radu wouldn't let it go to waste, not all of it. While there was yet a pulse in his victim's neck, he sank a wolf's fangs into it to draw off the remainder of Ion's life. And drank long and deep, giving nothing of himself but taking all from the other, even the very last dregs.

Blood . . . it was what he'd needed, what his vampire leech had needed. It was the nectar of life . . . it *was* the life! And it was the drug that very nearly killed him, because he almost—but not quite—let himself drown in it. Because the sheer unbridled pleasure of it almost—but not quite—numbed him to everything else. Until, as if in a dream, he heard a startled gasp as someone cried:

"There! But look—only *look*, will you!''

Radu knew the voice: Rakhi Ferenczy, the younger of that degenerate pair. Knew the next voice, too, as that of Rakhi's brother, when Lagula answered: "I see him—and I've *got* the moon-crazed bastard!''

He surfaced from his delirium of bloodlust, straightened up from slaking his monstrous thirst, and shook his head—to clear his swimming senses and red-drenched vision both . . .

. . . And moved—but not fast enough!

Lagula's bolt burned his neck, cut a shallow groove in it before burying itself inches deep in the tree. Radu laughed, a great bark of a laugh . . . until Rakhi's bolt bit deep into his left thigh, scraped bone and jammed there, midway between knee and buttock.

Radu had fired his last bolt. He had nothing to fight back with except his fierce Wamphyri strength. He *would* have fought, certainly, if his leech had let him. But survival was uppermost in the symbiont's "mind"; its host's survival, and its own, of course.

The werewolf let himself fall to the forest's floor, went three-legged, limping through the undergrowth, but still with the sinuous, flowing motion of the Wamphyri. And this time he breathed his mist in earnest, knowing what he did, to obscure him as he fled. Not far from Ion Zirescu's dangling, ravaged body, he found the machete where it had fallen, and for a moment considered standing and fighting. But a greater wisdom (or a more sinister, insidious instinct?) forbade it. For the time being, survival was everything.

Once, near the edge of the clearing, Radu paused to look back, and saw the Ferenczys still blundering about in his mist, searching for him (but searching oh so carefully!) in the undergrowth on the fringe of the stand of trees. The fools, to have let him slip through their fingers like this! Didn't they know, didn't they realize, that he'd be back for them? Obviously not. Radu thought to remind them, and as the moon tumbled from view behind the treetops, he threw back his head and howled.

And from now on, whenever the Ferenczy brothers heard the howling of a wolf, they would automatically tremble and reach for the nearest weapons . . .

In the western foothills, well away from the camp of the Zirescus, Radu cut the flights from the bolt that transfixed his thigh and drew it out head-first. At first there was pain, but as he gritted his teeth the pain faded to a dull throb, and in another moment all that remained was an insensitive numbness, as if his thigh were asleep.

There were medicinal leaves Radu knew of that would help in the healing, but he didn't bother with them. Something told him they weren't necessary. It was his leech, already at work on him with its vastly superior metamorphic processes.

Radu was a changeling creature now, but in the main his mind remained the mind of a man, and in his sleep he was visited by nightmares. He dreamed of the Thing that he'd become, and woke up cold and shivering, unwilling to accept the fact that he was no longer entirely human. His vampire, of course, worked on him to subdue all such fears and regrets. Dimly, he was aware of its influence: the small urging voice of some subconscious "conscience" that nagged or advised him; no voice at all, but in fact chemical agents and catalysts in his blood and his brain, changing the way he thought. Eventually he succumbed to suggestion, stopped fearing and lost interest in it; finally he accepted that he was what he was—without considering that he was what his leech wanted him to be.

When the moon was down or on the wane, he was a man—a wolfish-looking man, by all means—but a man. When the moon was up and full, then it was hard to remain a man. But at all times he was Wamphyri, even though he still didn't understand or recognize his condition . . .

He dwelled for some years between the foothills and the barrier mountains, sleeping in deep caves or crevices by day, and wandering gradually eastwards by night. And despite that his work wasn't finished in the camps of the Szgany Zirescu—by now the Szgany Ferenczy—and that it never would be while Rakhi and Lagula lived, still he put distance between. He knew that to return now would mean certain death; the entire tribe would be watching out for him, doubtless with orders to shoot on sight. And in any case he needed time to explore his amazing powers: his mentalism, metamorphism, and the source of his boundless, surging energy. As for the wound in his thigh: that had healed in a night and a day; there was scarcely a scar to show for it.

Adept at avoiding the encampments or settlements of men, he continued to do so; alas that they couldn't avoid him. But the farther east Radu journeyed, the more surely he was aware of a change. Not in *him*self this time, but in the Szgany, in Sunside's people *them*selves.

Thus far, avoiding men, he had also avoided their challenge, or rather the challenge of his bloodlust; he had slaked his thirst (and that of his parasite) on the raw red flesh of creatures of the wild. In this respect, and without even knowing it, Radu had pitted himself *against* his leech! But as well as tenacity, the vampire has all the patience of centuries of life as yet unlived. With a vampire's longevity, it's not too hard to be patient.

And meanwhile: Radu was allowed to believe that the pleasure he'd derived from slaughtering Ion Zirescu and drinking his blood had lain in the killing, while in fact it had lain in the drinking! Revenge? That had been *his* motive, but necessity had been his leech's. Well, Radu would learn in time. And meanwhile his vampire must be satisfied with the blood of beasts. Except, and as has been noted, there are beasts and there are beasts.

And indeed *great* beasts had come among the Szgany of Sunside, which was the reason for the changes that Radu had noted in them. For now during the long hours of daylight, there were grim-faced, determined men on the flanks of the barrier mountains, hunters who pursued and butchered . . . men! Aye, and it *was* butchery. For with his own eyes, Radu was witness to it.

It happened at a time perhaps two years and nine months (one hundred and thirty-five or thirty-six sunups) after he'd taken his revenge on the Zirescus in the westernmost woods . . .

It was the twilight before the true dawn, and the tumbling moon was already reduced to a pale stain of a disc high in the amethyst sky over Sunside. Soon the furnace sun would be up, but it wouldn't find Radu wanting. For by now his photophobia was full fledged; he knew that direct undiluted sunlight would kill him, even if he still didn't understand the reason.

But no sooner was he settled in the back of a shallow cave, where a single stratum of soft rock had weathered out from the face of the cliff, than he heard a panting and scrabbling from beyond the rim of his shelter. It was a man in full flight, exhausted from his exertions and hoarse from the terror of pursuit. Dried up and beginning to blister even in the first faint rays from the southern horizon, he came stumbling, croaking his relief, into Radu's cave.

Hidden in a dark corner, Radu shielded the luminous yellow glare of his eyes and waited until the man—a ragged-looking Sunsider, possibly a loner— had himself under partial control at least. And when the other's panting had slowed and his whimpering ceased, then, speaking softly, Radu asked: "Who pursues you, and why?"

At the first word the other had jumped a foot, gasped out loud, spun about where he sat upon the dusty floor. "What?" he croaked. "Who?" And then he saw Radu's eyes, and the dark shape of a man sprawled on a bed of heather in the back of the cave. Radu's crossbow was loaded; aiming it at the man, he eased himself erect—or partly erect, because of the low ceiling—and went to where the newcomer cringed against the wall of the cave. The man seemed speechless; his throat throbbed and his Adam's apple went up and down, but he merely gurgled. And finally he pointed at Radu's face, at his eyes. .

"Eh?" Radu growled, rapidly losing his patience. He wanted to know what was going on here. If this man was a fugitive, he wanted to know why, from what cause. "Are you deaf or daft, or both? I asked why are you running?"

"Y-*you*, ask that?" Finally the other had found his voice.

And perhaps Radu understood at that. He narrowed his feral eyes, sniffed his suspicion. "Are you a Ferenczy, is that it? Have you heard about me and what I've done, and what I'll do!" He pointed his crossbow direct at the other's throat. But even in the act of speaking the words, he knew he was mistaken. The Ferenczys had become an obsession with him, that was all.

"A F-Ferenczy?" The fugitive frowned. "No, I'm a Romani—Bela Romani, of the Szgany Mirlu. Or I was . . ." And now the sob was back in his voice.

"Are you an outcast then? What, a leper?" The Zirescus had used to banish anyone even suspected of leprosy. And they'd put a bolt through him and burn his body if he tried to return!

"Leprosy?" The other looked at Radu through haggard, red-rimmed eyes. "Ah, no. Worse than that!"

Radu backed off a pace. What? Could anything be worse than leprosy? "Explain!" he barked.

"Who . . . *what* are you?" Now it was Bela Romani's turn to be curious. "A loner? A wild man of the mountains? Where have you been that you don't . . . don't *know* of these things?"

"Of what things?" Radu was exasperated. "Enough of riddles! Can't you explain yourself?"

The other crouched back away from him. "I'm speaking of . . . of the Wamphyri!" But the *way* he spoke that last word, or name!

"Wamphyri?" Radu repeated him, and frowned. "Who are they?"

The other licked his lips and shook his head. "But you . . . your eyes! Are you saying that you're not . . . not one of them?"

And for the first time Radu pondered it. He was more than a mere man, for sure. But Wamphyri? "Tell me about them," he gave a nod of his huge gray wolfish head. And Bela Romani told him:

It had started in the east, beyond the great pass into Starside and the barren boulder plains. There were rearing stacks out on those plains, vast carved buttes, some a kilometer high, either weathered from the mountains over countless millennia or thrust up from below by some colossal, forgotten prehistoric upheaval. The boulder plains were empty of life, cold and dead, for which reason men never went there.

Or at least, that was how it had used to be; neither the Szgany nor any other beings had dwelled there, except leathery trog unmen in caverns under the barrier mountains. But for some years now there'd been rumors of lights in those rearing rock castles, and gray smoke issuing from fissure chimneys, and flying things that soared in the winds off the northern Icelands, around the summits of those mighty aeries of . . . of what?

And a hundred sunups ago the first of *Them* had come raiding on the Szgany camps. They came in search of provisions for their manses in the towering stacks, thrall recruits for their aeries, and fodder for their beasts. But they themselves, the Wamphyri, were the greatest beasts of all: blood-beasts out of Starside!

Huge men all, the Wamphyri looked human but were *in*human. Their strength was unbelievable! They took strong Szgany youths for their lieutenants and thralls, and beautiful girls as their odalisques. Chiefest among them was One whose nature had rapidly become a byword for everything evil: Shaitan the Unborn! He was beautiful as a golden man, but deep and dark as the swamps that spawned him. And his lust was insatiable.

At first Shaitan had restricted his raids to regions east of the great pass, and had set up tribes of Szgany supplicants there. But as other monstrous Lords had ascended to their aeries, and the needs of the Wamphyri had doubled and redoubled, so the raids had spilled over from the eastern lands into Zestos, Lidesci, Tireni, and Mirlu territories west of the pass, and sometimes to points even further west. But the Szgany Zestos, the Lidescis, Tirenis, Mirlus, were not supplicants; they fought back! And now during the daylight hours they traveled— they had *become* Travelers—as a matter of survival, and not merely to beat the bounds. But during the nights:

"We hid in deep caves or in the woods, with never a fire for comfort or light," Bela continued. "But still the Wamphyri would find us. Last night—following immediately on the evening twilight—they found us again! There was some fighting, but what can men do against *Them*? The Szgany Mirlu scattered . . . I ran, too, into the woods! But I was caught anyway.

"Hengor 'the Gust' Hagi, a blood-soaked barrel of a man, got me, clubbed me unconscious, drank blood from my veins and infected me with his poisons. When I came to in the twilight before the dawn, I remembered his instructions as in a dream: that I must go to him in Starside, and be his thrall in Hengstack. *Never!* I would return to my wife and children, and be a Mirlu! Oh, really? *Hah!*

"I was—I *am*—a vampire creature, in thrall to Hengor the Gust! The sun is my mortal enemy, the night my only friend. As the poisons take hold, so my condition will worsen. I tried to return to the Mirlus; they saw the mark of Hengor's bite on my neck; now if they find me—they'll kill me! But you, your looks," Bela turned imploringly to Radu. "We are the same, I'm sure. Except . . . you seem to have learned to live with it!"

Radu shook his head. "I don't know. But one thing is certain: I won't die with it! While you were talking, I was listening, but not as you listen. And you're right: Mirlu hunters are coming. And this cave . . . is mine. I was here first."

Bela's eyes went wild in a moment. Drawing his lips back from snarling needle teeth, he made to spring at Radu—

—Who simply caught him up in one hand, dragged him to the mouth of the cave and tossed him out!

The entrance was fringed with a little undergrowth and a few trees, and the sunlight didn't strike at Bela immediately. He tried to stay in the shade, searching for a way up the cliff. There was a goat track; he might even make it! He scrambled up above the tree level, and so came into view of the men who had followed him up through the scree jumbles of the foothills.

Crossbows twanged and bolts buzzed like angry wasps. Radu saw it all: the way the fugitive was swatted like a fly against the cliff, his feet sliding on the narrow track, his back arching like a bow, as he was struck time and time again. His body crumpling, then toppling, and turning lazily end over end, and slamming down hard into the sharp rubble and scree at the foot of the cliffs.

Anyone would think that would be enough, that Bela's pursuers would be satisfied; apparently they weren't. They took his body, drove a stake through his heart and cut off his head, and built a fire to burn him to ashes! Which apparently *was* enough. It would have to be, for there was nothing left of him. It took a while but finally the men left, and Radu crept back into his cave to sleep in safety from the sun.

Getting to sleep took a while, too, for there was a great deal on Radu's mind. Yet somehow, while he slept, a good many problems were resolved. And it might even be said that he resolved some of them himself . . .

In the twilight before the true night Radu awakened, felt the lure of the fading moon and left his cave to worship a while. And as his eerie, ululant howling echoed up into the mountain heights and down into Sunside, he knew. Knew finally and for certain that he *was* Wamphyri! An eater of men, aye, a Great Vampire. But more than this: he was a werewolf! A man half-human, half-wolf, with the brain of the one and all the speed and cunning and killer instinct of the other. And if changeling men—mere men!—could make it on Starside, where the sun never shone, and be Lords and masters of the great aeries there, then what of Radu? And so, turning his back on Sunside (for now, at least), he climbed for the peaks and headed for Starside and the destiny that waited for him there.

And there was such a monstrous joy in Radu—the joy of darkling knowl-edge, the hideous *anticipation* of living off the life-blood of others—that he could scarcely contain it. For Bela Romani had had it quite wrong, and Radu wasn't like him at all. Oh, the same fever was in his blood, certainly, but where Bela had been a mere thrall infected with the disease of vampirism, Radu *was* that disease! By virtue of his parasite he *was* Lord Radu Lykan! And he knew it.

For welling up from deep within his werewolf body and vampire heart, it was as if he heard the first discordant notes of a strange, savage, and wonderful song. And *how* that silent song of blood and eternity thrilled him to his core, when at last he came padding, panting through a high mountain pass, and fi-nally gazed down on Starside.

Starside, aye. And faint with distance yet darkly foreboding against a back-drop of writhing northern auroras, there in the cold blue light of the Northstar . . . the mist-wreathed stacks of the vampire Lords! But however awesomely bleak, the scene wasn't weird or cold to Radu. Indeed it felt . . . familiar? No, much more than that: it felt like home!

And as he turned his face to the sky and vanishing moon, and gave voice from a throbbing throat, it seemed to Radu that even his howling carried a new note and was more surely a song, albeit a song that was awesome and terrible:

Wamphyri! *Wamphyyyyri . . . !*

EXILED—TO EARTH!

GOING DOWN FROM THE HEIGHTS OF THE BARRIER MOUNTAINS INTO STARSIDE, Radu came upon a ragged handful of pitiful "survivors" of last night's vampire raid: men of the Mirlus, like Bela Romani, and of the Szgany Tireni and Szgany Zestos. He told them who he was and what he intended to do: lay claim to an aerie among the several as yet vacant stacks, and people it with thralls of his own. They were reluctant to join him; they "belonged" to Hengor "the Gust" Hagi, or Lord Lankari, or the Drakul brothers, or—Lord Lagula Ferenczy!?

What? Lagula, a Lord of the Wamphyri? But . . . the *same* Lagula? Well, Radu must wait and see. But meanwhile he offered the vampirized group a choice: he would guarantee them his personal "protection," swear them to his service, and proceed with them across the boulder plains . . . or they could die the true death right here in these barren foothills, with crossbow bolts skewering their poor decapitated bodies. And without more ado they went with Radu.

Their presence was observed; giant Desmodus bats from the various aeries reported their progress; they were in any event "poor quality" thralls who had not warranted transportation on the backs or in the belly pouches of their masters' flyers. But when they headed for a middling, unoccupied stack in the outer circle of great upthrusting aeries, *that* attracted rather more attention. Too late to do anything about it, however, for Radu and his followers had taken all of the long Starside night to come across the mountains and boulder plains, and already the sun was burning on the higher ramparts of the greater stacks.

This was the time when the Lords slept, normally in north-facing rooms on the permanently dark sides of their aeries. It was *not* a time when they would launch out on their flyers simply to investigate the odd behavior of a handful of "branded" thralls! Perhaps the thralls themselves were merely being cautious and taking shelter from the sunlight. All well and good; this was a sign of some intelligence among them at least! Come sundown they'd doubtless proceed to the stacks of their rightful Lords, who had recruited them in Sunside.

But they didn't. Radu, less fearful of the sun than most vampire Lords, had put his men to work at once. They had inhabited a cave near the foot of the stack, fortified its entrance, found bolthole passageways onto other levels and down onto the boulder plains, and generally made themselves as "comfortable" as possible. Cold comfort, true, but Radu was still learning the way of things.

And a lot more to learn yet, be sure . . .

Sundown, and Lord Egon Drakul sent a thrall and flyer to see what was what. He had beasts to feed and two of these errant thralls were his, destined for the provisioning of Drakstack. The thrall landed his mount at the foot of the suspect aerie, went striding into the scree jumbles, and disappeared. And in a little while, a strange, long-haired figure was seen seated awkwardly astride the flyer, putting it through its paces over the knobby dome of the new aerie! But what was this? Some raw recruit fresh out of Sunside, who yet fancied himself a Lord?

Klaus Lankari sent two thralls to investigate. These were bold, burgeoning lads who aspired to lieutenants . . . the result was the same. By now Shaitan the Unborn himself was interested; he watched and "listened" keenly from afar, as Hengor Hagi flew out with his chief lieutenant from Hengstack. Ah, but the Gust was careful to remain airborne as his man Emil landed in soft, sliding scree at the base of Radu's aerie, and continued afoot to put matters right. But shortly:

My Lord? Emil Hagisman sent, with a slight but patently nervous tremor in his Gust-oriented, feeble mental probe.

Aye? The Gust circled on a flyer that was all muscle and manta wing, to take his great weight. *What's the word?*

My Lord, a man is with the recruits who says he is Wamphyri. In fact he has the looks, and I smell it on him. This one has a mature leech!

Oh, really? Swamp-born, was he? With no egg-sire? So he's Wamphyri, so what? He hasn't ascended; we haven't accepted him. Not yet, anyway. Nor are we likely to, since he's a thief! The recruits you speak of belong to me, to the Ferenczys, to Klaus Lankari and the Drakuls. What, is he herding them for us—if so, well, that's damned kind of him! But it's another matter if he intends to keep them for himself.

But now a different "voice" joined in, that of Radu. *Hengor, I can do many things for myself, including speak! I don't need an interpreter. I have a leech; I'm "swamp-born," aye, if that's the term, but that was some time ago. Oh, I know: this stack I've chosen for myself isn't nearly as grand as some of your soaring aeries, but it's a start and I will ascend! If I need your recognition, then I'll wait for it. If it's not forthcoming . . . well, I'm here anyway! Meanwhile, what's mine is mine. Nor am I a thief in respect of these thralls: a middling lot at best! I need them for now, that's all. But in due time I'll gladly repay whatever and whoever I owe, with interest.*

Oh, indeed? The Gust sent back. *So you take and then say you've merely borrowed, eh? And the flyers you've commandeered, are those yours, too?*

For now, until I've learned the way of making my own. And that includes this one of yours . . . but I'll give you your man Emil back. He's loyal to a fault, and therefore useless to me.

Really? Hengor couldn't make up his mind to roar his rage or laugh out loud! But he found himself liking this one—his audacity, anyway—without that he'd even met him as yet. *And if I sent another flyer for Emil Hagisman, will you keep that, too?*

(A mental shrug, and): *He can fly or he can walk. That's your problem.*

Do you know, said Hengor, beginning to enjoy this now, in the perverse fashion of the Wamphyri, *but without ever meeting you in the flesh, already I like your colors. And I fancy I'll like them even more—when I use them to decorate the walls of my great hall in Hengstack!*

Have I slighted you? (Radu's voice showed mild surprise—feigned, of course.) *Then come down and let's settle it.*

Well, bugger me backwards! the other burst out, but he was no longer amused. *A challenge, is it? Listen, upstart: between the Ferenczys, Drakuls, Klaus Lankari and myself, we have four hundred men, thirty-two flyers and seven fighting beasts! How do you think you and your handful of fools would fare against those odds, eh?*

Badly, Radu answered, *which is why I've taken the time to parley.*

But here yet another mental voice in Starside's aether, a voice as powerful and authoritative as it was sinister, interrupted and came between the two; the voice of Lord Shaitan the Unborn: the devil himself!

What's all this about a swamp-born Lord, Hengor Hagi? Do you frown on a man because he had no egg-sire? Is a spore any less than an egg or a leech? Now, let's face it: whether a vampire is born of a woman, or changed by a spore or a leech, or by a bite, we're all of the one source, the one origin, which is the swamp. It's not the route *we take, which is a decision of fate, but the* getting *here that counts. Well, so this one has got here . . .*

Hengor seemed more than a little surprised. *What, and do you accept him, Lord Shaitan? On his word alone? Why, we don't know what we have here! But a thief and a loudmouth upstart—we know these things for sure!*

Oh? (Now Shaitan's mental voice was a sneer.) *But aren't we all thieves? Don't we all steal, out of Sunside? As for his braggart's mouth: is it any bigger than your own? Or mine? Or anyone's? Nor is his status suspect: we most certainly* do *know what we have here: a Lord of the Wamphyri, and one to watch out for, it's obvious! But if you disagree, take a look at the evidence. He plays a decent word-game—better than you, Hengor, for it was you who lost your temper! Also, your own man says he has a leech; neither spore, egg, nor mark on his neck but a mature leech! And he has made his way into Starside to occupy his own aerie; oh, a hovel of a place, granted . . . as yet! So there you have it: he* must *be a Lord. Moreover, he has mentalism, which many of our colleagues lack, or possess to a lesser degree. But this one's mentalism is a power; I felt it!*

Shaitan grew thoughtfully quiet, perhaps inviting comment, and the telepathic aether came alive in a moment:

Klaus Lankari now speaks, said a wooden, almost mechanical, yet somehow doom-fraught voice. *What's to be done? Something must be done, for this newcomer appears to have taken a thrall of mine, which I recruited in Sunside.* Klaus was an ex-loner, not much known for quick-thinking. But he *was* a great and monstrous destroyer of life and drinker of blood.

He has men of ours, too, the Drakuls spoke up, in voices that hissed their telepathic venom. *Is he to simply keep them, and get away with it? We say let's take them back, right now, and him, too! So he has a leech—so what?*

All the better, in fact, said the Gust. *For there's nothing quite like the juice of another vampire—especially his leech! And since I'm closest, I lay claim to it!*

And finally Radu's turn again. *What? Don't the Ferenczys have anything to say? Don't they want their peck at me, too? If so, well fine, for I certainly want my peck at them!* There, it was out in the open, his hatred—the blood feud—between him and the Ferenczys. And better to do it this way, bold and swaggering, as befitted the image Radu would convey. For there was that in their voices (and in his own dark heart) that told him it *was* their way, the way of the Wamphyri. They seemed to take pleasure in words: perverse, convoluted argument and contradictions. Not so strange, really; why, they were themselves contradictions—of Nature!

But so was Radu, and just as devious as the worst of them. He had flyers now and could ride them in a fashion; if he were attacked in force he could flee to the barrier mountains, find a place to hide and consider his position. And he would take a handful of thralls with him, and so retain at least the nucleus of an aerie. Thus his braggadocio wasn't all it might seem. He wasn't about to stand and fight a veritable horde of Wamphyri Lords and their followers, but he *was* ready for flight at a moment's notice!

As it happened, the way he'd acted was the best thing he could have done, said, thought. Shaitan the Unborn was fascinated, intrigued; it set his own more than devious mind working overtime. What, some bad blood between this one and the Ferenczys? The brothers were fairly recent among the Wamphyri, true, but already they posed a threat; they were like stormclouds on Shaitan's horizon, roiling and issuing stabs of lightning, and inevitably heading his way.

For one thing there were two of them, and as a team they were closer far than the Drakuls. Shaitan remembered how they had ascended:

Two years ago Lord Petre Stakis had taken a small party of lieutenants, thralls, and an aerial warrior west along the spine of the barrier mountains and down into previously unexplored regions of Sunside. Unexplored, aye . . . Odd, then, that he should receive such a warm welcome! But such appeared to be the case. For it seemed that the Szgany of those western parts had been ready, waiting and prepared for just such an invasion—or for something in the nature of an invasion, at least! The Ferenczy brothers had been members (indeed, they'd been the recently elected leaders) of the same tribe, formerly the Szgany Zirescu. And that night . . . well, Lord Stakis had been unfortunate, to say the least.

His warrior had developed a temporary fault, which caused it to land badly in the mountain peaks. Leaving two of his lieutenants to see what could be done, Stakis had gone on with his reduced force, homed in on the smoke of a Szgany campfire, and landed in the lower foothills. On foot and engaged by a ferocious fighting force under Rakhi and Lagula, Stakis had been shot once through the eye and twice through the heart. His leech had reckoned he was done for, and made ready to exit his body; the Ferenczys had been on hand and would make perfect hosts.

But even in his death throes, still Stakis was a force to be reckoned with. Grabbing Rakhi when he drew close to inspect his body, Stakis savaged him, transfusing essence of his blood into Rakhi's system. Lagula, seeing his brother grappling for his life with a "dead" man, set about Stakis with a machete and decapitated him—and likewise fatally injured his leech, which at that very moment was attempting to make an exit through its host's throat! Dying, the leech issued an egg which transferred to Lagula. Thus Lagula was Wamphyri, and his brother a vampire in the making. Two birds with one stone, as it were!

So much Lord Shaitan had had from a spy of his among Stakis's thralls. The rest of the story—how the Ferenczys had holed-up in the dark woods, slept the Sleep of Change, and the next night set about "recruiting" as many of the former Zirescus as they could find; and how they'd then made their way back to Starside in a body—was unimportant. The rules of the game were as simple as Shaitan himself had made them: it wasn't the route men took but the getting there that counted.

Well, they had got here, since when they'd made their presence felt . . . almost as a thorn in Shaitan's side! He was sure they worked against him, or would if given the opportunity. He was glad that they had no mentalism to speak of, which was the reason of course that they hadn't been privy to what was going on here. And now the coming of this one, and bad blood between them, or so it would appear. All in all an interesting situation, and something to be fostered. For if the newcomer and the Ferenczys were at each other's throats, they wouldn't have the time to be at Shaitan's. Which was why he now proposed a solution to the problem posed by Radu:

Hear me out, he said. *Let's give this one the benefit of the doubt. He says he'll repay your losses. Very well, and if he forgets his promise, time enough then to sort matters out, and take back—and take* all—*of what he's accrued. Except . . . we cannot continue to think of him as he. Among the Wamphyri, I am the only* He, *the first and only Lord of Lords. You, stranger, do you accept that? If so, tell us your name, and how you come to be here.*

And Radu answered: *My only desire is to be accepted among my peers. Since you appear to be the greatest of them, be sure I'll agree to anything you propose—on the understanding that you leave me the means to live and prosper, of course! My name and status: I'm Lord Radu Lykan, who fused with a leech in the swamplands far to the west.*

All of which seems only right and reasonable to me, the unseen Shaitan answered, eager to be done with the preliminaries. *Very well, then we will trust you—but it's a trust you must repay in kind. If I were to offer you audience in Shaitanstack, would you attend me, come up to my manse and enter of your own free will?*

Previously, there had been a subdued but very real background "babble" in the psychic aether; now, as Shaitan made his invitation, this faded to an almost electric air of expectancy, a *hush* as of held breath. And Radu sensed that the question of free will was of vast importance to the Lords—as indeed, for some ill-defined reason, it was to him. In effect, Lord Shaitan had offered him the ultimate test (or ultimate challenge?), and if nothing else, Radu's answer would decide his suitability one way or the other. Which was why he said:

My Lord, merely tell me the hour of my audience, guarantee my safe access and egress, and give me a route . . . ?

And: *A lot of "merelys"!* Shaitan answered. *But . . . so be it.* And so it would be . . .

The time was set: three hours before dawn. That was Shaitan's choice, of course, and a good one for him. That close to sunup, he could be sure that the affair wouldn't be a long one, therefore that it wouldn't get too heated. For of course this was to be more than any mere audience: it would be in its way a reception for the newly ascended Lord Lykan. While Shaitan had failed to mention it to Radu, the other principal Lords—and at least two of the Ladies—would also be there. Indeed they would demand invitations, ostensibly as a matter of protocol, but mainly to ensure that no deal would be struck between Shaitan and the stranger without their knowledge. With the Wamphyri, suspicion was a way of life . . . not to mention a way of undeath and true death.

Radu still didn't know too much about the Wamphyri. Since Hengor seemed reluctant to send down another flyer for his lieutenant, Radu used the long night hours to question Emil Hagisman and familiarize himself with vampire codes and customs. And oddly (or perhaps not) he approved almost everything he learned of them; for after all he was Wamphyri, too! But in fact their nature was much as he'd expected it to be—as he was or would be himself in the fullness of time.

They were proud, vain, lusty, greedy and devious, and they were bestial beyond the beasts, cruel beyond human cruelty, and bloody beyond the deepest gutters and vats of the worst possible charnel house. Their conceit and various vanities were perhaps their weirdest aspect. Every one of them considered him or herself "handsome" or "beautiful" to a fault—except they had no faults, not to mention, and certainly none of their own making! Any shortcomings were blamed on their "worthless" eggs or leeches, while every triumph however small was as a direct result of their own efforts. It was an utter contradiction of the so-called "free-will code" that governed their every interaction with and treatment of their contemporaries, thralls, beasts and victims. Since the Wamphyri *themselves* enjoyed no free will as such, the ideology or concepts of freedom and self-determination in others was paramount. If lesser men controlled their own destinies, then surely the mighty vampire Lords controlled theirs? Why, of course they did . . . !

The Wamphyri were bloodbeasts. The blood was the life, and the life was or could be eternal as far as was known. Youth and blood went hand in hand; if a Lord wished it, he could keep his "looks," hold back the years and retain his sexual potency forever. Lesser men could—indeed *must*—shrivel under his bite and die the true death if nothing of him got into them, or rise up again undead and renewed, vampirized and enthralled by their Lord's essence; while he would go on unchanged, except he would be stronger (made stronger by their loss), and so continuously evolving through his victims' devolution, always.

And people, the Szgany of Sunside, and their produce . . . were for using. They were no more than very temporary vassals (or vessels?), from which all the good things of life including life itself might be taken wholesale as by right, or gradually siphoned off, as was more frequently the case. And the Wamphyri could do no wrong, not in their own red and rapacious eyes, for they were mainly without conscience! Perhaps the first handful of changeling Lords—with the exception of Shaitan—wondered about it from time to time: how they who *had been* Szgany could now live like parasites off their former kith and kin, and put them through such travails of terror. *Perhaps* they pondered it . . . but infrequently. For while their own parasites held sway, the host bodies would be and do as their leeches willed it . . .

* * *

Next, Radu learned about the individual Lords and Ladies:

About Shaitan the Unborn, so called because he had neither father nor mother (not that he remembered), but seemed to have bred himself out of the vampire swamps! . . . And why not, since he was the original vampire Lord? No such creature before him, and none since except he made them or made those who made them, or they had followed him out of the spore-laden western swamps. He alleged that he was the victim of some Great Expulsion, but from where or when he knew not; his persecutors had robbed him of all memory of previous existence! But he believed that his "crime" had been his pride and awesome beauty: he had dared to be more beautiful than the masters of that unremembered place, which to them was unforgivable.

And in fact Shaitan was "beautiful," as handsome a Lord of Vampires as could be imagined. "Judge for yourself," Emil Hagisman told Radu, "when you go up to see him. Why, Shaitan is so good-looking you just know he has to be the worst! He makes no pretense of it but calls it the 'perfection of evil': when the external or visible image reaches a peak such as his, then the rot must commence invisibly from within. And Lord Shaitan has been rotting since his very first moment of being!"

Shaitan was the overlord here, the uncrowned King of these beings. But among his closest contemporaries ("peers" he would never allow) it was generally suspected that just such a crown, and a throne, were his ambition. Therefore, because he was so powerful, his allies were few. Perhaps that was why he seemed so eager to accept Radu . . . as a future ally? But in any case, Lord Lykan would do well to watch his step in Shaitanstack.

As for the rest of the Wamphyri: Radu paid some attention to what Emil Hagisman told him—especially with regard to the Ferenczys—but their descriptions, habits and origins, could only come as something of an anticlimax after Shaitan himself.

There was Hengor, called the Gust for his girth, thunderous outbursts, and bellowing laughter. Not that there was very much of "merriment" in him; his angers were frequently as violent as his "mirth," while his vampire appetite— for anything unholy—matched the size of his belly. Hengor was not a true Hagi; he took his surname from the Szgany Hagi, the first Sunside tribe visited by Shaitan the Unborn during his journey of discovery from the western swamps into Starside. Among the unsuspecting Hagis, the Lord of Vampires had seduced a girl, who later converted Hengor among others before the tribe's leader, Heinar Hagi, put her down. Hengor had dwelled in Starside only a year less than Shaitan himself; his aerie rivalled Shaitanstack in its colossal if morbid grandeur. And meanwhile, the Szgany Hagi . . . were probably no more.

Klaus Lankari was a mountain man, a loner and dullard who had thought to explore the swamps . . . only to return from them something other than a man. Less "scrupulous" than Shaitan and the others, most of his thralls were trogs recruited from caverns under the barrier mountains. He kept trog odalisques, too, and was pleased to admit that during his years in the wild he had shagged far worse than these.

As for Thereza "Three-Eyes" Lugosi: she would be a gross mistake in any world! Born a freak, as a Sunsider child she'd been fortunate to escape with her life. The Szgany had enough to do in those days of restructuring without the extra burden of caring for monstrous children. But her parents had pleaded her case; however grudgingly, they had been granted the right to care for her; fearing for her safety anyway, they'd become loners in Sunside's foothills and mountain passes. The source of her eventual vampiric contamination was unknown except to Thereza herself, but that her doting parents had paid in full for letting their deformed ogre of a child grow to full maturity was scarcely a matter for conjecture: she kept their teeth and finger bones on a gold chain around her neck!

Thereza's deformities were several. One shoulder appeared to be missing entirely; she held the good one high, which gave her the appearance of a hunchback. Her left arm was of normal length, but the right dangled to her knees. Her breasts were dissimilar flaccid dugs, and all of her skin was mottled with purplish blotches and birthmarks.

But her third eye was the worst of her blemishes. She'd been born with an extra orbit in the back of her skull, and a rudimentary eye skinned over in its socket. Since her change, Thereza had developed this abnormality into an actual optical receptor, an eye which gazed out lidlessly—if not vacantly—from the spot where she kept her hair shorn. Which was perhaps a measure of her *real* monstrousness: that with her metamorphism, while she scarcely required to remain ugly at all but might easily remodel herself, she *preferred* it that way! As to the eye: she declared that of all the Wamphyri, she alone possessed the means of watching her back at all times . . .

Then there was the Lady Rusha Basti, by all accounts gorgeous as a peach! Except, by whose account? To Emil Hagisman's knowledge no one had ever seen her entirely . . . what, exposed? Not even her occasional lovers! Rusha's hair was red as flame and longer than her ample body, and she wore it in several sensuous designs, strategically bunched, or shaped with clasps to cover or expose her various parts according to her mood. Sometimes she would leave a breast bare, now and then her back and buttocks, or her long and alluring legs . . . but *never* her face. Perhaps she was a hag after all; rumor had it that she detested her eyes—which were red as her hair, of course—and her nose, which had a flange and was convolute beyond her ability to mask it with vampire metamorphism. A rarity, Rusha actually admitted to these small flaws—or rather, she would *not* admit to them, and so must keep them covered. With luck, Radu might find himself "on a good thing" with the Lady Rusha Basti. With the exception of Lord Shaitan the Unborn, who preferred absolute control over his odalisques, and Hengor Hagi, because he had the bulk of a bull shad and Rusha would not suffer the necessary bruising of such an affaire, she'd had all the Lords worth mentioning as lovers. Indeed, she loved them and left them as easily as snapping her fingers!

But on the other hand . . . Rusha was not so easy as might at first be reckoned. Stolen out of Starside just four or five years ago, she had ascended in very short order. And the young Lord who had taken her . . . well, where was he? She had his egg, be sure, but did she also have his head? According to Rusha he had died of some wasting disease in her loving embrace. And if so, then he'd probably expired happy—but *expired*, definitely! Emil Hagisman had heard of certain female spiders, who . . . but he'd made his point, and Radu assured him he need say no more.

Then there were the Drakuls, Karl and Egon. They had been among the first-established in Starside. The younger bloodsons of a loner family vampirized in the swamps, they'd been obliged to care for themselves almost from infancy. For the Drakul family had dwelled in the mountains, where as long as they stayed Starside of the peaks they'd been able to eke out something of an existence.

But allegedly, in those days there had been dog-Lords in the hills—men much like Radu, but with a great deal more of the wolf in them and far less of intelligence—and these and the Drakuls had feuded. One night, hounded by these wolflings, the man, his wife, and one older son had been driven over into Sunside in the twilight hours before the dawn. Unable to find shelter, they'd perished in the blast from the rising sun. But the infant brothers—twins, which were not uncommon among the Szgany—had been left behind and raised half by the wild dog-Lords, half by a pack of common gray brothers.

When they were old enough (and they were only youths even now, perhaps seventeen or eighteen years old, but precocious far beyond their years), then they had come down into Starside to build an aerie among the menhirs of the Wamphyri. Demoniac fighters, both of them were viciously territorial, even more so than the Wamphyri in general. Perhaps it was only natural, for after all their mountain-dwelling parents had had nothing. Currently the brothers occupied Drakstack, which Egon had claimed as his own; wherefore his twin was already at work on nearby Karlscar. Both of these stacks would make tremendous aeries, which together might house vampire armies to rival anything of Shaitan's making. Shaitan, however, was aware of Drakul rapaciousness; needless to state, the brothers were not his favorites among the lesser Lords. Nor were they anyone's, for even by Wamphyri standards their ways were dark . . .

And finally the Gust's lieutenant went on to tell Radu of Turgo Zolte, Shaitan's so-called "son." But discovered by Shaitan in an act of black treachery, Turgo had been thrown out of his "father's manse" onto the boulder plains, to exist as best as possible in the scree and the rubble and the dust. It was said he dwelled now in Sunside, sleeping out his days in deep caves where the sun couldn't find him, and constantly on the run from the Szgany. If so, then he was fortunate indeed—and far more so than his co-conspirators. One of these had been tossed into the Starside Gate, and so banished to unknown hells; the other lay undead in a deep grave on the boulder plains, slowly stiffening to a stone among stones . . .

As for the lesser Lords and Ladies: they were diverse as all of the aforementioned, but Emil Hagisman would gladly say on if Radu wished it. He didn't, for in the newfound conceit or self-assurance of his own strengths and talents, he wasn't much interested in the lesser personages. Certain things, however, continued to puzzle him; not least how for so long he'd been ignorant of the Wamphyri's presence here.

"The Lords lived on trogs for long and long," his informant told him. "Until their stacks were established. And it's only recently that Lord Shaitan bred his first flyers and warriors, thus prompting the others to follow suit. But now . . . they're moving that much faster. They've organized supplicant tribes east of the great pass, who make their battle gauntlets for them, and other supplicants who . . . are simply flesh. They take tithe from the poor bastards, even as

I was taken. Raids west of the pass have been few and far between; certain of the Szgany tribes fight back! The Lidescis in particular are vicious in their defense of Sunside! And you say you were a loner, who dwelled in the mountains and kept apart from men? Plainly you were, for there's that of the great wolf in you. But the barrier mountains are a mighty range; it's not surprising you didn't sight the Wamphyri on their infrequent raids. Ask yourself this: why should they raid west of the pass when there's easy meat in the east? Also, why should they be in a hurry to show themselves? What is time to them? But that was then, and this is now; Sunside will come more and more under attack . . .''

And one other subject:

''Mentalism,'' said Radu. ''Do they all have it? Who is the craftiest thought-thief, whom I must watch out for? And who is least talented, that I can spy on his mind?''

''You could get me killed!'' Emil Hagisman protested. ''Perhaps I've said too much already!''

''And why have you?''

''Something about your eyes, their penetrating stare. Or your open attitude . . . your 'innocence,' perhaps? You treat me as a man, not as a slave. I suspect it's because you are new to all this—ah, but you'll be a true Lord soon enough! Perhaps it's because you have more than mere mentalism. They say that Rusha Basti is a beguiler, too.''

''A beguiler? Hypnotism?'' Radu hadn't realized it, not in himself.

''There's that in your voice that lulls,'' said the other. ''It makes me weary and lures words out of me.''

Radu held him close and stared deep into his eyes, which were feral even as Radu's own, but without his scarlet cores. ''Then say on, and tell me what I would know,'' he said.

And Emil Hagisman told him—or would have. But at that very moment one of Radu's thralls came scrambling down from a high vantage/viewpoint looking northeast on the greater stacks of the Wamphyri. He was pointing back over his shoulder, gabbling, ''Lord Lykan! There in the sky around one of the mightiest aeries: aerial warriors, and flyers bearing armored men! They swarm even now, perhaps against us!''

In moments Radu and the Gust's lieutenant had climbed up into a viewing niche, where they gazed out through a wide and jagged crack in the stack's outer sheath, upward and into the heart of the nest of sky-scraping towers. And in one sense at least Radu's thrall was correct: a swarm of men and creatures were massed about one of the central aeries. Except they were not descending from it, but attacking it.

''Shaitanstack!'' Emil Hagisman gasped. ''Shaitan, the Lord of Vampires himself, is under attack!''

Radu looked at him. ''In two more hours I was to meet with him. Now . . . it would seem not!''

''It was probably his invitation to you that started this going,'' the other told him, shielding his eyes from the northern auroras as he tried to identify the shapes darting around Shaitanstack.

''Oh? How so?''

''A distraction, of course. The perfect time to launch a pre-emptive strike!

What, a reception in Shaitanstack? Why, the Lords are all busy prettying themselves up, not to mention the Ladies! Proud, aye! And Shaitan himself, proudest of them all: he'll want his place to look its very best. Oh, they don't get their heads together very often, these vampire Lords, but when they do . . . it's a grand contest of words and gestures, poses and postures!

"All for me?"

"For them! Half-hinted taunts and challenges, threats and insinuations. They thrive on it. But at a reception: no weapons allowed. They can crow, preen and bluster all they like, and no harm done. Until later, possibly."

"You make them sound . . . what, like fools? Buffoons!"

"Among themselves, so it would ofttimes seem—for they have each other's measure, after all. Well, more or less. But among humankind? Ah, no. Great bears play rough-and-tumble in the foothills of Sunside, and no harm done. But if they played with men like that, they'd break all of their bones." Emil saw something and pointed excitedly. "Ah, see!"

Radu looked. "See what?"

"More flyers going up . . . from Kirkscrag, Antonstack, and Wenskeep. Reinforcements! And look, a crippled flyer heads this way. It is one of Lord Ehrig's creatures; I cannot be mistaken, for his sigil adorns its flank. Lord Shaitan's enemies are . . . Kirk Nunosti, Anton Zappos, and Ehrig the Wen!"

"Lesser Lords, all?"

"Aye," Emil nodded his head in great excitement. "All lesser Lords—all joined together now against Shaitan—and all losers, too!"

"Losers?"

"He has their measure!" Emil pointed again, and Radu saw.

With a stuttering and coughing of bio-propulsive orifices, *Things* had emerged from Shaitanstack's launching bays. And even at this distance they were far more awesome constructs than the ones ranged against them. Other bays issued flyers with lieutenant and thrall riders; their polished leather armor and iron weapons glinting blue in the sheen of the stars. There followed a scattering as of leaves in a sudden gust, as Shaitan's forces fought and tore and ravaged amongst their enemies. And shortly, in the space of only a minute or two, the *debris* of Lords Nunosti, Zappos, and Ehrig the Wen's shattered forces began spiraling, drifting, or plummeting down onto the boulder plains.

Some survivors—a very few, the merest handful, all of them in wild disarray—made to fly home to the lesser aeries of Kirkscrag, Antonstack, and Wenskeep; Shaitan's superior forces harried them all the way. "If the errant Lords themselves are among the survivors," Emil husked, "Shaitan will hang them in silver chains from his ramparts, and fry them in the golden fires of sunup."

Suddenly, there were flurries of activity in the launching bays of the other manses and aeries. Where previously the greater Lords had looked on, perhaps even wagering on the outcome of this insurrection, now they seemed eager to show their solidarity with Shaitan. Flyers launched as "anxious" Wamphyri Lords and Ladies made to attend their overlord. But he would have none of that.

Radu jerked back from his natural viewport as great gonging thoughts rang in his (and in all) vampire minds: *Keep back! Who dares come here now comes at his own risk! My blood is up! I am betrayed! And who can say but that these were only dupes, playing out the moves of some sneaky, cowardly gamesmaster? Is there no honor among the Wamphyri?*

Of course not, and Shaitan knew it . . . knew also that the others would protest his insinuation—indeed his accusation—anyway. But before their denials could get underway, Shaitan's "voice" rang out again: *Shaitanstack is now inviolate. I shall not suffer any of you to come here. All invitations and engagements are canceled. Now I go to make assessment of my losses—and my not inconsiderable gains! Also to think what must be done—and against whom! First, however, I require a show of allegiance. Answer me now: who stands with Shaitan, recognizing him as his one and true Liege Lord?*

Radu answered at once: *I, Radu Lykan, stand with Shaitan.* (In truth he didn't care who he stood with, just as long as he was accepted with a minimum of trouble.)

From the others there was momentary silence . . . until the Lord of Vampires said: *Any who do not stand with me, naturally stand against me . . .*

At which there was a concerted babble of nightmare voices, as they sought to "guarantee" their allegiance. For if not, why, Shaitan could pick them off one at a time! And they had already seen what lesser alliances were worth.

The mental gabble picked up, until again Shaitan broke in:

Radu Lykan—Lord *Lykan, as you are now—you were first to side with me. Since it seems I now hold sway, I hereby testify to your ascension . . . you are Lord Lykan! Moreover, he who would harm you, harms me.* (He paused.) *Except . . . I would hazard from your wolfish ways, and the bark in your mind, that you are a dog-Lord?* (And after another pause, a mental shrug.) *Just so. Well, and as the dogs of the Szgany are faithful, so shall I expect faithfulness of you. So be it . . .*

But from the other Lords:

What? He has ascended? Just like that? This bold thief of a wolf out of Sunside?

And Shaitan laughed and told them: *Aye, and he keeps what he has taken! No payment or repayment due! What? But your losses are small! For only think what you might lose, should I pursue . . . certain investigations? As it stands, the uprising has been put down. Those Lords who were caught red-handed will pay for it, and let that be the end of it. Shaitan is merciful . . .*

As the psychic aether fell silent, Radu said to Emil Hagisman, "Now you can take your flyer and return to the Gust. If he asks you what transpired, tell him you told me nothing, and be sure I'll never give you away. Also, if at any future time something should befall Hengor Hagi, you know there's a place for you with me. Only tell me one more thing before you go."

"Name it," the other's relief was plain to see.

"In all of this so far, I've haven't heard a single word out of the Ferenczys. Are they without mentalism, or what?"

"Apparently," Emil nodded. "It will doubtless come with time, as all Wamphyri talents do—though slower in some than in others—but for the moment the Ferenczy brothers are deaf and dumb in the art of telepathy."

"They'll know nothing of my presence here?"

"Oh, be sure they'll know you're here, if not who you are. And they'll know that soon enough, for others are bound to tell them. Then there's the question of Lagula's stolen thralls. But you have Shaitan's protection—for now, at least."

"He's changeable?"

"As the wind off the Icelands, aye!"

"The wind off the Icelands—" Radu repeated him, nodding thoughtfully and stroking back his mane. But then he grinned in his wolf fashion, clapped Emil on the shoulder, and barked: "—Which currently blows in your favor! So be off now to Hengstack, and give my regards to the Gust. Tell him I admired his word-game, and that I look forward to taunting with him again sometime . . ."

Thus Radu Lykan ascended to Wolfsden in Starside, in those earliest days of the Wamphyri . . .

The rest is known.

Radu rose in the ranks of the Wamphyri, and acquired all the "natural," monstrous instincts of a Lord almost as a vampire born. Eventually he incurred the wrath of Shaitan, by which time he was equal in stature to even the greatest of the lesser Lords, and Wolfsden was insufficient to contain his army. Territorial, he looked at the other stacks—all of them occupied now—but *especially* he looked at Ferencscar!

Let the bloodwars commence! Radu allied himself with Hengor Hagi, Klaus Lankari, and Thereza Lugosi against the Ferenczys, who were now legion. Lagula Ferenczy had sired a bloodson, Nonari the Gross, and a daughter, Freyda Ferenc, both of whom had ascended in their turn to occupy their own aeries. Rakhi Ferenczy had likewise ascended to a Lord (albeit a lesser one); for Petre Stakis's last bite had been virulent indeed, transfusing or conferring upon Rakhi all the ingredients of a Lord. In short, he had developed a leech of his own.

Still Rakhi fell first. Radu beheaded him, tore out his parasite and devoured it. Rakhi's men and beasts were divided between the victors; straws were drawn for Rakstack, which went to the Gust, who at once gutted the place; Radu and his allies again turned their eyes on Ferencscar, Nonspire and Freydastack. But Freyda, a so-called "Mother of Vampires," was no more; she had died spawning a deluge of eggs, all of which save one were diseased and likewise expired.

Ferencscar fell, and finally Lagula Ferenczy—the lone surviving member of that band who had ravaged Radu's innocent sister—must pay the price. A hundred and seventy years had passed since then, but Radu had forgotten and forgiven nothing. The Wamphyri do not forgive. He cut through Lagula's tendons to weaken his joints, put his neck in a silver noose, skewered his limbs with iron hooks, and had him drawn and quartered between straining flyers, so that his blood and his bits fell like red rain down onto the shuddering boulder plains . . .

And that would have been that, except now Lagula's bloodson, Nonari the Gross, swore vengeance on Radu and death to his kith, kin, and spawn for all time to come. The impassioned vow of a Lord of the Wamphyri, which might outlast eternity itself. They would have gone at it at once, except a greater peril now united all the Lords, even Radu and Nonari, against a yet more pitiless foe—whose name was Shaitan!

The Lord of Vampires had stood aloof from the bloodwars . . . until now. But finally, when all the others were weakened, Shaitan swooped on the lesser stacks and ate them up in a veritable frenzy of conquest. Until shortly, only two camps left: Shaitan on the one hand, and his Great Enemies on the other.

The stacks under Shaitan's control were many; flesh of his flesh, his own bloodsons and daughters, inhabited them. But one of these (Shaitan's "true" son, or egg-son, the once-Turgo Zolte, long returned from banishment and grown mighty in Starside) joined now with his father's foes in the longest and bloodiest bloodwar so far . . . which in the end Shaitan won.

Then the reckoning, when Hengor Hagi, Klaus Lankari, and Thereza Lugosi were buried alive out on the boulder plains, to stiffen to stones, and Turgo Zolte was banished into the northern Icelands; except he reneged on his punishment and fled east over the Great Red Waste, out of his father's jurisdiction, and presumably to his death. And the Drakuls, Nonari the Gross, and Radu were hurled, along with a handful of surviving thralls and supplicant Szgany, into the Hell-lands Gate; many of whom resurfaced in a land called Dacia by its Roman overlords, on a great river called the Danuvius, in a world an entire dimension's remove from Starside, in the year AD 371.

They emerged close to a harbor, where Roman merchants and the soldiers who protected them, along with local Dacians, gathered to buy or barter, and to trade in slaves. And because they arrived by the light of the full moon it was a joyous time for Radu, when he and his ran free and amok among the sparse local populace . . .

Eventually, the Drakuls and theirs went up into the mountains (later the Carpathians), to find or build an aerie; Nonari "the Gross" Ferenczy fled east from Radu's wrath and took a new name; and Radu crossed the river with his followers, who spread out into all the lands around. And in an age of legends, it was the beginning of a new legend—indeed, of several. The legends of the vampire and the werewolf, and the dark things of night.

As for the place of Radu's resurgence, the barter-camp of the Romans and Dacians, it would have many names down the centuries. But to the superstitious people of that region, who had long memories, it would always be known as Radujevac:

"Where Radu came forth," of course . . .

DREAMS IN RESIN.

RADU DREAMED HIS OLDEN, LESS THAN VIVID DREAMS, AND STROVE TO REIN-state, restructure them, in the eye of memory. He dreamed of ages past and of the life he'd known then, and of the many lives he'd consumed since then. Crimson dreams of his genesis as a man in a far vampire world; of his monstrous conversion into something other than a man during his time of banishment; of his everlasting (and soon to be ongoing) revenge on those who had dared to rape and ruin what little he had loved.

Less than vivid, these dreams of his, aye—unless they were recounted, reinforced, revisited time and again to bring them into nightmare definition in a yet more nightmarish mind. For time has the power to blur and even erase, and these were things that Radu desired to remember forever. During his sleep of centuries they had been his one recourse, his only means of keeping his hatred alive while he waited out his time undead.

He recalled names out of the fading past, names that were cursed for all time to come. Such as the Zirescus: Giorga, Ion, and Lexandru—and the Ferenczys, Lagula and Rakhi, once Lords in Olden Starside. Except all were dead in another time, even another world. Dead by his hand, aye! And Radu relished resurgent memories of how he had dealt with them who had borne those names, and how he would *next* deal with any survivor, any descendant, when once more he was up and abroad in this new world where his dreams would become the new reality.

True, the resolution of ancient blood-feuds was but a very small part of the overall schemes he'd schemed in his immemorial sleep . . . but a delicious part! And it would be for any survivors just as it had been for their ancestors, or worse.

His "immemorial" sleep . . .

Well, immemorial to those he'd left behind—Szgany supplicants, thralls to remember and restore him when his time was nigh—but not to him. For despite the fact that Radu's dreams and memories required constant restoration, still they remained his one true anchor on the dimly echoing past, his one guide to an ever-expanding future . . . and *still* they were red! He saw it even now in the eye of memory: how it had been in another time, another world. And how it was yet to be in this one:

Giorga, that cruel old bastard! *Bah!* For his death had been too easy . . . *Flopping about in his own blood, awash in a crimson flood that pulsed from his gaping throat and punctured gut. Air whistling in and out of his sliced windpipe, forming bright red bubbles into a livid froth that stained his beard and speckled his madly puffing face. But the spurting of his life-blood and all his jerking and twitching quickly slowing down as life ebbed. Much too quickly!*

And Giorga's son, Lexandru: *who had raped Radu's sister, sharing Magda's body—even when life had fled it—with his brother Ion and the Ferenczys. He too had died far too quickly, with a bolt from Radu's crossbow buried in his black heart and Radu's name spraying in red from his disbelieving lips.*

And Ion, last and most loathsome of a brutish line:

Ion, with one bolt through his right arm, and another in his shoulder pinning him to a tree. But Radu had promised himself that this time the payment would be cruel as the crime—*even so cruel, just so cruel!* Magda had been raped, deflowered even unto death, her innocence crushed and ravaged from her as if torn out. So be it . . .

Ion, hanging there helpless from a crossbow bolt, while Radu's taloned hands caressed him in his body's most delicate parts. Then . . . all of Radu's rage and Wamphyri passion flowing in a single moment into his arms and hands!

In that same moment Ion Zirescu had lost everything, even the lower pipes of his body: dislocated, wrenched out of place, and left dangling like lumpy red rags! Not surprisingly, he had lost consciousness, too, and would have gone on losing enough blood that he would never wake up—except Radu would not let it go to waste, not all of it. And while there was yet a pulse in his victim's jugular, he had buried a wolf's fangs in it to draw off the remainder of Ion's life.

Ah, how he had slaked his awful thirst, giving nothing of himself but draining all from the other, even to the dregs . . .

Blood! It was what Radu had needed, what his parasite vampire leech needed. It was the nectar of life—

—It had *been* the life, and would be again, when he was up, up, *up* from his gluey grave! No, not a grave but a refuge, a sanctuary. From men, and from ancient enemies who were other than men, and from time itself. But especially a sanctuary from that Greatest of all Destroyers, which had finally determined his fate. Black it had been, and Black its name. Black as the swarming rats that brought it out of the east . . .

As for men: they'd been naïve as children when first Radu and the others out of Starside came among them. Their sciences were young, their superstitions many, and their blood sweet as any to be found on Sunside in that far vampire world of Radu's youth. Even so, their weapons had been deadly, and their courage unbelievable. In the first hundred, two hundred years, the vampire and werewolf had flourished; aeries and lairs had been erected or excavated in the mountains, and men had shunned the wooded foothills of the Carpatii Meridionali and lands around.

In the beginning, ranging far and wide, Radu and his various packs had ravaged among the colonial settlements north of the Danube—even to the point of harassing a Roman garrison's three cohorts, which were permanently stationed there to man forts strung out between the river and foothills, protection for the trade and supply routes. A fairly easy target, the garrison was residual of a much earlier XIIIth Legion; its soldiers had mainly settled the land around; they were as much "locals" as the Dacians themselves.

But despite that they were only three cohorts of the original legion, the title "the 13th" stuck, and the troubles Radu brought them quickly earned them a prefix: the "Unlucky" 13th. From which time forward that number had been known as a symbol of ill-fortune among the Romans and others, and eventually the entire world, even as it had been in Sunside/Starside.

Night-skirmishing with legionnaires along the river and in the Dacian hamlets: ah, but *that* had been a grand and dangerous game! One time, Radu had been taken in an animal trap.

. . . Given a knock on the head that near-brained him, he'd come to on a Roman ship on the Danube, on course for the Black Sea and eventually Rome itself, and doubtless the Games! Several of his pack were with him, taken with common wolves in nets or pitfalls. Perhaps their captors considered them a new species! Well, so they were, in a way. There were also caged bears, and wild boars from the woods of eastern Pannonia, chests of local gold in thumb-sized ingots, barrels of spices, and wines galore in racks of amphorae. A varied cargo.

But the wolf is a wily beast, and the werewolf even more so; while the sheer physical *strength* of a Lord of the Wamphyri . . . is awesome! The oak-staved cages were like so much kindling in Radu's hands. And above decks a full moon rode high in the Dacian skies, and the night was by no means done . . .

The ship had beached itself near Zimnicea; its crew, and a handful of legionnaires retiring out of the army and returning to their homelands, were found hanging by their heels from the rigging, naked, pale and bloodless. But despite that their bodies had been ripped apart and their throats torn out, there was little of actual blood to be discovered. Later, local Dacians had paid for this atrocity; a hamlet in the foothills, well known for the rebellious nature of its citizens, was put to the sword and razed to the ground.

It still amused Radu to think of it: how he had freed the wild creatures to swim ashore, stolen much of the wine and destroyed what couldn't be carried away. As for the gold . . . well, in his way Lord Radu, too, had been naïve in those early times. And gold had been common in Starside. He'd seen no use for the heavy stuff; his thralls had thrown a fortune overboard! There it had stayed (for all he knew) in the silt of a shallow reach of the river for over fifteen hundred years. If ever he revisited those parts, he would know where to find it again.

But there had been two other items of cargo that Radu had found much more interesting, which years later he had cause to remember and utilize: several amphorae filled with a glutinous golden liquid, at first mistaken for honey; and . . . a chest of yellow stones? The first was resin, used throughout the Mediterranean as a preservative in wine, and the second was *fossilized* resin, turned hard as rock and rounded by the Baltic into polished amber pebbles. And Lord Radu—originally an untutored nomad, little more than a savage from the woods of a parallel world, then a mutated Lord on the dark side of that world, now finally a werewolf in *this* world—had seen the connection between the two, and might well have been one of the first men ever to see it.

For on Starside it had been the practice of certain Lords of the Wamphyri to bury defeated enemies alive (or undead) out on the boulder plains, to "stiffen to stones" and fuse with the earth in their deep and inescapable graves. But in this case it was different—here the preserving resin *itself* had stiffened, keeping *intact* whatever was caught within. For the translucent, softly glowing pebbles had contained flies and beetles trapped in the exuded life-fluids of coniferous forests dead and gone for countless years.

Radu had no idea of the span of time, of the aeons it had taken to turn resin to amber, but the principle had astonished him all the same. Especially when he examined some of the specimens locked in the amber: such as a perfectly preserved dragonfly, or an ant with a fragment of leaf still clearly visible in its mandibles. These creatures were dead, of course, and in the terms of men might well have been dead "forever." But what if a Lord of the Wamphyri should choose to preserve himself in this fashion? What, a metamorphic vampire, with self-regenerating flesh? And from that time forward Radu had worn an amber bauble, with its captive insect intact, on a slender chain of gold around his neck . . .

Amber: the ultimate end product of resin.

Resin: the blood of great pines . . . which fifteen hundred years ago, and indeed in far more recent times, had covered the mountain slopes like winter fur on a beast's hide; not only the granite mountains of inhospitable Scottish regions but those of far, foreign parts as well. No shortage of resin, no! Two centuries after Radu's coming, all the Greeks in the Mediterranean had been using countless tons of the stuff just to cure their wines! And if Radu's "contemporaries"—the Drakuls, for instance—had thought to bring native earth from their aeries in Starside for their beds here in *this* world, then why not a bed of amber for a sleep of centuries?

For long and long, years without number, the idea had lain dormant in Radu's head without his even suspecting it was there. But when he'd needed it . . .

Resin: a preservative with medicinal properties. A shield against the ravages of time. Perhaps even a cure for a terrible curse that in this world was as devastating as leprosy in Starside. Well, that last wasn't proven as yet, but—

—*What was that . . . ?*

Radu's "dreams" were more nearly conscious thoughts now, so that the very slightest of tremors which he'd felt through the walls of his sarcophagus and the near-solid matrix of his resin cocoon had seemed like a presence entering the room of a man on the verge of waking. He had sensed—something! Or someone? Or perhaps it was merely the mountains settling onto their foundations, as they had been doing for all of the six hundred years he'd lain here. He hadn't called, had he? It wasn't time yet, was it? Soon, but not yet. So . . . could it have been his creature, stirring with hideous life where it waxed in its own great vat? Possibly. He would "feel" such motions, certainly, for its mind and flesh were of his making. And so:

Gently, little one, gently, Radu sleepily sent. *Your time is soon, be sure . . . but not before mine. So have no fear, for your master shall be there to bring you forth . . .*

There was no answer, and Radu hadn't expected one. It was simply a tremor in these old and fractured rocks, that was all. He could go back to his dreaming: of men and monsters, time and the plague, and of his eventual flight from all these things.

Men . . .

The Romans. But the Empire had been on the wane, at least in the parts where Radu and the others came forth. Aye, for the Goths were coming, and they were only a very small part of what *else* was coming! Such wars, such battles, such blood! The blood was the life! And the *diversity* of blood, in this new world! No wonder that at first these hell-lands had seemed like some sort of Wamphyri heaven or paradise. Oh really . . . ?

Men, and their wars . . . (Radu gradually settled back into his sleep of centuries.)

During long years of upheaval, the Wamphyri had moved into the mountain heights and spread out into the lands around, even into other lands across the sea; indeed, into all the shores of the Mediterranean and its islands. For they had seen the folly of their ways when first they came here; they had been too bold and had become legends which would not fade quickly in the memories of men. But if they desired long lives here, they must be (or at least appear to be) as one with the world and its people and not apart from them. And slowly but surely they had come to a mutual understanding: that in this bloody and war-torn world, they would use to best advantage such cover as the wars established for them. And indeed a cover had been required.

For already it was seen how men reacted to the Wamphyri presence: fearfully at first, in a world rife with superstition—but then, like the Szgany of Sunside, they fought back! For while men may suffer their lands to be stolen, their children to be eaten and their wives seduced away, when finally they have nothing left, then there's nothing left to lose! And then *any* man will fight!

That was how it had been: the alien invaders of Earth had thought to rule by terror, as they had in Sunside/Starside. But even there they had not had it all their own way. Through seemingly endless days the sun had forbidden entry into Sunside; in the dark of misty nights the Szgany had hidden themselves away, or if they could not hide had taken up arms. Likewise in this world, except here it was worse. Here the nights were fleeting things and allowed so little time for the vampire Lords to establish themselves; and the days . . . were terrible! The furnace sun passed directly overhead, and there were no barrier mountains to contain its searing rays, or the rage of vengeful men.

Oh, there were mountains, to be sure—and *such* mountains: the vast horseshoe of the Carpatii in the east, and the mighty Alps in the west—but unlike the barrier mountains of Sunside/Starside, the solar orb was not restricted by them, and at its zenith burned down on all and everything indiscriminately. As for the great armies of nomad tribesmen that were sweeping the world at that time: where mountains could not be climbed, they could always be circumvented . . . and they were. By warriors!

By men who had known how to destroy their enemies, even the Wamphyri, and destroy them utterly; known how a bolt or a lance through the heart would kill a man, and how his *head* on a lance would *guarantee* he was dead . . . then how to reduce his castle and its contents to ashes, until nothing of him or his survived. Such methods were simply the way of the warrior, and by no means reserved for the Wamphyri and their followers. For in a majority of cases the invaders who used them—first the Goths, later the Visigoths and Avars—did not even know they went up against the Wamphyri! No, for they were merely mur-

236 / Brian Lumley

dering rich Dacian landowners in their gloomy castles, or strange, savage gray halflings in their foothill keeps and caverns.

And because of the times, times of change, tumult, and crisis—indeed the crisis of an entire Classical World—the as yet young legend of the Wamphyri, of the blood-crazed vampire and werewolf, was *almost* eradicated. What need for monstrous myths in a world that was *in reality* a bloodbath? Forty years after Radu's coming the Visigoths had sacked Rome itself, and forty-five years later it had fallen again, to the Vandals; except on that occasion Radu had been part of it. For like most of the Wamphyri exiled from Starside by Shaitan, he was unable to resist blood, certainly not in such copious amounts.

War, to which he was drawn as a lodestone is drawn north. And such wars to be warred as nothing conceived in Starside by even the mightiest of the Old Lords. And down all the years and decades, Radu was a great mercenary washed hither and to by the tides of war and blood. He used his gift of oneiromancy— not uncommon among dog-Lords—to scry on future times and know in advance which side to join in the great wars to come. And likewise he remained alert for word of those olden enemies who came through the Hell-lands Gate with him. And time and again Radu cursed himself that he'd not dealt with them then, on the very threshold of this new world, when they were at their weakest. But then, he had been at his weakest, too, for a time.

Rumors found their way to Radu. Employed as a mercenary warlord by the Vandal Gaeseric (who dubbed him "Radu, Hound of the Night," because he preferred guerilla warfare by the light of a full moon), he learned of the alleged death of one "Onarius Ferengus," a provincial senator (what, Roman?) murdered by pirates in his villa at Odessus on the Black Sea ten years earlier. This he had from a Numidian slave-girl, Ulutu, set free when Gaeseric's forces sacked Rome. Upon a time she'd belonged to Onarius, but she had fled from the fire and the fighting on the night he was killed. And from Ulutu's descriptions of her ex-master . . .

. . . Radu had little doubt but that he had been none other than Nonari the Gross Ferenczy!

And in Radu's keeping, where he and his pack spent their days in a den under the *Colli Albani* twelve miles out of Rome, Ulutu fell under her new master's spell (and Radu, to a lesser degree, under hers); and they were lovers. But because he had enough of "pups" up in the mountains of Dacia, now Goth territory, and because he had learned that anonymity and insularity were synonymous with longevity, he made sure that Ulutu stayed entirely human; which is to say that for all that he was into her, nothing *of him* got into her. And at times, lying spent on their bed of cured furs, at Radu's request she would tell him various things about her former master.

Just how Nonari the Gross had gained elevation to the rank of a Roman *Senator in absentia* during the eighty-odd years sped by since the coming of the Wamphyri into Dacia—that was anybody's guess. But the way the girl described his castle, backed up to a great cliff, with his private chambers facing away from the sun and always in the shade; and his servants, "like mists over a bubbling swamp, drifting, pale and ghastly, yet smiling with strong white teeth . . . all wafting and weaving, hastening to Onarius's beck and call, yet shuddering to his touch so cold and menacing; and his right hand like a club, with its fingers all welded into one . . .''

He had called her "his little trog," and had told her that he'd known trogs before, in the dank caverns of a far forbidden world. Except they had been shambling leathery creatures, while Ulutu was graceful and her skin so soft. It had never ceased to amaze him: that she'd been browned by the sun, "but yet was not burned up!" But Onarius's odalisques were white—Arabs, Britons, and Syrians—and he had no time for dalliance with trogs, even if they were as beautiful as Ulutu. And so she had carried water, cleaned Onarius's chambers, and been grateful. For she knew how he dealt with them with whom he "dallied." Or rather, she did *not* know, for he was wary of prying eyes.

But she had seen the evidence of his passion, apparent in the feral yellow eyes of his male and female thralls alike, and in their "wafting and weaving" after only a very short space of time spent in his service; even in certain of the villa's children, which were gross. She had seen how rapidly his odalisques aged and his thralls were worn down—"sucked dry, until they were no more,"—and how when they died he buried them deep in the earth where the rocky land sloped down to the sea, with the rush and roar of breakers to deaden . . . *other* sounds.

Onarius had a son in the mountains far to the north, in a place called the Khorvaty in Moldavia. (Here Radu had paid more attention. What, another *living* Ferenczy?) He was called Belos Pheropzis (not Ferengus? No, of course not, not if one desired to hide one's true kith and kin away!) and kept a great castle in the heights, on the very borders of the Empire's territory. All secret from Romans and nomad invaders alike, the place was to be Onarius's bolt-hole, in the event he should need one.

As to how Onarius's "little trog" had known these things: she had feared this Belos mightily when he visited his father, because of the way he looked at her—the way he looked at all females, even his father's thrall mistresses! Yet at the same time she had been fascinated by him: his dark good looks, hawkish features, massive yet proportionate stature. Keeping well out of sight, she'd listened to their conversations, mainly to ensure that Belos did not ask for her. For if he had, then she would have run away.

But when Radu had queried her one time, about this attraction that she'd felt toward Belos:

"No, my Lord," Ulutu had told him, lying sprawled between his legs and fondling his now flaccid rod, squeezing its glans between her dark breasts, and kissing its tiny lips, "perhaps I have given you the wrong impression. It was not so much fascination as terror that I felt. For this Belos was like one of the great warhorses that draw the Roman chariots . . . and what was I but a tiny black mare? I was a slave, and if this son of Onarius had wanted me . . . I scarcely believed I could contain him in my small body!" (At which she had seen her mistake at once, for Radu was fiercely prideful.) "—*But*, since it seems I contain *you* well enough, my Lord, obviously I was mistaken! Whichever, this Belos frightened me, seeming more creature than man, more animal than human."

"What, even as I am more creature than man, more animal than human?" Radu had reached down to fondle her soft breasts and draw Ulutu effortlessly up onto his belly, where he could squeeze her dark and rounded buttocks.

"You are a wolfling, as I've seen," she had told him then. "But Belos . . . was other!" And Radu had felt her small shudder.

Aye, and Ulutu was right: Belos *was* "other." No slightest shadow of a doubt, he was this Onarius's (or Nonari's) egg-son. Wamphyri! Which perhaps explained his looks and appetites, and the reason why he and his damned father were so close. Or maybe that last was as a result of the wars, the shaken, perhaps even crumbling Roman Empire, the unstable skein of things in general. For even the best Wamphyri relationship could scarcely be described as "close," not in normal circumstances. But that apart, quite obviously this . . . this *scum* of Starside had bred one of its own here in this world! An egg-son for Nonari! A Ferenczy!

Well, so be it. It simply meant there'd be one more Ferenczy for Radu to hunt down when all wars were won and times were right, and the world was quiet again. And as for this so-called "Onarius Ferengus" . . . dead, was he? Radu didn't think so. More likely it was some grand contrivance, the entire scenario, some scheme of Nonari's to vanish a while, and come back later under a new name and in a different guise. The idea was interesting, something Radu could even try for himself in some future time, when it might seem to some that he had lived too long . . .

Radu's dreams had set his juices working however sluggishly. Dreams of his undying hatred for the Ferenczys, his charnel love of the battlefield, but especially his carnal memories of Ulutu.

Ah, Ulutu! She had loved his horn, and it had been hard to will his spunk lifeless when he spurted in her. But if she had fallen pregnant . . . then she had also fallen dead, be sure! For Radu was not like Nonari, making vampires left, right and center, to plague him in a later age. His pups were enough for him. They had known his bite and bore his curse—that of the moonchild, the changeling, the werewolf—but not his seed. There would be time for blood-sons, and eventually an egg-son, later, when he could afford the time to train, control, and bend them to his will. But in that savage world of fifteen hundred years ago, Radu Lykan had control over nothing! Even kings and emperors had controlled nothing! Only the restless forces of Nature, Change, and Chaos had any control at all . . .

But Ulutu: Radu had bitten her during intercourse, a love bite, but much too deep. She would never be Wamphyri—well, not for a long, long time at least, if she lived that long—but she would be a wolfling, bound to Radu as his thrall. Very well, she could run with the pack and be his mate, for as long as it lasted. Alas, but that hadn't been long. Gaeseric's advisers, who earlier in the campaign had welcomed Radu's pack as "mercenary warriors without peer— men who fight like dogs of the wild!" now gave their lord different advice. Oh, it had seemed a grand irony at first, a marvelous jest, that a great city founded by wolf-suckled brothers should be brought to its knees in part by a wolfish man, this so-called Hound of Night, with his band of howling berserks. But the city had fallen now and Radu and his lot had been paid off. And who could say, perhaps they had even been paid . . . too well?

For what were they after all but mercenaries? And only a handful by comparison with the true Vandal army. No match for Gaeseric, if he should decide to take back what tribute he had paid them. Aye, and these wolves of war kept many comely women plundered out of Rome, and measures of good red wine likewise sacked from the city, which they held in their cavern lair in the mountains with the rest of their loot . . .

A man of Gaeseric's had come to Radu in the early evening with news of a legion mustering in the north, and Roman galleys from the Eastern Empire putting men and ordnances ashore south of the Tiberis. And these were Gaeseric's orders:

Radu was to send one-third of his men to spy out the land to the north, and he and the rest were to harass the sea-borne invasion at the mouth of the river; which in the same night he set out to do . . . only to discover that there were no such reinforcements for the ravaged city! Nor had there been. Then he remembered how he'd dreamed dreams of treachery, and saw when he rushed back to his lair under the mountains how his dreams were true: smoke and fire issuing from the great cavern's outlets, and the ravished bodies of the pack's women strewn among the coarse grasses at the mouth of the cave! Even Ulutu, with blood under her nails from the fight she'd put up.

At which it was as much as Radu could do to keep himself from screaming aloud. It was not that she was dead—he might even have killed her himself, had circumstances required it—but more the *way* of her death. For it brought back to him memories of his own sister's rape and murder at the hands of Zirescu and Ferenczy scum, in Sunside in a different world.

And finally he did scream, except it was a *howl* that went vibrating up to the sinking moon. And a full moon, at that . . .

There were Vandals in the heights around the cavern and in the defile that led to it. They had thought that Radu would not be back until full daylight, which would be to their advantage for he was a night fighter. Yet here he was, albeit weary from his abortive journey to the coast and back. By comparison Radu's hundred was a handful, while Gaeseric's ambush party, a formidable assault unit, outnumbered them four to one.

But despite that the two sides were unequal, and that the Vandals held the high ground, still their advantage was not so great as might be reckoned. Not against furious, vengeful men, and men who were werewolves at that! So the battle was joined, as bloody as might be imagined.

It was the twilight before the dawn, when the eyes of men may not be trusted. But the eyes of wolves are feral; they see in the twilight just as well as in the night. Also, a mist was rising . . . a vampire mist, conjured out of Radu's pores and up from the bone-dry earth! But all in vain; the pack was beaten from the start, almost before it began. For they must strike up at the ambushers, while the Vandals need only strike down. And Radu's wolflings fought in ragged clothes, with staves, knives, axes, and their bare hands and fierce teeth; while the Vandals had leather armor, lances, bows and primitive crossbows. (And that last was an irony in itself, for it had been the Wamphyri who brought the first crossbows with them out of Sunside/Starside. In their world the crossbow had been a Traveler weapon, which the vampire Lords had neither the skill nor the patience to duplicate or manufacture for themselves in this one. As for the few entirely human Szgany thralls they had brought through with them: they had become scattered among the peoples of this new world. Aye, and all their skills with them. Hence that the Vandals had crossbows.)

Yet still Radu's pups slew three to one, except there was always a fourth to come. And pierced by lances, feathered with red-streaming shafts, one by one they went down. And all their tribute stolen, their women raped and butchered, finally their very lives forfeit to the treachery of the Vandals . . .

The sun rose on a hillside that seemed to smoke from all the blood and urine, all the sweat and guts and foulness that had been spilled there; four hundred and ten bodies reeking under the hot sun. But Radu and two of his lieutenants had survived; seeing how all was lost, they'd crept away through Radu's mist to find refuge in a deep dark crevice till nightfall.

And coiled like a snake in the cool dank of their hiding place, and willing his leech to heal his several wounds, Radu had vowed a Wamphyri vow where he sheltered—not only against Gaeseric and the Vandals but against mankind in general. For so far Radu had been the most "lenient" of all the Lords, the most "human" of an inhuman lot. But that was over now. What, treacherous, the Wamphyri? *Hah!* For now it seemed to Radu that those old Starside Lords had been the veriest beginners in the ways of the traitor! And as for cruelty . . .

The lust of the vampire was that of a man, increased tenfold by his parasite. When he raped it was because he *must!* His passions, rages, delights, all of his emotions were larger than life or even undeath. He could no more turn away from a shapely woman than a drunkard refuse a jack of wine, or the furnace sun hold still in the sky. He could no more resist blood than a fly avoid fresh dung, or the tides resist the pull of the moon. For the blood was the life! But the men of *this* world—Romans and barbarians alike—they fucked simply because it was there; not because they were driven to it, but because it was right of the conqueror! To the victor the spoils!

And while the vampire as often as not created life—or undeath—the men of *this* world invariably destroyed it. Radu had seen how it was when Gaeseric and his Vandals stormed Rome; he had *seen* how inhuman were these humans. And as for the "civilized" Romans: why, in the Eastern Empire they would crucify a man for stealing a loaf of bread!

Well, Radu was halfway between the two, or so he'd like to fancy. As much wolf as man, yes, but *more* wolf than vampire. That was how he'd seen himself: greater than a mere man by virtue of his strength and awesome vampire powers, yet superior to the Wamphyri by virtue of the last lingering traces of his humanity! A paradox but a fact. Oh, really? And again, *hah!* Well, so much for humanity! And this was the final change, the *true* change, the last straw that turned a man to a pitiless monster.

But naïve? Aye, he'd been that. In Sunside, naïve. Looking back, he knew that he'd always had the measure of the Ferenczys and Zirescus. But he'd been a mere youth and inexperienced. And in his Starside aerie, naïve: to believe he stood the slightest chance against Shaitan the Unborn, yet still he'd gone against him. Finally in this world, oh so naïve. The golden ingots he'd thrown in a river believing them worthless—while in fact men would kill for them! The way he'd made werewolves to run with him, when he should have stayed a loner. Last but not least, to have sold himself to a warlord, and think he'd actually be *paid* for his services and accepted as an equal!

What, an equal? Radu Lykan? But he had the measure of all these so-called "warriors." Their only advantage was that they were men, and could live here as men. Ah, but in the long term time was on Radu's side. He could outlive them all . . . if only they would let him!

And so, with all such notions as "honor," "trust," and "faith" put aside forever, a new strategy was needed. From now on Radu would *honour* neither man nor creature, but only his own vows. He would *trust* no one, not even his pups, but continually assert his will and ensure that his word was law. He would have *faith* only in himself, and in the blood which is the life. And above all, he would be the most secretive and watchful of men, so that no one could know him, or come upon him unsuspected.

So, perhaps old "Onarius Ferengus" had got it right and Radu should find himself a position, elevate himself, and prepare bolthole dens and lairs along the way, with caretakers to keep them in his absence. Then, like Nonari the Gross Ferenczy, he would be able to venture forth in the world as before, indulging himself as *never* before, but always knowing there would be a refuge in needful times, or when the number of his years was such that he should "retire" a while.

Or perhaps he misjudged Nonari and that one had not gone into hiding since his "murder" as a Roman senator but was out and about, revelling in all the great reel and roil of things. If so, no doubt he'd come to Radu's attention again, when the time was ripe for him to rise up in other parts. And who could say, perhaps then the time would also be ripe for "Onarius" to vanish forever? Likewise his egg-son, this Belos Pheropzis.

These were some of Radu's thoughts, and some of the plans he made, while hiding the day away in a hole in the ground . . .

Came the night. One of Radu's pups had died of too many cuts in his side, which had leaked all his blood away. He had gone uncomplainingly, simply stiffening where he crouched. The crevice would make as good a grave as any; Radu and the other survivor of Gaeseric's treachery had dropped stones on him from on high, to block the crevice and keep away any lesser wolves and wild dogs from the body of their ex-colleague.

Then away into the night under a moon that was still full, heading north for the Appenino heights that stretched the full length of Italia. For in a land overrun by Vandals, that would be the safest route out.

Werewolves run swift. The next night, up in the mountains, the pair met up with other survivors, men of the pack that Radu had sent north to spy on the alleged legion massing there. They had their own story to tell: of a vile ambush not twenty miles along the river north of Rome, which had left forty-two of them dead. Only eight had been lucky; they'd somehow managed to swim to safety across the river, and left Gaeseric's lot bogged down in their armor with all their weaponry. After that, like Radu, the eight had made for the heights, for they'd known that they were dupes.

So ten of them now, ten of a hundred and fifty. Well, and that must suffice, for Radu would make no more werewolves for a while . . .

* * *

He started . . . a nervous twitch of his limbs that spent itself uselessly in his resin matrix. Not enough to wake him entirely, but enough to make certain subconscious connections, so that he dreamily wondered: *What . . . ?*

But is there someone here, someone coming? What was it he thought he had heard, footsteps? But *footsteps,* in this riddled rock, which barring the furtive creep of spiders and flutter of bats had been so long silent? Perhaps a stone had rotted out of the high ceiling, and the thunder of its fall had caused him to dream of a past age when he had piled boulders on the body of a dead colleague . . . and secondary shocks had caused him to start? Yes, that must be it.

Yesss. That must . . . be . . . it . . .

After Rome Radu had taken his much reduced party north to the Danube, then east through the forests and mountains, and eventually down into the Dacian territories that they knew so well. This was Lombard, Ostrogoth and Hun territory now, but south of the river the people were mainly Christian. Radu himself had no religion except blood; the superstitions and beliefs of local Dacians made little or no difference to him, except Christian-held land made safer journeying than land under the control of the barbarians.

In any case it wasn't his intention to stay south of the river; finally he headed north again for the mountains of what would much later become Wallachia. For he believed that in taking the high ground he would be secure a while from the bloody tides of war washing all around on the fertile plains below.

In this he was correct. The mountains were mainly barren and inhospitable. Unattractive to invaders, they contained little or nothing of value; Radu knew he could safely recruit the hardy locals for the building of a castle, an aerie of his own in a place as high and inaccessible as he could find.

That would require funds, of course, but he had learned a valuable lesson: that while wine and women can do a man a power of good, gold can do him even more. And on his way from Rome to Dacia he had not been remiss in accumulating monies. There had been Romans fleeing the barbarian slaughter of their land; Radu had slaughtered them, for their wealth. There'd been parties of Vandals scathing in the land around; he'd done some scathing of his own, taking back what they had stolen. Finally, on the Danube, there had been a last handful of Roman merchants and traders. Radu had traded death for their blood and their gold.

And journeying through the nights and paying his way during the days in Christian camps and villages, he'd listened to rumors and learned a new word which the local folk associated with the devil and every evil thing. But this word was in fact a name, one that had filtered through the high passes and from far across the mountains. It was the name of a family—or of a curse now—and one that was by no means new to Radu:

The Drakuls!

Upon a time Karl and Egon had been Radu's allies against Shaitan the Unborn; now they were his greatest threat, in that they continued to scourge among the horseshoe of the high Dacian mountains, so bringing themselves into unnecessary prominence. Unlike Radu—who had developed a certain tolerance for weak sunlight, until he could abide to venture out in a hooded cloak—the Drakuls were true children of the night; sunlight would kill them instantly. But they'd developed their metamorphism to such a degree that like Shaitan the Unborn they could shape themselves into bats to fly out in the night and so take their prey. And they'd been doing it ever since. Moreover, in Starside they had been reared by wolves. They *knew* wolves, and in this world kept gray brothers as familiar creatures. Wolves of the wild kept watch for them, by means of which the Drakuls were secure in their aerie and feared no man.

For the moment it worked for them, hence the rumors now finding their way to Radu. For the barbarian invaders who were settling the plains north of the mountains were no less superstitious than the locals they usurped. And when their wives or children died mysteriously or vanished in the night, then they knew who to blame: the winged devil in his mountain retreat—the "obour" or "viesky," the vampire—the Drakul! The brothers had long since built a castle or castles in no-man's-land, at least one of which aeries stood on a rocky promontory over a chasm.

This much Radu learned, and no more. Sufficient to determine him to avoid the error of bringing himself into prominence. And he kept reminding himself: anonymity and obscurity are synonymous with longevity. The Drakuls were true legends now; when all the fighting was over and done with and Dacia was united as a single tribe or country, then the people would remember these monsters and go looking for them. But even if the locals should forget, be sure that Radu Lykan would not. Territorial the Wamphyri, aye, and this place was where Radu had come forth.

And anyway, there'd never been much love lost between him and Karl and Egon in the first place.

Ever vengeful—and smiling grimly, if only to himself—Radu dreamed on . . .

PART 4

Wamphyri: Ancient and Modern.

MORE OF RADU'S STORY.
BONNIE JEAN: SHE VISITS HER MASTER.

I N THOSE DAYS IF YOU WOULD LIVE, THE HIGH MOUNTAINS WERE MOST PROBA-
bly the safest place to do it. And for the time being the werewolf Radu Lykan
had had his fill of war. In the last quarter of the year 467 A.D., he and his small
pack wintered down in what was to be their lair for the next sixty years.

The place was a great cavern in the mountains of western Moldavia, not far
from a scrabbled-together "town" or village, more properly a makeshift encampment of refugees, called Krawlau by its one hundred and fifteen polyglot
inhabitants.

As to why he chose this place: Radu's reasons were several. For one, the
heights were inhospitable and almost inaccessible. To gradually establish one-
self there would be one thing, but for any would-be invader to launch an attack,
or even want to? . . . That seemed unlikely. Two: being simply a hollow crag, the
redoubt would not *invite* attack in the manner of an "aerie" or castle; and at its
rear, its lowest crevice exits opened on the shore of a broad, bitterly cold lake. In
the event that he *was* attacked, Radu could easily slip away by boat to the far
shore. For while it was a time of relative quiet, there would continue to be sporadic invasions from the east (Radu's dreams were full of them) . . .

Three: while a true aerie would be his first choice for a permanent dwelling
place, its construction would prove prohibitively expensive. The cavern on the
other hand required no actual or external building as such but only some interior works, and what monies Radu had amassed were better put aside against the
vagaries of an uncertain future—his precognition was by no means infallible.
Four: an entire work-force, with which to make the crag habitable, was immediately to hand in the shape of the folk of Krawlau. These former farmers—driven
into the mountains by war and the collapse of the Eastern Empire's borders in
the face of invading Asiatics—had no work. Like Radu, they were simply winter-
ing out the bad times. In order to survive they'd become scavengers, hunting
the land and fishing the lake for food. Which was why, when first Radu found
them, they saw him as a godsend.

At first, aye . . .

And when he was established . . . then they saw him almost as a god! Oh, it was in his bearing when he walked among them: his penetrating gaze and lordly mode of speech, his attire and generosity. Obviously, with his dark, wolfish good looks—standing tall and lean as a tree, and equally strong—this was no ignorant, guttural farmer born in the fields but a gentleman landowner, a *boyar* removed from his own place by those same savage forces that had removed them. And he had gold, and the wit to fashion himself a fortress from a raw crag! His money was of little value now—not in these naked mountains where there was nothing to buy—but it would be when the land was quiet again. As for Radu's cavern: when all of the work was finished and if the winters were hard, then it would provide refuge for all of them. This was his promise.

Oh, Radu knew he shouldn't bring himself into prominence, but up here in the heights that was in any case a near-impossibility. Who was there to see him or his, or know what they were about? No one but these low persons in their sod-roofed, timber huts. Radu hired them by the dozen, and chose men to watch over them while they turned the great cavern into a lair. When a man joined him, Radu would state his wages and promise him a bonus if he should later decide to go his own way, perhaps back down to his ruined fields to start again.

In that first winter, when the snow lay deep, a good many of them did just that: approached Radu and told him they'd left families in Moldavia, and would now return to see if they survived . . . and if so provide for them out of the monies Radu had paid them, and the bonus he still owed them. For his part, he would always require one last day's work of them before paying them their due, wishing them well and seeing them on their way in the dusk of evening. But in the dark of night he would send members of his pack loping after them, to make certain no word of him and his works—and none of his money—found its way down out of the mountains.

And because new refugees were arriving day after day, and others trying to leave, there was a steady turnover of workers and no lack of . . . provisions. (Likewise, there was no gradual trickling away of Radu's funds.)

The keep took shape. He would go among the workers directing them, so that every stone was laid in accordance with his design (even as it had been in Wolfsden in Starside in another world). Massive timber lintels for the several "doors" that he left open, and piled boulders in other holes that Radu desired closed; archways with keystones to bolster the dripstone ceilings where they were eaten with rot, and stone staircases leading to ledges, lesser caves or high "window" observation ports in the rough outer walls; the levelling of various floors, and laying of an uneven but serviceable paving of slate slabs. And so to the fireplaces and ovens, and the flues to channel smoke to the rear of the crag, there to drift with the mists rising off the lake.

And while all such works were in progress to make the cavern liveable if not "comfortable," Lord Radu was not remiss in seeing to its defenses:

Outside, between the natural spurs of the crag, he built awesome death-trap gantlets for would-be invaders; on high, he piled rocks behind logs stopped with chocks that were easily knocked away in the event of an invasion. And at last Radu saw that his lair was safe. But in any case these were no puny castle's walls to fall to the first assault of an enemy's battering rams—they were the walls of the mountain itself! And as each external work was completed, so Radu would disguise it as living rock, in imitation of its surrounding formations.

But inside:

In strategic places Radu buttressed certain works of stone with good timber; which would seem odd to some, for obviously the wood could not outlast the stone. But Radu reasoned that when the time came for him to leave his mountain fastness, then by lighting a handful of fires behind him he could easily topple it, or at least reduce it to the original shell. Wamphyri and savagely territorial, he could not bear the thought of another dwelling in a place that his hands had wrought. But by the same token he also knew that if ever he desired to return, then that he had the knowledge and skill to put the place back to rights.

Radu's "pups" worked side by side with the men of Krawlau, showing never a sign of their lupine natures except perhaps in their silence and the feral intelligence of their eyes. The ex-farmers saw nothing peculiar in it; they'd seen wave after wave of slant-eyes (and of yellow-eyes, and—skins, too) long before Radu came on the scene. He and his retainers were from foreign parts, that was all. Plainly this rangy *boyar* in his fur boots and jacket, with his long, gray-to-white hair falling on his collar, and golden crescent moons in his fleshy ears, was some rich expatriate. Certainly he was "Lord" Radu to his men!

And he was fair to a fault. When his hunters went out and killed a pig in the night (though where they were able to find such game up here in the mountains was a mystery) then there'd be meat off the bone for the common workers too, be sure! And Lord Radu laughing and joking with them as they sucked at the sweet, smoking flesh.

Radu "recruited" the strongest of them—but by the light of a full moon, and not as workers! For while earlier he'd determined to "make no more werewolves," still he was on the lookout for men of quality. The ones he chose from these ex-farmers were hard as men come; they'd make superb lieutenants when next he went out into the world . . .

So the dog-Lord proceeded.

A long, hard winter came and went, and several more like it, before finally "Wolfscrag" was finished to Radu's satisfaction. But only Radu himself, and those who were his, knew what he'd named it.

By then the men of Krawlau were much reduced in numbers; they worried about the fact that of all their fellows who had left Radu's employ, not a one had been known to return to it. They went down from the mountains to the steppes—aye, allegedly—but they never came back! Not a one? And this so-called "Lord" in his lair of a cavern: why, his looks were more wolfish than ever! And his men . . . *their* looks, too. The way they loped like upright dogs!

As for the three or four ex-Krawlau men who had actually joined Radu and dwelled with him now in his great cavern: why, they were visibly changed! As quickly as that, they had become indistinguishable from the rest of his retainers. Loping, long-haired and wild . . . their eyes were feral in the night . . . and when they grinned their upper lips wrinkled back, curling like the muzzles of snarling wolves!

Thus legends that were already one hundred years old—which had been almost but not quite forgotten—were re-born and lived anew.

Radu heard their whispers where the men of Krawlau crept about like so many mice, putting the final touches to his den. Well, let them whisper; he had other problems. The sixth winter was on its way, provisions were low, and the dog-Lord had no more use for clods such as these . . .

. . . No, not so: there was *one* more use for them, yes!

As to why they'd so suddenly become aware or at least suspicious of their danger: Radu had relaxed certain strictures on himself and his pups both, until they went about more nearly as "nature" intended. Now it was plain to see that nature had *not* intended, that these were by no means natural men. Yet in some respects they were all too natural.

For years now they had gone without good wine and woman-flesh, and all the other small comforts that men—even men of war—might easily grow accustomed to when they are not about their business. Radu was scarcely ignorant of his men's needs, for he felt them, too. But now that he was set up . . .

Earlier in the year, aware that the Huns had had the run of the Moldavian steppe for decades and wondering if their supremacy was holding, Radu had dispatched scouts east to discover the state of things. He had also sent men west through the high passes and all along the twin spurs of the horseshoe range, and a spy into a handful of villages where they clung to the flanks of the mountains not too far removed from Wolfscrag. These latter places were small, isolated, self-supporting townships. But if Radu's long-term plan was of merit, in time they might also support him. Now he waited for his scouts to return and report to him . . .

When the first snows came, Radu went down into Krawlau personally, to invite the last half-dozen of his former workers into the great cave for the winter. They thanked him, however cautiously, and told him they would take advantage of his offer . . . perhaps tomorrow? Radu sat by their fire a while—long enough that they noted the red cores of his eyes, and his talon hands which he made no effort to hide—and when all grew silent he left.

But within the hour, panting as they dragged their scant belongings behind them on makeshift sledges, the ragged survivors of Krawlau were off down the mountain trails. Except they were survivors no longer. They got to the first pass . . . where they found Radu and the pack waiting for them.

Which saw to the provisioning . . . for the next week or so, at least.

One by one as winter laid its white cloak on the land, Radu's scouts returned. Utterly in thrall to their dog-Lord, they had given him away neither by word nor deed. But they brought home to him various items of information and all manner of rumors.

Information:

There were trappers, at least four teams of them, working along the river where it wound to Iasi in the east. These were good clean, hardy folk; they'd make for good recruiting . . . or eating, whichever. They'd made their winter camps, and because the Moldavian steppe was still volatile they had brought their families—and more especially their women—with them!

There was a man with his two sons—aye, and a fine fat daughter, too. Another couple had *two* grown girls, who helped out with the skinning, curing and what all. Oh, and there were others, eating good red meat and taking pelts for the trading. Radu's informant had seen these people from the tree-line over the river. He had noted their locations, discovered their rude lodges in the rocks, but done nothing to alert them to his presence. They were only a few miles away, seven at a guess. Why, he could lead a party back there this very night . . .

Radu himself led the raiding party, and at last there was woman-flesh in the dog-Lord's cavern manse. Naturally, he took "first fruits" of the women; he had all of them that were worth having, kept the one he considered best for himself—the only one who'd tried to have his eyes out . . . at first, anyway—and gave the rest to his men. They'd fight over them, he knew that, but it was only to be expected. Indeed, Radu watched the rough-and-tumbling with great interest, in order to discover the most worthy fighters. These were his lieutenants, after all . . .

Another scout came in, bringing more information:

He had gone into the mountain hamlets in the guise of a beggar (but in fact as a spy) and seen how they were ripe for conquest and destruction. Why, the people were so soft he had no doubt they could even be herded, like so many cattle! Isolationists, pacifists, they had cut themselves off completely from the outside world, from all the surrounding war-torn regions of Dacia and the great battlefields under the mountains.

Radu couldn't really say he blamed them, and in any case it wasn't conquest that was on his mind; or perhaps . . . a very subtle conquest? No, these people didn't need a conqueror but a savior! He would not kill them, not yet, but instead offer them his services as a mercenary warrior, their *Voevod* against who or whatever might brave these mountains and attack them. A grand scheme, and a safe one at that; for indeed it seemed that the dog-Lord had been right and the mountains were impregnable. What? But only thirty years earlier Attila himself had had his headquarters at the foot of these very mountains—but even he had skirted them to continue his assault on the west!

And since Radu first commenced building Wolfscrag here? Six years sped by, and not a single invader had ventured into these heights. Or perhaps . . . could it be that the threat from the east was finally over? Uneasy precognitive dreams told him "no, not yet!" But Radu's dreams weren't always right. Or they were, but rarely worked out the way he thought they would. The future seemed a very devious thing. And just how long *was* the future, anyway . . . ?

Finally all of Radu's scouts returned, including the man he'd sent down onto the steppes to see how things stood. And now it was known for a fact: the last of the Huns had either retreated back into the east or settled the plains to the north. For the time being, locally at least, the fighting was over. Wherefore it seemed a good time for expansion. Now Radu's Wamphyri territorialism could come into play.

Obviously these mountains belonged to no one. They might be temporarily "annexed" now and then, by this or that regime, but no one held physical sway over them. It could be said that they belonged to the Dacians, the Ungars, the

Romans, whoever; but who was there here to protect them? No man . . . except Radu Lykan. And what is a mountain if not an aerie? And these horseshoe mountains, rearing like a buttress against the east?

Inhospitable, were they? What, like the colossal stacks of Starside? Ah, but there's inhospitable and there's inhospitable! By comparison, these mountains were sheerest luxury. And inaccessible? Aye, to an invader—but not to a man already in residence. And Radu was that man.

Very well. Hamlet by hamlet, village by village, town by town, these unconquered Dacian mountains would come under his control. At first he'd be the Voevod Radu, then a princeling, finally a king of his own land—*this* land! It might take all of fifty years, even longer, but what was that to Radu? Wamphyri, he had hundreds of years behind him, and an incalculable number ahead. His original men, those thralls and lieutenants who had come through the Gate with him: where were they? Gone down into the earth, or gone up in smoke and reek on some battlefield, that's where. Why, even the longest-lasting of them had been dead for twenty years! But Radu—he looked a young thirty; younger, if it so pleased him! Anonymity? *Bah* to anonymity . . . for now, anyway. But insularity? Ah, *yes!* He would protect the mountains, and the mountains would protect him.

So be it . . .

Rumours. One of Radu's scouts had heard it that a Ferenczy was in league with the Vandals. *Hah!* Well good luck to him, whoever he was, be it Nonari the Gross—if in fact he still lived—or this son of his, this Belos Pheropzis. For if that bastard Gaeseric dealt as badly with all of his mercenaries as he'd dealt with Radu . . . well, that was one Ferenczy he needn't hunt down!

As for the Drakuls:

They held fortress castles ("aeries," of course) in the western reaches of Dacia: in the Zarundului Mountains and the northern Carpathians. Perhaps they were enemies now; certainly they had put space between them! All the better when the time came for Radu to deal with them; he could take them out one at a time. And because they'd brought themselves into prominence and were become "legends"—*viesky* or *vrykoulakas,* who descend like bats in the night, to drink their victim's blood or steal his wife and children—it shouldn't prove too hard to recruit an army of locals to go against their castles. Oh, Radu looked forward to it! But all in good time.

And meanwhile he had work to do . . .

Radu had reckoned on fifty or more years to make himself Lord or "king" of the horseshoe mountains. It took all of that and would have taken more, if ever he'd been able to complete the job. But fate, history, and ancient enmities intervened. Despite earlier vows, he brought himself into prominence, became less than anonymous, set himself up as a target.

Fifty years to spread out into all the mountain hamlets, villages, towns. A half-century to become Voevod of the horseshoe range—in its eastern reaches, anyway—during a period in history when warlords or princelings were the last thing it needed. He had werewolf lieutenants in every town, with dozens of thralls to back them up. He knew every pass, track, route, and short-cut through the eastern heights, and could move his men with incredible speed from place to place. Of course he could, for there was that of the wolf in all of them. And indeed Radu and the pack were fearsome warriors . . . or would be. But where was the war? Never up here.

And Radu had been wrong, too, in his belief that the Drakuls would be hated. They were, by those they wronged, but they were worshiped by others! Indeed, in a hundred and fifty years they had infiltrated, corrupted and vampirized the populace of their own western mountain areas to such an extent that entire townships were now in thrall to them, including *all* of the hamlets on the approaches to their aeries!

Moreover, the Drakuls had recruited and turned loose many thralls to become their "emissaries" or servants (or more properly their spies) abroad in the world. These had become wanderers, Gypsies, and "Travelers" here no less than in Starside, in another world. And the Drakuls had engineered all of this a hundred years ago, when the Empire held sway over these Dacian parts. Why, men of the Drakuls had even crossed the borders to become true citizens of Rome—"sleepers," as it were, in the so-called "civilized" regions of a barbaric world. Romans, aye . . . or Romani? *Romany!* The source of yet another legend.

And so the Drakuls had become almost invulnerable, impervious to attack except perhaps in the drone of hot summer days when they slept in the deeps of their castles, in "native soil" brought with them out of Starside.

But Radu knew none of that, not then.

He knew where they were situated, but *not* their situation, how powerful they'd become. He might have guessed something of it when, well past the fifty years of his earlier reckoning, he sent spies to map out the land in the heart of Drakul territory . . . and they never returned. But Radu had grown powerful in his own right, until he believed that *he* was invulnerable. And perhaps this had made him lax . . .

Meanwhile, in the outside world beyond the mountains—beyond Dacia, beyond the Danube—history was passing him by. The Western Empire had crumbled away entirely; an Ostrogothic kingdom had been established in Italy; only the Eastern, "Byzantine" Empire, with its capital at Constantinople, survived intact. He knew of these things, for he was not without external intelligence; perhaps he even pined a little, for all the blood spilled on the reeking battlefields of the world. And all gone to waste, without that he'd been part of it.

And Gaeseric the Vandal king: dead and gone these forty-odd years; and Radu's Wamphyri vow of vengeance gone with him, for he'd not been a part of *that* either! Oh, it was maddening! Which was when he realized how bored he'd become. Well, enough of all that! And he promised himself that when finally he was established *throughout* the mountains, and not just in the east, then he'd find time to venture forth and play the warrior again.

But now, in order to bring that time forward—also as an exercise in preparation for it—*now* it was surely time for a grand expansion west, against the Drakuls!

Except . . . the Drakuls moved first, against him.

There had been warnings. In retrospect, looking back on the far past—still dreaming his unquiet dreams in the semi-solid matrix of his resin "tomb,"—

Radu knew it well enough: that there had been unsettling occurrences in his many outposts strung out north and south along the legs of the horseshoe range . . .

In the northern Carpathians, the Voevod Radu (occasionally "the Wolf") held sway in villages as far removed as Rakhov, and in the south as far as Turnu Rosu, where the hurtling waters of the Oltul had long since carved a pass through the mountains on their way to the Danube more than a hundred miles farther south. But many miles *inside* these far boundaries—deep in the Wolf's heartland—even there his outposts had had their problems. And not hard to guess what sort of problems.

He prepared expeditions to Iacobani in the north and Ruckar in the south, to see what could be done. Radu himself would lead the southern expedition; it would consist of some forty of his men, and one hundred more to be gathered along the way. Two of his bravest lieutenants—true werewolves or "pups"—would head north for Iacobani, and likewise collect a small army en route. These detachments of Radu's main mercenary force, whose nucleus was still centered in Wolfscrag and the hamlets around, should suffice to sort out the problem. Which was this:

Villagers and their wives and children in Ruckar, Iacobani and neighboring towns were being picked off by the *viesky,* the *Drakul* who fell upon his prey out of the night sky. People—mainly women, but occasionally children—had vanished without trace; other victims had been found drained of their life's blood. Mumbled prayers were said over them before they were put down into the ground . . . but they would not *stay* down! Those of Radu's lieutenants who were permanently stationed in the plague towns knew well enough how to deal with these undead "droppings" of the Drakuls—the stake, the sword, and the fire—but were at a loss as to what to do about the nightly attacks. They were werewolves and ran on the ground, while the Drakuls were flying creatures who struck out of the sky!

And so it was seen how the Drakuls' methods were the very opposite of Radu's. For despite that he was no longer "anonymous," still he kept the facts of his vampirism—the fact that he *was* Wamphyri, and especially the fact of his lycanthropy—fairly well hidden; whereas the Drakuls scathed openly abroad as vampires and revelled in their power. And where he used his military might and prowess to keep a tight rein on the peoples who came under his control and within his sphere of influence, they used fear pure and simple. Also, where Radu recruited men only in such numbers as were sufficient to resupply or complement the pack, and killed only strangers, wanderers, outsiders, and beasts of the wild for the provisioning—but *never* people under his "protection"; or rarely, when they were rebellious, or openly suspicious of him—the Drakuls not only recruited their thralls in outrageous numbers but were using their vampirism to infiltrate the enemy camp and destroy opposition from within. So that in a way their blunt methods were subtle after all: first convert Radu's people, and when his power base had been destroyed . . . then attack him!

These had been the Wolf's thoughts on the matter, and in his mind's eye he'd seen the gradual eastward creep of the Drakuls—their eating-up of his towns and villages—until at the last, as leaders of two vast vampire hordes, they'd join forces in a mass attack on Wolfscrag itself . . . and discover Radu and the remnants of his pack trapped in the cavern manse.

Then . . .

. . . Perhaps it was only the morbidity of Radu's old memories (for in their subconscious minds, even creatures who are grown evil and monstrous beyond words may be terrified anew by nightmares out of their past; even the horrific may be horrified) but suddenly he gave an involuntary shudder; a tremor ran through him in the semi-solid resin of his vat.

Or was the tremor in the resin itself?

What? A sound! A reverberation, however faint—or furtive? Now surely *the Drakuls were upon him . . . !!!*

But no, no, for that was only an old dream out of the distant past, while the sound had been here and now . . . immediate and threatening. And this time he could not be mistaken. There was someone here! Or . . . someone coming? Well, of course someone was coming, eventually. A delicious someone who always came. So perhaps that was it: anticipation, or wishful thinking. Imagination.

Ah, yesss! But it was much too early . . . she wouldn't be here yet awhile.

Anticipation, yesss. But not yet . . . awhile.

No, not yet . . . a . . . while . . .

Slowly Radu relaxed into resurgent dreams, allowing them to foam up again over his anxieties to drown them. And however uncertainly, however reluctantly—having come that much closer to a true awakening this time—his mind returned to its state of hibernation, its contemplation of bygone centuries . . .

At that time, in the mountains of Moldavia, Radu had scarcely realized the urgency of his situation; he had seen the gradual encroachment of the Drakuls across the Transylvanian mountains into Moldavia as just that: gradual. But in fact their plan had been more immediate, and their campaign not merely one of territorialism but also of destruction.

Radu's destruction, and now!

Partly, it was the enmity which exists between all great vampires. A hatred which had existed since the building of the first Starside aeries, which had been wrought in all the bloodwars of a parallel world, and which would now continue in this world until the end of time, or until no one was left to carry it on. It was the knowledge in the dark heart of every Lord of the Wamphyri that if he would live he must do to others of his kind before they did to him.

But from the Drakuls' point of view, it was also the need to clear the way for expansion. For it seemed to them that they had proved a point: that they *could* live as vampires here without hiding themselves away. Anonymity was no longer a requirement, no longer synonymous with longevity—but invincibility was!

They were not visionaries, the Drakuls, no; but planners, certainly. For the time being, for now, these soaring mountains were vast. But in some future time, would there be room for all the Wamphyri yet to come, those as yet unsired out of women, or brought about by transfusion of vampire eggs or poisoned blood? Which of them were destined to inherit this earth, these gaunt and gloomy mountains? The egg- and blood-sons of noble Drakuls, or the spawn of miserable dog-Lords? And what of the Ferenczys? Well, for the moment the Ferenczys were not part of the equation, but Radu Lykan most definitely was . . .

Radu's expeditionary forces were ready; he was on the point of sending them westward through the high passes when he heard a rumor—but *such* a rumor that it at once rooted in his imagination and grew there until he couldn't ignore it. Then, sending the Iacobani contingent north, he took his own party with him down into the steppe, to Bacau where this whisper had its origin. And now the truth was learned: how the Emperor Justinian had commissioned a fleet under the general Belisarius, to strike at the Vandals even across the Mediterranean, in north Africa and other parts . . . and take back the Western Empire.

The Vandals! and Radu's old vow still unfulfilled! And a *Ferenczy* among the treacherous scum at that! Old Gaeseric may have gone the way of all—or most—flesh, but at least one Ferenczy remained. And even after all this time any surviving member of the Ferenczy dynasty was far and away Radu's direst enemy, spawn of those olden destroyers of his dearest love in another world, another time. And all of it like yesterday to Radu.

His blood was up at once; he saw all kinds of possibilities: join with the Byzantines as a mercenary under Belisarius, distinguish himself in the field of battle, eventually return to these desolate heights, but as Voevod of all Dacia—and all with the Emperor's approval! And then see to the Drakuls, with an entire legion, perhaps, to back him up.

Grand schemes, except . . . no, it could never be. For his plans were made and his mind set. And in the west the Drakuls were waiting even now. Also, who could say how the Byzantines would come out of this new venture? What if they should lose? Indeed, it would be to Radu's advantage if that were the case (especially if he was not with them), for he would rather protect his mountain territories against some future invasion by Vandals than the reborn, restructured might of Rome!

And so, torn two ways, Radu returned to Wolfscrag in the heights. Or to what had been Wolfscrag. But now . . .

It might easily be a different place. Radu scarcely recognized it. But he did recognize his error, or something of it. His dreams of warfare in these mountains: not against invaders out of the east but the Drakuls; not against a horde of nomad warriors but a swarm of vampires! Under the gray cloud ceiling of early winter, there had been no sun to fear; they had flown by day, attacked by night. And, but for the fact that he'd gone down into the plain, Radu would have been part of it. But from the sheer *scale* of the devastation he knew that even he could never have survived it.

The gantlets were undermined, toppled inward. In several places the ceilings—even the sides of the crag, of the mountain peak itself—had fallen in, where black smoke roiled and the occasional tongue of flame still belched up from the fires within. Fifty years' work gone up in smoke. The scene was very nearly volcanic; certainly it burned in Radu's heart.

The Drakuls! Evidence of them and theirs was everywhere, but they had not had it all their own way. A half-dozen common thralls stood gaunt as sentinels in the early morning light, like mind-blasted, yellow-eyed totems on the slopes of ruined Wolfscrag; but a handful of grim, grimy, surviving lieutenants tumbled mangled vampire bodies down into the fiery vents, the while inhaling gustily on the reek of their burning.

Ah, Radu's dream was real as life, as death, as undeath! So that he sniffed, too— with his mind, *for his great wolf's nostrils were plugged with resin—and for a moment he could even smell the roasting meat . . .*

. . . Until he smelled something else!

Smelled—heard—sensed—something else!

A presence! An intelligence!

And this time he simply could *not* be mistaken. Footsteps, running. A mouth, gasping. A heart, pounding.

Radu's heart pounded, too, but just once: a single great throb in his breast, finally bringing him awake . . .

Bonnie Jean came to the place of her Master. She came panting, with pictures of the vat-creature's slit of an alien eye still burning on the eye of her own mind. And she came pondering the question of her own presence here. It was hardly the first time she'd so pondered, and it wouldn't be the last. But did it constitute uncertainty, making her unworthy? Surely not. Surely it was part of the ritual: not only to perpetuate Him but her own faith in Him. For after all she was *of* Him, however, many times removed.

And the creature in the vat? Was that *of* Him, too? Bonnie Jean knew that it was, and once more was set to wondering: what *sort* of a future world would it be, when He came up to elevate mankind into His kind? What part could a *Thing* or things such as the vat-creature play in the dark and deadly future world of her Master's forevisioning? His guardian creatures? But against what, in a world where the dog-Lord was the ultimate power?

At the western extreme of the lair she recognized her location, came to a halt, controlled her breathing. It would never do to approach Him in this agitated state, showing signs of her uncertainty. But as she waxed more and more *like* Him, the more fearful she grew . . .

. . . And *that* was a thought to give pause, too! What, Bonnie Jean Mirlu, His from birth, fearful? And of Him? Ridiculous! It was this place, playing on her nerves, her mind; it was the creature in its resin vat; it was . . . anxiety, yes! The advent of Harry Keogh, and the watcher in Edinburgh, and recent events in general. But most of all it was awareness of the fast-approaching time of her Master's awakening, when He would be up again. A time of change, when her oh-so-long established way of life must *of necessity* change, to accommodate His.

For at present He was only her Master *in absentia,* and she was the "wee mistress." But . . . how much influence would Bonnie Jean retain when the Master was back? And if it's true that when the cat's away the mice will play, how "playful" the cub when the Wolf is not to house? Would her Master have given thought to such, or was it beneath Him? Could He consider such things, in His long sleep, and why did she give thought to it? *Had* she been unfaithful, if only in her mind, in her thoughts? Bonnie Jean didn't think so; but in any case never seriously, and *never* maliciously!

But then, she would be *Wamphyri! And they were ever prideful, territorial . . . and this had been* her *territory for close on two hundred years!*

What!?

She couldn't go to Him thinking these thoughts! She hadn't intended to think them! It was this place, her mood, the question of her own continuity, when all that should concern her was His!

How would it be when He was up? What would be allowed, and what disallowed?

Men? Oh, she'd known men over the years. But that had been entirely compatible with her faithfulness to Him. Indeed He had *required* that she know men, so that she might be experienced in all things. He wished no wilting, virginal hand-maiden sitting at His right hand in that dark, future world of His visions but an experienced woman. No naïve, blushing bumpkin but a scholar in all Man's ways, in his emotions as well as his sciences. For the more a man (or a woman, or a changeling creature out of the myths and legends of the past) knows his enemy, the more easily he may dispose of him.

Intelligence . . .

Aye, intelligence, that was it! . . . To gather knowledge of the world around, for His sake. And surely to have intelligence was to *be* intelligent and to question things? Even such questions as Bonnie Jean had asked herself? But they were not symptomatic of treachery. Never that.

Intelligence? . . . A presence? . . . Bonnie! Bonnie Jean! (A grunt, almost of pain, finally of recognition, but sounding in her mind!)

And then B.J. reeled as if struck in the forehead, as she knew that the words in her head were not hers but His. *She* was the intelligence, that presence He referred to; for her Master had sensed her here! But how long had He been listening, while she thought . . . *such* thoughts?

She cleared her mind; indeed her thoughts were driven out, if only by her utter confusion. And: "Master, I am here." She gasped the words out, concentrating only on Him.

Bonnie! Bonnie Jeeeeean! (A grunt, a snarl, finally a sigh. Then a vast and terrible sniffing, like that of a great hound—*the* Great Hound—as He tracked her essence through the shuddering vaults of her mind.) And echoing there: *But I had thought . . . an intruuuuder!*

She was in control of herself now. "No intruder, no." She shook her head, then lifted her gaze up, up, taking in the outline of his great stone sarcophagus, like an altar at the apex of a granite jumble: the source of these, His thoughts. "No intruder, my Master. Just me."

(Another rumbling sigh, and His thoughts coming clearer to her as the mental connection strengthened, as His concentration centered upon her.) *Ahhhh! Bonnie Jeeeean! But . . . did I call you? It seems . . . too soon?*

"You did not call me, my Master." (Bonnie Jean had caught her breath now; she was fully in command of the situation, of her words and thoughts alike.) "But I came in a hurry, before my time. If I have disturbed you, then I am sorry, but events were such . . ."

Eventsss?

"Yes," she nodded, climbing the crazily angled jumble of the steps. "Yes, there have been . . . occurrences. A watcher in Edinburgh—some kind of spy, perhaps—and a mysterious stranger. Perhaps these things mean nothing, I can't yet say, but I thought it best that you should know."

But just as quickly as Bonnie Jean had regained command of her senses, so Radu had come fully awake. And as she stepped up onto the platform of his sarcophagus, so she felt the intensity of his thoughts—his mental frown—right through the stone slab walls of his coffin. *A spy, in Edinburgh?* (His "voice" was sharp, severe.) *And a mysterious stranger? And yet you saw fit to come here? What, and would you place me in jeopardy, Bonnie Jean?*

"Never that, my Master!" She shrank back from his severity. "For am I not your guardian, set to watch over you? And I have watched most diligently. I have served you faithfully. Why, my blood is in you, as yours is in me! But now I need advice, and who else can I go to?"

(Radu's grunt by way of reply. And after a moment's consideration): *First tell me about this watcher, this spy. Could it be . . . Them? Do you think they seek me out?*

"I think it must be them, yes," she answered, and she told him what Harry Keogh had told her. It wasn't much, but it worried him nevertheless. When she was done:

But what if you were followed on your way here? How do you know your precautions were sufficient? At least one Drakul survives; so I believe, for I have dreamed it. Aye, and more than one Ferenczy! And here am I, a weak, shriveled old thing like . . . why, like a fly in amber! I am not ready to be up, Bonnie Jean. I cannot protect myself. And you . . . are only a girl.

At which she bridled a very little, and knew that he would sense it as surely as if they were face to face. Then, climbing onto the piled slabs toward one end of the sarcophagus, she leaned over the rim to gaze down on him; so that now they *were* face to face. But his form was indistinct, obscured by the resin where dust had settled on its crusted, wrinkled surface. She stared harder, until slowly the thing in the resin took on an awesome outline.

His eyes were closed, of course, as they had been for all of the two hundred years she'd known and served him. But behind them, as ever, Bonnie Jean saw, sensed, but couldn't quite feel their heat. Oh, but it was there, subdued but not quenched: the flickering heat of life—or undeath—suspended to the limit. Moreover, it was as if something of the fire of those eyes had spilled out onto their sunken orbits, to turn them and his hollow cheeks ruddy against the sick-yellow pallor of his face in general.

Her Master, despite that he was not *all* man, was a veritable giant of a man. He must be almost seven feet tall, and in his heyday, full-fleshed, he had been more physically powerful—and more dangerous, certainly—than any intelligent creature the world had ever known. He'd had the speed and cunning of the wolf, the intelligence of man, the strength of the Wamphyri!

And will again, Bonnie Jean, and will again, he told her. And in a moment: *Very well, I can see that I have offended you. And I accept that you came here in all good faith, and that you have taken all necessary measures to keep me safe. And truth to tell, I have been feeling . . . weak. Which has made me impatient and less than agreeable. Is that so hard to understand? I think not. The years of waiting have been long, and what am I become but a wraith of my former self? And you are right: your blood has kept me warm, kept me alive. So, this time you are early; perhaps it is as well, for my spark flickers low, Bonnie Jean. But you . . . shall rekindle it yet again.*

At that last Radu's "voice" had fallen to a low, guttural, almost a lustful growl, which Bonnie Jean had answered with an involuntary shudder (of immeasurable horror . . . or unthinkable pleasure? She couldn't say), for his meaning was clear enough.

That, however, will have to keep for now, the thing in the resin quickly went on, and his voice was normal again. *Aye, for we have other things to do, to discuss. Problems have presented themselves; but until I know their extent, I cannot know how to counter them. And there have been other problems, which remain . . . unresolved? What about the girl? A whole year, Bonnie Jean. Is she still missing? Is there no news of her? If not, we must assume the worst: that* They *took her! Wherefore, they could be that much closer to you, and to me . . .*

But: "No," B.J. shook her head, and knew he would sense it. "She didn't know this place; she'd never been here. Nor did she know *you,* my Master."

But she knew of *me. And certainly she knew of you.*

"She was sworn to silence," B.J. countered. "She was beguiled, hypnotized . . . she could *not* speak! None of us can, and myself least of all; you *your*self have seen to that, my Master. An enemy might contrive to steal me away—though not without a fight—but he could never make me talk . . ."

Huh! (A wry, dry, barking chuckle.) *But you do not know the Wamphyri, Bonnie Jean. With them, you must always assume the worst. However, let us put that aside for now and go on to this other thing. You have told me about the watcher. We will talk about him—what to do about him—again. But you also made mention of a mysterious stranger. What, and have you let a man into your life, Bonnie Jean? Into our lives? Ah, and you seem to consider him important! I can even feel your . . . what, excitement? Very well, and now perhaps you will tell me about him.*

Yesss, tell me all about your mysterious stranger.

Or better still, show meeee.

And she did. For long minutes the story flowed from her mind to his, just as she remembered it. And while it answered certain questions he hadn't yet asked—such as the result of her quest for a bogus werewolf in London, which she had undertaken on his behalf—it prompted others which he'd scarcely conceived *ever* to ask her.

And now Radu's excitement was as great as hers . . .

BONNIE JEAN: HER DUTIES.
THE DOG-LORD: HIS SOLUTION.

T *HIS MAN,* (RADU'S "VOICE" WAS EAGER, ALMOST PANTING, IN BONNIE JEAN'S mind), *this Harry Keogh. I have seen him with your eyes and know how he strikes me. But how did he strike you?*

B.J. didn't quite know how to answer. "As . . . mysterious," she finally said, and tried to suppress her involuntary shrug. "As if he hid secrets where there couldn't possibly *be* secrets, because he was beguiled. He struck me as a man who has seen and experienced things no other man ever saw or experienced. He was warm, gentle, human . . . and yet he was cold, hard, and—"

Inhuman? (The Great Wolf sniffed in her mind, literally a *blood*hound on the trail.) *Yet still you tell me that he's not one of them!*

"He *is* human, my Master," she told him. "I would stake my life on it."

Oh, but you already have, he answered with a low, rumbling growl. But as B.J. recognized the threat, he quickly added, *All of our lives!* Which served to relieve something of the onus he had seemed to place on her.

"Master," she set out to convince him, "this man had me in his power, however briefly—but long enough to kill me, certainly! Instead he kept me from trouble, from harm. He admits to skills that would be of great benefit to you. He has worked for . . . a covert agency" (she was finding difficulty in describing Harry's duties; and no wonder, for she scarcely understood them herself). "He was . . . *above* the laws of the land. Now, as *your* agent, he could prove invaluable. As a fighter, he's quick and strong. And as a thinker, deep, I think. If there's more to him than I have found, I know you can find it where I have failed." There was nothing more she could tell him.

After a while:

As to how he struck me: forcefully, Bonnie Jean. He struck me powerfully, and with more than any normal power. Why, I felt it in your mind! He was beguiled, aye, but he likewise beguiled you! You were attracted to him as a man, not so? Don't deny it, for even though you won't admit it to yourself, you cannot lie to me. I have felt it: your fascination for this . . . this mysterious one, aye.

"But . . . but . . . !" B.J. sputtered, because her Master had seen what she had not, or what she had refused to accept.

Oh? Ha-ha-ha-ha! Radu's laughter was a staccato barking that stabbed briefly, harshly in her mind . . . before coming to an abrupt halt. *And is that why he's still alive, Bonnie Jean? Because you desired to feel him in your body, his root burrowing in your soil, seeking to seed itself in the garden of your sex? Is it so? Did you desire to fuck him, Bonnie Jean? Or for him to fuck you?*

"My Master, I . . ."

Then you should have! *For there are more ways to enslave a man than by sharing your blood, your essence; better ways to enthrall him than by a bite; other ways to seduce than by addiction to poisoned wines.* His voice fell to a whisper, a whine, a fetid panting. And it seemed that he stripped her to the soul as he informed, *Why, your woman's body would more than suffice to enslave a man—any man, or creature—I am sure. Your soft breasts and thighs would enthrall, enfold him. And the suction of your sex would be a greater addiction, a sweeter poison far than any wine, however strange and rare . . .*

Bonnie Jean got down from the rim of his sarcophagus, stood with her head bowed, and stared at the buckled flags supporting his great coffin. She felt shame, for plainly her devotion had been to other than her Master. But it had taken Him to identify emotions that she had rejected. Radu felt B.J.'s confusion, her dejection, and said:

No, Bonnie Jean, you are not at fault. You're a woman, destined to be more than a woman. And you have suppressed emotions that are instinct in you as they are in me. In so doing, you've also proved a point: that you are not yet *Wamphyri! For the Wamphyri may not* suppress *their emotions. If they could, then were they unstoppable, unbeatable! Aye, and that is important to me, Bonnie Jean: that you are* not yet *of that high station. For the . . . condition* of the Great Vampire is such as to make it, well, let us say *undesirable, at this time.*

He fell silent (musing, she thought.) But his meaning had not escaped her . . .

After a while—if only to change the subject and divert his thoughts—B.J. felt it prudent to prompt him: "Master, I am here early, that's true. But in any case it is close to the time of your renewal. While you give thought to the things I've told you, we should see to your replenishing. Also to the needs of your creature . . ."

My warrior? He was at once interested. *Is the beast well? Does the great vat support him? Does he wax and quicken? Surely it is so. For since he is of me, he too must feel the time narrowing down.*

"He waxes, my Master. He . . . *quickens* in his vat, yes."

See to it, then, he told her. *Tend the beast first, while I lie here and think, and consider . . . oh, a great many things. But hurry, Bonnie Jean, for you have awakened me and my time is nigh. And I hunger like a helpless child stirring in his crib, but the faithful little mother is at hand to bare her breast . . .*

B.J. went out onto the bald, doomed roof of Radu's redoubt and followed a southwesterly route that she'd known for the better part of two centuries. Indeed to her keen eyes and senses there was now a clearly discernible track between scattered boulders, across gaping fissures, and through the treacherous screen jumbles of the high, narrow passes.

Her camouflaged denim suit was crag-gray and lichen-green, matching her surroundings. Over her left shoulder, tied across her back, she carried a rope; also on the left, two small grappling irons dangled from her wide leather belt. A crossbow hung on her right thigh, and was strapped just above the knee so as not to swing with her movements. These things, plus a knife in a leather sheath, were all that Bonnie Jean carried.

To her relief, the sun was hidden behind bank upon bank of clouds sweeping in from the west, across the Monadhliath Mountains and the Spey. It was mid-afternoon, creeping toward evening; the shadows of the crags beginning to creep, too, but that meant nothing to B.J. Her eyes were feral as the wilds she traversed; they saw the wildcats sporting in the heather before the cats saw her. Only the eagles, circling on high, had any great advantage. But she wasn't interested in cats and eagles. Both were difficult, and both dangerous until stone dead.

But on the penultimate, false-plateau of a series of mighty terraces east of Loch Insh, B.J. knew there were near-inaccessible woodlands and copses in the lee of the upper heights. Knew, too, that she'd find deer there—indeed, a small herd of deer. Her kill would not be missed; these were creatures of the wild; she was the only one who had ever culled them. And she required just one, a fawn; not for sweetness but size. It must be easily portable, back to the lair.

She came to the rim. The forest-belt sprawled a dark, misted green all of seven hundred feet below, and the chimney of a teetering stack was her route down.

At the top of the last stage of her descent, B.J. used her rope to form a hoist and lowered the grapples, and without further pause went hand over hand to the bottom. Her prey had long since sensed her and fled, of course; in this place, there were no sounds extraneous to nature. Any sound that was strange was also dangerous.

So she tracked them through the woods. And from then on, never a snapped twig or the swishing recoil of a brushed-aside branch to give her away . . . until the last moment, when the gut of her crossbow thrummed and the lethal bolt hissed unerringly to its target . . .

Paralysed, with its spine almost severed at a point one inch forward of the flanges of its shoulders, the buck merely trembled as B.J. used the rope and grapples to hoist it by stages up the cliff. The animal had voided itself in the woods and so didn't foul her. Then the four-mile trek back to the lair, with the shuddering buck on her shoulders, and B.J. hoping against hope that it wouldn't die along the way. No, for at the vat of Radu's beast she would require the engine of its pounding heart to beat to the very last.

At the lair, she lowered the animal into the vent closest to the great vat, followed it into darkness. Shortly, she ascended the ramp to the rim of the vat and tossed the buck down onto the yellow, semi-solid surface. Then back down and around to the rear of the vat, where a copper implement was stored in oiled wrappings. It was a hollow tube three feet long, three-quarters of an inch in diameter, with a trumpetlike funnel at one end. The pointed end had been cut through diagonally, like the tip of a hypodermic needle.

Back up the ramp to the buck, where B.J. moved the paralyzed animal aside in order to drive the sharp end of the funnel down into the resin . . . at which the obscure outline or silhouette of Radu's creature *stirred visibly,* however sluggishly, in the gelatinous soup of its vat womb! For the fluids in the sacklike core were not alone of resin and therefore less resistant. She saw the sudden movement, which caused her to start. It was the first time in *all* B.J.'s time that this had happened. And it meant that her Master was right: his beast was indeed quickening!

Then, without further pause (or, if anything, more urgently, while yet her mood was right for it) she worked the copper tubing down into the gummy resin, a good two-thirds of its length, until the funnel stuck up like a pouting mouth. And grimacing a little, but with no other sign of reticence, she cut the buck's throat and held its body steady on the rim, watching its life's blood spurting into the obscene bell-mouth of the funnel, from there to gurgle its way to the thing in the vat.

Down there, there might be a rudimentary mouth or mouths. B.J. didn't know, couldn't say. She only knew that the living blood of the buck would be absorbed into her Master's creature. A quart of blood, maybe. So little for so much, but enough. And only a little less for Radu, despite that he had only one-tenth of the vat-thing's bulk. But then, Radu needed—or demanded—so much more. And *not* deer's blood . . .

In a while (surprisingly long minutes later, when the flow was less than a clotting trickle), B.J. dragged the buck's body to one side and drew out the long funnel. Taking it to a place where water fell vertically from above, and cascaded into conjectural depths below, she washed the funnel out, replaced it in its wrappings, returned it to its niche behind the vat.

Then she cut out the raw, fresh heart of the buck to take with her, and toppled the stiffening carcass down the dark and unknown course of the waterfall. And now it was time to attend Radu.

· The day had seemed very short; it was the season, and B.J. had had much to do. Outside, the sun was setting, the light fading. Her eyes readily adjusted to the gloom of the cavern complex, as she returned to the sarcophagus, kindled a fire of bone-dry faggots from a pile of prepared wood, boiled water on a tripod and brewed tea. Hungry herself now, and succumbing at last to her own needs, she ate the buck's heart raw with teeth that formed razor cusps even as they worked at the wild flesh. Jaws like a steel trap finished the job in short order: not much by way of sustenance, but the heart's dark muscle had been strong and B.J.'s system would make best use of what little there had been. She could have saved more of the buck, but hadn't wanted to glut herself. No, for now she must stay alert, and not give in to the inevitable drowsiness of her imminent . . . depletion.

Her depletion, yes, for her Master would have it no other way. How often had he told her: "The flesh and blood of one's own must always be the dearest, as it *is* always the sweetest!" His meaning had never been entirely clear—at best it sounded sinister—but B.J. had taken it to mean that the blood of men and women, human beings, was the natural fare of the werewolf. And apart from a handful of occasions when she'd brought various thralls and recruits here, this perhaps dubious duty had been hers alone.

Fortified by her meal, now it was time . . .

Radu's funnel was of soft beaten gold; only its needle tip was of copper. B.J. took it from its secret place, carefully wiped it clean, carried it up to the rim of his sarcophagus and gazed down on him. "Master, I am ready."

As am I, Bonnie Jean! His answer rang at once in her mind. *As am I, yesss. And I have given thought to everything you've told me. Now, as you attend me, I shall tell you what must be done. For time is narrowing down, and my dreams scan ahead of me to strange new tomorrows. Nothing must be allowed to interfere with my . . . my resurrection? And everything must be done to enhance it. For while I have "seen" to that point, beyond it lies uttermost confusion. The future of all men and creatures was ever a devious thing, Bonnie Jean. And mine—and yours—no less. But for you I have seen a full and glorious moon: a wondrous good omen, yesss! While for myself, I shall be bright as a star! And so our places in tomorrow's firmament seem fixed, which is the where and the when of it. But as to the* how *of it: that remains to be seen . . .*

While he "talked" to her, B.J. busied herself. She pushed the feeder into the resin crust of Radu's sarcophagus and used her weight to drive it slowly but surely deeper into the semi-congealed stuff within. A gauge-mark scratched into the golden tube, coming level with the surface of the resin, told her precisely where to stop. Any deeper and the sharp, hollow "knife" point of the funnel would drive right into Radu's face.

About the watcher, Radu continued, as she prepared a tourniquet on her left arm, but left it slack. *If this is no innocent or coincidental thing, then it can only be one of extreme menace. And indeed I feel* menaced! *This watcher is a thrall: a Ferenczy, or a Drakul, aye. He watches you to discover me. And he* will *discover me, if he can, and lead his master here to my lair—through you, Bonnie Jean, through you! And so there is only one answer to it: dispose of him. But not now, not yet.*

First learn all about him; know him as you know yourself, if that is at all possible, so that he may not creep up on you unannounced. Then, closer to the time—but only when I give the word—then see to him! For if he were to suddenly disappear, now, immediately . . . why, his master would surely understand that he had found me, and that I had found him!

And shortly thereafter there would be two watchers, then three . . . until in the end I would starve up here, because you could not come to me. Or if and when you did, my enemies would follow you and find me helpless here. And be sure, Bonnie Jean, that they would deal just as cruelly with you as with me. For you are a woman and comely, and they . . . are Wamphyri!

B.J. sat beside the rim of the sarcophagus with her back to an angled slab of stone, but not too comfortably, and without glancing away made one slicing cut through the arteries of her left wrist with the razor-sharp blade of her knife. Indeed it was so sharp that she scarcely felt its bite—or only very briefly—and the cut was so clean that for a single moment it remained closed. Long enough for her to lean forward over the rim and direct the first sudden spurt into the golden funnel.

But Radu had "heard" the *hiss* of air between her clenched teeth, felt the sting in her mind, sensed the tightening of her stomach, and knew what these things meant. And, *Ahhhh!* he said, as the hot, red, salty stream commenced to flow down the golden tube to his encysted figure. Then, to cover the unmistakable lust that suddenly burned like fire in his thoughts (and must surely burn its way into Bonnie Jean's), he forced himself to continue with his instructions:

. . . So then, he barked, *we have dealt with this watcher. Or we will, eventually. But always remember, Bonnie Jean, that revenge is a dish best served cold. Revenge? Oh, yesss! for I have seen in your mind how he has worried and angered you with his snooping. And I know that you would be avenged, even as I must avenge myself against his master, one of mine own enemies out of ancient times. But attend me well, Bonnie Jean. It can be nothing dramatic, nothing spectacular. When the time comes this watcher should simply . . . yes, disappear! Let his master wonder but never know. That way, by the time he must know the way of it, and when his curiosity brings him to seek me out, I shall be up and about in the world. Time then for my revenge, aye! But only think, Bonnie Jean: if such as you have felt the urge to strike at our enemies—and for what good reason, eh? The small irritation of covert observation? The shuddering anticipation of some unknown, unspecified DOOM waiting just around the corner—then what of my passions, whose torment has lasted for two thousand years? Huh! Well, let me tell you: there were blood-feuds before mine, and bloodwars since. But the next one will be hot, be sure. As hot as every hell that men have ever dreamed . . . !*

Then a pause so sudden, so sharp it was almost a gasp in B.J.'s mind, as the first drop of her blood, then a gush—a crimson, bloating bubble in the yellow envelope of fluid surrounding him—stained and suffused the area of Radu's weird wolf head. And:

Ahhhh! It was almost a sob of pain, but an agony so sweet that it vibrated like some unbearable note struck on the chords of the mind. And in B.J.'s mind it was the rushing, irretrievable cry of climactic sex, the nerve-wrenching howl of a shovel in clay-cold ashes, the joy of the full moon when its call can no longer be denied. It was all of these things, and more. It was the blood that is the life.

Her blood, and Radu's life, as the influx, the monstrous infusion, commenced.

And it was always the same: as if her Master were a live, alien current, which the conductor of her blood carried back to Bonnie Jean. For once the connection was made, the current came flowing back up the life-stream and into her. It *leaped* to her, quick as light, with the speed of an electric arc: the incredible, terrible fact of Him! And as always—if only for those first few unutterable, unbearable seconds—she knew the *truth* of Him. That there was no truth *in* Him!

It came and it went, and left her floating, drifting on a sea of unknown emotions, no less than his bite would have done. For one brief moment the agony of Truth . . . and for the rest of time the inescapable acceptance of a Great Lie. And before she could consider the difference, or even the existence of a difference:

Yesss! (His hiss sounded that much clearer in B.J.'s innermost being.) *Ah, yesss! Child of my children, my life is in you, as you were in me. My life is you, as yours will be mine. But not yet awhile, not yet . . .*

And as something of his unthinkable pleasure receded, and he accepted the renewal of his hideous life:

As for the girl, gone for a year and never to return: we must accept that she is no more.

At best she has become one of theirs: a Drakul or a Ferenczy, aye. More likely, she's a husk, drained of knowledge and life both. Let us assume that you are right and she could not talk. Still she "told" enough to interest them; hence the watcher. Or has he been there a long time, Bonnie Jean? Longer than you suspect? Even years, decades? The latter, I think. If not, then how did they know to take one of yours in the first place? What came first, the egg, the spore, or the leech? It is a riddle; it moves in a circle and is best left alone. Likewise the girl . . . forget her. She is no more.

B.J. listened with the one part of her mind that remained alert. As for the rest: her eyes were closing, her head nodding until she struggled to keep it upright. Drowsing, she was carried on the current of Radu's life, and was nothing without that she belonged to him. It was his art, his hypnotism, the beguiling. She had it, too, but by comparison was an infant where he was the old, old Master . . . but a master of more than mere hypnotism.

And B.J.'s heart thudded, her blood pumped, and her mind listened . . .

Finally we have this . . . this mysterious one (Radu eventually continued). *Of whom you admit to wondering: perhaps the Mysterious One? Yesss, Bonnie Jean, and you have set me to wondering, too. For I have seen him in my dreams these many ages, and the one whom you have shown to me is not dissimilar. But in my dreams . . . strange, but I never saw him clearly. While I was given to know of him, I was never permitted to know him. He was blurred, aye, or at best ill-defined, as all dreams of the future are, only more so. And so I came to think of him as The Man With Two Faces, because while he remained the same . . . his face changed! Not that he was "two-faced," as in the common usage of that term, you understand. No, for this has nothing to do with simple treachery.*

So . . . what does it mean? For I have read it in your mind, that you, too, Bonnie Jean, have seen another side of him—as if some other were looking out through his eyes? But could that other be me, in some future time? If so, then indeed he is the Mysterious One of my dreams. Or—

—Is it all a trick, a trap, a clever subterfuge? (Radu's mental voice was suddenly sharp as B.J.'s knife.) *He helped you when he could have killed you, you say. But I remember how, in the Greek Sea, the fishermen would bait their hooks with little fishes—to catch big ones! And this "covert agency" he worked for. Whose agency, I ask? The powers that be, you say. For what good purpose, I ask? To which you answer, "to usurp the laws of the land, and supplement them where they will not suffice!" Eh? Usurp the laws? I am astonished! For this agency must be powerful indeed, that it works outside of governments and laws! Very well, then who were this Mysterious One's masters? Alas, here we have no answer, for this was a line you did not pursue. Ah, but be sure that I will . . . !*

Radu paused, probed a moment with his vampire mind, and immediately, worriedly inquired: *Is all well, Bonnie Jean? Do you hear me? Best attend me, for my needs shall go on beyond today. And I would that you go on with them!*

B.J. jerked awake. She had *been* awake, the part of her that listened, at least. And she saw that the funnel was overflowing into the sarcophagus, where her blood pooled on the crusty resin. Like the gauge-marks on the stem of Radu's funnel, this was her warning, telling her, "this far but no further!"

It was not the first time that this had happened, nor that her Master had "saved" her life. But then, what would become of him without her?

She tightened the tourniquet on her arm, watched the spurting slow to a sporadic spatter, willed her metamorphic flesh to action. *Heal me!* Then, as she got stiffly down from the sarcophagus, a last twist on the tourniquet, which she taped in position. And finally the slow, awkward business of bandaging her wrist with dressings from her pack.

While she worked, Radu talked to her:

How many times had I expired without you, Bonnie Jean? How often have I escaped the true death? But the sweet hot spark of your life's blood rekindles mine and I live anew . . . if such as this may be considered life. (A creature of moods, now her Master was sour again. And B.J. knew why. It was always the same when his needs had been satisfied—or his immediate needs, at least.)

Ah, you read me well, he told her. *For I would be up again, and abroad in the world of men. I would be up, even now, except pestilence put me down. And so I stay here, waiting out my time. And I keep myself quiet, lest my thoughts go out into the world and others hear them. And I dream my red dreams, and keep them quiet, too, for the same good reason. And my bones stiffen, and my flesh sags, and even my memory fades a little, for time is a long, long thing. So that sometimes I wonder at the purpose of it all . . .*

. . . Until you return to me, and then I know the purpose of it all! For once I was as men and lived with men. I fought side by side with men, as were they my equal. I tried to be the same as men, but was different. I reined back on my spirit, which is a roaring fire that devours!!! *And I quenched it as best possible. But I was wrong to try, Bonnie Jean. Aye, for to be Wamphyri is to be other than men, more than men.*

Oh, I have a man's appetites, be sure. Indeed, I have them tenfold! I do not love but lust; which is better than love, for when love lies spent lust drives on. And the strength of a man? Why, in these hands of mine strong men have snapped like twigs! As for the span of a man: what mere man has survived for thirty lifespans? And as for a man's passions: who before me has hated for twenty long centuries, and will continue *to hate so long as his enemies survive, even to the end of time?*

And my thirst, my thirssst! Ahhh! Do you recall how it is when the day is hot and the way is long, and there is no water? And then the sparkle of a stream . . . your hand trembling as you lift the water to your lips? Well, I have thirsted for six hundred years, *Bonnie Jean! Ah, no, I am not ungrateful, and you have sustained me . . . but a quart? Sometimes I think I know the source of these measures: for is not a quart one fourth part of all your blood? Close enough, I think. But a quart! Why, I have* bathed *in blood, the blood of whole men, and women, and babes—and* still *I wanted more!*

Men? With their puny needs, they are as ticks on the back of a goat. But I am a wolf, and the field is filled *with goats! Except I am crippled, trapped, immobilized. Why, I lie so still they don't even suspect I'm here at all. Only the other wolves know. Only my own sort, aye . . .*

He rambles, B.J. thought, unmindful of her own thoughts as she rekindled her fire, with which to warm a can of soup. *He is delirious on my blood, like a man who has drunk too much strong liquor. These are only his frustrations coming out of him, and nothing more. This is* not *the way he will be.*

WHAT? Her Master at once shouted, or snarled, in her mind. *And is it for you to say how I will or will not be?*

"Forgive me," B.J. answered wearily from where she sat by her fire. "I . . . I think I must be delirious, too, for it seems you've had more than a quart, my Master. And I have rarely felt so tired . . ."

He was at once solicitous. *Ahhh! Bonnie Jean, Bonnie Jean! It is my fault, my fault! But I hungered so . . . I let it go too long, too long.*

"No harm done," she sighed. "I have Auld John's soup, his strong tea. I'll stay here the night, and rest."

Aye, he answered, *aye. The way down is hard, and you must be strong for it.*

"The way is nothing," B.J. shook her head. "The climb is child's play. But in the dark I could slip, and the way I feel right now . . ."

Best rest, he told her. *Best rest . . .*

But in a little while, spooning soup as she huddled beside her fire in a blanket, B.J. was curious to know something. "My Master, how would it have been? What would be the result if you had not roused me up? Not death, I know. Not the true death."

Indeed, no, my Bonnie, he answered, so low it was a coughing rumble in her mind. *Never the true death, not for you. For you, undeath. But* with *you . . . quite unnecessary. You are what you are. A throwback? No, a throw forward! That is the way of it. Blood tells, Bonnie Jean, and in you it runs true.*

"I would be . . . Wamphyri?"

Will be, perhaps. (But now she sensed a seething darkness in his mental voice.)

"Perhaps?"

Her master at once came alive again, and the darkness receded. *Time will tell, my faithful one,* he said. *Aye, time alone will tell . . .*

B.J. gave herself a shake, as the dog-Lord abruptly inquired: *Where . . . where was I? For it appears you were right, and I rambled? Certainly my mind has wandered.*

It was as if he, too, had been asleep; his thoughts were dull, uncertain, groping in her mind.

The lair was so much darker now; B.J.'s fire burned low; a sappy branch crackled and popped, and sent a few last sparks flying. Through the rocky tangle of the high crystalline vaulting, a lone star glittered like an eye frozen in a stony orbit.

"The Mysterious One," B.J. reminded her Master. "Have you reached a solution?"

I remember, Radu's "tone" was more focused now. *But you are mistaken; I had already reached a solution, but I had not voiced it. I must see him—talk to him with my own "voice"—have him here, where I can decide for myself his value . . . or his threat? But not yet. Not yet a while. So, my solution:*

He has things to do, you say. Then let him do them. For a year, even two years. He would search for his missing wife and child? Good! let him search. Ah, but he is resourceful; he has talents. Excellent! Let us put them to use. We are agreed that my enemies seek me out. Very well: let this "mysterious" Harry Keogh seek them out! Let him locate them for us. Then, when or if they do not see fit to come to me, I can always go to them! So, how is that for a solution?

"And if he draws attention to you, what then?"

Huh! But their attention has never been absent! They have sought me for long and long! And as always, I shall rely upon you to hold them at bay.

"And if he places himself in jeopardy, maybe gets himself killed?"

What is that to us? Or should I say, to me? For plainly it is a great deal to you! But I take your point. You are asking: why sacrifice a valuable ally? Is that it? Well, for one: his value is not yet proven. This could be the ultimate test. And for two: if he is indeed my Man

With Two Faces—the Mysterious One of my dreams—then he'll suffer no harm. How can he, and still come to me at the time of my coming forth?

"But . . . before he can seek them out—the Drakuls and the Ferenczys—he must know of them. And you have always forbidden me to speak of them. As you lie secret in the world, my Master, so must they, else alert men to the presence of us all!''

A good argument (Radu seemed genuinely pleased with her). *But a false one. Do you think I would let someone loose in the world with that sort of knowledge, without that we place certain strictures upon him? Of course not! You have told me he is in thrall. True?*

"Beguiled," she nodded. "And by now addicted to your wine. He knows nothing at all of you; nothing of me, except that I am an innocent, a friend, and possibly—''

A lover?

B.J.'s silence answered for her.

All to the good. For I tell you, Bonnie Jean, that if he is not your lover, or does not at least aspire, then he is not a man by my books. Which means he is not my *man!*

"And if he does . . . aspire?''

What? And should I send you out to whore for me? (But seeing her confusion): *Oh, ha-ha-ha! And now you would tell me you have no mind of your own, and that you are guided in all things by me.* (His sarcasm smoked like acid as the laughter faded from his thoughts.) *Huh! And you know how I cannot abide a liar!*

"You . . . you're playing with me." She stuttered. "This . . . this has to be a word game. It must be!''

Indeed! Radu growled. *And if you cannot win them, then do not play them! Certainly not with me . . .*

B.J. waited, tried not to tremble, and eventually he said: *Very well. And did I not hint—and more than hint—that you should use your woman's ways, your female wiles, on him? Better ways than poisoned wine? Other ways to enthrall a man? Aye, but use them on* him, *Bonnie Jean, not on me!*

"Yes, my master," she bowed her head.

See to it, then, and when next you come make report.

"Yes, my master." She curled herself up.

And Bonnie Jean, do without the wine. If you have weaned him on it, now wean him off. Doubtless it served its purpose, but an end to that now. I want a man, not a sot. And finally—in the event that you do seduce him, or he seduces you, whichever—one last thing. Be sure, absolutely sure, *that nothing of you, of us, gets into him. Above all else, be sure of that. For when he comes to me, he must be human—*all *of him.*

"I understand.''

So be it. And now sleep well, my Bonnie.

"And you, my . . . my . . . my Master." (His final words had been a command, and she was his thrall. Already B.J. was yawning, her eyes closing.)

And as he felt her slipping away, and knew that she would not hear him: *Aye, sleep well, Bonnie Jean. For if I was up—or when I am up—there shall be no sleep for you, but a night such as you never imagined. Indeed, a night to die for! One of us, anyway . . .*

* * *

In the gray dawn B.J. woke up, changed her dressing, saw that the scar was knitting and no fresh blood flowing. There was a cold cut of cooked venison in her pack, courtesy of Auld John. Washed down with strong tea, it served as breakfast. Then she saw to the cleaning of Radu's feeder and stored it away. She should have attended to it last night but had been too weary. And finally she took her departure. As she left the lair, the psychic aether was empty of her Master's emanations. He continued to sleep his sleep of ages.

Coming up, her spirits had been high; she had revelled in the climb. Going down, she took the easiest route; her mood was different and she must think things over . . . about her Master's instructions, of course. (Oh, yes, for she was still too close to him to think . . . other things.) Confused, disorientated in all manner of ways, finally she did little thinking at all but concentrated mainly on her climbing.

She was not naïve, Bonnie Jean—with so many years behind her, how could she be?—but she was enthralled, beguiled. Radu held her in his spell no less than she held Harry Keogh. And as his thrall she must always obey him. But as a Lady of the Wamphyri . . . ?

Except that was a thought she must *never* think, and so she didn't—

—Until midday, back at Auld John's place, when he noticed a spot of blood on her dressing and changed it for her. Then he had cause to remind her.

"Why, Bonnie Jean!" he exclaimed. "It's no more than a wee scratch. Ye must have stretched it a bit, that's all. But . . . I never saw healing like it! Surely ye could'nae hae gone so deep this time?"

"Deep as ever, John," she told him. And in the next breath, "But we all heal quickly. It's part of us—part of you, too."

"Aye, but never like this!" For a moment in awe of her, he stepped back and gaped. And then, eagerly: "But he did promise ye, after all. And we've always known that sooner or later—"

"Later, John, later!" she hissed, suddenly angry, but with herself as much as with him. "When he's up . . . when *he* says so, and not before. So don't you say it, nor even think it!"

"No, no!" He blinked rapidly, licked his lips, peered at her. "Ye're right, of course ye are, but—"

"No buts, John!" She cautioned him. "There can be no buts. I told you: don't even think it, because I *daren't* think it!"

But later, in his tiny bathroom, after she had bathed and when she applied a minimum of makeup:

B.J. paused, then stood stock still in front of the small mirror. Mirrors hadn't much bothered her before; they had never been a problem. But now, for the first time . . . was there something wrong? Or not wrong but different?

She stared harder at her own image. The gray in her hair. Not a premature gray but the natural color of wolfish fur. It *wasn't* fur but hair, but the color was all wolf. Much more so than before. And her eyes: their slant, the golden rim of their cores. And her ears: elfish before, but now . . . longer?

And when she put up a hand with a square of tissue to dab pale lipstick from the tip of an eyetooth . . . surely her teeth were longer, too? And behind her teeth . . .

B.J. held her breath, bared her teeth, all the way, then flicked her tongue over them—or *flickered* it, like a snake's tongue. Her *cleft* tongue!

Not all the way, not yet. But indented at the tip, beyond a doubt. And suddenly her blood was singing in her veins, singing a strange, savage song. But one that she must not, dare not sing! She remembered how easily she had changed for Harry Keogh. And how she had *known* she could do it. Oh, she had known before him, but always at the time of the full moon. Now, apparently, she could do it any time. It was simply a matter of will.

And standing there, before the mirror, she willed the gray from her hair, willed her tongue to its human shape, willed her eyes and her ears back to normal. And they were . . . normal?

Well, yes, for a normal human being, anyway . . .

That afternoon she slept. She didn't need it, but made herself sleep. That way she was out of Auld John's way; he couldn't ask her things, and she wasn't tempted to think or experiment.

As night fell she set out, with John as back-up in a battered old car he'd owned for years, doing the same job her girl had done two nights past. Through Pitlochry she saw his headlights blink twice, and his car quickly faded in her rearview. Then she was on her own, on her way home.

And no time to spare, because B.J. had given the "Mysterious One," Harry Keogh, specific post-hypnotic instructions to call her early tomorrow morning before the three-week stricture she'd placed on his departure was up. She had supposed that by that time she would know better what to do about Harry; which she did, courtesy of the dog-Lord Radu. Now she had other, more important orders to pass on, and she *must* speak to Keogh before he commenced his search abroad, which from now on would be that much more important and so much more dangerous. But she daren't miss his call, in case this close to the full of the moon Harry took this to be his "obligatory" call—in which case it could be the last opportunity she would have to speak to him for more than a month, until the *next* full moon.

Full moon, aye, in just a few days' time. B.J. could even feel it, tugging at her mind. But these sudden complications in what were once long-established, uninterrupted routines. Harry Keogh; and Radu's—what, churlishness?—his impatience, anyway; the changes taking place within herself, of which she was ever more aware. And the unknown watcher, this Drakul or Ferenczy thrall. And all of it weighing on B.J.'s shoulders.

Upon a time, no problem. She could have dealt with all of this and much more. She *had* dealt with many problems, down the decades. But her system, thought processes, mutating emotions, were badly out of kilter. And even if Radu hadn't detected it—even though he might deny it—still B.J. *knew* what was happening to her. But she, too, must deny it . . . or deny him! And after all this time, that last was unthinkable.

She wasn't giving her best concentration to the road, her driving; her hands were too loose, or occasionally too vicious, on the wheel; her speed was too great for the bends and uneven camber. When the front offside tire blew it was as much as she could do to hit the brakes before the car skidded off the road, smashed through a fence, nose-dived down a grassy decline, and slammed to a halt in the pebbles of a sluggish beck.

On impact, B.J.'s head snapped forward, banged down hard on the center of the steering column—

—And for quite some time that was all . . .

So maybe Radu was right after all. For would a little knock like that have put a true Lady of the Wamphyri to sleep? Even as B.J. realized that the thought was her own, she felt a hand fumbling on her shoulder through the shattered mess of the driver's window. And as the hand went round her neck, seeking her pulse, she wrenched herself free and snarled, *"What?"* And then, in a more reasonable, even a pained voice—feeling the aching in her neck and head, and turning the latter to squint into the early morning light—"W-what?" It had to be six or six-thirty in the morning. She must have been out for hours!

A policeman stood beside the car, ankle-deep in the cold water of the beck. His face was full of concern. "Dinna try to move, miss," he told her. "We're calling help right now. Ye'll be out o' there in no time."

He was right, and sooner than he thought! "I'm . . . okay," B.J. said, unfastening her seatbelt and wrenching at the handle of the door, which at once sprang open. "I'm all right. Just a bit shaken, that's all."

There were two of them, the second one leaving his vehicle to come scrambling down the bank. They assisted her back up to the road and into their police car. "How long were ye there? We would'nae hae known if not for the broken fence. We'll take ye into town for a checkup," the driver glanced back at her. "That bruise of yours—"

"—Is just a bruise," she told him, then smiled. "Look, the last thing I need is a checkup. I'm fine. As for my car: a tire burst. But if you really want to be helpful, you can take me on to Perth where I can get a taxi. I've an important appointment in Edinburgh, and I'm late already."

They looked at each other. B.J. dug in a pocket, produced documentation. "Details of the car," she said. "Insurance documents, for your notebooks. I hired the car. You could do me a favor and let them know. It's their . . . *junk*, after all! Their problem to recover it. My name and address are on the agreement there if you should need to contact me later."

One of the officers scratched his head. "Ye're an awfy cool lassy, for someone just out o' an accident."

"Accidents happen!" B.J. snapped, then bit her lip. "Look, I really am in a hurry. I'm sorry if I appear ungrateful . . ."

Too late. Her attitude had been all wrong and sorry wasn't going to put it right.

In the police station in Perth they recorded her statement and had a doctor look at her anyway, if only to cover themselves. Which meant it was after ten before she could call a taxi and get under way again . . .

A PICTURE OF THE MIND, A PHOTOGRAPH OF THE FUTURE.

I N CASE HER PLACE WAS UNDER OBSERVATION, BONNIE JEAN RODE THE TAXI TO within a quarter mile of "B.J.'s," paid her fare, then walked or was blown the rest of the way. It was a little after midday, raining, and blowing a gale. Buffeted along the slippery pavements, she thought: *The windy fucking city, indeed!*

Furious by the time she arrived at the bar—mainly with herself, but also with the way things were or were not working out—she had to call one of her girls down from her bedroom, from where she was *supposed* to be watching the street outside, to let her in!

"Didn't you see me arrive?"

"I . . . I was using your toilet," the girl told her.

Two other girls, who were in the vicinity and witnessed B.J.'s arrival, reported to her in the bar as she was towelling her hair and trying to dry out.

"Any luck?" She glared at them. "What of the watcher? Has he been back? And Harry Keogh? Have you found him?" But seeing the negative look on their faces: "Let's get this place tidied up, sorted out. We open tonight. If we stay closed any longer, it will only attract attention. I'll make adjustments to your duties as soon as I get the chance." And finally, as she made to head upstairs: "Any calls?"

"A few," the girl from her bedroom told her. "They're on your answering machine. I didn't monitor them. You didn't tell me to . . ."

B.J. rushed through the bar and up the stairs to her bedroom. There were three calls from regulars wanting to know when the bar would be open again, and two more from someone or ones who said nothing, but the next and last—

—Was from Harry:

"B.J.?" (He sounded unsure of himself, tinny, distant.) "I said I would call you before I went off. So, I'm calling. Tried to get you twice already—nothing doing. Too early, I suppose. Sorry about that. So, I'll be away maybe a month, I'm not sure. About a month, yes. I don't know why I'm bothering you, really. That's it, then . . ." But after a long pause:

"Oh, and by the way, that Greek wine of yours is . . . good stuff? Well, let's say it's an 'acquired taste,' eh? But a damn good way to get to sleep nights, when your mind just can't stop ticking over! Know what I mean? No, I don't suppose you do . . ."

(Another pause, then):

"I'll be in touch . . ." And again a long silence before the 'phone went dead.

And: "Damn!" B.J. said under her breath, expelling all of her air in a heavy sigh before taking her first deep breath for what seemed like the first time that day.

She breathed in . . . and held it. Now what in all—?

Aftershave? Old Spice? Harry's aftershave? It must be. But lingering on, all this time since he'd been here? Except . . . he hadn't been here, not "up" here, not in her bedroom! Or was it just his voice that had set it off? But damn it all, she could *smell* him—*him*, and not just his aftershave! He was *that* real, that vivid, tantalizing, in her mind . . . And in her room?

B.J.'s eyes were suddenly feral in the gloomy quiet of her room, with the curtains drawn and the rain pattering on the window panes. Her nostrils gaped; she turned her head sharply this way and that! She sniffed, as she tracked the essence of a man, his scent, his odor. But *here*, in her bedroom . . . where he had never been.

Oh, really?

She flew down one flight to her livingroom. Nothing! His scent wasn't here—or if it was, it was just the merest trace. He may have been here, but he hadn't lingered here. He'd gone . . . up to her bedroom!

She bounded back up the stairs. And there it was again . . . like a familiar perfume, hanging on the air. His scent, and the sweet human smell of her girl. Hers, and his.

B.J. called for her, screamed for her, down the stairwell. "Moreen! Come up here! Come *now!*"

She came, looking confused, frightened, astonished. B.J. took her by the shoulders and shook her. "He was here! He was here—with you!"

"He what? Who?" Moreen was a stunning redhead, twenty-two or twenty-three years old. Her green eyes were wide, amazed, disbelieving. Finally she broke free. "B.J., no one was here. Not while I was here, anyway!" And she shrank away from the other, especially from her looks. "You look like . . . like a wild thing!"

And B.J. knew that she did, that she was. But at least it was controllable. She pulled herself together, willed the thing hiding within her to subservience, then slumped on her bed. "He *was* here," she said, mainly to herself. "Maybe not with you, if you say so. But here, certainly."

"The watcher?" Moreen was genuinely mystified. "You think I would invite—?"

B.J. shook her head. "Not the watcher, no. Damn, we don't even know if the watcher exists, not for sure! I'm just taking Harry Keogh's word for it. *He's* the one I'm talking about. Him, Harry Keogh himself, who tossed Big Jimmy about like a sack of coal that night!"

"The one we're looking for?"

B.J. bared her teeth. "I can smell him, right here."

"Then you're mistaken." The girl tossed her head almost defiantly, and sat down beside the bed on a chair.

B.J. sat up, took hold of Moreen's shoulders again, more gently this time. "Look, this is important. Were you here all the time?"

"Why, no, of course not. How could I be?" the other said, and gave a defensive shrug. "I mean I had to eat, sleep, attend to various other things. But when it was important to be here, then I was here."

"When it was important? When, exactly?"

"I sat at that window," the girl pointed, "oh, until two or half-past two each morning, just watching the road outside. And you have no idea how boring that can get to be, B.J. But I did it anyway, for you."

"And then you slept? Where, and how long?"

"Wrapped in a spare blanket, in the barroom beside one of the big radiators."

"Downstairs, you're sure?"

"Yes."

"And if someone had got in?"

"But that's *why* I slept down there!" Moreen was close to tears. "Any burglar or intruder would have had to get past me. I'm usually a light sleeper and would hear him. But I was up each morning by six-thirty, so as to come up here and check if anyone was watching us in the early mornings—this morning especially . . ."

B.J. was quick to catch that one. "Why? What was so special about this morning?"

"There were two calls. I heard the 'phone ring before your answer machine took over. I seem to remember checking the time; the first call was, oh, about five-thirty I think, and the second maybe fifteen minutes later. That one woke me up more yet. I tossed and turned a bit, then must have dozed for a few minutes. But about six o'clock, I thought I heard something."

"What did you hear?" B.J. tightened her grip.

"I heard the boards creak, somewhere up here. But it was windy and raining; it was just the old house protesting."

B.J. thought about it. Harry could have called from any telephone. A telephone box in the street, even. He'd called twice, got no answer, given up and come here personally. But how had he got in past Moreen? And more importantly, what did he want? Suddenly the answer was clear in her mind.

As clear as his voice on her answering machine . . .

"Go down and help the others," she said, standing up. "I . . . I'm sorry I was so excited, sorry I shouted. Things could be working out better, that's all. You understand?"

The girl looked worried now. "B.J., are we in trouble?"

"Not if I can help it," she shook her head. "Do as I say, and don't worry about it."

But as soon as the girl was gone she turned to her bed, stooped and reached underneath, and drew out a three-by-four cardboard wine crate. There were three bottles of her "Greek" wine sitting neatly in their sockets in the last row. Three, yes. But B.J. knew there should be four!

Oh, she'd weaned him on, all right, this oh-so-talented Harry Keogh, this "mysterious" Mr. Keogh! And the longer she knew him the more talented and mysterious he got to be . . .

It wasn't quite a month before Harry was back; in fact, it was twenty-five days. And B.J. needn't have worried about weaning him off her wine—Radu's wine, actually—for Harry had been doing that, or trying to do it for himself, and fairly successfully. A single shot on a night, before sleeping, was all he'd allowed himself. And he'd tried tempering the stuff with other brews. Jack Daniel's Old No. 7 had been one such: a top-quality liquor whose potency should leave any mere wine standing at the post. But that stuff of B.J.'s was definitely . . . oh, something else! It was very much to Harry's taste—or Alec Kyle's taste, whichever. Its only drawback was what it did to him: his stinging eyes, dry throat, fluffy head; all the symptoms of a heavy cold, for which *it* seemed to be the only cure! There was a word for it: addiction, which Harry realized well enough. It was why he would only take it on a night, and then only one small shot.

Even so, it interfered with his search. Except (as he had come to realize by the end of his three weeks and four days in Seattle, Washington, USA), his "search" was a joke. And a joke that he was playing on himself.

Of course, with the Möbius Continuum at his fingertips—his to command—he hadn't needed to *stay* in Seattle. He could come and go as he wished; spend every night at home in Bonnyrig if he so desired. But he hadn't desired.

Truth to tell, the old house where his beloved Ma had died and his murdering black-hearted bastard of a stepfather, Viktor Shukshin, had continued to live—until his past and Harry had caught up with him, at least—was a cheerless sort of place, ominous and full of evil memories. It would be a long time, if ever, before the Necroscope could think of it as "home" in the truest sense of the word.

Which was why he'd hired a so-called "house"-boat down on the waterfront in Seattle, paying a month's rent in advance for far less comfort and only half the space he'd been used to even in his and Brenda's tiny garret flat in Hartlepool, in the . . . in the old days. But the flat had worse memories than the house in Bonnyrig, which was one of the reasons he had got rid of it. He'd thought about taking a hotel room, or a suite. Why not? He could easily stay at the city's finest, if he fancied; and just as easily skip out without paying the bill when it was time to Möbius on. Except hotels weren't him.

But, "the old days?" Funny, that it seemed so long ago! Funny, yes . . . for a man whose incorporeal, metaphysical mind had once had access to all of the past, and all of the future, and as much of space as he or any man could live in or explore even in an eternity of lifetimes!

And the funniest thing of all—or the most ironic—was that he still had it but couldn't use it. Not to its, or his, best advantage. Not until he'd found Brenda and the baby.

The past? That was over and done. There was nothing there to help him now, even if he had access to it. Which he didn't; and that, too, was funny. Incorporeal, he'd been able to "immaterialize" in the past. But now if he went there, he'd be like a toy man on a toy train that went in a circle—or figure-of-eight loop?—and never stopped; with all the stations passing him by, but never able to get off.

And as for space—which in this case meant the total of all the places, the geographic locations, in the world—well, he had access to those, certainly. But there were millions of them, and Brenda and the baby were only in one of them. Which one was anybody's guess. The Great Majority couldn't help him, because they had no contact with the living except Harry himself. And the living . . . ?

Of all living people, the E-Branch specialists—Darcy Clarke's espers—should have been able to tell him something. Yet they'd told him nothing. And he believed them; they simply didn't know. So where did that leave Harry? What chance did he stand? A very slim one, at best.

Yet there he'd been in Seattle, Washington, USA (why, he couldn't say), allegedly "searching" for two people who were, or should be, very dear to him. And he wasn't even sure about that last part, either! Love Brenda? But she didn't love him, didn't even *know* the him he was now! And love the baby? What, little Harry, who knew more than he did about everything that made him what he was?

And yet Harry must search, if only to find out *why* they'd left him. No, not even that, for he knew why: because he wasn't him, and because the things he'd done—and others he might yet do—were dangerous. The baby loved his Ma, that was all, just as Harry loved *his* Ma. Except *this* baby wasn't about to let anything happen to Brenda.

And so back to that word: "search." Big joke! In England it had seemed to make sense. Close to Brenda's source, she had felt more real, she'd seemed feasible. Here she seemed impossible. So what it boiled down to was Harry wandering about in a strange body in a strange city in a strange land, praying he'd somehow collide with someone who was trying her best to avoid him! And she had a million other places in which to do it. And things were mainly a blur anyway, because he felt like hell . . .

Maybe if he hadn't run out of B.J.'s wine he would have stayed on even longer, doing nothing much. But it was starting to look like the wine wasn't the only thing that had him under its spell. B.J. herself kept coming back to mind: some beguiling thing about her, some promise he'd made, or she'd made. Or maybe some unspoken promise that he wished they'd made.

Harry wasn't too pleased with himself that he had stolen B.J.'s wine, but whatever else he did he knew (or hoped) that he wouldn't have to steal any more. With any luck it was out of his system now. And truth to tell his "problem"—his, or Alec Kyle's alcoholism—had narrowed itself down, become specific. For it was now an established fact that the Necroscope couldn't or didn't want to drink any other kind of liquor. What was the point when it had little or no effect on him, except in massive doses? So maybe that was why he'd come home at this time: to be closer to B.J., and to her wine. Hell of a note!

And what the hell kind of alcoholism was this anyway? Was it possible for a smoker to be addicted to just one brand? What if they stopped making it? After he'd finished his last pack of Brand X, what then? He'd never smoke again? The Necroscope had never heard of anything like it. And neither had his Ma.

Have it analyzed, she told him. *See what's in it. Maybe it has an antidote.*

Harry was sitting on the river bank where he had materialized, his first port of call upon his return. It had been just after six A.M. in Seattle when he'd woken up, lifted his head, and looked at an empty bottle sitting there on a shelf at the side of his bookcase headboard. An empty bottle and an empty glass. And his first thought had been that he had used up the wine and there'd be none for tonight. That had been some twenty minutes, a wash, shave and a good stiff toothbrushing while he was still brave enough to put something in his mouth, ago—plus a minute or two to get dressed. While here in Scotland it was mid-afternoon. A decently warm spring day; the sun shining, birds singing and all . . . and Harry feeling rotten.

"Möbius-lagged!" he grumbled, and at once bit his tongue. He shouldn't be talking about that stuff to anyone—or even thinking about it where the dead were concerned. Even his Ma. He'd have to learn to guard his thoughts about . . . about that sort of thing.

Nonsense! his Ma answered. But she was talking about his comment, not about his regretting it. *You're not any kind of lagged! You're hung over, that's all.*

He was glad to change the subject. "Yes, probably. Except it doesn't go away."

So do as I tell you! And anyway, if that's the end of it, it's the end of it. Thank goodness for that.

"But I know where there's more." And again he could have bitten his tongue, for she was on him like a ton of bricks:

Leave it alone, Harry! That's all I can do, advise you. You have a mind, and therefore you have a choice: be an alcoholic or don't be. It's one or the other. To be or not to be. It's up to you. No one can order you not to drink, but by the same token no one can make you drink!

But in the back of the Necroscope's head, a voice seemed to say, "Oh, really?" Harry didn't know what it meant, and so ignored it. "Anyway," he said out loud, "credit where credit's due: I'm fighting it. It's just this last wrinkle in my—or Alec Kyle's—gray matter. It needs ironing out, that's all. It's something that's residual of him, like his precognition. But I can feel it adjusting to fit me, I think. And if I don't use it, don't pander to it, it will . . . I don't know, atrophy? It's just a matter of time, I'm sure."

His precognition? She repeated him, as glad as he was to change the subject. *Have you been having more visions, then?*

"No," Harry shook his head—

—And at once reeled, and grabbed at the root of a tree to keep from toppling from the bank! For his Ma's question had seemed to bring something on, a scene obscured by what appeared to be mental static—until the Necroscope realized that he was seeing it through a blizzard!

A frozen monochrome landscape, like the roof of the world, and a gaunt range of mountains marching against gray skies that went on forever. It was cold—a biting cold— that was so real Harry could even feel it gnawing at him; and the snow slanting down like a million white spears, piercing his warmth as they landed and formed an ever-thickening layer on his being, his mind, his psyche . . .

. . . It was gone, leaving him shivering and reeling, while his Ma's dead voice cried in his mind: *Harry! What on earth—?* But what she should have been asking was where. Where on earth? For Harry had seen nothing like it; he'd never been in or imagined being in such a place. He gasped for air, could scarcely believe that he was warm and the sun still shining down on him. It had been so very real. And damn it, he could feel it coming back again!

He had let go of the root but now clutched at it again, as the thing invaded his senses and tore him from his reality into its own:

The iron-gray mountains, snow-capped, ridged with carved, drifted snow; and the valleys and passes between the spurs and peaks full of it, like white dunes rolling to rearing horizons of stone. But to Harry's right . . . what, a city? A walled city, yes, protected in the lee of the mountains and by a long, snaking wall—like a miniature version of the Great Wall of China—with gaunt square towers, battlements, mighty gates. But the old, cold city was dead and empty; it huddled down into itself behind the wall, and kept its secrets . . .

It was much like a scene from some old geography book in Harry's secondary modern school at Harden. And once again the thought struck him: the Roof of the World, yes! But . . . Tibet? Why was he seeing a scene out of Tibet?

The blizzard had fallen off a little. (Harry felt the familiar river bank under his thighs)—*but he also felt the cold of the snows gnawing in his bones, and saw a scene from incredible distances of space, or even out of future time, enacted on the screen of his mind. But Harry was the Necroscope and could handle it, perhaps even better than Alec Kyle himself. And finally accepting it, no longer fighting it, he shielded his eyes against the falling snow and stared harder.*

Out there on the white waste . . . movement? Single file, a line of seven people—antlike figures, at this range—were making their way across the snow. They were robotic in their movements, like a military drill routine—left, right, left, right, left—but rapid and shuffling. The three in front were dressed in red, also the three bringing up the rear. But the one in the middle was all in white. And as if from a million miles away, the Necroscope could hear the chiming of tiny golden bells . . .

. . . The cold receded, was gone from mind and body in a moment; the river swirled below; Harry swayed like a drunkard, and his Ma had time for a single word—*Son!*—before Alec Kyle's talent struck again.

It was no longer snowing. Harry saw the six—what, monks? And one initiate?—out on the snows, tramping single-file as before. But the walled city was no longer in sight; the location was different. This time, in front of the six, the base of a sheer cliff reared like a titan face. It was a face: carved out of the rock! But if the location was cold, that great grim visage in the rock was colder still.

It could only be a temple (a monastery?), with huge steps carved from the bedrock leading up to the entrance: the yawning mouth of the great face. And up the steps the seven went, to where a portcullis was lifted and the throat became a passageway into the monastery. Then:

Sheer fantasy!

For as the seven disappeared inside . . . so the face became flesh! The great jaws snapped shut, and the eyes opened wide to burn crimson as hell! And suddenly the no-longer-stone face was smiling the devil's own smile!

Harry couldn't believe his eyes. He blinked—

—And stared up at a blue sky, where wisps of cloud drifted across a blinding sun. He'd toppled over onto his back, and was lying there on the river bank with his mouth wide open. Dazzled, Harry blinked again—and at once gritted his teeth, cringing down into himself in anticipation of another shift. But no, it was over now, and it gradually dawned on the Necroscope that he *knew* it was over.

Then, struggling to sit up, and gasping the words out, he began to ask his mother, ''Ma, did you—?''

Of course I saw it! She cut him short. *We're in contact; I saw what you saw. But Harry, what does it mean? What was it?*

Harry stood up and shakily, absentmindedly brushed himself down. Finally he shook his head. "Whatever it was, it certainly wasn't delirium tremens!"

But it's all tied up, isn't it? It's all one and the same! Harry, are you into another of these . . . these things of yours? Her dead "voice" overflowed with concern.

"Things?" Harry's mouth was dry; he hadn't quite given up expecting something else to happen.

You know what I mean, his Ma insisted. *Are you in trouble again, son?*

And for the first time the Necroscope wondered, *Am I?*

But out loud, without really considering what he said, he answered, "Ma, to the best of my knowledge, I'm not in any real 'trouble' trouble. I don't think so, anyway. And that's fine by me, because I've got enough problems as it is. So don't you go wishing any more on me, okay?"

And yet again he could have bitten his tongue, because what he'd said wasn't nearly what he'd meant. But too late now.

Well! his Ma said, in a certain way she had, making that one small word an entire statement on its own. Following which she wasn't much inclined to talk to him any more . . .

Harry walked the river path to the arched-over gate in the garden wall, and letting himself into the garden became aware of a car's engine fading to silence at the front of the house. Since the rest of the houses in this once select, now neglected location were derelict, this could only be someone visiting or delivering to him.

Avoiding the brambles as best he could, Harry ran up the garden path and quickly let himself in. He could have taken the Möbius route, of course, but the more sparing he was in his use of the Continuum, the less likely he'd be to give away its secret inadvertently. In a few seconds he was through the house to the front, where it took only a moment or so to unlock and open the door. Outside, a tall, slim young man was already halfway back down the walled yard to the gate that he had left open. In his hand was a large manila envelope. Beyond the gate, a black car stood waiting on the rutted service road. Hearing the door of the house open, the man turned and saw Harry.

"Delivery," he said, showing Harry the envelope. And trying hard not to show too much interest, his keen, curious eyes looked the Necroscope over.

Harry returned the other's cautiously appraising look and said: "You don't much look like a typical postman." And it was true, he didn't. No uniform for one thing, and the car outside wasn't a post van, and the envelope had no address or stamps.

The other shrugged. "Well then, let's say it's 'special' delivery. Or better still—"

"—E-Branch," Harry's mouth turned down at the corners as the man started back up the path. "Do I know you?" He held the house door open to let his visitor in. They both had to avoid trampling a month's worth of mail—most of it junk—on the coconut-fiber mat just inside the door.

The other shook his head, held out his hand, which Harry pointedly ignored. He'd told Darcy he was finished with all of this. "Munroe," the stranger let his hand fall. "James Munroe. And no, we haven't met. I'm usually on embassy duties here and abroad, 'checking out the talent,' so to speak. I'm a spotter, only recently returned from Italy to home duties—rotation of embassy staff, and what have you. Today I sensed you were back at last . . ." He paused and frowned. "But I'm puzzled you didn't answer the door sooner. Is there a problem, Mr. Keogh?"

"No problem," Harry led him through the house to the room he'd designated as his study, whose patio doors looked out over the garden, directed him to a chair and seated himself. "I was out in the garden, that's all. But did you say 'back at last?' How long have you been waiting for me, then?"

"For a fortnight. In Edinburgh, coming out here each day to see if you were home yet."

As they talked, Harry had checked James Munroe over. He would be six foot one or two, twenty-six or twenty-seven years old, one hundred and forty-five pounds maximum. His face was angular: jutting chin, pointed nose and ears, and jet-black hair, swept back and lacquered down. His eyes saved him from looking cynical, or even sinister; they were wide, brown, penetrating and honest. The sort you could look into and not worry about what was going on in there.

"A fortnight? Coming out here every day? It's that important?"

"To you, I believe." Munroe shrugged. "And possibly beneficial to the Branch, too, but I'm just guessing. It's the way we work, as you know." He was staring, and Harry was suddenly uncomfortable.

"Is there something?" he snapped.

"Eh?" the other sat up straighter, was at once startled. "Oh, I'm sorry! I was staring, right? It's just that when you asked if you knew me, I almost answered, 'No, but I once knew you.' But Darcy Clarke has told me you're touchy about that."

Harry sighed, nodded and said, "Alec Kyle. Yes, I'm sometimes touchy about it. But I'm getting used to it—to him—to certain aspects of him, anyway." He was nervous. This was getting too close to stuff he couldn't talk about.

"It's funny," the other said, "but on you he looks—oh, I don't know— younger?"

"Oh? Well, he *feels* ancient!"

"I meant younger . . . *overall,*" Munroe hurriedly corrected himself. "I mean, it's like I can sense a younger man shining through. But shining too brightly, maybe? Burning up?"

"What are you, an empath, too?"

The other's turn to sigh. "I'm sorry, but I'm really fucking this up, right? But I've read your files. You're the Necroscope, and I expected . . . no, I didn't know *what* to expect! And I didn't mean to say *that,* either! I mean—you know— I'm not usually a rude person, Mr. Keogh . . ."

And now there was an awkward silence, until:

"Harry," the Necroscope said at last, his unnatural antagonism collapsing. "Call me Harry, please. And I'm afraid I *have* been rude, so don't you go apologizing. Just recently I've been doing more than my fair share of tripping over *my* tongue!" And changing the subject: "So what's in the envelope?"

Munroe shrugged. "I wasn't told what's in here." He handed it over, and Harry looked at it with an almost accusing expression. This could be some kind of hook, and him the fish. But on the other hand . . . it just *might* be news of Brenda.

And as he tore it open: "I imagine Darcy tried to get me on the telephone, right? And when he found he couldn't get me, then he sent you?"

"Your listed number?" Munroe shook his head, and smiled. "But we're E-Branch, Harry. No such things as listed numbers, not to E-Branch. Darcy Clarke could 'phone you, if he wanted to. I suppose he's doing his best to respect your privacy."

The Necroscope said, "Huh!" He took out a single, double-folded sheet of A-4 from the envelope. A letter, probably, but there was something stiff inside it—a photograph, maybe? And because it might be about Brenda, he wanted to open it at once. But because it mightn't be, he didn't.

"It doesn't make sense," he finally shook his head. "Darcy can get me on the 'phone and doesn't. Or he could just write me a letter, asking me to contact him. But he doesn't. Instead, he sends you." He glanced at the contents of the manila envelope—the letter, or whatever—still folded in his lap. "So what do you reckon, James? Was your journey really necessary?"

The other raised a querying eyebrow. "I'm sorry, but—"

"See," Harry cut him short. "I'm not going to look at this—this whatever it is—until I know why you had to deliver it personally. In fact, if you don't tell me, and in the very near future at that, say the next five seconds, I'll simply set fire to it and dump it in the fireplace there. And you'll have to go back down to London and tell Darcy Clarke what happened."

He looked around for his table-lighter, began to stand up, and Munroe said: "Okay! You're right. Darcy wanted me, or someone, to see you personally. Yes."

Harry sat back again. "Why?"

"Just to see how you, well, looked . . ."

"He's . . . what, worried about me?"

"Maybe about how you're taking things. Maybe he feels responsible. Guilty . . ."

Harry jumped on that. "Guilty? And maybe you're right. So what would he have to feel guilty about?"

Munroe shrugged again, perhaps desperately this time, and said, "Harry, I'm just a messenger, that's all. But Mr. Clarke did say he was concerned about your general health. I mean, he knows your problems better than I do, right? So why don't you read the letter? Maybe it's all in there."

And in any case, despite his threat to burn it, the Necroscope had to know. So he unfolded the single sheet of A-4, laid the small envelope inside to one side for the moment, and read what was written in Darcy Clarke's spidery script:

Harry—

First things first. Still nothing on Brenda, I'm afraid. And I suppose if you had heard anything, you would have told me. Don't worry, we're still on it.

Last time we spoke, you said you were thinking of taking a long holiday, except you were short of funds. So it could be you would take a sort of working holiday? You asked if I'd check a few places out for you. Well, I've found a place you might like—in the Mediterranean. The weather would be beneficial I'm sure, and the deal could work out really cheap . . .

Oh, and you asked about exchange rates? Well, they are pretty good, too. So why don't you contact me and we'll talk?

I enclose a photograph. Nice place. I think you'd enjoy working there . . .

All best—
Darcy.

The Necroscope knew what Darcy was talking about; he remembered how he'd suggested doing a job on the Russian repository in Moscow, or maybe on some other outfit or organization in the Branch's bad books, for monies to fund his search. *Damn!* Was that all this was? Darcy scratching his back—and maybe hoping to get a job done for free—all the time knowing it would put Harry in his debt, so that at some future time the Necroscope might feel obliged to do a little back-scratching in return? A sort of two-birds-with-one-stone scenario?

"So why don't you contact me and we'll talk?"—Indeed! E-Branch! It was typical! The nerve of the double-dealing . . .

He almost ripped the photograph from its envelope . . . and then sat there frozen, staring at it!

For a moment Harry thought it must be one of Alec Kyle's "things" again, his precognition. Hell!—it *was* one of Kyle's things, but this time it was real! As real as this photograph, anyway:

The stark yellow and white cliffs, colored by sunlight. And the squat, white-walled castle, mansion, château, whatever it was, perched there on the edge of oblivion. A fortress on a mountainside, at the rim of a sheer drop. The scene was Mediterranean; yes, of course it was, and Harry had seen it before. All sun-bleached rocks, brittle scrub, a few stunted pines; he could almost taste the salty tang off an unseen ocean.

Finally he moved, rocked back in his chair, and James Munroe was at his side in a moment. "Harry? Are you okay? I mean, your face. You looked stunned . . ."

Harry got a grip on himself. He didn't know what all this meant, but he would soon damn well find out. "I . . . I'm okay," he said. "It's . . . something you wouldn't understand." *Because* I *don't understand it!* "Look, you get on back to London. Sorry I can't be more hospitable, but I've things to do. Especially now. And don't worry, you've done your job. I'll be getting in touch with Darcy Clarke and E-Branch, yes."

And after he'd seen Munroe off, he did just that . . .

The Necroscope could have just telephoned Darcy, but there was a better, almost an easier way. And anyway, face to face Darcy wouldn't be able to hide too much. That is, assuming there was anything to hide.

Not so long ago, using the Möbius route to E-Branch would have been *much* easier, but Harry couldn't do that now. Part of him realized that Darcy knew all about it anyway, but he still didn't like the *idea* that he knew—Darcy or anyone else, for that matter! And so he was restricted in his use of the Continuum; he couldn't do it in front of people. So there was no way he could simply materialize in Darcy's office.

But that was all right, for there was another way. Harry doubted if they would have converted his room just yet; Darcy had told him they'd keep it for him just the way it was, even if he never had cause to use it again. So he couldn't see any reason why he shouldn't use it now, one last time.

He did: used it as one of his Möbius co-ordinates—

—And a moment later stepped out through the door of his old room into the main corridor of E-Branch in central London.

About half-way to Darcy's office, situated at the far end of the corridor, two Branch agents were talking to each other. Harry headed their way, and for a moment they scarcely noticed him. But as he passed the open door of the Duty Officer's room he heard someone say, *"Holy shit!"* and guessed he'd been recognized. So, in another five seconds maximum Darcy Clarke would know he was here, too. Then, as he closed with the two espers, they finally saw him, snapped erect as soldiers on parade, and slid to one side out of his way. Harry was aware of their surprised glances, at him and at each other, as he passed by.

Darcy's office was full of security gadgets; the Necroscope knew that if he just barged in, he would probably set some of them off. So he went to knock . . . but before his fist could strike home the door was yanked open from within.

And Darcy was there—in his shirt-sleeves, open-mouthed—beckoning him to come in. "Harry! It's . . . really great to see you! In fact I was just talking about you—"

"—With Munroe, on his car-phone?" the Necroscope nodded. "Or with the Duty Officer?" He tossed Darcy's letter and photograph down on the Head of E-Branch's desk. And without further ado: "Would you care to explain this?"

Darcy moved to close the door. Before he could close it all the way, Harry looked back down the corridor and saw half-a-dozen faces peering from their respective offices. Darcy saw his raised eyebrow and knowing, even scornful expression, gave a shrug and said, "Er, word travels fast around here."

"In some cases as fast as thought," Harry nodded. *"Especially* around here!" He placed extra emphasis on the "esp" of "especially." "So how will it be? Can we have some privacy for once? I mean *complete* privacy?" He sat down in a chair facing Darcy's desk. "You have more than your fair share of listening devices around this place, Darcy: gadgets and ghosts and what-all. But your people would do well to remember how curiosity killed the cat. Maybe the two-legged variety could use a reminder now and then?"

Darcy sat down in his own chair, flipped a switch on the desk and said, "All stations. We have a guest who's a personal friend of mine, and of the Branch. You all know who he is, and of course he's to get the same degree of respect that we give each other. So this is private—and that's a capital 'P.' "

As he switched off again, Harry nodded and said, "Gadgets and ghosts, yes. Machines are easy to switch off. But minds . . . are something else, right?" He glanced about the office. "Well, nothing seems to have changed much around here."

"Er . . . how's it going?" Darcy rubbed his hands in a businesslike fashion. He was lost for words if only for a moment. "So, where have you been, Harry? And for that matter, *how* have you been?"

"How do I look?" The Necroscope was unsmiling.

"Fine!" Darcy answered, then slumped and shook his head. "Hey, we're friends, Harry," he said, his tone of voice flattening out a little, losing its bounce. "I'd like to think so, anyway. And in that respect I'm pretty much like Ben Trask: I don't like to lie."

"So don't."

"You look about the same as last time," Darcy told him. "You've lost weight, gained a few wrinkles, and you seem very tired. But at the same time—I don't know—somehow you look more like you, too? But you don't *talk* like you. I mean, I've given a lot of thought to that conversation we had about Alec Kyle— could he have been a secret drinker and so forth? That was pretty strange stuff! So, you know, apart from Brenda and the baby . . . what is it that's troubling you, Harry? I mean, I'd really like to help, if I can."

And suddenly the Necroscope felt he could relax a little. Darcy's friendship was genuine. Oh, there would always be this E-Branch thing, but that aside Darcy was real, and Harry felt able to talk to him. About certain things, anyway. And he did talk to him:

Told him about Alec Kyle's precognition, how he seemed to have inherited it, and something about his strange new problem with drink. He didn't go into details on the latter, but enough that Darcy got the message. Certainly he got the message on the other thing.

"About Alec drinking; I still think you're wrong," Darcy said, when Harry was through. "And even if you're right, it's amazing to me that he hid it so well! As for this," he picked up the picture from his desk. "You say you've seen it before?"

The Necroscope nodded. "Yes. A scene, or sudden vision—in my head— but absolutely real. Actually, it was during our conversation about a Russian Fort Knox. Do you remember?"

"Of course, as a result of which I sent you the picture."

"Right, but my mind—or maybe Alec Kyle's mind, the last wrinkle in his gray matter?—had *already* sent it to me! Only I didn't recognize it, didn't know what it meant."

Darcy nodded. "That's how it was with Alec, too," he said. "He rarely understood anything he saw but simply had to run with his visions to see how they worked out. He had to wait until he caught up with the future."

"Me, too," Harry said. "Except this time I've been given more than just a precognitive glimpse, more than a mental clue. I have your photograph, too," he leaned forward and tapped his index finger on the picture. "And I know that *you* know quite a bit about this . . . what, target? So I won't be going in blind, because now that I'm sure this place is waiting to happen to me somewhere in my future, you'll be giving me all the details."

"As much as we have," Darcy said. "Certainly. But even so, it's still *fait accompli*. You *are* going to do it."

"So it would appear," Harry's face was grim. "So maybe we can start with you telling me who it is I'll be doing it to . . ."

DARCY'S TARGET.
BONNIE JEAN AT HARRY'S.

FIRST THE PLACE," DARCY PUSHED THE PHOTOGRAPH BACK ACROSS THE DESK closer to Harry. "We don't know much about it; its history is vague at best. But you can probably find out more locally if you're so inclined." (In fact the "probably" was redundant, for Darcy knew that the Necroscope could do just that—could actually talk to the original owners or builders, if he so desired—but he didn't want to broach that subject.)

"Anyway," he went on, "it's called Le Manse Madonie, named after the mountainous region in Sicily where it stands. It was built about four hundred years ago on the foundations of a castle dating back to crusader times. And like most ancient properties, it's been added to and subtracted from for centuries.

"As to what it was originally: a watchtower looking out over the Tyrrhenian? Possibly. The redoubt of some princeling? We don't know. And actually it mightn't be so easy to find out after all—not from books, at least—because as far as we're able to discover most of its historical records have been destroyed. I mean, utterly.

"The one sure thing we do know is that it's stayed in the hands of the same family for centuries. Their line goes back a long way, you might say immemorially. But records?—forget it! Where they exist they've been altered, updated, rewritten from scratch. Not that there's much we can deduce from that; quite a few old families have skeletons in their closets. These people have cleared them out, that's all. Or maybe that's not all. It could be they were simply making room for a few new ones . . ."

"These people?" Harry sat wrapped in his own thoughts. He had absorbed all that Darcy had told him, which wasn't much so far. "Well, it seems obvious to me that you've been interested in 'these people' for quite some time. And that's E-Branch I'm talking about, *keenly* interested! So who are they?"

"They're called the Francezcis," Darcy told him. "That's their family name, anyway: the current owners and occupiers of Le Manse Madonie. But as I've said, it's been Francezci family property, oh, since the year dot. They're brothers, twins, but not identical. Anthony, or Tony, and Francesco Francezci. That is *who* they are, but it's *what* they are that interests us."

Harry nodded. "So what are they?"

"First the facts," Darcy answered. "Let me tell you what we know for sure, and then what we suspect. And finally we'll be down to best bets. The Francezci brothers are the sole surviving heirs to one of the richest families in the world. You can measure their wealth . . . well, in billions! So we believe. Okay, okay!" He held up a hand. "I said I'd tell you only what we know, and we *do* know. But it isn't easy to tie these people, or their assets, down. Put it this way: if you could calculate their wealth in terms of the Italian economy—if you could find a way to put back half of what they have taken out—then Italy and Sicily wouldn't be in half the shit they're in now."

Harry could see where they were going. "Mafia," he said, very simply.

"*Shhh!*" Darcy put a finger to his lips and pulled a mock-horrified face. "What, the Francezci brothers? But that's akin to blasphemy, Harry! Even suggest such a thing in polite Italian society, you'd be ostracized in a moment—and later you could end up circumcised, too, from the neck up! No one talks about them in such terms, but we're pretty damn sure it's how people *think* of them. Except . . . well it's amazing how things get warped with the passage of time. I mean, look at the so-called "legends" of Robin Hood, Jesse James, Ned Kelly—all the murderers and thieves who've become folk heroes."

As he paused for breath, Harry said, "Are you telling me the Francezcis are heroes?"

Darcy grinned, or grimaced, and said, "But when you're powerful enough you can be what you want to be. I'll give you an example of what I'm talking about. Some forty-odd years ago it was a Francezci—allegedly one 'Emilio' Francezci, a shady 'uncle' to Anthony and Francesco—who helped to organize the collaboration of a then underground Sicilian Mafia in the American invasion of 1943. That was a joint effort that came about as a direct result of an old debt owed by Emilio to Lucky Luciano, who was then rotting in an American prison cell.

"It was Emilio's 'suggestion' that in exchange for Luciano's freedom and later extradition to Italy, Lucky might like to contact several Sicilian 'ex'-*capo* friends on behalf of the American invasion force, and request that they and their 'ex'-Mafia soldiers—who were still scattered throughout Sicily's villages—tighten the screws on what remained of Il Duce's armed forces and make them an offer they couldn't refuse: life if they ran away, death if they chose to remain at their posts. Except while a clean sudden death as the result of an American blitzkrieg couldn't be guaranteed, a very ugly one on the cutting edge of some *mafioso* guerrilla's garrotte most certainly could!

"The reason for all those 'ex's is simple: you've got to remember that at the time, Mussolini was hanging *mafiosi* from whichever handy lampposts he could find, and so it was a very good time to refute or better still cancel your membership in that organization! But the Mafia never dies; it might go away for a while, but it always comes back. And Il Duce, by standing against them, had put himself in their line of fire. They wanted rid of him—and they certainly didn't want Hitler!

"Thus the American invasion of Sicily was a walkover, and the course of the war—and a great many world-shaping events since—was altered. And so while this Emilio Francezci might be a difficult man to trace, by which I mean that we know *absolutely nothing* about him, still he could become one of those fake folk heroes I was talking about. But then, I'm told that there are people who idolize the memory of Al Capone, too . . .''

Harry was silent a while, then said: ''But we *are* talking about Italy, or more properly Sicily, which is a place apart, surely? The way I understand it, graft, political corruption, crime in general, these things are almost a way of life. Just because this one Francezci—this 'Emilio'—had bad connections, does that mean they're all tarred with the same brush? I mean, isn't everyone in that sort of culture tainted or at least touched by it, from the politicians down? . . . Or up, as the case may be? What else have you got, Darcy? Why don't you tell me what brought about E-Branch's interest in the Francezcis in the first place?''

''Cut straight to the point, right?'' Darcy answered. ''Okay, let's try that. E-Branch's interest in the Francezcis:

''Harry, I have prognosticators, people like Alec Kyle, yet unlike him, who are mainly interested in the future. The future of this country, and its welfare— and, I hasten to add, of the world as a whole. But charity begins at home. So what do I mean, these people are like Alec yet unlike him? Well, you were with us long enough to understand that no two sets of ESP skills are exactly alike. The talents of my precogs don't work like Alec's did, that's all. But they *are* skilled at making damn good guesses. Except as any precog will tell you, the future is devious as hell and therefore hard to gauge. But they do their best.

''The point is, as an island and a race we're moving closer and closer to Europe. Not in the physical sense, no, but ideologically, politically, and financially. So it would seem, anyway; so my precogs—my futurologists—have predicted. Well, if that's how it will be, it's how it will be. But in a future world where we are tied to Europe, we'd like to give ourselves the best possible advantage. Just because we happen to be divided from Europe by the English Channel and the North Sea—a situation which has given us a positive advantage in the past— doesn't mean we have to be some kind of poor offshore relative, some sort of bare-arsed cousin!''

The Necroscope was quick on the uptake. ''Your—futurologists?—foresee financial difficulties?''

Darcy was impressed. ''Among others,'' he answered. ''French governments come and go like day follows night, and the French franc fluctuates accordingly. Then there's the deutschmark . . . except there we're more worried about the *past* than the future! The old deutschmark may look good now, but it has one hell of a bad record, Harry. And as for the lira and the drachma? I mean, seriously, the pound sterling should end up tied to currencies such as those?''

''So, you've gauged something of the future, you're mindful of the lessons of the past, and you're now considering the present, right?'' Harry nodded. ''So that you can discover where the rot has set in, and stop it from spreading over here? Which led you to the Francezcis.''

''Among others, right. But we've had to tread oh-so-carefully. The Francezcis seem immune from any kind of accusation. I can give you several examples in the last decade where Italian governments have fallen just because they *looked* like they were pointing a finger in their direction! E-Branch is E-Branch, yes, but on an international scale even we don't have that kind of diplomatic clout. Let them get wind of the fact that we've been checking on them . . . why, even our plug could be pulled! And the intelligence of these people is awesome.''

Darcy had gone too fast. "Hold it!" Harry held up a hand. "You could get the plug pulled? Cease to function? But surely, you're first-line national security?''

Darcy sighed. "We're E-Branch. There are people who should know better who still don't even believe in us, and others who want to cut our expenditure . . . and we exist on a fucking shoestring anyway! And it isn't just idle flattery when I tell you that you, personally, have saved our skin time and again. *You*, your successes, are what's kept us afloat. We are ahead of The Opposition, which means we're successful. Ergo: we are allowed to exist. But the Francezcis are just too *powerful* for us. As a covert organization, we simply can't go against them. If we're right about them, we lack the clout to do anything about it. And if we're wrong and get found out—they'd have us by the balls . . .''

Harry was thoughtful. "Two brothers, that powerful? Just the two of them? What's their power-base—I mean, apart from money.''

"Well, of course, that's the most powerful force on Earth!" Darcy exclaimed. "But okay, apart from money:

"Harry, they're like an octopus, with tentacles all over the place, in every kind of sinkhole. I mentioned their intelligence. Well, in the main that's their power-base, too. Except the rest of this is really deep and you might find it difficult to believe, even hearing it from me, even here at E-Branch HQ.''

"Try me, anyway," the Necroscope answered. "See, I have a very open mind." He actually smiled, and for a moment looked even more like the old Harry Darcy had known. And Darcy could see the humor of it: someone trying to tell Harry Keogh that something might be too hard to believe! And that someone just happening to be himself, Darcy Clarke, who could walk through a minefield blindfolded, in snowshoes, and come through without a scratch. So that Darcy smiled, too, then chuckled, and the tension was that much more diminished.

But in the next moment it was back to business, as Darcy said: "Okay, then listen. These people, the Francezcis, aren't just a couple of big-time hoods. They've got the weight of the Mafia behind them—the total weight! Of course they have, for they're *advisers* to the Mafia, like Dons of dons, or Godfathers of godfathers! But that's not nearly the end of it. For *through* the Mafia they're also advisers to the KGB and, on occasion . . . to the CIA!''

The Necroscope looked blank, as if he hadn't heard. But as it sank in, he cocked his head on one side and said, "They're what?''

Darcy nodded. "You can't see it. Well, that's understandable. But remember the Lucky Luciano story, and then ask yourself why the Mob is still alive and well and living in a great many places even today, when every 'straight' body in this big wide world would love to put them out of business for good.''

"But the CIA?" Harry still needed convincing. "I mean, the first is acceptable, even plausible; naturally Mother Russia would love to undermine western capitalism. And what better way than by the corruption at its root? But the CIA?

What kind of 'advice' would the Central Intelligence Agency take—what kind would they even *want*—from people in bed with the Mob?''

"Go back a step," Darcy told him. "First the KGB. I never said they were giving orders to the Francezcis. I wasn't hinting that they were sabotaging or manipulating financial institutions, or anything of that order—though they could well be, or at least setting up the machinery for it. I said the Francezcis were 'advisers.' The key word is 'intelligence!' And as I told you, the Francezci intelligence machine is awesome! Which is why the CIA uses them; their information is *that* good. But as to the *kind* of advice they offer . . ." Darcy shrugged. "The Branch isn't privy to that information. But it won't be small potatoes, you can bet on it. As to how it works: they'll tell the KGB stuff that doesn't conflict with CIA interests. Likewise, they'll offer information to the CIA if it doesn't drop the Russians in it. And the Mob benefits both ways by knowing what's going to go down world-wide. And everyone involved is grateful to the Francezcis. That's power, Harry.''

Harry was silent a while, then said: "So, they're 'advisers' of a sort to the Mob, the KGB, even the CIA . . .''

". . . And through them, advisers to their governments—just as Emilio Francezci was, when he advised that collaboration between the American invasion force and Sicily's Mob-in-Waiting.''

"Information of that order," Harry mused.

"Yes . . .''

"Intelligence is the key word," the Necroscope continued to mull it over. "Okay, so what *is* their intelligence machine? How do they organize it? What's the source of their information? Maybe they're simply the Mob's *own* CIA: the nerve-center in a spiderweb of international crime and corruption?''

Darcy shrugged again. "Possibly. But unlikely. For let's face it, the Families aren't that . . . well, *familiar* with each other. There are Mob wars going on even now in the USA; probably in Italy, too. They're not united. It isn't in their genes. But here's something to think about:

"Our precogs tell us that Communism is on the wane, certainly in Russia. So maybe the Francezcis are preparing the way for the Mob, or a faction of the Mob, in the USSR? That's a lot of turf, Harry! The point is, whatever they're doing, you can guarantee they're not up to any good.''

"And you—or the Branch—want me to throw some spanners in their works?''

Darcy held up his hands in protest. "Hey, I told you we can't be involved! You asked me if there was someone you could hit for funds. Which suggested to me that maybe there was a way we could both benefit from . . . well, from what you do best. But if there's any fall-out from anything you do, the Branch can't be implicated. We aren't part of this scene.''

"What if I don't need the money that badly?''

"Then let it go.''

"The fact is I *don't* need the money that badly, or haven't so far.''

"You asked me to do something for you," Darcy said. "What can I tell you? I've done it. Now all I'm saying is this: that place in the photograph, Le Manse Madonie, houses money, treasures, gold, beyond your wildest dreams. Because we're sure that quite apart from what these characters have stashed away in the world's banks, they're also magpies. They—their family—have been accumulating goodies for a couple of hundred years! A lot of the wealth of Europe that vanished into Nazi coffers during World War Two still hasn't been accounted for. Hell, it never will be while it's tied up in that place!''

"Oh?" The Necroscope raised a querying eyebrow. "So even now I don't know it all?''

"I would have told you," Darcy said at once. "That's the whole idea of talking like this, surely? But so far we've just been kicking it around, right?''

"What about plans of the place?''

"I thought you weren't interested?''

Harry grinned, however tightly. "But we're just kicking it around, right?''

"No plans. And their security is second to none. The space center at Baikonur in Kazakhstan would be easier! That's probably an exaggeration, but I'm sure you take my point.''

"The Château Bronnitsy was secure, too," Harry answered.

Darcy nodded but made no reply. He didn't want to mention Harry's 'talent' for getting into and out of places . . . or the damage the Necroscope had done to some of the places he'd been into. The Château Bronnitsy—*once* the headquarters of Soviet ESPionage—was only one of them. And Bronnitsy was no more.

"But that place was the very seat of evil," Harry went on, "while I'm not yet convinced that these Francezcis are anything but big-time crooks.''

"I'm not asking you to destroy anything," the Head of E-Branch shook his head. "In fact, I'm not asking you to *do* anything. If you do, it's your business and I don't even want to know. I'm just pointing out the bull's eye in case you should ever want to do a little target practice, that's all.''

"And if during my 'investigations' I should discover the Francezci's oracle, the source of their intelligence . . . ?''

"We'd be grateful, of course. Because if we could tap into that source . . . it goes without saying that we'd put it to better use than they do.''

"And maybe queer their pitch at the same time?" Harry was on top of it. "But you're not in any kind of hurry?''

"No. Honestly, Harry, this was for you. If you use it, then you use it. And if you don't . . . well, it's your choice. But as you say, if it's also of benefit to us so much the better.''

The Necroscope gave it another moment's thought, said, "Do we know what these brothers look like? Or their people? You've told me their security at Le Manse Madonie is good. So what do they have up there?''

"Their own private 'staff,' " Darcy answered. "Not massive by Mob standards—but, as I've said, the Francezcis aren't Mob. They're bigger than that. They just pull strings; others do the twitching. And an army wouldn't be necessary anyway, not in a place as inaccessible as the Madonie. They have guards, their 'servants,' a four-seater helicopter, and various types of surface transport. Locally, they like to travel in a stretch limo: which is about as close as they come to emulating their nearest and dearest!''

"Yes," Harry nodded. "The Mafia. And Sicily is still Mafia HQ?''

"But definitely!" Darcy said. "If the Francezcis ever required it, they could call up a lot of heavy-duty help. But not in short order. It takes time to get from Palermo into the Madonie—for some people, anyway." With his last comment he averted his face, dug in a desk drawer, and came out with a handful of photographs which he tossed onto the desk top. "Pictures of our friends," he quickly returned to the original subject. "Not very good ones, I'm afraid. But the Francezcis appear to be the world's least photographed—and least photogenic—people!"

"Can I take these with me when I leave?"

"Sorry," Darcy shook his head. "Memorize by all means, but that stuff stays right here. I'll say it again: officially, we aren't even interested in these people. We can't be identified as a source of information in this respect."

Harry frowned. "You make it sound like the Francezcis have influence over here, too."

Darcy said nothing.

"What, with the British Government? Are they 'advising' our intelligence agencies, too? Another reason you're interested in them?"

"We don't know *what* the Francezcis are or aren't into!" The other threw his hands wide. "But with their intelligence, there has to be a real chance that they're players on our side of the pond, too. Not big as yet, but—"

"—Up and coming," the Necroscope finished it for him. And: "I have to admit, you've got me interested. I'm not keen on the idea of my country's strings being pulled by some kind of super-criminal puppet-master, not now or in the future."

He looked at the photographs.

Three of the five pictures were of the same two men, taken from the same angle, same location. They'd been snapped in gray evening light leaving a typically Italian or Sicilian building, descending a wide flight of steps. Other people were following on behind them but out of focus. In the first picture, the two were glancing directly at the camera, their eyes unseen behind the dark lenses of sunglasses, their handsome faces twisted by shock or surprise.

In the second picture they loomed much closer, one of them pointing at the camera, his slash of a mouth barking some sort of question or order. In the third picture the pair were almost totally obscured by the five fingers of a gloved hand, reaching to cover the lens of the camera.

In all of the photographs their features—while appearing handsome in an almost stereotyped Mediterranean fashion—were very indistinct, blurred; possibly by motion, or by the nerves of the cameraman. Dark hair brushed back, large ears lying flat to their heads, long, slender faces. Also, they appeared taller than the average Italian. Harry knew he would retain these lasting impressions of the Francezcis . . . and one other: their lack of color. For Italians, or Sicilians, they didn't seem to have too much color . . .

"A couple of cold-looking customers, right?" said Darcy, his voice reaching Harry as if from a million miles away.

The Necroscope looked up. "Hmm?" he said.

"Crawly types." Darcy pulled a face. "The result of misspent youths. Pale as a pair of long-time hustlers; spawn of the back alleys and the billiard halls—or in their case, of the dimly lit, echoing rooms of Le Manse Madonie."

"Being a bit theatrical, aren't you?" Harry frowned, and his thoughtful or faraway expression disappeared. "And anyway, I thought you didn't know anything about Le Manse Madonie?"

"No, but I know something about them. They have a congenital disorder, a kind of photophobia: allergy to strong light. Which means they keep pretty much to home. It's one of the reasons why we don't have better pictures. No one has better pictures. Another good reason is that they don't like people *taking* pictures! The fellow who took these . . . he *was* paparazzi, at the time of that nasty Aldo Moro business. It seems amazing to me that he ever got these pictures out of Sicily. Anyway, that's not all he got."

"Oh?"

Darcy shrugged, but in no way negligently. "He was found hanging from a bridge in Naples a month later. Suicide—apparently."

Harry looked at the other photographs. One of a squat man in a flying suit, and the other of a cadaverous type in a valet's uniform. "And these people?"

"The little stubby one is their pilot," Darcy said. "His name is Luigi Manoza. Until a couple of years ago he was working for one of the New York families. A local war took out his employer, and there were threats on Luigi's life, too. He fled to relatives in Sicily, ended up working for the Francezcis.

"The other one is their chauffeur, Mario. He doesn't have a second name—not that he's telling anyway. But he's a dead ringer for a certain 'Mario' who was a highly paid hit man for the Scarlattis in Rome in the late Sixties. He was 'the best' at his infamous job; just the right sort of chap to be driving for the Francezcis!"

"Nice," said Harry. "But something seems wrong. I mean, for people who want to appear divorced from the Mob, these Francezcis seem to employ an awful lot of ex-soldiers."

Darcy shrugged. "In Manoza's case, he was on the periphery. So he's a pilot, but he could just as easily be a gardener. The Mafia employs ordinary people, too, you know. As for Mario: he has no criminal record, was never brought to trial. It's hardly surprising: 'the best' never are."

The Necroscope dropped the photographs back on the desk and stood up. He held out his hand and Darcy shook it. But as Harry headed for the door:

"Harry," Darcy said. "I can still find you some clean money if you want it."

Harry paused. "I'll make out," he said. "I'm not short, not yet anyway. It depends how long it takes to find Brenda and the baby—*if* I find them. You're sure there's nothing your end?"

Darcy shook his head. "But we're keeping our eyes and our ears wide open."

He watched Harry open the door and step out into the corridor. He wanted to call him back, but didn't. He wanted to ask after his health again: were there any other problems—inside his head, maybe? But he didn't. It was always the Branch first. And if the Necroscope had looked back, seen Darcy's face right then, he would have known something was wrong. And maybe Darcy wanted him to. But Harry didn't look back.

Instead, over his shoulder, he said, "Thanks, Darcy. It's as much as I can ask."

And then he closed the door behind him . . .

* * *

That night, Harry called Bonnie Jean. Why, he could never have said. Maybe it was the three-quarters full moon hanging in the sky over the budding trees beyond his garden wall. (Though why that should be a motive was just as big a mystery.) Or maybe it was simply that he'd run out of B.J.'s wine, which was probably why he'd left Seattle and headed for home in the first place.

But these were arguments the Necroscope had had before, if only with himself. And Bonnie Jean . . . was just another of the mysteries of his life. Or was she more than that? An innocent? Harry was sure she was. But how innocent can someone who goes out intent on murder be? Except Harry wasn't allowed to think that way, and so he settled for innocent. Also, she was a damn good-looking woman and someone to talk to. Company, yes. Well, if she wanted to be.

And it looked like it could be a long night, spent tossing and turning. Especially if Harry didn't have anything to drink. And damn it, he intended *not* to have anything to drink! So why call Bonnie Jean?

But he called her anyway.

First he got one of her girls, then Bonnie Jean. She was in the bar, said she'd take it upstairs. (For privacy, he imagined. She wanted privacy, to talk to him.) And she must really have flown up those stairs, for after a few seconds:

"Harry? Is it really mah wee man himself?" Her voice—or words—were like warm fingers driven home through his butter brain, pressing buttons, switching channels, conjuring a different him. Then B.J. dropped the accent but retained her husky breathlessness: "Funny, but I've really missed you, Harry . . ."

And whatever misgivings he'd had—if he had had any at all—were at once forgotten. "Well, I'm back," he found his voice. "For the time being, anyway. And you told me to stay in touch . . ." It seemed a weak, ineffectual way to broach what was on his mind. But the words just slipped off his tongue as if they were someone else's.

"And if anything, your call is early," B.J. said, without really thinking what she was saying. But it was a fact that the full moon was still a week away. Immediately realizing her mistake (why did this bloody man have this *effect* on her?), she went to add something, anything, but Harry beat her to it:

"I know what you mean," he said, without really knowing. "I seem a bit eager, right? Well, maybe it's the moon."

That shocked her rigid, so that she found difficulty in answering: "The moon?"

"Over my garden wall," he explained. "I seem to have this tune in my head: 'Give me the moonlight, give me the girl, and leave the rest to me.' Well, I have the moonlight, but . . ."

She sighed her relief, inaudible to Harry, and said, "But no girl, eh?" And before he could answer: "Where are you?"

"Pretty close. I'm home. Five or six miles."

"Did you find them? Your wife and child?"

"No," the Necroscope answered, his voice showing no emotion one way or the other. B.J. wouldn't be able to tell if he was glad or sad. And the fact was that right now, Harry didn't know either.

"It's a quiet night," B.J. said. "We'll be closing around twelve . . ."

It wasn't much, Harry thought, but she seemed to be saying so much more. And: "That's more than three hours," he answered.

"Too long?"

"Yes . . . no . . . I don't have much to do. I mean I'm alone and . . . lonely, I suppose."

"Do you want to come here?"

"I can if you—"

"—No, don't. Look, why don't you tell me where you are, and I'll come to you? I'll take a taxi. The girls can take care of things here for one night."

"You'll come now?"

He sensed her shrug. "I could use a break. Have you eaten?"

"Not in a while." (It was true, he was starving!)

"Do you have any food in?"

"No food," he shook his head, despite that she couldn't see him. "No drink either . . ."

She answered pause for pause and finally said, "I'm sure we can fix that. I mean, I'll pick something up on the way. So . . . what's the address? Oh, and Harry, give me your 'phone number, too, in case I'm delayed. The number I have doesn't work."

And he told her both his address and telephone number. Why not? It seemed the most natural thing in the world to do . . .

Harry's address was scarcely the easiest place in the world to find. It was one of four Victorian houses standing in an uneven cluster on a riverbank a mile or two out of Bonnyrig, with undulating patchwork-quilt fields on three sides, dotted with dark copses here and there, and, during daylight, the rare hazy view of a distant steeple or square church tower.

Just why any specific area falls derelict is hard to say, but this district definitely had. Three of the once-proud, even grand old houses were terraced and stood in high-walled gardens extending almost to the river. The two outer houses had been empty for years and were beyond redemption; their windows were gaping holes and their roofs were buckling inwards. They had been up for sale for a long time; every so often someone would come to look at them, and go away shaking his head. They were not "desirable" residences. The central house was Harry's place. It was lonely, but he could talk to his Ma in private here and never fear that anyone would see him sitting on the river bank mouthing nonsense to himself.

Glimpsed through the trees lining the river bank, Bonnie Jean's first view of the house was from a road on the far side of the river. She had asked the driver of her taxi to halt, and sat there a while just looking across the river. It was obvious which house was occupied: the ground floor lights were on; they flooded out and lit the sprawling garden, lending the place an eerie illumination. The house was alive, barely. But by comparison the others were stone dead. Yet oddly enough, B.J. didn't consider the place as a whole at all out of keeping with Harry Keogh's character. Indeed, she thought it suited him.

The reason she had caused the driver to stop was simple: she'd wanted to observe the house from a safe distance. But it was what it was, an old house on its last legs: hardly a "safe" house as she would imagine such a place to be. And in any case, since Harry's people, his ex-employers, already knew about her—or something about her—it made little difference. But he had told her they were finished with him and that they'd have no further interest in her. Following which she'd made doubly sure by giving him certain post-hypnotic commands. But he was no ordinary man, this mysterious Harry Keogh, and it was something she'd have to check up on anyway.

After a while she'd told the driver to carry on, and a minute later the taxi had crossed the river by an old stone bridge onto a rutted service road. The row of houses lay at the end of the road, and B.J. dismounted and paid her fare outside Harry's address: Number 3, The Riverside, the one with the lights.

As the taxi pulled away, B.J. walked the moonlit ribbon of paving stones to Harry's door, which opened as she reached it. And Harry was there.

Taking the brown-paper, Chinese-motif takeaway bags out of her hands as he ushered her inside, he looked harassed and was instantly apologetic about the state of the place. He had obviously been busy; his brow was damp with perspiration.

"But . . . you seem in a bit of a state!" she said, looking all around his spacious if sparsely furnished study, the only room that he'd spent any time on, and that nearly a month ago. "What on earth have you been doing, Harry?"

He grimaced. "Er, tidying up?"

"Really?" She couldn't help but smile. "Then I'd hate to have seen it when it looked rough!"

He nodded glumly. "A mess, right?"

She shook her head in bewilderment. "And you live here?"

"Is it *that* bad?" He looked around, licked his lips nervously, nodded again. "Yes, it is that bad. Well, actually, the house isn't *too* bad at all. It's been a decent old place in its time and was built to last. Which is as well, because it's seen some neglect. But the site . . . is a mess, yes. The main thing is, this place is mine, and I can do it up. I've only been here a while, after all. And I've been busy. But the place has had a survey and doesn't seem to have any problems. I mean, structurally," Harry opened his arms expansively, setting the Chinese takeaway bags swinging, "it's just fine! I'll replace the carpets . . . well, eventually. And a few floorboards kind of creak. Er, the *décor* could be improved, I suppose. And I really don't know where all the dust comes from." He sighed, and his poorly-feigned optimistic air disappeared in a moment. "Then there's the paintwork, and a handful of roof tiles, and . . ." Shrugging, he fell silent.

"But why this place?" There had to be a reason.

"It was my Ma's," Harry said. "Then my stepfather's. They . . . are dead now. It's just a place to be, I suppose, now that I'm on my own."

Listening to him, B.J. had felt his loneliness. She'd been lonely, too—albeit in a different way—for a very long time now. "Outside, from across the river, I thought it looked like you. The house, I mean. From a distance, it's still—I don't know—rich?"

"I'm not rich," Harry shook his head.

"I mean its character," she said. "In the night, it looks like it has style."

"Do I have style?"

B.J. nodded and cocked her head on one side. "Well, you've certainly got something, Harry Keogh. Else I wouldn't be here." Which was the truth, however she meant it. And, before he could answer: "Where's the kitchen?" she asked, as she took the takeaway bags back from him. "Or don't I want to know?"

But thank God, the kitchen had been modernized . . .

They ate. Discovering that he really was hungry, Harry set to with a will. B.J. watched him mainly, and toyed with the smaller portions of Chinese food that she had served herself. She had also been watching him as she'd unpacked and reheated the food in his microwave: his keen interest in what there was to drink, and his obviously disappointed frown on sighting a bottle of liebfraumilch.

He didn't want any (for which she was glad), settling for a can of Coke instead. But as she poured herself a glass, she said, "The red wine is gone. What was left, anyway . . ." And the pause was pregnant as she stared at him.

Harry was ready for it, but still he glanced at her before looking away. "That was bad of me," he said. "Would you believe me if I said I came to see you? I mean, you'd asked me to stay in touch, and here I was about to go away. And I couldn't contact you."

"But why break in?"

"Break in? As in burglary?" He shook his head. "I didn't have to break anything. I told you: this is what I do best. It was my job, remember? And your place is a walk-in, believe me! From the back, anyway."

"Oh?" She'd thought she was so secure, but the fact was that she had been advised to employ more security at the rear of the premises. "It was that easy?"

"I'll show you some time," he said, hoping he would never have to. And he carried on eating.

"And you got past one of my girls," B.J. wasn't finished.

"I move very quickly, and very quietly," Harry said, knowing that she couldn't argue with that.

"But it was very wrong of you, anyway! What would I have thought or done, if I had been in and you had suddenly entered my bedroom? And as for stealing a bottle of my wine . . . !"

Harry grinned in what he hoped was a disarming manner. "I left a calling card, that's all. You must have seen that ad on TV. You know the one: 'and all because—' "

" '—Harry Keogh loves red wine?' "

"Something like that, yes. But you know that stuff really did have an adverse effect on me? And didn't I read something recently—about a mass-poisoning or some such—where certain European vintners were accused of topping up their wines with antifreeze? And now you tell me it's gone? What, did you actually *sell* that stuff?"

What? Bonnie Jean could hardly believe it! Now *he* seemed to be accusing *her* of something! Also, this was beginning to sound a lot like one of Radu's word-games . . . and if so, then Harry Keogh was good at them! But she kept her temper, answering: "You know, you could be right? I tried it myself and the next morning felt like you looked that time. But no, I didn't sell it. I gave it to my customers to try—and they didn't like it either."

"And so it's gone?"

"Finished, yes."

Against his will, Harry felt himself gritting his teeth. He didn't quite know whether to be glad or mad. He should have taken all the bottles when he had the chance. But no, of course he shouldn't! It had to be for the best that the vile stuff was finished. And with it the "after-image," or whatever, of Kyle's alcoholism, obviously. For Harry was damned if he could fancy B.J.'s liebfraumilch! Exactly how it all tied up he couldn't say, but now, at last, it was over. It had to be over, because there was no more of B.J.'s wine.

And as if someone had pulled a plug in his brain, most of Harry's frustrations, anxieties and self-doubts went flooding away down the drain of his mind, leaving him relieved and cool where a moment ago he'd been burning up. For perhaps, after all, he was that one smoker in ten million who could only smoke one brand . . . and at last they'd stopped making it! Yet even now, in the depths of his subconscious mind, a small voice was asking him: "Oh, really? But what about Greece? I'll bet you can get it in Greece . . ."

And there it was: *the* question right there on the tip of his tongue, making ready to blurt itself out: *That friend of yours, the one who brought it back for you? You wouldn't happen to know where he got it, would you?* Except he mustn't ask it! Never! Not if he would be his own man again.

She came to his rescue, saying: "All I knew was that someone had been into my place. I didn't think of you at first, but wondered if maybe it had been this organization you worked for. Maybe they were checking me out or something."

For a moment that caught him off guard; he had quite forgotten the story he'd told her about the Branch wanting him to clear up a point or two. But now she'd brought it all back to mind, and since in fact E-Branch knew nothing at all about her: "No, B.J., no one's out to get you," he said. "Like I told you, the people I worked for aren't police, and in fact they're not even remotely interested in you. Not any longer. Nor in me for that matter. And believe me, I really am sorry I caused you so much concern . . ."

They finished the rest of the meal in an awkward silence, just mulling things over. But when Harry finally sat back, he sighed and said, "You want to know something? I think this is the first time in—God, I don't know how long!—that I've felt relaxed. Your choice of food was just great. And you . . . are just great, too. Wrong-headed, maybe, but great. And anyway, who am I to talk?"

"Who indeed?" she said, something like his Ma might, but with an entirely different feel to it. "Was that a compliment?"

Harry laughed and rubbed his chin. "I'm not sure," he answered, "but it felt like a whole series of them!"

"Your best line? Your idea of chatting me up? Seduction, even? To tell me that I'm great despite that I'm wrong-headed? Well, I have to say I've heard better!" The way she said "Well," it really did sound like his Ma.

The idea of red wine was now rapidly receding in the Necroscope's mind. B.J. had spoken several key words—words that had nothing to do with previous post-hypnotic commands—which Harry had picked up on. And now he realized what else he'd been missing in the last eighteen months, other than his own body.

Taking up the used plates and cutlery, and fumbling it a little, he said, "Do you feel cold? Is it cold in here?" There had been a fire laid in his open fireplace ever since he moved in, but the Necroscope hadn't felt the need to light it. Normally he didn't like it too warm, and perhaps surprisingly the house's oil-fired central-heating system was working very well.

She had seen his eyes rove over the hearth and had perhaps read something of what was on his mind. "A little chilly, yes."

"Then toss a match on the fire while I wash up."

"All right," she said. "And . . . I'd like to wash up, too."

"Ummm?"

"The bathroom, is—?"

"Off the landing, upstairs," he answered. "The shower is . . . very good."

"But I bet your bedroom's a mess, right?" The direct way was usually the best and easiest. Even so, B.J. was surprised to find herself breathing a shade too fast.

"Actually, no," Harry answered, his voice a little husky. "No, it's . . . pretty tidy. I, er, tidied it?" He paused in the doorway and looked back to where she was standing by the fireplace. Their eyes locked, and for a moment it was like it had been in her barroom. There was this magnetism, which had nothing to do with the art of beguilement . . . or on the other hand, it was that entirely natural, mutual beguilement, the electric moment, when a man and woman know that it's going to happen.

"But now that the fire's lit," she tore her eyes from his, struck a match and tossed it onto a base of crumpled newspaper and kindling, "I think I would be just as comfortable . . . down here?"

And beginning to burn as quickly as the fire, and just as hot, Harry husked, "Then after you've showered, bring down the quilt and soft top blanket from my bed."

Then he was off to the kitchen, and B.J. licked her lips. The dog-Lord was right: there were other ways, better ways, to enthrall a man. With the lights off and the curtains drawn, in the red glow of the fire, it would be just like a warm, secret cave in here.

Yes, it would be just like a lair . . .

ONE OF THE OTHER WAYS.
TRUTHS, HALF-TRUTHS, AND DAMNED LIES.

IT WAS TWO A.M. BEFORE HARRY FELL ASLEEP IN HER ARMS, BUT THE NIGHT time was B.J.'s time and she didn't feel the need. She needed, oh yes, but not sleep. And as the time crept inexorably closer to the full of the moon, that need was ever more insistent. But she had long since learned to deny herself, so that Harry was never in any real danger. Especially Harry, who impressed her more and more as the Mysterious One, Radu's "Man With Two Faces."

Well, his ways weren't quite so mysterious now. One facet at least had revealed itself to her. And in his way, he had initiated it. Shy to begin with (scarcely a Don Juan!), his prowess had improved with experimentation. And, unlike most men the first time they are with a woman, Harry had felt driven to satisfy her; he'd quickly discovered her preference.

A moon child, with that of the wolf—a great deal of the wolf—in her, B.J. had "submitted." And with her breasts flattened to the soft blanket, and her face turned to the red glow of the fire, she'd felt the delicious thrusting, the hammering home of Harry's turgid flesh in the heart of her womanhood. Oh, he had gone without for . . . a *long* time, that much was obvious. But so had she, and could take all that he could give. Yet despite the fact that she sucked on him desperately with her sex, still he had held back until he first felt *her* shuddering, and heard *her* moaning, before firing into her his long, hot bursts. And Bonnie Jean Mirlu had never felt so well satisfied. Not in that respect, anyway.

For him, their sex was a jammed floodgate finally opened. Pouring himself into her, the rest of his pain—his grief?—and all of his anxieties and frustrations were temporarily suspended. Time itself seemed suspended, in the oblivion of those briefly blazing seconds as B.J.'s sugar, the searing and singing of her flesh, saturated his psyche and melted in his mind. And the second time he came, such was B.J.'s pleasure that as they disengaged she turned him on his back and kept his shaft moist and throbbing in the soft sleeve of her mouth . . . until he was ready again.

But throughout she had been aware of the danger, and mindful of Radu's warning: "Be sure—be absolutely *sure*—that if he gets into you, nothing of you, of us, gets into him!"

Of course not, for he wanted Harry for himself, to use . . . however he would use him. He wanted him pure, human. At first, anyway. As for Radu's purpose with Harry:

B.J. knew of it (the dog-Lord had explained something of it, at least) but for the moment did not want to think about it. For the moment she wanted only to lie here, warm and drowsy, with Harry's arm draped over her and his sleeping, no longer intense but oddly innocent face resting against the resilience of her breasts, and her thigh between his legs where his rod, all flaccid now, twitched occasionally, perhaps from the "memory" of its mounting. For while he had pleasured her with his body, it had not stopped there: he now pleasured her with his presence. Yes, she . . . *liked* being there with him! And it was also a curiously pleasant thought that he'd shot his seed into her—despite that she had been obliged to kill it.

Contraception? Pills and plastic and senses-stifling rubber? Unnecessary. Her body, her system, was its own protection. There was that in her blood—the same alien essence that defended her against Man's common ailments, time's deterioration, and even physical injuries—that would not allow of the invasion of his sperm. B.J. need only call on it, think it into being, and her system would, or had, responded to destroy all of Harry's myriad squirming tadpoles of generation.

It had taken but a thought, a command issued from B.J.'s mind to her own innermost organs and tissues, to the immature leech which she even felt growing within her despite that her Master had denied it:

Other than you, there is that in me which is alive. I do not wish it. Cleanse me of this infestation. So be it. And it was done.

Except the other way was much harder: to keep that alien essence to herself, and not transmit it, or allow it to transmit itself, into her partner. She wanted him enthralled in the one sense, but not as a true thrall in the other. B.J. herself, *she* might have wanted him so, but the dog-Lord did not. No, for Radu wanted him for himself. Again, it seemed a contradiction:

That her Master would insist she was *not* Wamphyri, but at the same time worry about her passing on anything to Harry, to his Mysterious One. Herself a thrall (*if* that was all she was), B.J.'s bite would make him a moon child—aye, to be stricken by the moon at its full, and held in awe of unnatural urges—but never a true wolfling. Only by transfusion of Radu's blood, his saliva, his sperm, his essence, could that be accomplished. Or by his leech or its vampire egg. But surely, during all the years that B.J. had served him, sufficient of her Master must have found its way into her? No, not so; Radu had it that the giving was a one-way thing; B.J. got nothing back . . .

Oh, really? Then why was it that she always felt—what, an electric *connection?* An inner awareness, anyway—as Radu's funnel filled and he began to consume her life's blood? Bonnie Jean knew why, or supposed she knew. But she scarcely dared to admit it, not even to herself. For if she was wrong . . .

How great his wrath, to discover that she had somehow imagined herself magically endowed—indeed Wamphyri—without that he had engineered it!

Well, he need not worry, for it was not her intention to make a vampire, a wolf, or any other creature out of Harry. It *was* her intention to obey her Master and eventually have him up out of his resin grave; for as much as Bonnie Jean had been the dog-Lord's champion, she sensed the day coming when he must be hers. The Drakuls and Ferenczys and their thralls were abroad in the world; as yet B.J. was more woman than composite creature; Radu *must* survive, at least until she had learned all she could from him, and with that knowledge became more capable of managing, of engineering . . . her own . . . dynasty?

And so it was out in the open at last, in the open of her consciousness, her self-understanding, at least. Not treachery, but survival! Her own survival. More proof—and possibly the best yet—that she was or would soon be what she'd suspected for the last forty years at least: Wamphyri! So for now, Radu would continue to be her Master, and his word law.

And until he was up again, and for as long as the Drakuls and Ferenczys were a threat, she would suppress it as best she could; and as he had used her she would now use others, and so prepare her own way in the world.

As for the dog-Lord's plans for Harry—his so-called Mysterious One, his "Man With Two Faces,"—B.J. could now look at those in a different light, from Radu's point of view. For what he would do now, she herself might yet be obliged to attempt in some far-distant future time . . .

Radu had not gone down into the resin of his own volition. Not entirely. He had thought that he sickened; he had believed that the Black Death held *him* in thrall, and knew from experience that he could not beat it. With his own eyes he had seen his pups develop those hideous black pustules, and die. He had *felt* the disease inside him, and knew the struggle his essence put up against it, in vain. And he'd cursed his leech for its weakness, its idle inefficiency, that it could not combat the creep of this insidious thing.

But the 1340s was a decade not only of plague but of famine and unrest. Simple movement throughout Europe had been the most difficult thing in its own right. Even a rich Boyar's entourage, fleeing before the all-devouring scourge from the east, could scarcely expect to find it an easy passage. Radu had got into a fight, suffered a sword thrust in his side. Normally his vampire leech could easily handle, quickly heal a simple wound. But his parasite was already battling the plague within Radu's system; a fight it couldn't hope to win, not as long as he was up and about, engaging in other activities.

He had hated it, but there was no other solution. So that finally, in Scotland in 1350, the dog-Lord's long-laid contingency plan for continuity must be brought into being. The pack had built him a makeshift lair in unexplored mountain heights, and Radu had gone down into the resin.

A drastic solution, perhaps, but this was what he'd seen in precognitive dreams: that he *must* go down for long and long—six hundred years and more—and rise up in a future world, even in another body! Metempsychosis: the passing of his Being and Personality into the body of another. Moreover, he had long dreamed of this Mysterious One, who would be there at his awakening; and of himself as the avenger out of time, destroyer of his olden enemies, burning bright as a star in the final hour of his triumph!

With these things in mind it had been easier to submit to the sarcophagus of soft, suffocating resin. The wine of desert-bred wizards had helped; the coma it induced had been like unto death itself, but in fact was the dawn of a radically extended undeath. And immobile in his state of suspended animation in a gluey grave in the Cairngorms lair, he had commenced to dream.

And now that Radu was no longer active, consuming energy and making demands on his leech, his vampire could concentrate on its real battle, directing all of its efforts to combat the virus raging in the dog-Lord's heart. Just how that battle had gone . . . who could say? Radu slept; and even when his mind was awake, still in a way it was detached from his body. He would not know he was a whole man again until the two came together, which would be on the day when B.J. melted away the resin and set him free.

And if he was not the whole man? If his parasite had lost its fight and the fever rose up in him again, resurgent after all these years? That was where Harry Keogh came into the picture; it was the role that Radu saw him playing in that final scene. Metempsychosis, aye.

Because in the year preceding the dog-Lord's awakening, he would use his superior powers of beguilement—that hypnotism which was his art above all others—to transfer his *detailed* memories into Harry's mind. And if when he arose he discovered his body riddled with disease, about to succumb and suffer the true death, then he would cause his leech to flee his body into Harry's. Indeed, he would scarcely need to "cause" it, for the natural tenacity of the parasite—its lust for life—would see to that. And if by chance the leech itself could not transfuse, if it should be obstructed, then it would issue its egg, swiftest and surest of all carriers of vampirism!

But in the moment of transfusion, by whichever method, the dog-Lord would attempt his greatest wonder. Radu *was* an incredibly powerful mentalist, a telepath without peer. And with his own uniformly scarlet gaze, he would burn out Harry's mind and project himself through Harry's own honey-brown eyes into his mentality. He would *be* Harry Keogh.

Or more properly, Harry would *become* him. With Radu's egg, or leech, all of his memories and his mind entire . . . he would *be* Radu. Why, eventually, through metamorphism, he would even come to look like him, would wear the dog-Lord's face. The Man With Two Faces, aye.

That was Lord Radu Lykan's plan.

But on the other hand—if he should rise up again a whole man or creature, free of the plague—then there would be other uses for the Mysterious One. And they were far less of a mystery. For one thing, there'd be a hungry warrior to see to . . .

It was 2:30. Harry stirred and mumbled something in his sleep, and it was as good a time as any.

B.J. shushed him, checked that he was still deeply asleep, reached across him and toppled a smouldering block of firewood, oak, she thought, from the back of the deep old-fashioned fireplace into the glowing embers. Then she slid out from under the blanket that she'd drawn over them, crossed the room and turned on a reading-lamp at Harry's desk. And aiming it directly into Harry's face, his shut eyes, she at once blocked the beam with her naked body and quickly returned to him.

Then she lay beside him and propped herself on one elbow, turned and looked at the lamp. And narrowing her eyes to close out the rest of the room, she nodded and congratulated herself that the glowing sphere of light looked not unlike a full moon, the principal image, the trigger, that was already implanted in his mind. The rest of it was down to power of will, the intensity of her own eyes and voice and mind, to which he'd already succumbed on previous occasions.

And she breathed, "Harry, mah wee man. Are ye listening!" It was a deep, purring, penetrating Scottish brogue, which she breathed into his nostrils as well as his ears. Her scent, her musk, infiltrated Harry's system, his dreams and subconscious, and for a moment his eyelids fluttered, then were still, as he mumbled:

"Y-yes."

"Good," she purred. And dropping the accent: "Harry, you *will* listen to me, and you *will* obey me. Is that understood?"

"Y-yes."

And as quickly, as easily as that, she had taken command of his mind. It still seemed amazing to B.J. that control was so simple over a mind she'd suspected of being so complex! And so far she'd used only the *human* side of her will, while there was that in her which was much stronger and far and away superior to anything human. But now, because of the ultimately esoteric nature of what she must tell Harry—as a prelude to what Radu would eventually instil into him—B.J. had need of that greater, alien strength of will.

Again leaving their makeshift bed before the fire, she went to the patio windows and opened the curtains. High over the garden, a three-quarter-full moon poured its silvery light on her, which pooled around her and turned her to an alabaster statue. She opened her arms wide, sighed, and reached up, letting the moonlight flood her psyche and drawing strength from it. And this time her metamorphosis was that much easier.

Colors flowed, flesh rippled, moved, rearranged. There sounded a crackle of static electricity as fur bristled, stood erect, and settled down on B.J.'s flanks. And drawing the curtains again, and falling to all fours, she went back to Harry.

And cradling him, and lusting after his flesh (but denying herself, because her lust was no longer sexual), she commanded that he open his eyes and gaze upon the glorious moon, and that he *see* only her eyes, in the moonlight flooding from his reading-lamp. Then, burning the message home with her furnace gaze, she told him what he must know if he was to go out into the world as the dog-Lord's spy, to seek out the Drakuls and the Ferenczys: knowledge he would retain in his innermost being without even realizing it was there. Likewise any information he might gather: no other would be privy to it—Harry himself would scarcely be aware of its existence—until B.J. or Radu Lykan drew it out of him.

And as her husky, she-wolf's voice coughed, rumbled and occasionally whined through the long night hours, telling its truths, half-truths, and damned lies—mainly as she herself had heard the story from the dog-Lord Radu, and employing his mode of expression—so the Necroscope absorbed all that she told him, soaking it up as a bone-dry sponge soaks water . . .

* * *

Haaaarry! Harry Keogh, listen to me. Listen, and remember all that I shall tell you. But these are secret things—this is secret knowledge—for you and you alone. Retain it, and use it when the time is right. But at other times forget it, lest it harm you irreparably.

Harry, there is a world other than this world. A place, a space, other than ours. It has a name, Sunside/Starside, where there are men . . . and other than men. There are barrier mountains, which keep the two races apart. Sunside of the mountains dwell men; Starside is home to the Wamphyri. The Wamphyri were men, but no longer. Now they are greater than men; they are the vampire Lords of a vampire world.

In the earliest times of the vampire world, Lord Shaitan of the Wamphyri was the greatest of the Starside Lords. The others rose up against him, and he defeated them. Many of them whom he took prisoner were executed in various ways; they were put into deep graves to stiffen to stones in the earth, or were banished into the bitter-cold Icelands. But others were thrown into the Starside Gate, which was thought to be the throat of a vampire hell. In fact it was a true Gate . . . to this world, our world! Except having come here, they could not go back, for the Gate had closed behind them.

Among them who came through with their thralls were several of the vilest of men, creatures whose evil was quite beyond the imagining of mundane minds: the Drakul brothers, Karl and Egon, and Nonari the Gross Ferenczy. And these awesome Lords were destined to become the forebears of vampirism in this world, even as they had been among its first progenitors in Starside.

But there was one other who was banished with them, and He was honorable even among the Wamphyri, where true honor never existed. His name was Radu Lykan, a so-called—"dog-Lord," whose mistress was the moon, and whose shape and affinity were more like unto the noble wolf than the ill-omened bat. Oh, Radu was Wamphyri, but in his nature he was above them as men are above rats.

And for a thousand years Radu ran with the wolves and was one with the wild of this world . . . a creature of Nature, aye, and different from the vile and terrible Lords who came out of Starside with him. He desired only to go his own way, doing no harm to men but living alongside them, unseen in the woods and mountain heights. His prey were the wild things, and his drink was the clean, clear water of mountain streams.

But as for the Drakuls and Ferenczys: they were—they are—a monstrous scourge and the source of a legend as wide as a world. The legend of the vampire! And Radu, because he is Wamphyri, has been tarred with their brush. In that ancient world where he came forth out of Starside, down all the years of his freedom in the wild, even unto these modern times, he is known by a terrible name and an undeserved reputation: werewolf! And despite that he was never guilty of Drakul and Ferenczy excesses and atrocities, he bears the selfsame taint and his memory is likewise cursed.

His memory, aye . . .

Because he is no more, nothing in this world but an ancient creature in a cavern lair. Nothing but a bad dream, which was never given the opportunity to clear its name. Because he was driven into hiding, made to seek refuge and relinquish his life in the wild as a veritable Force of Nature, by his olden Starside enemies. Six hundred years ago, in a time of war and famine and pestilence, they sought him out, to pursue him and put him down. But he evaded them and theirs by hiding himself away in a mountainous redoubt. Except it is a redoubt in name only. Untenanted, unprotected, it is more a lair, a sanctuary—a place of refuge—than a fortress.

But even there the dog-Lord Radu is not safe. Even there, even now, he is "dogged" by the sons of the sons of his olden Starside enemies. For while the descendants—the spawn—

of vile Drakuls and Ferenczys are ignorant of Radu's whereabouts, still they know that he is not dead but undead, dreaming in a place of his own, and they cannot bear that he yet abides.

For when Lord Lykan's sleep of centuries is done, he will be up again and return to his woods and mountains. Except this time he will not suffer such as his enemies to live. This time he will seek them out, wherever they are disguised as men, and deal with them as they would deal with him.

But . . . it will not be easy. For even in those bygone days six hundred years ago, already the Wamphyri were adept at hiding themselves away among men! And the Ferenczys especially so. Let me tell you what I know of their history, Harry, as it was told to me by my Master, the dog-Lord Radu Lykan. But remember: as a family-tree of infamy, this history of the Wamphyri is incomplete; it ends where Radu retired to his mountain hideaway. And in all the time gone by since then . . . ah, but who can say what is become of such creatures now, their place in the world today? Well, I can say. Something of them at least.

First the Drakuls:

As told, there were two of them came through the Gate with Radu: Karl and Egon. Black Karl, as he was known—not for the color of his skin but that of his heart—met up with Radu in Ain Jalut in 1260. Karl was with the Mongols (as was a certain Ferenczy, who ran off when he saw how all was lost; I will tell you about him later) and Radu with the Mamelukes, who were triumphant. Wherefore we needn't any longer concern ourselves with Karl! Thereafter, however, Egon Drakul was far more mindful of a Wamphyri maxim here in this world: that anonymity is synonymous with longevity! Perhaps it was because Radu was actively hunting the Drakuls down—perhaps Egon had simply had enough of the slaughter of the times?—whichever, he disappeared for a while, and for long and long Radu could discover nothing of his whereabouts . . .

. . . But some ninety years later Radu's spies reported Egon's presence in Poland! Alas, Radu only learned of this when he was in France en route for England, fleeing from the scourge of the Black Death, else he would have gone to Poland at once.

Too late . . . He fell ill . . . Even as the Black Death began to burn itself out—in its initial manifestation at least—so the dog-Lord went into "hibernation" in his secret mountain refuge. But he left certain tried and trusted thralls behind, to look after his interests down the centuries . . .

Of the latter: there weren't many. Most of his "pups" had been taken by the plague; others had died building his retreat; only the hardy descendants of Mirlus and Tirenis, recruited out of Sunside in the vampire world, when Radu was a Starside Lord, lived to survive him—and then only by virtue of their isolation, the inaccessible mountain heights in which they worked.

But when Radu was safely asleep in his great sarcophagus, then they went down into Scotland to settle the land around, or to wait out the last days of the plague before returning abroad to more familiar lands and territories. Ah, how could they know that the plague wasn't finished with them, that scarcely a decade would pass for the next four centuries without it returning again and again to scythe among them? For since they were moonchildren all, and of Radu's blood, its contagion was deadly to them no less than leprosy to the vampire Lords of Starside.

Well, if there were survivors, I do not know of them . . .

But of that handful who remained local and loyal to Radu, a few did survive. Aye, and six hundred years ago, an ancestor of mine, a Mirlu, was one of them. We had to *survive, else Radu himself could not. For who would there be to . . . to* tend *him in his secret lair? To listen to him dreaming? To reassure him, if only by our presence, of the time of his return? To . . . to* console *him, in his long, lonely sleep?*

My ancestor, aye. He, or more likely she, lived and died a moon child—but not without leaving an heir to her duties. And there would always be an heir down the centuries. For four hundred years, Harry—a Mirlu to care for Radu in his immemorial tomb! Until there was me . . .

And surely that is the true miracle: that to know him and be faithful to him—indeed, to dedicate one's life to him—is to extend that life indefinitely! Longevity beyond the wildest dreams of the boldest men of science and medicine! And yet Radu has it, Harry, and so do I. And so can you!

But I fancy I've strayed . . . I was speaking of Egon Drakul . . . let me continue:

In Poland the Black Death had little impact. Why? Who can say? The plague was carried by rats of Asiatic origin; perhaps there were too many rivers to cross: the Danube, the Elbe, the Oder. Anyway, and despite that one third *of the European population succumbed, Egon Drakul survived. Or if not Egon himself, a blood- or egg-son, certainly.*

Now, the Drakuls had been driven out of their foothold in Transylvania many hundreds of years earlier by successive waves of eastern invaders. Their influence in that mountainous region had been eroded; they'd been less than covert in their activities; the legend they originated was eradicated—almost.

But six hundred years ago, in the wake of plague, famine, war, and civil unrest in general—after the decimation of Europe—it was time to return to the source land, the mountains that Egon knew so well. Why, upon a time he'd even been a Lord there, no less than in Starside in another world! So much I've gathered . . . for in two hundred years I have been something of a far-traveler myself, when times have allowed. And on my Master's behalf I've done what you will do: sought evidence of his olden enemies; sought to locate them, so that when Radu returns he'll know their numbers and whereabouts.

And this much I have learned:

That indeed there was a Drakul in his Transylvanian castle until a time as recent as a hundred years ago! An "aristocrat," aye—a Count! The people around knew him, however, and eventually it was his time to move on again. But was it Egon Drakul? Egon himself? Oh, I think so. And I have my reasons.

Radu had killed Egon's brother Karl, then "gone to earth" in Scotland. Perhaps Egon sought revenge. Perhaps he would even seek out my Master! However it was, he had his thralls in England—"sleepers," if you will—and went there. Now down the years this Drakul's mentalist talent had grown; in order to inform his English thralls of his imminent arrival on their soil, he reached out to them with his mind . . . and in so doing, likewise alerted Radu where he lay dreaming in his mountain refuge! And Radu alerted me . . .

A hundred years ago, aye. Can you imagine how things have changed, Harry? There were no airplanes in those days; now men have walked on the surface of our mistress moon, and sent their messages out to the stars! The sciences were still *young, while superstition was still rife. There were alchemists, and others who remembered and believed in the old legends. And there were some I feared, because of what they believed. But there was no other way and I must protect my Master.*

There was a much-traveled man, a doctor, who knew—who believed—the legend of the Wampir. *And before the Drakul was able to set up a colony in England, I made known to this doctor his presence here. It was easy . . . a letter . . . a warning. And it coincided with a spate of strange deaths and deteriorations. Also, Egon had come aboard a ship; well, how else? But a plague ship by the time it wrecked on the north-east coast! And so my doctor was convinced.*

He put paid to Egon's plans, pursued him back to Transylvania, brought him up out of his coffin into sunlight. It was the end of one of the original Lords of the Wamphyri, brought about by my hand! . . . As instructed by my Master, of course.

But it was the way of it—the way of his true death—that convinced me it was Egon Drakul and none other, no matter what names he may have used. To surrender to the sunlight like that, and devolve into so much dust. Ah, but he had been Wamphyri for long and long . . .

And what an opportunity, eh? I couldn't resist it: a trip to my Master's country, where first he entered this world. And from there into the hinterland, where at least one ancient Drakul castle is standing to this day. My duties were such that I could afford ninety days, no more: barely sufficient time. But I went anyway—to the castle of the dead Drakul.

What, on a whim? Never! My Lord Radu Lykan sent me, and with specific instructions at that. For he knew that the Drakuls had been creatures of habit, by which I might know for certain it was Egon we had killed. And in the dank and gloomy dungeons, in the spider-haunted vaults of that hated place on its gaunt promontory, I found the evidence I sought:

A bed of earth in the crumbling debris of an antique coffin. Earth out of Starside, in a vampire world. But a coffin? One coffin? Ah, no . . . there were two coffins!

The one, the old one, bore a motif in the shape of a riven man. And according to my Master Radu, it had been a Drakul punishment in Starside to tear enemies asunder and let their guts rain down onto the boulder plains beneath the great aeries. The other coffin was newer. Some two or three hundred years old, it carried no special sigil but only these initials: "D.D." Surely the second of the two must stand for Drakul?

There were Szgany around, Szekely. Apparently they were in thrall in one degree or another to the now absent Drakuls. They kept the castle, and sheltered within its structure through bad winters. Me they hated on sight, but I am what I am and was not concerned. They melted away into the country around, leaving me to my own devices. But before departing for England I . . . found a Szkeley youth who was . . . not adverse to talking to me.

And the youth told me that indeed the great Boyar's "son" had set out with his retainers and journeyed east, at the self-same time as his "father" had ventured westward. So then, Egon was dead, but his son—egg- or blood-son, I can't say—had fled east. But "east" is a big place and too far away in those days for me to visit. And it seems that this most recent Drakul had learned the lesson his forbears forgot or ignored: the maxim which has it that longevity is synonymous with anonymity. For in all the years since I've heard no more of these terrible Drakuls. Except from Radu, who assures me that at least one of them survives still. "D.D." of course.

Well, so much for them, who were in any case the least of Radu's enemies. As for the worst of them: they were—they are—the Ferenczys!

Let me tell you what is known of them, but in order to do so I must go back a long, long way . . .

Now in the vampire world, Radu and the Ferenczy clan had been enemies from the start. Theirs was a bloodfeud that began long before they were Lords, when they were Szgany in Sunside. Radu was a mere youth when the brutish Ferenczy brothers, Lagula and Rakhi, not only murdered his human father but raped to death his sister, the only creature he'd ever cared for in all Sunside. When she was dead . . . then he cared for nothing much. Nothing but revenge.

No, not true: he was also fond of a she-wolf who wandered the Sunside hills with him during his days as a mountain man, a loner without a tribe, neither family nor friends, only the sun to warm him and the stars for guide at night. Radu and his she-wolf, aye. But she was infected with vampirism and had a leech; the parasite vacated her for Radu, who was a stronger, cleverer host. Thus he became Wamphyri.

But when Radu crossed into Starside, he found the Ferenczys already there, vampire Lords of their own great aeries. So their bloodfeud continued, becoming part of the greater Wamphyri bloodwars. Eventually Radu conquered and killed both of the Ferenczy brothers, but not before Lagula had sired Nonari "the Gross" Ferenczy, whose left hand was like a club, with all the fingers fused into one.

And so the bloodwars went on, year in year out, for decades, until Starside was drenched in blood! But in the end the only real victor was neither dog-Lord, Ferenczy, Drakul, nor any "common" Lord. No. It was Shaitan the Unborn, first of them all, who had the wit to pick them off one by one when they were weakened by the fighting. Then, when it was over, Shaitan banished them through the Gate for their troubles. Thus Radu came into this world, and his most hated enemies with him—especially Nonari the Gross.

They could have settled it then, but they were strangers in our world with troubles enough. So they went their own ways; Radu adventuring in the world, and Nonari . . . doing whatever he did. But Nonari had sworn vengeance on Radu, his kith, kin, and spawn for all time to come, for the deaths of Lagula his father and Rakhi his uncle: the impassioned vow of a Lord of the Wamphyri, which might even outlast eternity! And down all the years and centuries Radu stayed alert, and kept an ear cocked at all times for word of Nonari Ferenczy.

He heard certain things. For instance:

How one "Onarius Ferengus," the Roman Governor of a small province on the Black Sea, had died in the Year 445 or thereabouts, at the hands of unknown barbarians. That was when Radu had been a Vandal, before they turned on him and drove him out of Italy. But he had also heard how this Onarius had a son in the mountains north of Moldavia, in a place called the Khorvaty. And this son's name was Belos Pheropzis.

Down the years, as time and his travels allowed, Radu made inquiry but learned little. A hundred years later, when he was a Voevod in the eastern Carpathians, he even tried to discover the whereabouts of this castle of Belos Pheropzis. Events intervened; his duties called him away; the search must wait. Centuries later he did come across the castle in the Khorvaty, but found it deserted and falling into ruin. Fortunately the people of the region kept records, and they remembered.

Belos Pheropzis had been a great and terrible Boyar, and his mountain retreat secret and near-inaccessible, as Radu had discovered. He, too, had a son, called Waldemar Ferrenzig, and a daughter who never ventured out from the castle. It was rumored that Belos slept with her, a not uncommon practice among the Wamphyri.

Belos had finally come to grief fending off a party of Bulgar raiders; his castle was saved but he lost his life; surviving Bulgars likewise expired, in an avalanche brought about by Waldemar. And thereafter Waldemar slept with his sister . . .

There were two sons (but one of them might have been Waldemar's egg-son, who knows? Wamphyri bloodlines are intricate as their histories are complex; even what I've told you so far is hearsay and unproven!). But at least one must have been a bloodson, by

Waldemar, most likely out of his sister. Well, brother murdered brother in an argument, and the survivor inherited the castle from Waldemar. But as to what became of Waldemar himself . . . again I am at a loss.

The brother who inherited the Khorvaty castle was called Faethor, and he reverted to the original family name: Faethor Ferenczy . . .

B.J. paused as Harry's body spasmed in an apparently involuntary (and inexplicable) jerk. It felt like the kick of a recumbent man in the moment before he falls asleep, which will often wake him up again. Except Harry's "sleep" was a state of deep hypnosis, and his reaction outside of B.J.'s previous experience.

"Are you . . . cold?" (For now she felt a shiver, or even a shudder, running through him.) Kneeling over him, B.J. stirred blackened cinders to life and placed kindling and a small log where the embers were still hot. By which time Harry had settled down again and she could continue:

Faethor was a strange one. He would stay at home in his castle for decades at a time, but always in the end the blood would draw him out, and off he'd go adventuring in a war-torn world. In the two hundred years preceding the Fourth Crusade he used a great many pseudonyms. He was, for instance, "Stefan Ferrenzig," then "Peter," "Karl," and "Grigor," He became his own son time and time again, for he knew that a man may not be seen to live too long among common men—and certainly not for centuries!

At various times he was a Crusader, an Uighur warrior, a warlord under Temujin; then a general under Genghis's grandson, Batu. As "Fereng the Black, 'Son' of the Fereng," under Húlegú he played a part in the extermination of the Assassins, and he was there at the fall of Baghdad in 1258. Why, the dog-Lord has even reasoned it out that it was this Faethor who fought on the side of the Mongols and Karl Drakul at the battle of Ain Jalut! Ah, but what a pity that Radu killed Karl and missed him, this damned Ferenczy!

And so, yet again, we see how the histories of the Wamphyri are complex . . .

But let me get on:

Faethor had two sons that Radu heard of in his time, though he never came up against them. They were Thibor, Faethor's egg-son—a fierce Wallach who was a Voevod *for the rulers of both Russian and his native land—and Janos, a bloodson out of Gypsy stock. The last my Master heard of Thibor was in the late 1340s, shortly before the plague drove him to seek refuge in the resin. At that time Thibor was a Voevod in Romania.*

In the last two hundred years, however—certainly in the last hundred, excluding the war years—it has been easier to travel in Europe. On behalf of my Master, Radu, I've done some research abroad and believe I know something of Thibor.

As stated, Thibor was a Voevod for a long line of Wallachian princes: the Mirceas, Vlad Tepes (whose evil reputation had a great deal to do with Thibor, I fear), Radu the Handsome—but no relation to my *Radu, be sure—and finally Mircea the Monk, who seems to have been sore afraid of him . . . too afraid to let him live, perhaps? At any rate, that is where Thibor's trail ends, as a warlord in the service of Mircea the Monk.*

And then there was Janos Ferenczy, who first made himself known as a young man in the early part of the 13th century. He was a thief, a pirate, a corsair on the broad bosom of the Mediterranean. During the Christian-Moslem conflicts of the Crusades, he was one of the petty princelings looting them who had looted others! He had a castle in the Zarundului heights (his father Faethor spent many years there, too), to which he would return periodically. And there is evidence to suggest he was a necromancer, for which there might be a simple explanation. As Faethor's bloodson, Janos could use this necromancy to en-

hance or supplement his meager Wamphyri powers, which are frequently weaker in blood-than in egg-sons or -daughters. Not that it could have done him much good; he seems to have disappeared at the end of the 15th century, about the same time as Thibor.

So, it's my conclusion that Faethor, Thibor, and Janos are all dead and gone. My Master . . . isn't so sure. He tells me the Wamphyri have a habit of turning up in the strangest places, at the most inconsiderate times. And he's certain that Ferenczys—more than one, and at least one Drakul: this "D.D.," of course—survive to this day . . .

But now there are more complications and we're obliged to go back, back, all the way back to Waldemar Ferrenzig. Waldemar was a lusty one and fertile, and his sister wasn't the only one he slept with. There were records in a museum in olden Moldavia that I read all of sixty years ago. Alas, when I went back recently the museum was no more; what they'd missed in World War I they hit in World War II, and the museum was a burned-out ruin. But I remember what I read originally:

That before Svyatoslav, in Kiev, there was a Boyar like a prince who was banished out of the city west, "to the farthest corners of the land," who built a great house "under the mountains on the border of Moldavia" . . . the Khorvaty! His name was "Valdemar Fuhrenzig," but I can only believe he was Waldemar. As to why he was sent out of Kiev . . . well, he was Wamphyri!

Those were Viking days, and the Varyagi *were establishing their trade routes to the Greeks along Kievan Russia's eastern rivers. Well, despite that Waldemar was banished from the land, he liked to go into the woods for days on end, hunting boar in the great forests that sprawled west of the River Bug. And one day he came across a Varyagi encampment.*

Normally there would be no trouble; oh, they were fierce men, these Vikings, but they were traders, too. And the Ferenczy had a party of retainers, his thralls, along with him. But this time it was different. The Vikings were heading north for the Baltic and home, and they had a beautiful woman with them, stolen out of some port on the Black Sea. So far, she had suffered no harm; they would sell her back home, to be some Prince or King's raven-haired, dark-eyed wife.

She implored Waldemar's help as a gentleman. Obviously he was a Boyar, for he had his men with him, his dogs, his hawks. But the Ferenczy's men were thralls, his dogs were wolves, and his hawks as bloodthirsty as he himself!

Well, there was no more of the story in the old Moldavian museum, but at least I was able to ascertain this lady's name. She was a Sicilian Princess, or at least of royal blood. Alas, she was also illegitimate, with no actual claim to the region from which she took her name: Constanza de' Petralia. And Petralia is a village or town in Sicily's Le Madonie.

It was worth a trip to Sicily; I spoke to several historians; the code of silence is extensive! But finally I was able to consult certain records. Constanza de' Petralia had returned to Sicily in 866. No sooner was she home than she gave birth to twin boys, one of which was hideously deformed and destroyed at birth. The surviving child was named—of all things—Angelo! Far more important, on coming of age he changed his surname: to Ferenczini! His mother came into property, money. She was overindulgent with her son, who was much-traveled: Corsica, Italy, Romania and Moldavia. But there the trail peters out, and to my knowledge there are no more Ferenczinis today. As for Ferenczy: it's a common name in all regions throughout and bordering the Carpathians. But—

—The real *Ferenczys are still out there somewhere . . .*

* * *

B.J. was finished with that part of it. Harry now knew (to the best of her knowledge) as much as she knew. In fact the Necroscope knew a great deal more; so much more that *he* could easily have told B.J. what had become of Faethor and Thibor Ferenczy! Except it wouldn't be easy, couldn't even be dragged out of him if it also meant compromising his talents. But in any case she didn't ask, for that was something she would never have suspected in a million years. Why should she?

B.J. was tired now; it had taken a massive effort of will to maintain her wolf-shape and the energy of her scarlet Wamphyri eyes. But she had needed to be sure that the knowledge she imparted would sink in, stay there and not get misrepresented. For he was a strange one, this Harry Keogh, and B.J. couldn't afford any more episodes or mistakes like the telephone farce.

And on that subject, after she had relaxed a fraction and flowed back into human form:

"Harry, about your telephone. Why change the number? What was that all about?"

He stared unblinking into her eyes, feral now in the dark blot of her head, where it was silhouetted against the glowing halo of his reading-lamp across the room. "I was scared of it," he croaked from a bone-dry throat.

She said: "Salivate, moisten your throat, feel well, and talk normally. But remain asleep, and hear and obey."

"Of course," he answered after a moment, when the knob of his throat had stopped bobbing.

"But why were you frightened of the 'phone?"

He shrugged (because hypnotized or not, he really didn't know.) But he could guess. "Bad dreams, maybe? I don't want to hear anything bad about Brenda and the baby . . ."

B.J. could understand and accept that. But it couldn't be allowed to go on; she must have contact with him. "Get an answering machine," she said. "If you start to hear something that you don't like, you can switch it off. Or you can monitor your calls, and simply cut them off as and when it suits you."

"Good!" Harry nodded.

"But of course you won't switch off when it's me on the line, because our little rule still applies. You'll hear—"

"—Is that mah wee man?" Harry cut in, talking normally.

"And you'll see—"

"—The moon, your eyes—"

"—And a wolf's head in silhouette, yes."

"Radu's head," he nodded.

"Indeed." B.J. was pleased. "But now we really must talk about this search of yours—for Brenda and the baby, I mean." But that wasn't what she meant at all; in fact she didn't even want him to find them. He needed a new direction, that was all, to which his "search" would be peripheral. His conscious purpose would seem the same to him, but subconsciously . . . ?

"Also, you're not as fit as you should be. We have to get you in shape."

"I've been intending to," Harry answered.

"And I have a sneaking suspicion that you've been having a hard time of it with alcohol?"

A frown at once etched itself deep into Harry's forehead. "Alcohol? Well, not so much booze in general as that damned red wine of yours! It seemed to have . . . something for me?"

"Something for you?" B.J. shook her head. "Not any more, Harry. As of now it's something you can do without. From this moment on you don't need it; indeed, the very thought of it is enough to make you feel sick! Is that understood?"

"Oh, yes!" Harry breathed his relief—but a moment later his face turned pale, his stomach lurched and he belched.

"It's okay now. Put it out of your mind and you'll be just fine." She had to smile as he sighed and snuggled closer to her warmth, her "safety." "And after we've talked over these other things—your search and what-all—then we'll be able to get some sleep."

"Afterwards, yes," said Harry, and she felt the need building in him, beginning to swell against her thigh.

She might have laughed—in surprise, delight, whatever—but knew it would only sap her concentration. And with him she needed all the concentration she could muster. With him, yes.

With this oh-so-mysterious Harry Keogh . . .

PART 5

Manse and Monastery: Aeries!

BONNIE JEAN: BIRTHDAY PARTY. HARRY: GETTING IN SHAPE, AND FUNDING HIS SEARCH.

N THE MORNING, B.J. WAS UP FIRST. IT WAS A FEW MINUTES AFTER SIX, AND THE light still burgeoning from the east. In the garden the birds had been twittering for some time: enough noise to wake the Necroscope up, albeit gradually.

He came awake knowing that it was going to be hell again, and was pleasantly surprised, or more properly relieved beyond measure, to find that it wasn't. No headache, no fluff in his head where his brains used to be, no sore throat, and no great urge to drink . . . anything! Except maybe a mug or two of black coffee. At which he remembered that both his pantry and fridge were empty.

B.J. was upstairs; he could hear the shower. He dressed quickly, made a Möbius jump into town, the local newsagent's, which doubled as a grocery-cum-post office, and just three or four minutes later was unloading stuff into the fridge; which, as B.J. came down and found him in the kitchen, looked like he was taking stuff *out* of the fridge, to prepare breakfast.

"You have a wash, brush your hair, clean your teeth—and whatever—while I do it," she said.

"Yes, Ma!" He cocked his head on one side, raised an eyebrow, asked: "Any other instructions?"

"Oh, you're okay," she laughed. "But in bed you're a ten, so why lower your average when you're up?" And eyeing his groceries, "Funny, last night when I was getting supper, I didn't think you had anything in."

"You didn't look in the freezer compartment," he mumbled, waved his arms. "The cupboards . . ."

She shrugged. "I'll manage something." And, as he headed upstairs: "And buy a new toothbrush. That one tastes awful!"

Make yourself at home! he thought. But he knew he should feel pleased. So why didn't he? Maybe because he—his place—had been invaded? This had been a private place. He and it could be as they were here. Now he had to be someone else; and there it was again: the reminder that he *was* someone else!

And it was possible he even felt guilty, too. But why, he couldn't honestly say. For after all, he wasn't the heavy in the piece. It was Brenda who had left him . . .

Breakfast was good, very. And for the first time in God-only-knows how long—with most of his guilty feelings and doubts melted away—the Necroscope actually *felt* good! But then, as the sky turned a lighter shade of gray, and B.J. made ready to leave him, he didn't. For with her out of the way he'd be back to thinking in ever-decreasing circles again, and doing nothing much else . . .

. . . Or perhaps not. For in fact it seemed he did have a few things to do now. They were there in the back of his mind, anyway, probably headed-off down the diversion that was B.J. But he knew that if he concentrated he'd get back on track again.

"I'll call one of my girls," B.J. said, breaking into his thoughts. "Sandra. I'll catch her before she sets out for work. She lives not too far away."

"Sure, if you like," Harry told her. Which satisfied her that this really was his place and not some kind of safe house for the people he had used to work for. If it had been, surely he wouldn't want too many people to know about it. But no, he fitted in here; the house had Harry Keogh written all over it.

"Or I can take a taxi?"

"Whichever suits you," he shrugged. "I'll call one, if you like? Whatever is best for you. Just don't forget where I live, right?"

And to B.J.'s mind, that settled it. "Not just a one-night stand, then?" Waiting for his answer, she dialed a number and spoke briefly to someone at the other end of the line, then put the 'phone down and turned to him.

Looking down in the mouth again, Harry was standing close to her. "I suppose it should be," he said. "A one-night stand, I mean. Or rather it *shouldn't* have been, shouldn't have happened at all. But it did, and frankly I'm . . . I'm upside down, messed up. That's the truth of it: I'm messed up."

She nodded. "Well, perhaps I am, too. But I'd better tell you now, Harry Keogh: I can't see myself as part of an eternal triangle thing, in the role of 'the other woman.' It's not my scene, and it certainly isn't my style."

Harry shook his head. "This wasn't a cheap thing. Not for me. It's just that I don't know how I feel. I did a moment ago, but now I don't. As for Brenda and my son: this search is something I have to do, even though I know I won't find her. Oh, I might find them . . . but I won't *find* her. Brenda doesn't know me any more."

"Neither do I, scarcely."

"But time is on our side," Harry said.

She looked surprised. "Time? What, from what was possibly a one-night stand to a long-term relationship—all in one quick move?"

"I told you I was messed up."

B.J. almost felt sorry for him. She knew why he was messed up. Something of it, anyway. And leaning forward, giving him a brief, brushing kiss: "Let's wait and see how it all works out, okay?"

He nodded and said nothing.

And they waited for her girl to come . . .

* * *

B.J. hadn't been gone ten minutes before Harry made a jump and bought himself a telephone answering machine. And a bicycle, to be delivered. The first so that he could monitor calls, and the second so that he could get himself in shape. Himself, yes. For he'd finally decided: this was *him* now, and he'd have to accept it. And it (*he*, damn it to hell!) couldn't really be that bad, after all, because B.J. for one had accepted him—with a vengeance!

It was only after the bike had arrived that he realized he could have ridden it home, along the Möbius route. Why not? He could easily have pedalled down a back street, through a door, and so home. He knew the co-ordinates of the service road, and the road across the river. It would have been the easiest way. He wouldn't have had to pay for the delivery, either.

Next up on his search itinerary was Northern Ireland. He would give himself a week or so here at the house, settling in and adjusting to a new regime, make a list of places to visit, then go and do it. And he wouldn't any longer be alone . . . not while he was at home, anyway. B.J. would be here. He just knew she would come to him, or he could go to her. He couldn't say how it would work out, didn't even want to think about it. It was just the way it was.

The day had cleared up; the sun was peeping through tufts of fluffy cloud; *next thing you know, it'll be spring!* Harry thought. And time for spring-cleaning.

Had B.J. mentioned that? Spring-cleaning? He thought she probably had— told him the house could use a little dusting, polishing, scrubbing—but couldn't think when. Or had it been sparked by the shame he'd felt when she first walked in and saw the place? But if it *was* her, then she'd been wrong: the house could use a hell of a *lot* of dusting, polishing and scrubbing! His "study" . . . wasn't even a room yet! It was a jumble.

So why not start now! A little hard labor would pass for getting himself in shape, wouldn't it? But first he had something really important to do: a mind to put at rest . . .

Down on the riverbank Harry was wrapped warmly for once. But more importantly he felt warm on the inside, too. And his Ma felt the difference in him as soon as she "heard" him in her mind. "I've been bad, Ma," he told her, but she could feel the grin on his face. One that slipped a little as she answered:

In how many ways, son?

"Er, I meant about the doctor. I didn't go to see one like I promised. But listen, whatever the trouble was, it's gone."

No more drinking?

"Couldn't face it." He shook his head. "The very thought's enough to make me want to throw up!"

It was the last of Mr. Kyle, then . . . which you've finally kicked out. You've rejected what little was left of him to make room for you. I can feel that you've more or less settled down with yourself, son. At least, I think so. I hope I'm right . . .

"I feel a lot better all round, yes." He said, but even now couldn't be sure. Maybe she sensed that, too. Even as an expert at talking to the dead—*the* expert, the Necroscope—Harry knew how hard it was to fool his Ma.

And Kyle's talent? This precognition thing?

"Not for a while now," Harry answered. "But that could be my loss. I didn't understand it, but it might have given me a few pointers. Anyway, the main thing is I feel . . . good. And I'm determined to get myself back in shape. I've bought myself a bicycle—for exercise, lots of it—and when I'm finished talking to you, I'm going to tear the house apart.'' He sounded really enthusiastic, if a bit jumbled.

You'll what? Tear the house apart? With a bicycle? Now she sounded more than a little alarmed.

"I mean I'll rip the place apart—dust, polish, scrub. It can use it. Spring cleaning, Ma!''

Yes, she said, after a moment. And thoughtfully: *Why, I do believe I can smell it! Springtime, when a young man's thoughts turn to . . .*

". . . To spring cleaning!'' Harry stopped her.

Among other things, his Ma said, but very quietly.

It was Harry's cue to leave. "I'll let you know how I get on,'' he said, turning away from the river.

But you started this conversation by telling me you've been bad, Harry. (She wasn't about to let him go.) *And I asked you, in how many ways?*

Harry guarded his thoughts. "I meant two things, Ma. About not seeing a doctor, and about being neglectful.''

Of me?

"Of course!''

Not of Brenda? (She was sharp as a tack.)

"Ma?'' And now he was doubly cautious, defensive.

You haven't mentioned her once, Harry . . .

"Ma,'' he was momentarily lost for words, "I feel . . . like we're drifting.''

Drifting apart?

He nodded. "I mean it's not just that Brenda is lost; she lost herself, after all. She, or the baby, wanted to get lost, or they wanted to lose me. But it goes deeper than that. It's that we're strangers now . . .''

He sensed her understanding, or at least that she was trying to understand. And in a little while she said: *Well, let's not you and I go the same way, all right? I mean, there's nothing you can't tell me, Harry. We're too close for that. I was there at the start of you . . . and you're here at the end of me! I'm not some kind of ogre that you have to hide from, now am I?*

She had sensed that his guard was up, and it saddened her. But from Harry's point of view there was no help for it. There are some things you don't tell anyone.

And especially not your Ma . . .

Once he got started on the house there was no stopping him. He wanted it in order before he saw B.J. again. Two days went by, three . . . a few more and there'd be a full moon. What that had to do with things Harry couldn't say, but he knew that he must speak to, must see B.J. again, and soon.

Finally he couldn't fight it any longer. Right or wrong he wanted her in his bed again, maybe even in his life. Damn, she *was in* his life! He called her at the wine bar, got one of her girls—who told him that B.J. wasn't available right now.

Then would she please tell B.J. that he'd called?

Of course. Would he be around if B.J. called back later?

Yes, he would, and it didn't matter how much later.

And that night, dozing on the couch in what really was his study now, he felt the light of the full moon flooding through the patio windows into the room, and wondered why it felt like B.J.'s eyes on him. But she was busy right how; she had a life of her own and he had to understand that. Maybe she would call him later.

God, he hoped so . . .

B.J. *was* busy, or was about to be. It had been a six-month and her needs, and that of her girls, must be attended to. Discretion was the name of the game. It was like fishing, or hunting, for that matter; or better still, poaching. Make too much noise and you'd scare away the game and perhaps attract unwanted attention. Use the wrong lure and the fish wouldn't bite, or the game would ignore the trap.

Tonight, Zahanine was the lure. She was black and she was beautiful, and she was one of Bonnie Jean's: a moon-child, and hungry as the rest of them. Oh, she ate and she drank the same as anyone else. Except it *wasn't* the same.

It was Zahanine's night off . . . That was what she told Big Jimmy Lee when he walked into the lounge of the Fiddler's Elbow down the road from B.J.'s. The place was almost empty; with her round, perfect backside seated on a bar stool, and her long legs crossed and swaying to a juke box tune, Zahanine stood out like a sore thumb, or a green light.

Big Jimmy bought himself a drink, hesitated a moment and bought another for the girl, before eyeing her up and down in an openly suggestive, pig-eyed fashion, and saying: "But ah'm surprised ye're still on speakin' terms wi' such as me, since ye're boss, that bleddy Bonnie Jean, kicked me oot-a there."

"Big Jimmy," she said, her voice as soft as her dark skin and seductive as her dark eyes, "you were out of order and well you know it. You used threatening behavior against a customer, disturbed the other members, and wrecked a table. Now tell me, how is B.J. supposed to run a decent bar with all that stuff going on? Until that night you were a valued customer . . . she's said so herself."

"B.J.? Oh, really?" He looked doubtful.

Zahanine nodded. "She's looked for you coming back, even had a new member's card made out with your name on it. But B.J. isn't the sort to beg. If you want in again it's up to you. No more trouble, though, or the next time's final."

"A new card?"

"I've seen it myself," she told him, then fell silent as the barman headed their way picking up empty glasses. But when he went into a back room: "You should drop by."

"Ye think so?"

"I know so. And tonight would be a good time."

"What? But does she no close up around now?"

Zahanine glanced at her watch. "Half an hour, yes. That's when you should come, after I've had a chance to speak to her."

Big Jimmy frowned. "Come again? Ah'm no wi' ye."

"Party time," she explained. "After hours. Staff only—just B.J. and the girls—and maybe you, too, if you think you can mend your ways. One of the girls is having a birthday. Why else would I be here on my night off? Free drinks,

Jimmy! Not something that happens every day! I'm on my way in a minute or two. So what do you say? Should I tell B.J. you'll be dropping by?'' Standing up, she leaned forward and put her index finger in the cleft of his chin. "Frankly, I've missed you, too."

He was genuinely taken aback. "But ah . . . ah didn'ae ken ye cared!"

"Maybe you've been chatting up the wrong girls," she said, and headed for the door. "Thanks for the drink . . ."

"Ye'll speak to her?" Big Jimmy called after her.

Zahanine turned back, stepped closer. "But remember," she whispered, "this is a private party. You've been quite enough trouble already, so don't go blabbing it all over Edinburgh or B.J.'ll lose her license for sure!"

Big Jimmy nodded. "No a word!" he promised.

"Then wait half an hour and come on along. Just give the usual ring, and I'll let you in."

"Ye're sure it'll be okay?"

"Positive. But we'll be late finishing. Maybe you'd be a gentleman and see me home afterwards?"

He grinned. "Oh, ah'm no so sure aboot the gentleman bit, but ah can see ye home, definitely!" His voice was now rougher than ever, with anticipation.

She smiled knowingly and left, and he watched her out of the door and saw her distorted shadow pass by the small-paned, smoked-glass windows. But the memory of Zahanine's deliciously wriggling backside stayed with him for the next half hour . . .

. . . Until he pressed the bell outside B.J.'s and fidgeted under the dark archway until the door was opened. Zahanine was there, and one of the other girls. They took his coat and would have led him inside at once, but B.J. stepped from behind the door to caution him:

"Ye're privileged, Jimmy. Don't mess it up, now."

"Oh, no fear, mah Bonnie lass!" he told her.

"But ye know ye're drinkin' after hours and shouldn'ae be here? If I let ye in it's on ye're own head, of ye're own free will."

"What? Why, all the polis in Edinburgh couldn'ae keep me away!" he declared. And, smiling, B.J. took his arm and marched him down the corridor.

All four girls were in the bar; five, if Jimmy included Zahanine. Apart from her, they all wore their black stockings, short, flouncy dresses, high heels, blouses that were open way too far in front, and showed lots of flesh at the back. Owing a lot to Playboy attire, all they were missing were the fluffy bunny tails and ears. And they were obviously in party mood.

Poppers went off left, right, and center as Big Jimmy Lee appeared with B.J. and party; he was covered in paper streamers, slapped on the back, made welcome as a prodigal son, told "Good to have ye back, Big Jimmy!" by all and sundry.

"Damn, but ah'm fair knocked out!" he declared. "The only thing tha's missin' seems tae be the fatted calf!"

"Later, Jimmy," B.J. told him. "We'll eat later. But for now there's the drinks. Wine's ye're tipple, is it no?"

"Wine, whiskey, whatever!" he said, as she directed him to a stool at the bar. And Zahanine perched herself alongside, her swinging leg stroking his thigh. "Damn me!" he said. "But ah'd swear this was all for me!"

B.J. poured red wine ("My own special reserve, Jimmy!") which he swigged back almost without tasting it, and the party got underway. The girls took turns to flank him, rubbing themselves against him, all tits and smiling teeth and temptation. And Big Jimmy had never resisted temptation. It was wonderful! He was the only man here, and though he'd heard of parties like this, he'd never imagined he'd be the centerpiece at just such a one. A gaggle of stacked women, all bent on plying, pleasing, and plundering him of his vital fluids.

The lights were low, the juke box played some old bluesy stuff, and the girls seemed more gorgeous with every taste of B.J.'s red wine. As for Bonnie Jean herself:

She disappeared momentarily; Jimmy scarcely noticed; he was having a hard time loosening the last button on one of the girls' blouses, but finally succeeded and gawped as her ample breasts lolled free and available. He would have availed himself, too, except B.J. was back, and dressed in a flimsy see-through baby-doll nightie!

By now Big Jimmy was certain-sure what kind of party this was, and despite that the room spun a little when he moved too fast, and that the bar stool seemed to sway under his backside so that he must constantly maintain his balance, his blood was pounding as he dazedly wondered which of the girls would want him first.

As it happened, they all did.

"So," B.J. said, standing a little apart from him along the bar, "was it worth coming back to us, Jimmy?"

"Ah wouldn'ae missed it for the world!" he tried to answer, but all of his words came out sideways. He tried staring at B.J., tried to focus on her breasts, the dark V of her pubic region under the gauzy nightgown, but his gaze kept sliding off first to one side, then the other.

Behind the bar, Zahanine poured him the largest measure of whiskey he'd ever seen, said: "This will straighten you up, Big Jimmy. It's more what you're used to."

"Right!" he said, and actually managed to grasp the glass, and tilt its contents down his throat. As Zahanine refilled it, two of the other girls wheeled a long trolley up behind Jimmy, positioning it precisely to his rear. Head lolling, he glanced around and took in the scene as B.J. and the girls stood chairs around the trolley, three to a side. Decked with a tablecloth, the trolley was quite empty. Obviously they'd be bringing food and a birthday cake out from the kitchen. Obviously, yes.

"Whose f-f-fuckin' birthday is it anyway?" Big Jimmy slurred, tilting more whiskey down his throat. But this time as he went to put the glass down he missed the bar and sent the glass crashing to the floor. It pulled him together momentarily, long enough to look from face to face, stupidly, as he waited for an answer. And eventually B.J. said:

"Birthday? Why, it's yours, Jimmy!"

"Aye!" Big Jimmy rocked on his stool and tilted it back a little way, but just a little too far. "Tha's a good'yin, that is!" he roared. "Mine, by fuck!" And he teetered there.

"Except it's not exactly a *birth*day," B.J. said, and her voice was quite different now, as she touched his shoulder to apply the very slightest pressure. Losing his balance and toppling over backwards, he scarcely knew he was falling. Several pairs of hands took his weight, lowering him on to the top of the trolley—or rather, to the hardwood draining board, for one of the girls had whipped away the cover.

"There are two big days in a man's life, Jimmy," B.J. said where she stood looking down into his quivering face. "One's at the beginning, and the other's at the end. Well, you've had the one, and this is the other."

"Wha'?" he said. "Whazzat?" As the girls strapped him down, hands and feet. And: "Eh? Eh?" he queried, as they used knives as sharp as scalpels to cut away his clothing. And however ridiculously, Big Jimmy was still grinning, for this could only be some kind of weird sex game, or an even weirder dream, as someone turned the lights down more yet and B.J.'s eyes—and the eyes of her girls—became yellow triangles in the gloom.

Then there was more yellow—the glitter of golden instruments—as B.J. passed around slender tubes with trumpetlike mouthpieces, similar to the funnels she'd used in Radu Lykan's redoubt. Except the feeders had been for the giving, and these smaller versions were for the taking.

Big Jimmy only noticed them in passing, however, because he wasn't able to take his eyes off B.J. herself. Bonnie Jean, who might just as well be naked for all her nightgown hid, standing there in the gloom, with her yellow eyes—no, her *scarlet* eyes now—burning into Jimmy's soul!

All feeling had fled him; Jimmy was as drunk, or as poisoned, as any man had ever been and remained conscious. Oh, he had a powerful constitution, but not powerful enough. He could still hear, see, think (though not much of the latter), but he couldn't have moved a muscle, couldn't speak any more, didn't understand that the crimson pounding in his skull, his heart and his veins wasn't sexual potency but an effect of the drugged wine.

And the ceiling was revolving, first this way, then that; and the faces of the girls looking down on him were foxy, wolfish, lustful; and B.J. herself—

—Wasn't Bonnie Jean!

What she was exactly Jimmy couldn't have said. But as the nightgown slid from her slender, furry form, and her soft dark muzzle wrinkled back in a half-snarl, half-smile, he thought:

What a bitch! Which was perhaps as close as he would ever come to the truth of it. Or to anything. Ever again.

When the siphons sank in, Jimmy barely felt them. He felt the warmth leaving him, and the cold seeping in, and a tide as dark and darker than the deepest ocean floor rolling over him, washing him to and fro, and gradually dissolving him all away . . . but that was all.

At 2:30 in the morning Bonnie Jean got Harry out of bed to answer the door; Sandra had dropped her off. There had been an after-hours birthday party for one of the other girls. B.J. was sorry, but she hadn't been able to get out of it. Anyway, here she was. Or, if it was too late. . . ?

Too late? Harry told her she must be joking, made her a coffee in the kitchen while she watched, had a hard time keeping his hands off her but managed it somehow. And he even made small talk, until she asked him: "Can't we talk in bed?"

Then he almost had her on the kitchen table, and she was equally wanton on the stairs, until finally, in the bedroom . . . getting her out of her clothes was a frenzied affair, for both of them.

Afterwards . . .

. . . Harry lit one of his very rare cigarettes, and eventually B.J. said, "Don't think me vulgar, please, but that was a fuck. That wasn't just making love . . ." And replete—in every way replete—she was asleep before he could think her vulgar, or think anything else of her.

Before sleeping himself, he touched her body all over, but very gently so that she wouldn't know. Maybe it was to reassure himself that she was there. But it felt like he was making sure that she was . . . she? What *that* was all about, he couldn't say.

In his bed, she smelled of woman, and warm flesh, and sex, and—something else. Her breath? Copper? Salt? Or was it just the sex. Hah! *Just* the sex! But she'd been like an animal: vibrant, writhing, crushing him in her coils. He had found himself thinking on several occasions that she would draw blood—with her nails or her teeth—but she hadn't. He believed he'd actually felt her holding back; he *knew* there had been a repressed violence in her (purely sexual, he thought), which had inspired the same sort of frenzy in him. But now:

Now, despite that he felt exhausted, it was hard to get to sleep. Something was bothering him. Finally Harry realized what it was: the light of the full moon, pouring its rays in through his bedroom window.

So he got up and drew the faded curtains . . .

Life became a blur. Space, time, places, faces: Harry couldn't say where they came from, or where they went. He even began to forget where he'd been; would have forgotten, he was sure, but for the list he kept of the places he'd visited. Spring turned to summer. The seasons were turning, and Harry frequently felt that his mind was turning, too . . . from sanity to full-fledged madness. Yet when he was with B.J. he knew he was sane. Indeed, those were the only times when he did know it.

Upon a time he'd had difficulty accepting his body; he had felt that when it was hurt—despite that it *had* hurt—that it really didn't matter because it wasn't his body anyway. But those times were past now. That had a lot to do with B.J., too, the fact that she had accepted him. She'd become his anchor on an increasingly ephemeral world. She'd anchored his body, anyway. But his mind was something else.

Frequently he would wake up furious, frightened, unable to remember the nightmare that had awakened him, but thinking, *someone is fucking with my mind!* And promising himself that when he found out who it was, then there'd be hell to pay. But as the waking world took over, so the anger would recede. Yet the feeling persisted: that while his body was very definitely his now, his mind was someone else's.

His memory, for one thing—or memories, recent memories, anyway—was or were totally up the creek. Sometime around the middle of May he'd mentioned it to Bonnie Jean when they stayed late in bed at his place one Sunday morning:

"Do you remember when I did Ireland?" And he had felt her drowsy attention sharpening, rapidly centering on him.

"Yes. You've not long since finished. What of it?"

"Well, I don't! I don't remember it!"

She had slipped out of bed in a moment, gone to a dresser, returned with his notebook and opened it at the relevant pages: his Irish "itinerary." And she'd read from a list of places in his handwriting, starting at Belfast and working down the coast to Dundalk before he stopped her.

"That's right! That's right!" He was excited, frustrated. "Downpatrick and Newry and Kilkeel, and half-a-dozen more. You think I don't remember?" His jaw was tight where he scowled at her almost accusingly.

She sat beside him, looked down on him curiously with her head cocked on one side, and said, logically, "But didn't you just say that you *don't* remember?"

And she was right. It was a contradiction, a confusion, a confounded nonsense! He had shook his head, flapped his hands, said: "Green fields; emerald green, in fact! Greener than England. Irish accents—'Top o' the mornin' to yeh, sor!' Little pubs with ocean outlooks and peat fires. Shillelaghies and all that shit. Picture book stuff. Toss in a pixie or two, and . . ."

"Harry!" she'd stopped him. "What *is* all this?"

And the look on her face had said it all: that it wasn't rational talk, and hardly reasonable behavior, that he should take this out, whatever it was, on her.

After that they hadn't seen each other for a week or more. Finally he'd called her and apologized for his irrational accusations, which had been directed at the world in general, never at Bonnie Jean. She had seemed uncertain and he'd said he would come and see her at B.J.'s. She had stalled him and come to him instead. For which he was grateful, for she really had become his one anchor on the world . . .

No, for there was one other, of course, but Harry hardly dared speak to his Ma anymore. And (mercifully) he knew that she wasn't likely to sneak up on him at an awkward moment. She knew he liked his privacy and would wait until he came to her, to the riverbank. He hoped so, anyway.

But a new idea had occurred to Harry, and he felt stupid that he hadn't thought of it earlier. He'd been relying on his own skills and the extraordinary talents at E-Branch to turn up something on Brenda and the baby. But wasn't that exactly what the missing pair would expect? Harry Jr. was a Power in his own right and would know how to avoid that sort of detection. And he could move his mother at will any time he wanted to. As to providing for her, or for both of them . . . well, who could say what he was or wasn't capable of? He would provide for his Ma what she couldn't provide for herself, and vice versa.

So, they would naturally expect the very sort of approach that Harry was employing: the esoteric, the gadgets, the ghosts of E-Branch. But what about a more *mundane* approach? Every major town and city in the Yellow Pages of the whole wide world—certainly the Western World—listed scores of detective agencies! And here was Harry Keogh, Necroscope, trying to cover all of that ground himself. Which he could do, of course, given an eternity of time! Stupid!

And if he should ever be lucky enough to get close and they spotted him . . . then the whole wild-goose chase would have to start all over again.

But to have fifty detective agencies all on the job at the same time, in fifty different places—

—would cost a hell of a lot of money! And Harry's funds went only so far . . .

. . . *His* funds, yes.

But there were others who could well afford it. According to Darcy Clarke, anyway . . .

By the middle of June Harry had set up the mechanisms for putting his battalions of detectives in their regiments of agencies in England, France, Germany and the USA, to work. All he needed was the funding: *at least three and a half million pounds sterling,* or the equivalent in whatever currency was available, to guarantee he could bankroll the thing for just the first three months of its operation! Meanwhile Darcy Clarke had put him in contact with a Swiss bank used by E-Branch, and Harry had made a ridiculously small deposit—a few hundred pounds out of his remaining few thousands—to open a numbered account.

Now he could get on with the more serious stuff . . . So he thought. But Bonnie Jean Mirlu had other plans.

She had decided it was time that Harry went into training in earnest. Real training.

For a man in his early thirties (she of course worked on the not unnatural presumption that his body was his own, that his mind and body were the same age) Harry hadn't been in the best possible shape. Concern over his wife and child might explain some of that, and long idle periods between jobs would account for the rest: the fact that he'd done little or nothing in his field since his people ditched him.

But when he was working . . . well, she had evidence of his general efficiency. The way he'd been able to handle that situation in London; the episode with Big Jimmy (who would never be a problem to anyone ever again); the fact that he had been able to enter secured, guarded premises—*her* premises—find what he sought and get out again without being detected . . . it said a lot for his skill in every department. And even B.J., who had known a good many men in her vastly extended time, had to admit that he was good in other departments, too. So good indeed that she considered herself genuinely fond of him. Or as fond as she could be of someone with his strictly limited future potential.

But the thought of actually sending him out into the world—into Radu's world of hideous dangers such as he "could never imagine," except as she had told him about it—was a matter of some concern. Not so much for Harry (if he failed and fell foul of Drakul or Ferenczy, so be it) as for herself and her Master. Not that he could talk about them . . . he didn't even *know* about them, not consciously. But anyone who cared to backtrack Harry Keogh's recent activities was bound to come across B.J. somewhere along the line, and possibly, in the course of things, Radu Lykan. On that front the secret watcher was problem enough (despite that his purpose was as yet undetermined) without any further complications.

Also, B.J. hadn't yet quite satisfied herself that Harry was all he appeared to be, or something more. She had reasoned that he wasn't in thrall to any Other . . . or if he was, then it was beyond her power to detect. Radu, however, would soon sniff out whatever she might have missed. Nor was she convinced that his previous employers were quite done with him—or with her. What if she was being watched through Harry—without his consent or knowledge? With that in mind she had ordered him not to scrub messages on his answering machine, which so far were few and far between. And then she'd monitored them for coded or in any way cryptic content. But so far, nothing.

As for E-Branch itself: well, he'd said it was an esoteric organization, one of the "secret" services. And so it appeared; she'd been unable to discover anything at all, not a single reference or clue, to any such authority. And despite that Harry was completely in B.J.'s thrall—beguiled at the snap of her fingers, or the utterance of a simple phrase, "Mah wee man"—still he refused to divulge anything more than he'd already told her. He would simply tense up, sweat, tremble, and offer no further information. If they'd brainwashed all of their operatives the same way, it was hardly surprising that this E-Branch remained secret! But there again, the dog-Lord Radu had his own methods; if there was something her Master should know, be sure he would get to know it.

Except, of course, she must first get Harry into the lair. He must somehow be made to climb into the "unexplored" heights of the Cairngorms, along with B.J. Which was why she'd needed him fit, and why she must now train him . . .

In early July Harry woke up one morning to find B.J. gone from his bed. It was a Wednesday; she'd recently been a little neglectful of work in the wine bar; he found her note in the kitchen, where she'd thoughtfully laid out the makings of his breakfast:

Harry—

What with your home-maintenance drive, your cycling, and all your fit-making activities, you are almost a new man. I want you to give serious thought to what we talked about—that holiday in the Highlands? It will be different, something for me, really. But something I would like to share with you. Surely you can afford a few days, before you start searching again? After all, I don't know that if you're successful, it won't be the end of us. Do I?

All Love—

B.J.

The conversation she mentioned sprang immediately to mind (though he couldn't remember where or when they had had it.) A holiday, yes, in the Highlands. B.J. liked to hunt, climb, live off the land: healthy exercise, for body and mind both. And she had suggested that he might like to go with her, live rough for a long weekend, make love under the moon and stars. Especially the moon . . . or was that last one of Harry's inspirations?

It inspired him to go, anyway. Thus it was *his* decision to go, if only to please her. So he thought.

The Wamphyri have long believed that wherever possible the destiny of men should be in their own hands: that whatever they enter into, it should be of their own free will. But no harm on occasion to offer a little encouragement along the way . . .

Later he rang her and they set a date: a month from now, in August. Meanwhile, they'd practice at least once a week in some good spots in the Trossachs, just a few hours out of Edinburgh. B.J. knew a lot of good rock climbs that would be ideal for an enthusiastic amateur. Well, maybe so, but the Necroscope didn't intend to be *that* much of an amateur.

Also, she'd only asked him to put off his search for a while; which to his mind didn't include his planned operation to *fund* that search. And in any case, it was something that would only take a day or two, depending on circumstances yet to be encountered in Sicily. Since he was seeing her only once or twice in any week, it was something he could fit in in between dates.

As for his preparations: they were simplicity itself. The Necroscope made a jump to an Army Ordnance Depot in the south of England, entered in the dead of night via the Möbius Continuum, and equipped himself with a lot of devastating weaponry. He could have gone to Darcy Clarke for his supplies but wanted to avoid implicating E-Branch in anything he did. This wasn't simply because Darcy had asked him to, but mainly because he'd quit the Branch and couldn't afford any more favors. He'd managed to keep himself out of debt so far, and liked it that way. Even if they found Brenda for him they would only be balancing the books on what he had done for them.

The Necroscope was scrupulously fair-minded. At the ammo depot, he knew the squad on duty would catch hell; they'd be in it up to their necks. So before getting out with his heavy-duty loot he deliberately tripped an alarm. Let the M.O.D. and Military Police try to figure out how it had been done. That's what they were paid for. Doubtless they'd blame the IRA.

Next (and most obvious and easiest), he obtained a recent map of Sicily, and more especially of the mountainous Madonie. Then, the next night, riding the Möbius Continuum to the Mediterranean in a series of cautious exploratory jumps, he checked flight ETAs at the sleepy airport in Catania, and synchronized his watch to local time.

Finally he used the toilets in the reception area, secured his stall's door on the inside, made doubly sure of his co-ordinates and returned home.

And when he'd very carefully packed his suitcase, then he was ready . . .

An hour later, at 9:30 that same night, he 'phoned B.J. to tell her he'd be away for a day or two.

"Looking for Brenda?" She seemed anxious, maybe even suspicious.

"No, other things. Business . . ."

"I didn't know you had any 'business.' Not any more."

"This is financial. I have to move my bank accounts, sort things out in general. I've got nothing fixed up locally. It's your fault, in a way. You've occupied my free time, not to mention my thoughts. I'm doing some important personal administration, that's all. Stuff I've let slip. But it doesn't interfere with anything, and I'm not due to see you until Saturday."

There was a long pause, until B.J. very softly said: "Are you sure? That it won't interfere with anything?" And before he could answer, even as he framed words to answer: "Now listen to me, mah—"

"—Of course I'm sure!" he cut her off, and was surprised to find himself perspiring. "B.J., it's Thursday night. I'll be back tomorrow night, or Saturday morning at the latest."

And after another pause: "Very well—but remember, Harry, we're climbing this weekend."

"I wouldn't miss it for the world," he told her . . .

After that:

Briefly Harry gave thought to what he was doing. Something puzzled him, and he couldn't figure out what it was. Eventually it came to him. There had been a time when he would have simply used the Möbius Continuum to jump straight into Palermo. Now—

—It seemed he'd developed a real need for his little subterfuges, the secrecy, this esoteric camouflage for his metaphysical talents. But that was ridiculous: *of course* he needed to keep his skills secret! *Obviously* he did—but to this extent? It was odd; he was more concerned now about someone discovering his talents than ever before in his life. But why now (he kept asking himself), in a time of relative safety?

Safety? Scarcely that, considering what he had in mind!

But if there was an answer to all of this, it was going to have to wait. His course was set, his plans made. For the next few days, at least.

It was 9:45 in Edinburgh, 10:45 in Sicily.

Harry made an international call to the airport at Catania to check the sitrep on the incoming flight from Athens. It was descending, starting its approach run. He allowed it forty-five minutes to land and commence discharging its passengers toward customs, then took the Möbius route directly to the stall he'd booked in the men's toilets. Two or three minutes later he was queuing to change pounds into lira at the cambio, then walking out of the airport reception area into the Sicilian night with a handful of rather more mundane travelers.

Now he was just another tourist with a heavy suitcase.

Heavy for its size, anyway . . .

DAHAM DRAKESH—
LE MANSE MADONIE—DEAD SILENCE.

THE NECROSCOPE TOOK A TAXI TO PATERNO, PAID FOR A ROOM AT THE HOTEL Adrano two nights in advance, and by 12:30 was taking a shower before retiring. With a little luck, the fan above his bed would keep him cool in the seventy-plus degrees of heat . . .

Hot in Sicily, yes . . . but some four and a half thousand miles away, on the Roof of the World, it was anything but hot; indeed, on Tibet's Tingri Plateau at 7:00 A.M. the temperature hovered just one degree above freezing. But the sun was bright where its burgeoning golden blister threatened to burst on the eastern horizon, and Major Chang Lun was comfortable enough in his winter-warfare uniform, fur-lined boots and hooded jacket.

He and his Corporal driver had set out from the barracks at Xigaze ninety minutes earlier because they knew they had to reach Drakesh Monastery within an hour or so of the sun clearing the horizon. Any later and they'd be denied entry. No one was allowed to enter the monastery at Drakesh in full daylight. Daylight was for contemplation, worship; darkness was for mundane thoughts, the maintenance of the body as opposed to the soul. The Major must consider himself fortunate indeed that the High Priest of the sect, the enigmatic Daham Drakesh, had seen fit to grant him audience during daylight hours.

Such would be the opinion of outsiders, anyway. *Hah!* Well, Major Chang Lun knew differently. Powerful as this monkish creature was in his own spheres, the so-called "People's" Army of Communist China was more powerful yet. But Chang Lun was under orders and must play Drakesh's game.

The Major's vehicle was a two-seater halftrack, a snow-cat equipped for the plateau's uneven terrain. His driver parked it in the lee of boulders close to steps leading up to the monastery's foreboding entrance, covered it with a tarpaulin, finally came erect and saluted. Chang Lun nodded his curt approval, turned and bowed from the waist to the string of red-robed priests where they stood stock still, arms folded, patiently waiting.

There were six of them; they indicated that the Major and his driver should take their places centrally in the line. And with three priests leading and three bringing up the rear, the string set out at what was to the Chinese soldiers an awkward, unmilitary shuffle, climbing the steps single-file to the yawning stone mouth that formed the entrance to the monastery. The leading priest held his left arm tucked into his waist at the elbow, with the forearm held stiffly out in front. His jogging motion caused tiny golden bells to chime where they were stitched into the seam of his robe's extended sleeve.

And so into the Drakesh monastery. As they entered, Chang Lun looked back. In the middle distance, glowing yellow where glancing rays of sunlight struck through the shade in the lee of ragged mountains, a nameless city stood gaunt and deserted behind high fortress walls. If it weren't so remote the place would make an excellent military base, but what purpose would it serve to station soldiers in a region as barren and inhospitable as this? The southern borders with Nepal, Bhutan, and India were no longer in dispute.

Then a portcullis of massive timbers was lowered, shutting off the view and Lun's thoughts both. The tinkling of the bells receded, along with the soft flutter of monkish robes; darkness settled; the silence was near-absolute. And as the Major's eyes began to adjust, he saw that he and the Corporal were alone . . . if only for a moment. Then:

"Welcome to Drakesh," said a voice as dark as the surroundings. It spoke a sibilant Chinese but yet without a trace of dialectal accent. "You have entered of your own free will—or rather, at the command of your superiors! Well, so be it." The voice held a none too subtle sarcasm.

Abruptly, a torch was lit; the shadows were at once thrown back, and flickering light illumined the face and form of Daham Drakesh.

Chang Lun had met him before but the physical appearance, the *presence* of Drakesh, never failed to impress him. At sixty-eight inches in height, the Major himself was taller than average for his race, but he felt dwarfed in the presence of Daham Drakesh. The man must be all of six and a half feet in height! But thin to the point of emaciation, he looked almost skeletal where the light of his torch showed through his shift and silhouetted his pipestem body. His hands were freakishly long and tapering, their pointed fingers tipped with thick yellow nails hooked into claws; his shaven skull was thin at the front and lantern-jawed, long at the back and bulbous as the head of an insect on a scrawny neck.

But for all that Daham Drakesh seemed fragile as porcelain, his eyes—eyes luminous and yellow as molten sulfur—gazed on Chang Lun and the Corporal, and seemed to gaze through them, as if *they* were the ephemeral ones, not he. They felt paralyzed by that gaze, until finally Drakesh's lips cracked in a ghastly smile and he said:

"Come. I have prepared a room for your man in the left eye of the carven face. There he may enjoy the daylight, forbidden to me and mine, sip tea, break bread, take his rest—and wait for you, of course. We require no underlings to attend our discourse." He smiled a mirthless sideways smile down on the Major and moved silently, flowingly ahead of his guests, leading them through the labyrinth of rock-hewn halls, galleries and tunnels which was the monastery. "Alas, you and I may not rest, Major" (again his loathsome smile, directed at Chang Lun.) "The wicked are not permitted to rest, ever—by which I mean that we have matters to discuss, of course."

"Indeed we have," the Major snapped, feeling (as he always felt) intimidated by this creature in this place and determined to regain the upper hand. "Grave matters, which have brought me here on the orders of my superiors!"

"Aye, and your timing—or the timing of your masters in Peking—is faultless," Daham Drakesh answered, as he rushed his visitors along gloomy stone corridors, with his torch held high in front. "For just as you have your orders, so I have my . . . shall we say, requirements? Who can say, perhaps there are higher powers at work? Certainly it seems that your coming at this time was inevitable. For if you had not requested an audience, I most certainly would have summoned you."

"Summoned?" Chang Lun gasped. "Why, you . . . !" But there he paused with his mouth agape, his slanted eyes opening wide.

In the last few moments, a massed moaning had become apparent; the Major had thought it might be some acoustic effect of the wind on the outer shell of the monastery. But now, in addition to the moaning, he could discern a regular whistling or slicing sound, like the *crack* of a lash splitting the air, or of several lashes in unison. And he had seen its source.

They had reached a central gallery deep in the mountainside. Lit by flambeaux, still the light failed to illumine the high ceiling or reach into every corner. The place was an amphitheater, with stone steps descending to a level central area. But while the rest of the hall, cave or excavation was poorly lit, that central area was all too clearly illumined. Burning braziers suspended on chains from the ceiling cast their flaring light on a scene that Bosch might easily have omitted from some hellish triptych. Emerging onto a perimeter walkway, the Major had come to an abrupt halt. Drakesh immediately gripped his elbow in a surprisingly powerful hand. "Ah, no!" he whispered. "Be silent, I beg you. Do not disturb them. They are at worship . . ."

"They" were the monastery's priests, the sect's devotees, the acolytes of the faith. They were naked; their red robes of priesthood lay folded on the lower tiers of the amphitheater's encircling steps; their pale, cringing bodies thronged around the central dais—no, *the long stone trough,* as Chang Lun now saw—but those who stood upon or in the trough were clad in red nevertheless. The red of their own blood!

Heads down, in single-file, they trudged in their shuffling flip-flop fashion from one end of the trough to the other, while the "brothers" all around flailed away at them with long black—and red—metal-tipped whips. The blood streaked them; it rained from them; their feet were stained crimson where they slopped through an inch of plasma like men treading grapes! Yet never a cry of pain from a single "brother" but that low, concerted moaning, not least from the ones with the whips . . . who knew it was their turn next.

And the blood in the trough: it drained away through boreholes to a sluice, and went steaming down a chute into unknown darkness. Those who had offered up their blood stepped from the trough at its far end, and went stumbling, reeling down an exit tunnel, presumably to a place of rest and healing. While at the other end untried brothers took their places, stepped into the trough and commenced the ordeal of blood. And in the outer circle, the last of the priests were even now disrobing, accepting whips from flayers who chose their own places in the shuffling, moaning line.

"Worship?" The Major was aghast, and his driver trembling, where Daham

Drakesh hurried them around the perimeter and under an archway marked with an ankh: a symbol of long life, as Chang Lun was aware. But long life, in a place like this?

"But what of the blood?" The Corporal's face was now a far paler shade of yellow. "Where does it all go? All of that blood, all of that . . . life?" For some time there was no answer, just the flaring of Drakesh's torch as he forged ahead. Then finally his voice came echoing back to the pair hurrying after him:

"The blood returns to the earth . . . eventually. Surely it is better to offer it fresh than rotting in corpses? Men take from the soil and the rivers, giving nothing back but piss and shit until the end. But here we observe our duty to Nature."

"Huh!" the Major couldn't suppress a derisory snort. "And do you bleed with them, Daham Drakesh?"

Drakesh rounded on him in the doorway to his quarters and for a moment seemed to rear taller still. Then the fire dimmed a little in his eyes as he answered, "With them? No, Chang Lun, I bleed *for* them, for they are sinners all! In the night, they have sinned. Even their dreams have been foul, and full of the vices which are in men. They have dreamed of women, and some of men. They have plied their own flesh, making it despicable. But in this place we are of the spirit, not the body. Which is why, periodically, we suffer their vile bodies to be purged; not by the release of base fluids but the essence of life itself. And so you see, your driver was right: the blood *is* the life . . ."

At which a red-robed priest stepped forward from the shadows, and Drakesh turned to the shivering Corporal. "Go with the brother here, who will see that you are comfortable." When they were gone, he stood aside and ushered the Major into his chambers . . .

Daham Drakesh had been here a hundred years. At the time, this had seemed the only place in the world that no one wanted. But now men wanted everything, everywhere, even a wasteland as barren as this plateau.

When first he came here there was the walled city and its people, nothing else. But in twenty-odd years the city was forbidden and its people in thrall, and in another twenty most of them had died in the excavation of the "monastery." It pleased Drakesh to call it a monastery, which was in fact an aerie. As for the survivors of the great task: their children were still in thrall to Drakesh in his aerie, in one of the highest, most remote places on Earth. But it had not been remote enough.

Even that mighty fang *Qomolangma*, Everest itself, one hundred and thirty miles away, would not be remote enough. Men had conquered its topmost peak; they had come out of foreign lands to plant their sigils there. Usually they hailed from the west, but in older times they had come from the east, too. Except those earlier conquerors had had scant interest in Everest.

History repeats. Those same slant-eyed warriors were back again. Not the Hsiung-nu or Avars nor even the Huns, but their descendants certainly, and with the same fierce blood in them. But where before they had skirted the Great Plateau, this time they had taken it. Well, and Daham Drakesh, last of his line, was of an alien blood, too—of a *truly* alien blood, aye! This would not be the first time his kind had been swayed, usurped, even decimated by human invaders. But never exterminated. Nor would it happen now.

It had been the same in Dacia, Eflak, Wallachia, Transylvania (the same in "the source-place," under whatever name the pages of history ascribed to it), in those earlier times. Daham had heard it from his egg-sire, Egon, who had lived through all of those long centuries of war to become the survivor of survivors, oldest of all the Wamphyri . . . Well, save one:

How nomadic invaders from the east had driven the vampire Lords from their ancient territories time and again, not least when they had considered themselves secure. And now? Was it to be the same again? Not if Daham Drakesh had his way.

He had come here those hundred years ago to remove himself from the actions of his father. Bored by isolation in his Transylvanian keep, and aware that an ancient enemy lay asleep in a secret place in the west, the "Count" had determined to venture out and broaden his interests in the world; he had lain low for far too long. Daham Drakul (now Drakesh), Egon's "son" by transfusion of his egg, had been left to care for the keep: "in command," as it were, of a handful of itinerant Szekely serfs and thralls. Huh! What was that for power?

But treachery was ever the way of the vampire, and no one hates a Master Vampire, a Lord of the Wamphyri, more than his own flesh and blood, his own egg-son. By virtue of Egon's egg, the burgeoning leech within him, Daham *was* Wamphyri; he would be a Lord in his own right. But not here in Transylvania, not in another Lord's castle. Wherefore he must remove himself to some far place and find or build an aerie of his own. A handful of soil out of Starside (his "birthright") and six Szgany thralls vampirized into lieutenants, were all Daham took with him. Oh, and some monies in ancient golden ingots stolen from his father's treasury.

And so to the Roof of the World, and to this place—

—Where eight years later he'd learned of Egon's death at the hands of some merely human adversary. But by then a return to the Transylvanian keep had been out of the question, for it had been recognized as a source of great evil; the local administration would never allow another Drakul to take up residence there. It were best that the legend die again, only to rise up in other parts when the time was ripe.

And so the decades had flown, but what is time to a Lord of the Wamphyri? Time is nothing . . . but ennui is. And just as Egon had become bored, so was his "son" bored by his existence in this place. Except he must wait out his time; or rather, he must wait out the time of Another, until He was up again.

Daham knew about Radu; knew *who*, if not *where* he was. At least he knew as much as Egon had known, before his ill-fated sojourn in England. He also knew about the "Francezcis" (more properly the Ferenczys), and had watched from afar while they grew powerful in the world. For just as they had their sources, so Daham had his. Indeed they were often the same sources! But more than this, he had his eyes and ears out in the world, his red-robed thralls and "Emissaries of the Message," ostensibly a message of love and peace . . .

In reality they were his spies pure and simple, and their message a sham. Or rather, they were his *not*-so-simple and far *less* than pure agents. But as well as

information, they sought out vampires, too—common vampires like themselves, or less than themselves—to learn from them . . .

. . . And then to destroy them!

It was part of the ages-old scheme of things, a rule as valid as it had been
fifteen hundred years ago: that obscurity and anonymity are synonymous with
longevity. A simple code of existence that Egon Drakul had forgotten or put
aside once too often. But his son Daham would not make the same mistake. For
he knew that if man discovered vampires in the world—and if man believed in
them—he would not rest until they were destroyed, every last one, including
Daham. Which was why he sought out and killed these lesser creatures first.

As to who they were:

Spawn of Ferenczy, Lykan, *and* Drakul, errors from a time lost in history.
The sons of the sons and daughters of daughters of supplicant Szgany come into
this world with Radu Lykan, Nonari the Gross Ferenczy . . . yes, and with Karl
and Egon Drakul, too, out of a far strange place. They were not Wamphyri, no,
but they were of the blood. And their source had been Sunside/Starside in a
vampire world. Daham had learned something of that place from his father,
and of blood-feuds so terrible that they would outlast time! Moreover, he knew
it was only a *matter* of time before just such a feud erupted here.

He knew, because down the years his "disciples" had come across descendants of Radu's thralls—lycanthropes with eyes full of moonlight—who told of a
legend sleeping in a mountain far in the west. This was the same rumor Egon
had heard a hundred years ago, that sent him plunging headlong into England
. . . to his eventual death. And who could say that Egon's death had not been
wrought by Radu, or those he'd left behind to tend him through his long sleep?

Radu Lykan, and the Ferenczys, and the Drakuls. But *that* had been a
feud—and would be again, when Radu was up! As to the when of it: soon, if
Daham could believe his sources. And he did believe them. The Ferenczys had
had thralls in England for long and long; for what good reason, if not to track
Radu to his lair? And just as Daham's people had researched the so-called "Ferenczinis," and later the "Francezcis," so had some other agency *out* of England! Daham knew it; his eyes and ears were out there, not always in the guise
of red-robed priests! Radu's thralls protected and looked after their sleeping
master even now, and in their turn sought out his olden enemies until the time
of his return.

And when he returned, what then? And what of Daham Drakesh, Wamphyri, in this remote but not inaccessible place? How long before Radu found
him? Or—if the Ferenczys should find and destroy Radu first—how long before
they found him?

. . . Or (and this was surely the worst possible of any and all scenarios), what
if they had *already* found him . . . ?

Well, he had no proof of that, nor even a shred of evidence as yet. But there
was always tomorrow, and Daham Drakesh was a sincere believer in another old
edict: that a stitch in time saves nine.

Egon had told him how, upon a time in the vampire world, the great Lord
Shaitan the Unborn had stood off and let lesser Lords fight a great bloodwar,
until all of them were depleted, made weak by their efforts. Then how he'd

picked them off one by one, until he was the undisputed Lord of Lords. It had been a story worth listening to, and a lesson worth learning.

But how much better, how much more ironic, if Shaitan the Unborn had *set* those lesser Lords to fighting, if he had deliberately planned it so that they performed the bulk of his work for him? And who could say, perhaps he had! And perhaps Daham would do the same. The ultimate *agent provocateur*, yes.

History repeats . . .

All of which were thoughts that passed fleetingly through the vampire Lord's mind as his visitor, Major Chang Lun of the People's Army of Red China, tried in vain to make himself comfortable in the austere cavern that served the last Drakul for living space.

There was an alcove cut back into one wall. Within it a long, lidded box like a linen chest fitted snugly into the seven-by two-foot recess. A bench, its polished top was scattered with cushions of a coarse local weave. This was where Drakesh had seated the Major, upon his own bed in fact—which was *inside* the box. Normally at this hour, Drakesh would be inside, too. Alas that on certain rare occasions, such as this one, he was obliged to make allowances.

And while Chang Lun's "host" brought tea and foul Tibetan biscuits from a secondary cave, the Major sat and narrowed his oval eyes, staring all about the dim, somehow smoky interior of this place. It *wasn't* smoky, he knew, yet seemed full of drifting shadows and the shimmery mobility of a scene viewed through smoke. Perhaps it was an effect of the indirect daylight filtering in through narrow slits hewn right through the great thickness of the far wall, the only indication that Daham Drakesh's apartments were on the outer extremes of the monastery.

Chang Lun had inquired about those narrow windows before. In other keeps in other lands they might easily be mistaken for ancient arrow slits, but in fact they were Drakesh's clock. The light crossed the room in dim, barely perceptible bars, forming patterns on the wall above the alcove where Chang Lun sat. According to the shape and brightness of the patterns and the time of year, Drakesh could immediately determine the hour to within two or three minutes.

"And at night?" (the Major had asked him one time.)

"I have a certain affinity with the night," Drakesh had at once answered. "It is an art of mine *instinctively* to know what is the hour. I take pride in it—a vanity, I know. But as the setting of the sun is a marvel, and its rising even more so, we should likewise pay attention to the darkness that lies between the two." Pseudo-mystical garbage . . .

. . . The Major felt himself slumping and sat up straighter. It was always the same: this place seemed to drain him of life. Huh! "The blood *is* the life," indeed!

"Tea," said Daham, entering as if from nowhere, and causing the dingy air to shift and shimmer into new patterns. "And there are Somangha biscuits, should you require refreshment."

"The tea is welcome," the Major offered his curt nod. "As for Himalayan grass seeds in milk paste—"

"—Each to his own," Daham nodded his understanding and placed a brass tray on a circular wooden table. Then he pulled up a three-legged stool and seated himself facing his visitor. "Soup, cheese, biscuits, bread: you would probably starve on a diet such as that. But to the Tibetan, more than sufficient."

The Major smiled thinly. "But you are not Tibetan."

"Polish, originally," Drakesh was frank. "When my mother died and my father returned to his native Romania, I went with him. There I—what, heard the call?—I knew I had a mission in life. And so I came here and built *this* mission, this monastery. Think what you will of it, and of me; I have my devotees. You saw some of them at a phase of their devotions."

"Indeed I did!" Chang Lun grimaced, and quickly diverted the conversation. "So, you built your monastery. Then we came, and one by one the temples began to topple."

"But not this one," Drakesh's eyes had narrowed. "Those troops who preceded you—warriors, and not merely an occupying force—they saw that I was different, and that the mysteries of the Drakesh Sect were real. They made report, and an officer—ah, a full *Colonel*, Chang Lun!—came from his headquarters on Kwijiang Avenue, Chungking, to see me. Do you know the significance of that? Perhaps you will understand me better if I speak of the British E-Branch, or their Russian equivalent at the Château Bronnitsy near Moscow? Oh, yes, Major! There are forces in the world greater than all the armaments of war. Some men understand such things, and I, Daham Drakesh, am one of them. But that is my pride speaking, and pride is a sin. Indeed, it is one of the original sins. But . . . perhaps I'm boring you?"

Chang Lun shook himself. This man was hypnotic; his voice lulled; his eyes drilled into your soul. And as if he knew the Major's innermost thoughts, Drakesh was even now smiling that ghastly smile of his. "No," the Major protested. "What, bored? Not in the least! So tell me: what did the Colonel from Chungking want?"

Drakesh nodded. "I know that you already know," he said, "and that you think me a fraud, a *fakir,* and Colonel Tsi-Hong a gullible fool. But I'll tell you anyway. He wanted to see me melt a block of ice—from within! He wanted to know how I can see in the dark, without the aid of nitelite binoculars. He was fascinated that I could fast for thirty days and nights without even water or a crust of bread to sustain me, then walk naked, ten miles out into the snows, to meditate. And having heard certain truths and untruths about me in Lhasa, he was especially interested in my longevity, the fact that I've been here for a hundred years!"

Chang Lun nodded. "Metaphysics," he sniffed. "Longevity. ESP. On Kwijiang Avenue, in Chungking, they study such things. Also genetic mutations and such. I say it's a fad. What weight can a thought carry? And what use to breed freaks? But we *know* the weight of a tank, and how deadly a gun is in the hands of a well-trained soldier! So . . . for the moment Colonel Tsi-Hong is in favor. Indeed, he has been in favor a good many years. But he has superiors, too, and men want results. As for genetics: the Russians have bred a super-pig. The beast can't walk, its flesh is vile, and its shit stinks!"

"But on Kwijiang Avenue in Chungking," Drakesh's voice had fallen to a whisper, "they are not breeding pigs . . ."

And now, finally, it was the Major's turn to smile. He just couldn't resist it.

"On Kwijiang Avenue," he said, letting each word sink in, "they are no longer breeding anything!" Reaching inside his uniform, he produced a heavy, "sealed" manila envelope, which he handed to Drakesh.

Without a word or change of expression, Drakesh opened the envelope with a hooked fingernail. The "seal" sprang open at a touch, which scarcely surprised him. Where Major Chang Lun was concerned, the word privacy wasn't in his vocabulary. What was written was lengthy and very complicated; Drakesh's eyes swept the crackling pages at incredible speed. He nodded his acceptance of the contents. And:

"I told him as much nine years ago," he said. "So now we'll do it my way." As he placed the envelope in his robe, his face was entirely emotionless.

Chang Lun made no attempt to disguise his knowledge of his host's subject. "They wanted tissue samples . . . you refused to cooperate. They wanted blood . . . you said it was your 'life,' and you could not part with it. They wanted *you!* As a sample of something alien, extraordinary, they would dissect you like a frog, disassemble you like a watch to see what made you tick. Oh, no physical damage, neither scar nor puncture hole to tell the tale, but small bits of you removed all the same. You bluffed them; you said you would rather die first, told them you'd will yourself to death. Tsi-Hong believed you—why, he might even learn something from watching you do it!—but then you offered him an alternative."

"My seed," Daham Drakesh nodded. "It seemed abhorrent to me that pieces of me, however small, should die on their telescopic slides and in the chemicals of their experiments. I did not want myself . . . examined. But I could find no logical argument against the *promotion* of life, from the ugly, wriggling, otherwise useless hordes of my loins."

"You came in a bottle for them," Chang Lun, too, could be cold, emotionless. "They froze your sperm and took it away . . ."

"To Chungking," Drakesh whispered.

"Indeed. And that was nine years ago."

"And fifty came forth!" Drakesh's eyes seemed afire in the cave's weird light.

"Out of the flower of China's womanhood, yes. You, father to a horde, when loyal, weeping Chinese parents were strangling their babies in the name of the People's Republic!" (Chang Lun was merciless, by his lights at least.) "To what end, Drakesh? What of Colonel Tsi-Hong's genetic experiments now?"

"I told him how it would be," said the other. "That one may not grow exotic orchids in a paddy field; that they will come up twisted and strange. But if they are tended by caring gardeners, watered by familiar rains, and reared in their natural, their *native* soil . . ."

"In other words, you'll 'grow' them yourself. What, here? And how will the brothers react to that, Daham Drakesh? A monastery, or a harem? A holy place, or a place of holes?"

"If it's your intention to offend me, your time is wasted here," Drakesh answered. "What will be will be . . . not necessarily because *I* want it, but because your leaders want it. And if in order to exist I must obey, then I will obey. I will not be forced out of being, driven from my place."

"You don't fool me," Chang Lun shook his head. "Your so-called 'emissaries' are out in the world even now, to what end if not to find a new place for you? I fancy you'll flee before your deceptions are discovered. Let's be clear on this: I consider you a fraud, yes. But I also consider you evil. This . . . this *spawn* that they bred by artificial insemination in Chungking is proof of it. Sooner or later even Tsi-Hong will recognize the truth, and what of you and yours then? I don't know what you are, Drakesh, but you're no holy man. And you're not up to any good, I'm sure. As for this monastery: do you think I can't see why you chose this place, so close to so many borders? Even now your boltholes are ready to receive you, when you are found out!"

Drakesh touched his robe, the place of the letter. Major Lun's raving didn't concern him; his mind was on other things. Fifteen of his "children" deformed, destroyed at birth. He had known about that long ago, of course. But fifteen out of fifty? It was hardly surprising: freak births and nightmarish malformations had been all too common among the Wamphyri of Starside; So Egon had informed him. As for grotesque autisms—bone and brain disorders—tendencies to extreme violence and madness—"unnatural" lusts: what else would one expect? These children, these creatures, had been vampires! Daham's blood-brood, *his* creatures, aye . . .

"The last six escaped," Chang Lun broke into his thoughts, made no excuse for knowing every smallest detail of the letter. "Only eight years old, and apparently perfect apart from their accelerated growth rate. They killed their keepers and instructors; they not only bit the hands that fed them . . . but fed *on* them! Drinkers of blood, cannibals, homicidal maniacs! In only eight years they'd grown to men, and sexually voracious women! Finally they were hunted down to the last one, and eradicated. But it wasn't easy . . ."

And again Drakesh said, "I told them how it would be. But this time we'll do it my way." His whisper was a hoarse rustle in his pipestem throat. "My way, yes . . ."

All of his "children" gone now—the nucleus of an indefatigable army, which Tsi-Hong had tried to create as a unique breed, protectors of China—all gone now. But Drakesh knew no pain. He *had* known what the outcome would be. Tsi-Hong had tried to teach them to be human; Daham would teach them to be what they were, and to *hide* what they were until he was ready!

It was what he had wanted from the beginning. It had been the way of the Drakuls since a time beyond memory—to infiltrate and eat out an enemy's heart from within. But China, the enemy? Not at all; the enemy was Mankind! China was merely the greenhouse for the next and last generation of Great Vampires, and Daham Drakesh would be their unholy priest—their bloodsire, aye—in the vampire world of tomorrow! But for now:

"You asked me certain questions," he reminded the Major. "Unless they were frivolous, I would answer them. Indeed, I am obliged to answer them, so that you may take my answer back to Tsi-Hong. 'Would I make this place a harem?' you asked." Drakesh shook his head. "No. The brothers will make ready the city in the lee of the mountain. And the lascivious among them will repopulate it. But I shall be the true father of the brood!"

"I know that place," Chang Lun answered. "I visited it—but briefly—the first time I came here. Its doors are still daubed with plague markings."

Drakesh shrugged. "Whatever the plague was . . . it is gone now." And changing the subject: "There was something else that you said: that I would flee when I was discovered, and that my emissaries were out in the world even now, seeking new places for me. Well, you were right in one thing, at least. But quite wrong in another . . ."

"Oh?" Chang Lun prompted him.

"Boltholes—*hah!* If ever I had intended flight, surely by now I would have fled?" Drakesh cocked his knobby head on one side and smiled. "What? Only sixty miles to Nepal, and the same to Sikkim or Bhutan? And I am still here? No, don't pride yourself that I would ever flee from such as you, Major." And before Chang Lun could answer:

"As for my emissaries: you don't know the half of it . . . But Colonel Tsi-Hong does! Over the roof of the world—across the Himalayas—is the easiest route into 'friendly territories,' it's true. Ah, but not for me! For my 'emissaries!' "

Chang Lun frowned, and for the first time began to feel a little unsure of himself, a little uneasy. "Go on," he said.

"Who better to look into the affairs of the outside world—not only the religious affairs, but also the social, political and economical—than harmless monks of an obscure Tibetan order? *Spies*, Chang Lun! Not only for me but also for the much-reviled Colonel Tsi-Hong. And by whom reviled? By you! And you dare to threaten me? By all means do so. But remember, you may well be threatening China herself! My emissaries, yes . . . spies for China. Ah, and very necessary, Chang Lun! Never more so than now. Doubtless you read in this letter how the Château Bronnitsy is no more, reduced to rubble some two years ago? But how was it wrought, for what reason, and by whom? And what if a similar establishment on Kwijiang Avenue in Chungking should be next? Metaphysics, a fad? Do you still think so? Well, others in the world take it far more seriously. So now you see the entire picture; you've become one of the privileged handful who *do* see it. And perhaps one too many . . . if I were to let slip the fact of this new knowledge of yours, and of your opinions, to a certain Colonel in Chungking . . ."

Chang Lun came to his feet at once! But slowly, oh so very slowly, he sat down again. "I . . . seem to have underestimated you," he said. "Worse, it seems I was mistaken—about certain things."

"You were suspicious of what you did not understand," Drakesh told him. "But now you do understand . . . something of it, at least. Well, no harm done." He smiled that smile of his and stood up. "Now you will excuse me while I write my reply. This time, perhaps the seal will remain intact . . . ?" And once again, before the Major could answer or protest, if he intended to:

"But let's have no secrets, you and I. My letter will list my requirements, the equipment needed to make Drakesh City inhabitable again . . . Which the military, your forces in Xigaze, will transport as it is made available. Also, I shall require more freedom, the necessary visas, to send my 'emissaries' out into the world in greater numbers. For troubled times are coming, and I—or should I say we?—would be well advised to prepare for them now." It was all true as far as it went; logically, it fitted the scenario perfectly. But none of it was for China.

Drakesh turned to go, turned back again. "I will send for your driver; no need for you to wait on your own. Meanwhile, I thank you for your understanding, Chang Lun. May you always be at peace with yourself, if not with the world.''

Then, with a last enigmatic smile, bowing from the waist, he retired into his inner sanctum in a swirl of red robes . . .

The Necroscope's dreams were and always had been strange. Now more than ever before he found himself unable to recall their substance when he was awake. This morning was no different; he came awake in his bed in his room at the Hotel Adrano sweating, panting, fighting with his bedclothes in a frenzy of fear, yet a moment later was lost as to the cause. But the fear had been real, as the continued trembling of his limbs and pounding of his heart testified . . .

Something about B.J., about the moon, about wolves, about a place like a skull on a frozen plateau . . . about dark forces gathering in all the unquiet places of the world. It was there and it was gone. Something about himself: that he was two men in one body, with two sets of thoughts? When he was the other he didn't know his *own* mind, and when he was him—

—When he was him? . . . Now what the hell?

When he was him!? What? Was he back to that again? Well, he *was* him, and he was *satisfied* with him, now!

With which the rest of the dream blinked out and disappeared entirely, and Harry was left to locate himself physically, in three dimensions, as opposed to the fourth and purely mental dimension of his mind, in this first day of the rest of his life . . . in the Hotel Adrano, in Paterno, Sicily. And having fixed that, the rest of it fell into place and he knew why he was here. Set a thief to catch a thief? Well, not quite. But set one to steal from one, or from two . . . ?

That was why he, the waking him, was here.

But the subconscious Harry Keogh—of whom he wasn't even aware—was here for another reason. Yet no confusion of purpose physical or otherwise; *both* purposes locked together like the two halves of one brain! And B.J. could not have planned it better even if she'd known everything; but if she had, the Necroscope wouldn't be here in the first place, or any other place by now. Except maybe in a no-place, the last place on or under the earth: talking to his dead people in their *own* place, face to face as it were. But Harry didn't know that.

He called for coffee, breakfast, and when it came had no taste for it. By then he'd washed, shaved and dressed. So he ate anyway, and chewing over his food, likewise chewed over his plans. In doing so, the two halves of his mind found a meeting place. His business here was to "break into" Le Manse Madonie, of course, and steal back from the Francezci brothers some of their ill-gotten gains. But it could do no harm to do a little research first: in fact, to research the Francezcis.

Not from any library or registrar's office, but from the dead themselves. For who would know better about the history of a family and its ancestral home than that family's progenitors; or, if they were unwilling, its servants? And where better to find the latter than at Le Manse Madonie itself?

Except here . . . something extraordinary, that the Necroscope never before in his life stumbled across. Two extraordinary things, in fact.

One: thinking of Le Manse Madonie, his mind had conjured the photographs that Darcy Clarke had shown him at E-Branch HQ in London; more, it had superimposed them over that precognitive vision of the place, as shown to him by some residual echo of Alec Kyle's talent. This combination, a sort of mental triangulation, had the effect of locating the building *exactly* in his memory . . . and in his mind! Astonishingly, he "remembered" his co-ordinates from a flash-forwards!

The idea at once struck him that using the Möbius Continuum he could go there right now, without further ado. It would be as simple as that. He had his room's co-ordinates; if he was mistaken, or if something were to go wrong, he could return at once to the hotel in Paterno, or even further afield to any of the old co-ordinates he knew so well. But if he was right—if he could make one unbroken Möbius jump directly to the Madonie, without ever having been there physically—then the experiment would provide irrefutable proof that indeed he'd inherited some gradually fading trace of Alec Kyle's metaphysical skill.

And after Le Manse . . . there were *other*, perhaps far more important places.

It was completely irresistible. Placing his breakfast tray outside his door and locking it, Harry forced his mind's Möbius maths to a familiar configuration, conjured a door, stepped across the threshold and—

—Went there, to the mountains of the Madonie! It worked!

There had been two locations, one of them at a lower elevation, well away from the place, and the other close up. Harry had materialized at the first one, thus keeping a healthy distance between himself and the actual house. But there it was, just as he had seen it in his vision:

He craned his neck to look up and up, at stark yellow and white cliffs—yellow in sunlight, as he now saw,—and at the squat, white-walled castle, mansion, or château, perched there on the rim of oblivion. A fortress on a mountainside from the Necroscope's viewpoint, where he stood on a winding road halfway between the sea and the sky.

The sea, of course! He remembered how, during that brief, earlier "visit," he'd smelled the Tyrrhenian at his back. And now he could turn and take it in: the great sweep of Sicily's northern coast against the blue dazzle of white-flecked ocean, hazing toward Palermo in the west, and curving over the distant horizon to Messina in the east.

There were cars and a bus groaning their way up the steep road. Harry didn't especially care to be noticed; turning his back to the vehicles, he looked again at Le Manse Madonie:

That somehow foreboding mansion, built on the edge of a sheer drop that must be almost four thousand feet to the sloping scree of a rubble-strewn gorge. And the great cliff of the mountainside itself, all sun-bleached rocks, brittle scrub and a few stunted Mediterranean pines . . . exactly as he'd seen it before. Déjà vu indeed!

But in reverse? *More like Vega du!* Harry thought, drawing himself back to the present.

The vehicles had disappeared around a bend, been eaten up by a spur of the mountain where the road had been cut through it. The Necroscope was quite alone. He found a flat-topped rock by the side of the road and sat down. Now, with a bit of luck, he should be able to find someone who could help him.

Yet even as his mind slipped into its familiar mode, that weird telepathic talent which allowed him to talk to the dead, something warned him that he should guard his thoughts. It was the place . . . or rather, it was *that* place up there, teetering on the rim of the cliff like that. Oh, yes, it was as well to whisper, in the presence of the unknown. But a place is only a place after all; so why was Harry sweating? It was a hot day, certainly, but it didn't feel like that kind of sweat. And if it had been *other* than day—

—The Necroscope scarcely believed he'd want to be here at all. But he would have to be. Indeed he would have to go *in* there, into that place. Tonight . . .

Which made it imperative that he know something about it. And he would also like to know something about the Francezcis—something about their background, their history—something other than Darcy had told him. Though why he couldn't exactly say . . . call it for future reference.

Harry's thoughts—even his most recent, guarded, inward-directed thoughts—were ''audible'' to the teeming dead. They always were, except when he shielded them or aimed them at an individual. By now he would normally have expected someone to answer him, inquire as to his presence here. He was the Necroscope, after all. But no, the telepathic ''aether,'' his lines of communication, seemed to be down. No one was interested in him. Or if they were, they weren't expressing that interest.

And yet he knew they were there; he sensed them like phantom callers on a telephone; they ''breathed,'' however silently, in his weird mind. But it wasn't Harry who was afraid, it was them. And because they were, and after listening to their silence for a while, so was he . . .

. . . Harry?

He jumped a foot! ''What? Who . . . ?'' With all of his experience, still the Necroscope spun around; and despite that everything was bright, hot, dazzling sunlight, and that sweat (good old honest-to-goodness, physical sweat now, as well as a trace of the other sort) rivered his back, still he shivered. Until: ''I . . . I'm sorry,'' he finally gasped. ''I suppose I should have been expecting you. I mean, I *was* expecting someone. But this silence, this dead silence, is sort of unnerving.''

And that was it, the second extraordinary thing: the fact that with the exception of this one dead voice, the Great Majority were ''dead silent.'' Oh, they were here, but they weren't saying anything.

Nor will they, said the one lone voice in Harry's metaphysical mind. *You're forgetting something, Harry: that what the dead did in life, they continue to do in death. Isn't that how it goes?*

''Why, yes, but—''

—*But this is Sicily,* said the as yet unknown other, as if that were explanation enough. *It's a place apart, Harry. It has its own special code.*

And indeed the Necroscope did understand. ''A code of silence?''

That's right, he sensed the other's incorporeal nod. *It's a code they adhere to. And never more so than here.*

''Here?'' Harry knew what the answer was going to be in the selfsame moment he framed the question.

Right here, yes, said the dead voice. *In this very place. In the shadow of Le Manse Madonie . . .*

HUMPH, AND OTHERS.
IN THE VAULTS BENEATH.

WHO ARE YOU?" HARRY WOULD HAVE LIKED A PROPER INTRODUCTION, BUT it seemed that in this place he wasn't going to get one.

Who was I, do you mean? The other was open about it; he'd obviously had plenty of time to get used to the idea; he wasn't one of the recently dead, but more properly a long-time member of the Great Majority. *I was J. Humphrey Jackson Jr.—"Humph" to my friends. An American, yeah. As for what I did: I used to build safes.*

"Safes?"

That's right. For banks, for rich folks, and sometimes for thieves who were worried that someone might try to steal it all back. I designed and installed safes, strong-rooms, vaults. Big steel piggy-banks for little greedy piggies.

"Well, I'm very glad to meet you, Humph," Harry told him. "Especially since no one else around here seems interested!"

Oh, they're interested for sure! Humph told him. *But talk about close-mouthed? Cliques, Harry, a whole bunch of cliques, clans, families. Why, they talk to each other all the time—or rather, they whisper! But if you're an outsider . . . forget it.*

"But . . . in death, too? I would have thought silence was the last thing they'd want."

Well, you don't know much about the history of this island, do you? (Humph gave an incorporeal snort.) *It's a bloody place, Necroscope. Me, I sort of found out the hard way—and so could you. That's why I spoke up. See, I was beginning to fall into their ways. I mean, there are people here I can speak to, sure, but recently I've been as tight-assed as the rest of them! Then I sensed you'd come on the scene; you could only be the Necroscope because you were warm and I could hear you thinking—and what you were thinking about: Le Manse Madonie.*

"That's why you spoke to me?"

Mainly, yes . . . The dead man's thoughts were suddenly hard, cold. His was an uneasy spirit; in life, he'd either left something undone, or there had been a great injustice. Giving him a chance to organize his thoughts, Harry said:

"You sound pretty close, Humph. I mean, is there a cemetery close by?

Where's your grave? I could come and talk to you there. It seems only right."

Grave? Step to the other side of the road, Harry. And look down.

Harry crossed the narrow road and came to a halt at a knee-high metal safety barrier that didn't look any too safe.

That wasn't there in 1938, Humph told him. *No black-top on the road, either. Just a potholed track. An easy place to take a dive into the next world, if you were a careless driver—or if someone figured your time was up . . .*

"You crossed the wrong people?" The Necroscope took a cautious step over the barrier, one leg only, and looked down. Two or three hundred feet of thin air to a scree-strewn slope that went down to the next loop of road.

That's where I ended up in my burned-out wreck, Humph told him. *Right there on that stretch of road. Mercifully, I didn't feel a thing after the first bounce. And no, I didn't cross the wrong people . . . I worked for them!*

Harry guessed what was coming next. "The Francezcis?"

Absolutely. Three months to put in their vault—I supplied the brain, they supplied the brawn—and this is how I got paid off. A couple of their boys, their soldiers, flagged me down on my way off the mountain; they rapped me on the head hard enough to knock me dizzy, took the brake off, pushed me over. An "accident," of course.

"But why?"

Two reasons (Harry sensed a shrug.) *One: they took back my cash payment before I went over . . . miserable bastards! And two . . . Two has to be obvious.*

"You were the only one who knew about their strong room?"

That's how I figure it, yeah.

"Murder." Harry's voice had been quiet enough before; now it was the merest murmur.

Most foul, Humph agreed. And a moment later; *So, my bones went into a grave somewhere, but I hung about down there, where it happened. And what do you know, forty-odd years later, along comes Harry Keogh, Necroscope! Enough to make a man believe in God. Vengeance is thine, sayeth the Lord!*

"Except that's not what I'm here for," Harry told him.

And after a moment's silence: *Then maybe we should forget I ever spoke to you . . .*

". . . But I'll see what I can do." Humph's lead was too good to let go of. It might be exactly what Harry was looking for.

Promise?

"Absolutely."

How? I mean, how will you get my own back?

The Necroscope's turn to shrug. "They robbed you . . . it's my intention to rob them."

They killed *me, Harry! And I don't go for this turning the other cheek stuff! I mean, I've been hearing some things in the last couple of years; like, you're a man who believes in an eye for an eye?*

"That's true enough," Harry answered. "But I also need to believe in what I'm doing. And as yet I don't have much information on the Francezcis. I'm pretty sure it's within my parameters to *steal* from them, but as for anything else . . . try to put yourself in my position. There's no way I can right *every* wrong that's ever been done to the dead. Not on my own. There are an awful lot of you, Humph—you're of a very large, even a Great Majority—and I'm only one. But yes, when I can see the whole picture, then I'll see what can be done."

(A thoughtful pause, and): *So what can I tell you?*

"First, do you know anything about their family history?"

What? (Utter bewilderment.) *I mean, what the hell would I know about family histories? I build safes, Harry! Or I did.*

"Is there nothing you might have seen inside that place?"

Shit, I wasn't allowed to see anything inside that place! I had a room. I could go from my room to my place of work, and from my place of work to my room. And also to the place where I ate, always alone. Oh, and the grounds; it was okay if I wanted to walk around the grounds. Layout? Oh, I can tell you the layout, roughly. I can tell you where their treasury is, for sure! But history?

"Very well, let's settle for the layout. For now, anyway."

And Humph told him. Taking it all in, the Necroscope listened intently as he moved out of the glaring sunlight into the shade of an embankment where the winding road had been blasted through the solid rock of the spur.

It had been some time since Humph was inside Le Manse Madonie, but it had been on his mind ever since. Also, his description was enhanced by pictures straight out of his dead mind, so that Harry was enabled to "see" the route he had taken from his room to the vault that he'd been securing in the bowels of the place as if he himself were walking it. He could actually get the feel of the place, take co-ordinates.

"Right down in the bedrock," he eventually commented.

No, Humph told him. *Deep, but not right down. There were other levels below that one. I just sort of happened to stray down there one time. I can't remember if I lost my way or if I was just curious. Probably the latter—no, definitely the latter. Anyway, I found a place with a steel-barred door hooked up to a generator. Electrified! Oh, yeah! 1938, but Le Manse Madonie had its own juice. That was something in Sicily in those days.*

"Maybe that was the old strong room that yours was replacing?" Harry reasoned.

Maybe, but I don't think so, Humph's thoughts were very dark now. *There was just something down there that they didn't want anyone to see . . . Not anyone. Anyway, a guard caught me, gave me hell, frog-marched me in front of Emilio Francezci, my employer.* (Harry caught a "reflection" of the man from Humph's mind—and gave a start.)

Oh? Humph said. *Something up?*

Something was up, yes. This could easily be one of those photographs that Darcy Clarke had shown him. The family resemblance was *that* close! And like the photographs, this picture from the mind of a dead man was somehow blurred, indistinct.

I know what you mean, Humph said. *These people were shady characters in more ways than one. I never could remember precisely what they looked like. Funny, eh? But in no way funny ha-ha . . .*

"You say this Emilio was your *employer,* singular," Harry frowned, felt a little confused. "But you've also been talking in the plural: 'they,' and 'these people.' "

Emilio's brother, Humph explained. *He was a big cheese in Le Manse Madonie, but didn't go out much. Never, that I saw. I saw the pair together, though, frequently. Brothers, but definitely. Twins, even, if not identical.*

Darcy had said exactly the same thing, but about the *current* owners of Le

Manse, the current generation of Francezcis. And this time it was Humph who saw their pictures in the Necroscope's mind.

That's them! he said at once.

"Can't be," Harry shook his head. 'These are Francesco and Tony, or Anthony . . . today people. What you're seeing is from a recent photograph." He felt Humph's astonishment. And:

You know something? the dead man said, very quietly. *Emilio's brother was called Francesco . . .*

"Well, why not?" Harry wanted to know. "Names can carry on down the generations as well as family resemblance. And anyway, I'm not so much concerned with the current family as with the historical . . ." (But for the life of him he couldn't say why, even to himself!)

I don't know anything about that, said Humph, stubbornly.

"Maybe you do. Let's go the route again, from your room to the tunnel where you were putting those vault doors in." He had remembered seeing something and wanted to see it again.

Humph took him back along the route, from his first floor rooms in the manse, down a winding marble staircase into a huge hall or ballroom. And on the walls—glimpsed however dimly in the eye of the American's memory—rich, gilt-framed portraits of . . .

. . . *Francezcis!* Humph had surprised himself. *Hey, I remember now! Why, there's a whole damn family tree on those walls! Except . . . I'm sorry, Harry, but I can't remember what a single one of 'em looked like.*

"Try to look a little closer," the Necroscope begged him.

And Humph obliged. As he had said, these people were shady characters in more ways than one; even their brooding portraits seemed obscured, either by Humph's memory or the patina of age, or . . . whatever. But the family likeness was there in every one of them, certainly.

Harry leaned against the rocky wall of the cutting through the spur and closed his eyes the better to see through Humph's. And he saw—

—A woman. Misty in Humph's memory, but still beautiful. She was long-necked, had an elegant or perhaps haughty tilt to her head, and was classically Sicilian. And under the picture, her name on a brass plate, swimming up uncertainly in the eye of the dead American's memory:

Constanza . . .

Constanza de . . .

Constanza de' Petralia . . . ! And this time Harry's start was violent indeed. Humph felt it, and moving on to the next portrait asked:

Are you okay, Necroscope? Are you getting all of this?

Harry nodded, knew Humph would sense it, peered yet more intensely through his incorporeal eyes. And next to Constanza's portrait, that of her son, Angelo as a young boy. But the very next frame was Angelo again, this time as a young man. And now he had changed his name. To Angelo *Ferenczini*, of course!

The Necroscope withdrew, crashing out of Humph's mind as if all the devils of hell were after him. Well, they weren't, but evidence of them was in there for sure. Even as they were in—*still* in—Le Manse Madonie!

Harry? Humph queried as from very far away. *You okay, Necroscope?*

Harry knew what he'd seen and recognized, but already the information was subsuming itself into his inner identity, into his subconscious mind. It wasn't for him, this information, but for some other. He was only the one who gathered it. He mustn't allow it to register. That part of his mind—or Bonnie Jean's part—was like her personal computer. What was in there would not be activated until *she* pressed the right keys.

Hearing the warning toot of a car's horn, Harry opened his eyes. He'd staggered out into the middle of the road, and a car was coming through the cutting. Slowing to avoid him, it pulled to a halt and the driver leaned out of his window and made some inquiry in Italian. Harry stumblingly apologized, shrugged, got out of the way. And the car rolled forward, picked up speed and set off again down the mountainside.

Harry? J. Humphrey Jackson Jr. called again, a faint cry from a long, long way off as the Necroscope deliberately tried to shut him out entirely. He felt ill and didn't know why. Sunstroke? Possibly. But suddenly his entire being seemed to reel like a drunkard. What in hell had happened—*was* happening—here? What was happening *in his head?*

He had felt this before, when that lunatic telepath "wolfman" had invaded his mind. But that had been in London and this was Sicily. Was someone trying to get at him, or get through to him? Normally Harry could guard his thoughts to exclude whoever he wanted to. But something—some shock or other—must have thrown him out of kilter, off balance. However temporarily, his mind was wide open.

And they came . . .

. . . *Whoooo? Whoo? Who? Who are you? Who? Yes, who? Who are you???* A dozen of them, all speaking at once.

Whooorrrr? A growl.

Who? A small, timid, pleading voice.

Whoooooooooo!? Like some young girl's shriek of agony.

Who? Who-ho-ho? Ha-ha-ha-haaa! A burst of crazed laughter, fired into the Necroscope's mind like a stream of bullets from a machine-gun.

And finally: *WHO? . . . WHAT? . . . WHERE . . . ?* But unlike the previous voices—and despite that its source was the same—this one was utterly alien and totally menacing. And Harry felt himself reeling again from its sheer terror, from the *touch* of its mad blind groping in the innermost whorls of his brain.

Run! (The lesser voices whispered as one dead voice in his head.) *Oh, run, run, run!*

NO! WAIT! Mad mental "hands" were reaching, clutching for him. He clapped his own hands to his ears and ran!

His knees hit the crash barrier; his body pivoted; he toppled forward, and felt the air whistling in his clothes, plastering back his sweat-wet hair. Harry opened his eyes—saw the cliff and the sky and the distant sea, all revolving—and saw the rocks and rubble waiting for him below. In a moment, sanity returned, and in the next he conjured a Möbius door immediately beneath his falling body . . . and fell through it.

The Continuum! Safety! His co-ordinates! Paterno—

—He stumbled from the Möbius Continuum into his room at the Adrano, crumpled to his knees, and was at once sick in the middle of the beautifully carpeted floor . . .

* * *

Harry must have been down for a couple of hours. When he awoke he remembered being sick but not what had caused it. Sunstroke, it could only be. He'd cleaned up the mess before collapsing on his bed; thank goodness he didn't have to face that! The room's air-conditioning had dispersed the stale smell.

But turning his mind to Le Manse Madonie . . . he remembered everything Humph had told him, including the dead man's tale of a forbidden place with an electrified door deep in the bedrock, but nothing after that. No big deal; he knew where the strong room was, the Francezci treasury, and that was why he was here.

The only reason? The only reason, yes. *So why was he shivering?*

It was a momentary thing . . . it came and it went . . . possibly, even probably, it was whatever had made him sick. Well, probably. He shivered again, which triggered something else out of the past. Not what had made him sick but a scene of bitterly cold wastelands, and a stony face carved on the stonier face of a mountain.

As quickly as that the Necroscope's computer mind—but a computer "damaged" or "diseased," not only by Bonnie Jean's virus but also by Dr. James Anderson's—had managed to switch drives and thrown him off what could easily have become a very dangerous program or train of thought.

And Harry was quick to grab hold of something—anything solid—that might steady him up and give him a focal point to revolve around, instead of all this dizzy spinning he was doing now. And he remembered an idea that had flashed across his mind on discovering that he had Le Manse's co-ordinates without ever having been there in the flesh: that if it could work for that place, maybe it would work for those *other* places, too.

Why not? Alec Kyle's power had been to look into the future, but without ever knowing just exactly what the things he saw meant. And something of that power had come down to Harry in the contours of Kyle's brain. He'd "seen" Le Manse Madonie as part of his future, but his own weird talent had complemented Alec's; his metaphysical mind had instinctively recorded the co-ordinates!

And there *were* other places. The stone-faced—what, temple?—in the mountains was one of them. And the other:

Was or might be where Brenda was!

High passes and fang-like mountain peaks, and stars like chips of ice glinting with a frozen blue sheen in an alien sky. And down below, a barren plain of boulders reaching to a shimmering horizon under the weave of ghostly auroras . . .

Harry gave himself a shake. Brenda and the baby could be there? Yes, they could be—*if* it was a scene from his future and not just the leftover of some fanciful dream.

Well, he'd already proved the theory by going to Le Manse Madonie, and so would feel safer using it to visit these other places, too—wouldn't he? Only one way to find out.

First the temple or monastery, or whatever it was . . . but not before he felt a little better.

He took two Alka Seltzers, let them go down, and waited a few minutes until his stomach felt settled. Then he threw cold water in his face over his wash basin, patted himself dry with a fresh towel. And after lying on his back on his bed with his hands behind his head for half an hour, just thinking it over, finally he was ready.

He pictured the place in the frozen wastelands, the location from which he'd viewed the temple, and tried to remember the co-ordinates. No problem: they were waiting right there in his mind. This was it. He got up from his bed, conjured a Möbius door, and went there:

—And again it worked!

A little after twelve noon in Paterno, Sicily—five in the afternoon at the Drakesh Monastery on the Tibetan Plateau.

And there the place was, exactly as Harry had seen it in that previous visitation. Indeed this *was* that visitation; it was his future caught up with him, or him with a precognitive glimpse out of the configurations of a brain not yet conforming to his patterns:

The unseasonal blizzard had fallen off; fresh snow glistened softly in sunlight glancing through a gray cloud blanket; and out there on the white waste . . . movement? Of course: ant-like figures at this range, making their way across the snows. They were robotic in their movements, like some physically punishing military drill routine—left, right, left, right, left—rapid and shuffling. The three in front were dressed in red hooded robes, also the three bringing up the rear. But the one in the middle was clad in pure white. And coming to the Necroscope across a half-mile of gradually melting snow, the chiming of tiny golden bells . . .

Harry wasn't dressed for this. ''Summer'' it was, even here, but the elevation more than compensated. The Roof of the World, yes. And shivering again—this time from the cold—he conjured a door and returned to Paterno.

The heat struck him an almost physical blow as he stepped from nowhere into his room. And a maid was banging on the door, the *real* door, asking if she could ''makes it da-cleanings.''

He let her in, showed her the stained carpet and said he'd spilled coffee, let her get on with her tut-tutting and frantic cleaning. And sitting in a corner out of the way, watching her, he wondered what the stone-faced temple on the cold plateau was all about, and how it featured in his future. One thing seemed certain: Brenda wasn't there. There had been no ''sense'' of her presence, and there'd be no sense *to* it. Not in that place.

But mainly he wondered about the *next* place, and how that featured.

—*A garden in a fertile valley between ruggedly-weathered spurs, where dusty beams of sunlight came slanting through the high passes during the long daylight hours, and the stars glittered like frosted jewels at night, or ice-shards suspended in the warp and weave of ghostly auroras . . .*

Was Brenda there?

Just thinking of the place, weird co-ordinates surfaced on the screen of Harry's mind. Weird, yes, like nothing he'd ever seen before. So strange that he was given to wonder: were they real, or were they simply the co-ordinates of fantasy, the ephemera of dreams? Was that it, wishful thinking? Had he wished or dreamed too hard of an unattainable location somewhere over the rainbow?

Well, the Necroscope didn't have any ruby slippers, but he did have the Möbius Continuum.

Finally the maid was finished. With many nods, smiles, and a mouthful of unintelligible pidgin-English, she backed out of the room and was gone. Harry waited no longer but conjured his Möbius door, and in the primal darkness of the Möbius Continuum he pictured the esoteric symbols, the weird equation that would signpost his destination, and went . . . nowhere.

It had been after all a dream, a wish, a forlorn hope. And the co-ordinates had failed because they, too, were an invention of his wishful imagination and meant nothing.

He was wrong, of course, but had been perfectly correct to think of the co-ordinates as alien. For in a parallel dimension beyond space as we know it, Harry's "weird" co-ordinates would have taken him directly to his target. There was nothing wrong with them at all . . . *except* that they were alien.

Enough of experimentation, discovery and disappointment; right now, despite that he had rested, still Harry was tired. He was emotion-lagged, time-lagged, even Möbius- or spacetime-lagged. But later tonight he would need his wits about him, need to be physically and mentally fit for the job in hand. He had all the information he needed about Le Manse Madonie; his new knowledge with regard to the inhabitants of that place had sunk into and locked itself away in post-hypnotic vaults of the Necroscope's mind; it would remain there, beyond recall until some other—Bonnie Jean, or Radu Lykan—pressed the right buttons. As for conscious apprehensions: they were natural enough considering his mission. So he told himself.

He slept like a small child, for once undisturbed by the whispering of the dead in their graves. If they were talking, they were very quiet about it. But this was Sicily after all . . .

Waking about six in the evening, Harry felt a moment's disorientation before his mind cleared. It was still broad daylight, would be for another two to three hours.

Showering to shake off the last effects of dull sloth, he made a desultory meal in the hotel restaurant—a "something" Genovese—and at once returned to his room.

Now the Necroscope was just about ready and it was only a matter of time. Now, too, he realized how little he knew about Le Manse Madonie, its occupants and staff . . . Like how many of them, for instance, and what their duties were. But in a place like that—a fortress in its own right—there would be little or no requirement for security in the form of guards. A night watch, possibly, but on the perimeter. Even then it seemed unlikely that there would be too many people up and about in the wee small hours.

Oh, really? (Harry frowned to himself, at the niggling little voice in the back of his mind.)

Well, if they *were* up and about, his plan was designed to take care of that. They would be buzzing like wasps once he'd set the thing in motion, but on the outside. A distraction was what they required, something to divert them from their normal routine. And a distraction was what he intended to deliver.

As for the vault doors: they were combination-locked. He wasn't an expert safe-breaker, but he *was* an expert at getting into places without going through doors. Or rather, he was the only one with the combination to his doors. In fact it worked very much in Harry's favor, that Humph's steel vault doors—two of them—took time to open; he'd be out of there before anyone else could get in! Why, they might not even try to get in; probably wouldn't, because Humph's doors were alarmed. And Harry wasn't going to set off any alarms—not on the outside, anyway.

It was time he checked out his distraction. He hung a "do-not-disturb" sign on his doorknob, double-checked that the door was locked, got out his suitcase and opened it on his bed. Four T-shirts, a black track-suit, a pair of soft black canvas shoes (a bit scuffed), a light-blue summer jacket, and . . . an ex-Army web belt, with canvas pouch attachments, a box of six tear-gas canisters, and nine fragmentation grenades, packed like dully glinting, blued-steel eggs in a three-by-three plywood nest of straw-stuffed compartments. The mere presence of the last couple of items would suffice to make most people extremely nervous, but the Necroscope had played around with far more deadly things in his time.

He put the stuff away again, went down to the bar, drank mineral water and sat alone, determined to remain mainly unnoticed. Beyond patio windows a swimming pool's lights came on. A party of British tourists was out there, hooting and splashing about. A pretty blonde girl came in with a towel wrapped round her, ordered drinks, smiled at Harry and said, "English?"

"Nicht verstehen," he told her, went back to his room and fidgeted. But on his way to his room he remembered to stop off at the gift shop and buy a pencil-slim flashlight . . . he might well need it, in the treasure vault under Le Manse Madonie.

His room had a small balcony; he sat out there under brilliant stars and counted satellites tracking the sky, until just after one o'clock in the morning when his patience ran out. It was still early, but it would have to do.

He put on the track-suit and black shoes, fitted the belt and attachments to his waist, stuffed the pouches with canisters and grenades, then tested their weight and his own freedom of movement. Everything was just right, yet still he felt . . . not unlike he'd felt before he "invaded" the Château Bronnitsy for the first time. But surely it wasn't as bad as that? Then: Harry had been full of mayhem, bloodlust; he had been going up against Boris Dragosani, a vampire. This time: it was "just" a couple of Godfathers . . . Wasn't it?

Also, Dragosani had been expecting him, and these people weren't.

But in any case, Harry's course was set; too late to have second thoughts now; he had to fund his search for Brenda and the baby—and fund it big—and the Francezcis were crooked as they come, and murderers to boot. That last couldn't be proved in a court of law, no, but the Necroscope was satisfied to take J. Humphrey Jackson Jr.'s word for it. He'd rarely known a dead man to lie. *Some* dead things lied, but not men.

He conjured a Möbius door and "went" to Le Manse Madonie, to that spot under the walls of the place whose co-ordinates he remembered from his second flash forward. And without pause he jumped again—this time a half-mile away across rugged, barren terrain, to where uneven fang-like outcrops of rock jutted from the stony, desiccated mountain soil like shattered teeth. That was far enough.

Using his flashlight, he climbed a few feet to a good vantage point and looked back at the dark, squat silhouette of Le Manse. There were just a handful of dim lights shining out from rooms built into the walls—servants quarters, Harry supposed. But the arched-over entrance to the inner courtyard was lit up by a battery of spotlights. That was okay; he wasn't going in through the main door. He had his own doors.

"Humph," he said, under his breath, "are you out there?"

Hey, I've been expecting you, Necroscope! The other came back at once. Then the excitement ebbed as the American asked him: *What happened, Harry? I mean, when we were talking? You were there and you were gone. You sort of faded out, as if you were being* blocked *out . . . but by what?*

The Necroscope frowned, shook his head. "I'm . . . not sure. I don't remember. I get this feeling occasionally that someone is messing about with my mind, and when I find out who there's going to be hell to pay! But for the moment . . . I think maybe I'd better keep a tight rein on *this* conversation at least. So it'll be just you and me this time, Humph."

How can I help you?

"Show me the route to the vault again—not from your room but just the underground part, the tunnels in the bedrock."

Humph was puzzled. *But with your talents, why not go right on into the vault?*

For the life of him, Harry couldn't think why not! He only knew he had to take a closer look at the subterranean layout of the place, "Maybe it's for later," he shrugged.

Humph answered shrug for shrug, and said, *It's your game, Harry.* And without more ado his dead mind lit with all the details of the snaking tunnel labyrinth through the bedrock under Le Manse Madonie. The Necroscope memorized all the co-ordinates he needed—including those of that forbidden nether tunnel in the very bowels of the place, where Humph had earned himself a reprimand.

Got what you want, Harry?

"Let's hope so," the Necroscope answered, and excused himself. He was going to be busy now.

Good luck then, Humph told him, his dead voice fading into nothing.

Harry got down from the rock. It was time for his distraction, a diversionary tactic. He took three fragmentation grenades from his belt pouches, pulled their pins, lobbed them left, right, and center as far as he could throw. Then he ducked down in a cluster of rocks and counted off the seconds.

In the silence of the warm Mediterranean night, with only the frying-fat sounds of a hundred cicadas, and the *toot-toot!* of owls to disturb it, the abrupt triple blast of the grenades going off one, two, three, sounded like the beginning of World War III. Shrapnel whistled overhead.

Harry waited until the echoes came rolling back from the mountains, then stood up. Sulfur and cordite stench came drifting on orange and gray clouds, while across the false plateau the lights of Le Manse Madonie blinked on one by one until the entire façade was lit up like the esplanade of Edinburgh Castle during the annual tattoo. There was even a searchlight beam in one of the corner towers, that began to sweep the ground immediately outside the walls. Whoever was awake—probably all of them by now—they'd heard the blasts but hadn't detected the source. And that wouldn't do.

Harry gave it a count of ten, then lobbed another grenade off to his left. This time, after the flash and the bang, the searchlight beam came lancing right at him. He sat down in the rocks and let it pass overhead. Unless these people were equipped with something extraordinary in the way of night-sight binoculars, they wouldn't see anything at this range.

A minute passed, and another; the beam flashed to and fro; a motor coughed into life and a vehicle—probably a Landrover, four-wheel drive engaged—roared into view from under the arch of the entrance. It came bumping across the rough terrain, headlights blazing. Then another motor snarled into life, and with a rising whine and the unmistakable *whup, whup, whup* of rotors, a helicopter hovered into view from behind Le Manse's walls.

Harry wasn't about to let these vehicles get to him, only to where he had been. By now every occupant of Le Manse Madonie would be looking—and thinking—out. It was the Necroscope's time to go in. He conjured a Möbius door, and jumped . . .

. . . To the location, the co-ordinates, that had come over the clearest (and the darkest) from J. Humphrey Jackson's memory: a junction of rock-hewn tunnels deep under Le Manse Madonie. Darkest, because this was a place that Humph hadn't much cared for. The Necroscope had felt it as the dead American had guided him along the route: his reluctance—even in death, and after all this time—to have to visit this spot again, however briefly. It was easy to see why.

The place was claustrophobic, soulless, empty . . . there was nothing here, except the junction of tunnels itself. Yet it was as if something listened. So that Harry found himself listening back, to nothing. Maybe it was just the knowledge of the *weight* of rock overhead—claustrophobia, yes—and the sudden notion that if Le Manse were a beast, these tunnels were its jaws; and the waiting for them to close. It was an oppressive place, evocative of morbid thoughts . . . but no more so than any deep, dark, deserted mine shaft. So Harry thought, as he deliberately shook the feeling off.

The gouged, arched ceiling was low, no more than six and a half to seven feet. Every fifteen paces or so, dim naked light bulbs were strung to the walls, bending away horizontally with the curvature of the tunnel. The illumination they offered was eerie at best: more a haze than true lighting. This was a meeting point for five tunnels. Stone steps going up, to the basement of Le Manse, Harry knew. And others descending, to forbidden regions, apparently. It was down there that Humph had got himself in trouble. Just for being there, without having seen anything. But Harry *must* see—eventually.

(*What?* But his reason for being here was money, surely? It was to fund his search. The two halves of Harry's mentality—conscious and subconscious, or post-hypnotic—met in momentary conflict, confusion, then canceled the problem out, solving it with a soft solution: the Necroscope's need to explore this place was just his natural curiosity, that was all.) But right now his need was to be into the Francezci treasure vault.

Yet still he paused, if only for a second, to fix this co-ordinate indelibly in his metaphysical mind. *These steps coming down from above, and others descending steeply into the echoing bowels of the place . . . And three other tunnels joining horizontally . . . The place was a labyrinth, just as Humph had said . . .* They *and* theirs *had been hollowing it out for centuries.*

Harry gave his head an angry shake, blinking his eyes rapidly, worriedly in the poor light. But the information had sunk in, buried itself in his secret memory. And now he could get on with the job in hand.

Seconds had passed, that was all. Up above, there'd be a lot of activity by now. But down here all was silence, or near-silence: the soft susurration of ventilation systems, a sighing of air through the tunnels, the muted throb of unseen machines. And the pressured tonnage of the solid rock overhead, of course—with all the additional weight of Le Manse Madonie on top of that—which *felt* like a sound in its own right: the mute but ever present groaning of stressed strata . . .

Two of the three horizontal tunnels were unknown quantities; Humph had never explored them. Harry "knew" the route that lead upward into Le Manse, also something of the route leading down . . . to whatever. The third horizontal tunnel led straight to the strong room, to the massive steel doors installed by the dead American some forty-odd years ago. But Harry needn't waste time following the tunnel. He could "go" directly to the outermost door.

He thought to contact Humph again, to check the co-ordinates, then changed his mind. Not in this place. He wouldn't want to disturb the psychic aether in this place. And so the Necroscope was on his own here; it was as simple as that. He went via the Möbius route to the vault's outer door—and discovered it exactly as Humph had described and pictured it: a hinged, circular, six-foot "plug" of shining stainless steel, set in a wall of rough-surfaced blued steel whose four unseen edges were sunk deep and concreted into walls, floor and ceiling. The great airlock of a plug was fitted with a combination lock and a massive wheel to slide the hidden bolts. You could only go through that door if you had the lock's combination, or a thermal lance with an unlimited power source, or quite a few well-placed high velocity tank shells. That was it. There was no other way—

—Except one. Harry's way.

To anyone watching, it would seem he simply disappeared . . . and reappeared, in the utter darkness on the other side of the door. He breathed dead air, used his flashlight, took two paces to the inner door, then a third pace into another quite invisible door which he conjured over the impervious metal . . . and so into the treasure vault of the Francezcis, the fabulous loot of centuries, the greedy black "heart" of Le Manse Madonie.

And in the first thin beam from his flashlight, as he swept the room, or rather the cave—the treasure cave, yes—behind Humph's less than impenetrable doors . . .

. . . The Necroscope had known something of what to expect, but that something was nothing compared to the reality. Wealth? Monies? The illicit proceeds of ten, twenty, or thirty years of Mob graft and greed, vice and crime, overseen or advised by the Francezcis? Well, in that case they had a hell of a lot of crime on their hands! But deep inside—in a forbidden place within himself, which was as much a sealed vault as this place—Harry knew better, knew it was more than that. Much more.

That *some* of this unthinkable, some might say obscene spoil was garnered recently was obvious. For one thing, there must be millions, if not *billions,* in high denomination notes of almost every modern currency: certainly the wages of crime—for what did the Francezcis *do*, that they could possibly have earned all of this legitimately? And if it was legitimate, then why was it here?—but that was only the actual money, and by no means the treasure. As for that:

Some of it was *literally* centuried. There had been pirates on the Mediterranean since the early tenth century, when Genoa and Pisa raided the Saracen shipping routes. Later, the Crusaders themselves had been attacked as their ships lolled westward loaded down with the loot of fine cities; and some of that loot was here. Statuettes in rare marbles and gold, crude ingots of that same precious metal, treasures from every era of Mediterranean history. But there was more recent treasure, too. Harry's flashlight illumined chests clearly marked with the swastika—some of which were as yet unopened! But of those that had been opened:

Harry knew of a wartime legend that Rommel's forces, pinned down in Tunisia in May 1943, had moved an immense hoard to Corsica in the hope of using it to galvanize the German war effort. The treasure was in the form of gold, ivory, works of art, jewelery; all of which had been "accumulated" in Tunisia, Libya, and northern Egypt. But none of it had ever fueled the war, if indeed it ever reached Corsica. The Necroscope knew now that it never had—for it was here!

But his flashlight wasn't enough, couldn't show him enough. Harry's mouth was dry; his hands trembled and he felt the sweat of fever on his brow; even the Necroscope wasn't immune to this. For it was greed—like the insatiable, incredible lust of the Wamphyri themselves—treasure fever!

To be here, alone, surrounded by . . . by a world's ransom! For a moment he could actually feel it: the way *They* must feel in all their power, their strength, their gluttony. And it was seductive.

Then, sweeping the metal shelves, chests, naked walls with his slender beam, Harry saw what he needed: electrical conduits looping down from the ceiling, with wires leading to light switches on a panel mortared to the wall between racks of shelving. It pulled him together, let him get a grip on his emotions, his greed-stricken senses. It separated his two parts, his two purposes. So that while he *knew* about the Francezcis in their modern role, he also knew about the Ferenczys in all their ancient horror:

Knew that the historical treasures gathered here had been amassed by the brothers' father—who or whatever he was—and before him by *his* forebears all the way back to Angelo Ferenczini, bloodson of Waldemar Ferrenzig and Constanza de' Petralia. As to how *many* forebears . . . that was beyond even Harry's mathematical powers to calculate, a matter for conjecture. But certainly this mad, magpie's nest was not the work of one man but generations. Generations of vampires!

The knowledge was there—clear as crystal in the Necroscope's mind—but only for a split second. Then it sank down into the limbo of B.J.'s beguilement and was gone. And, frowning to himself, Harry hit the light switch.

In the dazzle of the bright lights, for the first time he saw the full extent of it . . . and in his turn was seen!

In a tower security room, a guard stared from a half-open window across the plateau of the Madonie and watched the helicopter sweeping the far jumble of rocks and blasting clouds of dust over the sheer rim of the canyon. Then, sensing the glare of a viewscreen brightening to unaccustomed life on the security console, he blinked tired eyes and turned to see what was happening. What he saw froze him rigid, if only for a moment:

It was the strong room; its lighting system could only be activated from within; it *had been* activated, else the screen would be in darkness. But that was okay; it must be one of the brothers; *must* be one of them, because no one else was allowed in the strong room, ever. Except . . . the brothers were down at the arched entranceway, waiting for reports on the explosions!

A shadow—a male figure, dark-suited—flitted across the viewscreen, paused at one of the racks, picked up a small burlap sack and spilled some of its contents. Gold burned silver on the monochrome viewscreen as coins rolled this way and that. The intruder was plainly astonished; he picked up handfuls of heavy coins, standing stock still to let them trickle through his fingers.

Unaccountable blasts . . . both of the Francezcis in plain view out there in the night . . . strong room . . . *intruder!*

It all came together in the disbelieving watchman's mind. His jaw had fallen open; he snapped it shut to bite off a half-hissed, *"Shit!"*—then grinned as a red flashing light on the console told him that the vault's cameras had been activated along with the lights. Whoever it was down there, he was having his picture taken! One way or the other, he was already a dead man. And sliding the window open all the way, the guard shouted down to the Francezcis: "Intruder! In the vault! *Intruder!"*

At first they failed to hear, or perhaps they didn't understand, accept. But who would? Then it sank in. "What?" Anthony Francezci called up, as he and Francesco glanced frowningly at each other and began walking, then running, toward Le Manse's main doors. "What's that you say? In the vault? *What* vault?"

"He's on-screen!" The guard's voice was hoarse with excitement. "He's in the strong room!"

The brothers knew what it meant. Of course they did. It was one of theirs, could only be one of theirs. The bomb blasts had been a decoy. Treachery! But it was unheard of, unthinkable. To a man, these people were all in thrall. In any case, how could anyone even *think* to get away with it?

"Weapons!" Francesco called out, his voice booming into the night. He snatched his dark glasses from his face, and his eyes were scarlet. "Everyone up and on the alert. Man the walls. Any stranger you see, take him alive—or if you can't, then shoot him dead! In or out of the house." And pointing at the security guard in the tower window: "You—what about the cameras?"

"They're activated, yes." The guard shouted back.

But by then the Francezcis were into Le Manse and gone from view . . .

The Necroscope hadn't noticed the cameras in the ceiling. Since switching on the lights he'd noticed nothing, except the extent of the hoard. And even then his mind couldn't take it in, only the fact that it was massive and ill-gotten.

From stacks (literally stacks) of "lost" Old Masters—one or two of which, in rich gilt frames, were actually hanging on the naked rock walls—to the coins of forgotten realms; from the books and illuminated manuscripts of antiquity, to the jeweled ornaments of Byzantium; from pirate gold to modern paper money in bundles inches thick, Harry's eyes were drawn this way and that as the *mass* of it sank in.

It was far more than Darcy Clarke had hinted, because Darcy hadn't known. But the Necroscope did know, and knew what he must do.

The place had ventilation; he could hear a faint whirring and feel a gentle current of dry air being circulated. And when he looked closer, sure enough there were ducts behind the racks. Doubtless the system was an extension of Le Manse Madonie's air-conditioning. Harry grinned (for what felt like the first time in a very long time), and thought *Well, and why not add insult to injury? This is for Humph. Something of what he's owed, anyway.* He took two tear-gas canisters from his belt attachments, positioning them on shelving close to the ventilation ducts . . .

. . . But first he had his own needs.

He unzipped the top half of his track-suit and stuffed it to bulging with wads of deutschmarks, sterling, dollars; filling the jacket until it bloated obscenely on him and threatened to split at the seams. Then he took up two small, ridiculously heavy burlap sacks and hung them from hooks on his belt. It was as much as he could manage; it would have to do.

He yanked the ring-pulls on the gas canisters, backed off across the concrete floor and turned his face away. There came the threatening hiss of hot gases expanding under pressure.

Harry conjured a door and held it steady. He took two grenades from his belt, armed them, tossed them among the shelving. Wanton destruction of priceless treasures, but so what? No way the Francezcis were ever going to release any of this stuff or let anyone else see it, or even admit that it was here! It was here because it was theirs; ownership was everything.

He stepped through his door, exiting the Continuum *between* Humph's doors, in the airlock section. Quickly, he fiddled with the combination, until a red light began flashing . . . the alarm system, obviously. Then he heard the *crump! crump!* of his grenades from within the vault, and felt the bedrock give a shudder under his feet.

Another jump took him into the outer passage on the other side of the first door, where again he fiddled with the combination . . . and once more the red flashing light—

—Which was when he heard the shouting, and saw powerful torch beams turning the dim light almost to daylight where they lit up the bend in the tunnel. As to why he'd bothered to mess with the combination locks: he'd definitely developed a "thing" about protecting his talents. This way he was making it "obvious" that somebody had *physically* broken into the strong room. And thus it would be far less obvious that the someone in question was purely and not-so-simply a magician!

But in order to protect his talents yet again it was now time for him to move on, before the people with those powerful hand torches came into view around the bend. And anyway, there was somewhere else he wanted to see.

He didn't quite know why, but—

—There was definitely somewhere else he wanted to see . . .

THE PIT-THING—
THE CLIMB—THE EXAMPLE.

HARRY WAS BACK IN HIS HOTEL ROOM. HE DUMPED HIS SMALL BUT HEAVY BUR-lap sacks and unzipped his jacket into a wardrobe, deflating himself like a marquee with a snapped kingpost. Then, moving at a frenzied pace, he was out again.

At Le Manse Madonie: only nine or ten seconds had passed; the Francezci brothers were at the outer vault door, where Tony expertly spun the combination lock in a sequence that disarmed the alarms. But already Francesco was asking: "Why did he lock the fucking place up again? And how did he—how *could* he—get past us on his way out? Or . . . is he still here, one of us?" He glared all about, at the small party of thralls gathered in the tunnel.

They stared back at his writhing features, the unequivocal guarantee of murder written clear in his scarlet eyes and flaring, convoluted nostrils.

Tony had the outer door open; he made to step through into the airlock section . . . paused, lifted his head, and sniffed at the air. And, nostrils gaping, he inhaled frantically, disbelievingly—then choked and grabbed his brother's elbow.

They all smelled it at the same time: gas!

Tear-gas, in the ventilation system!

The lieutenants and thralls reacted instantly: they stumbled about in the tunnel, coughing and choking, blinded by their own tears, as the atmosphere became tinged with a trace of yellow from the tunnel's ducts. But a trace was enough.

Not enough for the Francezcis, however. Not yet. Wamphyri, they had more control over their bodies. The gas couldn't hurt if they didn't breathe it in. Their eyes wouldn't sting if they shuttered them with transparent membranes. The *membranes* would sting, but sight would remain unimpaired for a while at least.

Francesco put the second combination to rights as his men began to leave the tunnel, staggering away through the reek of the place, colliding with each other, their torches probing the misty-yellow, gradually thickening atmosphere. He spun the dial this way and that, and finally swung the door open—on an inferno!

Hot metal had set fire to paper money and burlap; shelving sprawled in twisted disarray; art treasures lay blackened, broken in the roil of dense smoke and fumes. Electrical conduits burned, sparked, sputtered. Flames licked up the rear wall and gouted on the ceiling, emitting the greasy black smoke and gut-wrenching stench of destruction, as fabulous oil paintings submitted to the heat. A *wall* of heat came scorching out of the strong room!

There were fire extinguishers, but many of them were damaged, blasted loose from their seatings on the walls. It took quite some time for the Francezcis to find two that were still working, and a lot longer to bring the wreckage of the treasure vault under a semblance of control. And of course they must do it themselves in the stinging yellow fog, through all the tears and blood and rage of their hellish vampire eyes—for as yet their thralls were only human after all . . .

Harry emerged from the Continuum at Humph's co-ordinates deep under-ground—where the American's unauthorized explorations had been chal-lenged more than forty years ago, and from which he'd been marched under escort before his employers—in that wide, spiraling stairwell that led upwards to the junction of five tunnels and downwards . . . to what? A secret place that no one was allowed to see. Which was why the Necroscope must see it.

It was very confusing. He told himself it was to satisfy his "natural curios-ity," but in fact it was to satisfy B.J.'s post-hypnotic command that he seek out the Wamphyri. Oh, she'd yet to turn him loose *officially*, but he knew her pur-pose, and it had become his. It would have been his purpose anyway, whatever the circumstances; but at the same time he'd been ordered to store away what-ever information he discovered—to "forget it," place it in limbo—until B.J. or Radu brought about its resurgence.

The result of which was that he was now here, investigating a monstrous survival, a powerful and esoteric branch of the most dreadful "dynasty" to ever infest mankind with its evil—the Ferenczys. And on this level he worked without conscious thought with regard to any outcome, but certainly with regard to his own safety. He was in thrall, but he was still Harry Keogh . . .

Down here, there was as yet no tainted air. In these nethermost extremes of Le Manse Madonie, the performance of the air-conditioning system was at its slowest, the circulation languid at best. But up above . . . Harry could hear the hoarse shouting, the crying of men scrambling for fresh air. And they wouldn't find it until they were out of the building proper, out in the night. That was good, for they wouldn't be coming down here.

On the other hand Harry knew his own limitations, too. He was sure that the tear-gas would soon find its way through the system and back to him. Where-fore time was of the essence.

He went down the spiraling steps through several complete revolutions, until he arrived at a door formed of parallel bars of steel set in vertical stan-chions. A warning sign—an openly displayed red lightning flash—warned that the bars were electrified. Beyond the door the floor was fairly level but uneven, and showed the natural stratification of rock; the place was a cave at the terminal point, the very lowest level, of Le Manse Madonie's excavations.

Well back from the bars on Harry's side of the door, there were twin, rubber-handled switches set in a panel bolted to the wall. One of these was marked with a lightning flash; the other was likewise pictorial, showing a series of horizontal bars. It couldn't be simpler. Harry threw both switches, waited until a mechanism hummed and the bars slid from left to right through the housing stanchion. The door stood deactivated, and open.

Of course the Necroscope could have simply taken the Möbius route into the natural cavern beyond the door, but he'd been interested in the operation of the mechanism; plainly the technology here antedated Humph's vault doors. Also, *this* door was never intended to keep people out—which gave Harry pause as he stepped across the threshold into the dimly-lit cave beyond.

There was a nest of supplementary light switches mortared to the wall; when he switched them on, a battery of spotlights high in the walls lit the cave with a brilliance that was dazzling. It took a few moments for Harry's eyes to adjust. Then he saw that the main focus of the spotlights was the mouth of a great circular well whose wall was of massive blocks of old hewn masonry.

The Necroscope took it all in at a glance: the well, its electrified wire-mesh cover, the hoist with its metal platform, throwing a gallow's shadow across the mouth of the well . . . or the pit? And the deeper shadows, sharp-etched, marching away into the cavern's unseen corners. But the walled pit was definitely the place's center of focus. And perhaps "well" was a better description after all; Harry could make out a thin mist issuing from its throat, vaporizing on contact with the cover.

That this place was a facility, that it was used, however infrequently, was obvious. The door, spotlights, hoist, electrification . . . all of these things spoke volumes however inarticulately. But what was it used for?

In the very instant of his inwards-directed question, the Necroscope was warned not to ask it. Too late; Harry's "natural curiosity" had let him down; his mental *guard* was down, and his every thought was like a spoken word to the dead. Of which Le Manse Madonie—and the "pit" in particular—had more than its fair share. They might have remained silent, but his query: "What was this place used for?" galvanized or even shocked them into grotesque activity. It had been akin to showing the long-healed victims of some hideous torture the implements of their suffering. Except it was much worse, for *these* victims were not yet healed.

The use of this place, of the pit? But they had been part of its use—as they were even now part of the creature *in* the pit! And while he, *it*, was not quite insane, they were—*driven* mad, because they remembered what they had been, and knew what they'd become.

The Necroscope gaped; his jaw fell open in that same split second; the short hairs stood up stiff at the back of his neck, because he sensed the coming onslaught. But this time—however strangely, inexplicably—he was ready for it. He somehow *knew* these people . . . he had heard their dead voices before, but had forgotten them because they were part of something that he had been *ordered* to forget. Now, however, he was once more performing in that earlier "mode," so that for the time being his subconscious memory was intact again. And:

Him! (The one with the small, timid voice.)

He was here befooooore! (The one who growled.)

He's back! back! back! (A voice that seemed to echo.)

He didn't listen, didn't run! (The agonized girl, her pain still fresh in her incorporeal mind.)

He must be as mad as we are—har, har, haaarrrrgh! (The utterly crazed one, whose "laughter" had sounded like bullets, and now sounded like a soul tearing.)

But all of them beating on Harry's metaphysical mind simultaneously, so that he had difficulty sorting them out; beating almost physically, great hammerblows of passion, rage, or terror. And not only for themselves but for him.

"Dead!" the Necroscope heard himself gasp out loud. "But where? How?" Again that question. And in answer:

Here! (All of them in unison, explaining the where of it.) *In the pit!* And another voice—like the breath of hell, like the croak of some gigantic, obscene toad—that cowed them all to silence in a moment, explaining the how of it:

IN ME . . . !

Contact with the group had been through Harry's talent: he was the Necroscope and conversed with the dead. But this other contact was different. It was telepathy, which Harry recognized in a moment. But how could it be, when its source was the same? They had the answer to that, too:

But we're part *of Him,* the terrified girl, perhaps not so terrified after all—or simply stronger, more determined than the rest—told him. *The Francezcis . . .*

BE QUIET!

. . . They fed us to *him!* She finished in a whisper.

He. Him. Something in the pit. Something that breathed air, creating the miasma rising from the throat of that now terrible hole. But . . . something alive? Obviously—yet when Harry had spoken to them in his unique fashion, *it* had answered him back.

THEY'RE DEAD! The thing told him at once, its massive mentality gonging in Harry's mind. BUT THEIR MINDS LIVE ON IN ME . . .

And because telepathy and the language of the dead frequently convey more than is actually said, now Harry had the whole picture, or thought he did:

The Francezci brothers—Wamphyri, last survivors of the dread Ferenczy dynasty—had *grown* something in this pit, even as Yulian Bodescu had grown that Other thing in the cellars of Harkley House in Devon, England. But where Bodescu's beast had been a mindless monstrosity sprouted of his own vampire flesh, a thing of little or no original intelligence, this construct of the Ferenczys was *hugely* intelligent! It gathered knowledge from the minds of those it consumed. It was powerfully telepathic; it was *in* Harry's mind even now, leeching his knowledge. He could *feel* it—its eagerly groping fingers—and slammed the doors of his mind on it, to shut it out before it learned too much! Its hold was broken; Necroscope and pit-thing stood off, "face to face," as it were, weighing each other up; Harry felt its awesome vampire probes fumbling at the outer reaches of his identity.

But while telepathy is one thing, communication with the dead is something else; while the thing in the pit could "hear" Harry and its "own" absorbed vestigial multi-minds speaking—and while it might occasionally cow those consumed identities, or shout them down—it was mainly incapable of anything but threats. For you can't any longer hurt the dead. And the girl, the one whose agony was still so fresh, seemed finally to have recognized that fact and *was* talking to Harry, begging him to:

Run! Oh, run! You're warm and alive . . . you don't want to be like us, cold and dead! So run!

"But I have to know," Harry told her, as he sniffed the first faint reek of gas. "What . . . what *is* he?"

He is their seer, their scryer, their crystal ball. He's their machine: they aim, direct him, and he gathers knowledge for them. Even from across the world! He is their oracle! *And more than that, he—*

—I WAS THEIR FATHER! The great voice was back, breaking through all Harry's barriers. But now there was a gasping sob in it, an all-consuming grieving, a sense of great loss, like the loss of being—or of the *control* of being. I WAS ANGELO FERRENZIG, FERENCZINI, FRANCEZCI. AND I *WAS* THE MASTER OF METAMORPHISM—UNTIL METAMORPHISM MASTERED ME!

Again, more was conveyed than was spoken. Much more:

The Necroscope's skin crept as he saw the seething horror of a grotesque birth . . . *twins, one of which was a monster from first gasp and destroyed at once. The other was Angelo, bloodson of Waldemar, and apparently normal . . . A thousand years of vampire life, until his metamorphism ran rampant, became a disease, reduced or exploded him to what he was now.*

If Harry had wondered how many generations of Francezcis?—then he wondered no longer. The answer was one: the brothers themselves, twin sons of Angelo Ferenczini, born toward the end of his time as . . . as a man! For as his disease had taken hold on him, he had determined to extend something of his loathsome existence into the future. Or . . . perhaps he had hoped to do a lot more than that, which was why he was now trapped down here and not free-roaming. For Harry had ample evidence of the tenacity of the Wamphyri; he knew that if there'd been any way for this creature to continue as "a whole man," then that he would have found it—*or would yet find it!*—perhaps in one of his sons, if they'd not seen fit to trap him down here first.

So, how long had he been here? Two, three, four hundred years? And all that time his sons inhabiting Le Manse Madonie, sometimes as one person and at others as brothers. Little wonder there was a long history of twins—for they were the *same* twins! They would live here for a while (until one of them had to "die" and for a time live elsewhere), then reverse the process, "rejuvenate," come together as sons and brothers again. And always there would be at least one "keeper" here.

But their father was Faethor Ferenczy's brother, or half-brother, out of a different mother, Constanza de' Petralia. Had Angelo not known—didn't he *know?*—of his sibling in a different time, a different land? And what of the long-dead Faethor? Did *he* not know of Angelo? He had never mentioned him to Harry. But then, Faethor had usually kept himself apart; his interests had been limited, divided between war and his mountain territories, and bitter hatred of his egg-son, Thibor the Wallach. Or perhaps the two *had* known of one another but simply stayed well apart. And anyway, what would it have profited Faethor to speak of this Angelo, whom he never met? And if he *had* spoken of him, would it have been the truth? For of all liars, there is none like a vampire: fathers not only of monsters, but of lies!

Harry gave up on it; there were discrepancies enough in the history of the Wamphyri, as the Necroscope had long-since discovered . . .

But though all of this—these incredible revelations, and the presence of the thing in the pit—was mind-staggering, still Harry had to know the worst of it. And through the first faint wisps of a yellow mist, he stumbled to the rim of the pit, avoided the wire-mesh, ignored his stinging eyes and gazed down the throat of the awful shaft.

Down there, looking back up at him through its own miasma, something with burning sulfur eyes quivered and surged . . .

Get out of here! the multi-minds urged him, while the Necroscope reeled with the knowledge—the vision—of what had driven them half or wholly mad. But: OUT OF HERE? Angelo Ferenczy was quieter now, his "voice" dripping sarcasm. OUT OF LE MANSE MADONIE? BUT CAN'T YOU SEE? HE CAME OF HIS OWN FREE WILL—AND UNINVITED. THERE'S BUT ONE WAY OUT, WHICH HE WILL FIND BARRED, I AM SURE! AND EVENTUALLY . . . AH, IT WILL BE A PLEASURE SPEAKING TO HIM AGAIN, BUT MORE INTIMATELY NEXT TIME! OH, HA HA HAAAA!

Dizziness, nausea, that same mental confusion which had left Harry so helpless on the road below Le Manse Madonie the previous afternoon, struck again! But this time he knew what it was. The mental *power* of the thing in the reeking pit—of Angelo Ferenczy, or what was become of him—was awesome. The Necroscope could only think of his own safety now. And he knew that the multi-minds of those that the thing had devoured were quite right: he should run, get out of here with all speed.

Harry staggered back from the pit amidst thickening clouds of yellow and conjured a Möbius door. It took unaccustomed effort . . . the gas was in his eyes and lungs; the multi-minds were shouting at him, telling him to run, run; and the ancient, hideously mutated Ferenczy was tearing aside the Necroscope's mental barriers like so much tissue paper.

Panic set in. Confused, Harry saw half-a-dozen co-ordinates displayed on the screen of his mind, places he could escape to. Such as his old flat in Hartlepool; or better still the Hartlepool cemetery, for the flat was probably occupied by now . . . or (most obvious) his hotel room in Paterno . . . or his study, garden, or bedroom at the house in Bonnyrig . . . Except he could no longer think of that last without B.J. Mirlu also crossing his mind. Everything was so confused and confusing!

The pictures in the Necroscope's mind were automatic, instinctive; lacking an explanatory "narrative," they gave little or nothing away. But the girl—the *mind* of the dead girl who had not yet forgotten the agonies of her dying—seized upon one of them and clung to it.

And: *Bonnie Jean!* she cried. *B.J. Mirlu sent you!*

And because she was part of Angelo Ferenczy, he heard her, too. MIRLU? RADU LYKAN'S THRALL? THIS ONE IS . . . ONE OF RADU'S? Then, his awful mind registered utter terror! His mental probes were immediately withdrawn;

they released their grip on Harry's mentality, writhing back from him as if he were suddenly white hot. And in a way Angelo was right: Harry *was* one of Radu's.

Go! The girl cried. *Hurry! You can't help me. No one can. So go now, if you still can. And tell B.J.—tell her . . .*

But Harry never found out what he should tell Bonnie Jean, for at that moment Angelo exerted his telepathic power over all the shrieking multi-minds and closed them down, and the psychic aether was empty as deep space. By which time—

The Necroscope was in even deeper space: that of the Möbius Continuum, where he twirled aimlessly for what seemed a long time, before a co-ordinate surfaced from the whirlpool deeps of his metaphysical mind and he fled to its source:

His room at the hotel in Paterno . . .

Harry woke up from an instantly forgotten nightmare, woke with a splitting headache, sweating and shivering and nauseous. But he fought it down and lay still, and in the light of a bedside lamp took in his surroundings. The hotel, yes. His room at the Hotel Adrano. In Paterno. Sicily.

It all came flooding back—or it didn't, not all of it:

Le Manse Madonie, the treasure vault, the tear-gas—*and the money!*

At that he came off the bed so fast it set his mind, and his body, reeling again. And his clothing stank of gas. God—no wonder he felt nauseous! He'd been hit by his own tear-gas! But the money . . . was it real? Nothing *felt* real. It all felt like some badly fragmented dream, as if something was missing. So what else was new? He hadn't felt right from the first moment he got to this fucking place!

But after he'd opened the windows to his balcony, and then opened the wardrobe . . .

It was no dream, and nothing was missing. Not of his loot, at least. A burlap bag slumped over on its side, and a handful of gold coins slipped from the rim and set off on their diverse courses, wobbling across the polished boards. Their milled rims purred on varnished pine; they thumped heavily where they collided with the carpet trim and fell on their sides.

And in the wardrobe where he'd emptied his jacket—*bundles* of high denomination notes! A suitcase full. Pounds, deutschmarks, dollars, in fifties and hundreds. And the Krugerrands: twin burlap sacks weighing at least thirty pounds each! Sixty *pounds* of solid gold!

And all of this money here in his room, in the night, in Sicily. Harry broke out in a sweat again. He wasn't a thief—but he was now! But so were the Franceszcis. And what the hell, he'd known what he was doing. And what it was for. But . . .

. . . He had to get it *out* of here!

He did, to the old house in Bonnyrig. Then returned to the Hotel Adrano, and lay tossing and turning all through the rest of the night, unable to sleep.

Rising with the sun, Harry checked out of the hotel. He didn't dare simply disappear, for that would be to invite investigation. But having checked out, *then* he disappeared—

—back to his home in Bonnyrig, where at last he would be able to set the wheels of a real search in motion.

In his house—which felt unaccountably strange and empty now, as if he'd been away for a week at least—Harry secreted the money away and began to feel a little easier. And then, to make up for the deficiencies of last night, he slept . . .

. . . But only for an hour, until the sun rose again for the second time in just sixty minutes.

It was the telephone that brought him awake; Bonnie Jean's husky voice inquiring oh-so-knowingly, "Is that mah wee man?"

And oh, yes, it was him. And he was hers, beyond a doubt:

The full moon, its golden light streaming down . . . B.J.'s strange eyes, undergoing an even stranger metamorphosis . . . and a wolf's head in silhouette, dark against the disk of the moon.

Harry said nothing, because her words hadn't been a question but a trigger. On the other end of the line B.J. understood his silence, smiled at it and asked him: "Well, did you get your finances sorted out? You can answer normally, Harry."

"Er, yes," he said. "I'm all fixed up now."

"And ready for a weekend's climbing?"

"Ready as I ever will be," he answered.

"Good!"

She arranged a meeting for lunch: 12:00 noon, at a little place she knew outside Falkirk, about half-way to where they'd be climbing. And she finished by asking him, "How will you get there?"

"I'll bike it," Harry answered. "Looks like a nice day. I should enjoy the ride." It was no lie; he would bike it—some of the way, anyhow.

He sensed B.J.'s surprise. "But that's—I don't know—maybe fifteen miles?"

"I'll be setting out about 9:30. Plenty of time."

"I'll have my car. I could pick you up?"

"I . . . think I'll enjoy the fresh air."

At last he sensed her shrug. "Well, okay, just as long as you save *some* of your energy. Er, for the climbing, I mean . . ."

"Oh, I'll have enough of energy."

"Very well then," she laughed. "I'll see you around midday. Afterward, when we're done, we can always put your bike on the roofrack and I'll drive you home . . . mah wee man."

Which left Harry feeling as if the world had blinked and for a moment he'd felt the darkness. But all he could remember was that he had a date with Bonnie Jean, and that she was innocent, of course.

But innocent of what . . . ?

At Le Manse Madonie there was hell on. There had been hell on all night. And unheard by the brothers' lieutenants and common thralls (their servants or "soldiers,") and ignored for now by the Francezcis themselves, because they were busy, the ancient thing in the pit had wailed piteously, continuously to itself for hours now.

And one by one the interrogations went on: the "household staff" were called forward one after the other into Francesco's private rooms; he and Anthony talked to them, threatened them, required them to admit responsibility for last night's damage and robbery. Or if they weren't directly responsible, to admit that they'd been seduced by some outside agency, and were part and parcel of the break-in. To no avail; but the brothers had known that from the start; it was simply something that had to be done.

Finally it was done. Le Manse's staff, sufficiently cowed but all perfectly "innocent"—or as innocent as vampires can be—were back at their duties; the Francezcis could now begin to consider, or at least attempt to consider, the mechanics of this thing. Which had to be the most frustrating, infuriating part, for it was patently impossible.

Francesco paced, while Tony sprawled in an easy chair. The latter looked entirely exhausted, but his looks were deceptive. Wamphyri, he was simply exhausted of ideas. But in fact he was the most "sensitive" or "passive" one, while Francesco had all the aggression.

"We should have Guy Cavee in again!" Francesco burst out. He strode to the hugely heavy curtains, looked for a moment as if he might draw them, tear them aside. But out there, all was brilliant sunlight. And throughout Le Manse Madonie all of the curtains would stay closed until sundown. The Francezcis had a woman whose sole responsibility it was to open and close curtains. No one else touched them, not even the brothers.

"The night watch? To what end?" Tony lolled in his chair. "He gave warning, while still the intruder was in the vault."

"We don't know that!" Francesco rounded on him. "If Cavee is lying, the thief could have been in there—and out of there—before he called out. If there was a plot, he is the obvious one to have been in on it."

"But if he is lying," Tony waved a slender, languid hand, "then he's also planning his escape from this place. Indeed, he would *be* fled by now, or dead by his own hand. For he must know that when, if, we discover the truth . . ."

"In any case," Francesco stopped pacing. "We have to make an example of someone. And again, he is the most obvious one."

"You're saying that whoever did this, he can't be seen to get away with it entirely? Someone must pay?"

"Exactly."

"But it will make no difference. We still won't *know* who did it, or how he got into the strong room without tripping an alarm, and out again—and out of Le Manse—without anyone so much as seeing, hearing, or even smelling him!" Even Tony was beginning to show his agitation now.

"Oh, I smelled him well enough!" Francesco shouted. "Tear-gas! In the ventilation! And grenades, in the vault! Uncounted—literally *uncounted*—billions in marks, lira, francs, dollars, and treasures, destroyed or stolen. From under our noses. At least a quarter of everything we held down there. And as if that weren't enough, he actually locked up before leaving! The impertinence of this bastard! Unbelievable!"

"Impertinent, yes," his brother agreed, scowling. "And we sit here impotent."

Francesco ground his teeth, and repeated: "We should have Cavee in again."

Tony's shrug. "He knows nothing. One look at his face says it all: why, he thinks he should be *rewarded;* he was that quick off the mark!"

"Rewarded!" Francesco snarled.

"And the cameras, ruined," Tony slumped more yet. "It was hot in there."

"Not necessarily ruined," Francesco answered. "They think they can save one of them—or rather, its contents. We can at least *hope* that we have this dog on film!"

"We do have Cavee's description."

"Hah!" Francesco snorted. "What, a true description? If he was in on it? And if he wasn't, what was that for a description anyway? A face and figure, seen distorted, in monochrome and at an angle from above?"

Tony stirred himself, stood up. "You know, of course, that *He* has been crying out all this time? There was gas down there, too. And he is, after all, our greatest 'treasure.' For without him, where would we be?"

"I've heard him, yes," Francesco rumbled. "But then, who could avoid hearing him? Raving, babbling about bloody Radu, at a time like this!" But he knew that it must have been worse for his brother, for Anthony and his father were closer. Then, in a moment, Francesco's expression changed. And turning to face the other, his eyes narrowed more yet and became red-burning slits in his dark face.

"Oh?" said Tony, wonderingly.

"We have to make an example of someone," Francesco growled. "We can't be seen to be . . . impotent, as you put it. Our dear father is ever hungry. And if Guy Cavee has knowledge of this thing . . ."

"He's a lieutenant," Tony pointed out. "Junior, but—"

"No, he is our *example!*" Francesco cut him off, grinning darkly. "Our important example. We can always promote another junior lieutenant, but we shall never be able to make a better example—of anyone."

Again Tony's shrug. "Well, at least it's a course of action," he said. "Certainly we need to do something. But I can't see that it will produce anything of a solution. However, and since you seem determined . . ." Grudgingly, he nodded his head. "So be it . . ."

By 11:30 the Necroscope was cycling through wild and gorgeous country somewhere west of Edinburgh. He wore his track-suit; a pack on his shoulders contained a pair of decent climbing shoes and some spare items of clothing; he supposed B.J. would see to anything else. Himself: Harry had already seen to something and got himself some expert tuition; or he'd arranged access to it, at least.

Not wanting to make a total fool of himself in the hills, this morning he'd spoken to the dead in a Bonnyrig cemetery and got some leads. The man he had been looking for was in a graveyard in Dalkeith. Harry had gone there along the Möbius way and introduced himself in his fashion; when the excitement had died down, he'd explained his reason for being there. Now he felt a lot happier that he could look after himself on a cliff face.

The dead man he'd spoken to had been a climber of the old school. Not a mountaineer as such, no, but someone who had made himself something of a local legend in his lifetime, as a rock-climbing man without peer. *No nylon ropes in they days, Necryscope,* he'd told Harry. *And I wouldn'ae be caught dead—ye'll excuse mah language—with hammer and piton in mah hand! Lord, no! All that cack wiz fer the so-called "professionals." Ah wiz no professional—but man, ah could monkey up a sheer slab o' a rock like a wee lizard! Lookin' back now, all eighty years and more—ah can't say, ah don't know—ah think it wiz the view pure and simple. Tae look doon on the world frae on high, frae a new place, ye ken, and ken that only the eagles had ever perched there afore a man? Ah, that wiz something!*

"Will be again," Harry had told him from his seat on the old lad's sarcophagus in the shade of a tree, breathing in the cool, calming quiet of the cemetery. "You can see it all again, through my eyes; though I can't promise you the climb is going to excite you. I'm only a beginner. I don't suppose my guide will be letting me tackle anything too adventurous."

A beginner, is it? Well, ye're in good hands, be sure, I wouldn'ae dare let anything happen to ye! The dead man had assured him. *Me, but ah traveled tae do mah climbing, Harry. Ben Nevis, the Peak District, North Wales, Derbyshire, the Dartmoor Tors, the Cornish and Pembrokeshire sea cliffs . . . you name it! But a wee climb will be better than none at all! Just gi' me a call, and ah'll be there fer ye. And don't fret none . . . ah'll no be letting ye down, Necryscope. No wi' a bump, anyhow!*

"Good!" Harry told him. "See, this lady I'll be climbing with is good at it. I don't want to be made to look, you know, stupid, that's all."

Eh? A wee lassie, is it? Aye, well there were a few good ones in mah day, too. Ah mind one who . . . oh, it's a long time ago. But she wiz the only one who ever beat me up a crag, ah'll tell ye that . . .!

And shortly it had been time to go.

It was only after the Necroscope had left that his new friend recalled the name of the girl from his time, eighty years ago, who had "beaten him up a crag." Then, he'd thought to call out after the Necroscope, but Harry's Ma had got to him first:

Don't, she told him. *My son . . . is in trouble. But we have it under control. We think so, anyway. The thing is, if he were to hear that girl's name . . . we really don't know what it would do to his mind. So let it be for now. There will be time later, if it comes to it . . .*

The old climber had asked no questions. Like most of the Great Majority, he'd heard of Mary Keogh and knew her reputation; that whatever she did on Harry's behalf would be for the best. But he really couldn't understand her concern. Why, that young lassie he'd remembered, that Bonnie Jean Mirlu, would be a long time down in the ground herself by now! What, after all these long years? Of course she would.

But because Mary Keogh had spoken, these were thoughts he would keep to himself, always . . .

The Necroscope had long since mastered the technique of vacating the Continuum astride his machine: it was just a matter of balance, of going from metaphysical to physical, weightlessness to gravity, darkness to light—"simple" things, to Harry. But he still had his other thing—about someone seeing him in the moment he emerged into this space-time. He had become *that* concerned with keeping his esoteric talents secret.

On this occasion, though (and oddly enough, *because* he was riding a bike), he didn't worry. For it's one thing for a man to suddenly appear out of nowhere, but quite another for a man *on a bicycle* to spring into existence. For a bicycle is such a mundane thing that if a man on a bike comes from nowhere, then it's a trick of the light, or the eye, or the mind. But it certainly can't be weird or supernatural.

Thus in only ten minutes Harry was able to cover the distance from his house on the outskirts of Bonnyrig to his rendezvous with Bonnie Jean at a pub on the approaches to Falkirk, by "jumping" stretches of the road ahead for distances of anything from a hundred yards to half a mile. If he could see the way was clear ahead—see with his own eyes the place where he would like to emerge—it was as good as a co-ordinate, and he could simply "go" there.

Finally the picturesque little pub was in view; he spied the place from the crest of a low hill, jumped to a paved service track at the rear, and emerged as from an avenue of tall, fully clad chestnut trees that made for a perfectly concealed "landing." A moment more and he had cycled round to the front of the place, parked his machine and entered.

Bonnie Jean was seated at a table in an alcove at one end of the bar. A shame, because it was gloomy; she could have chosen a window seat; but in any case the day was overcast. Maybe she wouldn't want to climb after all. But no such luck.

He slid into his seat beside her, said, "Hello," and: "It doesn't look any too hot out."

"It's ideal." She gave him a kiss on the cheek. "We won't have the sun in our eyes." He couldn't know that she had been keeping abreast of the weather forecasts and so had been fully aware that there'd be little or no sun from noon today.

They talked, about nothing much in particular, ate a light lunch, and Harry paid the bill. "A man of means," B.J. commented.

"Er, you could say that," he answered. "I'm solvent again, anyway."

She pulled a wry face. "I wish I could say the same. That place of mine scarcely pays for itself. In fact, I'm in debt." Then she bit her lip, for she hadn't meant to tell him that.

"How much?" he asked her.

"Too much," she told him. "Three and a half thousand too much!" And she sighed and shrugged. "It might mean becoming a pub instead of a club after all."

Harry felt sorry for her, said, "Oh, you never know. Something could turn up." In a way he felt guilty; for she'd been spending quite a lot of her time, her nights, with him. Well, he certainly had the means to put that right . . .

The climb B.J. had chosen was further than she had thought; it was some time since she'd been out this way, and never by car. Something like sixty years since the last time she'd practiced her climbing here . . . but the scenery hadn't changed that much. The place, in the sprawling foothills of Ben Vorlich, was

dramatically beautiful: Loch Lubnaig gleamed silver-gray under the low, unseasonal cloud ceiling, and Ben Ledi across the loch was a hazy blue silhouette like
a squat mushroom—the bulk of the mountain holding aloft a massive gray cap
formed of dirty sky.

"Shoes," B.J. commented, eyeing Harry's feet as they made their way diagonally across sliding scree to the foot of a jagged rock outcrop that rose almost
sheer for a hundred feet, to a saddle between awesomely carved spurs. "Boots
were better—climbing boots—but as you can see, I don't wear them either. Anyway, it's the soles that count. Good, gritty rubber to grip the rock. Boots do
protect the ankles, though. You'll remember, if you get a sprain."

"Thanks," Harry told her. "I'll try not to." But, as they arrived below the
crag: "Are we climbing *this?*"

B.J. grinned at him. "For starters," she said. "But don't worry—this time
next year, this will be like a Sunday afternoon stroll! And anyway, I'll have you
on a rope—this time. So for now, why don't you just sit there and watch while I
get the gear ready? I'll be a minute or two, that's all."

She shrugged out of her pack, turned her back on him, and went down on
one knee.

Harry wandered off around the base of a chimney that rose half-way to the
summit. Out of sight of B.J., he spoke to his friend in the cemetery in Dalkeith.
How about it?

The other looked out through his eyes, answered: *Damn me, but ah've climbed
here before! Ben Vorlich, am I right?*

Absolutely.

Well, are ye ready?

Harry peeped around the base of the stack. B.J. was still busy with her pack,
her back still turned to him. *Yes, why not?*

Off we go then. A piece o' cake. Just you leave it tae me, Necryscope.

And the Necroscope left it to him—but not entirely. He felt what the dead
climber felt, every nuance of the climb. And of course he learned as they went;
for it was his arms and muscles taking the strain, easing him up, ever up within
the cleft of the chimney; his eyes scanning the way ahead, taking in each and
every detail of the route; his brain, recording it all for later. And the old-timer's
narrative to guide him all the way:

*That crack there—a good wee hand hold, three fingers at least. And that split oppo-
site: ye can get ye're toe in there—but mind ye dinnae twist ye're foot! and that wee ledge,
Necryscope: aye, park ye're arse right there a moment . . . but on'y a moment! And alwiz
keep moving—on and up! And breathe, laddie, breathe! For it's the air that powers ye.
Breathe easy, Harry, in and oot. Ah! And see there: a piton! But dinnae ye touch it!
That's cheatin'!*

They were through the chimney and onto the outer face, and Harry felt
like he was actually haring for the high horizon of the topmost rim. Then he
scuffed loose a pebble that went clattering all the way down the sheer face, until
it hit the scree and bounced up between B.J.'s legs, where she'd just that instant
straightened up from her pack. Laden with a rope, hammer, pitons, she
frowned, turned, saw a trickle of dust from above. And she looked up.

Then . . . she would have called out—in astonishment if for no other reason—but was afraid to do so in case she distracted him. The *idiot!*

But "the idiot" was hauling himself up onto the rim, to sit there with his legs dangling, waving down at her! And B.J. too sat down, with a bump, on the scree, stared up at Harry and for the first time in as long as she could remember felt dizzy—from the angle of her neck, and from the thought of Harry's "solo" climb: the speed of it!

Then anger replaced her astonishment. The clever bastard! Letting her think he was new to all this!

Quickly, she shed her gear, grabbed her pack, set off back the way they had come. Thus she failed to see Harry reeling on the rim, and almost falling before he could regain his balance. Except it wasn't him but his guide: the fact that the old climber's mind had seemed suddenly to go blank, so that the Necroscope had been left alone, as it were, on a knife-edge of vertiginous rock.

Following which . . .

. . . The way down took a deal longer, and Harry could feel something of a tremble in his guide's suddenly uncertain mind. At the bottom he asked him: "What was all that about?"

A sick spell, the other lied. *That's what stopped me frae climbing, Necryscope: dizzy sickness. Er, vertigo? Aye, and it got me in the end, sure enough. Ah got dizzy once too often . . .*

"You fell?" Harry's jaw fell open. He couldn't believe it.

So ah did. But it's how ah lived; ah cannae complain; it's how ah died, too.

And Harry sighed deeply, closed his eyes and thought: *Now he tells me!* But he kept the thought to himself.

Likewise his guide. He, too, kept his thoughts to himself. The fact that he now knew something of what Harry's Ma had been talking about. For in fact his "attack" had come when Harry had looked down at Bonnie Jean. The old climber had seen her, too—through the Necroscope's eyes—that lass who eighty years ago had beaten him up a crag!

Well, and finally he'd got his own back . . .

By the time Harry reached the car, B.J. had almost, not quite, forgiven him. Her tone was severe as she told him: "I've a mind to make you cycle home."

"You've got it all wrong," he lied, but in a way told the precise truth. "I've never done it before. It just seemed—I don't know—so natural, that's all. Sort of instinctive?"

And by the time she'd got him home she was half-convinced.

They made love through the evening, but as night came on she had to go. "I've missed too many Saturday nights," she explained. "My regulars expect to see me behind the bar."

But as she kissed him and got into the car, Harry pressed a velvet gift sacklet into her hand. "Oh?" B.J. looked at him curiously, surprised at the weight of his present.

"It's very practical," he told her. "A little something I feel sure you can use."

And it was. In her room above B.J.'s, she untied the ribbon and turned out the contents onto her bedspread: twenty golden Krugerrands. B.J. knew their value! Her mysterious Mr. Keogh certainly seemed to have got his finances sorted out—not to mention hers . . .

* * *

At Le Manse Madonie, the "cleansing" of Guy Cavee's person had taken all day. He'd been kept fully conscious most of the time—a torture in itself; the Spanish Inquisition could scarcely have been more cruel—and like the Inquisition, at each stage of the process he'd been given the opportunity to confess. If he had been able to tell the Francezcis anything, certainly he would have done so. And in the end he did: let them so much as make a suggestion—he agreed with it. So that even then they couldn't be sure he was entirely innocent.

But they knew how to *make* sure. In the moment of his absorption into Angelo, the truth would be known. After that . . . his mind, or what was left of a mind, would be mainly his own again. But his body—well, there would be no body. Angelo's digestive system was that of the Wamphyri carried by his rampant metamorphism to its absolute limits. Literally absorption: he would not so much "digest" the ex-lieutenant as render him liquid, suck him up like a sponge, add his mass to the bulk of the unthinkable abnormality that was Angelo Francezci, Ferenczini, Ferenczy. A process of simultaneous internal and external homogenization: to make Cavee as one with the *active* body, the substance, of the pit-thing. The utter and utterly destructive rape and *reduction* of a person to protoplasm of . . . of a different nature. But the mind, thoughts, memories, would be there, not alive but incorporated into Angelo's mentality, giving him something of access, as to a piece of unfeeling computer software. Incorporeal, and therefore unfeeling, yes, but not without emotion and not without memories. Guy Cavee, like all the others before him, would know exactly what was become of him.

As for the thing in the pit: Angelo had been "silent" for hours; even Tony Francezci had heard or sensed nothing of his father since midday. It was possible that the intruder's tear-gas had entered the Thing's system, rendering him ill or even unconscious. But his metamorphism—which was all he was now, *a* metamorphism—would have no trouble dealing with that; and his mist, his miasma, rose up from the pit as before.

Tony had tried "speaking" to him, told him what had happened and what he and his brother were doing about it; hoping to bring him round, he had even asked for his advice in the matter—all to no avail. But as the brothers had had the now unconscious Cavee placed on the crane's platform and swung out over the open pit, Tony had felt a psychic tingle of expectancy and had sensed an incredible hunger; so that he'd known his father was silent for his own reasons.

Therefore, before bringing Cavee awake with an ampoule and lowering him into the shaft, Tony had tried one last time:

"Father, we need to know if this man is a traitor. We need to know who coerced him, turned him against us, against you. I know you are hungry, but if he is a dupe we need his thoughts. We need the names in his head."

Nothing—only the miasma thickening—as the brothers, and their lieutenants and senior thralls, edged back from the mouth of the pit. And then Francesco, ever impatient, stepped forward and broke an ampoule under Cavee's nose, committing him to hell.

The platform descended; the miasma rose thicker yet; Cavee began screaming as he came awake to his worst nightmare. He was tied down; his screams, denials, confessions, pitiful pleading, couldn't help him—nothing could. Then the choking, coughing, gurgling, and the soggy splitting sound . . . like meat wrenched from a bone, or wet leather tearing; and in a little while the mist rising from the mouth of the pit turning pink. Then:

AN INNOCENT, their father's doom-fraught voice rang in the brothers' minds. MORE INNOCENT THAN THEM WHO LEFT ME DOWN HERE TO CRY OUT, NOT KNOWING THE WHYS OR WHEREFORES OF IT! THE SAME ONES WHO NOW BEG ME FOR *MY* HELP! . . . *HAH!* BUT YOU MERELY SEEK ANSWERS, WHILE I ALREADY HAVE THEM . . . !

Tony waited awhile, then said: "Father, what threatens us threatens you. We need to know, else we can do nothing."

AH, ANTHONY, MY ANTHONY! AND FRANCESCO; I SEE THAT YOU ARE HERE, TOO. BUT DID YOU NOT HEAR ME CALLING OUT TO YOU? I CALLED FOR LONG AND LONG. AND DID YOU NOT HEAR THE *NAME* THAT I CALLED?

The brothers glanced at each other, and Francesco finally grunted and said, "That again: Radu, Radu, *Radu!* But he's long gone to earth and won't be up for a while, if ever. What has he to do with anything?"

OH YOU FOOL! said that awful "voice" from the pit, quietly but scornfully. WHY, UPON A TIME YOU BROUGHT ME ONE OF HIS—A GIRL—TO QUESTION HER. I LEARNED A LITTLE; NOT MUCH, BECAUSE UNLIKE *MY* THRALLS, RADU'S THRALLS ARE STRONG. SHE WAS BEGUILED; HER MIND WAS CLOSED; SHE COULDN'T SPEAK. BUT SHE WAS ONE OF HIS . . . AND *YOU* TOOK HER!

"Because you pressured us into believing that when he was up again he'd come looking for us!" Francesco snarled, displaying his objection to being called a thrall. "Because *you* fear this dog-Lord bastard, and transferred your fear to us!"

And after a moment's silence: FEAR HIM? WHY, I FEAR *EVERYTHING!* TRAPPED DOWN HERE AS I AM, I AM VULNERABLE! EVEN MY OWN SONS HAVE POWER OVER ME. BUT NOW THERE'S ONE WHO MAY WELL HAVE POWER OVER ALL OF US.

"His name?" Tony was eager now.

AYE, I SAW THAT, IN HIS MIND. IT WAS . . . IT WAS HARRY!

"And is he invisible, this 'Harry?' " Francesco snorted his sarcasm.

APPARENTLY—OR *NOT* APPARENTLY! The Thing had its sense of humor.

"And his master, the people he works for?" (From Tony.)

HOW CAN YOU BE MY SONS, AND DEAF, DUMB, AND BLIND, TOO?

Again the brothers glanced at each other. And: "Are you saying—" Tony began, only to be cut off at once by a howl of rage, frustration:

HE STRIKES BACK, EVEN FROM HIS LONG SLEEP! YOUR INTRUDER WAS NO COMMON MAN—WHAT, BUT HE SPEAKS TO THE DEAD!—AND HE WORKS FOR NO COMMON MASTER. YOU TOOK ONE OF *HIS,* AND THIS WAS HIS REVENGE . . . OR *PART* OF IT. Angelo was mistaken, in part at least, but his logic was perfectly sound.

"Radu?" And now there was a tremor in Tony's voice.

THE SAME, his father answered. HE FLEXES WASTED MUSCLES, AND TESTS OUR METTLE IN ADVANCE OF HIS RETURN, AND HE HAS FOUND IT WEAK!

Tony grabbed Francesco's arm. "I think he's right. I *know* that he believes it!"

"I need proof!" the other snarled. "Oh, I know we can move on our father's word, bring about mayhem in England or wherever, perhaps track this Radu to his lair and destroy him there—and perhaps expose ourselves, too! Not to any old vampire Lord, but to the authorities! What, centuries of secrecy wasted? Ah, and how many of our good *friends* across the world would 'flock' to our assistance then, do you suppose? No, before I make another move, I need proof."

I, I, I. It was always "I" with Francesco and never "we." Tony narrowed his eyes. But before he could answer, there came a shout from the stairwell:

"Francesco, Anthony! Sir, and sir!" A man in a white smock waved something excitedly. "Photographs! The intruder! We have him on film!"

And: "Proof?" Tony said, his red eyes lighting like lamps. "Well, perhaps now we have it!"

And behind them as they left the place, the ancient thing in the pit thought: IT BEGINS!—then relapsed into gibbering and darkness . . .

PART 6

Harry Keogh, Catalyst.

THE CALM BEFORE THE STORM.

I N THE PRIVACY OF FRANCESCO'S ROOMS, THE BROTHERS STUDIED THE PHOTO-graphs at greater length; but even at first glance in the cavern of the pit that housed their terrible father, Francesco had gasped, *"What in the—?"* before showing the badly mottled pictures to his brother. Tony's reaction had been more or less the same: not shock but dismay, that it appeared the pit-thing, old Angelo Ferenczy, was right. For he had to agree with Francesco that for all the distortion of the grainy prints he, too, was certain they'd seen images of this man before.

Some months earlier their sleeper in the British Isles—a trusted, senior lieutenant—had sent them a series of snaps taken outside "the woman's place" in Edinburgh. Just like these current pictures they too had been badly lit, mono-chrome, spur-of-the-moment efforts; scarcely studio quality. But then, they weren't required to be. They had been obtained "for information only," items destined for the brothers' file on one Bonnie Jean Mirlu, whom they had long suspected of being in thrall to Radu Lykan.

Now the contents of that file lay sprawled across a massive desk; one picture uppermost, where Francesco had thrown it in a rage. For it was clear to both men—or monsters—that the man in the Edinburgh photograph, and the in-truder pictured inside their treasure vault, was indeed one and the same man.

"A *dead* man!" Francesco snarled for the third time. "Him, the woman, Radu too! All of them!"

"You agree that our father was right, then?" Tony made no attempt to hide his smugness; he took pride if not pleasure in the fact that he'd been wise to take Angelo's side in this matter.

"Eh?" Francesco rounded on him. "And what difference does it make if that . . . that disgusting *Thing* was right? Yes, yes, of course he was right—but isn't he always? It's his function to be fucking right! And yours to bolster his bloody ego, or so it seems to me!"

Tony smiled thinly and said, *"We* were right, then." And before his brother could rage again: "Which seems to mean that we now have a feud on our hands.

You and I, and the people we control—all of us, under the, er, *Thing's* guidance, of course—against this elusive character in the photographs, his mistress Bonnie Jean Mirlu and her people, and the sleeping but by no means silent Radu Lykan.''

"Because of that girl we took?" Francesco was trying hard to control himself.

"That's what Angelo said," Tony nodded.

"This Radu: he goes to war over a thrall, while he himself is still in hibernation or whatever?''

"So it would seem."

"Then he must be pretty damn sure of himself!" Again Francesco's outburst. And again his brother's nod:

"Pretty damn sure of his thralls, anyway. What are we up against, brother? Oh, we now know what our intruder looks like—but how did he do it? Where did he come from, and where did he go? And how? Angelo says he talks to dead people!''

"Angelo babbles!''

"Frequently, yes. But at other times he's perfectly lucid. Today . . . he seemed lucid enough to me."

"Lucid *and* devious," Francesco snarled. "He took Guy Cavee knowing that he was innocent. This intruder had no inside help, and our bloody father knew it!''

"He was hungry," Tony shrugged. "As always. And anyway, it was your idea. Cavee was *your* example . . .''

Pacing to and fro, Francesco scowled and nodded grudgingly *"Yesss,"* he hissed, "he was! But anyway, it did produce results of sorts. We appeased the old bastard and he did speak to us—if only to talk rubbish.''

"Some of it, maybe. But we do know the intruder's name, at least. What, Harry? British, isn't it?''

"Probably." Francesco picked up the vault photographs from a corner of his desk. "He looks British, anyway."

Tony took the initiative. "Let's take a look at what we've got and try putting it all together. We've been watching Bonnie Jean Mirlu for years, but from a distance. Recently, because of Angelo's warnings, we've been taking a lot more interest in her. We could have had her taken out a long time ago, but that would have alerted Radu's other thralls and it still wouldn't tell us the location of his lair. So, we waited. More warnings from our father in his pit; we saw an opportunity to grab one of Mirlu's people, the girl. We got very little out of her—yet in a way we did. At least she showed us how strong Radu's power is over his people. Even our father failed to get into her . . . well, in one way at least. Or perhaps she didn't know a lot? But in any case she was only a thrall. Oh? But she was one of *his,* Radu's. And apparently he cares for his own, even from his secret lair. How we were traced, tracked down, and discovered after all this time . . . who can say? But we were. And last night the dog-Lord struck back, hit us where it hurts most. So, what use is money to such as him? But as you and I know well enough, in this modern world money is all-important! Especially to someone attempting to re-establish himself, who will doubtless build his own power base, his own army.

And what a wonderful irony—to fund it with the proceeds of a strike against his greatest, his oldest enemies!''

"But we were *not* his enemies!'' Francesco burst out. "After two thousand years? Radu's enemies were all dead long before we were born!''

"Perhaps you should have paid more attention to our father when . . . when you could have,'' Tony told him. "For to the Wamphyri, the blood is the life. And a blood-feud is a blood-feud, unending until . . . until it ends. This Radu *will* seek to avenge himself. Yes, even for alleged crimes committed against him in another world, another time, by an earlier generation.''

"Another world, another time!'' Francesco mimicked. "Myths and legends—and lies, of course. And tell me, how would our dear father know about that, anyway! What? Why, he never knew *his* father, Waldemar Ferrenzig! So what are his sources to all this Wamphyri history? What makes *him* such an authority?''

Anthony smiled wryly at what he could only assume was his brother's naïveté, his stupidity, his petty, argumentative nature. "Now I know that you are playing word games,'' he said. "Or you are being stupid and arguing for argument's sake. Our 'dear father,' as you have it, had centuries in which to research his forebears. I'll tell you something you don't know, for you were away at the time in the USA, Rome, Berlin. That was a most difficult period, as you'll perhaps recall?''

"What, the Second World War?''

"Exactly. You remember the American invasion?''

"Of course I remember. Wasn't I your go-between, 'Emilio' Francezci's spokesman in America? Didn't I bargain for Luciano's freedom, in return for a 'soft landing' for the American invasion force? And also to ensure that no shells fell in the vicinity of Le Manse Madonie?''

Tony smiled. "That wasn't all you bargained for, or with. Our dear father had told me about a plan he'd been working on: a saturation air-raid on Nazi-held territory north of Ploiesti in Romania. It called for pin-point bombing.''

"I remember,'' Francesco answered. "There was to be a top-brass meeting of German strategists, to re-direct the course of the war they were losing. This was a valuable piece of information that Angelo wanted passed on to the Americans. The meeting place would be the target for the bombers, who would then head south and raid the oil installations at Ploiesti. What of it?''

"There were no German strategists north of Ploiesti on the night of the 1st August 1943,'' Tony told him. "Just a village, or a huddle of rich homes and fine gardens. And in one of those houses . . . a Ferenczy!''

"What?'' Francesco frowned. "What are you saying?''

"Our father's brother, a bloodson of Waldemar, but out of a different mother—which is to say our *uncle,* Francesco!—lived there. As he had lived there for hundreds of years! His name was Faethor, and he was or might possibly become a threat. *Such* was our father's research, brother, that he was aware of Faethor without that Faethor ever knew of him! And such was—such *is*—his wicked intelligence, that he had Faethor removed without that he, or we, could ever be shown to have been involved. That way if Faethor had survived, he would never know that the bombs that night were intended specifically for him! But in any case, he didn't survive.''

"And I never knew about this? I was never informed?" Francesco's brows were black as thunder.

Tony held up a hand placatingly. "You were the negotiator. You were our liaison with the Americans—among others. If you had known, would your story have held the same conviction?"

"I arranged for the death of my own uncle?"

"Before he could discover you and arrange for yours, yes."

"I don't know how I should take this . . ."

"Take it as it was intended. Angelo—he and I—was protecting you, us, the Franczezcis."

"Without my knowing? All these years . . ."

"You were *away* for years! It was one thing, one incident. Why, I wouldn't have remembered it myself, if you hadn't questioned our father's authority in such matters. But it's as I've said: he *is* an authority, mainly as a result of research in his youth. Such research as led him to the conclusion that this was the way forward: *his* way—and *our* way."

"Our way?"

"Strength in riches, in secrecy, in ritual silence, Francesco. Why are the Sicilians the way they are? *Omerta!* Because of the Mafia. Why *is* the Mafia? Because of the Franczezcis. Why were we—until last night—untouchable? Because we are the heart of a secret empire of terror. And why all or any of this? Because of Angelo Franczezci's talents! What? But he knew something of everything, even of the future. And he knew that the bloodwars were not finished!"

"Huh! Francesco snorted. "The sins of the fathers, indeed. But out of another world and time? Did we inherit that, too?"

"Apparently, along with everything else. Haven't you enjoyed it, then? What? And isn't it worth fighting for? You say we weren't the dog-Lord's enemies . . . oh, really? but the Ferenczys have been his enemies as long and longer than you or I can possibly remember. When we took that girl, to examine her, we rekindled an old fire, lit an old fuse. Yes, and it's burning down even now, Francesco . . ."

"We have to find him," Francesco was paler than ever.

"Him?"

"The intruder. Find him, extract every ounce of knowledge, and kill him!"

But Tony shook his head. "No, we have to find *them.* And I mean all of them. The Lykans, the Drakuls, their aeries, their thralls to the last man. And we have to do it soon. Then—and only then—can we move against them. And even then in stealth and secrecy."

"A blood-feud," the other mused.

But again his brother disagreed. "I would call it a bloodwar," he said. "Oh, yes, for that's how hot it could get to be! Yet on the surface all must appear calm—the world can't know. We must use our wits, as Angelo used his. It must be something like that bombing raid on those 'German strategists.' "

"It is definitely coming, then?"

"It has come. And no use to plead innocence or ignorance; for just like last time, we Ferenczys are the ones who started it."

"Damn it to *hell!*" Francesco slammed a clenched fist down onto the desk top, scattering papers.

"To hell, yes," Tony agreed. "Or maybe to glory? We have the advantage, brother. Radu isn't back yet, but we're already here! Not only do we have the intelligence of a certain—what 'disgusting thing?'—but also of the Mafia, the KGB, and even our several contacts in the CIA.

"As for this Harry person, whoever he is: he'll be out of Sicily by now. But we know where to find him: with Radu's lady lieutenant, Bonnie Jean Mirlu! And we certainly know where to find her—and through her Radu himself."

"All very interesting," Francesco told him. "But haven't you forgotten something—like our vulnerability? We've been hit once. So what's to stop them doing it again? I mean, this 'Harry' fellow has to be a ghost! Indeed we have our father's word for it that he 'talks to dead people!' *Hah!*"

"We *were* vulnerable, yes," Tony answered. "But no more. From now on there'll be day and night patrols, guards outside the vault, men on the walls and at every access or egress; Le Manse Madonie has to become a fortress. And after that, if we so much as smell a stranger within a mile of the place . . ." He left the threat unspoken.

Finally Francesco was convinced. "Everything you've said makes sense," he said. "Especially what you said about intelligence. So why not put our contacts to use? In the past we've been in the business of selling them information, so why don't we buy a little back? Let's not stick our own necks out—or, at least, not too far—but have the KGB and CIA do it for us. Our father tells us this Harry is no common man . . . *Huh!* As if we didn't have proof enough already! But doesn't that mean he should be on record somewhere?"

"Good!" Tony was enthusiastic. "Send out copies of these photographs. If he's known, then we'll know him too. And meanwhile I'll look to the security of this place. We have a network, brother, so let's use it. But slowly, oh-so-slowly. And let me emphasize it again: the world must *never* suspect, must never know of our secret war. For if it did know, be sure the world would go to war, too—against us, all of us! Our father says two to three years before Radu Lykan is up again. That is when he will be at his weakest, in the hour of his resurgence. Well, two to three years should be time enough to find him. So I repeat: slowly, slowly does it. And let's be sure that whatever it is that's going down, we're not going with it . . ."

Harry Keogh, Necroscope, woke up in his house on the outskirts of Bonnyrig one morning and discovered that two years had gone by. He had known they were going, of course, but still it surprised him. From autumn to autumn to autumn, as if in a single night. It was the color of the leaves that told him; some of them were turning again—just as they'd been when he and B.J. had first started climbing together.

But two years? As long as that? Maybe it was only one!

And feeling disoriented—but even so, knowing what he would find—he checked his calendar. Two years, yes.

And again he wondered about his memory. Alzheimer's? God, no! He was too young for *that!* Echoes of Alec Kyle: his talent, and all his problems? Was Harry compensating for those glimpses of the future by losing fragments of his past? But Kyle's "problems"—in particular his drinking—had disappeared, merging with or being subsumed into Harry's stronger identity; and his dubious talent hadn't recurred. Not so far, anyway.

But two years! And as he got dressed, Harry tried to fill them in. He had done a little searching, for his wife and baby of course. Except now . . . he sometimes forgot what Brenda had looked like; and this time it wasn't any kind of defect in his memory. Not long-term, anyway.

He remembered her as a girl, in Harden on the coast; and school holidays . . . on the beach . . . the woods . . . long walks . . . their first fumbling attempts at making love. Then a blank. It was grief, but Harry didn't know that. It was as if Brenda had died, and his mind had found ways to forget. Forget what she'd felt like in his arms, what he had felt like in her. The adult part, the meaningful part, had been closed down. *He* had found ways to close it down, to forget—if only to get to sleep at nights—when he was on his own.

As for the baby: nothing. Harry just didn't know, couldn't remember a single feature of the baby. But except to a mother, aren't all babies like that? A baby is a baby. And what the hell, Harry Jr. wasn't a baby any longer (and had he ever been one?). He was an infant, almost four years old now: lost years, from his father's point of view. And Harry wondered: would he even recognize Harry Jr. or his mother if he were to pass them on the street?

But in any case, he *had* done some searching—personally, that is, and keeping it quite separate from the army of private investigators who were now working on his case. The west coast of England: Maryport to Blackpool . . . the Derwent at Workington . . . ''grockles'' in kiss-me-quick hats on fifty different promenades. Blackpool and the illuminations, and the tower like some garish beacon, its lights liquidly mobile on a rainy night. And of course, the east coast again: Whitley Bay, Seaton Carew, and Redcar; Marske and Saltburn-by-the-Sea; Whitby and Robin Hood's Bay. But all stereotypes—images, unreal somehow— scenes that drifted on the surface of his memory, unable to anchor themselves, as if he had never been there at all! Except he must have, for they were all places he'd struck from his itinerary. Yet if he tried to focus on any specific place or moment: nothing. And time and again he remembered catching himself thinking: *someone is messing with my mind!*

In the end he'd given it up: his search, the personal side of it. He would let the professionals do it. Except they seemed to be having as little luck as he himself. And of course he had to fund them all the way. Or someone must fund them, if not the Necroscope.

And a good many someones had; including the most powerful of Japan's Yakuza ''families,'' whose illicit earnings were such that they operated their own bank, and several oil-rich, potentially dangerous potentates, and a Czechoslovakian arms manufacturer notorious for his dealings with terrorists. So far it had cost twenty million pounds, or the equivalent, and the end was nowhere in sight. Another two or three months, Harry would have to top-up his fund yet again. But since there was no lack of rich villains, that shouldn't be too hard . . .

But the idea of ''villainy''—the word itself, the thought of it—was sufficient to bring on other emotions. First among them (again), Harry felt *himself* victimized; by whom or what he couldn't say. Worse, he, too, felt like something of a villain. It wasn't his series of grand larcenies (his ''fund-raising activities,'' as he liked to think of them), because in that regard he felt more like some modern Robin Hood; no, it was his adultery. It was his guilt.

And no matter how many times he reminded himself that his wife, Brenda, had deserted him, still *he* felt like the villain of the piece; like some kind of animal, yes. The Necroscope had never considered, had never thought of people as animals before meeting B.J., but he did now. For his sexual appetite when he was with her was certainly animal. Likewise hers! Love? Perhaps he was in love with her, and she with him. But wild? No "perhaps" about that! Together, they were wild! Harry told himself that for him it was a sort of frenzied making up for lost time—the taking back of something stolen from him, if only by circumstances—but at the same time he admitted to a fascination he'd never known before. No doubt about it, B.J. *was* fascinating.

And for her? What was in it for her? Just lust? Maybe in the beginning, but Harry felt it was deeper than that now. How much deeper, then? What if he *were* to find Brenda now? What if she should change her mind, decide to come back, and suddenly appear? Where would B.J. fit in the scheme of things then? And would he even want Brenda back?

Thus his guilt complex—if that was what it was—ran in circles. And the idea of himself as some sort of lustful animal who cared only for his own sexual fulfillment was reinforced. It perhaps explained his dreams . . .

Harry's dreams—specifically his nightmares—had always been complex things, but never more so than now. While he could never remember the substance of certain parts, the animal motif was always present; the wolf fetish (inspired no doubt by those events in London almost three years ago) featured strongly.

He would dream of B.J., usually when he was alone, and the nightmare would start when she was in his arms, gazing into his eyes. The moon's rim would rise above the window-sill, shining into *her* eyes. And they would change . . .

. . . *From slightly slanted hazel ovals, to feral yellow triangles, then from the color of gold to that of blood. And finally . . . finally they would* drip *blood! Then a swirl of strange motion, and dark against the disk of the moon, a silhouette . . . always the same silhouette . . . a wolf's head, thrown back in a full-blooded howl!*

Thinking about this fragment (for that was all there was to it) was sufficient to bring it back into focus, and sufficient to chill the Necroscope to the bone even though the morning was warm and sunny. Brilliant sunlight streamed in through his bedroom window, pooling on the polished boards of the floor, while Harry sat and shivered, and listened to an ululant, fading howl conjured from a dream . . .

He gave himself a shake, slid his feet into shoes, tried physical as opposed to mental activity. He knew what he would *like* to do today: talk to his Ma. (God, something else to feel guilty about!) How long had it been? Far too long he was sure. She would be feeling neglected. But how could he talk to her? There were questions she was bound to ask that he couldn't possibly answer. And if he guarded his thoughts she would know it at once, would think he was hiding something. And of course he would be; he'd be hiding B.J.

Bonnie Jean. The woman was always on his mind. Especially at this time of the month. Tonight was a full moon: he wouldn't be seeing B.J. After two years he knew . . . that she had her own moods—did her own thing, whatever it was—at the full of the moon. She was a woman; it was all part of her cycle, Harry told himself. And every three-month without fail, he could guarantee she'd be off to her beloved Highlands for three or four days on her own. Climbing, and hunting, no matter the season. He remembered her promise: to take him with her one of these days. And, in fact, they had already set the date: just a month from today. Well, at least it would be something to do, other than check the mail for endless negative reports on the whereabouts of Brenda and the baby. And so he looked forward to it—

—And yet, at the same time and without knowing why—he didn't . . .

. . . And neither did B.J.

But the two-year period of probation was up. She was satisfied that Harry had no ulterior motive, that he was under no other's influence. He was fully trained in her climbing techniques; not that she believed he'd needed extensive training, but at least it had been an excuse to keep him from the most dangerous climb of all . . . until now. For Radu had finally decided it was time he met his "Man With Two Faces," this oh-so-Mysterious One, in the flesh. Even knowing that this was not the safest of times, still the dog-Lord had insisted that B.J. bring Harry to the Cairngorms lair; and she knew that he'd ordered it in spite of the danger, because he now felt obliged to advance the hour of his resurgence.

Dangerous times, yes—for Radu, and for Bonnie Jean, and not least for Harry.

For Radu, because of his vulnerability. For B.J., because she suffered agonies of indecision, the frustration of her own burgeoning vampire, which constantly strove to defy and undermine the authority of her Master. And for Harry because he was the catalyst; several kinds of catalyst.

For one thing, Harry worked on Bonnie Jean. She was used to him now, wanted him for herself; she was unwilling to envisage a future without him in thrall to her—and herself partly in thrall to him? Well, possibly. And for another he worked on Radu. For the dog-Lord saw Harry as his future; as an alternative to the possibility of a crippled, diseased, incapacitated body. And finally he had worked, and was working still, on the Francezcis . . .

Harry's "watcher" had been seen again, indeed on a number of occasions over the last two years. Bonnie Jean had even seen him for herself; she had spied him one night through the gauzy curtains of her garret bedroom—an ominous shadow lurking in the dark doorway across the street, keeping his furtive vigil. And her girls had been followed to and from their various lodgings, so that all of their comings and goings, the tracks and trails of B.J.'s small pack were known.

Occasionally one or another of the girls would report seeing a certain figure and face on a crowded street in the gloom of a warm evening. It was festival time, and the tourists were here in their thousands; the Castle on the Rock was lit like a Christmas tree. Normally, it would be a good time for B.J. and the pack. This or that lone stranger could so easily disappear in the thronging night. Bonnie Jean's girls were good-lookers all. But now they were wary as never before. It was that face, that figure, that watcher whom they feared; for B.J. knew him. She'd seen him before—oh, ten, twenty, thirty *years* before.

Bright bird eyes in a rheumy wrinkled old face; eyes that one second looked gray and the next shone dull silver, like an animal's at night. B.J. understood that well enough. For they were feral eyes—thrall eyes! The heavily veined nose, flanged at its tip, and the too-wide loose-lipped mouth and aggressive jaws. And the gray, aged aspect of the face generally. But just like herself he never changed or got any older, and until now had been cautious not to show himself too frequently.

She had passed on details of this suddenly increased surveillance to Radu, of course, which had perhaps determined him to accelerate his rising. And now he would examine Harry, find out if he was a fit vessel for his resurgence, and also to discover whether in fact he could be sent out into the world as an agent and put to good use prior to . . . to his *primary* use. And even though B.J. was worried about the possible loss of her lover in various ways, the dog-Lord wasn't. For if indeed this Harry Keogh was the key to Radu's future . . . why, then it was already decided.

If he was the one foreseen, then surely he *must* be there at Radu's rising. Between times, no harm could possibly befall him . . . Not *between* times. Oh, the dog-Lord knew only too well that the future was a devious thing, but what was foreseen was foreseen; as fixed as the moon in its orbit. And nothing could change that . . .

These were "facts" which Radu impressed upon B.J.'s mind, just as she had impressed her own "facts" upon Harry's. It had become necessary, for the dog-Lord had seen the way things were going with his long-lived—perhaps too long-lived—lady lieutenant. As the seasons passed and the hour of Radu's true awakening drew ever closer, so with each successive quarterly visit she paid him, the dog-Lord had felt B.J.'s reluctance, her resistance to his beguilement . . . the way she seemed to be turning *away* from him.

He had known for many years, of course, that she was Wamphyri. But while he was fixed in the resin—helpless, vulnerable—it was something he'd been obliged to keep from her. Not that he doubted his own powers, but that he was unable to assess the growing potential of hers. For B.J. was that rarity among Great Vampires: she had achieved her ascension neither by transfusion of an egg, migration of a leech or the breathing of spores; nor by a "bite of conversion" (near-total loss of blood and its replacement by copious amounts of metamorphic vampire essence, the "natural" result of which would be undeath and true vampirism); nor even as her birthright. (For all that Bonnie Jean's parents had been "of the blood," moon-children, they'd also been common thralls and for the greater part human. Much like Auld John.)

No, none of these things had brought about Bonnie Jean's ascension. For she had simply willed it. Oh, there'd been more to it than that—the fact that her blood was "tainted" by more than four centuries of ancestral thralldom; her regular contact over two more centuries with a source of "purest" vampirism and lycanthropy, in the shape and form of Radu; the indefinite extension of her own existence at the expense of others—but in essence it was the truth. Bonnie Jean had willed it. Which was perhaps a measure of the vampire Lady she could become, *if* her Master were to allow it. Which of course he would not . . .

In the past—*for* the past two hundred years—B.J. had been Radu's lifeline, without which he could not exist. By now, but for her ministrations, he would be a shriveled, truly dead thing. In some millions of years when his mountain den had collapsed and his remains were excavated, men would wonder at this bony relic out of time, of which there was no other fossil record; this dog- or wolf-like man—Homo lupus?—preserved in amber. But that time would never come, for which he should be grateful to her.

On the other hand, she had outlived her span by a hundred years at least, and was still young; so *she* should be grateful to him! Well, and she had been, and loyal to a fault . . . until recently. For at last she had started to feel the influence of her own creature.

Radu had sensed it in her, he had tasted it in her blood: how she was torn two ways, between obedience to him and obedience to her "instincts," her burgeoning parasite. But more than this, he had sensed her uncertainty, her fear. Her uncertainty with regard to the future: B.J. knew that the Ferenczys and at least one Drakul were out there waiting; would she be capable of handling them without Radu? . . . And her fear of him. Oh, he had promised her the moon, but that was when she was a thrall. Now she was a Lady! And what about her Harry? How would he fare when Radu was up again? Was he to *be* Radu? And if so, in whose design? Would he have his man's body and aspect . . . or the dog-Lord's?

Bonnie Jean was a Lady, aye, but her thoughts and tumultuous emotions were as yet a woman's, set to raging by her parasite. But a vampire is a vampire, and a Great Vampire is Wamphyri! Already she had doubts . . . and in a hundred years? The time would come when Radu must deal with her, he knew it. So why not in the hour of his resurgence, when his need would be greatest?

The idea was nothing new; he had considered it before. But now it was more than merely a notion, it was a necessity. What? But she loved a man! A mere man! Radu had only told her to give her body, not her soul! That was his; or if not his it belonged to whoever it was who gathered them, when they were fled . . .

Now that it was decided, definitely decided, the dog-Lord looked forward to it: that marvelous feast to come! Oh, he had sipped of Bonnie Jean's nectar before, but to take it all—to take *her*, as he had so often dreamed of doing—to fill her on the one hand while draining her on the other . . . The thought was delicious! But he would save the most prized delicacy, the gobbet of true delight, until the last: B.J.'s immature parasite itself, to break a fast of centuries . . .

So he lay in the yellow glue of his sarcophagus, and surrendered himself to his leech's lust. For, of course, these were not the dog-Lord's plans alone but mainly those of his vampire, from which creature sprang everything that he was. Through his leech's talent, or its vampire influence on his, Radu *knew* how the future would be; something of it at least. For he had been given to see it:

The Mysterious One (this Harry Keogh?), *his eyes full of a weird and wonderful passion: his new knowledge—his new being, perhaps—in the wake of Radu's metempsychosis? And the thrall, Bonnie Jean: a pallid husk, all drained away to nothing . . . And Radu Lykan, risen from the resin, burning bright as the moon in his glory! And the world of men trembling, tumbling, thundering to its knees in the face of such a plague as to make the Black Death seem the most trifling thing . . .*

But not a man of them would die from Radu's plague, or not for long. For they would all be *undead!*

Not *a man* would die, no—

—But as for those who were *already* undead: the Ferenczys and Drakuls,

Radu's ancient enemies out of time, or their descendants . . . well, of course they *would* die, most certainly. The true death at last, for them.

For a solution had dawned on Radu; even a "final solution" to a problem as old as olden Sunside/Starside. That in a vampire world, which this world would be, the only safe course for a Lord of vampires was to be the only one! Let there be vampires galore, aye, but only *one* Lord. Lord Radu Lykan:

Wamphyri . . .!

The Ferenczys and the last Drakul had their own problems, one of which was common to both: Harry Keogh—except they didn't know him under that name. Or rather the Ferenczys did, through their father in his cavern pit, but Angelo Francezci seemed to have given them the *wrong* name!

Two years ago the Francezcis' many contacts had responded to a rare reversal, when the brothers had sent out pictures of their intruder, the thief in their treasury, *requesting* information! And over the next few months the answers had commenced to come in:

From long-established "Families" in Italy and America, and also from more recent branches in Europe: nothing. To the Cosa Nostra, the man in the photographs was an unknown quantity; he wasn't on file. From the brothers' contact in the CIA; nothing. Indeed, "their man" in the CIA returned their substantial "gift" in crisp dollar bills with the recommendation that the Francezcis "suspend their inquiries" concerning this man—which only served to make them more curious yet. And from their long-time contact and senior lieutenant in Edinburgh: a very disappointing nothing. He had seen this man only once, since when Bonnie Jean Mirlu had tightened her security. It was now more difficult than ever to keep track of her and the members of her pack. And as for the man in the pictures—he left no tracks at all! The Francezcis had answered by telling him to try harder, which accounted for his increased surveillance; and so far only sheer misfortune had kept him from tracking B.J. from her wine bar to the Necroscope's house near Bonnyrig. Misfortune, and the fact that she was now doubly vigilant.

But from the KGB, some eleven months after the Francezcis dispatched their initial request for information, at last a positive but baffling response. Yes, their high-ranking go-between with the KGB knew the man in the photographs; to prove it, he enclosed a microfilm of his own. The pictures had been taken two years earlier in the Château Bronnitsy, the Soviet ESPionage center, on the night of the Château's destruction by some unknown agency. As for the man in these pictures:

He was Alec Kyle, Head of E-Branch, the British equivalent of the Russian organization whose HQ had been the Château Bronnitsy! As a result of "extreme methods of interrogation," Kyle had been brain-dead (which, with no life-support system, meant as good as physically dead) when the pictures were taken. But he had been *most certainly* dead later that same night, when the Château was reduced to so much rubble, and a great many of its staff with it! There was no way he could have avoided *that* holocaust! As for the cause of the destruction: it remained to be ascertained, but sabotage seemed probable.

And a connection, however tenuous: the name "Harry" rang a bell. One Harry Keogh had been an agent of this same E-Branch, but he too was dead.

And as circumstances would have it, he too had died at the Château Bronnitsy, also during a time of crisis and sabotage in which he had definitely been instrumental. But that had been prior to the actual destruction of the place. The two incidents were probably connected, but if so the connection was "restricted beyond this agent's need to know." In short, he didn't have access to the relevant files . . .

The brothers had pressed for further information on British E-Branch. Three months later, a list of names (Branch operatives and contacts) had arrived at Le Manse Madonie—and also a warning: this organization was the most secret of the British secret services, and certainly the most effective. In the field of extrasensory or parapsychological intelligence-gathering, no comparable opposition existed; not since the destruction of the Bronnitsy complex—which perhaps said a lot in itself. But in any case, these people should be considered untouchables.

Which gave the brothers pause. Until now they had thought that their organization—their web, with their diseased father at its center—was the only one of its sort. And so it was, in the field of *criminal* endeavor. Indeed the report in its entirety gave them pause. For unless the man pictured on a mortuary trolley at the Château Bronnitsy had an identical twin, he was quite definitely the intruder in their subterranean vault; *and* he was the man in the street outside Bonnie Jean Mirlu's place in Edinburgh!

But if the report was wrong and Alec Kyle was still alive—and perhaps alive in his capacity as Head of E-Branch?—then what was he doing with B.J. Mirlu? Was it possible that the dog-Lord Radu Lykan had started recruiting in advance of his return, and that he was recruiting such as these top-level British espers? What if the Bronnitsy affair had been some kind of elaborate subterfuge to make it *appear* that Kyle was dead? And on the subject of death, what had been their diseased father's meaning when he said that this "Harry" spoke to dead people?

One further request of their Moscow contact—with regard to the Harry Keogh mentioned in the first report—produced a yet more thought-provoking result. Their informant was "embarrassed" that he must pass on such dubious information; but then, in his estimation, the whole world of ESPionage was a very gray and dubious area. The brothers could readily understand his reluctance. As a hard-boiled KGB double-agent, a very much down to earth secret policeman, his mundane perception of such matters was bound to be a narrow one. But to them . . . his information was worrying indeed.

For this dead Harry Keogh, an ex-member of E-Branch, was believed to have been a necromancer: a man gifted or cursed to commune with the dead in order to know the secrets of the tomb! The coincidences were too many; and anyway, the brothers Francezci were no firm believers in coincidence. Whatever was going on here it involved them, B.J. Mirlu, the dog-Lord Radu Lykan in his secret lair, and apparently certain members—dead or alive—of Britain's security services.

Enough! It had been time to set wheels turning. Eighteen months had gone by since the incident in their treasure vault, and their progress toward a solution and retribution seemed slow indeed. They had to know more about this E-Branch, about Alec Kyle, and about Harry Keogh.

·   But how might they investigate E-Branch, an organization of trained espers, without alerting them more substantially to their presence and their interest? Their father could probably help . . . the Old Ferenczy in his pit was after all their seer, scryer, oracle. But he was ever more difficult, given to rambling, less in control of himself. And if Angelo knew anything at all, why hadn't he already told them? They must see if they could find some special tidbit for him, something to goad him to greater effort.

Also, there was the list of E-Branch operatives and contacts, and on that list the name of a man who was not an esper as such but who was very skilled in the art of hypnotism. Sufficiently so that E-Branch used him from time to time. Surely he would know something about the organization? And if he did . . . then the Francezcis could *get* to know about it.

His name was Doctor James Anderson . . .

And meanwhile, on the Roof of the World:

Daham Drakesh, the last Drakul, had a certain advantage over the Ferenczys. He had known of the world's ESPionage organizations from the start. Indeed, he was ostensibly "employed" by one such: the People's Army's Parapsychology Unit in Chungking, under the command of Colonel Tsi-Hong. Through Tsi-Hong, he had been one of the first outsiders to learn of the destruction of the Château Bronnitsy. Also, he had been kept up-dated on what little was known of the activities of British E-Branch. This last was very important to him, for Radu Lykan lay sleeping somewhere in the British Isles. While seeking out his den, Drakesh must take care not to cross tracks with E-Branch. For just like the Ferenczys, he knew what would result if men suddenly became aware of the "monsters" in their midst! Until now Drakesh had been the most anonymous and secure of them all; he would like to keep it that way.

But some two years ago—by some weird process of synchronicity, at about the same time the Francezcis had been studying grainy photographs of their intruder—Drakesh had likewise received a set of pictures, a series of snapshots, from members of his "sect" in England. And he had at once recognized several faces: Darcy Clarke, current Head of E-Branch, Trevor Jordan, a Branch telepath, and—

—*Alec Kyle?* . . . But that was impossible!

Comparisons with photographs in one of Drakesh's numerous files had decided the matter. Despite a deal of evidence to the contrary, Alec Kyle wasn't dead. And the last Drakul had jumped to an understandable but incorrect conclusion: that for reasons known only to E-Branch, Kyle was now working undercover. In all likelihood he'd been "killed off" to free him from mundane duties and obscure the fact of his involvement with more important matters—or perhaps he had "died" in order to protect himself? But from what?

It had been a mystery that not even Tsi-Hong could solve; but then again, British E-Branch was a mysterious organization. And since Drakesh was in no way involved, the pictures and the report that accompanied them—about a peculiar event in London's Oxford Street—had been filed for future reference . . .

. . . Until recently.

But now, suddenly, E-Branch was hot again. The Ferenczys were known to be buying information on Alec Kyle and other members of E-Branch from their contacts worldwide; they had even sent two of their lieutenants into England to strengthen their presence there.

Drakesh had started to put two and two together:

One: the dog-Lord's rising was close now, he could feel it in his vampire bones. Two: the Ferenczys must likewise be aware of this. Three: for some time now the British E-Branch had involved itself in a great many hush-hush affairs— not least the Bronnitsy thing. Now they'd attracted the attention of the Ferenczys, in what connection Drakesh couldn't say. And in conclusion, four: since from now on it might well prove too dangerous to keep an eye on E-Branch, Drakesh should watch the Ferenczys' people in England instead.

Drakesh's emissaries, expert in discovering vampires, had found little difficulty in tracing the extra thralls sent into England by the Ferenczys. Through them they had also found the Ferenczy sleeper, and through him Bonnie Jean Mirlu. Moreover, they had succeeded where the sleeper had failed—for through Bonnie Jean they had also found Alec Kyle!

Both Radu's keeper *and* the supposed "ex"-Head of E-Branch together! Now finally it all made some kind of sense, and Drakesh believed he had the whole picture:

E-Branch was indeed aware of the menace in the midst of humanity!— something of it, anyway—aware of Radu and possibly the Ferenczys, too. But E-Branch did not yet know Radu's whereabouts, else they would have put him down and all subterfuge done with. Alec Kyle was their undercover agent, who had somehow found his way into the female thrall's confidence. Or, Kyle had been recruited by her . . . and if so, how many *others* of these damned espers had Radu got at? As for the Ferenczys: perhaps they were still safe, and were simply keeping a wary eye on the whole thing to see which way it went.

Well, Daham Drakesh *knew* which way it would go. It would appear that he was the only unknown factor in this entire equation, and he intended to stay that way. But for some time now he'd searched for a way to play the role of *agent provocateur,* and finally the opportunity had fallen right into his hands.

He had a triangle of forces here, all in deadly opposition, just waiting to be unleashed at each other's throats. The dog-Lord Radu Lykan in his unknown den, the enigmatic E-Branch, and the so-called Francezcis. If Drakesh could somehow bring matters to a head and set two out of three to fighting, the third might easily get caught in the crossfire. Drakesh himself would be waiting in the wings to pick off any survivors.

His "disciples" were in situ even now. It only remained to choose the right place and time.

But sooner rather than later . . .

"IT BEGINS . . ."

SEPTEMBER . . . HARRY AND BONNIE JEAN WERE DRIVING NORTH THROUGH the Grampians, en route for the Cairngorms. In the boot of her hired car: surprisingly little by way of climbing gear; Harry had turned out to be "a natural," and B.J. was mainly scornful of such equipment. And in any case she was planning to use the easy route to Radu's lair, on the Badenoch flank of the Cairngorms. That way she could save time by making a kill, food for Radu's waxing warrior, on the way up.

Harry was in "conscious" mode; he was for the moment himself, and not under any mental constraints other than the deep-seated post-hypnotic commands of James Anderson, and those of Bonnie Jean herself, of course. In short, he continued to hide his talents as best he could, and B.J. continued to be an "innocent" but strong- or wrong-headed young woman. She was also his lover, and Harry was loyal to a fault, or things might not be so easy for her . . . or so hard. Radu had been partly right: there *were* other ways to enthrall a man—but some swords are two-edged.

Physically, the Necroscope was fit and well. But mentally or subconsciously . . .

He was constantly uneasy. His worries, mainly unspecified—which seemed something of a contradiction in itself!—were many. And despite that he hid it from B.J. as far as possible, he often felt . . . paranoid? That was the only way to describe it: the omnipresent feeling that he was the victim of some malicious plot. His memory, however, was much improved—especially since giving up his search for Brenda on a personal level. On the other hand, his sleep continued to be plagued by grotesque nightmares he could *never* remember in his waking hours but which he knew had grown worse than ever.

All he ever recalled of them was that they involved the Great Majority, the teeming dead, who were desperately trying to convey some message which he wasn't allowed to receive; and a picture of his beloved Ma, her face filled with concern, and her arms thrown wide open as if to protect him from the tumult of their thoughts. And lingering over as he struggled to bring himself awake, always there would be that familiar moon *motif,* with a howling wolf's head in silhouette.

Oddly, these dreams didn't come when he slept with Bonnie Jean; she seemed to act as a buffer against them. And something of a paradox, too, that in the conscious, waking world he found the dead less inclined to his company, while sensing in them an air of expectancy hard to define . . .

"Penny for them?" said Bonnie Jean, luring the Necroscope from his inward-probing thoughts. She spoke mainly to fill the unaccustomed vacuum between them, an emptiness which—in her case, at least—felt like an ache in her bones, growing there from the moment Radu had told her to bring Harry to him.

"A total blank," he lied, not wanting to worry her. "I was just lying back enjoying it."

"The ride? You can drive if you like." (On the other hand, it would be better if he didn't. They were traveling north and it was past noon. If she let him drive, she would be uncomfortable in the warm sunlight coming through his window.)

He shook his head, elevated his seat a little, sat up and glanced out of the window. Almost unnoticed, summer had slipped quietly away and made room for autumn. The trees were beginning to shed their leaves: red, gold, and umber, slipping by outside the car, and the occasional glossy blur of an evergreen. "Where are we?"

"I chose a different route . . . er, from my usual one," she began to explain, then realized there was no need; Harry hadn't been out this way before. Anywhere north of the Firth of Forth would be new to him. "I just thought—I don't know—a change of scenery?" She fiddled with her sunglasses, adjusting them on the bridge of her nose. The real reason she was taking a different route was to break the routine and confuse anyone, such as the watcher, who might try to follow her. Also, since she had rarely if ever sensed an intrusion during daylight hours, it had seemed a good idea to make the trip in daylight.

"A change of scenery?" he said. "Well, that's *why* we're here. But I asked where."

"We're through Blairgowrie, heading for Pitlochry," she told him. "Does that help?"

"Shouldn't have asked," he shrugged. And, showing a rare flash of humor: "It's all Irish to me!"

"Scottish!" she admonished. But the smile as quickly fell from her face, too. And she wondered what he was really thinking, the man *inside* this man. For the man inside knew why they were here, where they were going, and who he would be meeting. But the man inside was a prisoner in his own mind-cell, and he couldn't be set free—couldn't think his real thoughts—except by special command.

To Bonnie Jean . . . suddenly Harry seemed much less than a whole man. He felt like some kind of zombie sitting here beside her—or a puppet waiting to jerk into life the moment she pulled his strings—and *she* felt guilty; she didn't like it. But the fact of the matter was he would only become a zombie, or a puppet, if and when she commanded it. Then he would know, would remember, everything she had told him . . . and not be able to do a damned thing about it! He was so *much* under her control that she felt sorry for him.

But at the same time . . . maybe something of understanding had surfaced at that. The atmosphere between them felt unusual, uneasy, unnatural. And now and then, if she looked at him suddenly out of the corner of her eye—

—Was that an accusing look on Harry's face? If she were a faithless wife, it might be just exactly the sort of curious, vaguely doubting look she would expect from a husband who half-suspected. Or was she just imagining it?

"Oh?" Harry raised an eyebrow. He'd caught her giving *him* just such a look as she'd imagined!

"Just wondering," she said. And before he could ask what: "After Pitlochry, within the hour, we should be back on my usual route and into the Forest of Atholl. Plenty of places along the way to stop and picnic, if you like? Or maybe a little café in the woods, for tea?" It all sounded so weak, so . . . treacherous? Even to her own ears, yes. Or especially so.

"Whatever you say," he said—which for some reason irritated her out of her mind. Bad enough that it was "whatever she said" when he was totally under her influence. But here he was like . . . like a *lamb* on his way to the slaughter! And maybe not now, not this time, but soon, too soon, he really would be!

"Do you put that much bloody faith in me, then?" she blurted, glaring at him. "Whatever I fucking say?"

He was taken by surprise. "Why, yes. Why not?"

Oh, mah wee man! B.J. cried out . . . to herself, yet still managing to surprise herself. If only it were possible to break the chains on his mind and set it free— set him free—to fly, fly like a small frightened bird! It would be worth . . . almost anything! She thought it, and at once denied the thought:

What, and betray a cause she'd worked for for two hundred years? And defy her master, Radu? And throw away her own chance of immortality? And prove once and for all and beyond any reasonable doubt that she could never be a Lady, Wamphyri, but must always be a sniveling . . . woman!? Ridiculous!

It was her immature leech fighting back; fighting for its life against a power as strong as anything it ever met before, which it didn't, couldn't possibly, understand. Bonnie Jean's emotions boiled over; she glanced at Harry; he had turned his face away to look out of his window. Damn, he was simply ignoring her outburst! As if she were a child! Probably because he subconsciously understood only too well what was going on.

And there and then—in broad daylight, even at the wheel of the car—B.J. felt the change coming and couldn't stop it. It was as though she stood outside herself, watching in horror, frozen by her own hypnotic talent! She could even *feel* the eye-teeth—her *dog*teeth—curving up through pink-sheathing gums, cutting the flesh! She could taste the blood on her gums. *Her* blood, as yet . . .

Harry glanced ahead, jerked upright, cried: "Christ—*the road . . .!*"

And the Lady in her was banished, and B.J. back in charge. For now at least.

She slammed on the brakes, hauled on the wheel, almost physically dragged the car round a sharp left-hand bend. Harry was thrown against her, and as they collided B.J. came close to losing her sunglasses. She knew her eyes would be crimson, but had to put every effort into bringing the car to a halt. The right-hand wheels bumped up onto the grass verge; the hedgerow made a sharp scraping against her window; her driving mirror was bent back. And the car stopped . . .

The Necroscope collapsed his Möbius door where he had instinctively conjured it across the dashboard. It had been a close thing. If they had crashed, been thrown forward . . . by now they would be in the Möbius Continuum! Nothing he could have said or done would have fooled Bonnie Jean this time. No "drug-induced hallucination" would have covered it.

He wiped the sweat from his brow and said, "Did I say something?"

B.J. thumped the steering wheel with both hands, glared at him—and burst out laughing! Then, in the mirror, she saw the blood on her lower lip and sucked it inside her mouth.

"Hurt?" he said, at once solicitous.

"I bit my lip," she lied. "You?"

He shook his head. "What happened?"

"I wasn't paying attention to my driving," she answered. "I suppose I'm just a bad driver, that's all." *A bad-tempered driver, anyway.*

"Let's get on to the Forest of Atholl, then," he said. "I could use a cup of tea now—not to mention a leak!" Which set her off laughing again.

A few minutes later, cresting the next wave of foothills, B.J. saw the rim of a full moon, so pale it was almost transparent, rising over a hazy, blue-pastelled horizon. Perhaps it explained something. She hoped so, anyway . . .

They found a tea shop, sat outside under the trees, relaxed a little. And as they sat there, Bonnie Jean sighed and surrendered her problems to fate. What would be, would be. And anyway, who could second-guess the future? But this man, this Harry—oh, his attraction, his *power* over her was strong. She knew it could be argued that hers over him was stronger, but hers was artificial. Some of it. How much was real, she wondered?

She lay back in her chair, eyes closed behind the lenses of her sunglasses, and said, "Harry, you know you haven't mentioned her in a long time."

When he failed to answer, she opened her eyes a crack to squint at him. He was frowning, staring at a long low station-wagon where it had just pulled into the car park opposite the tea shop. She followed his gaze. "Something?"

Harry didn't answer, just sat there staring. But as the occupants of the vehicle got out and headed up the path under the trees to the tea house, he averted his eyes, turning them on Bonnie Jean instead. And when the shuffling single-file of red-robed Asiatics had passed, he said: "I saw this bunch, or one like it, in London once. Other places, too."

"Hari Krishna types," she said, shrugging. "Pretty harmless, really. Do they bother you?"

The tinkling of tiny golden bells faded and died away as the group went into the café. Harry came back to life, smiled and said: "Bother me? Not much. They don't talk to you or look at you. There's no eye-contact. They just do their own thing."

But after that he couldn't seem to relax, and by the time the red-robes had come out of the tea shop and found themselves a table he was ready to move on. And B.J. noticed as they drove away how the frown was back on his face . . . how he kept staring into his rearview mirror long after the tea shop sign had disappeared into the distance behind them . . .

The roads were good and traffic light to nonexistent, but after their near-accident B.J. was taking it easy. If there was even the suspicion of a scenic "short-cut" she would take it. And the closer she got to her destination the slower she went, stopping off at the slightest excuse—for the view, or a chance to dabble her feet in cool water over rounded pebbles—whatever. They even pulled off the road and slept for an hour, cuddled up on a patch of heather in the lee of tall rocks, where Harry had to fix a blanket over a couple of dead branches for shade. He'd done so protesting that there was hardly enough heat in the sun to bother with it, but B.J. was "afraid of sunburn."

Finally, as they covered the last few miles to Inverdruie, the light began to fade, the mist crept up from the streams and writhed in the copses, and the wooded slopes took on a cloaked, mystical look out of legend. The lights of cottages clustering at junctions and crossroads twinkled like elf-fires, while the backdrop of the mountains, black against an indigo "v" of starstrewn sky seen through the pass, might easily be the façade of a gigantic set on some cosmic stage.

"The gloaming," B.J. commented, as she pulled off the road and turned tightly behind Auld John's cottage, parking the hire car in the shadows of birch and rowan.

"In which," the Necroscope whisperingly answered, "all the Jocks go a-roaming!"

"The wee lads and lassies, aye!" Laughing lightly, she got out of the car. (Ah, but if only her heart were as light as her laughter.)

And what about his . . . ?

Harry didn't quite know what to make of Auld John, but then he didn't quite know what to make of anything right now. His heart seemed to spend most of its time in his mouth (which was why he made jokes whenever he could), and his nerves were stretched to breaking. He supposed it was some kind of paranoia, the latest attack of this ridiculous persecution complex.

But Auld John was . . . something else. B.J. had told Harry that the old gillie used to work for her uncle—the one with the hunting lodge—and that while he was very respectful and trustworthy he was also very proper. And maybe just a bit peculiar? Understatements on all counts. Harry thought.

The old man didn't grovel but he came close. And not just to Bonnie Jean but also to the Necroscope. Bowing and scraping, he was very nearly obsequious—almost like a cringing dog who wants so badly to be petted but thinks he might be kicked. But as for proper: no doubt about it!

When Bonnie Jean went up to her tiny garret bedroom, the old man stayed downstairs with Harry; in B.J.'s absence he referred to her as "the wee mistress: a *verah* special lady!" Well, and so she might have been once upon a time, Harry supposed—when she'd used to stay at her uncle's lodge . . .

After a while B.J. called Auld John upstairs and for ten minutes or so Harry could hear them talking but couldn't make out what was said. Then Auld John came down again and offered him a nightcap—"A wee dram shid put ye away nicely, aye! A guid nicht's sleep cannae hurt a man.'' Maybe not, but the Necroscope refused anyway. If he was climbing tomorrow, he would need a clear head.

And when Auld John took Harry upstairs, he made a point of showing him the toilet, directly opposite the Necroscope's tiny room. ''Just so's ye cannae be mistaken . . . ye ken?'' Yes, he kenned well enough. And the wee mistress's room was at the other end of the corridor, with all those creaking floorboards in between. Wherever Auld John was in the house, he'd be sure to hear those boards.

But in fact they didn't creak once. B.J. was far lighter on her feet than Harry. And the way she was able to maneuver her way around a dark house was quite remarkable.

So thought the Necroscope . . . while deep inside he didn't find it remarkable at all. But he was glad she came anyway, on this night of all nights. It seemed to have meaning other than sex. Indeed it must have, since they didn't make love but were content enough simply to lie in each other's arms . . .

The morning was gray, overcast, and B.J. seemed pleased and in fairly good spirits. Pleased with the weather, anyway. The Necroscope couldn't say how he felt: ''odd'' might best describe it. They breakfasted, took Auld John's car—B.J. didn't say why—and headed southwest along a road that paralleled the Spey on their right and the Cairngorms on their left. It was early and the roads through the valley were empty.

''How far?'' Harry asked as they turned onto the main road. His voice and mood were very subdued.

''Just three or four miles,'' she told him . . . and then because she had been doing a lot of thinking and dreaming during the night, she abruptly changed the subject. ''Harry, would you mind telling me your thoughts about life?''

''Life?'' He was looking in his rearview mirror again.

''Birth, life, death: the whole thing. I mean, how do you view it? You're still young—*we* are young—but we get old, we die, and it's all over.''

Harry knew all about that—knew how wrong she was, that death wasn't the end, and it wasn't ''all over''—but that was something he couldn't talk about. Right now, though, he *could* lie; because without consciously thinking about it, *he* was in control of himself. But maybe he didn't have to lie. ''That's a bit morbid, isn't it?'' he said. ''What's brought this on?''

''Oh, I don't know,'' she answered, trying to find a way to explain. ''It's just that as we get older, we seem to leave so much behind. Family, friends, even lovers—especially lovers. One partner is older, or gets old faster, and dies faster, and leaves the other to go on. It seems unfair, makes having someone to love seem pointless. Doesn't it?''

''Is this us you're talking about? Are you worrying about the future?''

She sighed and said, ''I ask a question, and you answer it with a question!'' She could switch him on, of course, and find out how he felt that way. But in their situation that would be . . . unfair? And what if she didn't *like* the way he felt? But:

''Very well, if it's important to you,'' he said. ''The way I see it, life is some kind of learning process. We are born, and we don't know anything except we're hungry. We grow older, and we start to learn things. Eventually we're 'educated'; we figure we know everything! Except life isn't like that. The older we get the more there is to understand, and less time to understand it. So that by the time we die—" (which was something he knew all about) "—we're only just coming to the conclusion that we don't know any fucking thing!" *And then we really wise up—except it's too damn late! For by then we can't tell anyone how clever we are . . .*

"But what if we didn't get old?" B.J. said. "I mean, what if we didn't have to, if there was a way to avoid it?" She knew she was treading on thin ice. She must be careful not to bridge the gap between Harry's conscious and unconscious knowledge. It wouldn't do to have the two start leaking into each other.

She needn't have worried, for Harry wasn't listening. Suddenly his knuckles were white where his fingers gripped his arm rest, and his gaze was riveted to his rearview wing mirror.

B.J. glanced in the central rearview mirror . . . and gave a start! "What the . . . ?"

The station-wagon from yesterday, with at least two occupants from the red-robe troupe, was bearing down on them like a hawk stooping to its prey. And the way it was coming, it seemed aimed *at* their car, at them! So that a thought flashed unbidden through Harry's mind:

Is this it? I saw their monastery. That was Kyle's talent, warning me about my future. Are these people the end *of my future? A bunch of kamikaze monks trying to force us off the road? Is it as simple as that? And is that what's been bothering me, somehow knowing that this was creeping up on me?*

The car behind pulled out, looked like it would overtake. And B.J. gasped, "Is that what they are—all they are—roadhogs? What *idiot* issued a driving license to this maniac!" She gave way and applied her brakes . . . which probably saved their lives.

As the station-wagon rocketed forward and overtook them, it swerved violently to the left, cutting in on their vehicle. The collision between the rear end of the station-wagon and the front of Auld John's car threw the latter to the left. The road ran parallel to a grass- and weed-grown ditch on that side, but right at this point there was a rickety wooden bridge that went angling off over the ditch to a woodlands track. Just how B.J. managed to control the steering and turn onto the bridge, Harry couldn't say; it seemed more likely that the shock of the collision was responsible, that it had physically shifted the front of their car to the left. In another moment the bridge's boards were rattling and shuddering under B.J.'s wheels, and then they were into the woods and slowing down.

"Bad driving?" she gasped. "That wasn't bad driving. That was fucking *deliberate!*"

Harry was looking ahead. "The track curves right, probably back onto the road. Don't stop but follow it through the trees. If it was deliberate they may be waiting for us."

"So what good will that do?"

He gritted his teeth and said, "At least we'll *know* it was deliberate. We'll know to protect ourselves—and maybe to hit back."

"Hit back?" She stamped on the brakes, stopped and threw open her door. "How? Harry, we're in the middle of nowhere and unarmed. Well, with one exception." In the boot of the old car: her crossbow. She got it, came back to her driving seat, passed the weapon to Harry.

He looked at it, and almost had to shout, "What?" Because the ancient engine had decided to start racing.

"You'll want to hit back, won't you?" she yelled. (For it had sunk in that they really might have to. She'd been expecting something like this for as long as she could remember; had known it must come eventually. But like this?)

"Bonnie Jean, what the hell's going on?" he said, grating the words out. (Did it have to do with him—Alec Kyle's talent—or with her? And if with her, why? She was an innocent, wasn't she? But again, innocent of what?)

"Oh, load the fucking thing!" she snapped.

And as he made to do so:

Honk! Hoooonk!

They looked back. And there it was: the long, black, low-slung, now sinister-looking station wagon. It was maybe ten to fifteen paces behind them, half-hidden in dangling foliage, its front doors open. And leaning on the doors, the driver and his front-seat passenger. Even as Harry and B.J. stared, the driver reached inside the car and honked again, then cocked his head on one side and smiled.

Harry looked at their faces—eye-contact—and knew from that moment that whatever this was it was life-endangering serious. In the dappling of the trees, their eyes were feral, full of yellow, shifting light. And their grins were almost vacuous, like the grins of crocodiles or hyenas . . . filled with malice!

Almost unnoticed, B.J. had taken the crossbow from him. He saw the grins slip from the faces of the red-robes as they fell into crouches behind their doors, saw their slanted eyes narrow, heard the vibrating, electric *thrummm* of the crossbow's string. And in the next split-second B.J.'s bolt slammed home into the panel of the driver's door, burying itself deep.

The driver was inside the car now; straightening up behind the wheel, he called out to his passenger. That one had reached inside the car, come back out with . . . a machine-pistol? Almost of its own accord the Necroscope's Möbius math commenced evolving on the screen of his metaphysical mind. But before he could conjure a door—

—B.J. had the car in gear, fishtailing as the rear wheels threw up a screen of dirt. Then they were round a bend, bumping through birch and rowan, and onto a bridge in worse repair than the first one! And finally back onto the road. Then as B.J. put her foot down, without saying a word Harry took up her crossbow and reloaded it. But as he slowly, carefully put it down again, he said:

"I thought they might have something against me, but now I'm not sure. *You* were sure! You must have been, because 'innocent' people don't go shooting at people for being bad drivers! So what's going on, B.J.? What do these men have against you?"

She didn't answer but looked in her driving mirror—and saw at a glance that it was time to switch him on. Definitely, because the black station-wagon was coming at them again, and B.J. knew she couldn't handle this on her own. "Harry, mah wee man!" she yelled as the rear window shattered, showering diced glass inward, and something hot buzzed and spanged inside the car. "Are you listening? Do you understand? You can talk normally."

"Listening, yes," he mumbled dazedly as the moon blinked out, the wolf quit howling and the inner man surfaced. "Understand, no." His voice was like a child's: uncertain, afraid.

"I told you the time might come when I would send you out after them, the Ferenczys and the—"

"—Drakuls," he cut her off.

"Well, now they've come for us!"

"Vampires!" Harry said. And as suddenly as that, his voice had changed. This was the man she'd first seen in a dark garage in London—the one in the alley, after he had got her out of trouble—the one who had faced up to Big Jimmy in B.J.'s wine bar. Then for the first time in a long time she remembered just who he was supposed to be: Radu's Mysterious One! Maybe he was, at that! So it should come as no surprise that *this* Harry was a very hard, very cold one.

Up ahead, the road narrowed to a single lane on the left. The right-hand lane was coned off for some forty or fifty feet where the surface was badly pot-holed; but it was a Sunday and no one was working. Also on the right, a wooden fence guarded the road from a steep descent to the river. If a car went over, it would keep right on going until it hit the water.

Just as B.J. entered the defile, Harry reached his foot over and stamped on the brake. The car behind was almost on top of them. It skidded right, then sharp left; its nearside tires skipped over the ditch, which was shallow here, and it ran nose first into a clump of springy saplings that bent over with its weight and finally stopped it. It would take a little while to untangle.

But: "Shit!" Harry said, as he released the brake and B.J. shot Auld John's car forward again.

"What?" She was jubilant. "But we stopped them!"

"Only for a little while," he said.

Then they were round a slight left-hand bend and the road ran straight ahead for maybe a mile or more. At the end of the mile, the road was cut into the hillside on the left at another left-hand bend, while on the right the drop was sheer to dense woodlands. "Drop me here," Harry said.

"What?" She looked at him out of the corner of her eye.

"Drop me *here!*" he repeated, harshly.

She gave a snort. "What, and do you think you're the lone highwayman, or something?"

"Or something," he nodded.

"You'll jump out and surprise them, will you?"

"Drop me now, before they come round that bend back there and see us," he said.

She saw that he was serious. "They'll kill you."

"No, they won't," Harry shook his head. "This is what I do, remember?" So she dropped him.

But as the Necroscope headed for the trees at the side of the road, he called out, "Now go like hell! That car of theirs is more powerful; if they're not back on your tail in a couple of miles you'll know I got them. Then you can come back for me. And if they are . . ." He left it at that, and watched from cover as B.J. drove away . . .

* * *

Harry fixed the contours of the forested hillside ahead in his mind's eye and registered the co-ordinates. He would have liked to double-check them but didn't have the time. Then, conjuring a Möbius door, he made a jump to the attic of his house in Bonnyrig. It took only a moment or so to collect what he needed and make a return jump back into the trees at the side of the road.

Speeding southwest, Auld John's car had almost reached the place where the road was cut into the hillside. But in the opposite direction—just coming into view and rocketing down the road—the black station-wagon! At the speed they were going, they'd catch her in about two minutes.

Harry stepped back under the leafy cover of the trees and a moment later felt the blast of pressured air as the black car swept by. He had forty seconds . . . but needed only nine or ten. One: took him to a location on a bald bluff high over the road, midway between the two cars. Two: took him down again, to where the road bent under a rocky, wooded, almost overhanging granite formation. And three to ten saw him climbing just a few feet to a ledge where daisies sprouted in the cracks, where he was able to crouch down out of sight but yet keep an eye on the road.

In that position, by reaching out a hand, he would be able to touch a passing car. But simply to "touch" the station-wagon wasn't his purpose. He had just less than thirty seconds. B.J. was a half-mile farther down the road, and her pursuers were on their way. Harry peeked out around the rim of the rock and calculated time and distance.

Twenty seconds . . . fifteen . . . ten. The Necroscope's calculations were almost perfect. He took a combination of deadly items from his pockets and armed them, then held them a little awkwardly both in one hand. And his time was up; no more than two or three seconds left when he leaned out and swung his arm toward the open car window, releasing the grenade and CS canister into the blurred interior.

In the last moment the occupants of the station-wagon had seen him; the passenger—the red-robe with the machine-pistol—was on Harry's side. He had jerked the top half of his body back into the car as the Necroscope swung at his window—but he had seen what had flown inside! After that:

The activity in the station-wagon became frantic, a blur of motion, all to no avail. In just a moment the car began to swerve left and right as its interior filled with yellow gas, and the red-robe with the gun reached out and grabbed hold of the roof-rack, trying to drag himself out through his window! Then—

—The windows blew out and the roof blew off, taking the one with the machine-pistol with it! The vehicle had traveled maybe a hundred and fifty feet beyond Harry's position; but he threw up an arm to shield himself anyway, as the blast licked out and thunder shook the air, and the echoes started to come bouncing down from the valley walls. And when he looked . . .

The car's top looked like it had been peeled or cut loose by a giant can-opener. It was floating in the air over the car, turning lazily like a leaf, and the red-robe had let go of his gun and was hanging onto the roof-rack, clinging to it for his life. But both the car and roof were still traveling at more than sixty miles an hour, and though the bend in the road was slight it certainly wasn't a straight line.

The station-wagon went through the wooden safety fence as if it were balsa wood, then seemed to very gradually nose-dive into the canopy of trees; and the roof with its hanger-on went fluttering after. The Necroscope half-expected a second blast but it didn't come; just the sound of branches shattering, followed by the squeal of wrenched, twisting metal, several dull thuds, and silence . . .

Harry found a way down to the wreckage. He could have used the Continuum but wasn't in too much of a hurry. Despite the blast, that red-robe who had been clinging to the roof as if it were a life-raft had still looked fairly agile. A vampire, it was possible he'd survived the fall. He would have come down on top of the car, however, which wouldn't have made for a happy landing.

The trees were dense and the way dark beneath them. Birds, mainly wood pigeons, were starting to settle in their branches, and cheep and coo again after the initial shock. Maybe that was a good sign. Looking back, Harry could just make out the broken fence through the foliage canopy; and looking ahead through the undergrowth down the steep, leaf-mold slope under the trees, a flash of bright water caught in a stray sunbeam.

When he stepped over the freshly fallen branch of a tree, its bark ripped back, he knew he must be close. The slope was very steep here; lots of leafy debris had come down from above; the Necroscope began skidding on his heels, deliberately aimed himself at the bole of a huge tree—an oak, he thought, well over three feet in girth—to slow himself down. Above him the canopy was dense, with patches of daylight showing through . . . and one unmistakable large patch of dangling, broken branches.

Using the great gnarly roots of the oak as hand and footholds, Harry scrambled around the bole of the tree . . . and was there. Directly overhead, trapped in a tangle of branches, the twisted, dented wreckage of the station-wagon's roof lay horizontal on a platform of crushed foliage, like a metal blanket flung carelessly into the tree. And down below—

—The vehicle was standing on its nose, which had dug in, then crumpled as the soil compacted. Its rear end was trapped, compressed in a fork of mighty branches, else the impact might easily have caused the petrol tank to explode. *Maybe better if it had,* the Necroscope thought.

Better for the driver, anyway.

For the driver was still in the car, pinned like a fly on the column of his stripped steering wheel, where the blast of the grenade had thrown him. His face had come forward so that his chin was resting on the frame of the shattered windscreen, and crimson trails were seeping from his ears, nose, and mouth down the vertical, crumpled bonnet and dripping into the dark soil. But his yellow, Asiatic face was mobile, drooling, grimacing, and even as Harry watched his eyes opened. Inverted but on a level with his own eyes, they looked straight at him, and he saw how red they were in their cores . . .

Then the mouth blew red bubbles and made a noise, and a bloodied, broken hand twitched up onto the window sill of the sprung door. It jerked and trembled there, making feeble beckoning motions. And those awful eyes pleaded. The red-robe was asking for help.

"Oh, sure!" the Necroscope said, and stepped back a pace. But even if this one had been human—or especially if he were human—there'd be no helping him. Several pulsating loops of lacerated intestine were dangling out from under the driver's door, dripping blood.

Somewhere overhead, back through the tunnel of trees, the drone of a car's engine coughed into silence, and in the next moment a shout came echoing on the suddenly still air. "Harry! Where are you?" B.J.—she must have seen the broken fence and guessed something of what had happened.

"Down here!" Harry called back—which startled the wood pigeons again, set them fluttering, and broke the awe-stricken mood of the place. "Be careful how you go. It's steep . . ." And the thought struck him: *just like we were out rambling!* Except they weren't out rambling, and there was monstrous danger here. What about the other red-robe?

Then, smelling a new but no less lethal danger, he stepped back another two paces and began circling the suspended vehicle. Along with the blood seeping into the soil there was a shimmering pool of vaporizing fuel in the area of the buried fender. A trail of petrol led back to the fractured tank . . .

He became aware of B.J.'s sounds as she descended toward him through the trees. But suddenly everything felt wrong. What about the vampire who had been clinging to the roof? Where was he? And just *who was it* who was coming down the slope under the trees anyway?

Thinking of the one who had been on the roof of the station-wagon had caused the Necroscope to glance up into the tree again. At which precise moment there was movement; the twisted blanket of metal tilted a little . . . and a tattered, blackened sleeve, once red, came into view. But the hand projecting from the sleeve continued to hang on to the roof!

The roof tilted more yet and the red-robe came fully into view. He was conscious, furious! He saw Harry directly beneath him, and snarled; his eye-teeth were fangs! Then he let go his hold, slid from the roof face-down, and fell directly toward the Necroscope!

Harry hurled himself backward, missed his footing, tried to conjure a door. The vampire was on all fours, muscles bunching to spring. His robe was in tatters, limbs and body a mass of cuts and scratches. And his face was a mask out of hell!

B.J. stepped over Harry, aimed her crossbow almost pointblank, squeezed the trigger. The bolt sprang free, buried itself to the flights in the red-robe's heart. He had seen her at the last moment and had started to come erect; her bolt seemed to knock him backward, limbs flailing as he collided with the door of the station-wagon and slid to a sitting position. Then his mouth spat a stream of bloodied froth, his eyes closed and his head slumped onto his chest.

And B.J. panted, "Harry, your lighter . . ." She was shaken, yes, but there was a snarl in her voice, too.

Harry collapsed the invisible door he had conjured a little way down the slope, into which he'd been about to hurl himself. He fumbled out a cheap cigarette lighter, flipped its top and struck fire. He knew what B.J. would do; as they scrambled away from the car and its occupants, he did it for her:

He tossed the lighter in a lazy arc into the pool of vaporizing fuel. It hadn't even hit the ground before blue flames licked up, enveloped the car, making a *whoosh!* and a roar that threw out a wall of heat. B.J. and Harry kept going; they were into the trees, covered by the mossy boles of a clump of birch trees when the tank blew. And when they looked out the car was an inferno. The explosion hadn't shaken it loose, but already the foliage around was on fire, burning furiously. Nothing was going to get out of that hell alive, but still they kept watching.

"Look and learn," B.J. said, hoarsely. "One of them must be a lieutenant. A job like this could never have been trusted entirely to mere thralls." Harry knew she was right, and knew which one was the lieutenant.

"The driver," he said, remembering how his eyes were crimson in their cores.

She glanced at him, frowned and said, "Oh?" She might have been about to say something else, but a sudden commotion in the blazing car stopped her. It was the driver. For while his passenger was content to sit there and melt and drip, he wasn't.

Through the envelope of blue-shimmering heat, the lieutenant's red-robed, blazing figure was plainly visible. Twitching and jerking, with all his limbs spastically threshing, he lifted his head from the window sill and seemed to look out through the wall of fire. But his eyes were peeled white things with no sight in them.

"Dead," B.J. grated, "but his metamorphic flesh won't accept it. It wants to go on, wants more."

Even as she spoke, the chest and guts of the thing in the burning vehicle *erupted,* putting out corpse-white tentacles or feelers to lash in the super-heated confines of the car. Bunching together, they blossomed outward through the stripped roof and upward into the fiery slipstream, and floated there in the furnace updraft like the arms of some crippled anemone.

Other tentacles uncoiled out of the door, opened at their tips, and pissed an orange fluid all around that steamed where it fell to earth. Then the thing gave in, withdrew its melting appendages, crumpled down into itself and began to slop out of the door around the shoulders of the blazing thrall. Body fats were on fire now and the stink of roasting flesh was sickening. It masked what was left of the CS smell, which B.J. had taken to be part of the natural stench of the accident.

"That one had been a vampire . . . oh, for quite some time," she said. "If he wasn't Wamphyri, it was close. Now we have to go. It's over, and we don't want to be found here."

And Harry, who could still converse normally, said, "This was just two of them. There are four more that we know of."

"I know," she said, taking the lead and heading back up the slope under the trees. "Our trip is off. I have to talk to Auld John—but by telephone! They might have tailed us from his place! If they'd held back just a minute or two, they might even have followed us to . . ."

". . . To Radu in his lair?" Harry said.

She heard the confusion in his voice, looked back and saw it in his face. And she believed that she understood. Right now he was "switched on" to the reality of things; he knew that she was in thrall to Radu Lykan, Wamphyri! He knew that *he* was working for Radu's agent, Bonnie Jean, against those of other vampire Lords. The "myth" of their mutual affection—the bond he and B.J. had established—might have been compromised; Harry might have begun to suspect that he was being used.

Therefore . . . perhaps she would be wise to erase this entire episode from his mind. But not here. Indeed the sooner they got away from this place the better. And so:

"It's okay," she told him over her shoulder. "I'll explain things in the car. Then anything you don't understand will seem . . . oh, very much simpler."

And there might be one or two things she would like him to explain to her, too . . .

. . . Like: "How? How did you do it?" They were heading south for Dalwhinnie.

Despite that Harry was still under her spell, he couldn't answer her. Anderson's directive came first: that he must protect his talents at all cost. Wherefore he must lie. Beginning to sweat, he said, "I played the highwayman, as you suggested, left it to the last second and jumped out on them. If the driver had had a moment to think . . . he might have recognized me, run me down. But he didn't. He tried to avoid me, swerved, and never regained control."

"But . . . are you crazy?" She gasped. "You could as easily have died!"

"If they'd kept coming, I was ready to jump back into the bushes. It was them or me—or you."

"You did it for . . . ?" But there she paused. For she really didn't want to know this: that Harry had done it for her. She preferred to believe he'd done it because of her hypnotic programming—didn't she? But in any case, his answer had thrown her completely off track. So that she didn't think to ask how he had covered the mile from the place where she'd dropped him to the spot where the station-wagon had gone over the edge.

And she didn't even wonder why he'd been so quick off the mark with his cigarette lighter. But the Necroscope knew why:

He hadn't wanted to give her time to notice the *condition* of the wrecked car's interior, the fact that he had bombed it. That would only have led to more questions, and he wasn't sure he'd have any satisfactory answers.

But in any case there were no more questions, never could be in connection with this episode. For long before they got to Dalwhinnie B.J. had already wiped it from the Necroscope's mind, told him it had been a nightmare to merge with all the others, and that he should simply forget it . . .

Unnoticed by the pair as they had pulled away from the "accident site," another car parked on the grass verge three hundreds yards back from the bend had come to life, pulled out onto the road, rolled silently forward, and stopped where the fence was shattered and black smoke climbed in a column from the canopy of riverside trees to the blue-gray sky.

The driver—a slight man dressed in a lightweight black raincoat buttoned to the neck, a huge white hat with a floppy brim, and side-shielded sunglasses—got out and made his way quickly down into the woods. Following B.J.'s and the Necroscope's tracks, and his nose, he was soon at the scene of fiery devastation.

The fire was burning uphill through the tinderlike undergrowth, toward the road which would form a natural firebreak. Thus the blazing vehicle, clearly visible as the source of the fire, was approachable. Likewise visible were the two blackening corpses, one slumped behind the wheel and the other seated upright beside the sprung door.

Keeping well back from the fire, the slight man swept the scene with eyes that were bird-bright, yellow in the shade of his hat. A glistening black, steaming object roughly the size and shape of a cucumber hissed and made crackling noises some distance from the inferno. It shuddered and lay still even as the slight man took up a dead branch to prod it. Between this object and the car, a trail of sticky slime suggested that it had made its own way to where it had died.

It *was* dead, yes, but it couldn't be left lying there. Or sooner or later someone would be sure to examine it. And that wouldn't do at all. So using his branch, the man in the raincoat twitched the leech back into the inferno, into the furnace heat of the red-glowing car. That should do it.

Then without further ado the little man made his way back to his own vehicle, and drove quickly away from the scene. It was time he made report to his Masters in Sicily . . .

In Dalwhinnie, B.J. 'phoned Auld John and told him what had happened, told him to bring her car, where to leave it, and where he would find his own car. And when he'd got that straight she said, "And now it's up to you, John. Are you up to it?"

"The weather's guid," he answered, barely managing to contain his elation, "and ah'll take the easy way up. Dinnae fret, mah Bonnie lass . . . Auld John'll be just fine! Why, ah believe ah'm even looking forward tae it—tae see Him again!"

"But the feeding, old friend, the feeding. You must promise me you'll be careful?"

"No need tae bother ye're mind," he told her. "Ah ken well enough. It's near His time and He'll be hungry. But ah'll be on mah guard."

"Good. And make sure—make absolutely *sure*—that you're not followed. They may be onto you as well, John!"

B.J. could picture his wolfish grin as he answered, "Aye, but ah'm no so an easy target. And mah old shotgun's loaded wi' silver shot, as well ye ken."

"Good luck, then. And talk to me when it's done."

"Be sure ah will."

"So be it," said Bonnie Jean, and put the 'phone down . . .

EPILOGUE

I T WAS STILL THE EARLY HOURS OF THE MORNING IN DALWHINNIE, IN SCOT-
land; but some two hours earlier in the Drakesh Monastery, on the Tingri
Plateau, it had already been midday . . .

The white-robed initiate whom Harry Keogh had seen tramping the white waste
to the face in the rock was at last ready. Ready to face (as he saw it) his final
challenge, the last rite of "purification," and long-awaited acceptance into the
Drakesh Sect.

He had been cleansed of all earthly sins, all vices of the flesh, the mind and
the soul. He had endured all the rigours of life in the monastery—its austerity,
celibacy, secrecy; its lack of communication, which was forbidden—all of the
self-denial of the brotherhood without being a part of that brotherhood, without its acceptance. In short, for the two long years that he had lived here . . .
he'd lived a lie.

For unknown to him and two others just like him, they were the *only* ones
who had suffered the austerity, celibacy and silence. As for the rest of the brothers: they had survived *their* initiations long ago. Now they had their Master,
Daham Drakesh, to give them succour; now they bathed in the blood which is
the life, the tainted blood of their own; now they had each other. Moreover,
they had the women of the Drakesh Township: the produce of their farm and
fields; the warmth of their cringing bodies (while yet they *remained* warm) in the
dark of night; their blood, in however small a measure, to provide at least a taste
of the feasts to come.

Ah, for their Master provided for them in this monotonous white wilderness no less than he would provide for them in the outside world, when at last it
was his . . . when it was theirs! And except that they must not impregnate the
women—or drain them to death or undeath, or weaken them beyond their capacity to work—*nothing* was forbidden to the brothers. But the only, the ultimate, the unforgivable sin would be the denial of the vampire Lord Daham
Drakesh himself. And its punishment . . .

. . . But there were diverse ways in which sinners, or even innocent men—such as initiates—might serve in the monastery of Daham Drakesh.

This initiate—that figure in white whom the Necroscope had seen marching with three priests in front and three behind—was ready for his final ordeal. In the preceding two years he had fasted for weeks at a time; at other times he had survived on yak's milk, coarse bread, and pale honey. For a month now his diet had been such that he'd lost ten pounds in weight and now weighed a little over one hundred and five pounds. And this was a young, previously healthy man of eighteen years.

His ordeals had been fasting, freezing, loneliness, celibacy (which scarcely counted, since he'd never known a woman in his life), self-denial, hard work—and fear. The last because there were . . . *sounds* in the monastery, and an aura . . .

Work had been the first, when for months he must toil to dig his own cavelet from the solid rock, because he was forbidden to have a bed until he had a place to put the bed. The rest had been likewise obligatory: he could only eat what the brothers gave him, speak if or when spoken to, masturbate at his own peril. The *sensitivity* of the brothers, and especially of Daham Drakesh, was frightening. They could smell sex; they seemed to have the power to smell the very thought of it!

But he had been cleansed of outside influences, his body reduced and refined, his mind numbed. And Daham Drakesh—who was skilled in the arts of seeing without being seen, of knowing without being known, and of hearing without being heard—found him pleasing. Drakesh took pleasure in purity and innocence, perhaps because he had never had any of his own. But he knew where to get it.

The High Priest took his time arriving at the room of the rite. First he visited the cavern of the creatures: hybrid vampire things waxing in their vats. They would be warriors eventually, the first of many. Then, as it had been in Sunside/Starside, so it would be here. And every high place an aerie, each deadly day a time of curfew, and the nights . . . ah, the nights would belong to Daham Drakesh! In five, ten, fifteen years? A long time, aye, but what is time to the Wamphyri?

The cavern of the creatures: no one was allowed down here but Daham Drakesh himself and a handful of his lieutenants. If any common thrall should enter this place, he would be fortunate indeed to leave. Drakesh looked down into a vat, its gelatinous surface surging with long, slow ripples. They waxed, his beasts; they could be brought on quickly, if need be. Or they could lie here another hundred years, waiting to be born.

Then he looked at the trough-like conduits that serviced the vats, rust colored runnels carved in the rock, umbilical sluices to feed the foetal abnormalities being bred here. That fool in Chungking, Colonel Tsi-Hong, would have Drakesh breed *human* warriors. Well, and so he would—so he was, as witness the brotherhood—but Tsi-Hong knew nothing of such as these.

As the Lord of Vampires inspected his vats, so there had commenced a familiar combination of whistling, cracking sounds from somewhere overhead; the acoustical quality of the monastery's chambers was remarkable. And now it came, a trickle at first but gradually swelling: the red tide. The life-blood of the brothers, given of their own free will, gurgling down the sluices to the vats. Then, in the heart of every liquid womb, a sluggish stirring as vaguely outlined occupants sensed the flow of rich red food.

Daham Drakesh smiled in his fashion and moved on; he had seen all of this before.

He left the foetal vat-things to their gluttony, climbed stone stairs to the chamber of the trough, the long-accustomed scene of silent, ritual flagellation, and from there took long, loping, forward-leaning strides to the room of the last rite of initiation. He was eager now; the sight of the crimson flow in the cavern of the creatures, and the blood-tinged mist over the trough of silent agony, had set vampire juices working. Drakesh had his own needs no less than the waxing creatures in his vats of metamorphic creation. Except his needs were more selective.

The initiate was waiting; clad in white, kneeling between a pair of red-robed acolytes (Drakesh's lieutenants), he elevated his eyes as the Master entered—and at once lowered them. The room was small, square, high-ceilinged. At one end, a near-vertical, flue-like slot had been hewn into the solid rock wall. Six feet high from the floor, this chimney was sealed by a massive block of stone, stepped on one side like a dais. A pulley-system in the ceiling dangled long ropes of chains fitted with claw-like grapples. To one side, a cart was piled with blocks of ice that were slowly welding themselves together. A stairwell in the opposite wall went down into darkness.

With the sinuous ease of the Wamphyri, Drakesh moved to a position in front of the initiate, placed a slender hand on his bowed head, and said: "My son, are you sure? Are you prepared?" His voice was almost gentle, almost compassionate. "Do you desire to exchange your white robe for the red robe of a brother?"

"Indeed, Master." The initiate's voice was no more than a squeak. His fear was such that he might almost have said no . . . but he would not give in now, especially not in the presence of Drakesh. In *his* sight, he would never dare to admit defeat.

"Look at me," the Master of the Monastery commanded.

The face of the initiate was drawn; his eyes were hollow, his yellow skin pale as saffron parchment, with fine blue veins showing through. He smelled of youth, innocence, and everything that Drakesh was not. And the vampire smiled—

—And began to explain the test. "The chimney will house you standing upright with your head bowed to your chest—as if you bore the weight of the world! But nothing so great, be assured. These brothers will place blocks of ice above you, two or three depending on your . . . fortitude? This room is not especially cold and the ice will melt soon enough. But the process will be greatly accelerated by the generation of heat from your own body. This, then, is your ordeal, my son: the weight of the ice; its slow cold drip; the confines of the chimney. All these things against your determination, your force for life. Finally, when the last few shards of ice slip down around your feet and you climb out, it will be over and you . . . will be a brother!" he clapped his hands. "No more explaining. Into the chimney!"

The red-robed acolytes climbed the dais with the initiate and helped him down into the chimney. Drakesh stood watching as they operated the pulleys, began loading blocks of ice onto the shoulders of the youth. But . . .

"Master!" that one called out, the sound of his voice muffled now. "There are tiny holes in the floor. A great many . . ."

"Certainly," Drakesh called back. "So that the water from the ice can flow out and the air can flow in. What, and should I let you drown, or suffocate?"

More blocks of ice went into the shaft. Stacked on top of each other, they fitted well; and because the chimney inclined back into the wall a little, they could not topple forward. All of their mass was focused on the youth, who now cried out:

"Master, the weight!" His voice was strained, his words a series of panting grunts.

"An ordeal is an ordeal," Drakesh's answer was cold as the ice itself. "Less than that, and it becomes a mockery." But his very tone of voice was a mockery, while his feral-eyed acolytes grinned and plied the pulleys.

The column of ice reached up eight feet above the hole in the wall now; its weight was that of five men. As another block was released from the grapples and slid into place, so the column settled an inch or two in its slot. And feeling the sudden, rapid compression of his body, the initiate panted so much faster and louder, his voice becoming a screech of protest:

"I . . . *cannot!* . . . Master, I'm being *crushed!* . . . my knees are against the wall . . . my back is breaking!"

"Cry out, my son," Drakesh called back. "It will ease your pain. Pant and groan, even as your mother groaned when her body opened to spit you into the world. She gave you life—as you now give it to me!"

And as the acolytes worked at the rattling pulleys, Daham Drakesh descended the stairwell into the room *beneath* this room of torture. It was cold, and as he disrobed he shuddered a very little . . . but not from the cold. It was an almost sexual shudder of anticipation.

Against one wall of this lower chamber, the floor had been scooped out into a shallow basin. As Drakesh stepped naked into the basin, he looked up. In the ceiling directly overhead, contained in an area of some eighteen by eighteen inches, a hundred small holes had been drilled through to the base of the torture chimney. Through these holes—through the very rock—he could hear the frantic screams of his victim. And coming to him from the stairwell, the relentless rattling of chains.

Finally there was one last recognizable word: a throbbing "M-m-*mother!*" Followed by a shriek to end all shrieks that echoed quickly into silence, and a splintering sound that went on and on. And all that remained was a slow crunching and squelching: the compression of flesh and bone into jelly. Then, as the rattling of the chains continued unabated, the warm red rain of Drakesh's shower commenced to smoke down upon him.

But a worse horror was yet to come. For as Drakesh opened his jaws in a yawning gape, turned up his face and threw wide his spindly arms to the crimson spattering deluge, so his parasite leech took over. And all semblance of control, of anything remotely human, was surrendered now as the thing *inside* Drakesh revelled in this its life-source, its being, its cursed continuation—revelled in the blood of an innocent!

Drakesh's olive-marble skin took on a mottled life of its own; his meta-morphic flesh *rippled* over the bones of his face, chest, body and limbs; the pores of his skin opened like small pouting mouths—like the tiny flowers of some hybrid cactus in a rare desert rainstorm—lapping with their own tongues at the juice of a man where it followed the contours of Drakesh's writhing, tormented form.

It went on for a long time . . .

After the pulley chains had stopped rattling and the acolytes were gone in haste from the upper chamber (for they would venture nowhere near their Master now, not in his passion); then, as Drakesh recovered from his awful ecstasy and staggered from the basin, and the tiny mouths closed and his skin flowed back into a corpse-like but *unblemished* whole—

—Pain! Such a burning *agony!*

Drakesh hissed his terror, fell back against the wall and gazed crimson-eyed on his burning flesh. What was this? Was it possible he'd made a terrible mis-take? Had the initiate been a leper, some kind of plague-bearer? But no, this wasn't his parasite complaining. The pain wasn't his—it was in his mind!

Mentalism. Telepathy. A sending from far, far away. But it was so real—so immediate, so psychically in tune with him—that it could have only one possible source. Flesh of Drakesh's flesh: his bloodson and chief lieutenant, four and a half thousand miles away in Scotland!

Drakesh opened himself to it, accepted part of the pain in order to enter the mind behind it. And he was right, it was his bloodson, sent out into a foreign land. And sent there to die, apparently:

The flames melting away his body, his vampire flesh, cutting into the very heart of him, to the creature inside. And his injuries, so great as to be almost irreparable; utterly *irrepairable, in combination with the fire.*

Hoping to discover the cause of his son's funeral pyre—its perpetrators—Drakesh attempted deeper penetration of the tormented mind. But even vam-pire flesh can be weak in the face of the ultimate truth, the true death. It would not be easy to communicate with the terrified mentality behind the dying. But still Drakesh tried.

Who? he sent. *And how? If you would be avenged, you must try to tell me, my son.* The how of it came at once, for it was there, fresh in the burning mind:

The senses-numbing blast of heat and light inside a speeding vehicle . . . the crash through a fragile fence, and headlong plunge into high branches . . . the jarring cessation of an illusory slow motion falling, as the wrecked car slammed down nose-first into earth. And at last it was time for the pain, for the knowledge of a devastated body to sink in and its agony to wash outward.

But before it could wash all the way to Drakesh, he sent:

And now, who?

The man, the woman, the answer came back from a mind even now boiling in its steaming skull.

Show me!

And Daham Drakesh looked out through a shimmering wall of blue fire at the faces and forms of his son's destroyers. The man in the London photographs, of course—this Alec Kyle?—and Radu Lykan's female thrall. Protectors of an ancient enemy . . . and one who must now be aware that *His* enemies were abroad in the world!

The faces, the identities were there, and they were gone, liquefying along with the mind that sent them. Last faint echoes of pain receding . . . the flames dying out . . . the sending ending, along with the sender.

Shocked, scarcely realizing the full gravity of the thing as yet, Daham Drakesh dressed himself. And his fingers trembled and he saw again the enigmatic face of the man in his bloodson's sending, and in the Oxford Street photographs: that oh-so-human face masking its oh-so-weird intelligence. And again the Master of the monastery shuddered; not from anticipation this time but from the cold. And no ordinary cold, but that of the alien void behind the man's eyes.

However briefly then, it was as if the vampire sensed the fall of a strange and threatening night, whose taloned shadows were reaching for him even now . . .

Two days later, but again early in the morning, the Necroscope Harry Keogh came awake to the ringing of his telephone. He had slept late and dreamed strange dreams—of the Great Majority, talking about him but not to him—and as he focused his eyes on his traveling clock, so the time clicked over from 9:44 to 9:45. The telephone extension beside his bed continued to ring, and Harry reached out and picked it up. He had long since lost his actual terror of the thing, despite that it still conjured fleeting, disturbing motifs. Now, as his dreams faded away and his waking mind sharpened, he grunted, "Uh?"

"Did I wake you?" For a moment Harry didn't identify the gravelly voice on the other end of the line, but then it registered and he said:

"Ben? Ben Trask?" And he thought: *E-Branch? Now what's up?* But what could be up, except that they'd maybe heard something. And sharper now, giving it all of his attention, he said: "Ben, is it about Brenda?"

"Sorry, Harry," Trask answered at once. "But no, it isn't about Brenda. We're still on it, of course, but . . . nothing so far. It's just that it's been quite a while now and we thought it was time we spoke."

"We?"

"Darcy and the rest of us . . . to find out how the world's treating you, you know?" It came hard for Trask to lie. A lie-detector in his own right, it went against the grain.

Harry nodded, despite that the other couldn't see him. "I'm okay, mainly. And you people?"

"Routine" (Harry sensed Trask's shrug.) "Not that anything ever *is* routine around here! And apparently there's some weird shit in your neck of the woods, too . . ."

So, this *was* something other than a purely social call. The Necroscope made no attempt to disguise his sourness as he inquired: "So what is it, Ben? Can we get to the point? And where's Darcy? Shouldn't he be making this call?" *Or are you trying to get at the "truth" of things, eh? And what would I have to lie about anyway?*

"An accident—well, an *incident*—up there in Jock territory," Trask answered. "Didn't you read about it?" But he made no comment on Darcy Clarke's whereabouts.

"I only get Sunday papers," Harry told him. "So what are we talking about here?" The Necroscope was curious now, and cautious. Whatever it was, why was E-Branch talking to him about it? Something he might have been involved in? He hadn't robbed any banks in Scotland, had he?

"An incident," Trask repeated. "On the Spey, north of the Forest of Atholl, just a couple of days ago."

"On the river? What kind of incident?" Curiouser and curiouser! Harry and Bonnie Jean had been up that way, until she'd cried off their climb. She hadn't felt up to it . . . or perhaps she'd thought he wasn't up to it.

"Near the river," Trask said. "A car went off the road and burned out. Its occupants, too. Horrific! But the police found a weapon, evidence of a fire fight. There were two bodies, members of a Tibetan sect. The Home Office seems to think there's some kind of sectarian war going on. There were already a dozen of these types in England and another six on their way in. They work—carrying "the word," or whatever—in teams of six. The ones on their way in have been turned back, six more in London have been told to leave the country. Which leaves four of these people still unaccounted for . . ."

"And?" the Necroscope said, when it seemed Trask was done. "What has all of this to do with me?"

A slight pause, and: "It's for information only, Harry. I mean, since you happen to be up that way . . . ?"

"I'm not your eyes and ears in Scotland, Ben. I thought it was understood? Now I'm out of the Branch, I'm gone for good."

Trask's voice was cooler as he answered: "We're not asking anything, Harry. Just passing something on, that's all."

"Well, thanks," the Necroscope told him, just as tersely. "And is that it?"

"That's it."

"Take care of yourself," said Harry, and without waiting for an answer put the 'phone down.

At the London end, Trask looked at Darcy Clarke standing beside him and growled, "I didn't much like that."

"I could see and hear," the other nodded. "I understand and totally agree. Now forget it and tell me what you think."

Trask shook his head. "It's a funny one," he said. "I got the impression he *thinks* he's telling the truth."

"Thinks?"

"From his point of view," Trask tried to explain, "he was telling the truth— he wasn't involved in whatever it was that happened up there. And yet . . . I can't swear. I've only rarely come across this complication before."

"A complication?"

"Where I trust someone's word implicitly, and so must consider my own talent suspect! Still, I agree with you: the whole thing up there, whatever it is, has Necroscope stamped all over it. And by the way: the same goes for you."

"What's that?" Darcy didn't understand.

"That complication I mentioned?" Trask stared hard at him. "When it comes to Harry, I get much the same feeling about you. I mean, *I* trust you all the way, Darcy. But somehow I get this feeling that you . . . don't!''

After Trask left his office, Darcy sat at his desk and thought about it, and sighed. For he knew that Trask's talent wasn't in question. The esper had been right: Darcy didn't trust himself. Or at least, he didn't trust the decision he had made that time more than three years ago. His loyalties continued to be divided between Branch security and the well-being of a friend. And Harry was still under those post-hypnotic strictures imposed by Dr. James Anderson.

Just how they were affecting his life . . . who could say? But on the whole, Darcy liked to believe that his decision had been the right one. This thing with these red-robed priests out of Tibet was a case in point. Okay, so Harry wasn't involved—but supposing he had been? What if these religious fanatics had known about his talents and had been hunting him down for their own purposes? Surely it was better for all concerned that Harry had been neutralized in that respect? Of course it was—

—Yet still Darcy felt guilty. Well, it was something he would just have to learn to live with.

In his house outside Bonnyrig, the Necroscope absent-mindedly heaped pillows and sat back against them, frowned at the telephone, and wondered what all of that had been about. Red-robed Tibetan monks? Of course he knew something about them . . . that in some way or other they or their monastery were tied up with his future. But that was all. Maybe in the not so distant future he would try to find out more. But as for the recent past:

A couple of corpses in a burned-out car, and evidence of a sectarian war? Was there a connection? If so, it wasn't even beginning to make itself apparent! For the moment at least, he must let it go at that.

It was all he could do, for the fact was that the conscious, waking Harry Keogh really didn't know a thing about it. It had been excerpted from his life like a page lost from a manuscript, and there was only one person who could rewrite it.

Since she wasn't likely to, or wasn't ready to, for now it had become a part of the lost years . . .

NEXT:
In the conclusion of
NECROSCOPE: THE LOST YEARS
Revivals—Resurrection—the *Real* Harry Keogh—
the Reckoning . . . and more!